Back to Barbary Lane

Back to Barbary Lane

ARMISTEAD MAUPIN

Tales of the City
BOOKS
4–6

HARPER PERENNIAL

NEW YORK • LONDON • TORONTO • SYDNEY • NEW DELHI • AUCKLAND

HARPER ● PERENNIAL

Back to Barbary Lane

Babycakes

For Christopher Isherwood and Don Bachardy
and in loving memory of
Daniel Katz
1956–1982
and
once again
for Steve Beery

Memo to Lord Jamie Neidpath

Easley House may bear a marked resemblance to Stanway House, but Lord Teddy Roughton is nothing like you. You and I know that. Now the others do. Cheers.

A. M.

When you feel your song is orchestrated wrong,
Why should you prolong
Your stay?
When the wind and the weather blow your dreams sky-high,
Sail away—sail away—sail away!
—NOËL COWARD

A Royal Welcome

She was fifty-seven years old when she saw San Francisco for the first time. As her limousine pulled away from the concrete labyrinth of the airport, she peered out the window at the driving rain and issued a small sigh over the general beastliness of the weather.

"I know," said Philip, reading her mind, "but they expect it to clear today."

She returned his faint smile, then searched in her handbag for a tissue. Since leaving the Reagans' ranch she'd felt a mild case of the sniffles coming on, and she was dashed if she'd let it get the best of her.

The motorcade veered onto a larger highway—a "freeway," she supposed—and soon they were plunging headlong into the rain past lurid motels and posters of nightmare proportions. To her left loomed a treeless hillside, so unnaturally green that it might have been Irish. There were words on it, rendered in white stones: SOUTH SAN FRANCISCO—THE INDUSTRIAL CITY.

Philip saw the face she made and leaned forward to study the curious hieroglyphic.

"Odd," he murmured.

"Mmm," she replied.

She could only hope that they had not yet arrived in the city proper. This tatty commercial district could well be the equivalent of Ruislip or Wapping or one of those horrid little suburbs in the vicinity of Gatwick Airport. She mustn't imagine the worst just yet.

Her original plan had been to arrive in San Francisco on board the *Britannia*—an operation that would have entailed the pleasant prospect of sailing under the Golden Gate Bridge. The sea had become quite treacherous, however, by the time she reached Los Angeles, and the same storms that had brought six California rivers to flood level would almost certainly have played havoc with her undependable tummy.

So she had settled on this somewhat less than majestic entrance via aeroplane and automobile. She would spend the night in a local hotel, then reinstate herself on the *Britannia* when it arrived in the harbor the following day. Since she was almost sixteen hours ahead of schedule, this evening's time was completely unclaimed, and the very thought of such gratuitous leisure sent surprising little shivers of anticipation down her spine.

Where would she dine tonight? The hotel, perhaps? Or someone's home? The question of *whose* home was a sticky one at best, since she had already received feverish invitations from several local hostesses, including—and here she shuddered a bit—that dreadful petrol woman with all the hair.

She dismissed the issue of dinner for the moment and once more turned her attention to the passing scene. The rain seemed to have slacked a tiny bit, and here and there in the slate-gray skies a few dainty patches of blue had begun to make themselves known. Then the city materialized out of nowhere—a jumble of upended biscuit boxes that reminded her vaguely of Sydney.

"Look!" crowed Philip.

He was pointing to a dazzling rainbow that hovered like a crown above the city.

"How perfectly splendid," she murmured.

"Indeed. Their protocol people are more thorough than I thought."

Feeling giddier by the minute, she giggled at his little joke. It seemed appropriate to commemorate the moment by a cheery wave to the citizenry, but public assembly was quite impossible along this major artery, so she ignored the impulse and set about the task of repairing her lipstick.

The rain had diminished to a drizzle by the time the motorcade descended from the highway into a region of low-lying warehouses and scruffy cafés. At the first intersection, the limousine slowed dramatically and Philip signaled her with a nod of his head.

"Over there, darling. Your first well-wishers."

She turned her head slightly and waved at several dozen people assembled on the street corner. They waved back vigorously, holding aloft a black leather banner on which the words GOD SAVE THE QUEEN had been imprinted in silver rivets. It was not until she heard them cheer that she realized they were all men.

Philip smirked sleepily.

"What?" she asked.

"Poofs," he said.

"Where?"

"*There*, darling. With the banner."

She glanced back at them and saw that they were standing outside a building called the Arena. "Don't be silly," she replied. "They're sportsmen of some sort."

Mrs. Halcyon's Scoop

To commemorate the coming of Elizabeth II, the Marina Safeway had run specials all week on English muffins, Imperial margarine and Royal Crown Cola. The Flag Store on Polk Street had reported a rush on Union Jacks, while no less than three bars in the Castro had set about the task of organizing "Betty Windsor" look-alike contests.

All this and more had been painstakingly documented by Mary Ann Singleton—and a thousand reporters like her—in the grueling days that preceded the royal visit. Mary Ann's own quest for queenly minutiae had led her from tearooms on Maiden Lane to Irish bars in North Beach to storefront bakeries in the Avenues where rosy-cheeked Chicanas made steak-and-kidney pies for "Olde English" restaurants.

9

It was little wonder that Her Majesty's actual arrival had come as both a profound relief and a disappointing anticlimax. Tormented by the incessant rain, Mary Ann and her cameraman had waited for almost an hour outside the St. Francis, only to discover (after the fact) that the royal limousine had ducked discreetly into the hotel's underground parking garage.

Mary Ann salvaged the story as best she could, telecasting a live report from the entrance to the garage, then dragged herself home to 28 Barbary Lane, where she kicked off her shoes, lit a joint and phoned her husband at work.

They made a date to see *Gandhi* later that night.

She was warming up a leftover pot roast when the phone rang.

" 'Lo," she muttered, through a mouthful of cold roast.

"Mary Ann?" It was the crisp, patrician voice of DeDe Halcyon Day.

"Hi," said Mary Ann. "Don't mind me. I'm eating myself into oblivion."

DeDe laughed. "I saw your newscast on *Bay Window*."

"Great," said Mary Ann ruefully. "Pretty insightful, huh? I figure it's all over but the Emmy."

"Now, now. You did just fine."

"Right."

"And we all loved your hat. It was *much* prettier than the mayor's. Even Mother said so."

Mary Ann made a face for no one's benefit but her own. That goddamn hat was the first hat she had worn in years, and she had bought it specifically for the royal visit. "I'm glad you enjoyed it," she said blandly. "I thought it might have been a bit much for a parking garage."

"Look," said DeDe, "why aren't you down here? I thought for sure you would be."

"Down where? Hillsborough?"

DeDe uttered an exasperated little sigh. "Trader Vic's, of course."

Most rich people are annoying, Mary Ann decided, not because they are different but because they pretend not to notice the difference. "DeDe," she said as calmly as possible, "Trader Vic's is not exactly a hangout of mine."

"Well, OK, but . . . don't you want to see her?"

"See *who?*"

"The Queen, you ninny."

"The Queen is at Trader Vic's?" This was making no sense whatsoever.

"Wait a minute," said DeDe. "You didn't *know?*"

"DeDe, for God's sake! Is she there?"

"Not yet. But she's on her way. I thought for certain the station would've told you . . ."

"Are you sure?"

"Somebody's sure. The streets are crawling with cops, and the Captain's Cabin looks like opening night at the opera. Look, Vita Keating told Mother, and Vita heard it from Denise Hale, so it must be the truth."

Mary Ann's disbelief lingered like an anesthetic. "I didn't think the Queen ever went to restaurants."

"She doesn't," DeDe laughed. "Vita says this is her first time in seventeen years!"

"God," said Mary Ann.

"Anyway," DeDe added, "we've got a ringside seat. I'm here with Mother and D'or and the kids, and we'd love for you to join us. You and Brian, that is."

"He's at work," replied Mary Ann, "but I'd love to come."

"Good."

"Are there other reporters, DeDe? Do you see any television people?"

"Nope. If you haul ass, she's all yours."

Mary Ann let out a whoop. "You're an angel, DeDe! I'll be there as soon as I can grab a cab!"

Seconds after hanging up, she phoned the station and alerted the news director. He was understandably skeptical, but assured her that a crew would be dispatched immediately. Then she called a cab, fixed her face, strapped her shoes back on, and scrawled a hasty note to Brian.

She was striding through the leafy canyon of Barbary Lane when she realized what she had forgotten. "Shit," she muttered, hesitating only slightly before running back home to get her hat.

As she climbed from the cab at the entrance to Cosmo Place, she marveled anew at the enduring mystique of Trader Vic's. When all was said and done, this oh-so-fashionable Polynesian restaurant was really only a Quonset hut squatting in an alleyway on the edge of the Tenderloin. People who wouldn't be caught dead amidst the Bali Hai camp of the Tonga Room on Nob Hill would murder their grandmothers for the privilege of basking in the same decor at Trader Vic's.

The *maître d'* seemed particularly formidable tonight, but she placated him with the magic words—"Mrs. Halcyon is expecting me"—and made her way to the banquettes near the bar, the holy of holies they called the Captain's Cabin. DeDe caught her eye with a sly Elizabethan wave.

Striding to the table, Mary Ann slipped into the chair they had saved for her. "I hope you went ahead and ordered," she said.

"Just drinks," answered DeDe. "Is this a zoo or what?"

Mary Ann looked around at the neighboring tables. "Uh . . . who exactly is here?"

"Everybody," shrugged DeDe. "Isn't that right, Mother?"

Mrs. Halcyon detected the irreverence in her daughter's voice and chose to ignore it. "I'm delighted you could join us, Mary Ann. You know D'orothea, of course . . . and the children. Edgar, don't pick your nose, dear. Gangie has told you that a thousand times."

The six-year-old's lip plumped petulantly. His delicate Eurasian features, like those of his twin sister, seemed entirely appropriate in a room full of quasi Orientalia. "Why can't we go to Chuck E. Cheese?" he asked.

"Because," his grandmother explained sweetly, "the Queen isn't eating at Chuck E. Cheese."

D'orothea rolled her eyes ever so slightly. "It was her first choice, actually, but they wouldn't take a reservation for a party of sixty."

Mary Ann let out a giggle, then squelched it when she saw the look on Mrs. Halcyon's face. "I would think," said the matriarch, casting oblique daggers at her daughter's lover, "that a little decorum might be in order for all of us."

D'orothea's eyes ducked penitently, but contempt flickered at the corner of her mouth. She realigned a fork, waiting for the moment to pass.

"So," said Mary Ann, a little too brightly, "what time does she get here?"

"Any minute," DeDe replied. "They're putting her in the Trafalgar Room. That's upstairs and it's got its own entrance, so I guess they'll sneak her in the back way and . . ."

"I have to piss." Little Anna was tugging at DeDe's arm.

"Anna, didn't I tell you to take care of that before we left home?"

"*And*," added Mrs. Halcyon, with a look of genuine horror, "little girls don't use such words."

Anna looked puzzled. "What words?"

"Piss," said her brother.

"Edgar!" The matriarch gaped at her grandson, then spun around to demand reparation from her daughter. "For heaven's sake, DeDe . . . tell them. This isn't my job."

"Oh, Mother, this is hardly . . ."

"Tell them."

"The French say piss," D'orothea put in. "What about *pissoir?*"

"D'or." DeDe discredited her lover's contribution with a glacial glance before turning to her children. "Look, guys . . . I thought we settled on pee."

"Oh, my God," groaned the matriarch.

Mary Ann and D'orothea exchanged clandestine grins.

"Mother, if you don't mind . . ."

"What happened to tinkle, DeDe? I taught you to say tinkle."

"She still does," said D'or.

Another glare from DeDe. Mary Ann looked down at the tablecloth, suddenly afraid that D'or would try to enlist her as a confederate.

"Come along," said Mrs. Halcyon, rising. "Gangie will take you to the little girls' room."

"Me too," piped Edgar.

"All right . . . you too." She took their tiny hands in her chubby, bejeweled ones and toddled off into the rattan-lined darkness.

D'orothea let out a histrionic groan.

"Don't start," said DeDe.

"She's getting worse. I wouldn't have thought it possible, but she is actually getting worse." She turned and addressed her next remarks to Mary Ann, shaking a rigid forefinger in the direction of the restrooms. "That woman lives with her dyke daughter and her dyke daughter-in-law and her two half-Chinese grandchildren by the goddamn delivery boy at Jiffy's . . ."

"D'or . . ."

". . . and she *still* acts like this is the goddamn nineteenth century and she's . . . goddamn Queen Victoria. Grab that waiter, Mary Ann. I want another Mai Tai."

Mary Ann flailed for the waiter, but he wheeled out of sight into the kitchen. When she confronted the couple again, they were looking directly into each other's eyes, as if she weren't there at all.

"Am I right?" asked D'orothea.

DeDe hesitated. "Partially, maybe."

"Partially, hell. The woman is regressing."

"All right . . . OK, but it's just her way of coping."

"Oh. Right. Is that how you explain her behavior out there in the street?"

"What behavior?"

"Oh, please. The woman is obsessed with meeting the Queen."

"Stop calling her 'the woman.' And she isn't obsessed; she's just . . . interested."

"Sure. Uh-huh. Interested enough to hurdle that barricade."

DeDe rolled her eyes. "She didn't hurdle any barricade."

D'orothea snorted. "It wasn't for lack of trying. I thought she was going to deck that secret service man!"

The air had cleared somewhat by the time Mrs. Halcyon returned with the children. Mary Ann submitted to polite chit-chat for a minute or two, then pushed her chair back and smiled apologetically at the matriarch. "This has been a real treat, but I think I'd better wait out front for the crew. They'll never get past the *maître d'* and I'm not sure if . . ."

"Oh, do stay, dear. Just for one drink."

DeDe gave Mary Ann a significant look. "I think Mother wants to tell you about the time she met the Queen."

"Oh," said Mary Ann, turning to the matriarch. "You've met her before?" Her fingers fussed nervously with the back of her hat. Being polite to her elders had been her downfall more times than she cared to count.

"She's perfectly charming," gushed Mrs. Halcyon. "We had a nice long chat in the garden at Buckingham Palace. I felt as if we were old friends."

"When was this?" asked Mary Ann.

"Back in the sixties," said DeDe. "Daddy used to handle the BOAC account."

"Ah." Mary Ann rose, still gazing solicitously at Mrs. Halcyon. "I guess you'll be seeing her later, then. At the state dinner or something."

Wrong. The matriarch's face became an Apache death mask. Aflame with embarrassment, Mary Ann sought DeDe's eyes for guidance. "The problem," explained DeDe, "is Nancy Reagan."

Mary Ann nodded, understanding nothing.

D'orothea's lip twisted wryly. "At least, we all have the same problem."

DeDe ignored the remark. "Mother and Mrs. Reagan have never been the best of buddies. Mother thinks she may have been . . . blackballed from the state dinner."

"*Thinks?*" snapped Mrs. Halcyon.

"Whatever," said DeDe, handling Mary Ann's mortification with a sympathetic wink. "You'd better scoot, hadn't you? C'mon, I'll walk you to the door." She rose, making it easier for Mary Ann to do so.

"Good luck," said the matriarch. "Look pretty, now."

"Thanks," she replied. "Bye, D'orothea."

"Bye, hon. See you soon, OK?" *Away from the old biddy*, she meant.

"Where is she going?" Edgar asked his grandmother.

"To be on TV, darling. Anna, precious, don't scratch yourself there."

"Why?"

"Never mind. It isn't ladylike."

"The kids are looking great," Mary Ann said. "I can't believe how big they're getting."

"Yeah . . . Look, I'm sorry about all that squabbling."

"Hey."

"D'or hates these scenes. She's OK when it's just Mother, but when Mother's with her friends . . ." She shook her head with weary resignation. "D'or calls them the Upper Crustaceans. There's a lot of the old radical left in her still."

Maybe so, thought Mary Ann, but it was becoming increasingly difficult to remember that the woman in the Zandra Rhodes gown with the understated smudge of purple in her hair had once toiled alongside DeDe in the jungle of Guyana. DeDe's own transition from postdebutante to urban guerrilla to Junior League matron was equally rife with contradiction, and sometimes Mary Ann felt that the embarrassment both women suffered over the monstrous inconsistencies in their lives was the glue that held their marriage together.

DeDe smiled gently at her own dilemma. "I didn't *plan* on having a family like this, you know?"

Mary Ann smiled back at her. "I certainly do."

"Anna called Edgar a faggot the other day. Can you believe that?"

"God. Where did she pick *that* up?"

DeDe shrugged. "The Montessori School, I guess. Hell, I don't know . . . Sometimes I think I haven't got a handle on things anymore. I don't know what to tell *myself* about the world, much less my children." She paused and looked at Mary Ann. "I thought we might be swapping notes on that by now."

"On what?"

"Kids. I thought you and Brian were planning . . . God, listen to me. I sound like Mother."

"That's all right."

"You just mentioned . . . the last time I saw you . . ."

"Right."

"But I guess . . . the career makes it kind of difficult to . . ." She let the thought trail off, apparently shamed into silence by the realization that they sounded like a couple of housewives pounding a mall in Sacramento. "Tell me to shut up, OK?"

They had reached the door, much to Mary Ann's relief. She gave DeDe a hasty peck on the cheek. "I'm glad you're interested," she said. "It's just that . . . things are kind of on hold for the time being."

"I hear you," said DeDe.

Did she? wondered Mary Ann. Had she guessed at the truth?

The rain was clattering angrily on the canopy above the restaurant's entrance. "Are those your people?" asked DeDe, indicating Mary Ann's camera crew.

"That's them." They looked wet and grouchy. She didn't relish the thought of making them wetter and grouchier. "Thanks for the tip," she told DeDe.

"That's OK," her friend replied. "I owed you one."

The Baby Thing

Brian Hawkins found his wife's note when he got home from work, and he went up to the house on the roof to await her appearance on television. The tiny penthouse had been his bachelor pad in the old days, but now it functioned as a TV-room-cum-retreat for all the residents of 28 Barbary Lane. Nevertheless, he still seemed to use it more than anyone.

He worried about that sometimes. He wondered if he qualified as a full-fledged TV junkie, a chronic escapist who needed the tube to fill a void he was no longer capable of filling himself. When Mary Ann wasn't home, he could almost always be found in his video aerie, lost in the soothing ether of the Quasar.

"Brian, dear?"

Mrs. Madrigal's voice startled him, since her footsteps on the stairway had been drowned out by Supertramp singing "It's Raining Again" on MTV. "Oh, hi," he said, turning to grin at her. She was wearing a pale green kimono and her hair hovered above her angular face like random wisps of smoke.

Pursing her lips, she studied the television, where a man in his underwear was threading his way through a forest of open umbrellas. "How very appropriate," she said.

"Really," he replied.

"I was looking for Mary Ann," the landlady explained.

It was a simple statement of fact, but it made him feel even more extraneous. "You'll have to wait in line," he said, turning back to the set. Mrs. Madrigal said nothing.

He was instantly sorry for his pettiness. "She's got a hot date with the Queen," he added.

"Oh . . . another one, eh?"

"Yeah."

She glided across the room and sat down next to him on the sofa. "Shouldn't we be watching her channel?" Her huge Wedgwood eyes forgave him for his irritation.

He shook his head. "She won't be on for another five minutes."

"I see." She let her gaze wander out the window until it fixed on the intermittent blink of the beacon on Alcatraz. He had seen her do that so many times, as if it were a point of reference, the source of her energy. Turning back to him, she shook his knee playfully. "It's a bitch, isn't it?"

"What?"

"Being a media widower."

He came up with a smile for her. "It isn't that. I'm proud of her."

"Of course."

"I had just . . . counted on being with her tonight. That's all."

"I know the feeling," she said.

This time he was the one who looked out the window. A small pond had formed on a neighboring rooftop and its surface was being pitted by yet another downpour. It wasn't night yet, but it was definitely dark. "Do you have a joint?" he asked.

She cocked her head and mugged at him—a reaction that said, "Silly question." Then she foraged in the sleeve of her kimono until she located the familiar tortoiseshell case. He selected a joint, lit it, and offered it back to her. She shook her head, saying, "Hang on to it."

He did so, without a word, for almost a minute, while Michael Jackson minced down a make-believe street protesting that "the kid is not my son." It wasn't all that hard to believe him, Brian decided.

"The thing is," he said at last, "I was going to talk to her about something."

"Ah."

"I was going to buy her dinner at Ciao and take her to *Gandhi* and talk to her about Topic A one more time."

She was silent, so he glanced at her to see if she knew what he meant. She did. She knew and she was pleased. It made him feel a lot better. If nothing else, he would always have Mrs. Madrigal on his side.

"You can still do that," she said finally.

"I don't know . . ."

"What do you mean?"

"I mean . . . it scares the hell out of me. I'm not sure it's a good idea to make her say no one more time. This time . . . it might sound like she means it."

"But if you don't at least talk to her . . ."

"Look, what good would it do? When would she find the *time*, for God's sake? Tonight is so fucking typical, you know. Our private life has to take a back seat to every dumbass little news story that comes down the pike."

The landlady smiled faintly. "I'm not sure Her Majesty would appreciate that description of her sojourn."

"OK. Maybe not tonight. The Queen is excusable . . ."

"I should think."

"But she's done this half a dozen times this month. This is *always* the way it is."

"Well, her career is terribly . . ."

"Don't I show respect for her career? Don't I? That can be her career, and the baby can be mine. That makes a helluva lot of sense to me!"

His voice must have been more strident than he had intended. She stroked him with her eyes, telling him to calm down. "Dear," she murmured, "I'm the last person who needs convincing."

"Sorry," he said. "I guess I'm practicing on you."

"That's all right."

"It's not like we have that much time. She's thirty-two and I'm thirty-eight."

"Ancient," said the landlady.

"It is for making babies. It's shit-or-get-off-the-pot time."

Mrs. Madrigal winced, then arranged a fold in her kimono sleeve. "Your metaphors need work, dear. Tell me, when exactly did you last talk to her about this?"

He thought for a moment. "Three months ago, maybe. And six months before that."

"And?"

"She keeps saying we should wait."

"For what?"

"You tell me. For her to become an anchor, maybe? That makes a lot of sense. How many pregnant anchors have you seen?"

"There must have been some."

"She doesn't want to," he said. "That's the bottom line. That's the truth behind the excuses."

"You don't know that," said the landlady.

"I know her."

Mrs. Madrigal peered out at the Alcatraz beacon again. "Don't be too sure about that," she said.

That threw him. When he looked for clues in her face, her brow seemed to be furrowed in thought. "Has she talked to you?" he asked. "Has she said something about . . . the baby thing?"

"No," she answered hastily. "She would never do that."

He remembered the time and reached for the remote control. At the slightest touch of his finger, Mary Ann's face appeared on the screen, only slightly larger than life. She was standing in an alleyway behind Trader Vic's, smiling incongruously in a deep blue sea of cops.

"My goodness," beamed Mrs. Madrigal. "Doesn't she look just splendid?"

She looked better than that. A rush of pure affection swept over him. He smiled at the set for a few proud moments, then turned back to his landlady. "Tell me the truth," he said.

"All right."

"Does she look like a woman who wants to have a baby?"

Mrs. Madrigal's forehead wrinkled again. She spent a long time scrutinizing Mary Ann's face. "Well," she began, tapping a forefinger against her lips, "that hat is deceptive."

Volunteer

Michael Tolliver had spent rush hour in the Castro, the time of day when the young men who worked in banks came home to the young men who worked in bars. He watched from a window seat at the Twin Peaks as they spilled from the mouth of the Muni Metro, stopping only long enough to raise the barrels of their collapsible umbrellas and fire at the advancing rain. Their faces had the haggard, disoriented cast of prisoners who had somehow tunneled to freedom.

He polished off his Calistoga and left the bar, then forked out three dollars to a man selling collapsible umbrellas on the corner. He had lost his last one, and the one before that had sprung a spoke, but three dollars was nothing and he embraced the idea of their expendability. There was no point in getting attached to an umbrella.

Deciding on a pizza at the Sausage Factory, he set off down Castro Street past the movie house and the croissant/cookie/card shops. As he crossed Eighteenth Street, a derelict lurched into the intersection and shouted "Go back to Japan" to a stylish black woman driving a Mitsubishi. Michael caught her eye and smiled. She rewarded him with an amiable shrug, a commonplace form of social telepathy which seemed to say: "Looks like we lost another one." There were days, he realized, when that was all the humanity you could expect—that wry, forgiving glance between survivors.

The Sausage Factory was so warm and cozy that he scuttled his better judgment and ordered half a liter of the house red. What began as a mild flirtation with memory had degenerated into maudlin self-pity by the time the alcohol took hold. Seeking distraction, he studied the funk-littered walls, only to fix upon a faded Pabst Blue Ribbon sign which read: DON'T JUST SIT THERE—NAG YOUR HUSBAND. When the waiter arrived with his pizza, his face was already lacquered with tears.

"Uh . . . are you OK, hon?"

Michael mopped up quickly with his napkin and received his dinner. "Sure. I'm fine. This looks great."

The waiter wouldn't buy it. He stood there for a moment with his arms folded, then pulled up a chair and sat down across from Michael. "If you're fine, I'm Joan Collins."

Michael smiled at him. He couldn't help thinking of a waitress he had known years ago in Orlando. She, too, had called him "hon" without ever knowing his name. This man had a black leather vest, and keys clipped to his Levi's, but he reached out to strangers in exactly the same way. "One of those days?" he asked.

"One of those days," said Michael.

The waiter shook his head slowly. "And here we are on the wrong side of town, while Betty is having dinner at Trader Vic's."

Michael skipped a beat. "Bette *Davis?*"

The waiter laughed. "I *wish*. Betty the Second, hon. The Queen."

"Oh."

"They gave her a fortune cookie . . . *and she didn't know what it was*. Can you stand it?"

Michael chuckled. "You don't by any chance know what the fortune was?"

"Uh . . ." The waiter wrote in the air with his finger. " 'You . . . will . . . come . . . into . . . a . . . great . . . deal . . . of . . . money.' "

"Sure."

The waiter held his hands up. "Swear to God. Nancy Reagan got the same thing in hers."

Michael took another sip of his wine. "Where did you get this?" This guy was awfully nice, but his dish seemed suspect.

"On the TV in the kitchen. Mary Ann Singleton has been covering it all night."

"No kidding?" *Good for her*, he thought, *good for her*. "She's an old friend of mine." It would tickle her to know he had bragged about that.

"Well, you tell her she's all right." The waiter extended his hand. "I'm Michael, by the way."

Michael shook his hand. "Same here."

"Michael?"

"Yep."

The waiter rolled his eyes. "Sometimes I think that half the fags in the world are named Michael. Where did they ever get this Bruce shit?" He rose suddenly, remembering his professionalism. "Well, you take care, hon. Maybe I'll see you around. You don't work in the neighborhood, do you?"

Michael shook his head. "Not usually. I did this afternoon."

"Where?"

"Across the street. At the switchboard."

"Yeah? My friend Max worked there for a while. He said it was exhausting."

"It is," said Michael.

"This one guy called every other afternoon, while his wife was at her Dancercise class. He usually wanted Max to be . . . you know . . . a butch trucker type. Max said it took him *ages* to come, and he said the same thing over and over again. 'Yeah, that's right, flop those big balls in my face.' Now, how the hell you can flop your balls in some guy's face over the *telephone* . . ."

"Wrong place," said Michael, feeling a faint smile work its way out.

The waiter blinked at him. "Dial-a-Load?"

Michael shook his head. "The AIDS hotline."

"Oh." The waiter's fingers crept up his chest to his mouth. "Oh, God. I am such a dipshit."

"No you're not."

"There's this phone sex place upstairs from that new savings and loan, and I thought . . . God, I'm embarrassed."

"Don't be," said Michael. "I think it's funny."

The other Michael's face registered gratitude, then confusion, then something akin to discomfort. Michael knew what he was wondering. "I don't have it," he added. "I'm just a volunteer who answers the phones."

A long silence followed. When the waiter finally spoke, his voice was much more subdued. "My ex-lover's lover died of it last month."

An expression of sympathy seemed somehow inappropriate, so Michael merely nodded.

"It really scares me," said the waiter. "I've given up Folsom Street completely. I only go to sweater bars now."

Michael would have told him that disease was no respecter of cashmere, but his nerves were too shot for another counseling session. He had already spent five hours talking to people who had been rejected by their lovers, evicted by their landlords, and refused admission to local hospitals. Just for tonight, he wanted to forget.

A Hard Time Believing

It was almost midnight when Mary Ann got home. A winter full of rain had left a moss-green scum on the wooden stairway to Barbary Lane, so she climbed it cautiously, holding fast to the rail until she felt the reassuring squish of eucalyptus leaves under her feet. She noticed that Michael's lights were still on when she reached the lych-gate at Number 28. For some reason, that worried her, activating an instinct that might roughly be described as maternal.

She hesitated on the second-floor landing, then rapped on his door. He appeared moments later, looking rumpled and a little dis-combobulated. "Oh, hi," he said, raking his hair with his fingers.

"I hope you weren't asleep."

"No, just lying down. C'mon in."

She stepped into the room. "Did you catch my little coup, by any chance?"

He shook his head. "I heard about it afterwards, though. The Castro was all abuzz with it."

"Really?" The upward inflection of her voice was a little too girlish and eager, but she was hungry for reinforcement. Her secret fear was that her performance had been clumsy and sophomoric. "What exactly were they saying?"

He smiled at her sleepily. "What exactly would you like them to say?"

"Mouse!" After seven years of friendship, she still couldn't tell when he was kidding.

"Relax, Babycakes. My waiter was raving about you." He withdrew from her slightly and gave her a once-over. "I'm surprised he didn't mention the hat, though."

That stopped her cold. "What's wrong with the hat?"

"Nothing." He stayed poker-faced, teasing her.

"Mouse . . ."

"It's a perfectly nice hat."

"Mouse, if every queen in the city was laughing at this hat, I will *die*. Are you reading me? I will crawl under the nearest rock and die."

He gave up the game. "It looks fabulous. *You* look fabulous. C'mon . . . sit down and tell me about it."

"I can't. I just thought I'd stop by . . . and say hi."

He regarded her for a moment, then leaned forward and pecked her on the lips. "Hi."

"Are you OK?" she asked.

He made a little circle in the air with his forefinger, giving her a rueful smile.

"Me too," she said.

"It's the rain, I guess."

"I guess." It had never been the rain, and they both knew it. The rain was just easier to talk about. "Well . . ." She nodded toward the door. "Brian must think I've dropped off the face of the earth."

"Hang on," said Michael. "I've got something for him." He ducked into the kitchen, returning seconds later with a pair of roller skates. "They're ten-and-a-halfs," he said. "Isn't that what Brian wears?"

She stared at the skates, feeling the pain begin to surface again.

"I found them under the sink," Michael explained, avoiding her eyes. "I gave them to Jon two Christmases ago, and I completely forgot where he kept them. Hey . . . not now. OK?"

She fought back the tears, to no avail. "I'm sorry, Mouse. It's not fair to you, but . . . sometimes, you know, it just creeps up without any . . . Christ!" She wiped her eyes with two angry sweeps of her hand. "When the hell is it gonna stop?"

Michael stood there, hugging the skates to his chest, his features contorted horribly by grief.

"Oh, Mouse, I'm so sorry. I'm such a turkey."

Unable to speak, he nodded his forgiveness as the tears coursed down his cheeks. She took the skates from him and set them down, scooping him into her arms and stroking his hair. "I know, Mouse . . . I know, baby. It'll get better. You'll see."

She had a hard time believing that herself. Jon had been dead for over three months, but she suffered the loss more acutely now than ever before. To gain distance on the tragedy was to grasp, for the first time, the terrible enormity of it.

Michael pulled away from her. "So . . . how about some cocoa, media star?"

"Great," she said.

She sat at the kitchen table while he made it. Still pinned to the refrigerator door by a magnetized seashell was the snapshot she had taken of Jon and Michael at a pumpkin patch in Half Moon Bay. Averting her gaze, she commanded herself not to cry again. She had done quite enough damage for one night.

When the cocoa was ready, Michael removed a blue Fiesta cup from the shelf and placed it on a gray saucer. Frowning slightly, he studied the pairing for a moment, then substituted a rose-coloured saucer for the gray one. Mary Ann observed the ritual and smiled at his eccentricity.

Michael caught her reaction. "These things are important," he said.

"I know." She smiled.

He chose a yellow cup for himself and set it on the gray saucer before joining her at the table. "I'm glad you came by," he said.

"Thanks," she replied. "So am I."

While they sipped their cocoa, she told him about DeDe and Mrs. Halcyon, about her rebellious crew and the rude police, about the few brief moments she had actually laid eyes on the Queen. The monarch had seemed so unreal, she explained, unreal and yet totally familiar. Like the cartoon image of Snow White, walking amidst ordinary human beings.

She stayed long enough to make him laugh out loud several times, then said good night to him. When she reached her own apartment, Brian wasn't there, so she left the skates in the living room and climbed the stairs to the house on the roof. There, as usual, she found her husband asleep in the flickering light of MTV. She knelt by the sofa and laid her hand gently on his chest. "Hey," she whispered. "Who's it gonna be? Me or Pat Benatar?"

27

He stirred, rubbing his eyes with the knuckles of his forefinger.

"Well?" she prodded.

"I'm thinking."

She smoothed his chest hair, following the lines of its natural swirls. "I'm sorry I broke our date."

He smiled drowsily at her. "Hey."

"Did you see me?" she asked.

He nodded. "Mrs. Madrigal and I watched."

She waited for his reaction.

"You were terrific," he said at last.

"You're not just saying that?"

He raised himself slightly on his elbows and rubbed his eyes again. "I'm never just saying that."

"Well . . . the fortune cookie stuff was pretty fabulous, if I do say so myself. Of course . . ." She was silenced when he reached out and pulled her onto the sofa next to him.

"Shut up," he said.

"Gladly," she replied.

She kissed him long and hard, almost ferociously, in direct proportion to the intensity of her workday. The more public her life became, the more acutely she relished such moments of unequivocal privacy. Within seconds, Brian's hands had found the hem of her tweed skirt and pulled it up over her hips. Lifting her gently under the arms, he propped her up against a nubby cotton bolster and began kissing her knee. She felt faintly ridiculous.

"Let's go downstairs," she whispered.

He looked up from his single-minded mission. "Why?"

"Well . . . so I can get out of this hat, for one thing."

A boyish leer transformed his face. "Keep it on, OK?" His head went down again, and his sandpapery cheek scraped against her pantyhose as he moved his tongue up the inside of her thighs. "What is this?" she asked. "Your Evita fantasy?"

He laughed, enveloping her in a wave of warm breath, then yanked off her pantyhose in a single, efficient movement. She laced her fingers through his chestnut curls and pulled his face into her groin, warmth into warmth, wetness into wetness. Moaning softly, she arched her neck and fell back into the embrace of the sofa. At a time like this, she decided, ridiculous was the last thing that mattered.

They were back at the apartment when she finally took off the hat. "The skates are from Mouse," she said. She tried to sound matter-of-fact about it.

"What skates?" He was sitting on the edge of the bed in his boxer shorts.

"In the living room." She avoided his eyes by pretending to arrange the hat in its box.

He rose and left the room. He was gone so long that she stopped brushing her hair and went to look for him. He was seated in the wingback armchair, staring into space. The skates were at his feet. He glanced briefly in her direction. "They're Jon's, right?"

She nodded, but moved no closer.

He shook his head slowly, a thin smile on his face. "Jesus God," he said quietly. He brushed a piece of imaginary lint off the arm of the chair. "Is Michael doing OK?" he asked.

"OK," she replied.

Brian cast his eyes down at the skates. "He thinks of everything, doesn't he?"

"Uh-huh." She moved to the chair and sat on the floor between his knees. He stroked her hair methodically, saying nothing for almost a minute.

Finally, he said: "I almost lost my job today."

"What?"

"It's OK. I didn't. I smoothed things out."

"What happened?"

"Oh . . . I punched out this guy."

"Brian." She tried not to sound too judgmental, but this had happened before.

"It's OK," he said. "It wasn't a customer or anything. It was just that new waiter. Jerry."

"I don't know him."

"Yeah, you do. The one with the Jordache Look."

"Oh, yeah."

"He shot off his mouth all day about one goddamn thing or another. Then he saw me eat a french fry off a plate that had just been bused and he said, 'Shit, man, you've played hell now." I asked him what the fuck he meant by that and he said, 'That was a faggot's plate, dumbass—your days are numbered.'"

"Great."

"So I pasted him."

She wrenched her head around and stared at him. "Do you really think that was necessary?"

He answered with a shrug. "I got a big kick out of it."

"Brian . . . they told you if it happened again . . ."

"I know, I know."

She kept quiet. These half-assed little John Wayne scenes were simply a reflection of his frustration with an unchallenging job. If she didn't tread carefully, he would use her disapproval as an excuse to remind her that fatherhood was the only job that really mattered to him.

"Did you ever read *Nineteen Eighty-Four?*" he asked.

The question made her wary. "Years ago. Why?"

"Remember the guy in it?"

"Vaguely."

"Do you know what I remember about him the most?"

She shifted uncomfortably. "I don't know. They put rats on his face. What?"

"He was forty," he answered.

"And?"

"I was sixteen when I read it, and I remember thinking how *old* the guy was, and I realized that *I* would be forty in nineteen eighty-four, and I couldn't imagine what it would be like to be that far gone. Well . . . nineteen eighty-four is almost here."

She studied his expression for a moment, then took the hand lying on his knee and kissed it. "I thought we agreed that one menopause in the family was enough."

30

He hesitated, then laughed. "OK, all right . . . fair enough."

She sensed that the crisis had passed. He seemed to know that this wasn't the time to broach the subject, and she was more than grateful for the reprieve.

Anna's Family

When Michael went down to breakfast, Mrs. Madrigal's kitchen smelled of coffee brewing and bacon frying. The rain that streaked the long casement windows above her sink only served to heighten the conspiracy of coziness that ensnared even the most casual of visitors. He sat down at the landlady's little white enamel table and sniffed the air.

"The coffee is heaven," he said.

"It's Arabian Mocha," she replied. "It's the sinsemilla of coffees." She tore off a length of paper towel and began laying the bacon out to drain.

He chuckled, but only because he understood exactly what she meant. If he was a true pothead—and sometimes he thought that he was—this fey sixty-year-old with the flyaway hair and the old kimonos was the fiend who had led him down the garden path. He could have done a lot worse.

She joined him at the table, bringing two mugs of coffee with her. "Mary Ann was up awfully early."

"She's in Silicon Valley," he said. "Mr. Packard is showing the Queen around."

"Mr. Packard?"

"The computer man. Our former deputy secretary of defense."

"Ah. No wonder I forgot."

He smiled at her, then picked up his mug and blew off its halo of steam. "He's giving the Queen a computer."

She made a quizzical face. "What does the Queen want with a computer?"

He shrugged. "It's got something to do with breeding horses."

"My word."

"I know. I can't picture it either."

She smiled, then sipped her coffee for a while before asking: "You haven't heard from Mona, have you?"

It was an old wound, but it throbbed like a new one. "I've stopped being concerned with that."

"Now, now."

"There's no point in it. She's cut us off. There hasn't been so much as a postcard, Mrs. Madrigal. I haven't talked to her for at least . . . a year and a half."

"Maybe she thinks we're cross with her."

"C'mon. She knows where we are. It's just happened, that's all. People drift apart. If she wanted to hear from us, she'd list her phone number or something."

"I know what you're thinking," she said.

"What?"

"Only a silly fool would fret over a daughter who's pushing forty."

"No I'm not. I'm thinking what a silly old fool your forty-year-old daughter is."

"But, dear . . . what if something's really the matter?"

"Well," said Michael. "You've heard from her more recently than I have."

"Eight months ago." The landlady frowned. "No return address. She said she was doing OK in 'a little private printing concern,' whatever that means. It's not like her to be so vague."

"Oh, yeah?"

"Well . . . not in *that* way, dear."

When Mona had moved to Seattle at the turn of the decade, Michael had all but begged her not to go. Mona had been adamant, however; Seattle was the city of the eighties. "Go ahead," he had jeered. "You like Quaaludes . . . you'll *love* Seattle." Apparently, he had been right; Mona had never returned.

Mrs. Madrigal saw how much it still bothered him. "Go easy on her, Michael. She might be in some sort of trouble."

That would hardly be news. He couldn't remember a time when his former roommate hadn't been on the verge of some dark calamity or another. "I told you," he said calmly. "I don't think about that much these days."

"If we had a way of telling her about Jon . . ."

"But we don't. And I doubt if we ever will. She's made it pretty clear that she . . ."

"She loved Jon, Michael. I mean . . . they squabbled a bit, perhaps, but she loved him just as much as any of us. You mustn't doubt that . . . ever." She rose and began cracking eggs into a bowl. They both knew that nothing was to be gained by pursuing the subject. All the wishing in the world wouldn't make a difference. When Mona had fled to the north, she had put more than the city behind her. Starting from scratch was the only emotional skill she had ever mastered.

Mrs. Madrigal seemed to share his thoughts. "I hope she has someone," she murmured. "Anyone."

There was nothing he could add. With Mona, it could well be anyone.

He tried not to think about her on the way to work, concentrating instead on the dripping wound in the roof of his VW convertible. A knife-wielding stereo thief had put it there three weeks earlier, and the bandage he had fashioned from a shower curtain required constant readjustment against the rain. It was no wonder the car had begun to smell like a rank terrarium; he had actually discovered a small stand of grass sprouting in the mildewed carpet behind the back seat.

By the time he reached God's Green Earth, the downpour was much worse, so he gave the plastic patch a final fluffing before making a mad dash to the nursery office. Ned was already there, leaning back in his chair, cradling his bald pate in his big, hairy hands. "That hole is a bitch, huh?"

"The worst." He shook off the water like a drenched dog. "The car is forming its own ecosystem." He peered uneasily out the window, beyond which the primroses had dissolved into an impressionistic blur. "Jesus. We'd better get a tarp or something."

"What for?" Ned remained in repose.

"Those bedding plants. They're getting beat all to hell."

His partner smiled stoically. "Have you checked the books lately? There isn't exactly a major demand for primroses."

He was right, of course. The rain had played hell with business. "Just the same, don't you think . . . ?"

"Fuck it," said Ned. "Let's hang it up."

"What?"

"Let's close for a month. It won't hurt us. It can't be any worse than this."

Michael sat down, staring at him. "And do what?"

"Well . . . how about a trip to Death Valley?"

"Right."

"I'm serious."

"Ned . . . *Death Valley?*"

"Have you ever been there? It's a fucking paradise. We could get six or eight guys, camp out, do some mushrooms. The wildflowers will be incredible after this rain."

He was less than thrilled. "How about during?"

"We'll have tents, pussy. C'mon . . . just for a weekend."

Michael could never have explained his panic at the prospect of unlimited leisure. He needed a routine right now, a predictable rut. The last thing he wanted was time to think.

Ned tried another approach. "I won't try to fix you up. It'll just be a group of guys."

He couldn't help smiling. Ned was always trying to fix him up. "Thanks anyway. You go ahead. I'll hold down the fort. I'll be glad to. Really."

Ned regarded him for a moment, then sprang to his feet and began rearranging the seed packets in the revolving rack. It struck Michael as a defensive gesture. "Are you pissed?" he asked.

"Nope."

"It just isn't there right now, Ned."

His partner stopped fiddling. "If you ask me . . . a good jack-off buddy would do you a world of good."

"Ned . . ."

"OK. All right. Forget it. I've done my Dolly Levi for the day."

"Good."

"I'm going, though. If you want to stay here and watch the roots rot, that's OK by me."

"Fine."

They had little to say to each other for the next hour as they busied themselves with minor maintenance chores, things that didn't get done when customers were there. After Ned had finished stacking pallets in the shed, he stepped into the office again and confronted Michael at the desk. "I wanted your company, you know. I didn't do it to be nice."

"I know." He looked up and smiled.

Ned tousled his hair, then reached for his flight jacket. "I'll be at home, if you change your mind. Go home, at least. There's no point in hanging around here."

He did go home eventually, and he spent the rest of the afternoon sorting laundry and cleaning his refrigerator. He was searching for another project when Mrs. Madrigal phoned just before five o'clock.

"Are you free for dinner, I hope?"

"So far," he said.

"Marvelous. I've found a festive new place for Mexican food. I want us all to go. We haven't had a family outing in ages."

He accepted, wondering if this adventure was being organized specifically for his benefit. His friends were awfully solicitous these days and he often felt enormous pressure to be visibly happy in their presence. The reborn joy they sought in his eyes was something he would never be able to fake.

Mrs. Madrigal's Mexican discovery turned out to be a cavernous room at the end of an alleyway near the Moscone Center. For reasons that no one could explain, it was called the Cadillac Bar. Its kitschy Lupe Velez ambience met with everyone's approval, and they guzzled margaritas like conventioneers on a three-day binge in Acapulco.

Maybe it was the liquor, but something about Mary Ann's demeanor seemed curiously artificial to Michael. She hung on Brian's arm throughout much of the meal, laughing a little too loudly at his jokes, gazing rapturously into his eyes, looking more like the Little Woman than Michael had ever seen her look. When her gaze met Michael's for a split second, she seemed to sense his puzzlement. "This place is great," she said far too breezily. "We should all be sworn to secrecy."

"Too late," he replied, parrying her diversionary tactic with one of his own. "Look who just walked in."

Both Mary Ann and Brian jerked their heads toward the door.

"Not *now!*" he whispered.

Mary Ann mugged at him. "You said to look."

"It's Theresa Cross," he muttered, "with one of those fags from Atari."

"Jesus," said Brian. "Bix Cross's widow?"

"You got it."

"She's on all his album covers," said Brian.

"*Parts* of her," amended Mary Ann.

Brian leered. "Right."

A cloud of confusion passed over Mrs. Madrigal's face. "Her husband was a singer?"

"You know," said Michael. "The rock star."

"Ah."

"She wrote *My Life with Bix*," Mary Ann added. "She lives in Hillsborough near the Halcyons."

The landlady's eyes widened. "Well, my dears, she appears to be coming this way."

Michael assessed the leggy figure striding toward their table. There were probably no twigs lodged within the dark recesses of her hair, but the careful disarray of her hoyden-in-the-haystack hairdo was clearly meant to suggest that there might be. That and her red Plasticine fingernails were all he could absorb before the rock widow had descended on them in a sickly-sweet aura of Ivoire. "You!" she all but shouted. "You I want to talk to."

The crimson talon was pointing at Mary Ann.

Clearing her throat, Mary Ann said: "Yes?"

"You are the best," crowed Theresa Cross. "The best, the best, the best!"

Mary Ann reddened noticeably. "Thank you very much."

"I watch you all the time. You're Mary Jane Singleton."

"Mary Ann."

Mrs. Cross couldn't be bothered. "That hat was the best. The best, the best, the best. Who are these cute people? Why don't you introduce us?"

"Uh . . . sure. This is my husband, Brian . . . and my friends Michael Tolliver and Anna Madrigal."

The rock widow nodded three times without a word, apparently regarding her own name as a matter of public knowledge. Then she turned her gypsy gaze back to Mary Ann. "You're coming to my auction, aren't you?"

So *that* was it, thought Michael. Mrs. Cross could smell media across a crowded room.

Mary Ann was thrown off balance, as intended. "Your . . . ? I'm afraid I don't . . ."

"Oh, no!" The rock widow showed the whites of her eyes, simulating exasperation. "Don't tell me my ditzy secretary didn't send you an invitation!"

Mary Ann shrugged. "I guess not."

"Well . . . consider yourself invited. I'm having an auction out at my house this weekend. Some of Bix's memorabilia. Gold records. The shirts he wore on his last tour. Lots of stuff. Fun stuff."

"Great," said Mary Ann.

"Oh . . . and his favorite Harley . . . and his barbells." The moving finger pointed in Brian's direction. "This one looks like he works out a little. Why don't you bring him along?"

Mary Ann shot a quick glance at "this one," then turned back to her assailant. "I'm not sure if we have plans that day, but if . . ."

"*W* is coming for sure, and the *Hollywood Reporter* has *promised* me they'll be there. Even Dr. Noguchi is coming . . . which strikes me as the very least he could do, since he was the one who broke the story when Bix . . . you know . . . bit the big one."

Michael listened with a mixture of fascination and revulsion. It was this kind of candid banter that had earned Theresa Cross a rung of her very own on San Francisco's social ladder. She might be a little common at times, but she was anything but boring. Besides, her husband's death (from a heroin overdose at the Tropicana Motel in Hollywood) had left her a very rich woman.

Whenever local hostesses needed an "extra woman"—as they often did in San Francisco—Theresa Cross could be counted on to do her part. Largely because of her public image, Michael had once referred to her in Jon's presence as "the fag hag of the bourgeoisie." Jon's reaction had been typically (and maddeningly) cautious: "Maybe so . . . but she's the closest thing we have to Bianca Jagger."

Unnerved by Theresa's "frankness," Mary Ann was still fumbling for words. "This place is really charming, isn't it?"

The rock widow made a face. "It was *much* more fun last week." Radar-like, her eyes scanned the room until they came to rest on a diminutive figure standing at the entrance. Everyone seemed to recognize her at the same time.

"Holy shit," Brian muttered. "It's Bambi Kanetaka."

"Gotta run," said Theresa, already inching toward her new quarry. "I'll see you at the auction."

"Fine," came Mary Ann's feeble reply.

Now two tables away, the rock widow yelled: "Ten percent goes to charity."

"Right," said Michael, unable to resist, "and ninety percent goes up her nose."

"Mouse . . . she'll hear you."

He snorted. "She's not hearing squat." He pointed toward the entrance alcove, where Mrs. Cross was already giving her pitch to Bambi Kanetaka.

Mary Ann's unfulfilled ambition burned behind her eyes like a small brushfire. "Well," she said dully, "I guess an anchorperson takes precedence over a reporter."

There was a long, pregnant silence, which Mrs. Madrigal punctuated by reaching for the check. "Not at our house, dear. Shall we pick up some gelato on the way home?"

When bedtime finally came, Michael slept fitfully, pestered by the alcohol and unfinished business. If Jon had been there, Michael might have woken him to say that Theresa Cross was an asshole, that he had always done fine without even *one* Bianca Jagger, that the nervous pursuit of chic was a weakness unworthy of a doctor of medicine.

He lurched out of bed and felt his way to the telephone. In the light of the streetlight on Barbary Lane, he punched out Ned's number. His partner answered on the second ring.

"It's me," said Michael.

"Hey, kiddo."

"Is it too late to change my mind?"

"About what?"

"You know . . . Death Valley."

"Hell, no. That's great. How about this weekend?"

"Perfect," said Michael.

Hello Sailor

While rain pelted the press platform at Pier 50, Mary Ann huddled under her cameraman's umbrella and scarfed down a breakfast of Cheerios and milk. "Where did *this* come from?" she asked, meaning the cereal.

"The local protocol people," answered her co-worker. "It's a joke."

She shot him a rueful look. "I'll say." She had long ago wearied of chasing this pleasant but lackluster Englishwoman through the rain. They could have done a helluva lot better than cold cereal.

Her cameraman smiled indulgently. "A *real* joke, Mary Ann. The Queen is leaving, see? We're saying Cheerio to the Queen, get it?" Her reaction must have registered immediately, for he chuckled sardonically and added: "Doesn't help a goddamn bit, does it?"

Mary Ann set the bowl down and glanced across at the *Britannia*. A band on deck was playing "The Anniversary Waltz"—an obvious reference to the Reagans, who had celebrated their thirty-first on board the night before. Soon they would emerge from the royal yacht, along with the Queen and the Prince, to board limousines bound for the airport.

While the *Britannia* sailed to Seattle, the Queen and her consort would fly to Yosemite to continue their vacation. The President would jet to Klamath Falls, Oregon, to make a speech about the decline of logging, and his bride would catch yet another plane to Los Angeles, where she was slated to appear in a special episode of *Diff'rent Strokes* concerning drug abuse among children.

Normally, such a hodgepodge of absurdities would have provoked at least a brief cynical monologue from Mary Ann, but she was far too absorbed in her own dilemma to wax witty about the Reagans. Instead, she set her jaw grimly and waited in silence for the final ritual of this inane tribal extravaganza.

The rain let up a little. A kilted band trooped bravely along the pier. Fireworks exploded in the pale gray skies, while a blonde woman in limp marabou feathers argued audibly with the guard at the entrance to the press platform.

"But I *am* with the press," she pleaded. "I just don't have my . . . uh . . . card with me today."

The guard was unyielding. "Look, lady. You got your job, I got mine."

Mary Ann went to the edge of the platform and shouted down at the sentry. "She's with me," she lied. "I'll take responsibility for it."

Elated, the wet-feathered blonde beamed up at her savior and yelled: "Mary Ann! Thank goodness!"

Mary Ann replied in a monotone, already embarrassed. "Hi, Prue."

It was a sad sight, really, this ersatz socialite looking like Big Bird in a monsoon. Prue Giroux had apparently come unglued since losing her job as social columnist for *Western Gentry* magazine. Her life had been built around parties—"events," she had called them—but the invitations and press passes had dried up months before.

Among the people who thought of themselves as social in San Francisco, no one was more expendable than an ex-columnist—except maybe the ex-wife of a columnist. Prue was obviously feeling the pinch.

Fluffing her feathers, she wobbled up the steps in spike heels. "You are so sweet to do this," she said, speaking much more quietly this time. "Isn't this just the most thrilling thing?"

"Mmmm," Mary Ann replied, not wanting to burst her bubble. Prue's naiveté was the only thing about her that invited respect.

"Look!" Prue exclaimed. "Just in time!"

Wearing a white hat and a beige coat, the Queen approached the gangplank on the arm of the President. As Mary Ann signaled her cameraman, thunderous applause swept across the pier and Prue Giroux sighed noisily. "Oh, Mary Ann, look how *beautiful* she is! She is truly beautiful!"

Mary Ann didn't answer, engrossing herself in the technicalities of her job. The entire spectacle took less than fifteen minutes. When it was over, she slipped away from Prue and the crew and downed a stiff drink at Olive Oil's, a waterfront bar adjoining the pier. She sat at the bar, beneath a row of signal flags, and watched the *Britannia* as it steamed toward the Golden Gate.

The man on the stool next to her hoisted his glass in the direction of the ship. "Good riddance, old girl."

Mary Ann laughed. "I'll say. Except the old girl isn't out there. She's flying to Yosemite."

Her barmate polished off his drink, then teased her with warm brown eyes. "I meant the ship." He had an English accent, she realized.

"You must be with the press," she said.

"Must I?" He was being playful again. Was he trying to pick her up?

"Well, the accent made me think . . . Oh, never mind."

The man laughed, extending his hand. "I'm Simon Bardill."

She gave him a businesslike handshake. "I'm Mary Ann Singleton." Her first real assessment of the Englishman made her realize how much he looked like Brian. He had the same chestnut curls, the same expressive eyes (though brown, not hazel), the same little tuft of fur sprouting beneath the hollow at the base of his neck.

True, his face was somewhat more angular—more foxlike than bearlike—but even a disinterested observer would notice the resemblance. There was an age difference, of course, since this man appeared to be in his late twenties.

He sensed her distraction immediately. "Uh . . . I haven't lost you, have I?"

She smiled apologetically. "For a moment, maybe. You look a lot like . . . somebody I know." To say "my husband" would have sounded far too intimate. Even so, the remark still came off like a pickup line, so she added hastily: "You must be from around here."

"Nope," he replied. "From there." He pointed a long, elegant finger at the departing ship.

She sensed that he enjoyed the mystery he was weaving. "You . . . uh . . . you're taking leave or something?"

He shook the ice in his glass. "Of my senses, perhaps." He peered out the rain-varnished windows of the saloon, fixing his gaze on the royal yacht, now a diminishing smudge of dark blue on the gray canvas of the bay. "There's a distinct possibility of that."

She blinked at him. "OK, *now* you've lost me."

Again, he rattled his ice. "It's simple, really. I jumped ship."

Her mind raced frantically toward an undesignated deadline. Had she stumbled across the only *real* story in this whole media circus?

"You know the expression?" he asked.

"Yes . . . of course. You're a crew member or what?"

"Oh, no no no. An *officer.*" He signaled the bartender by raising his empty glass. "May I?" he asked Mary Ann, nodding toward her glass.

"Oh . . . I'm fine." Was it too late to catch up with her crew? "Look, I'm sorry to be so thick about this, but . . . you were supposed to be sailing on the *Britannia* and . . . you just decided not to?"

"Precisely."

"You . . . defected?"

He laughed heartily. "From Mrs. Thatcher to Mr. Reagan?" He thought for a moment, stroking his well-defined jaw. "You're on the right track, mind you. I suppose one *could* say that I have defected. Yes . . . yes . . ."

He seemed to reflect on the concept, as if intrigued by it, until the bartender arrived with his drink. Hoisting it in her direction, he said: "To the new Simon Bardill and the lovely lady who shares his dark secret."

She lifted her empty glass. "I'm honored . . . what is it? *Lieutenant* Bardill?"

"Very clever. You even pronounced lieutenant correctly."

She bowed demurely, feeling curiously regal in his presence. "But you're not supposed to take ice in your drink, are you?"

His brow furrowed. "When were you last in England?"

"Never, I'm afraid."

"There's no need to be afraid." He smiled. "We keep ice on the bar now. *They* keep ice on the bar now."

"I see."

"A great deal has changed. A *great* deal." He gazed at the bay again, as if to assure himself that the last trace of England had vanished. It had.

"And to think," he said, turning back to her again, "I was going to be the last of the Snotty Yachties."

She smiled, eager to show him she recognized the nickname for the *Britannia*'s crew. "Aren't they going to miss you?"

"Oh . . . terribly, I'd imagine. I'm a likeable fellow, don't you think?"

"I meant professionally. What's going to happen when you don't show up at . . . wherever you're supposed to show up?"

"I'm a radio officer," he answered, "and it's already happened . . . whatever *it* is. I expect they've found another twit with breeding to take my place. Have you ever seen the city from Point Bonita?"

43

She missed a beat, noticeably, before she managed to reply: "Many times."

"Isn't it marvelous?" He intoned it so earnestly that she realized he had not been issuing an invitation but asking a simple question.

"Beautiful," she replied.

"You should never let people see San Francisco from Point Bonita if they're seeing it for the first time." He took a sudden swig of his Scotch, setting the glass down with deliberate grandeur. "They could very well run amok."

She smiled skeptically at this too-cute explanation. "So you did it for the scenery, huh?"

"In a manner of speaking."

"Would you mind telling that to a camera?"

He regarded her for a moment, then shook his head with a weary chuckle. "I should have known."

"I mean, it's really a fantastic . . ."

"What station do you work for?"

His tone somehow suggested betrayal. She resented that. They were just two people talking in a bar. "You don't have to, if you don't want to," she said.

The lieutenant ran his forefinger around the rim of his glass. "Do you want a story or do you want a friend?"

She answered without hesitation. "A friend."

He winked at her. "Excellent choice."

She knew that already. A friend just might relent and agree to a story after all. A friend who could trust her to present him in the best possible light. She explained her reasoning to Brian as they opened their Lean Cuisines that evening.

"He might be calling," she added.

"Calling? You gave him our number?"

She nodded. "I doubt if he will, though."

"But he might?"

"He might. He doesn't know a *soul*, Brian. I told him to call if he needed help with anything."

He nodded slowly. "Sort of a . . . Welcome Wagon gesture."

She glanced across at him, then blew on the surface of her steaming dinner. "You're not jealous. Don't pretend to be jealous, Brian."

"Who's pretending?"

"He'll be a nice new friend for both of us. He worked on the royal yacht, for God's sake. He's bound to be interesting, if nothing else."

He plunged a fork into his dinner. "So what's the name of our interesting new friend?"

"Simon," she answered grumpily. "Simon Bardill."

"What does he look like?"

"Gorgeous. Well, sort of gorgeous. He looks a lot like you, as a matter of fact."

Brian stroked his chin. "Why do I find that disquieting?"

She rolled her eyes in retort. "What in God's name would I do with a younger, English version of you?"

"The mind fairly boggles," he replied.

Campmates

As dawn crept over Death Valley, Michael stirred in his sleeping bag and catalogued the sounds of the desert: the twitter of tiny birds, the frantic scampering of kangaroo rats, the soothing rustle of the wind in the mesquite trees . . .

"Oh, no! The vinaigrette leaked!"

. . . the voice of Scotty, their chef for this expedition, taking stock of his inventory in preparation for breakfast. His plight provoked a burst of laughter from Ned's tent, followed by more of the same from the sandy bluff where Roger and Gary had slept under the stars.

"What's so fucking funny?" yelled Scotty.

Ned answered: "That's the nelliest thing that's ever been said in Death Valley."

"If you want butch," the chef snapped, "try the third RV on the right—they're eating Spam and powdered eggs. Us nellie numbers will be having eggs Benedict, thank you."

General cheers all around.

A tent was unzipped, probably Douglas and Paul's. Boots crunched against gravel, then came Paul's voice, froggy with sleep. "Does anybody know the way to the bathroom?"

More laughter from Ned. "You didn't really believe that, did you?"

"Listen, dickhead, you told me there was running water."

Roger came to the rescue. "All the way down the road, on the right-hand side."

"Where's my shaving kit?" asked Paul.

"Behind the ice chest," said Douglas.

Turtle-like, Michael inched out of his sleeping bag, found the air decidedly nippy, and popped back in again. There was no point in being rash about this. His absence from the banter had not yet been observed. He could still grab some sleep.

Wrong. Scotty's smiling face was now framed in the window of his tent. "Good morning, bright eyes."

Michael emerged part of the way and gave him a sleepy salute.

"Are you heading for the bathroom?" the chef asked.

"Eventually."

"Good. Find me some *garni*, would you?"

"Uh . . . *garni?*"

"For the grapefruit," explained Scotty. "There's lots of nice stuff along the road."

"Right."

"Just something pretty. It doesn't have to be edible, of course."

"Of course."

Garni in Death Valley. There was bound to be a message there somewhere—about life and irony and the gay sensibility—but it eluded him completely as he stood at a sink in the middle of nowhere and brushed his teeth next to a fat man in Bermuda shorts and flip-flops.

On the way back to the campsite, he left the path long enough to find something suitably decorative—a lacy, pale-green weed that didn't appear to shed—then decided on an alternate return route. He felt strangely exhilarated by the brisk, blue morning, and he wanted to enjoy the sensation in solitude.

They had pitched their tents along the edge of a dry creekbed at the northern end of the Mesquite Springs campground, where a kindly quirk of geography kept the neighboring RVs out of sight behind a rocky rise. As a consequence, he had trouble finding the campsite until he spotted the sand-colored gables of the Big Tent—a free-form communal space Ned had built with bamboo poles and tarps from the nursery.

Breakfast was a success. Scotty's eggs Benedict were a triumph, and Michael's *garni* received a polite round of applause. When the table had been cleared, Douglas and Paul began heating water for dishwashing, while Roger and Gary repaired to their corner to divide the mushrooms into seven equal portions. After each had downed his share, Ned proposed a hike into the Last Chance Mountains. "I have something to show you," he told Michael in private. "Something special."

Scotty stayed behind to fix lunch while everybody else followed Ned into the hills, stopping sporadically to exclaim over a flowering cactus or an exotic rock formation. (Douglas was positive he had seen hieroglyphics at one point, but his unimaginative lover assured him it was "just the mushrooms.")

They came to a windy plateau scattered with smooth black rocks that had split into geometric shapes. At the edge of the plateau, a six-foot stone obelisk rose—a man-made structure which struck Michael as considerably less precise than the landscape it inhabited.

Douglas stood and stared at the stack of rocks. "It's very Carlos Castaneda," he murmured.

"It's very phallic," said Gary.

"Well, don't just stand there." Ned grinned. "Worship it."

"Nah," said Gary, shaking his head. "It isn't big enough."

Their laughter must have traveled for miles. Ned began walking again, leading the way.

Michael caught up with him. "Was that it?"

"What?"

"The thing you wanted to show me?"

Ned shook his head with a cryptic smile.

They had yet another slope to climb, this one with a staggering view of the valley. Reddish stones arranged along the crest seemed to be fragments of a giant circle. "It used to be a peace symbol," Ned explained. "Remember those?"

As they scurried down the slope, Michael said: "That wasn't it, I guess?"

"Nope," answered Ned.

The terrain leveled out again, and they proceeded uncomfortably close to a crumbly precipice. The mushrooms were singing noisily in Michael's head, intensifying the experience. And distances were confusing in a land where the tiniest pebble resembled the mightiest mountain.

Suddenly, Ned sprinted ahead of the group, stopping near the edge of the drop-off. Michael was the first to catch up with him. "What the hell are you doing?"

"Look!" His partner laughed. He was crouching now, pointing to the valley floor beneath them where five brightly coloured tents squatted like hotels on a Monopoly board. Behind them, shiny as a Dinky toy, was Ned's red pickup. They had circled back to the ridge above the campsite.

"Well?" asked Ned.

Michael peered down at the tiny tribal settlement and smiled. He didn't need to ask if this was Ned's surprise; he *knew* what Ned was saying: Look at us down there! Aren't we magnificent? Haven't we accomplished something? See what we mean to each other? It was a grand gesture on Michael's behalf, and he was deeply touched.

Ned cupped his hand and shouted hello to a Lilliputian figure standing by the campfire. It was Scotty, no doubt, already making preparations for lunch. He searched for the source of Ned's voice, then waved extravagantly. Ned and Michael both waved back.

After lunch, the group became fragmented again. Some with-

48

drew for siestas and sex; others enjoyed the gentle downdrift of the mushrooms by wandering alone in the desert. Michael remained behind in the Big Tent, a solitary sultan engrossed in the silence. By nightfall, it seemed he had lived there forever.

He rose and walked toward the hills, following the pale ribbon of the creekbed through the mesquite trees. It was much cooler now, and fresh young stars had begun to appear in the deep purple sky. After a while he sat down next to a cactus that was actually casting a shadow in the moonlight. A breeze caressed him.

Time passed.

He got up and headed back to camp, almost mesmerized by the amber luminescence of the Big Tent, the faint heartlike pulse of its walls, the gentle laughter from within. As he was about to enter, one of the canvas tarps trapped the rising wind like a spinnaker on a galleon, then ripped free from its restraints. Several people groaned in unison.

"Can I help?" he hollered.

"Michael?" It was Roger's voice.

"Yeah. Want me to make repairs?"

"Fabulous. It's over here. This back part just flapped open again."

"Where?" His hands fumbled in the shadows until he found the hole. "Here?"

"Bingo," said Gary.

Bringing the errant canvas under control, he laced the twine through the eyelets and pulled it tight. Then he made his way back to the front of the tent and lifted the flap.

They had dispensed with the Coleman lantern, having learned the night before that it didn't have a dimmer switch. Paul's inspired alternative was a heavy-duty flashlight in a brown paper bag which was presently casting a golden Rembrandt glow on the six men sprawled across the Oriental rug Gary had received from his wife in their divorce settlement.

Gary sat against the ice chest, Roger's head resting in his lap. Douglas and Paul, the other pair of lovers, were idly rummaging through a pile of cassette tapes in the far corner of the tent. Ned was giving the hardworking Scotty a foot massage with Vaseline Intensive Care Lotion.

It was a charming tableau, sweet-spirited and oddly old-fashioned, like a turn-of-the-century photograph of a college football team, shoulder to shoulder, hand to thigh, lost in the first blush of male bonding.

"Thanks," said Gary, as Michael entered.

"No sweat," he answered.

Ned looked up from his labors on Scotty's feet. "You got some sun, bubba."

"Did I?" He pressed a finger to his biceps. "I think it's the lighting."

"No," Gary assured him. "It looks real good."

"Thanks." He entered and stretched out on the empty spot next to Ned and Scotty.

Scotty grinned at him blissfully. "There's some trail mix and cheese, if you're still hungry."

"No way," he replied.

After a brief exchange of eye signals, Roger and Gary rose, dusting off the seats of their pants. "Well, guys," said Roger, "it's been a long day . . ."

"Uh-oh," piped Scotty. "We just lost the newlyweds."

Roger's embarrassment was heartrending. With a sudden stab of pain, Michael remembered the early days when he and Jon had been equally awkward about this maneuver. "Give 'em a break," said Ned, laughing. "They don't have a tent. They have to have privacy *some*time."

"And they've been working like Trojans," added Douglas.

The departing Gary shot a look of amiable menace in Douglas's direction. "I'll get you for that."

"For what?" asked Scotty, after the lovers had left.

Douglas smiled. "Gary brought rubbers."

Three people said *"What?"* at the same time.

Douglas shrugged. "They don't call it a crisis for nothin'."

"Well, I know, but . . ." Scotty was almost sputtering. "Forget that. I'm willing to do my bit . . . but *c'mon.*"

Ned unleashed one of his mysterious grins. "I think they're kinda fun myself."

"Why?" asked Douglas. "Because they make you think of straight boys?"

"Marines," said Paul, embellishing on his lover's theme.

"I don't fantasize about straight men," Ned said flatly. "I've never sucked a cock that wasn't gay."

"So what's so great about them?" asked Scotty, his left foot still nestled in Ned's hands.

"Cocks?" asked Ned.

"Rubbers," grinned Scotty.

"Well . . ." Ned's nut-brown brow furrowed. "They're sorta like underwear."

"Calvin Klein Condoms," said Paul.

Everyone laughed.

"Why are they like underwear?" asked Scotty.

"Well . . . didn't you ever ask a guy to put his Jockey shorts back on just because it looked hot?"

"Yeah, sure, but . . ."

"And all there was between you and that incredible cock was this thin little piece of white cotton. So . . . that's kinda what rubbers are like. They get in the way, keep you from having everything at once. That can be the hottest thing of all."

Scotty rolled his eyes. "They are *balloons*, Ned. Face it. They will always be balloons. They are ridiculous things, and they are meant for *breeders*."

More laughter.

"I remember," offered Douglas, "when the rubber machine always said 'For Prevention of Disease Only.'"

Paul looked at his lover. "They still do, dummy."

"But they always scratched out the 'Disease' part and wrote in 'Babies.' Now straight people don't even use them anymore."

"Yes they do."

"No they don't. They use the pill, or they get vasectomies or something."

While Douglas and Paul continued with this halfhearted quarrel, Michael signaled Ned, to indicate he was leaving. He slipped under the flap and made a beeline for his tent, avoiding even the slightest glance at the rise where Roger and Gary were encamped. He was almost there when a voice called out to him.

"Is that you, Michael?" It was Gary.

"Uh-huh."

"Come on over," said Roger.

He picked his way through the darkness until he found the path leading up to the rise. Only the moon lit the faces of the lovers, snuggled together under a zipped-open sleeping bag. "See"—grinned Roger—"we didn't run off to fuck."

"It must be the mushrooms," said Gary. "We've been telling ghost stories. It's really nice up here. Why don't you get your sleeping bag and join us?"

He looked back at the dark dome of his two-man tent, sitting empty under the stars. "I think I'll take you up on that," he said.

They fell asleep, the three of them, after Gary had told the one about the man with the hook.

Michael dreamed he was once again on the ridge above the campsite, only this time it was Jon who knelt beside him. "Look," Jon whispered, "look who's down there." Mona emerged from one of the tents, so tiny she was almost unrecognizable. Michael waved and waved, but she never saw him, never stopped once as she walked into the desert and disappeared.

Mona Revisited

Seattle had once struck Mona as an ideal retirement spot for old hippies. Its weather was moderate, if wet, its political climate was libertarian, and a surprisingly large number of its citizens still looked upon macrame with a kindly eye. In the time it had taken Jane Fonda to get around to exhibiting her body again, almost nothing had changed in Seattle.

Almost nothing. The lesbians who had baked nine-grain bread in the sixties and seventies now earned their livings at copy centers across the city. Mona was one of those lesbians, though she was every bit as puzzled as the next woman by this bizarre reshuffling of career goals. "Maybe," she told a friend once, in a moment of rare playfulness, "it's to prove we can reproduce without the intervention of a man."

Mona lived on Queen Anne Hill in a seven-story brick apartment house the color of dried blood. She worked four blocks away at the Kwik-Kopy copy center, a high-technocracy in varying shades of gray. Neither place did very much for her soul but when was the last time she had worried about *that*?

"Cheer up, Mo. It can't be as bad as that." It was Serra, her co-worker at the neighboring copier. Serra, the perky young punk.

"Oh, yeah?"

Serra looked down at the huge manuscript she was collating. "It can't be as bad as this."

"What is it?" she asked.

"'A Time for Wimmin,'" answered Serra.

She made a face. "How is it spelled?"

"How do you think?" said Serra. "Maybe we should call the *Guinness Book*. If my hunch is right, this could be the longest dyke potboiler in the history of the world."

"Any sex?"

"Not so far," said Serra, "but a helluva lot of nurturing."

"Yawn."

"Really," said Serra. "What have you got there?"

"Much worse," she replied. "That queen from the Ritz Café is having a thirtieth-birthday party."

"An invitation?"

"A Xerox collage, no less. Featuring a lovely photo of his dick and some old stills from *I Love Lucy*. He's made me do it over twice."

"Of course," said Serra.

53

"The dick is too orange and Lucy's hair is too green. Or maybe it's the other way around. Who gives a shit, huh? Is this art or what?"

Serra laughed, but her face registered concern. "You need a day off, Mo."

She looked down at her work again. "I need a lobotomy."

"No, Mo. I mean it." Serra left her machine and moved to Mona's side. "You're pushing too hard. Ease up on yourself. Holly can spare you for a day or two."

"Maybe so," she retorted. "But Dr. Sheldon can't."

"Who?"

"Dr. Barry R. Sheldon," she explained. "A periodontist on Capitol Hill who's on the verge of repossessing my gums." She offered Serra a helpless smile. "As we speak, young lady."

Serra's sympathy seemed mixed with embarrassment. "Oh . . . well, if you need a loan or something . . ."

"That's nice." She squeezed Serra's hand. "It's a little more serious than that."

"Oh."

"I could use a little more overtime, as a matter of fact."

"I just thought . . . I thought you could use a change."

"You got that right," said Mona. "Your machine is jamming."

"Shit," muttered Serra, sprinting back to her post.

When noon came, Serra insisted on treating Mona to lunch at the Ritz Café, a perfect backdrop for Serra's squeaky-clean Kristy McNichol bob. They both ordered Pernod Stingers, and Serra raised hers in an earnest toast to Mona's recovery.

"Things will get better," she said flatly. "I really believe that."

"That's because you're twenty-three," Mona replied.

"Are things so different at thirty-seven?"

"Thirty-eight," said Mona. "And they're not a bit different. Just harder to take."

"I don't know about that," said Serra.

Mona made a face at her. "Tell me that again in fifteen years. It's OK to Xerox dicks when you're twenty-three. It's not OK at thirty-eight. Trust me. I wouldn't lie to you."

54

For a moment, Serra seemed lost in thought.

"What is it?" asked Mona.

"Nothing. Nothing yet."

"Now wait a minute . . ."

"It's just an idea."

"C'mon," said Mona. "Out with it."

"I can't. Not until I see if it's possible." She took a sip of her drink, then set it down suddenly. "Oh, God!"

"*What?*" asked Mona.

"Guess who our waiter is?"

The waiter recognized Mona instantly. "Oh, hi! The invitations look fabulous!"

She gave him a thin smile. "I'm glad you like them."

After lunch, they received a rush order for five hundred fliers announcing a "British Brunch" in honor of the *Britannia*'s recent arrival in Seattle. Mona glowered at the layout—Queen Elizabeth saying, "I just love a good banger"—then looked up and glowered at the customer.

"Would somebody please tell me why every homo in Seattle is so obsessed with this woman?"

The customer drew back as if he'd been slapped. "What arc you? The editorial board?"

She glanced impatiently at the clock. "I suppose you want this today?"

The man let his irritation show. She really didn't blame him; she had always been detached enough to know when she was being a bitch. "Look," he said, "tomorrow will be just fine. And I've had a bad day too . . . so slack off, will you?"

"Maybe I can help?" It was Serra, intervening as sweetly as possible.

Mona felt herself reddening. "It's no problem. I'll just fill out the . . ."

"Go home, Mo." Serra squeezed her forearm gently. "I can manage."

"Are you sure?" She felt like a real ogre.

"You deserve it," said Serra. "Go on. Scoot."

So Mona got the hell out, stopping briefly on the way home to write a bad check for tuna fish and detergent at the S & M Market. Once upon a time—three years ago, to be exact—she had gotten a big laugh out of the S & M Market. She had promised herself she would take Mouse there if he ever came to Seattle.

But Mouse had never come, and the irony inherent in the name of her corner grocery had faded like her California tan. They had drifted apart gradually, and she wasn't sure whose fault that was. Now the thought of a reunion was embarrassing at best, terrifying at worst.

Still, she couldn't help wondering if Mouse was doing OK, if he had found someone to hug him occasionally, if he would still call her Babycakes the next time they met. She had thought of phoning him three or four times, while on Percodan from her periodontist, but she didn't want his sympathy for her dud of a life.

When she reached her apartment, her neighbor Mrs. Guttenberg accosted her in the lobby. "Oh, thank God, Mona! Thank God!" The old lady was a wreck.

"What is it?" asked Mona.

"It's old Pete, poor thing. He's in the alley out back."

"You mean he's . . . ?"

"Some fool kid ran over him. I couldn't find a soul to help me, Mona. I've got a blanket over him, but I don't think . . . The poor old thing . . . he never deserved this."

Mona rushed into the alley, where the dog lay immobile in a light drizzle. Only his head stuck out from under the blanket. A rheumy eye looked up at Mona and blinked. She knelt and laid her hand carefully against his graying muzzle. He made a faint noise in the back of his throat.

She looked up at Mrs. Guttenberg. "He doesn't belong to anyone, does he?"

The old lady shook her head, fingertips pressed to her throat. "All of us feed him. He's lived here for ten years at least . . . twelve. Mona . . . he's got to be put out of his misery."

Mona nodded.

"Could you drive him to the SPCA? It's just a few blocks."

"I don't have a car, Mrs. Guttenberg."

"You could push him."

Mona stood up. "Push him?"

"In the shopping cart I take to the S & M."

So that was what they did. Using the blanket to hoist him, Mona laid Pete in Mrs. Guttenberg's shopping cart and pushed him six blocks to the SPCA. An attendant there told her there was no hope for the dog. "It won't take long," he said. "Do you want to take him back with you?"

Mona shook her head. "He isn't mine. I don't know where I'd . . . no . . . no, thank you."

"There's a surrender fee of ten dollars."

A surrender fee. Of all the things they could have called it.

"Fine," she said, feeling the tears start to rise.

Five minutes later, when the deed was done, she wrote another bad check and pushed the empty cart home in the rain. Mrs. Guttenberg met her at the door, babbling her gratitude as she fumbled in her change purse for "something for your trouble."

"That's OK," she said, trudging toward the elevator.

During her slow, clanking ascent, she thought suddenly of the maxim Mouse had called Mona's Law: *You can have a hot lover, a hot job and a hot apartment, but you can't have all three at the same time.*

She and Mouse had laughed about this a lot, never dreaming that one day, two out of three would be regarded as something akin to a miracle.

The lover part didn't bother her much anymore. By living alone she could maintain certain illusions about people that helped her to like them more—sometimes even to love them more. Or was that just her rationale for being such a crummy roommate?

The apartment part went straight to the pit of her stomach when she reached the fourth floor and opened the door of the drab little chamber she had learned to call home. There was something profoundly tragic—no, not tragic, just pathetic—about a thirty-eight-year-old woman who still built bookshelves out of bricks and planks.

She was on the verge of reevaluating the job part, when the telephone rang.

"Yeah?"

"May I speak to Mona Ramsey, please?" It was a woman's voice, unrecognizable.

"Uh . . . I'm not sure she's here. Who's calling, please?"

"Dr. Sheldon's bookkeeper."

Mona tried to sound breezy. "I see. May I take your number?"

"She's not there, then?"

"'Fraid not." Less breeze this time, more authority. This bill hound wasn't giving up without a fight.

"I tried to reach her at her place of business, and they said she had gone home sick today. This *is* her residence, isn't it?"

"Well, yes, but . . . Miss Ramsey has left for a while."

"I thought she was sick."

"No," Mona answered. "In mourning."

"Oh . . ."

"Her best friend died this afternoon." That sounded a little too conventional, so she added: "He was executed."

"My God."

"She took it kinda hard," she said, getting into it. "She was a witness."

This was almost overkill, but it worked like a charm. The caller audibly gulped for air. "Well . . . I guess . . . I'll call her when . . . Just say I called, will you?"

"Sure will," said Mona. "Have a nice day."

She set the receiver down delicately, then yanked the phone jack out of the wall. If periodontists had any link with organized crime, she was in deep, deep, trouble.

She made herself a cup of Red Zinger tea and withdrew to the bedroom, where she searched the mirror for even the tiniest clue to her identity. In an effort to be charitable, Serra had once told her that she looked "a lot like Tuesday Weld." Mona had replied: "I look a lot like Tuesday Weld on a Friday." Today, the wisecrack was all too applicable.

Her "character lines" made her begin to wonder if there was such a thing as too much character. What's more, the frizzy red hair had stopped looking anarchistic years ago. (Even Streisand had finally abandoned the rusty-Brillo-pad look.) Was it time to relent, to throw in the towel and become a lipstick lesbian?

Some of the most political dykes in town had already converted, tossing out their Levi's and Birkenstocks in favor of poodle skirts and heels. It was no longer a question of butch vs. femme, liberation vs. oppression. Clothes did not unmake the woman; clothes were just clothes.

The prospect of a total makeover was strangely thrilling, but she needed a second opinion. She went straight to the phone, plugged it back in, and dialed Mouse's home number, suddenly delighted to have such an off-the-wall excuse to break the silence between them. But Mouse wasn't at home.

Where was he, then? The nursery? Another call produced the same result. It was Saturday, for God's sake! Why would the nursery be closed on a Saturday? What the hell was going on?

The door buzzer squawked at her from the other room. She got up and went to the ancient, paint-encrusted intercom. "Yeah?"

"Is this Mona Ramsey?"

A moment's hesitation. "Who wants to know?"

"A friend of Serra Fox. She said I might find you here. I tried ringing you from . . ."

"Just a minute." Mona dashed to the window and peeped down at an elegantly dressed brunette waiting in the entrance alcove. She certainly *looked* like a friend of Serra's. The lipstick lesbians were everywhere.

Mona addressed the intercom again. "This isn't about money, is it?"

The woman tittered discreetly. "Not in the way you might

think. I shan't take a great deal of your time, Miss Ramsey." She spoke with an English accent.

Mona counted to ten and buzzed her up.

Private Collection

Brian was surprised to find himself thinking of Mona Ramsey when he and Mary Ann arrived at Theresa Cross's auction in Hillsborough. During the course of their half-assed little affair in 1977, he and Mona had shared a passion for three things: the movies *Harold and Maude* and *King of Hearts*, and Bix Cross's *Denim Gradations* album.

Mona's favorite song from that album had been "Quick on My Feet." Brian had found "Turn Away" more to his taste, and here, gleaming at his fingertips, was the platinum record heralding its success.

"Look at *this*," whispered Mary Ann, as they moved along the trophy-laden tables in the late rock star's screening room. "She's even raided the liquor cabinet." She lifted a half-empty bottle of Southern Comfort.

Brian read the tag on it. "Yeah, but he drank out of that with Janis Joplin."

"Big deal," murmured his wife. "Who cares?"

Was she spoiling for a fight? He cared a great deal, and she knew it. "It's history," he said at last. "For *some* people, anyway."

She made a little grunting noise and kept moving. "How about this?" she asked, indicating a broken toaster. "Is this history?"

The playful look in her eyes kept him from getting angry. "You'd sure as hell think so if this were Karen Carpenter's estate sale."

Her eyes became hooded. "That was *low*, Brian."

He chuckled, pleased with himself.

"And I wasn't *that* big a fan."

He shrugged. "You bought her albums."

60

She groaned as she examined a box of plastic forks. "I bought *an* album, Brian. Stop being so hipper-than-thou."

The debate was cut short by the arrival of their hostess. She swept into the room wearing a black angora sweater over black Spandex slacks. Mary Ann nudged Brian. "Mourning garb," she whispered.

"Hi, people!" The rock widow strode toward them.

"Hi," echoed Mary Ann, practically chirping. For all her private bad-mouthing, his wife was intimidated by Theresa Cross. Brian could always tell that by the tone of her voice, and it always brought him closer to her.

"Is your crew here yet?" asked Theresa.

"Any minute," Mary Ann assured her. "They must have had a little trouble finding the . . ."

"Did you see the Harley?" Now the rock widow was talking to him, having dispensed with media matters.

"Sure did," he replied.

"Isn't it the *best?*"

Mary Ann's cameraman appeared in the doorway. "There he is," she said.

"Fabulous," exclaimed Theresa. "It won't take long, I hope. *Twenty/Twenty* is coming at noon."

"Half an hour," Mary Ann replied. "At the very most. I just need to talk to him about the stuff I want." She turned to Brian. "Will you be all right for a while?"

"I'll take care of him," said Theresa.

"Great," said Mary Ann, backing off.

Theresa turned to him. "C'mon. I'll give you the grand tour."

She led him out of the screening room through padded gray flannel corridors trimmed in chrome. "Were you a big fan of my husband's?"

"The biggest," he answered.

She shot a wicked glance in his direction. "I hope that's not false advertising."

By the time he had figured out her meaning, she had brought him to a halt in front of double doors, also flannel-covered. "I'll show you something you won't see on *Twenty/Twenty*." She flung open the doors to reveal an Olympic-size bedroom lined with lighted Lucite boxes. Showcased in the boxes were dozens of pickaninny dolls—"coon art" from the thirties and forties. Cookie jars shaped like black mammies, Uncle Tom ashtrays, Aunt Jemima posters.

"This is amazing," he said.

The rock widow shrugged it off. "Bix was always just a little bit sorry he wasn't born black. That's not what I wanted to show you, though." She moved to a huge chest of drawers near the bed. "*This* is." With a flourish, she yanked open one of the drawers.

He was dumbfounded. "Uh . . . underwear?"

"*Panties*, silly."

He shifted uneasily. What the fuck was he supposed to say?

"From his *fans*," explained Theresa, removing one of them from a labeled Baggie. "This one, for instance, is from the Avalon Ballroom, nineteen sixty-seven."

His laughter was nervous and sounded that way. "You mean they threw these on stage?"

She winked at him. "You're a quick one."

"And he saved them?"

"Every goddamn one!" She ran a crimson nail across the panties, like a secretary explaining her filing system. "We've got your Be-In panties from Golden Gate Park. Remember that? George Harrison was there. An-n-nd . . . your basic Fillmore panties, nineteen sixty-six. That was a good year, wasn't it?"

He laughed, liking her for the first time. At least, she had a sense of humor. "These ought to be in the auction," he grinned.

"No way, José. These are *mine*."

"You mean . . . ?"

"You better believe it! I wear every goddamn one of them!"

This time he roared.

"I look pretty fucking wonderful in them too!"

He had already pictured as much.

"C'mon," she said. "You're starting to sweat. Let's get you back to the wife."

The Return of
Connie Bradshaw

Two days later, Mary Ann found herself on Union Square, shooting a promo for Save the Cable Cars. Since the cable cars were out of commission during their renovation, she was using the one that sat on blocks beside the Hyatt, a melancholy relic whose embarrassment she could almost sense, like the head of a moose on a barroom wall.

She delivered her spiel in a very tight shot, while dangling recklessly from the side of the stationary car. To add to her humiliation, a small crowd gathered to witness the ordeal, applauding her good takes and laughing at the fluffs.

When she was done, a pregnant woman stepped forward. Her condition, though easily discernible to the average idiot, was confirmed by a yellow maternity smock bearing the word BABY and an arrow indicating the direction the baby would have to go in order to get out.

"Mary Ann?"

"Connie?"

Connie Bradshaw squealed the way she always squealed, the way she had squealed fifteen years before in Cleveland, when she had been head majorette at Central High and Mary Ann had been a mildly celebrated member of the National Forensic League. Some things never change, it seemed, including Connie's inability to make it through life without things written on her clothes.

A clumsy embrace followed. Then Connie stood back and looked her former roommate up and down. "You are such a *star*!" she beamed.

"Not really," said Mary Ann, meaning it more than she wanted to.

"I saw you with the Queen! If that's not a star what is?"

Mary Ann laughed feebly, then pointed to the arrow on Connie's belly. "When did this happen?"

Connie pushed a tiny button, consulting her digital watch. "Uh . . . seven months and . . . twenty-four days ago. Give or take a few." She giggled at the thought of it. "Her name is Shawna, by the way."

"You already know it's a girl?"

Connie giggled again. "You know me. I hate suspense. If there's a chance to peek, I'll do it." She laid her hands lightly on the Shawna-to-be. "Pretty neat, huh?"

"Pretty neat." Mary Ann nodded, wondering when she had last used the phrase. "God, it's so easy to lose track of things. I didn't even know you were married."

"I'm not," came the breezy reply.

"Oh."

"See?" Connie held up ten ringless fingers. "Magic."

For the first time in fifteen years, Mary Ann felt slightly more middle-class than Connie.

"I got tired of waiting around," Connie explained. "I mean . . . hey, I'm almost thirty-three. What good is a bun in the oven, if the oven is broken? You know what I mean?"

"Mmm," answered Mary Ann.

"I mean . . . Jees . . . I want a baby a lot more than I want a husband, so I said to hell with it and stopped taking the pill. You can have a husband any ol' time. There's a time limit on babies." She paused and studied Mary Ann with a look of earnest concern. "Am I freaking you out, hon?"

Mary Ann laughed as jauntily as possible. "Are you kidding?"

"Good. Anyway, the father is either Phil, this software executive who took me to the Us Festival last year, or Darryl, this really super accountant from Fresno." She shrugged, having made her point. "I mean . . . it's not like they weren't both great guys."

In some ways, it made a lot of sense. Leave it to Connie to name the baby before she had named the father. "You look just great," Mary Ann said. "It really becomes you."

"Thanks." Connie beamed. "You and Brian got married, didn't you?"

The question came out of left field, but Mary Ann wasn't really surprised. According to Brian, he and Connie had slept together once back in '76. Later that year he had brought her to Mrs. Madrigal's Christmas party. Nothing had ever come of it. To hear Brian tell it, the interlude had meant a lot more to Connie than it had to him.

Mary Ann nodded. "Two years ago this summer."

"That's great," said Connie. "He's a neat guy."

"Thanks. I think so too."

"But no babies, huh?"

Mary Ann shook her head. "Not yet."

"Your career, huh?"

In a matter of seconds, Mary Ann weighed her options. It was time to talk about this to *someone*, and Connie suddenly struck her as a logical candidate. She was decent, practical and completely detached from the tight little family unit at 28 Barbary Lane.

"We need to catch up," said Mary Ann. "Why don't I buy you a cup of coffee?"

"Super!"

So they walked across the square to Neiman-Marcus, where Connie elaborated on the joys of impending motherhood. "It's like . . . it's like this friend you've never met. I know it sounds dumb, but sometimes I just sit and talk to Shawna when I'm home alone. And you know . . . sometimes she even thumps back."

Mary Ann set her cup down. "That doesn't sound dumb at all."

"I don't know why it took me so long to do it," said Connie. "It's the best thing that ever happened to me. I kid you not."

"Are you on maternity leave or what?"

Connie looked puzzled.

"Aren't you still with United?" asked Mary Ann.

"Oh." Connie let out a little laugh. "You *are* behind the times, hon. I quit that five or six years ago. The glamour was gone, if you know what I mean."

Mary Ann nodded.

"In my day, we were *stews*," Connie continued. "Now they have flight attendants. It's just not the same thing."

"Yeah. I guess that's true."

"I saved some money, though, so I have my own little house in West Portal. I manage a card shop there. You should come by sometime. I'll give you a press discount or something." She smiled wanly at Mary Ann, suspecting that it would never happen. "You must be superbusy, though."

"I'd love to come," said Mary Ann.

"There might even be a story in it. It's a cute place."

"Mmm."

Connie reached across the table and took Mary Ann's hand. It was a sisterly gesture, reminiscent of the days when Mary Ann had camped out on Connie's sofa in the Marina, crying her eyes out over rotten times at Dance Your Ass Off. Connie had been her only refuge, a benevolent link between Cleveland and her family at Barbary Lane.

"What's the matter, hon?"

Mary Ann hesitated, then said: "I wish I knew."

"About what?"

"Well . . . Brian wants a baby very much."

Connie nodded. "And you don't, huh?"

"No. I want one. Maybe not as much as Brian does . . . but I want one."

"And?"

"Well . . . I stopped taking the pill eight months ago."

Connie's mouth opened slightly.

"Nothing's happened, Connie. Zilch."

Connie cocked her head, showing sympathy. "And Brian is freaked, huh?"

"No. He doesn't know about it. I haven't told him."

Connie screwed up her face in thought. "I don't get it. You didn't tell him when you went off the pill?"

"I wanted it to be a *surprise*, Connie. Like in the movies. I wanted to see the look on his face when I told him I was pregnant."

"Like in the old days," said Connie. "That's sweet."

"Now I have to see the look on his face when I tell him I'm not."

66

"Bummer," said Connie.

"The thing is . . . it means so *much* to him." She chose her words carefully. "I think he's proud of me and my career—I *know* he is—but his self-respect has suffered a lot. He sees himself as the waiter who's married to the TV star. I mean, he's warm and kind and loving . . . and incredibly sexy, and that's always been enough for me . . ."

"But not for him," Connie added.

"Apparently not. This baby is a major obsession. I guess it's . . . something *he* could do, you know? A mark he could leave on the world. His own flesh and blood."

Her confidante nodded.

"Only it *can't* be, Connie. It can never be."

"You mean . . . ?"

Mary Ann nodded. "I've seen a doctor. It isn't me."

"And you're sure he's the one who's . . ."

"Positive."

Connie's brow furrowed. "But if they haven't tested his sperm yet . . ."

"Connie . . . they have."

"What?"

"They tested it at St. Sebastian's about a month ago. His sperm count is practically nonexistent. It just won't cut it."

"Wait a minute. I thought you said you hadn't told him."

She might have known it would come to this. "I did, Connie. But it's possible to have his sperm tested without . . . Oh, c'mon, Connie . . . think about it."

Connie thought about it, then said: "Jees. That must've been a bitch."

Mary Ann looked at her nails, saying nothing.

"How on earth did you . . . ?"

"Connie, please . . . don't ask, OK?" The last thing she needed was to rehash the horrors of that trying day: the mad dash to the bathroom, where she'd hidden the jar, the feeble excuse she'd made to get out of the house before breakfast, the Chinese funeral that almost kept her from making it on time . . .

67

"He isn't wearing Jockey shorts, is he?"

"What?"

"I read that in 'Dear Abby.' Sometimes they can cause sterility."

"No . . . it isn't that." She wondered momentarily if Brian had worn Jockey shorts when Connie had slept with him.

They both fell silent for a moment. Mary Ann knew what Connie was thinking, so she beat her to the punch. "Time to face the music, huh?"

Connie looked up from her cup with a game little smile. "Seems that way to me, hon."

Mary Ann suddenly felt silly. "I should have told him weeks ago. I just thought there might be some way I could spare him the . . . hell, I don't know. If I tell him what I did . . . you know . . . with the sperm and all . . ."

"Don't tell him that."

"But I can't make him go through it again. He'll insist on that, I'm sure."

"You could tell him *you're* sterile."

Mary Ann rejected the idea with a frown. That would jeopardize their relationship even more than the current bag of worms. It was better to stick with the whole truth . . . or wait for a miracle.

When she arrived home that night, she found Brian in the house on the roof, watching *Three's Company* in his KAFKA baseball cap. She had hated that stupid cap ever since Brian had read about it on a matchbook cover and mailed away for it, but tonight was hardly the time to tell him so.

"I brought us some Eye of the Swan," she said, holding up the bottle.

He peered at her over the back of the sofa. "Oh . . . hi. Great. What's the occasion?"

"No occasion."

"Fair enough."

She moved to the window. "The rain has stopped. See? There's even some blue over there. Shit!"

"What?"

"I forgot to bring glasses."

"No sweat."

"I'll run down and . . ."

"Mary Ann . . ." He caught her free hand. "Just relax, OK? We're fine. We can pass the bottle."

"It won't take a minute . . ."

"No one's watching, Mary Ann. This isn't a segment on *Bay Window*."

Thank God for small favors, she thought.

He tugged her back to the sofa. She set the bottle down and settled in with him, giving him a long kiss. Then she pulled back and looked into his long-lashed hazel eyes. "Do you realize how lucky we are?"

He regarded her for a moment, then said: "I do."

She picked up the bottle, took a swig from it, and handed it to him. He took a similar swig and gave the bottle back to her. "Why are we counting our blessings?" he asked.

She placed the bottle on the floor beneath their feet. "What do you mean?"

"I don't know . . . you always talk about how lucky we are right before you drop one of your bombs."

"No I don't."

"OK, you don't." He gave her his I'm-not-looking-for-a-fight smile.

"I just . . . well, as a matter of fact, I did want to talk to you about something."

He folded his arms across his chest. "Great. Shoot."

"Well, I thought it would be nice if we hyphenated our names."

"Huh?"

"You know . . . if I became Mary Ann Singleton-Hawkins."

Brian studied her. "Is this a gag?"

"No. I told you before I *feel* like Mrs. Hawkins. Keeping my own name was never a big deal."

"It was to the station," said Brian.

"OK. So if I become Mary Ann Singleton-Hawkins, they'll still

69

have their precious name recognition factor and . . . you know . . . it'll be more like I'm married."

He sat there slack–mouthed.

"Besides," she added, "I think the name's really pretty. It's distinctive."

Brian frowned. "Making me . . . what?"

"What do you mean?"

"I mean . . . what do I tell the guys at work? That I've just become Brian Singleton-Hawkins?"

That stopped her cold. "Oh . . . well . . . yeah, I see what you mean."

"What in the world are you . . . ?"

"Forget it, Brian. I didn't think it out. It was a stupid idea." She smiled sheepishly. "Gimme that bottle, handsome."

He did so. She took another swig. He reached out and touched the side of her head. "You know the name business doesn't bother me. I told you that a long time ago."

"I know."

He laid his arm across her shoulder. "Christ, I'm a modern sonofabitch."

The phone rang downstairs.

"I'd better get that," she said, grateful for the reprieve. She clattered down the narrow wooden stairway and caught the call after the fourth ring, gasping "Hello."

"Miss Singleton?"

"Yes."

"Simon Bardill here."

"Simon! How are you? Is everything going OK?"

"By and large. I'm in a bit of a scrape as far as accommodations are concerned."

"Oh . . ."

"Do you think I might solicit your advice at some point? At your convenience, of course."

"Of course! Hold on a sec, OK?"

She dashed back upstairs and confronted Brian. "It's that Englishman from the *Britannia*. I thought I might invite him to dinner tomorrow night . . . if you'd like to meet him, that is."

Brian's hesitation was almost imperceptible. "Fine," he said.

Simon's Proposition

He had already pictured the Englishman as a sort of latter-day Laurence Harvey, a spoiled aristocrat with pretentious airs and esoteric tastes. He couldn't have been more surprised when Simon Bardill ambled over to his record collection and perused the cover of *Denim Gradations*.

"A bloody shame," he said.

Brian was caught off guard. "What? Oh . . . his death, you mean?"

"Mmm. Free-basing, wasn't he?"

Brian shook his head. "Smack. According to the coroner."

"Ah."

"You . . . uh . . . you're a fan of Bix Cross?"

The lieutenant smiled dimly. "More of a freak than a fan. I played nothing else in my rooms at Cambridge." He held out the album so Brian could see it. "The lovely breasts belong to his wife, I understand."

Brian smiled back. "You understand correctly. I met the lady this weekend."

"Indeed?" If an arching eyebrow was any indication, the lieutenant was clearly impressed. "Katrina, isn't it? No, Camilla . . . something exotic."

"Theresa," Brian told him.

The lieutenant rolled the name across his tongue. "Theresa . . . Theresa." He turned and gave Brian a knowing, man-to-man look. "Is her face as delicious as the rest of her?"

"Better," said Brian. That was somewhat of an exaggeration, but he enjoyed being an expert on Theresa Cross.

The lieutenant breathed a sigh of relief. "Thank God!"

"Why?"

"Well, one doesn't enjoy seeing one's fantasies dashed on the rocks."

"Yeah." Brian nodded. "I guess that's true."

The lieutenant looked down at the album again. "I banged the bishop over *this* one more times than I care to count."

Brian didn't get it. "I think you'd better run that by me again."

The lieutenant chuckled. "You know." He made a jerking-off gesture with his fist.

Brian grinned. *"Banging the bishop?"*

"Right."

"Where did that come from?"

The lieutenant thought for a moment. "I haven't the foggiest."

They shared a brief laugh. The lieutenant returned the album to its place on the shelf. Brian decided to take advantage of the silence. "So," he said, "why aren't you in chains by now?"

The lieutenant seemed little disconcerted by his direct approach. "I think you've been reading too much Melville. The modern navy isn't nearly as stringent as you might think."

"Yeah, but . . . you jumped ship, didn't you?"

"More or less."

"Well, isn't that a court-martial offense?"

"Sometimes," answered the lieutenant. "It can vary, though, depending on the individual."

Brian looked him squarely in the eye. "You mean you have friends in high places?"

The lieutenant seemed tremendously uncomfortable. He was about to say something, when Mary Ann bounded into the room, letting him off the hook. "Well," she said, "I'm afraid she's not home yet." She glanced apologetically at their guest. "This is so disappointing. It's such wonderful stuff. She named it after the Queen Mother and everything."

The lieutenant looked puzzled.

Brian translated for him: "Our landlady names her pot plants after women she admires."

72

"I see."

Mary Ann turned to Brian. "I checked Michael's too. He isn't back from Death Valley yet. I could look for roaches in the ashtray in the car."

"Too late," he answered. "I did that last week. We'll just have to face your chicken straight."

She gave him an evil eye before addressing the lieutenant. "I can get you some wine."

"Lovely," he said.

Mary Ann disappeared into the kitchen. The lieutenant sidled to the window, turning his back to Brian. "That beacon must be Alcatraz," he said. He obviously had no intention of picking up where they'd left off.

"That's it," said Brian.

"They don't still keep prisoners, do they?"

"No. It's empty. Has been for a long time."

"I see. Lovely view from here."

"Yeah," said Brian. "It's not bad."

Mary Ann sailed into the room with the wine stuff on a tray. "Have you ever had Eye of the Swan?"

The lieutenant turned around. "No . . . I can't say that I have."

"It's a white Pinot noir. Very dry." She set the tray down on the coffee table, then knelt in front of it and began pouring.

"Glasses and everything," murmured Brian.

She handed him a glass, ignoring the remark.

"So," she chirped, giving the lieutenant a glass. "You've been having trouble finding a place to stay?"

"Not exactly," he replied. "I took a room at the Holiday Inn on Fisherman's Wharf."

Brian and Mary Ann groaned in unison.

The lieutenant chuckled. "Yes, it is, rather. I was hoping for something with a little more character. I don't fancy breaking that little paper seal every day."

"What seal?" asked Mary Ann.

"You know . . . on the toilet."

73

"Oh." She laughed a little nervously, Brian thought. "How long do you plan on staying?"

"Oh . . . about a month. I plan on returning to London several days after Easter."

Mary Ann frowned. "That makes renting a little difficult."

"Actually," said the lieutenant, "I was rather hoping for a swap."

"A swap?"

"My place in London in exchange for someone's place here. Could such a thing be arranged?"

Mary Ann was already deep in thought.

"It's a tatty little flat," added the lieutenant, "but it's in a colorful neighborhood and . . . well, it might be an adventure for someone."

Mary Ann looked at Brian with dancing eyes. "Are you thinking what I'm thinking?" she asked.

Settling Up

Ned's red pickup and its seven weary passengers had survived sandstorms in Furnace Creek, snowstorms in South Lake Tahoe, and a blowout near Drytown by the time their ten-hour trans-California odyssey had ended.

Michael climbed from the truckbed, hoisted his bedroll to his shoulder, and trudged up the stairway to Barbary Lane, stopping long enough on the landing to wave goodbye to his campmates.

Ned answered with a toot of the horn. "Go to bed," he yelled. Like a master mechanic who could diagnose an engine problem simply by listening, he knew that Michael's emotional resistance was down.

Michael gave him a thumbs-up sign and followed the eucalyptus trees into the dark city canyon of the lane. He whistled during this last leg of the journey, warding off demons he was still unable to name.

Back at the apartment, he dumped his gear on the bedroom floor and drew a hot bath. He soaked for half an hour, already feeling the loss of his brothers, the dissolution of that safe little enclave they had shared in the desert.

After the bath, he put on the blue flannel pajamas he had bought the week before in Chinatown, then sat down at his desk and began composing a letter to his parents.

The warming sound of Brian's laughter drifted through the window as a new moon peeked from behind the clouds. Then came another man's laughter, less hearty than Brian's but just as sincere. Michael set his pen down and listened to enough dialogue to determine that the visitor was British, then returned to the task at hand.

Boris, the neighborhood cat, slunk along the window ledge, cruising for attention. When he spotted Michael, he stopped in his tracks, shimmied under the sill and announced his arrival with a noise that sounded like a rusty hinge. Michael swung his chair away from the desk and prepared his lap for the inevitable. Boris kept his distance, though, rattling his tail like a saber as he loped about the room.

"OK," said Michael. "Be that way."

Boris creaked back at him.

"How old are you, anyway?"

Another creak.

"A hundred and forty-two? Not bad."

The tabby circled the room twice, then gazed up expectantly at the only human he could find.

"He's not here," said Michael. "There's nobody to spoil you rotten now."

Boris voiced his confusion.

"I know," said Michael, "but I'm fresh out of Tender Vittles. That wasn't my job, kiddo."

There were footsteps outside the door. Boris jerked his head, then shot out the window.

"Mouse?" It was Mary Ann.

"It's open," he said.

She slipped into the room, closing the door behind her. "I heard talking. I hope I didn't . . ."

"It was just Boris."

"Oh."

"I mean . . . I was talking to Boris."

She smiled. "Right."

"Sit down," he said.

She perched on the edge of the sofa. "We have this really delightful Englishman upstairs."

He nodded. "So I hear."

"Oh . . . we haven't been too . . . ?"

"No," he assured her. "It sounds nice."

"He's from the *Britannia*. He used to be a radio officer for the Queen."

"Used to be?"

"Well . . . it's a long story. The thing is . . . he needs a furnished apartment for a month, and he wants to swap with somebody from here. He's got a cute flat in Nottingham Gate . . . or something like that. Anyway, it's just sitting there waiting for somebody to come live in it."

"And?"

"Well . . . doesn't that sound perfect?"

"For me, you mean?"

"Sure! I'm sure Ned wouldn't mind if . . ."

"We're closed for a month," he said.

"So there you go! It *is* perfect. It's a ready-made vacation."

He said nothing, letting the idea sink in.

"Think of it, Mouse! England! God, I can hardly stand it."

"Yeah, but . . . it still takes money."

"For what? You can live as cheaply there as you can here."

"You're forgetting about air fare," he said.

Her shoulders drooped suddenly. "I thought you'd be *excited*."

She looked so crestfallen that he got up and went to the sofa, kissing the top of her head. "I appreciate the thought. I really do."

She looked up with a wan smile. "Can you join us for a glass of wine?"

"Thanks," he answered, tugging at the lapels of his pajamas. "I was just about to crash and burn."

She rose and headed for the door. "Was Death Valley fun?"

"It was . . . peaceful," he said.

"Good. I'm glad."

"Night-night," he said.

He made himself some hot milk, then went to bed, sleeping soundly until noon the next day. After finishing his letter to his parents, he drove to the Castro and ate a late breakfast at the communal table at Welcome Home. When the rain began to let up a little, he wandered through the neighborhood, feeling strangely like a tourist on Mars.

Across the street, a man emerged from the Hibernia Bank.

His heart caught in his throat.

The man seemed to hesitate, turning left and right, revealing enough of his profile to banish the flimsy illusion.

Blond hair and chinos and a blue button-down shirt. How long would he live before those things stopped meaning Jon?

He crossed the intersection and walked along Eighteenth Street. In the days before the epidemic, the house next door to the Jaguar Bookstore had been called the Check 'n Cruise. People had gone there to check their less-than-butch outer garments (not to mention their Gump's and Wilkes Bashford bags) prior to prowling the streets of the ghetto.

The Check 'n Cruise was gone now, and in its place had blossomed the Castro Country Club, a reading room and juice bar for men who wanted company without the alcohol and attitude of the bars. He sometimes repaired there after his stint at the AIDS switchboard.

Today, as he entered, an animated game of Scrabble was in progress. At the bar, two men in business suits were arguing about Joan Sutherland, while another couple rehashed the Forty-Niners' victory at the Super Bowl.

He found a seat away from the conversation and immersed

himself in the latest issue of the *Advocate*. An ad for a jewelry company caught his eye:

I'M SAFE—ARE YOU?

It was too much. He growled and threw the magazine on the floor, attracting the attention of the Forty-Niners fans. He gave them a sheepish grin and left without further explanation, heading straight for his car.

When he got back to Barbary Lane, sunlight was streaming into the courtyard for the first time in weeks. Wisps of steam, like so many friendly ghosts, hovered above the courtyard as he passed through the lych-gate. He stopped long enough to savor the sweet, wet, ferny smell tingling in his nostrils.

A figure rose from behind a low hedge, startling him.

"Oh . . . Mrs. Madrigal."

The landlady wiped her hands on her paisley smock. "Isn't it a grand day?"

"It's about time," said Michael.

"Now, now," she scolded. "We knew it was coming. It was just a question of when." She looked about her on the ground. "Have you seen my trowel, dear?"

He scanned the area, then shook his head. "What are you planting?"

"Baby tears," she answered. "Why aren't you going to London?"

"Hey." She had pounced without warning.

"Never mind. I guess I'm being selfish. Still . . . it would have given me *such* vicarious thrills." She fussed delicately with a strand of hair at her temple. "Oh, well. Can't be helped."

These days, Mrs. Madrigal almost never tried to pull off her helpless-old-lady routine. Michael couldn't help smiling at the effort. "I hope Mary Ann also told you it was a question of finances?"

"She did."

"So?"

"I'm not as gullible as she is." The landlady found her trowel and slipped it into the pocket of her smock. Then she removed a pale yellow parchment envelope and handed it to Michael. "So I'm hereby eliminating it as an excuse. You'll just have to come up with another one."

He opened the envelope and removed a check for a thousand dollars. "Mrs. Madrigal . . . this is awfully sweet, but . . ."

"It isn't a bit sweet. It's a cold-blooded investment. I'm commissioning you to go to London and come back with some happy stories for us." She paused, but her great blue eyes remained fixed on him. "We need that from you, Michael."

There was nothing he could say.

"But money's not the reason, is it? Not really." She sat down on the bench at the end of the courtyard and patted the place next to her. "You haven't finished settling up with Jon yet."

Typically, she had lured him onto the appropriate set. He sat down less than ten feet away from the brass plaque that marked the spot where Jon's ashes had been buried. "I'm not sure I ever will," he said.

"You must," she replied. "What more do you want him to know?"

"What do you mean?"

"I mean . . . if we had him back with us right now . . . what would be your unfinished business?"

He thought for a while. "I'd ask him what he did with the keys to the tool chest."

Mrs. Madrigal smiled. "What else?"

"I'd tell him he was a jerk for needing to hang around with pissy queens."

"Go on."

"I'd tell him I'm sorry it took me so long to figure out what he meant to me. And I wish we'd taken that trip to Maui when he suggested it."

"Fine."

"And . . . I wore his good blazer while he was in the hospital and somebody burned a hole in the sleeve and I never told him about it . . . and I love him very much."

"He knows that already," said the landlady.

"I'd tell him again, then."

Mrs. Madrigal slapped her knees jauntily. "Does that about wrap it up?"

"More or less."

"Good. I'll take care of it."

He blinked at her, uncomprehending.

"He'll get your message, dear. I talk to him at least twice a week." She patted the bench again. "Right here." She leaned over and kissed him softly on the cheek. "Go to London, Michael. You're not going to lose him this time. He's a part of you forever."

He clung to her, tears streaming down his face.

"Listen to me, child." Now she was whispering directly into his ear. "I want you to run along the Thames in the moonlight . . . take off all your clothes and jump into the fountain at Trafalgar Square. I want you to . . . have a wild affair with a guard at Buckingham Palace."

He laughed, still holding tight to her.

"Will you take the old lady's money?" she asked.

All he could manage was a nod.

"Good. *Good.* Now run upstairs and tell Mary Ann to make all the arrangements."

He had reached the front door when she shouted her final instruction: "The toolbox keys are on a hook in the basement."

This Terrific Idea

On the eve of Michael's departure, Mary Ann found herself on a vigil at the San Francisco Zoo, awaiting the birth of a polar bear. She and her crew had camped out for seven hours beside the concrete iceberg which Blubber, the expectant mother, was compelled to call home. As the eighth hour approached, so did a smiling Connie Bradshaw, hunched over from her own pregnancy like some noble beast of burden.

"Hi! They told me at the station I could find you here."

This was just what she needed. The Ghost of Cleveland Past. "Yeah," she said dully. "If it keeps up like this, it may be a permanent assignment."

Connie peered through the bars at Blubber's lair. "Where is she?"

"Back there." She pointed. "In her den. She's not real fond of the cameras."

"I guess not, poor thing. Who would be?"

Mary Ann shrugged. "Those women on the PBS specials seem to love it."

"Yuck." Connie mugged. "Screaming and yelling and sweating . . . then waving at the baby with that dippy expression on their face. Only people are that dumb."

"I'm sure Blubber agrees with you, but she hasn't got much of a choice. There are hearts to be warmed out there in the naked city."

Connie gazed wistfully at the iceberg, then turned back to Mary Ann. "Can you take a break and have a Diet Coke with me?"

Mary Ann hesitated.

"It won't take long," added Connie. "OK?"

"Sure," she replied, her curiosity getting the best of her. "Just for a little while, though. Blubber's looking close."

She told her cameraman where she would be, then joined Connie under a Cinzano umbrella near the snack bar. Her old high school

81

chum had rearranged her face into a mask of sisterly concern. "I'll get right to the point, hon. Have you broken the news to Brian yet?"

Mary Ann was beginning to feel badgered. "No," she said flatly. "I haven't."

"Super." Connie beamed. "So far so good."

Mary Ann clenched her teeth. What the hell was so far so good about that?

"I've been really thinking about this," Connie added, "and I've got this terrific idea."

Ever since the time she had taken Mary Ann to singles night at the Marina Safeway, Connie and her terrific ideas had been nothing but trouble. "I don't know," said Mary Ann. "If it's about getting pregnant, I'd just as soon . . ."

"Don't you even wanna *hear* it?" Connie was crushed.

"Well . . . I appreciate your concern . . ."

"Hear me out. OK? Then I'll shut up. It's not as weird as you might think."

Mary Ann doubted that, but she murmured a reluctant OK and fortified herself with a sip of Diet Coke.

Connie seemed enormously relieved. "Remember my little brother Wally?"

Why was it that people from home always expected you to recall minutiae from fifteen years ago, things that weren't even that important at the time? " 'Fraid not," she said.

"Yes you do."

"Connie . . . Cleveland was a long time ago."

"Yeah, but Wally used to deliver your paper. He delivered most of the papers on that side of Ridgemont."

The light dawned, however dim. A dorky kid with Dumbo ears and a bad habit of mangling the petunias with his Schwinn. "Yeah," she said. "Sure. Of course."

"Well, Wally's at UC med school now."

Mary Ann whistled. "Jesus."

"I know," Connie agreed. "Does that make you feel old or *what?* He's kind of a hunk too, if I do say so myself."

That was almost too much to imagine, but she let it go. She had a creepy feeling she already knew where this conversation was going to lead her. All she could do was pray that the polar bear would go into labor and rescue her from the embarrassment.

"Anyway, Wally and some of his friends make donations from time to time to this sperm bank in Oakland."

Right on the button.

"They're not exactly donations," Connie continued, "since they get paid for it. Not much. Just a little . . . you know . . . extra cash."

"Mad money."

"Right."

"Besides," Mary Ann deadpanned, "they're lying around the dorm all night with nothing to do . . ."

Connie's face fell. "OK. I'm sorry. Forget it. I shouldn't have brought it up."

She should never have used irony on Connie Bradshaw. "Hey," she said, as gently as possible, "I appreciate the thought. I really do. It's just not for me, that's all. The people at St. Sebastian's suggested it, but . . . well . . ."

"I thought it would be so perfect," Connie lamented.

"I know."

"They have these three cold-storage vats at the sperm bank— one for known donors, one for unknowns, and an extra one in case the freezer craps out. Wally's stuff goes into the 'unknown' vat, but I thought maybe we could get his number or something . . . or get him moved into the 'known' vat . . . so you'd know what you were getting."

"It was a sweet thought. Really." Not so sweet was the vision looming hideously in her brain: a turkey baster brimming with the semen of her former paperboy.

"Plus," added Connie, still plugging away, "it seems like the perfect solution if you want to get pregnant and you don't want Brian to know that he's not the father. There wouldn't be any strings at-tached as far as Wally is concerned, and . . . well, everything would work out for everybody."

And the blessed event would be Connie's niece or nephew. It was touching to think that Connie might regard this arrangement—consciously or unconsciously—as a means of cementing a friendship that had never quite worked out. It was downright heartbreaking, in fact.

"Connie . . . I'd go to Wally in a second, if I thought I could handle artificial insemination."

"It's not all that complicated, you know. They send you to this fertility awareness class and teach you how to measure your dooflop, and you just *do* it. I mean, sperm is sperm, you know?"

"I know, Connie. It also comes with an attractive applicator."

"What?"

"Don't you see? I know it's easy. I know *lots* of people do it. I can see your point entirely. It's the artificial part that stops me cold." She lowered her voice to a vehement whisper. "I can't help it, Connie. I want to be fucked first."

Connie's jaw went slack. "You want Wally to *fuck* you?"

"*No!*" She proclaimed it so forcefully that a Chinese woman at the next table looked up from her chili dog. Modulating her voice, she added: "I meant that in a general sense. I want a baby to grow out of an act of love. Or . . . affection, at least. You can blame my mother for that. That's what she taught me, and that's what I'm stuck with."

"This is amazing," said Connie.

"What?"

"Well . . . I've seen you on TV. You look so *hip*."

"Connie . . . it's *me*, Mary Ann. Remember? Vice-president of the Future Homemakers of America?"

"Yeah, but you've changed a lot."

"Not that much," said Mary Ann. "Believe me."

"*Mary Ann! She's doin' it!*" It was her cameraman, bearer of glad tidings.

She sprang to her feet. "That's my cue."

Two minutes later, the wet cub plopped onto the concrete floor without so much as a tiny grunt from his mother.

84

"Animals have it so easy," said Connie, watching from the sidelines.

Mary Ann spent the rest of the afternoon editing footage at the station. As she headed home at twilight, the security guard in the lobby handed her a manila envelope. "A lady said to give you this."

"What kind of a lady?"

"A pregnant lady."

"Great."

She didn't open it until she had reached the Le Car, parked in an alleyway off Van Ness. Inside the envelope were two brochures with a note attached:

Mary Ann—Don't get mad, OK? I'm leaving you these cuz I thought they might explain things better than I did. Just between you and I, Wally was a little ticked when he found out I didn't give you some literature first. Let's get together real soon. Luff ya. Connie.

She couldn't decide what annoyed her more—Connie's chronic breeziness (a style she had picked up years before from inscribing *dozens* of Central High yearbooks) or the realization that Brian's sterility was now a topic of major concern to the entire Bradshaw family.

She began to read:

We believe that women have the right to control our own reproduction and in doing so, determine if, when and how to achieve pregnancy. Donor insemination is a process of introducing semen into the vaginal canal or cervix with a device for the purpose of fertilizing an egg and achieving pregnancy. Fresh or thawed-out frozen semen can be used.

Its safety and effectiveness have been well established. Currently in the U.S., 15–20,000 children a year are conceived by insemination. Since WWII, well over 300,000 children have been born as a result of this method, and since

85

1776, when the technique of freezing sperm was developed,
over a million children have been . . .

Shuddering, she put down the brochure. Frozen sperm during the Revolutionary War? Where had *that* happened? Valley Forge? Brian had been right about one thing, at least; 1984 was almost here. Something had gone haywire if science had advanced to the point that babies could be made without sexual intimacy.

No. She couldn't do it.

If this was the future, she wasn't ready for it.

She would tell Brian the truth. They would go somewhere for the weekend. She would be gentle and loving and he would accept it. Maybe not at first, but eventually. He would *have* to accept it; there was no other way.

It was dark by the time she got home. As she fumbled for her key in the entrance alcove, she spotted yet another manila envelope, propped on the ledge above the buzzers. She was ready to scream when she realized it was addressed to Mouse. Taking it with her, she went upstairs and knocked on Mouse's door.

"Come in."

He was leaning over his sofa, arranging clothes in a suitcase. "Hi, Babycakes."

"Hi. Somebody left this at the front door." She laid the envelope on a chair.

He glanced at it, still packing. "Must be Ned's bon voyage package. He said he was dropping something by."

"Ah."

"Sit down," he said. "Talk to me."

She sat down, noticing another suitcase on the floor. "You're taking an awful lot for a month, aren't you?"

"Just this bag," he answered.

"What about that one?" She pointed to the suitcase on the floor.

"Oh." He grinned. "That's Simon's. He left it here a little while ago. He's having dinner down at Washington Square."

"I see."

He gave her an impish sideways glance. "Why didn't you tell me what a hunk he is?"

She shrugged, commanding herself not to blush. "You didn't ask."

"I was expecting one of those horse-faced dudes with big ears and crooked teeth. This guy looks like a skinnier version of Brian."

"You think so?"

"Now, don't tell me you didn't notice that."

"No," she replied. "Not really."

"Well, look again, woman."

"Are those jeans new?" she asked.

"These?" He held up the pair he was packing. "I got them today."

"They look black."

"They *are* black. All the rage. See?" He pretended to model them. "The Widow Fielding Goes to London."

She giggled. "You are the worst."

"Well . . . I figure they haven't got them there yet. I might be able to barter with them in an emergency."

"Sell your pants, you mean?"

"Sure." He folded the Levi's and placed them in the suitcase. "I remember when American kids used to pay their way across Europe that way."

"*Ages* ago, Mouse."

"Well . . ."

"When were you last in London?"

"Uh . . . late sixties."

"Late?"

"Nineteen sixty-seven."

"Right," she said. "And they called it Swinging London."

"OK."

"And Twiggy was around."

He pretended to be shocked. "Twiggy is *still* around, and don't you forget it!"

"How old were you?"

87

"Sixteen," he replied. "It was sixteen years ago, and I was sixteen. Half my life ago." He turned and smiled at her. "I came out there, too."

"You *did*? You never told me that."

"Well . . . had my first sex, anyway."

"Whatever," she said.

"Does Brian get along well with Simon?" he asked.

"Wait a minute. I thought we were talking about London."

He patted a side pocket of the suitcase. "I already have my instructions."

"What?"

"Simon left a small tome about the operation of his apartment."

"Have you looked at it yet?" she asked.

"Nope. Don't want to. I want it to be a complete surprise."

That made sense to her.

"Well?" he asked. "Do they?"

"What?"

"Get along well together."

"Mouse . . . what is this?"

"Nothing," he shrugged. "I'm just curious."

She hesitated. "I don't know. They seem to like each other. They both have the hots for Theresa Cross."

Michael made a face. "Brian told you that?"

"He doesn't have to. I know how he is. He's got a sleazy streak in him a mile wide."

He grinned at some private movie. "Yeah . . . that figures. Any man who would make you wear leg warmers during sex . . ."

"Mouse . . ."

His languid grin remained.

"I should never have told you that. I knew you'd throw it back at me. Besides . . . he doesn't make me do it. I do it of my own accord."

He nodded solemnly. "I admire a woman who takes responsibility for her own sleaziness."

"That's the *last* juicy tidbit you get from me."

"Juicy tidbit? You told me it was a transcendental experience. You said it made you feel like one of the girls from *Fame*."

She stomped into his kitchen. "I'm pouring myself some wine."

"Help yourself," he hollered back. "Pour me some, too."

She stood there for a moment in the light of his refrigerator, enjoying the afterglow of his teasing. She had loved this sentimental, funny, adorable man longer than she had loved Brian even, and it warmed her heart to realize they were getting back to normal again. Returning with two glasses of wine, she handed one to him and asked: "Aren't you going to open your package?"

He looked confused.

"The one from Ned," she added, pointing to it. She couldn't stand it when people didn't open things *immediately*.

"Oh." He set his wine down and reached for the envelope, tearing off the end. "And the winner *is* . . ." He peered down into it, then pulled out a note written on a card with a naked fireman on the front. " 'Don't do anything I wouldn't do. I'll miss you. Your buddy, Ned.' "

"That's sweet," she said.

He nodded, with a little smile.

"That's not all, is it?"

Another nod.

"Mouse . . . there's something in there."

"There is, huh?"

"I felt it moving around." She took the envelope from him and shook it over the sofa. Five foil-wrapped rubbers fell out. "Oops," she said.

Mouse just grinned at her. He didn't look particularly upset. "It's Ned's way of saying . . . you know . . . be careful and have a good time." He scooped them up in both hands. "Here . . . from me to you."

"What?" She was sure she was scarlet.

"C'mon. Take 'em. I'm celibate. You guys can use them more than I can."

"Uh . . . Mouse. Thanks just the same. OK?"

He looked at her for a moment, then dropped the rubbers back into the envelope. "Hooked on the pill, huh?"

She picked up her wine and downed it.

He sipped his slowly, peering at her over the rim. "Do I still get that ride to the airport?"

"Sure. You bet. What time?"

"Well . . . I guess we should leave no later than three-thirty. Just to be sure."

"Great." She pecked him on the cheek. "See you then."

When she got back to her own apartment, she found Brian washing the breakfast dishes. She leaned into his back and kissed his neck. "Mouse is so excited," she said.

"I don't blame him," he replied.

"Maybe we should do the same."

He dried his hands on a towel and turned around. "Go to London?"

She smiled at him. "Get out of town, at least."

"All right. Our savings account should get us as far as, say, Oakland."

She touched the tip of his nose. "*Exactly* what I had in mind."

"*Oakland?*"

"Sure. A weekend for two at the Claremont. All expenses paid."

"How come?"

She looked as cavalier as possible. "No reason."

"No. I meant: how come all expenses are paid?"

"Oh. I did a feature on them last month. It's a freebie."

"Not bad."

"I know. Jacuzzi, sauna . . . baking by the pool. Nothing to pack but swimming suits and something for the dining room."

"And leg warmers."

"And leg warmers," she echoed. "*Sold!* To the gentleman with the hard-on."

Pumping the Lieutenant

When she returned from the airport the next day, she found Simon sitting on the bench in the courtyard. He gave her a jaunty little wave as she passed through the lych-gate. "You look like you belong there," she said.

He smiled at her. "It certainly feels that way."

"Well . . ." She made a graceless gesture in the general direction of Daly City. "Mouse is off in the wild blue yonder." It sounded as lame as the gesture must have looked.

Simon pointed to the brass plaque in the garden. "Is this his lover?"

She nodded.

"His ashes?"

Another nod.

He shook his head slowly. "No wonder he wanted to get away."

She couldn't bear to think about Jon just now. "Simon . . . let me know if I can . . . you know . . . help with anything."

"Thank you," he said. "You've been a great help already."

"Well, hey . . . no problem . . ." She was *backing* toward the door, she realized, like some awkward teenager.

"Do you have a moment?" he asked, leaning toward her slightly.

"Sure."

"Wonderful. Come sit, then."

She joined him on the bench. "You're lucky," she said. "You're getting some of our sunshine. The poor Queen missed it completely."

He gave her a lazy smile. "I'm sure this irony isn't lost on Her Majesty."

She laughed uneasily. What did he mean by *that*? That the Queen had personal knowledge of his escapade? That she was envious of irresponsibility? "Is the Queen a nice person?" she asked.

A deep chuckle. "The Queen is a lovely person."

"Have you ever actually talked to her?"

"Oh . . . four or five times at the most."

"She doesn't seem to smile very much."

He shrugged. "Smiling is her job. When smiling is one's job, one is very circumspect about the way one doles it out. Otherwise, it means nothing."

"That's very well put," she said.

Another half-lidded smile. "It's our regulation answer."

"Do you have to be . . . like . . . a lord or something to be an officer on the *Britannia*?"

"Not at all."

"Are you, though?"

His laughter was hearty but not malicious. "You Americans just jump right in there, don't you?"

She was enough of a Californian to resent being called an American. "Well, I think it's only natural to wonder if . . ." Her search for the right words proved futile. She *was* pumping him, and it showed.

Simon leaped gallantly into the silence. "The only titled member of my immediate family is my aunt, my mother's sister, a grotty old duchess by marriage who wears waders and messes about in boats."

"The Queen does that," she put in.

"Not with *this* duchess, I assure you."

She laughed without knowing exactly why. "And your mother and father?"

"They're both dead," he replied evenly.

"Oh, I'm . . ."

"My mother was an actress in the West End. My father was a barrister who moved from Leeds to London after he met my mother. What about yours?"

She was thrown for an instant. "Oh . . . well, my father runs an electrical shop, and my mother is a housewife. They live in Cleveland." She reminded herself of a contestant on *Family Feud*.

"Cleveland . . . Indiana, is it?"

"Ohio."

He nodded. "They must be very proud of you."

"I guess they are," she said. "They don't see me on TV, of course, since I'm . . . you know . . . local. But I send them copies of *TV Guide* when I'm in it. That sort of thing. Your parents must've been young when they died."

"Mmm. Very. I was still at Cambridge." He anticipated her next question, looking faintly amused by her curiosity. "It was an automobile accident. On the M–One. Do you know the M–One?"

"A highway, right?"

"Right."

"Was your mother a good actress?"

He seemed to like that question. "As a matter of fact, I've wondered about that lately. I thought she was marvelous at the time. She was funny. And very beautiful."

"That makes sense," she said.

He passed over the ambiguous compliment. "When I was fourteen, she introduced me to Diana Rigg backstage at the Haymarket. I thought that was the loveliest thing any mother could do for her son."

"I can see how you would," she smiled.

A long silence followed, during which she remembered the joint in her purse. "I almost forgot," she told Simon. "You haven't sampled the Queen Mother yet."

"I beg your pardon?"

She giggled, holding up the joint. "Mrs. Madrigal's primo homegrown."

"Ah."

She lit the joint, took a toke, and handed it to him. "I rolled a couple for the trip to the airport. Mouse was feeling no pain when he took off."

He didn't respond, holding the smoke in his lungs.

She watched him, tickled by his dignity during the performance of this near-ridiculous ritual.

"Very tasty," he said at last.

"Mmm. Isn't it?"

"Do you still want that story?"

For a moment, she thought he was accusing her of weakening

93

his resistance with dope. Then she realized the question was in earnest. "Do you mean . . . ?"

"The one about me. 'Queen's Officer Jumps Ship in Frisco.'"

She smiled. "I think I'd handle it a little more tastefully than that."

He handed the joint back to her. "Do you want to?"

She hesitated. "Simon, I meant it when I said I wouldn't do anything if . . ."

"I know that. You've been perfectly honorable." He retrieved the joint and took another toke off it. "I've given this some thought, Mary Ann. Frankly . . . I don't see what harm it would do. If you're still game, that is."

She said nothing, wondering about his motives.

"Is it what you want?" he asked quietly.

She nodded. "Yes."

He smiled. "Then it's what *I* want."

"Simon . . ."

"I reserve the right to edit content, of course. I don't want to embarrass anyone."

"Of course not."

Another smile, a little warmer than the last. "Wonderful. It's settled, then?"

"You bet."

He returned the joint. "When shall we start?"

Brian materialized under the lych-gate, panting heavily in shorts and a tank top. Simon wasn't facing the gate, but he detected the change in her expression and turned around. "Oh . . . hello there."

"'Lo," said Brian, running in place.

"We're trying out the new weed," she offered cheerfully.

"I see." He was shaking out his arms now, like a marionette in a high wind.

"Do you run regularly?" asked Simon.

"Fair amount," Brian answered. He wasn't wasting an ounce of energy on friendliness.

"You must show me where you do it," said Simon. "I've been frightfully remiss in my own regimen."

"Sure thing," said Brian, loping past them into the house.

Simon turned to her with a rueful little smile.

"It isn't you," she said.

"I hope not."

"He's been . . . I don't know . . . not himself lately."

"Mmm."

The joint had gone out, so she lit it again and offered it to Simon. He shook his head. She took a short drag and extinguished it. "So . . . you're a runner, huh?"

He nodded. "Second generation."

"Really?"

"My father and I both ran at Cambridge."

"How *Chariots of Fire*," she said.

He laughed. "We weren't quite that competitive. It was mostly to keep fit. Ill health was considered very poor form in the Bardill family."

"Was?"

"Well." His eyes were twinkling again. "There's not that much left of the family, is there?"

44 Colville Crescent

The rain seemed to follow Michael to London. It clattered like spilled gravel against the great vaulting roof of Victoria Station as he grabbed his suitcase and scrambled toward the first available black cab. His driver, a sixtyish man the color of corned beef, touched the bill of his cap.

"Where to, mate?"

"Uh . . . Nottingham Gate."

"Eh?"

"Nottingham Gate." He said it with more authority this time.

"Sorry, mate. No such place. Now, there's a Notting *Hill* Gate . . ."

"The address is Forty-four Colville Crescent."

The driver nodded. "That's Notting Hill Gate."

"Great," said Michael, sinking down into burnished leather. "Thank God for that."

The flight had been a living nightmare. Despite the effects of the Queen Mother dope and the ministrations of a chummy gay flight attendant, he had been completely unable to sleep. When he arrived at Gatwick Airport, cotton-mouthed and cranky, he was detained for almost two hours while customs officials ransacked the luggage of three hundred African nationals who had landed at the same time.

After losing another hour as he waited to change money, he had boarded a packed London-bound shuttle train, where he shared a litter-strewn compartment with a brassy couple from Texarkana who insisted on talking about the Forty-Niners, despite his fearless display of indifference to the subject.

His driver glanced toward the back seat. "A Yank, eh?"

"Uh . . . right."

"See what we done to them Argies?"

RGs? A soccer team, maybe? "Oh, yeah . . . that was somethin.'"

A wheezy chuckle. "And we did it without the help of your bloody President."

It wasn't sports, then. It was politics.

"Mind you, you Yanks always come in late on the big wars. You come in late, or you don't come at all. Nothin' personal."

The light dawned. The Falklands war. The Argies were Argentines. Americans didn't call them that, because Americans had never cared. You had to start killing people before you took the trouble to give them nicknames. Japs, Krauts, Commies, Gooks . . . Argies. He had no intention of prolonging the war by arguing with this man. "I like your battle hymn," he said.

"Eh?" The driver looked at him as if he were crazy.

" 'Don't Cry for Me, Argentina.' Isn't that what the troops sang, or something?"

The driver grunted, apparently convinced that Michael *was* crazy. What did a bloody *song* have to do with anything? He stopped talking altogether, and Michael breathed a secret sigh of relief as the cab sped past the pale green blur of Hyde Park.

He had been away from this city for sixteen years, the longest time he'd been away from any spot on earth. He had lost his innocence here—or, more accurately, found it—at a time when mod was in flower and the streets were swarming with legions of white-lipped, black-lashed "birds." He had met a corduroy-clad bricklayer on Hampstead Heath and gone home with him and learned in an instant just how simple and comforting and beautiful real life could actually be.

The bricklayer had resembled a younger, leaner Oliver Reed, and Michael could recall every detail of that distant afternoon: the statue of David next to his bed, the brown sugar crystals he used in his coffee, the physique magazines he left lying around where anyone could see them, the silken feel of his hairless scrotum. Your first stranger, it seemed, is the one you remember for the rest of your life.

Where was he now? How old would he be? Forty-five? Fifty?

The cab veered left at Marble Arch, a landmark he recognized, then they appeared to follow the Bayswater Road along the edge of a large public garden. Which one? He couldn't remember. He was punch-drunk with fatigue and depressed by the rain, so he seized upon passing English icons to bolster his morale:

A shiny red mailbox.

A zebra crossing like the one on the *Abbey Road* album.

A pub sign banging in the wind.

The game became tougher when the cab moved into a region of plastic Pizza Huts and tawdry ethnic restaurants. It wasn't an unpleasant district, really, just surprisingly un-English—more akin to the Haight-Ashbury than anything he had experienced during his earlier visit.

Then the landscape became residential again. He caught glimpses of treelined streets and oversized Victorian row houses with crumbling plaster façades. Black children romped in the rain beside a yellow brick wall on which someone had spray-painted: STUFF THE ROYAL WEDDING.

He spotted a street sign that said COLVILLE. "Isn't this it?" he asked the driver.

"That's Colville Terrace, mate. You want the Crescent. It's just up the way a bit."

Three minutes later, the cab came to a stop. Michael peered out the window with mounting dread. "Is this it?" he asked.

The driver looked peeved. "You wanted Number Forty-four, didn't you?"

"Right."

"Then that's it, mate."

Michael checked the meter (a modern digital one that looked odd in the classic cab) and handed the driver a five-pound note with instructions to keep the change. He was overtipping, but he wanted to prove that a man who knew nothing about wars and streets could be generous just the same.

The driver thanked him and drove off.

Michael stood on the street and gaped at Simon's house. Its plaster façade, apparently a victim of dry rot, was riddled with huge leprous scabs which had fallen away completely in places to expose the nineteenth-century brick beneath. For some reason, this disfigurement went straight to the pit of his stomach, like bone glimpsed through a bloodless wound.

He dismissed a flickering hope that there might really be a Nottingham Gate and headed past overturned garbage cans (dust bins, the English insisted on calling them) to the front door of the three-story building. His dread became palpable when he found the name BARDILL printed on a card by the door buzzers.

He set his suitcase by the door, found the designated key, and wriggled it into the lock. A dark corridor confronted him. He located the light switch—a circular push thing—on a waterstained wall papered with purple roses. The door to Simon's ground-floor flat was at the end of the corridor on the right. By the time he had found the right key and slipped it into an obstinate lock, he was engulfed in darkness so complete that he thought for a moment he'd gone blind.

The light switch. Of course. It was on a timer. He recalled this sensible oddity of British engineering from his last visit. It had charmed him at the time, like electric towel warmers and teakettles that shut off automatically as soon as they whistled.

He turned the knob and pushed against the door with his shoulder, causing light to spill into the corridor from Simon's flat. A vile odor, like the halitosis of an old dog, rolled over him in waves. He held his breath and lunged for the nearest window, cracking it enough to let in a gush of rain-scented air.

As Simon had promised, the living room had fourteen-foot ceilings, which did lend it a certain aura of seedy elegance. *Tatty* was the word he had used, and that was a fair enough description for the lumpy, junkshop furniture grouped around the room's non-functioning fireplace. The pale green walls were dotted with tin engravings from Victorian times, the only visible concession to interior decoration. Simon's stereo and a stack of records completed the grim tableau.

Michael followed a narrow hallway in search of the bedroom. Once there, he dropped his suitcase and sank numbly to the edge of the bed, ordering himself not to jump to conclusions. He was bone tired from the ten-hour flight, so his mounting despair could well be a function of fatigue, not to mention the airline's Danish that flopped about in his stomach like a dying rodent.

It was noon now, he supposed. What he needed was a hot bath and a good sleep. When he awoke, the old wonderment would be back again, bringing with it his invaluable capacity for finding quaintness in hardship. What had he expected, anyway? Some sanitized, Disney-like version of English charm?

Yes, he decided, when he saw the bathroom. He had expected something along the lines of the cozy town house in *101 Dalmatians*. Something with roses in the garden and mellow paneling and—*yes, goddamnit*—towel warmers in the bathroom. What he found instead

99

was a cramped room smelling of stale pee and painted to simulate blue sky and clouds. Like the ceiling of an organic bakery in Berkeley.

The tub had legs, which scored a few points for quaintness, but the hot water ran out as soon as it reached the top of his knees. He lay there immobile, racked with disillusionment, and chastized himself for ever agreeing to swap apartments with a heterosexual he didn't know.

Moments later, he collapsed into bed, but he didn't fall asleep for at least an hour. As he finally drifted off, he had a vague impression of rain pounding on the packed earth of his "garden" and another, more rhythmic sound. Was it . . . drums?

It was dark when he woke. He stumbled about in search of a light switch, then went into the kitchen to take stock of the stuff he would need. There was no food, of course—except for some moldy noodles and a can of herring—and eating utensils were in sparse supply.

For starters, he would buy some cereal and milk, some bread and peanut butter. But that would be tomorrow. Tonight, he would find a neighborhood pub that served Scotch eggs and Cornish pasties and get just as shit-faced as the situation required.

Returning to the bedroom, he decided to make things official by unpacking his suitcase. He was almost done when he remembered the note from Simon stashed in the side pocket. He sat down on the bed and read it:

Michael—

I thought you might be able to use a few words of
advice about the many enigmas of 44 Colville Crescent:
The hot water (or lack thereof) is a bit of a nuisance, I'm
afraid. You'll find the tank in the nook between the lav
and the kitchen, should you have any serious problems
with it. (Truly serious problems should be referred to
Mr. Nigel Pearl, a plumber in Shepherd's Bush. His
number is posted on the door of the fridge.)

The automatic turn-off whatsit on the stereo does not turn off automatically. The central heating has been shut off for the season; I doubt you'll need it. There's an extra duvet in the bottom drawer of the cupboard in the bedroom. The bed, as you must have noticed by now, is propped up at one corner by my vast collection of *Tatlers*, which is quite the best place for them to be.

For basic foodstuffs, I recommend Europa Foods in Notting Hill Gate. For toiletries, try Boots the Chemist (a "drug store" in your quaint colonial parlance). For real drugs, try one of the black gentlemen in All Saints Road, but do not, under any circumstances, go there at night. Their grass is no match for Humboldt County's finest, but it does the job nicely if you lace it with hashish.

The gas cooker in the kitchen shouldn't present any problems. Trash is kept under the sink-basin, as is furniture polish, buckets, dustpan, etc. There is also a stopcock for the water. If there is ever any kind of flood, just turn that off (clockwise) and the watersupply is blocked.

The launderette (service-wash) and dry cleaners are round the corner at the junction of Westbourne Grove and Ledbury Road. The Electric Cinema in Portobello Road has good old movies, if you like things like *Glen or Glenda* (my personal favorite) and Jessie Matthews retrospectives.

A certain Miss Treves (Nanny Treves to me) will be popping in from time to time to keep an eye on things. Please introduce yourself and tell her you are a friend of mine. When she asks you about my ship-jumping caper (and she will, I assure you), feel free to tell her what you know and say I'll be home just after Easter. I'll give her the gory details in a letter. Miss Treves is a manicurist now, but she was my nanny for many years. She's fretted over me ever since I got away from her in the British

Museum (I was six), so she's likely to be a bit distraught. That's all you need to know about her except the obvious, which I'm sure you'll handle with your usual grace and gallantry. London is yours.

Simon

The note, rendered on flimsy blue paper in a spidery handwriting, gave Michael the soothing sensation of another human presence in the apartment with him. He could almost hear Simon's voice as he read it. When you came right down to it, the place wasn't *that* awful, he decided. All he really needed was a base camp from which to explore the city.

But what was the "obvious" thing he was soon to discover about Simon's former nanny?

And what the hell was a duvet?

To answer the simpler question, he checked the contents of the bottom drawer of the bedroom cupboard. There he found a threadbare quilt, faded from many washings. He held it against his cheek for a moment, like a housewife in a fabric softener commercial, feeling a rush of inexplicable tenderness toward this common household item. So what if the heat didn't work? He had his duvet to keep him warm.

He finished his unpacking, took inventory of his strange new money, and headed out into the night. It was roughly nine o'clock. The rain had stopped, but the fruit stalls in Portobello Road—empty and skeletal—were still beaded with moisture. As he left Colville Crescent and entered Colville Terrace, a corner pub beckoned him with yellow lights and the voice of Boy George.

Inside, he ordered a cider, the alcoholic English variety that had served him so well as a teenager in Hampstead. The other patrons were decidedly workingclass. Two pudding-faced men in tweed caps argued jovially at the bar, while a stately Rastafarian in dreadlocks nursed a dark ale at a table near the video games.

His cider was gone in a flash, so he ordered a second one to wash down a couple of Scotch eggs. By the time he had quaffed his third, he was winking playfully at a plump woman who sat across from him under a gilt-lettered mirror. She was well past forty and her makeup had been applied with a trowel, but there was something almost valiant about her cheerfulness as she drank alone, jiggling her large calves to the beat of "Abracadabra." She reminded him of one of those jolly barflies from *Andy Capp*.

He paid up at the bar and ordered an ale to be sent to the lady's table. Then, brimming with goodwill, he gave one last wink to his brave sister and stumbled out into the street to make his peace with London.

Time on His Hands

The lunchtime mob at Perry's had been even rowdier than usual, but Brian managed to cope with it by reminding himself that his weekend getaway to Oakland was less than four hours away. He was returning an order for a picky diner ("Surely you don't call that rare?") when Jerry of the Jordache Look sidled up to him with a greasy smirk on his face.

"Your wife is at my station, Hawkins."

"Make sure the goddamn thing is bleeding," Brian told the cook.

"You hear me, Hawkins?"

"I heard you. Tell her I'll be out in a minute." He checked two plates to see if they matched his orders, then shouted over his shoulder at the departing Jerry. "Tell her I'm up to my ass in customers."

"Don't worry," Jerry yelled back. "She's up to her ass in Englishmen."

He was still fuming over the remark when he stopped by Mary Ann's table ten minutes later. As reported, Simon was with her. She was autographing a menu for a fat woman at the next table, so she didn't notice him until Simon signaled her by clearing his throat.

"Oh, hi. Is this a bad time?"

"Busy," he replied. "I really can't talk."

"No problem." She gave him her secret Be Cool smile. "I just wanted Simon to see the place."

He addressed the lieutenant. "So what do you think?"

"It's . . . very jolly."

He nodded. "Like a Japanese subway."

Mary Ann and the lieutenant both laughed, but not much. She looked strangely ill-at-ease, and he was beginning to think she had every reason to be. What the fuck was she doing, anyway, bringing this guy here?

He turned to her. "Are we still on for tonight?"

"Of course."

"My wife breaks dates," he told Simon.

"Now wait just a damn minute!" she piped.

"There's always a good reason, of course. Earthquakes, queens, polar bears . . ."

"Excuse me . . ." The fat woman was back, this time tugging on Simon's arm. "I got so excited I completely forgot to get your autograph too."

Simon looked grossly uncomfortable. "Really, madam, that's awfully kind of you, but I don't see what possible . . ."

"Oh, *please* . . . My daughter will be livid if I don't bring her some proof that I met you!"

The lieutenant cast an apologetic glance at Mary Ann, then scrawled his name hastily across the menu. His face was bright red.

"Oh, thank you." The woman's upper lip was sweating as she added in a stage whisper: "My daughter is just gaga over men with hairy chests." Giggling to herself, she waddled back to her seat.

Simon shook his head slowly.

"The price of exposure," said Mary Ann.

"What does she have?" Brian couldn't help asking. "X-ray vision?"

Mary Ann laughed uneasily. "I did a little profile on Simon that aired this morning."

"Ghastly," mugged the lieutenant.

"With your shirt off?" asked Brian.

"Well . . ."

"Just for a jogging segment," Mary Ann explained. "We needed footage for a voice-over."

Brian became her echo. "Footage for a voice-over. That makes sense. Well . . ." He backed away from the table. "I think they need me in the Back Forty."

Moments later, as he'd expected, she cornered him in the kitchen. "OK. Why are you bent out of shape?"

He stepped out of the way of another waiter. "It'll have to wait. This is our busiest time."

"I did a little profile on the guy," she whispered. "Why should that freak you out?"

"It didn't freak me out. It . . . surprised me, that's all. You said he didn't want to be on TV."

She shrugged. "So I talked him into it."

"Right. And made him a beefcake star in the bargain."

"Oh, c'mon, Brian." She ducked as Jerry sped by with a tray. "What if I did? Hey . . . I did that story on the Tom Selleck look-alike contest and you didn't say a word."

He leaned forward and answered in an angry whisper. "The goddamn Tom Selleck look-alike wasn't living in our fucking house!"

She shook her head. "I can't believe you're threatened by this."

Her sanctimoniously modern tone annoyed the hell out of him. "I'd just like to know why you came *here* to celebrate your big media coup."

"Brian . . ."

"Just . . . go. It's no big deal."

"Brian, listen to me. I brought him here because I want you guys to be friends. I want the three of us to be friends. I just thought it would be fun if . . ."

"OK, OK."

She gave him a cautious smile, sensing the passing of his anger. "My timing was rotten, I guess. I'm sorry about that. Want me to pick up your laundry?"

He shook his head.

"I'll be home packing, if you need me." She kissed him on the cheek and walked out of the kitchen. When he returned to the front room three minutes later, she and Simon had already gone.

Back in the kitchen, Jerry was waiting for him. "Your wife's friend is a big tipper."

"He's my friend too," he answered.

"Really?" Jerry's lip curled.

"Yes, *really*, asshole."

Jerry nodded slowly. "Well . . . it's convenient, at least."

"What the hell do you mean by that?"

A surly shrug. "Look, man . . . I only know what I saw."

"Meaning?"

"Well . . . the guy bears a certain resemblance to you, that's all."

"So?"

"So . . . nothing." He walked away muttering the rest of it. "If the lady wants a matched set, it's none of my . . ."

He was cut short when Brian grabbed him by his collar, spun him around and rammed him against the wall.

"Watch it," said Jerry. "You know what Perry said. Do that in here and you're out on your ass."

Brian hesitated. "A very good point."

He secured a firmer hold on Jerry's collar, dragged him into the restaurant, and let fly with a right hook that sent his tormentor hurtling backward into a table full of empty plastic hamburger baskets. The table overturned, dumping Jerry on the floor. Customers scattered. A woman screamed. The fat lady with the autographed menu stood slack-mouthed at the cash register. Brian strode up to her, took the menu from her hands, signed his name with the ballpoint in his pocket, returned the menu, and walked out the door without looking back.

He didn't break stride until he had reached the top of Russian Hill, six or seven blocks away. His heart was pounding like crazy as he stopped for a moment outside Swensen's Ice Cream and considered his next move. He decided to maintain a normal pace for the last block or so. If his boss had already called, it would only increase his humiliation to arrive home out of breath.

When he got there, ten minutes later, Mary Ann was preoccupied with their escape to the Claremont. She was on her hands and knees in the bathroom, combing the cabinet under the sink for last year's Coppertone.

"I'm sure we can buy some there," he said.

"I know, but this was my number and everything."

"They'll have your number."

She stood up, brushing off her hands. "Aren't you off work early?"

He faked her with a smile. "They took mercy on me. I told them we needed to beat the Friday traffic."

"Perfect. Let's do it." She walked briskly into the bedroom; he followed. "You won't believe it," she said, "but I crammed us both into one suitcase."

"Great." He edged closer to the telephone, ready to grab it.

"I packed your sunglasses with the green lenses. I wasn't sure if those were . . ."

"They'll do fine," he said.

"Well, if you want the others . . ."

He hoisted the suitcase. "I want to go."

They had very little conversation until the Le Car reached the East Bay. "You know," said Mary Ann, keeping her eyes on the freeway, "I think Simon was hurt by your abruptness this afternoon."

He hesitated before answering. "Then . . . I'll apologize to him."

"Will you?" She glanced at him hopefully.

He nodded. "The minute we get back."

"Well . . . whenever. He likes you a lot, Brian."

"Good. I've got nothing against him."

She reached over and rubbed his thigh. "Good."

Minutes later, the Claremont materialized on the green hillside above them. "Isn't it wonderful?" gushed Mary Ann. "It turns seventy this year."

"It's a little too white," he replied.

"Well . . . tough titty."

"You know what I mean." He grinned. "It looks like a sanatorium in Switzerland. Sanitarium. Which is it?"

"Huh?"

"C'mon. One is for crazy people; the other is for face-lifts and stuff."

She shook her head. "They both mean the same thing."

"Nah."

She looked out the window. "Just drive," she said.

When they reached the hotel, they left the Le Car with the doorman and went straight to their room. It was sunny and spacious and overlooked the tennis courts. They smoked a joint and changed into their swimming suits, saying almost nothing for five minutes. Then they headed down to the Jacuzzi adjoining the swimming pool, where the sunshine and the dope and the jet of warm water pulsing at his back lulled him into the gentlest of reveries. The catastrophe at the restaurant seemed like a bad dream.

Mary Ann submerged herself completely, then rose like a naiad and gazed up at the old hotel. "Pink," she said finally. "No, *peach*."

He thought he had missed something. "What?"

"The color they should paint it."

He looked up at the hotel before turning to smile at her.

She returned the smile, then grazed his calf with the side of her foot.

"You know what?" he said.

"What?"

"I don't like anybody as much as I like you."

She skipped a beat before replying. "Then why don't you tell me the truth?"

The look on her face said it all. "You got a call?" he asked.

She nodded.

"From Perry?"

Another nod.

"Did he can me?"

"Brian . . . you broke the guy's jaw. They could just as easily have had you arrested."

He thought about that but said nothing.

"They took him to St. Sebastian's. They had to wire his jaw."

He nodded.

"What was it this time?" she said.

He had no intention of adding jealousy to his list of cardinal sins. "It doesn't matter," he said.

"Swell. Terrific."

"Look . . . he made another crack about a gay customer. He told an AIDS joke. I didn't mean to hit him hard. He'd been spoiling for it all day . . ."

"Why didn't you tell me about it?"

He shrugged. "I was going to. I didn't want to fuck up our weekend before it started."

She stood there blinking at him.

He still wasn't sure, as he asked again: "They canned me, huh?"

"Yes."

"I'm sorry you had to be there to catch the flak."

"He was nice about it," she said.

A small boy and his father, both brilliantly redheaded, trotted past his field of vision on their way to the locker rooms. The boy tripped on the laces of his Keds, and the father stopped to tie them for him. The tableau cut Brian to the quick, underscoring everything that was missing from his life.

"Earth to Brian, earth to Brian." Mary Ann coaxed him back into the here and now with a bemused smile.

"I'm sorry," he said. "What can I tell you?"

"I don't want you to be sorry. I want you to tell me the truth. Jesus, Brian . . . if we can't talk to each other, who can we talk to?"

"You're right." He nodded, feeling the weight of his guilt begin to lift.

"It's not just you," she said.

"What do you mean?"

"Well . . . I'm just as bad about that sometimes."

"About what?" he asked.

"You know . . . telling the whole truth. I gloss over things because I'm afraid of . . . damaging what we have . . . because I don't want to lose you."

He had never known her to lie, and he was touched by this unlikely confession. She wasn't explaining her own motivation so much as letting him know that she understood his. He cupped his hand against her wet cheek and smiled at her. She stuck her tongue out at him, ducked under the water, and goosed him. The crisis had passed.

He noticed that Mary Ann drank a little more wine than usual at dinner, but he matched her glass for glass. By the time their raspberries and cream had arrived, they were both just a couple of silly grins hovering in the candlelight. A gut instinct told him this was the moment to open Topic A again.

"I hated that job, you know."

She reached over and stroked the hair on the back of his hand. "I know."

"Sooner or later I would've quit anyway, and this way . . . wasn't half bad."

She waited awhile before saying anything. "I'm kinda sorry I missed it, actually. It didn't look dumb, did it?"

He shook his head.

"Heroic?"

He tilted his hand from side to side to indicate something in between. She laughed. "And now," he said softly, "I have all this time on my hands."

Her smile became a photograph of a smile. She knew exactly what he was saying.

"You said to tell the truth," he said.

She nodded. Her smile had disappeared.

"The way I see it, John Lennon was a househusband, and he did all right . . . and I bet he spent a lot more time with that kid than Yoko ever did . . ."

"Brian . . ."

"I'm not saying you wouldn't love the kid or anything. I just mean you wouldn't have to be as involved with it as I would be. Hell, women bore the brunt of that for centuries. There's no reason we can't make it work the other way around. Don't you see? Wouldn't it be great to have this little person around who's . . . a mixture of you and me?"

Her face was unreadable as she pushed back her chair and dropped her napkin on the table. Was she pissed? Did she think he had gotten himself fired to force her into this position? "What about our raspberries?" he asked.

"I'm not hungry," she replied.

"Are you . . . upset?"

"No." She cast her eyes at the neighboring tables. "I brought us here to tell you something, but I don't want to do it here."

"OK. Fine." He got up. "What about the check?"

"It's on the tab," she said.

They went back to their room, where she brushed her teeth and told him to put on his windbreaker.

"Where are we going?" he asked.

"You'll see," she said.

After slipping into one of his old Pendleton shirts, she produced a large brass key and opened the door leading to the suite above theirs in the tower. They passed through this space, climbing still another stairway in the semidarkness.

She flung open the last door with a flourish. They had reached a tiny, open-air observation deck at the summit of the tower. Before them stretched the entire Bay Area from San Mateo to Marin, ten thousand electric constellations glimmering beneath a purple sky.

She moved to the edge of the parapet. "This should do nicely."

He joined her. "For what?"

"Just be quiet now. You'll screw up the ritual." She unbuttoned the pocket of the Pendleton and removed a pink plastic case roughly the size of a compact. She held it up like a sacred talisman. "Farewell little Ortho-Novums. Mama doesn't want you anymore."

In a flash he realized what she was doing. "Jesus, you dizzy . . ."

"Shh . . ." Her arm swung forward in an arc, launching the pills into the night, a tiny pink spaceship bound for the stars. She cupped her hands around her mouth and shouted: "Did you see that, God? *Do you read me?*"

He threw back his head and roared with joy.

"You approve?" She was smiling into the wind, looking more beautiful than he had ever seen her.

"I don't deserve you," he said.

"The hell you don't." She took his hand and pulled him toward the stairway. "C'mon, turkey, let's go make babies."

Enter Miss Treves

Michael had always regarded jet lag as an affectation of the rich, but his first three days in London changed his mind about that forever. He awoke without fail at the magic hour of three o'clock—sometimes in the morning, sometimes in the afternoon. His disorientation was heightened by the fact that he found himself in a house where the telephone never rang and the drums never stopped.

The drums were actually next door, but their basic rhythms were easily audible at dawn, when he invariably lay in four inches of lukewarm water and watched the cold, gray light of another rainy day creep across the bogus blue sky of his bathroom ceiling.

In search of a routine, he touched base with his launderette, his post office, his nearest market. Then he trekked into other parts of town to check out familiar haunts from bygone times: a rowdy pub in Wapping called the Prospect of Whitby (more touristy than he had remembered), Carnaby Street (once mod and cheesy, now punk and cheesy), the charming old cemetery in Highgate where Karl Marx was buried (still charming, still buried).

When the skies cleared on the third afternoon, he ambled through Kensington and Chelsea to the river, then followed the Embankment to Cleopatra's Needle. As a sixteen-year-old, he had been intrigued by the Egyptian obelisk because the bronze lions flanking it—when viewed from a certain angle—had strongly suggested erect cocks. True, almost everything had suggested that when he was sixteen.

He left the river, mildly disenchanted by this reunion with the lions, and threaded his way through the streets in the general direction of Trafalgar Square. For reasons of economy, or so he told himself, he ate lunch at a McDonald's near the Charing Cross tube station, feeling wretchedly American about it until the man in front of him ordered "a strawbry shike to tike away."

Arriving in Piccadilly Circus, he bought a copy of *Gay News* and perused it amidst a crowd of German backpackers assembled at the foot of the Eros statue. Judging from the classified ads, gay Englishmen were perpetually searching for attractive "uncles" (daddies) with "stashes" (mustaches), who were "non-scene" (never in bars) and "non-camp" (butch). A surprisingly large number of advertisers made a point of saying that they owned homes and cars. On the women's news front, a group of North London lesbians was organizing a Saturday jog to the tomb of Radclyffe Hall, and everyone was looking forward to Sappho Disco Night at the Goat in Boots, Drummond Street.

Back at Colville Crescent, he did his best to rid the bathroom of its stench by anointing the ratty carpet with a concentrated room deodorant he had found at Boots the Chemist. (In some ways, English drugstores were the most unsettling institutions of all. The boxes and bottles looked pretty much like the ones in the States, but the names had been changed to protect God-knows-whom. Was Anadin the same thing as Anacin? Did it matter?) He shook the little amber bottle vigorously, releasing a few drops of the pungent liquid. It merged instantly with the pee smell, eliminating nothing. He flung the bottle into the waste-basket and stormed into the bedroom, where he searched his suitcase for the last of the joints Mrs. Madrigal had rolled for him.

He was on the verge of lighting it when a rude noise startled him. It took him several seconds to realize that he had just heard his door buzzer for the first time. Returning the joint to its hiding place, he left the apartment, walked down the dark corridor and opened the front door.

The woman who stood before him was about sixty. Her hair was gray and framed her face nicely with Imogene Coca bangs. She wore a brown tweed suit and sensible brown shoes. And that, as Simon had put it, was everything but the obvious. She was also no taller than the doorknob.

"Oh," she said in a startled chipmunk voice. "I saw the lights. I thought it best to ring first."

He sought to reassure her. "You must be Miss Treves. I'm a friend of Simon's, Michael Tolliver."

"Oh . . . an American."

He laughed nervously. "Right. We swapped apartments, in fact. Simon's in San Francisco."

She grunted. "I know all about the naughty lad."

"He's fine," he said. "He asked me to give you his love and tell you he's coming back right after Easter."

This news provoked another grunt.

"He just sort of . . . fell in love with San Francisco."

"That's what he told you, did he?"

"Well . . . more or less. Look, I'm not very settled in, but . . . can I offer you a cup of coffee? Or tea?"

She thought for a moment, then nodded. "Don't mind if I do."
"Good."

She led the way back to the living room and took a seat—her feet dangling just above the floor—in a low-slung chintz armchair. The slightly underscaled proportions of the chair seemed to suggest it had been provided specifically for her use.

Miss Treves brushed a fleck of dust off the armrest, then arranged her hands demurely in her lap. "Simon didn't tell me you were coming," she said. "Otherwise I might have tidied up a bit."

"I don't mind," he replied. "It's fine."

She looked around the room disgustedly. "'Tisn't a bit. It's perfectly vile." She shook her head slowly. "And he's supposed to be the gentleman."

Her indignation made him feel much better. He had begun to wonder if he was being too prissy about the apartment, too American in his demands. This second opinion, considering its source, reinforced his earliest suspicions about Simon's basic slovenliness.

He remembered the tea he had offered her. "Oh . . . excuse me. I'll put the kettle on for us." He spun around to make his exit, crashing ingloriously into a shadeless floor lamp. He steadied the wobbling pole with one hand, while Miss Treves tittered behind his back.

"Now there, love. You'll get used to it."

She meant her size, apparently. He turned and smiled at her to show that he was a Californian and knew his way around human differences. "What do you take in your tea?" he asked.

"Milk, please . . . and a tiny bit of sugar."

"I'm afraid I don't have sugar."

"Yes you do. On the shelf to the right of the cooker. I keep it there for myself when I stop by."

In the kitchen he ran hot water into the teakettle, removed a milk bottle from the refrigerator, and located Miss Treves's private cache of sugar. Sugar *crystals*, actually, like the stuff he had shared with his first sex partner, the non-scene, non-camp bricklayer from Hampstead Heath.

When he returned to the living room, he handed Miss Treves her tea and sat down on the end of the sofa closest to her. "So . . . Simon tells me he ran away from you once in the British Museum." It was a weak opener, but it was all he had.

She took a cautious sip of her tea. "He has a nasty habit of doing that, doesn't he?"

He assumed that was a rhetorical question. "He says you were a wonderful nanny."

She looked into her teacup, trying to hide her pleasure. "We made a sight, the two of us."

He started to say "I can imagine," but decided against it. "And now you're a manicurist, huh?"

"That I am." She nodded.

"Do you have a shop?"

"No. Just regular customers. I visit them in their homes. A select clientele." She cast a reproving glance at his hands. "You could use a bit of help yourself, love."

Embarrassed, he looked down at his jagged nails. "It's a new bad habit, I'm afraid. I had flawless nails for thirty years." He decided to change the subject. "How did you know that Simon had . . . left the royal yacht?"

She sighed. "Oh, love . . . The *Mirror* went daft over it. You didn't read it? It was just a few days ago."

"No . . . actually, I didn't."

"They made it sound as if he'd slapped the Queen."

He made an effort to look duly concerned. "It was nothing like that," he said. "He just got tired of the navy."

"Balls," said Miss Treves.

"Uh . . . what?" He wasn't sure he had heard her correctly.

"The navy is one thing, love. The *Britannia* is quite another. It's a terrible disgrace."

"How did the press find out about it?"

She growled indignantly. "Some bally woman on the telly."

"In San Francisco?"

She nodded. "Then the *Mirror* did their own snooping about and found his address. Printed it, if you please."

He thought about that for a moment. "Is Simon's family . . . upset about it?"

Miss Treves chuckled. "You're lookin" at it, love."

"Oh . . ."

"His mum and dad came to a tragic end when Simon was still at Cambridge."

"Oh . . . I didn't know that."

Her hands fidgeted in her lap. "Simon doesn't like to talk about it. A dreadful wreck."

He nodded.

"Don't mention it to him, will you? The poor lad has spent eight years getting over it."

"Who wouldn't?" said Michael. He had already begun to forgive Simon for the apartment and to regard this miniature nanny as a kind of guardian angel in tweeds. "He's so lucky to have had you," he added.

Her small pink rosebud of a mouth made a smile that was just for him. "Simon always has such lovely friends."

A Good Match

Mary Ann had left for the Peninsula to do a human interest story on the closing of an auto plant, so Brian sought tangible ways to celebrate his first official day as a househusband at 28 Barbary Lane: He trimmed the ivy on all the windowsills. He scoured the crud off the grout in the shower stall, then organized the cleansers and sponges under the kitchen sink. Slithering under the bed, he went after dust balls with the single-minded frenzy of a terrier routing a gopher from its lair.

He was working for three now. Every sweep of the dustcloth, every squirt of Fantastik, every mouse turd he banished from the pantry, made the house just that much safer for The Kid.

The Kid.

He capitalized it in his mind, paying superstitious homage to the seed which, even as he swabbed the toilet, could already be sprouting in Mary Ann's womb. The Kid was everything now. That incredible, microscopic little bugger had turned his life around and given him a reason to get up in the morning. And that was nothing short of a miracle.

He took a break and made himself a ham sandwich, eating it in the little house on the roof while a rust-red tanker slid silently across the great blue expense of the bay. Above the terra-cotta tile of the Art Institute, a rainbow-striped kite flickered in the wind.

There was so much to show a child in this city, so many commonplace glories to be seen again through the eyes of The Kid. The windmill in Golden Gate Park. Chinatown in the fog. The waves that come crashing over the seawall at Fort Point. In his mind's eye, they were frolicking on a generic beach, he and this little piece of himself, this bright and lovable boy-or-girl who called him . . . what?

Daddy?

Dad?

Papa?

Papa wasn't bad, really. It had a kindly, old-world ring to it—stern but loving. Was it too stern? He didn't want to come off as autocratic. The Kid was a *person*, after all. The Kid must never fear him. Corporal punishment was out of the question.

He returned to the apartment, dropped his plate into the sink, then decided to scour the sink. As he worked, he could hear Mrs. Madrigal going about her gardening chores down below in the courtyard. She was humming a fractured version of "I Concentrate on You."

He was dying to tell her about The Kid, but he squelched the urge. For reasons he couldn't exactly pinpoint, he felt the news should come from Mary Ann. Besides, it would be more fun to wait until they had some indication that Mary Ann was pregnant.

He wanted to show Simon that there were no hard feelings, so he went downstairs and invited the lieutenant to go running with him. Later, as they huffed and puffed past deserted docks toward the Bay Bridge, he was impressed by Simon's endurance. He told him as much.

"We're a good match," was the gracious reply.

"Not only that," Brian continued, "but you seem to do OK in other departments too."

"How's that?"

Brian cast a brotherly leer at the lieutenant. "I saw her when she left this morning."

"Ah."

"Ah is right. Where did you find her?"

"Oh . . . a little *boîte* called the Balboa Café. Do you know it?"

"Used to," he replied. "It's been a while. Was she good?"

"Mmm. Up to a point."

Brian laughed.

"No pun intended, sir."

"Right."

"She was a little too . . . uh . . . shall we say enthusiastic?"

"Gotcha," said Brian. "She bit your nipples."

The lieutenant was clearly dumbfounded. "Well, yes . . . as a matter of fact, she did."

"That's big with her," said Brian.

"You know her, I take it?"

"Used to. Before I was married. Jennifer Rabinowitz, right?"

"Right."

"Quite a lady."

"She's made the rounds, then?"

Brian chuckled. "She's the head shark in the Bermuda Triangle."

"Sorry?"

"That's what they call it," he explained. "The neighborhood where the Balboa Café is."

"I see."

The lieutenant seemed a little nonplussed, so Brian tried to buck him up. "I mean . . . it's not like she's the town whore or anything. She doesn't sack out with just everybody."

"Gratifying," said Simon.

They stopped running when they reached the bridge, then walked inland from the Embarcadero and sat at the base of the Villaincourt Fountain. A small Vietnamese child approached them, bearing a net bag. Brian waved him away.

"What was that about?" asked Simon.

"He wanted to sell us garlic."

"Why garlic?"

"Beats me. They get it in Gilroy and sell it on the streets here. Dozens of little Artful Dodgers hustling the white men who invaded their parents' country. Poetic, huh?"

"I should say."

"You're a great running partner," said Brian.

"Thank you, sir. So are you."

He shook the lieutenant's knee heartily. He liked this guy a lot, and not just because Jennifer Rabinowitz had made them equals. "You're looking at one happy sonofabitch," he said.

"Why is that?"

"Well . . . Mary Ann and I have decided to have a baby. I mean, she's not pregnant yet, but we're working on it."

"That's wonderful," said Simon.

"Yeah . . . it sure as hell is."

They sat there in silence, lulled by the splash of the fountain.

"Don't tell her I told you," said Brian.

"Of course not."

"I don't want her to feel like there's . . . you know . . . pressure on her."

"I understand."

"What will be, will be . . . you know?"

"Mmm."

"By the way, you're more than welcome to use the TV room whenever you feel like it."

"Thank you. Uh . . . where is it?"

"On the roof. All the way up the stairs. Everybody in the house uses it."

"Marvelous."

"I'll show you how to work the VCR. You might have some fun with that. I've got *Debbie Does Dallas*."

"Sorry?"

"It's a porn movie."

"Ah."

"I haven't played it very much . . . only when Mary Ann goes on assignment or something. Then I put that baby on and . . . wrestle with the ol' cyclops."

A slow smile spread across Simon's face. "You mean bang the bishop?"

"You catch on fast." Brian grinned.

Mirage

Michael's teenage sojourn in London had been spent with a family in Hampstead who housed him through a student program sponsored by the English-Speaking Union. Mr. and Mrs. Mainwaring had been childless, and they'd fussed over him as if he'd been their own, taking him to plays in the West End, plying him with shortbread at teatime, stocking the pantry with his favorite brand of thick-cut English marmalade.

He'd lost touch with them years before, so he couldn't help wondering if they were still watching their beloved telly in that snug little house off New End Square. Even if they weren't, the thought of seeing Hampstead again was wonderfully exhilarating. There was nothing quite like going back to an old neighborhood.

Leaving Simon's house, he wound his way through the vegetables and bric-a-brac of Portobello Road until he reached the ragtag commercial center of Notting Hill Gate. The familiar circle-bar brand of the London Underground beckoned him to a hole in the sidewalk, where he pumped coins into a ticket machine that listed Hampstead as a destination.

An escalator carried him still deeper, to the platform of the Central Line, from which he caught an eastbound train to Tottenham Court Road. Disembarking, he strode as knowingly as possible to the platform of the Northern Line, where a once-dormant signal in the back of his brain advised him that the Edgware train, *not* the High Barnet, would take him to Hampstead.

He loved the particulars of all this: The classic simplicity of the Underground map, with its geometric patterns and varicolored arteries. The warm, stale winds that whipped through the cream-and-green-tile pedestrian tunnels. The passengers—from skinheads to pinstripers—all wearing the same mask of bored and dignified disdain.

When the train stopped at Hampstead, his next route was indicated by a sign saying WAY OUT, a nobler phrase by far than the bland American EXIT. Since Hampstead was London's most elevated neighborhood, the lift to the street was London's deepest, a groaning Art Nouveau monster with a recorded voice so muted and decrepit ("Stand clear of the gate," it said) that it might have been a resident ghost. He remembered that voice, in fact, and it gave him his first shiver of déjà vu.

The streets of the borough were mercifully unchanged, despite the encroachment of fast-food parlors and chrome-and-mauve salons specializing in "hair design." He strolled along the redbrick high street until he came upon the hulking redbrick hospital that stood by the street leading to New End Square.

Four minutes later, he was hesitating in front of the house that had been his for three months in 1967. The chintz curtains that had once shielded the living room from the gaze of passersby had been replaced by Levolors. Did a gay person live there now? Had the Mainwarings retired to some characterless "estate home" in the suburbs? Could he deal with the changes, whatever they were? Did he really want to know?

He really didn't. Returning to the high street, he ate lunch in one of the new American-style hamburger joints, a "café" decorated with neon cacti and old Coca-Cola signs. Once upon a time, he recalled, Wimpy bars had served the only hamburgers in London, but they had hardly qualified.

He downed several ciders at an old haunt in Flask Walk, then considered his options for the afternoon. He could stroll over to the Spaniards Inn and down one or two more. He could look for the house where the inventor of the Christmas card had lived. He could wander down to the Vale of Health and sit by the pond where Shelley had sailed his paper boats.

Or he could look for the bricklayer.

Another cider settled the issue. Shelley and the inventor of the Christmas card were no match for the memory of a hairless scrotum. He breezed out of the pub and ambled along the pale green crest of the city toward Jack Straw's Castle and the Spaniards Road.

The heath was much as he had remembered it—rolling reaches of lawn bordered by dark clumps of urban forest. There seemed to be more litter now (which was true of London in general), but the two-hundred-acre park was still rife with the stuff of mystery. On his last visit, the sound of the wind in its thick foliage had instantly evoked an eerie scene from *Blow-Up*, a movie which meant London to Michael in the way that *Vertigo* meant San Francisco.

He entered the heath from the Spaniards Road, following a broad trail through the trees. When he reached Hampstead Ponds, he stopped for a while and watched a trio of children romping along the water's edge. Their mother, a freckled redhead in a green sweater and slacks, smiled at him wearily as if to thank him for the tribute he had paid her offspring. He smiled back and skipped a stone on the water, just to get a rise out of the kids.

It was here, he remembered, that a road led down to the south end of the heath and the street where the bricklayer had lived. *The street where he lived.* He laughed out loud at his gay rewrite, then began humming the tune from *My Fair Lady*.

The street was called South End Road. He remembered it because it intersected with Keats Grove, the street where the poet had lived, and Keats had been one of the things they had discussed after sex, along with Paul McCartney, motorcycles and world peace.

He found the place almost immediately, recognizing the nightingales in the Edwardian stained glass above the door. This was no time to think, he decided. He threw caution to the winds and rang the bell of the ground-floor flat. An old man in a cardigan came to the door.

"This is kind of unusual," Michael began, "but a friend of mine lived here a long time ago, and I was wondering if he still does."

The old man squinted at him for a moment, then said: "What was his name?"

"Well . . . that's the unusual part. I don't remember. He was a bricklayer . . . a big, strapping fellow. He must be about fifty now." *Come to think of it, I believe he did have a hairless scrotum.*

The current occupant shook his head thoughtfully. "How long ago was this?"

"Sixteen years. Nineteen sixty-seven."

A raspy chuckle. "He must be long gone. The wife and me have been here longer than the other tenants, but that's just eight years. Sixteen years! No wonder you've forgotten his name!"

Michael thanked him and left, accepting the futility of the quest. It didn't really matter. What would he have said, anyway, had he found his savior? *You don't know me, but thanks for being there first?*

The sun was quite warm now and cottony clouds were scudding across the sky, so he crossed the heath again and headed for the wooded mound that locals knew as Boadicea's tomb. No one really believed that the ancient queen was actually buried under the hillock, but the name endured nonetheless. He had gone there once at midnight, upon reading in *The Times* that the Order of Bards, Ovates and Druids would gather at the site for their Midsummer's Night ritual. The intrigue had vanished like ectoplasm when he saw for himself that the "Druids" were bank clerks in bedsheets and grandmothers in harlequin glasses.

As another chunk of the past slipped away from him, he sat down on the grass and tilted his face to the sun. Fifty yards below him, a large black sedan crossed the heath slowly, then came to a stop. A woman got out—blonde hair, white blouse, gray skirt stopping at midcalf—a striking figure against the endless green of the landscape. She turned in every direction, apparently searching for someone.

He observed her idly for a moment, then sprang to his feet, his mind ablaze with conflicting images.

"Mona!" he shouted.

The woman's head jerked around to find the source of his voice. *"It's me, Mona! Mouse!"*

The woman froze, then spun on her heel and climbed back into the sedan.

It sped out of sight into the trees.

Off the Record

The deluge of publicity that hit Simon after the broadcast made Mary Ann begin to wonder if it had been too much for him. He *seemed* to be all right, but he was a funny bird in many ways, and she could rarely tell what was really on his mind. The last thing she wanted was to alienate him.

When the weekend came, she waited until the time was right (Brian had gone to the laundromat) and invited the Englishman to join her on her shopping rounds in North Beach. Half an hour later, all she had to show for it was a pint carton of Molinari's pickled mushrooms.

"This is your *weekly* shopping?" Simon asked. They were walking up Columbus toward Washington Square.

She laughed, abandoning the pretense altogether. "I just needed an excuse to get out of the house. I've been feeling . . . cooped up lately."

"Shall we walk somewhere?" he asked.

"I'd love to," she replied.

"Where? You're the local, madam."

She smiled. She liked it when he called her madam. "I know just the place," she said.

She walked him up Union Street to the top of Telegraph Hill, then down Montgomery to its junction with the Filbert Steps. "The penthouse directly above us," she explained, "is the one that Lauren Bacall had in *Dark Passage.*"

He craned his muscular, patrician neck. "Really?"

"The one where Bogart has the plastic surgery that makes him look like Bogart. Remember?"

"Of course," he replied.

"My friend DeDe used to live there."

"Ah. Do I know about her?"

"The one who escaped from Guyana."

125

"Right."

She led him halfway down the wooden stairway, then brushed off a plank and sat down.

"This is not unlike Barbary Lane," he remarked, joining her.

She nodded. "There are places like this all over the city. This is technically a city street."

"The garden is magnificent."

"The city doesn't do that," she told him. "A precious old lady did that—this used to be a garbage dump. She was a stunt woman in Hollywood years ago, and then she moved up here and started planting this. Everybody just calls it Grace's Garden. She died just before Christmas. Her ashes are under that statue down there."

He looked faintly amused. "You're a veritable fount of local color."

"I did a story on her," she explained.

"I see." He was teasing her ever so subtly. "Do you do stories on everyone you know?"

She hesitated, wondering about his motives again. "Has it been too much?" she finally asked him.

The smile he offered seemed genuine enough. "Not at all."

"I hope not."

"I'm *astounded* there's been such a reaction. But it hasn't been unpleasant."

"Good."

"As long as you don't let any other journalists know where I am."

"Don't worry," she replied. "I want you all to myself."

He smiled again and bent a branch so that a large blossom touched the tip of his nose.

"They don't smell," she said.

He released the branch, catapulting the blossom toward the sky.

"It's called a fried egg plant," she added, "because it looks like . . ."

"Don't tell me, now. Let me guess."

She laughed.

"A bowling ball? No? A loaf of bread, perhaps?"

She shook his knee. "Stop teasing."

A silence followed. She felt awkward about her hand on his knee, so she removed it.

"Who lives in these houses?" Simon asked.

She was glad to take refuge in her role as tour guide. "Well . . . they're squatter shacks . . ."

"Really? I thought that was peculiar to England."

"Oh, no," she answered. "Are you kidding? During the gold rush . . ."

He cut her off with a brittle laugh. "We're in different centuries, I think. I meant *now*."

Thoroughly confused, she retraced her steps. "You . . . have squatters now?"

He nodded. "London is crawling with them."

"You mean . . . people just claim land?"

"Houses, actually. Flats. The hippies started it, back when the city allowed empty council flats to fall into disrepair. They moved in, fixed them up a bit . . . claimed them for their own."

"Well," she commented, "that sounds fair enough."

"Mmm," he replied, "unless you're the chap who goes on holiday and comes home to a family of Pakistanis . . . or what-have-you."

"Has that happened?"

"Oh, yes."

"They just move in? Take over the furniture and everything?"

He nodded. "To evict them, one must prove forcible entry. That's bloody difficult sometimes. There can be months of mucking about before they're booted out. It's a complicated issue, mind you."

"I can imagine."

"There are squatters in my building," he added. "They took over the vacant flat above me."

"You didn't see them do this?"

He shook his head. "I was on the royal honeymoon at the time."

"What are they like?"

"The Prince and Princess?"

She smiled. "The squatters."

"Oh . . . a middle-aged chap and his son. The father drinks too much. They're aboriginals. Half-castes, actually."

She had vague visions of grass-skirted natives with bones through their noses dancing around in circles, but she dismissed the subject in deference to a far more fascinating one. "OK. Now you can tell me about the royal honeymoon."

The smile he sent back was tinged with diplomacy. "I thought we covered that in the interview."

"That was the official stuff," she said. "Now I want the dirt."

He pulled the blossom into sniffing range again. "Off the record?"

"Of course."

"Off the record, there is no dirt."

"C'mon."

"My job was working with the radios. I saw very little of the honeymooners."

"Is she pretty?"

"Very."

"Beautiful?"

"You're on the right track." He smiled.

"Would she know you if she saw you on the street?"

He nodded. "I took her out once."

"You . . . *dated* her?"

"I escorted her to a David Bowie concert. Her flatmate knew a friend of mine. The four of us went. It was years ago . . . when she was only a lady."

She giggled. "You *double-dated* with Lady Di."

"So far"—he grinned—"there have been no medals for that."

"Was she really a virgin when she married him?"

He shrugged. "Insofar as I had anything to do with it."

She looked him in the eye. "Did you try?"

His lip flickered. "You don't give up easily, do you?"

"Well," she replied, "it's not like it's a big deal or anything. People do these things. Times have changed. Everybody does every-thing and nobody cares."

"And discretion," he added with a gentle smile, "is the last act of gallantry."

It was all she could do to keep from showing her relief. He had passed with flying colours. She conceded her defeat with a demure smile. "Never kiss and tell, huh?"

He shook his head. "I like kissing too much."

The screeching which prevented her next remark was so sudden and shrill that it took her a moment to realize what it was.

"Good Lord!" murmured Simon. That beautiful neck was once again arched toward the heavens.

"They're parrots," she said. "Wild ones."

"They're remarkable! I had no idea they were indigenous."

"They aren't. Not exactly. Some of them were in cages originally. The others are descended from ones that were in cages. They just sort of . . . found each other."

He turned and smiled at her. "That's a nice story."

"Yes," she replied. "Isn't it?"

English Leather

Five hours after his hallucination on the heath, Michael languished in a shallow tub back at Colville Crescent. It had been that dream, he decided at last—that Death Valley dream in which Mona had ignored his cries from the bluff. Something about the hillside on the heath, something about the blonde woman's stance or the angle from which he had watched her, had conjured up that dream again and caused him to lose touch with reality.

The woman hadn't *looked* like Mona, certainly. Not with that hair. And those clothes. Or even the way she carried herself. If anything, he had reacted to her aura—a concept so embarrassingly Californian that he vowed never to express it to anyone. This elegant stranger had simply touched a nerve somewhere, triggering his anxiety about a friendship which had all but collapsed.

He was determined not to think about that. He put on his black

Levi's and his white button-down shirt and headed into Notting Hill Gate, where he ate a curry dinner at a cramped Indian restaurant. Afterwards, he cashed a traveler's cheque at the local *Bureau de Change*, picked up a *Private Eye* at his newsstand, and returned to the house. Miss Treves, all three feet whatever of her, was crossing the front yard as he arrived.

"Oh, *there* you are, love."

"Hi!" It was pleasant to notice how much she felt like a friend. "I was just out having dinner."

"Having a marvelous time, are you?"

"Of course," he lied.

"Good. I brought my case. You don't mind, do you?" She held up a green leather satchel, roughly the size and shape of a shoe box.

He didn't get it. "I'm sorry . . . mind what?"

Her free hand, tiny and pudgy as a baby's, grabbed one of his. "These horrors. Something must be done about them. We can't have a friend of Simon's looking such a fright." She cocked her head and winked at him. "It won't take long."

He was both embarrassed and touched. "That's really nice, but . . ."

"I shan't charge you. You haven't plans for the evening, have you?"

He had toyed with the idea of exploring the gay bars in Earl's Court, but that hardly seemed an appropriate answer under the circumstances. "No," he replied, "not for the next few hours."

"Lovely," she chirped, turning smartly to lead the way into the house. Once inside, she opened her manicure kit and removed a newspaper clipping, tattered from many unfoldings. "This is a load of rubbish, but I thought you might like to see it." The headline said: ROYAL RADIOMAN ON FRISCO PLEASURE BINGE.

He scanned the piece quickly. Simon came off sounding like a thorough hedonist, a bratty aristocrat squandering the family fortune on nameless excesses in the "fruit-and-nut capital" of the western hemisphere. He returned the document with a discrediting smile. "You're right. It's a load of rubbish."

Miss Treves grunted as she poured a soapy liquid into a little bowl. He immediately thought of Madge the Manicurist on TV and wondered if he'd be soaking in dishwashing liquid. The whole scenario struck him as supremely funny.

She took one of his hands and placed it in the bowl. "Did you notice they printed this address?"

"Uh-huh," he said.

She said nothing.

"Should that be . . . a problem?"

"I don't know, love." She poked through her kit, searching for something. "You haven't noticed anyone snooping about, have you?"

What on earth was she getting at? "Uh . . . no. Not that I've noticed. You mean like . . . burglars or something?"

"No. Just . . . general snooping about."

"No. Not a thing."

"Good."

"Look, I'd appreciate it if . . ."

"It's nothing, love. I'm sure it's nothing." She began jabbing away at his cuticles. "When they print your bally address, it makes me nervous, that's all."

The manicure proved to be a reassuringly intimate experience. To sit there passively while this vinegary little woman repaired his nails gave him a sense of being noticed for the first time since his arrival in London. "Have you done this long?" he asked eventually.

"Oh . . . about fifteen years, I suppose."

"And before that you were Simon's nanny?"

"Mmm."

"Did you do nanny work for other families?"

"No. Just the Bardills. Let's have the other hand, love."

He obeyed as she repositioned the stool. "Did you always want to be a nanny?" he asked. As soon as he had spoken, he wondered if the question was too personal. He had never stopped to think about what career opportunities were open to a midget.

"Oh, no!" she answered immediately. "I wanted to be in show business. I *was* in show business."

"You mean like a . . . ?" A circus was what came to mind, but he knew better than to finish the sentence.

"A musical revue," she said. "A traveling show. A bit of song and dance. Readings from Shakespeare. That sort of thing."

"How fascinating," he exclaimed, captivated by the thought of a miniature Lady Macbeth. "Why did you give it up?"

She heaved a sigh. "They gave *us* up, love. The audience. The telly killed us, I always said. Who wanted Bunny Benbow when they could have *Coronation Street* for nothing?"

"Bunny Benbow? That was the name?"

"The Bunny Benbow Revue." She giggled like one of the mice in *Cinderella*. "Silly, isn't it? It sounds so old-fashioned now."

"I wish I'd seen it," he said.

"Simon's mum and dad took me in after we folded. Their friends thought they were daft, but it well and truly saved my life. I owe them a great deal, a great deal." She finished filing a jagged nail and looked up at him. "What about you, love? How do you put bread on the table?"

"I'm a nurseryman," he told her.

"How lovely." She stopped her work for a moment and stared misty-eyed into space. "Simon's mum had a splendid garden at our country place in Sussex. Hollyhocks. Roses. The dearest little violets . . ."

He noticed that her lip was trembling slightly.

She sighed finally. "Time marches on."

"Yes," he replied.

When she had gone, half an hour later, his spirits had improved considerably, so he decided to follow through with his original plan and check out the gay bars in Earl's Court. The tube brought him within a block of Harpoon Louie's, a windowless bar which flew a Union Jack in an apparent effort to show that poofters could be patriots too.

Inside, the place was self-consciously American: blond wood, industrial shades on the lights, Warhol prints. Perhaps in deference to the current occupant of Kensington Palace, the tape machine was playing Paul Anka's "Diana." The barmaid, in fact, looked like a chubbier version of the Princess of Wales.

The crowd was decidedly clonish—tank-topped, Adidas-shod, every bit as inclined toward attitude as a standard Saturday night mob on Castro Street. They smoked more, it seemed, and their teeth and bodies weren't as pretty, but Disco Madness (circa 1978) was alive and well in Earl's Court.

Finding a seat at a banquette against the wall, he nursed a gin and tonic and observed the scene for several minutes. Then he read a story about Sylvester in a newspaper called *Capital Gay* ("The Free One") and wandered into the back garden, where the smoke and noise were less oppressive.

He left as a clock was striking ten somewhere and walked several blocks past high-windowed brick buildings to a gay pub called the Coleherne. These were the leather boys, apparently. He ordered another gin and tonic and stood at the bulletin board reading announcements about Gay Tory meetings and "jumble sales" to benefit deaf lesbians.

When he returned to the horseshoe-shaped bar, the man across from him smiled broadly. He was a kid really, not more than eighteen or nineteen, and his skin was the same shade as the dark ale he was drinking. His hair was the startling part—soft brown ringlets that glinted with gold under the light, floating above his mischievous eyes like . . . well, like the froth on his ale. In his white shirt and bow tie and sleeveless argyle sweater he came as welcome relief from the white men in black leather who surrounded him.

Michael smiled back. His admirer kissed the tip of his forefinger and wagged it at him. Michael lifted his glass as a thank you. The kid hopped off his barstool and made his way through the sullen throng to Michael's side of the bar.

"I fancy your jeans," he said. "I noticed them when you came in."

Michael glanced down at the black Levi's. "Thanks," he said. "I'm breaking them in."

"You dye them yourself?"

"No . . . no, they come that way."

"Really?"

The upward lilt of his voice was almost Dickensian, and Michael enjoyed being reminded that a man who sounded like that could look like this. Up close, his full lips and broad nose seemed distinctly African, but his unlikely hair (lighter than Michael's own, he noted) remained a mystery.

"Mine's just the regular sort." The kid hooked his thumbs proudly in the pockets of his 501s. They seemed somewhat out of sync with the rest of his getup, but he looked pretty good in them just the same.

"You don't see many of those," Michael remarked. "Not around here."

"Twenty pounds in Fulham Road. Worth every penny, if you ask me. You fancy this place, do you?"

"It's . . . fine," was all he could manage. The room looked like a pub, at least. Just the same, there was something almost poignant about pasty-faced Britishers trying to pull off a butch biker routine. They were simply the wrong breed for it. He was reminded of an English tourist who had all but lived in the back room at The Boot Camp, but had never uttered a single word. That man had come to grips with the truth: Phrases like "Suck that big, fat cock" and "Yeah, you want it, don't you?" sounded just plain asinine when muttered with an Oxonian accent.

The kid gave the room a disparaging once-over. "They look like the dog's lunch to me."

Michael laughed. "I don't know what that means, but it doesn't sound good."

"It's not, mate, it's not. What part of the States are you from?"

"San Francisco."

"Well . . ." The kid rocked on his heels. "Poofters out the arse, eh?"

Michael smiled. "I guess you could say that."

"The Queen went there, didn't she?"

"Right."

"Rained like bloody hell."

"Still is," Michael said, "as far as I know. Just like here."

Still rocking on his heels, the kid gave him a half-lidded smile. "So . . . what say we have a go?"

"Uh . . . what?"

"Have a *go*, mate." He banged his pale palms together to show what he meant.

Michael chuckled. "Oh."

"What say?"

"Thanks, but . . . I'm off the stuff for a while."

"Don't fancy wogs, eh?"

His directness seemed designed to throw Michael off balance. "Not at all. I just haven't been very horny lately."

"Well, what are you doin' here, then?"

"Good question. Seeing the sights, I guess."

"OK, then . . . I'm one of 'em. My name's Wilfred." He extended his hand as an enormous grin spread across his face like a sunrise.

Michael shook hands with him. "I'm Michael."

For the next half hour, they remained side by side at the bar, but spoke very little. Meanwhile, the legions of would-be leatherettes grew shriller and smokier as rain sluiced noisily through the gutters outside the door.

"You didn't bring a brolly, did you, mate?"

"Nope. Like a dummy."

"C'mon, then. I did."

It sounded like another invitation to "have a go," so Michael took the easy way out. "Thanks. I think I'll just hang out for a little while longer."

"You'll be sorry," said Wilfred.

"Why?"

"Look at the time, mate."

A clock advertising Dane Crisps said ten forty-five.

"It's almost closing time," Wilfred pointed out. "It isn't a pretty sight."

"What do you mean?"

"They turn the lights up. If you think these blokes look grotty now, just you wait till eleven o'clock!"

Michael laughed. "A surefire way to empty the place."

"They know what they're doing." The kid grinned. "In straight pubs they turn the lights *down* at closing time. Who says we're just the same, eh? C'mon, now . . . what's your next stop?"

"The tube station. I'm going home."

"Super. So am I." He took Michael's arm and steered him through the crowd to the door, then opened his umbrella. "Here, c'mon . . . get under here, mate."

Since Michael was at least four inches taller than his escort, he held the umbrella while Wilfred acted as navigator and guide, his right hand snugly planted in the right rear pocket of Michael's 501's.

"Princess Diana lived down the way a bit . . . back when she was a teacher. Think of that, eh? Passing all these leather blokes on her way to the bleedin' kindergarten. Here! Mind the lorry!"

Michael jumped back onto the curb as a huge truck rumbled past, only inches away.

The whites of Wilfred's eyes flashed under the umbrella like a pair of headlights. "One more like that, mate, and we're married for all eternity." He pointed to white lettering on the street. "See? 'Look Right,' it says. We even paint it there for you bleedin' Americans."

They strode briskly past a newsstand, then a garish ethnic restaurant—Arabic, maybe—with the menu painted on plywood and a huge chunk of symmetrical mystery meat, floodlit by pink bulbs, spinning like a top on a vertical spit.

"Druggies eat there," said Wilfred. "It's open late. Do you have a lover back in the States?"

Michael laughed. "Nice segue."

"Nice what?"

"Nothing. Bad joke. No, I don't have a lover."

"Why not?"

He hesitated. "I used to have a lover. It didn't work out."

"A delicate subject, eh?"

"Yeah."

"I'd like to have a lover, I think, but I don't think I'm going to meet one at the Coleherne."

"I know what you mean," said Michael.

They rode the tube in virtual silence, as tradition seemed to demand, Wilfred's blue-denimed knee pressed against Michael's black one.

"What's your stop?" asked Michael.

"Same as yours, mate. Notting Hill Gate."

Michael was floored.

The kid grinned. "You've never even noticed me, have you?"

"I'm sorry. I don't know what . . ."

"I live upstairs from you, mate. Good ol' Forty-four Colville Crescent."

The final proof came when they reached the house and Wilfred produced a key that opened the front door. He flipped the timer switch before turning to peck Michael lightly on the lips. "G'night, mate. Thanks for walking me home."

Then he sprinted up the stairs to the second floor.

Cross Purposes

Like other things about her, Mary Ann's menstrual cycle was so regular that Mussolini might have included it on his train schedules. When the world was going to hell in a handbasket and chaos ruled the day, she could always count on the prompt arrival of her period—or, as her mother had once explained it, "the bloody tears of a disappointed uterus."

Her uterus had been unusually disappointed today, which meant that her midmonth pains were due in another fourteen days, give or take a day or so. According to her doctor at St. Sebastian's (and several authors she had seen on *Donahue*), those pains—*mittelschmerz* was the silly technical term—were the surest indication of ovulation.

While some women apparently showed no outward signs of

ovulation other than uncomfortable periods, Mary Ann had all the evidence she needed, thank you. Flipping through her *New Yorker* appointment book, she counted fourteen days ahead and found herself landing squarely on Sunday, April 3—Easter Day.

Eggs at Easter. Cute.

Brian never asked her about her *mittelschmerz*, apparently preferring to trust romantically in what he called "the good ol' hunt and peck method of making babies." The term had always annoyed her (why were men so *proud* of their obliviousness?), but she was suddenly grateful for his blind traditionalism.

She closed the appointment book and leaned back in her chair, suddenly thinking of Mouse. She had explained her *mittelschmerz* to him once, partially as a way of explaining her bitchy flare-ups, and he had never let her hear the end of it. ("Uh-oh," he would say, catching her with a frown on her face, "you're not having your *ethelmertz*, are you?") She giggled at the thought of that, and blew him a kiss across the world.

The rest of her day was horrendous. She argued for at least an hour with a director who wanted to score her baby bear footage with cutesy-pie Disney music. Then Bambi Kanetaka insisted on ditching Mary Ann's Wildflowers of Alcatraz story to make room for a sleazy feature on sex surrogates in Marin.

When she got home at eight o'clock, Brian was bustling around in his denim apron while an aromatic beef stew waited on the stove. He pecked her on the cheek, then saw the fatigue in her face. "A ballbuster, huh?"

"Yep."

"Well . . . this should cheer you up. We got an intriguing invitation today."

"Yeah? Who from?"

"Theresa Cross. She wants us to come hang out for a weekend. Use the pool, kick back . . . Who knows? Maybe even make a baby or two." Seeing her expression change, he added: "Hey, I know she's not one of your favorite people, but . . . well, it's kind of a nice gesture, isn't it?"

"Yeah," she conceded. "It is."

He looked relieved. "She's having some of her rock-and-roll friends."

"Great. When does she want us?"

"Easter weekend."

Of course, she thought.

"What's the matter?" he asked.

"Well . . . I can't, that's all."

"Why not?"

"I just . . . well, I have to work."

"On *what*?" he asked feistily. "It's Easter, for God's sake."

"I know, but . . . I promised to do the Easter feature for them . . . the sunrise service at Mount Davidson, that sort of stuff. I know it's a bummer, Brian. I meant to tell you earlier. Father Paddy is doing the sunrise service, and they want me to . . . you know . . . cover it for *Bay Window*."

He hung a scowl on his face. "Jesus," he muttered.

"I'm sorry," she replied softly, avoiding the Jesus jokes.

"*Easter*, for God's sake. Where do they get off telling you you have to . . ."

"Brian, it's my job."

"I know it's your job." His forehead was forming ugly little trenches, a sure danger sign. "Don't start with that it's-my-job crap. I know what your responsibilities are. And your priorities, for that matter. I'm just disappointed. All right? I have a right to that, don't I?"

"Of course."

"Forget I asked," he said in a calmer tone. "I'll tell Theresa we can't make it."

It jarred her to hear him call the rock widow by her first name—as if they were old buddies—but what else was he supposed to call her? Certainly not Mrs. Cross. "Don't do that," she said. "I think you should go."

He blinked at her.

"I *want* you to go," she added.

"I don't know . . ."

"Look, one of us should find out what it's like. Who's gonna be there, anyway?"

"Well . . . Grace Slick, for starters."

"Wow."

He eyed her suspiciously. "Since when did you say wow to Grace Slick?"

"That's not fair," she sulked. "I like Grace Slick."

"You do not like Grace Slick. You've never liked Grace Slick. Come off it."

"Well . . . I meant the wow for you. It was a vicarious wow. Oh, for God's sake, Brian, go to your rock-and-roll party. It's tailor-made for you. You'll be pissed at me forever if you don't go."

His eyes became doglike. "I wanted somebody to laugh at it with."

It was one of those moments of uncomplicated connection that made up for all the grueling compromises of marriage. She nuzzled his neck for a moment, then said: "We'll laugh about it later. I promise."

He drew away from her to add a missing detail. "She's asked her guests for overnight. I mean, like . . . the whole weekend."

She shrugged. Under the circumstances, she could hardly get huffy. "Fine. Great."

"Do you mean that?" he asked earnestly. "Or are you just being modern?"

"If she touches you . . ." She chewed her forefinger, pretending to ruminate. "I'll tear her tits off."

He laughed, then snapped his fingers. "I've got a great idea!"

"What?" He was making her nervous.

"I'll take Simon along with me."

"I don't know, Brian." She weighed several arguments and settled on one. "That's a little rude."

"Why?"

"Well . . . she invited the two of us. She doesn't even know Simon and . . . well, since it's our first real invitation, it might be a little pushy to drag along a perfect stranger . . . especially one who's kind of a groupie and all."

"That's what I thought would be perfect," he said. "He's crazy about her . . . and unattached."

"Yeah, but she's probably got a surplus of men as it is."

"Straight men?"

"Well . . . whatever. Don't fix them up, Brian."

"Why not?"

"Because . . . she's too much of a vulture."

He laughed. "I think Simon can take care of himself."

"Don't be so sure," she said, leaning against him again. "Have you forgiven me yet?"

"I'm working on it."

"Good. There's something else we can work on, too."

"What?"

"Save Palm Sunday for me, will you?"

"Why?"

"Because . . . the signs are good . . . babywise."

It took him a while. "You mean . . . *ethelmertz?*"

She nodded. "*Ethelmertz.*"

"Hot damn!" He held her closer. "That makes up for Easter, right there."

"Good," she replied. "I hoped it would."

The Kid Upstairs

Michael was feeling remarkably chipper when he awoke at eight forty-five in Simon's musty bedroom. A cement mixer gargled gratingly out in the street and someone was frying kippers across the garden, but nothing could shake his nagging suspicion that life was finally getting better.

He flipped on his bedside radio. A newscaster informed him that a schoolmaster had been found crucified on a moor in Scotland and that London bookmakers had opened bets on when the capital would have a consecutive forty-eight-hour period without rain. None of it bothered him a bit.

He was brewing a pot of tea when someone tapped on his door. To be almost certain who it was gave him the pleasant illusion of being at home.

"Mornin', mate."

Michael smiled at the kid. "Mornin.'"

Wilfred was wearing a variation of last night's ensemble—a bow tie (black) and sleeveless sweater (turquoise), with a white shirt and 501s. He had a "look," it seemed. Michael couldn't help remembering the porkpie hat he had worn all over London when he was sixteen.

"Tea?" he asked.

"Super," said Wilfred.

"Sit down, I'll bring it in."

He returned to the kitchen and came back with the tea things on a tray. "Why didn't you tell me you lived here?"

Wilfred shrugged, now sprawled on the sofa, one leg draped over the arm. "I didn't want to be the wog kid upstairs. I wanted to meet you . . ." He searched for the right words and couldn't find them.

"With our tribe?" offered Michael.

"There you go." Wilfred smiled.

"Did you follow me to the Coleherne?"

The kid's face registered mild indignation. "You're not the only bleedin' poofter who goes to the Cloneherne, y'know."

Michael took note of the pun. "The Cloneherne, huh?"

Wilfred twinkled at him. "That's me own name for it."

"Not bad."

"So what are you doin' in Lord Twitzy-twee's flat?"

"We swapped apartments. I gave him my place in San Francisco for a month and . . . Simon's a lord?"

"He acts like one, that's for sure. He's a poof, is he?"

Michael shook his head. "Nope."

"Didn't think so." Wilfred surveyed the room imperially. "Not very tidy."

On that point, at least, there seemed to be a consensus. "I don't think it matters to him," Michael said.

"Who's the midge?" asked the kid.

"The who?"

"The midge. The runt lady who visits."

"His nanny," Michael replied. "And watch your mouth."

"His *nanny*. My-my."

"What do you take in your tea?"

A powerful voice thundered in the stairwell. "*Wilfred!*"

"Jesus," muttered Michael. "Who's that?"

The kid was already heading for the door. "Look . . . meet me at the tube station in half an hour. I've got something special to show you."

"Wilfred, who was that?"

"Aw . . . me dad, that's all."

"Your *father?*"

"Tube station. Half an hour. Got it? You won't be sorry."

He dashed out the door, blowing a kiss as he left.

Michael listened to him clattering up the stairs, then sat down and poured himself a cup of tea. This was an entirely new wrinkle. If Wilfred lived with his parents, the last thing Michael needed was to come off as the foreign reprobate who had "recruited" their son. Daddy Dearest didn't exactly sound like a man of reason.

Fuck that. His life had finally begun to take on a momentum of its own, and it felt too good to turn back now. Or, as Mrs. Madrigal had once explained it: "Only a fool refuses to follow, when Pan comes prancing through the forest."

So he ate his toast and marmalade, made his bed, and strolled up Portobello Road toward the tube station. Wilfred was waiting for him by the ticket machines. "I wasn't sure you'd make it," Michael said.

"Why?" asked the kid.

"Well . . . your father sounded pissed."

Wilfred shook his head. "He doesn't start in drinking till noon."

Michael smiled, recognizing a language problem. "I meant pissed angry, not pissed drunk."

"Oh. Well, he's always pissed angry."

"About what?"

Wilfred thought for a moment. "Maggie Thatcher and me, mostly. Not necessarily in that order, mind you." He mimicked his father's booming basso. "'Oo needs a bleedin' Thatcher, when ya ain't got a bleedin' roof over your head? Eh? *Eh?*' That's his favorite joke."

Michael chuckled. "You do it well."

"I hear it enough," said Wilfred.

Following the kid's instructions, Michael bought a ticket to Wimbledon, the last stop on the District Line, south of the river. As they waited on the platform, he asked Wilfred: "Does this have something to do with tennis?"

"Just shut your trap, mate. You'll see."

"Yes, *sir.*"

Wilfred gave him an elfin grin. For just a moment, he reminded Michael of Ned in Death Valley, teasing his friends with the undisclosed wonders that lay just beyond the next bluff.

As the train thundered through the sooty tunnel, Michael asked: "Does your father know you're gay?"

Wilfred nodded.

"How did he find out?"

The kid shrugged. "I was busted for cottaging, mate. I think that gave him a clue."

"Cottaging?"

"You know . . . doin' it in a cottage."

Michael's confusion was obvious.

"A cottage," Wilfred repeated. *"A public loo."*

A woman across from them grimaced fiercely.

"Oh," said Michael, somewhat meekly.

"That's how I got tossed out of school . . . not to mention sacked from my job. I used to work down here in Wimbledon."

"We call that a tearoom," Michael pointed out.

"What? Where I worked? It was a bleedin' chippie!"

"No, a cottage. We call a cottage a tearoom." It was beginning to sound like a gay variation on "Who's on First?" and the woman across the way was the last to be amused. "I think we'd better drop this, Wilfred."

The kid shrugged. "Fine with me, mate."

When they reached Wimbledon, Wilfred bought a Cadbury bar at the station, broke off a chunk and handed it to Michael. "We've got a bit of a walk now. Let's hope ol' Dingo's still there."

"You bet," Michael replied, smirking a little. He had no intention of asking what that meant. It was amazing, really, how much Wilfred's technique resembled Ned's.

The kid made a beeline for a butcher shop, where he strode up to the counter and ordered half a pound of beef liver. When the order arrived, Wilfred handed the cardboard tub to Michael. "Take charge of this, will you? We'll be needing it later."

Michael give him a dubious look. "Not breakfast."

"Not ours," grinned Wilfred, leading the way out of the shop.

They walked through Wimbledon for five or six blocks. Twentieth-century Tudor alternated with bleak redbrick high-rises against a carpet of lush lawns. Michael was reminded of Kansas City, oddly enough, or a 1920s suburb on the edge of any Midwestern town.

Wilfred stopped at a vacant lot covered with brick and concrete rubble—all that was left of a house that had apparently burned to the ground. "They're building another one here next month. Dingo hasn't much time left." He stepped nimbly over the debris, approaching the end of the lot where the rubble was deepest. Then he snapped his fingers to get Michael's attention.

"What?" asked Michael.

"The *liver*, mate."

"Oh." He handed him the cardboard tub. Wilfred dumped the contents on a flat rock that appeared to have already been used for that purpose. "You're freaking me out," whispered Michael.

"Shhh!" Wilfred's forefinger shot to his lips. "Just hang on." They stood like statues amid the ruins.

"Here, Dingo," crooned Wilfred. "C'mon, boy."

Michael heard a scurrying sound beneath the rubble. Then a

pair of flinty eyes appeared in an opening adjacent to the flat rock. After a few exploratory sniffs, the creature scuttled out into the light.

"God," Michael murmured. "A fox, huh?"

"Very good."

"What's he doing here?"

Wilfred shrugged. "They're all over London."

"In the city limits, you mean?"

"Wherever they can make do. Right, Dingo?" Fifteen feet away, the fox looked up from his dinner for a moment, then continued to devour it noisily. "They'll level this spot in another month, and Dingo will be in real trouble."

"Why do you call him Dingo?"

Wilfred turned and looked at him. "It's what they call the wild dogs in Australia."

"Oh."

"I found him when I was working down at the chippie. One day at lunch I tossed him a bit of me fish-and-chips and he was so grateful that I came back the next day. But they gave me the sack, so I come down here on the tube when I can. It's been a while since the last time. You miss me, Dingo? Eh?"

They watched in silence while the fox ate. Then Michael said: "We have wild coyotes in California. I mean . . . they come into the city sometimes."

"Yeah?"

Michael nodded. "They raid people's garbage cans in L.A. People have seen them standing in the middle of Sunset Boulevard. They don't belong in the wilds, and they don't belong in the city either."

Wilfred nodded. "They're trapped in the mess we've made. They know it, too. Dingo knows it. All he can do is hide in that hole and wait for the end to come."

"Couldn't you . . . get him out of there?"

"And take him where, mate? No one loves a fox." He turned and looked at Michael with tears in his eyes. "I bought him something especially nice this time. I'm not coming back. Me nerves can't take it."

Michael himself was beginning to feel fragile. "He looks like he appreciates it."

"Yeah. He does, doesn't he?" He smiled faintly, wiping his eyes.

"How about you?" Michael asked. "Can I buy you breakfast?"

"Sure. Sure, mate." He glanced in Dingo's direction again; the fox was scampering away.

"Do you know a good place?" Michael asked.

"Yeah," the kid nodded.

It turned out to be a tiny Greek greasy spoon only two blocks from the fox's lair. Wilfred ordered for both of them, insisting upon the specialty of the house: fried eggs and bangers and a side order of stewed tomatoes. While they ate, the skies opened up again, varnishing the cast-iron blind child that was stationed outside the door.

Michael peered at the statuette through a rain-blurred window. "I've never seen anything like that," he remarked. "Do you drop money in his head?"

Wilfred nodded. "They have them for dogs and cats, too."

Michael gave him a sympathetic smile. "But not foxes."

"No."

"Have you ever seen a real dingo?"

"No. Me granddad told me about them once."

"He was . . . Australian?"

"Abo," replied Wilfred. "You can say it, mate."

"What?" He didn't recognize the word.

"Aborigines. You've heard of 'em."

"Oh."

The kid smiled impishly. "The ones the niggers get to pick on."

Michael felt instantly uncomfortable. "I wouldn't know about that."

"Well, I would." He sawed off a chunk of banger and popped it into his mouth. "Me grandmum was Dutch. Her and me granddad left Darwin during World War II . . . when you Yanks were all over the place and everyone thought the Japs were coming. Me dad was born in London."

"And your mother?"

"She ran off when I was eight."

"Why?"

He shrugged. "Sick o' me dad and his bleedin' port. I don't know. Maybe she didn't fancy me."

"I doubt that."

"*You* don't fancy me." He was looking at his plate as he said it.

"That's not true."

"You don't want to go to bed with me."

"Wilfred . . ."

"Just tell me why, then. I won't ask again."

Michael hesitated. "I'm not sure it makes a lot of sense . . . even to me."

"Try me."

"Well . . . my lover and I didn't split up. He died of AIDS."

The kid blinked at him.

"Do you know what that is?"

Wilfred shook his head.

"It's this thing that gay men are getting in the States. It's a severe immune deficiency. They get it, and then they catch anything that flies in the window. Over a thousand people have died of it." It felt strangely cold-blooded to start from scratch and reduce the horror to its bare essentials.

"Oh, yeah," said Wilfred soberly. "I think I read about that."

Michael nodded. "My lover weighed ninety pounds when he died. He was this big, lanky guy and he just . . . wasted away. I was sick myself about six years ago . . . paralyzed . . . and he used to carry me all over . . ." His tears tried to burn their way out. "And then he became this . . . ghost, this pitiful, pitiful thing . . ."

"Hey, mate . . ."

"He was blind the last two weeks of his life. On a respirator most of the time. The last time I saw him he didn't see me at all. All he could do was press his fingers against my face, feel my tears. I just sat there holding his hand against my face, telling some stupid joke I'd read in the newspaper . . . making plans for a trip to Maui." He snatched a napkin from a dispenser and dabbed at his eyes. "Sorry about that."

"I don't mind, mate."

"So I just . . ."

Wilfred finished for him. "You miss him."

"A lot . . . oh, a lot . . ." He began to sob now, in spite of himself. Wilfred came to his side of the booth and sat down, squeezing his shoulder. "So I'm just . . . treading water right now. I just don't feel like being with anyone in that way." He composed himself somewhat, taking another swipe at his eyes. "I'm not afraid of sex or anything. I just haven't been horny for a long time."

"Right," said Wilfred gently, "but doesn't your heart get horny?"

Michael gave him a bleary-eyed smile. "Sometimes."

"Well . . . a friend might help. Eh?"

The offer was so serendipitous that he almost started crying again. "Kiddo, I've never said no to that kind of . . ."

"Is there a problem here?"

They both looked up to see an enormous swarthy man, arms folded above his gut, glowering down at them.

"Sorry," said Michael. "If we're making too much noise . . ."

Wilfred bristled. "We're not makin' too much noise. We're makin' too much love." He stood the man down with his eyes, like a fox waiting for his next move. "Why don't you mind your own bleedin' business, eh?"

"Now, look," said the man. "You blokes have got your own places."

"Right you are. And this is one of 'em. So sod off."

The man glared at him a moment longer, then returned to his post behind the counter.

"Bleedin' Greeks," muttered Wilfred.

Michael was grinning uncontrollably. "How old are you, anyway?"

"Sixteen," answered the kid, "and I know how to take care of meself."

Her Little-Girl Things

Mary Ann's morning mail brought a number of oddities: a press release from Tylenol explaining their new "tamper-proof" packaging, a free sample of chewing gum sweetened with Aspartame, and a strange-looking plastic funnel called a Sani-Fem.

Dumping everything on her desk, she sat down and examined the Sani-Fem. *Ideal for backpacking*, the brochure trumpeted, *or when public toilet seats prove to be unsanitary.* The larger end of the funnel was contoured to fit snugly against the crotch.

She whooped at the wonder of it all.

Sally Rinaldi, the news director's secretary, stopped outside the door and peered in. "A raise or what?"

"Look at this thing," grinned Mary Ann.

"What is it?"

"It's . . . a Sani-Fem. It lets you pee standing up."

"C'mon."

Mary Ann handed her the brochure. "Read this." She picked up the Sani-Fem again. "I'm dying to try it out."

Sally backed away. "Well, don't let me stop you."

Mary Ann laughed. "In the bathroom, Sally."

"Go ahead."

"Right. And have Bambi walk in on me."

The secretary smiled. "Use the men's room, then. William Buckley might see you."

"Huh?"

"Larry's giving him a station tour. As we speak."

"William F. Buckley, Junior?"

"The very one."

God, what a pipe dream! Buckley and Larry Kenan against the wall, separated safely by a vacant urinal, shaking the dew off their respective lizards, when the girl reporter saunters in—natty in gabardine slacks and dress-for-success floppy bow and blouse. *Voilà!* Out comes the Sani-Fem. *"Morning, gentlemen. How's it hangin' today?"*

"Go ahead," coaxed Sally.

"You're crazy," said Mary Ann, dropping the funnel into the bottom drawer of her filing cabinet.

"You're too careful," winked Sally as she sailed out the door.

At the end of a do-nothing day, Mary Ann brought the Sani-Fem home with her. Finding Mrs. Madrigal in the courtyard, she showed the device to the landlady and gave a terse explanation of its function.

"Funny," said Mrs. Madrigal, her smile showing only in her eyes. "I had to wait forty-two years for the privilege of sitting down."

Mary Ann reddened. It was easy to forget that Mrs. Madrigal hadn't become female until roughly the time that Mary Ann hit puberty.

"Just the same," added the landlady, sparing them both the embarrassment, "I think it's a marvelous idea, don't you?"

"Mmm," said Mary Ann, adopting a quirk of Simon's. "I got a note from Mouse, by the way. He sends you his love."

"How sweet."

"He says Simon's apartment is kind of grungy."

The landlady smiled. "English aristocrats are proud of their squalor."

"Yeah. I guess so."

"It doesn't seem to extend to his personal habits, at least. He takes good care of himself, that Simon."

Mary Ann nodded. "You've spent some time with him?"

"Um. Some . . . Why?"

"No reason. I just wondered what your impressions were."

Mrs. Madrigal pondered for a moment, patting a stray wisp of hair into place. "Bright . . . I'd say. Quick. A little inclined to be vague." She smiled. "But that's part of his Britishness, I think."

"Yeah."

"But quite magnificent in the looks department. Or is that what you meant?"

There was something almost coy about the question that made Mary Ann uneasy. "No . . . I just meant . . . generally."

"Generally, I'd say he's quite a catch. For somebody."

Mary Ann nodded.

The landlady knelt and plucked a weed from the garden. "Sounds to me like you're matchmaking. I thought that was my job around here."

Mary Ann giggled. "If I find anybody good for him, I'll make sure you approve first."

"You do that," said Mrs. Madrigal.

The glint in the landlady's eye was more than a little disconcerting. *Be careful,* Mary Ann warned herself. *A nice old woman who used to be a man could very well know what's on everybody's mind.*

Heading upstairs, Mary Ann hesitated on the landing, then returned and rapped on Simon's door. He opened it wearing Michael's dark green corduroy bathrobe, loose enough to reveal an awe-inspiring wedge of thick brown chest hair. He was munching on a carrot stick.

"Well . . . hello there."

"Hi," she said. "I thought I'd just stop by on my way home. Is this a bad time?"

"Absolutely not. Here, let me pop into some trousers. I won't be a . . ."

"No. This is just . . . spur of the moment. You're decent. I've seen more of you in your jogging shorts."

He gave himself a split-second once-over, then said: "You're quite right. Well . . ." He welcomed her with a whimsical little flourish of the carrot stick. "Come in, won't you?"

The room, of course, still spoke loudly of Mouse, with its shelves of tropic-hued Fiesta Ware, its vintage rubber duck collection from the forties, its chrome-framed "Thighs and Whispers" Bette Midler poster. The only signs of Simon were the latest issue of *Rolling Stone* and a bottle of brandy on the coffee table.

He sat down on the sofa. "I was just about to pour myself a little nip. Will you join me?"

"Sure." She eased onto the other end of the sofa, leaving a cushion between them as no-man's-land. "Just a teeny one, though. Brandy gives me headaches."

He looked faintly amused. "Brandy takes a certain commitment." He poured some into a rose-colored Fiesta juice glass and handed it to her. "Bottoms up."

She took a sip. "By the way, I was wondering . . . have you made plans for Easter yet?"

He grinned.

"What's so funny?"

"Well, this is Lotusland, isn't it? I haven't given a moment's thought to Christian holidays." He chuckled. "Most of my celebrations have been pagan so far."

"I'm sure that's true," she replied, "but I thought it might be . . . you know . . . a good time for us to plan something . . . since you're leaving right after that."

He nodded thoughtfully. What was he thinking? "It's just the weekend after next," she added.

"Is it really?" He seemed amazed.

"Mmm."

He shook his head. "Time flies when you're pillaging a city." He turned and looked at her. "What exactly did you have in mind?"

"Don't laugh," she replied.

"Very well."

"It's . . . a sunrise service."

A moment's hesitation. "Ah."

"Was that a good ah or a bad ah?"

He smiled. "A tell-me-more ah."

"That's about it." She shrugged. "I'm supposed to cover it for the station. It's held at the highest point in the city, under this enormous cross. Everybody watches the sun come up over Oakland. It's kind of . . . caring-sharing Californian, but it might be a hoot for you."

"A hoot," he repeated. His smile had inched perilously close to a smirk.

"You hate it, don't you?"

"No . . . no. I wonder, though . . . how do we get up to this highest point?"

"Walk," she answered, "but not too far."

"Up Calvary, eh?"

She giggled. "Right."

"Well . . ." He tapped his lips with his forefinger. "I'm a foul-tempered wretch that early in the morning."

"I don't mind."

"Does Brian?"

"What?" He was making her nervous, but she hoped it didn't show.

"Mind getting up that early."

"Oh. Actually . . . he's not. He's going to a house party Theresa Cross is giving in Hillsborough. We were both invited, but . . . well, I got stuck with this assignment."

"I see."

"My motives are a little shaky, I guess." She gave him her best winsome smile. "I just wanted a little pleasant company during the ordeal."

"As Jesus said to Mary Magdalene." His eyes were full of mischief.

"Maybe it's not such a good . . ."

"I'd love to go," he said.

"You're sure, now?"

"Absolutely. It's settled. There." He punctuated the decision by clamping his hands to his knees.

She rose. "Great. I also thought we might have dinner together the night before. If you haven't got plans, I mean."

He gazed at her for a moment, then said: "Lovely."

As she left, she could feel his eyes following her. The sensation made her almost dizzy, so she went up to the roof to collect her thoughts before facing Brian. The night was clear and rain-washed. Beneath the new streetlight on Barbary Lane, the young eucalyptus leaves seemed pale as ghosts, the gentle gray-green of weathered copper. She counted four lighted vessels gliding soundlessly across the obsidian surface of the bay. The big neon fish at Fisherman's Wharf glowed pink above the water like a talisman from the Christians in the catacombs.

She sought out the North Star and made the only wish that came to mind.

"*Let me guess.*"

She flinched, startled by her husband's voice. He stood in the doorway, smiling at her.

"God," she said. "You scared the hell out of me."

"Hey. Sorry." He came up behind her and kissed her neck. "You were making a wish, weren't you?"

"None of your business, smartass."

He chuckled, nuzzling her. "I like it when you do those little-girl things."

She grunted at him.

"I've been thinking," he said, still holding her. "What about Sierra City?"

"What about it?"

"For our trip."

She drew a total blank.

"Don't tell me you've forgotten already."

"Well, don't make me guess."

"This weekend," he said. "*Ethelmertz* time?"

"Oh. Right."

"Or somewhere up the coast would be just as good."

"No. Sierra City is fine."

"Whatever," he said. "What's in the bag?"

Preoccupied as she had been, she had all but forgotten about the Sani-Fem. "Oh . . . it's a . . . never mind. You don't wanna know."

"Yes I do." He took the bag from her and removed the plastic funnel. "Christ almighty. What is it?"

She snatched the Sani-Fem from his hands and marched to the bay side of the roof.

"What the hell are you doing?"

She peered down into the dark tangle of shrubbery. "Nothing."

"Nothing?"

"Just one of my little-girl things." She dropped her slacks and pushed her panties down.

"Mary Ann, for God's sake . . ."

"Lower your voice," she said. "You'll attract attention."

That Woman Again

Wilfred's father was bellowing so ferociously that Michael awoke from a dream about bumping into Jon at a Buckingham Palace garden party. He sat up in bed, clinging to the fantasy like a comforter, while the patriarch slammed pieces of furniture against the wall upstairs. Amidst the cacophony, he could barely discern the shrill desperation of Wilfred's reedy, childlike voice.

"Poofter!" thundered the father. *"Bleedin' poofter . . . vile, filthy smut . . . I'll teach you, you little . . ."*

Something shattered against a wall.

Horror-struck, Michael jumped out of bed and slipped into Simon's red satin bathrobe. Opening the door to the hallway, he peered warily up the staircase just as the door upstairs opened, then slammed shut. He ducked back into his apartment, easing the door shut, and waited until he heard the father's leaden footsteps move down the stairs, through the hallway and out of the house. Hearing nothing else, he climbed halfway up the stairs and called: "Wilfred?"

No answer.

"Wilfred . . . are you all right?"

"Who's there?"

"It's me. Michael. Did he hurt you?" He continued to climb toward Wilfred's door.

"Wait there, mate. I'll be down in a bit. I'm all right."

So he returned to his apartment, where he brewed a pot of coffee and waited. When Wilfred finally appeared in the doorway, grinning valiantly, he was pressing a wad of toilet paper against his temple. "Sorry about the commotion, mate."

"Jesus," murmured Michael. "What did he do?"

"Aw . . . threw me against a cupboard."

"He *threw* you?"

"Is that so bleedin' difficult? I'm not exactly Arnold Bleedin' Schwarzenegger."

Michael smiled at him. "C'mere. Let's take a look at that. What did you do to piss him off, anyway?"

Wilfred came closer and lifted the wad of toilet paper. "He found me old *Zipper* in the dustbin."

"He did *what?*"

"It's a magazine with naked blokes."

"Oh. Jesus, that's gonna be a goose egg. Hang on . . . I've got some alcohol and Band-Aids in my travel kit." He found what he needed, then returned, dabbing the kid's forehead as he asked: "You read that stuff?"

Wilfred was aghast at his ignorance. "They're for wanking, mate, not reading."

Michael smiled. "I stand corrected."

"You never bought one?"

"Oh, sure. It's pretty popular at home right now. It's a lot safer to have sex with a magazine. Does that sting?"

"Like bloody hell," said Wilfred.

"Good. It's working. My friend Ned calls it periodical sex. I always thought that was kind of cute." He pressed the "flesh-coloured" Band-Aid into place, noting the careless injustice of that expression. "There. Almost good as new."

Wilfred sniffed the air. "Is that coffee?"

"Sure. Want a cup?"

"Super," said Wilfred.

Bringing him the coffee, Michael asked: "Got plans for the day?"

The kid shrugged.

"Great. Then take me to Harrods."

"Are you serious?"

"Sure. I need to buy some things for my friends back home."

So Wilfred obliged and led him to the princely department store, where Michael stocked up on treasures from the royal kitsch section: Prince William egg cups, Princess Diana dishrags, Queen Mum appointment books. He searched in vain for something with Princess Anne's face on it, but that visage seemed of little value to the British—camp or otherwise.

As they passed through the menswear department, Wilfred tugged on his sleeve. "Look, mate. Princess Diana."

"That's OK," said Michael. "I've already got the dishrag."

"No, mate. *Herself.*" He jerked his head toward a svelte blonde who stood at the counter examining a pair of men's pajamas. She was wearing a pale gray cashmere sweater above a pink floral Laura Ashley skirt. There were discreet little pearls at her ears and throat, and her feet were encased in black patent pumps.

Michael ducked behind a pillar and signaled Wilfred to join him.

The kid giggled. "Hey, mate, it isn't really . . ."

"Shhh. Don't let her see you."

Hugely amused, Wilfred whispered: "It's just a Sloane Ranger."

"A what?"

"A twitzy-twee bitch. They shop in Sloane Square. They all try to look like . . ."

"Wilfred, get back here!"

"Have you gone . . . ?"

"I know her," Michael whispered. "At least, I think I do. She looks a lot like an old friend of mine."

Wilfred rolled his eyes. "Why don't you ask her, then?"

"I tried that once and she ran away."

"When?"

"About a week ago. On Hampstead Heath. Oh, God . . . has she left yet?"

"Not yet. The shop assistant is showing her some more pajamas."

Michael strained to hear her voice, but it was obliterated by the stately din of the department store. "This is insane," he murmured. "She must be in deep trouble."

"Why?"

"I don't know. Why wouldn't she speak to me? Something is horribly wrong."

Wilfred shrugged. "She looks all right to me."

"I know," said Michael. "That's what's wrong."

The kid peered around the pillar again. "She's leaving now. What are you gonna do?"

"Jesus. If she sees me, we may lose her for good."

"What if I follow her? She won't recognize *me*."

"I don't know . . ."

"A wog would scare her off, eh?"

Michael frowned at him. "She's not like that. All right . . . go ahead. See what you can find out. Wait! Where should we meet?"

The kid screwed up his face in thought. "Well . . . the Markham Arms in King's Road . . . No, it's not Saturday."

"Huh?"

"It's only gay on Saturday."

"Screw that. I'll meet you there in an hour."

"Right. Markham Arms, King's Road."

"Got it," said Michael. "Don't let her see you, Wilfred. Just watch what she does, OK?"

The kid brought his fingertips to his Band-Aid and gave a jaunty salute, already moving toward his quarry. Michael waited fifteen minutes, then left Harrods and caught a cab to the Markham Arms. The pub was full of noisy shoppers, bordering on trendy, many of whom seemed to be in flight from the first major downpour of the day. He bought a cider and wedged himself in a corner as the jukebox began to play Sting's "Spread a Little Happiness" from *Brimstone and Treacle*.

Wilfred didn't appear at the appointed time, so Michael bought another cider and a package of vinegar crisps. He chatted briefly with a handsome businessman at the bar, who looked as if he belonged there on Saturday. They were discussing *Cats* when Wilfred pushed his way through the crowd and shook the rain off his golden-brown locks.

"In the first place," he announced, "she's an American."

"I knew it. What else?"

Wilfred grinned. "A stout would loosen me tongue."

"You got it." He signaled the bartender and ordered a Guinness and another package of crisps. "She didn't see you, did she?"

"Don't think so," the kid replied. "I kept me distance. It wasn't easy, mate. She kept a steady pace all the way."

"Where did she go?"

"Hey . . . me stout."

Michael turned and took the glass from the bartender, handing it to Wilfred. "There's a seat over there. Shall we grab it?"

"Good idea," the kid answered. "I'm exhausted."

Michael said "Take care" to the businessman and followed Wilfred through the raucous mob. When they were seated, Wilfred said: "She's a high-toned one, isn't she? She spent the whole bleedin' time in Beauchamp Place."

"Where's that?"

"Not far from Harrods. Off the Brompton Road. It's mostly for rich people and Americans. Poncy little shops . . . that sort of thing."

"Where did she go?"

"Oh . . . a shop called Emeline that sells jewelry. I don't think she bought anything, but it was hard to tell. I had to watch from the street. The shop was too small to do any proper spying."

"Good thinking."

"Then she went to a place called Spaghetti."

"A restaurant?"

"A dress shop. She didn't stay long. The rain started again, so she ran along the pavement for a bit. Some bloke on a motorcycle splashed water on her dress, and she stopped and gave him the finger. Said, 'Fuck you, mac.'"

Michael smiled. "It's her, all right."

"I waited a bit, then I tailed her into a shop called Caroline Charles. The bitch behind the counter gave me a dirty look, so I couldn't hang around too long."

"She didn't say anything? My friend, I mean."

"Not much. She bought a dress. Paid for it in cash with a great wad of bills she pulled out of her purse."

"Did she take the dress with her?"

Wilfred shook his head. "She wanted it mailed. Said she needed it by Easter."

"Great! Did she say where?"

"Sorry, mate. She wrote it down for the shop assistant."

"Did you follow her?"

Wilfred shook his head. "She took a cab when she left."

"What color was the dress?"

"Sort of pink," answered Wilfred. "No, peach, perhaps, with big puffy sleeves. Why?"

"C'mon, kiddo. Let's grab a cab. It's my turn to play detective."

Fifteen minutes later, he left Wilfred at a coffee shop in Beauchamp Place, then headed off to Caroline Charles on his own. The woman behind the counter was just as chilly as Wilfred had depicted her.

"Yes, sir. May I help you?"

"Yes, thank you. My wife just bought a dress here . . . about half an hour ago. An American lady in a gray sweater and pink skirt?"

"Yes."

"A peach dress. She asked that it be shipped."

"I recall it quite well, sir. What may I do for you?"

"Well . . . I know this sounds awfully silly, but she thinks she may have given you the wrong address. She's been . . . uh . . . ill lately and she tends to be rather absentminded, and she thinks she may have given you our winter address instead of . . . you know . . . our summer one, and, well, I thought it best to check."

The woman frowned at him.

"Frankly," said Michael, lowering his voice to a whisper, "if I could get her off Valium, we wouldn't have this problem. Last week she forgot where she left the Bentley and it took us two days to find it."

The saleswoman's lip curled slightly as she pulled out the order and laid it in front of Michael. As he read it, he burned the words into his brain:

Roughton
Easley-on-Hill
Near Chipping Campden
Gloucestershire

"Good," he said. "Everything's in order. I guess there's hope for the old girl yet."

By the time he got back to the coffee shop, the address had been reduced to gibberish in his head, slithy toves gyring and gimbling in the wabe. Spotting Wilfred, he silenced him with a wave until he had a chance to write it down. Then he showed it to him.

"Make any sense?"

The kid shrugged. "Gloucestershire does. I think I've heard of Chipping Campden, but the rest . . ."

"Is Roughton the name of a person or a place?"

"Could be either, I suppose. It's not hers?"

"Nope. Hers is Ramsey. Mona Ramsey."

"Maybe the dress was just a gift for someone. No . . . that's not likely."

"Why not?" asked Michael. The thought had already occurred to him. If she was being kept by a wealthy benefactress, she might well pick up a little something for her.

"Well," said Wilfred, "she tried it on, didn't she? Unless her friend is exactly the same size." He paused for a moment, apparently reading Michael's mind. "She fancies girls, does she?"

He smiled at the kid. "Most of the time. She's pretty much of a loner, though. She doesn't trust people. She thinks life is a shit sandwich."

"She's right," said Wilfred.

"She doesn't take any guff from people. She's like you in that respect."

"Nothin' wrong with that, mate."

"I know. I could learn that talent myself. I've never known a Southerner who wasn't too polite for his own good."

"You're from the South?"

Michael nodded.

"The Deep South?"

"Not exactly. Orlando. And stop looking at me like that. I've never lynched a soul."

Wilfred smiled and butted Michael's calf with the side of his foot. "What are you gonna do about her?"

"Well . . . I guess I could mail a letter to this address. Fat chance that'll do any good, since she ran away from me on the heath."

"Are you sure she knew it was you?"

"Positive. And I know why she ran away."

"Why?"

"Because I'm the closest thing she's got to a conscience."

"And she's doing something wrong?"

"Well . . . something she's ashamed of. She's even got a disguise for it. She doesn't usually look like that. Her real hair is red and frizzy, and she's never worn a string of pearls in her life. Not to mention *pink*."

"You've known her long?"

Michael thought for a moment. "At least eight years. My landlady in San Francisco is her . . ." He couldn't help chuckling, though it seemed faintly disrespectful to Mrs. Madrigal. "My landlady is her father."

Wilfred blinked at him.

"She's a transsexual. She used to be a man."

"A sex change?"

Michael nodded. "You hardly ever think about that. She's just a nice person . . . the kindest person I've ever known." He missed her, he realized, far more than he missed his real parents.

He was tired of fretting over Mona, so they returned to Harrods and resumed shopping. Two hours later they dragged wearily into 44 Colville Crescent, laden with royal-family souvenirs. While Michael examined his treasures, Wilfred pranced about the kitchen making sandwiches.

"This tastes wonderful," Michael mumbled, biting into a chicken-and-chutney on rye.

"Good."

"How's the noggin, by the way?"

"Aw . . . can't even feel it."

"Is it safe for you to go home?"

Wilfred looked up from his sandwich. "Sick o' me, mate?"

"C'mon. I was just worried about your old man. Does he stay mad for long?"

The kid shook his head. "He doesn't stay anything for long."

The door buzzer sounded, causing Michael to flinch. He rose and peered through the front curtains. The caller was a woman of thirty or so, looking soberly aristocratic in a burgundy blazer and Hermès scarf. Her box-pleated navy blue skirt appeared to conceal a lower torso so formidable that it might have done justice to a centaur. Her hair, dirty-blonde and center-parted, curved inward beneath her jaw, like a pair of parentheses containing a superfluous concept.

"Oh," she said flatly, when he opened the front door. "You're not Simon."

"Not today." He grinned. "May I give him a message?"

"He's still gone, is he?"

He nodded. "He'll be back just after Easter. We swapped apartments."

"I see. You're from California?"

"Right. Uh . . . would you like to come in or anything?"

She considered his lame offer, frowning slightly, then said: "Yes, thank you." She cast a flinty glance at two black children playing in the sand next to the cement mixer. "If nothing else, it's *safer* inside."

He had no intention of agreeing with her. "I'm Michael Tolliver," he said, extending his hand.

She held hers out limply as if to be kissed. "Fabia Dane." As she followed him into the corridor, her face knotted like a fist. "My God. That smell! Did someone park another custard in here?"

She meant puke, he decided, and he suddenly found himself feeling uncharacteristically defensive about the place. He loathed this woman already. "It's an old building," he said evenly. "I guess the smells are unavoidable."

She dismissed that thesis with a little grunt. "Dear Simon's problem is that he's never been able to tell the difference between Bohemian and just plain naff. One could certainly understand a grotty little flat in Camden Town, say . . . or even Wapping, for God's sake . . . but *this*. It must be awful for you. And those horrid abos with their drums going night and . . ."

Her diatribe came to an abrupt end as she barged into the living room and caught sight of Wilfred sprawled on the sofa. "Booga booga," he said brightly.

Michael grinned at him. Fabia turned to Michael with a granite countenance. "What I have to say is personal. Do you mind?"

Wilfred sprang up. "Just leaving, milady."

Michael saw no reason to humor her. "Wilfred, you don't have to."

"I know." He winked at Michael. "Talk to you later, mate."

As soon as he had gone, Fabia eased her centaur haunches into an armchair and said: "I'm sure Simon wouldn't appreciate that."

Michael sat down as far away from her as possible. "Appreciate what?"

"Letting that aborigine have the run of the house."

Michael paused, trying to stay calm. "He said nothing about that to me."

"Just the same, I would think that a little common sense might be in order."

"Wilfred is a friend of mine. All right?"

"They're squatting, you know."

"Who?"

"That child and his horrid father. They don't pay rent on that flat. They just moved in and laid claim to it. Never mind. I'm sure you think it's none of my business. I felt it only fair to warn you."

"But . . . if that's illegal, why hasn't . . . ?"

"Oh, it's perfectly legal. Just not very sporting. So-o-o . . . if Simon is cross with you, you'll know the reason why." She gave him the smug little smile of a snitch. Michael felt a sudden urge to wipe it off her face with a two-by-four. Instead, he changed the subject: "What is it you'd like me to tell Simon?"

"He's coming home in a fortnight?"

"More or less."

"He hasn't gone queer on us, has he?"

Not a two-by-four, a four-by-four. With a nail in it. "I haven't asked Simon about his private life," he answered blandly.

She studied him for a moment, then said: "Well, anyway . . . the message is that he missed a marvelous wedding." She paused, obviously for effect. "Mine, to be precise."

"All right."

"Dane is my new name. My maiden name was Pumphrey. Fabia will do, actually. I'm quite sure Simon doesn't know any others."

Michael was quite sure too.

"At any rate, my husband and I will be giving a little summer affair at our new place in the country, and it wouldn't be complete without Simon, God knows. The invitation will be coming later, but you might give him a little advance warning, so he can think up a truly masterful excuse."

The last remark was so full of poison that Michael wondered if she was a jilted lover. Did she stop by just to rub Simon's nose in her marriage?

"Come to think of it," added Fabia, "better make sure he gets the last name. I wouldn't want there to be any confusion. It's Dane." She spelled it for him.

"As in Dane Vinegar Crisps?"

"Yes," she answered, "as a matter of fact."

"No kidding?"

"That's my husband's company."

"How amazing. Wilfred and I had some of those just this afternoon."

"Wilfred?"

"The aborigine."

"I see."

Michael rose. "I'll give Simon your message."

Fabia regarded him coldly for a moment, then got up and went to the door. She paused there, apparently considering an exit line.

Michael folded his arms and squared his jaw. She gave him a faint, curdled smile and left.

Michael stood fast until she was outside, then sat down and finished his sandwich.

Wilfred returned ten minutes later. "She's gone, eh?"

"Thank God."

"What did she want?"

"Nothing. Nothing important. Just a message for Simon."

"It isn't us with the drums, you know."

Michael smiled at him. "I don't care about that."

"Just the same, it isn't me and me dad. It's those bleedin' Jamaicans across the way."

"Sit down," said Michael. "Forget about that harpy. Finish your sandwich."

The kid sat down. "You know there was a bloke watching your flat?"

"When?"

"Just now. A fat bloke. I saw him from me window."

"Oh," said Michael. "Probably her husband waiting for her." The all-powerful Mr. Dane, King of the Vinegar Crisps.

"No." Wilfred frowned. "Not likely."

"What do you mean?"

"Well, he ran off when she left the flat."

Michael went to the window. The children were still romping by the cement mixer, but there was no one else in sight. "Where was he?"

"Down there." The kid pointed. "Next to the phone box."

"And he was . . . just watching?"

Wilfred nodded. "Starin' hard at the window. Like he was trying to see who it was."

The Jesus Tortilla

Their Palm Sunday weekend was only hours away when Brian phoned Mary Ann at work. "I made a sort of unilateral decision," he said. "I hope you don't mind."

By now, she had grown extremely wary of new developments. "What is it?" she asked.

"I canceled our reservations in Sierra City."

"Why?"

"Oh . . . I thought we owed ourselves something a little fancier under the circumstances. How does the Sonoma Mission Inn sound to you?"

"Oh, Brian . . . Expensive, for starters."

"We can afford it," he replied, with somewhat less wind in his sails.

"Yeah, I suppose."

"You don't sound very excited."

"Sorry. I'm just . . . I think it sounds great. Really. I've always wanted to go there."

"I remembered that," he said.

She felt a nasty little twinge of guilt. She hated to see him make such elaborate plans on behalf of her fraudulent *mittelschmerz*. "Do we need to do anything special?" she asked. "Won't I need dressier clothes?"

"You've got time to pack them," he said. "They aren't expecting us until seven tonight."

"Great. I should be home no later than four."

She spent the rest of the afternoon tying up loose ends: editing footage for a feature on California Cuisine, making phone calls, answering memos that had languished on her desk for weeks. She was on the verge of making a discreet exit when Hal, an associate producer, caught sight of her in the hallway.

"Kenan's looking for you," he said.

"Shit. With an assignment, I'll bet."

Hal grinned at her. "No rest for the perky."

She weighed her options. If she walked out without checking with Kenan, she had no guarantee that Hal wouldn't rat on her. He was famous for that, in fact. So she gritted her teeth and stormed off to the news director's office, already stockpiling an arsenal of excuses.

As always, Kenan's inner sanctum was a hodgepodge of promotional media kitsch: miniature footballs imprinted with the station logo, four or five different Mylar wall calendars, a Rubik's Cube bearing the name and address of a videotape manufacturer. The only recent change was that Bo Derek had vanished from the spot on the ceiling above Kenan's desk, and Christie Brinkley had taken her place.

Arms locked behind his head, the news director eased his chair into an upright position, and fixed his tiny little eyes on Mary Ann. "Good. You're here."

"Hal said you wanted to see me."

His smile was a form of aggression, nothing more. "Do you remember . . . oh, way back when, when you first came to work for us . . . remember I told you a good reporter is the only person who is always required to respond to an Act of God? Do you remember that?"

"Sure," she said, nodding. For all she knew, even the janitors at the station were subjected to that asinine speech. "What about it?"

"Well, lady . . ." He was drawing out the suspense as long as possible. "I've got something for you that just might qualify."

When she broke the news to Brian, he was just as angry as he deserved to be. "Fuck that, Mary Ann! We've been planning this trip all week. You told them that, didn't you?"

"Of course."

"Well, why do they have to pick on you?"

"Because . . . I'm the lowest on the totem pole, and they know I'll do . . ."

"What's so goddamn important that they can't wait until Monday, at least?"

"Well . . . it's kind of an Easter story . . . Holy Week, rather . . . so they need it now, if . . ."

"*The Pope is coming? What?*"

"You'll just get mad, Brian."

"I'm mad already. What the hell is it?"

"A woman in Daly City. She thinks she's seen Jesus."

"Terrific."

"Brian . . ."

"Where did she see Him? On her dashboard?"

"No. On a tortilla."

He hung up on her.

She left the station minutes later and drove to Daly City. The site of the miracle was a tiny Mexican restaurant called Una Paloma Blanca. A white dove. Not a bad tie-in for the Holy Week angle. The cameraman was already there, fretting over technical problems with the tortilla.

"I'm telling you," he snapped, "it just won't read. Trust me. I know what I'm talking about."

"Look," she countered. "I can see it. See . . . there's the beard. That's part of the cheekbone. That wrinkle going left to right is the top of His head."

"Swell, Mary Ann. Tell that to the camera. There's not enough contrast, I'm telling you. It's as simple as that."

Mary Ann sighed and muttered "Shit" to no one in particular. This provoked a disappointed cluck from Mrs. Hernandez, the tortilla's discoverer. In anticipation of her television debut, the portly matron was decked out in her grandmother's lace shawl and mantilla.

"Excuse me," said Mary Ann, bowing slightly to underscore her sincerity.

"We could highlight it," the cameraman suggested.

"What?"

"The tortilla. We could touch it up."

"No!" She was feeling sleazier by the minute. Her perennial wisecrack about working for the "*National Enquirer* of the Air" contained more truth than she cared to admit, even to herself.

"But if we explained . . ."

"Matthew, *don't touch up the tortilla*, all right?"

He called for truce with his hands. "OK, OK." He looked around at the blackened pots and pans of the cramped kitchen. "Should we shoot it here?"

"She found it here, didn't she?"

"Yeah, but there's not enough room for the others."

"*What* others?"

He smiled at her lazily. "All those pilgrims in the front room. They came to be on TV."

"Well, they *can't* be!"

"Swell. You tell them that."

She groaned at him, then stomped to the pay phone in the front room. She called Larry Kenan and suggested that the story be scrapped. His response was clipped and vitriolic: "If it's too much for you, lady, I'll put Father Paddy on it. Wait there and don't touch that friggin' tortilla!"

Forty-five minutes later, the television host of *Honest to God* alighted cassock-clad from his red 1957 Cadillac Eldorado Biarritz. "Darling!" he beamed, catching sight of Mary Ann. "You poor thing! This is your first miracle, isn't it?"

"I'm not sure it qualifies," she muttered.

"Tut-tut. Miracles are like beauty, I always say. They're in the eye of the beholder. Where *is* the beholder, by the way?"

"In the back," she answered, pointing past the mob in the front room. "In the kitchen."

"Grand." Father Paddy glided through the throng like a stately pleasure craft, eliciting devout murmurs of recognition from the television viewers present. "The thing is," he told Mary Ann, "miracles are very, very good for people. We can't let a little faulty technology stand in our way. Some miracles are easier than others, of course, but I'm sure we can manage. Have you noticed, by the way, how it's always Jesus or the Blessed Virgin? *Good evening, my child, God bless you.* They *should* be seeing the Holy Ghost, since he's the ambassador-at-large, if you know what I mean, but no one ever spots the Holy Ghost on a tortilla—*God bless you, God bless you*—since no one has the faintest idea what the poor devil looks like. He gets no press at all. Christ, it's hot in here. Where's the tortilla?"

When they reached the kitchen, an elderly friend of Mrs. Hernandez was using the tortilla as a sort of compress against an arthritic elbow. "Oh, dear," said Father Paddy. "We may have lost Him."

A hasty examination of the tortilla reassured them that the holy features were still discernible.

"It won't show up on tape," said the cameraman.

Father Paddy gave him a knowing smile. "Backlight it," he said, "then tell me that."

"Huh?"

"You heard me, Matthew. Father knows best." He gave Mary Ann's hand a reassuring squeeze. "Never fear, darling. We're home free now."

He was right, it turned out. Backlighting the tortilla not only emphasized the color variations in the dough, thereby revealing the Christus, but also imbued the pastry with an inspirational halo-like effect. When the image finally appeared on the monitor, all twenty-three members of the Hernandez entourage uttered a collective murmur of appreciation.

"Perfect," purred Father Paddy. "Nice work, Matthew. I knew you could do it."

The cameraman smiled modestly, giving Mary Ann a thumbs-up sign. She was still uncertain, though. "They won't see the clothespins, will they, Matthew?"

"Nah."

"Are you sure?"

"I'll shoot just below them. Don't worry." He reached out and touched the length of twine from which the tortilla was suspended. "We wouldn't want Him to look like He's hanging out to dry."

She laughed feebly, hoping Mrs. Hernandez hadn't heard the remark. She was actually beginning to warm to this story. The face on the tortilla did look an awful lot like Jesus, if you discounted the lopsided nose and a dark spot that might be construed as an extra ear. She could already imagine the music she would use to score it. Something soaring and ethereal, yet basically humanistic. Possibly something from a Spielberg movie.

On the other hand, maybe the story was no longer hers. She turned to Father Paddy. "Will you be doing this for *Honest to God*?"

The cleric made a face. "What?"

"Well, Kenan sounded so pissed I thought maybe he had given you . . ."

"No, no, no. I'm just a consultant tonight. The story's all yours."

"Oh . . . well, in that case, maybe I should interview you about it. Just to get an official position from the church."

"Darling." Father Paddy lowered his voice and cast his eyes from left to right. "The church *has* no official position on this tortilla."

"What would we have to do to get one?"

The cleric chuckled. "Call the archbishop at home. Would *you* want to do it?"

"You don't have to declare it an official miracle or anything. Couldn't you just say something like . . ." She paused, trying to imagine what it would be.

"Like *what?*" said the priest. " 'My, what a pretty tortilla. Such a good likeness, too!' Come now. The archbishop has a tough enough time with the Shroud of Turin. The very least we can do is spare him the Tortilla of Daly City."

"Wait a minute," she said. "You called him for that statue story last December. I remember."

"What statue story?"

"You know . . . the bleeding one. In Ukiah or somewhere."

The cleric nodded slowly. "Yes . . . that's true."

"So what's the difference?"

Father Paddy sighed patiently. "The difference, darling girl, is that the statue was actually doing something. It was *bleeding*. The tortilla, for all its parochial charm, is simply lying there . . . or hanging there, as the case may be."

She gave up. "All right. Forget it. I'll wing it."

He ducked his eyes. "You're cross with me now, aren't you?"

"No."

"Yes, you are."

"Well . . . you were the one who called it a miracle."

"And for all I know, it *is*, darling." He chucked her under the chin. "I just don't think it's *news*."

She had come to the same conclusion when she dragged home at 10 P.M. and found Brian sulking in the little house on the roof. "I couldn't help it," she said ineffectually. "I know you're pissed, but these things come up."

"Tell me," he mumbled.

"We can still drive up there tomorrow."

"No, we can't. I canceled our reservations. We were damn lucky to even get a room. I had no way of knowing if you'd pull this again."

"So you thought you'd punish me. That's just great."

He turned and looked at her. "*I'm* punishing *you*, huh?"

Determined to salvage something, she sat down next to him on the sofa. "I've got an alternative plan, if you're really interested in hearing it."

"What?"

"Well, we could check into one of those tawdry little motor courts at the end of Lombard Street . . . we've talked about that before. And we could be there in fifteen minutes." She ran her forefinger lightly down his spine. "Wouldn't that work just as well?"

He made a grunting noise.

"And don't say it's a dumb idea, because you were the one who came up with it. Right after we saw *Body Heat*. Remember?"

He shook his head slowly, hands dangling between his knees.

"Besides," she added, "it strikes me that some sleazy neon would do wonders for both of us. Not to mention the Magic Fingers . . . and one of those Korean oil paintings of Paris in the rain. We can mess up both beds if we want to, and . . ."

"*Jesus!*"

The explosion really frightened her. "What on earth . . . ?"

"*Is that the way you want it to be?*"

"Well, it was only a . . ."

"Maybe I got it all wrong," he said. "I thought we were talking about bringing another life into the world! I thought we were talking about our kid!"

"We were," she replied numbly, "in part."

"So why the hell are you trying to make something cheap out of it?"

Her reserve flew out the window. "Oh my yes! Heaven forbid that Mommy should get a little fun out of the procedure. We're talking holy, holy, holy here. Tell you what, Brian . . . why don't you run out and gather some rose petals . . . and we can sprinkle them on our goddamn bed of connubial bliss, just so the little bugger knows we're good and ready for him . . . or her . . . or whatever the hell we're manufacturing tonight."

He stared at her as if she were a corpse in a morgue and he were the next of kin. Then he rose and went to the window facing the bay. After a long silence, he said: "I'm pretty thick, I guess, I've been misreading this all along."

"What do you mean?" Her voice was calmer now.

He shrugged. "I thought you *wanted* a baby. I really believed that."

"I do, Brian. I *do*. I just can't take it when . . . when you make it sound like that's the sole purpose of our sex, that's all. Hey, look . . . I came home from a horrendous day and you were sitting here like some spoiled kid with one more job for me to do. I'm sorry, but one miracle is all I can manage in a day."

"Miracle?" He frowned at her. "What's that supposed to mean?"

"Nothing. I just meant . . . I want you to want me for me, OK? I don't like being jealous of a kid who's not even here yet." She smiled faintly as a gesture of reconciliation. "That's all, Brian. Just for to-night, can't there be just two of us in bed?"

"Sure," he answered softly. "You bet."

"Do you understand what I'm saying?"

He nodded. "I'm sorry, babe. I didn't mean it to sound like that."

"I know," she replied. "I know."

They smoked a joint later and made love on the floor of the TV room. Perhaps because of the tension of her day, Mary Ann's orgasm eluded her until she took flight from the familiar and imagined it was Simon's body that was grinding her fanny against the industrial carpeting.

"You see?" said Brian, grinning at her afterwards. "Just the two of us."

Death at the Door

After some investigation, Michael learned that London's most fashionable dyke nightclub was a place in Mayfair called Heds. Tucked away discreetly in a basement, it was marked only by an understated brass plaque at the entrance: GENTLEMEN WILL KINDLY DISCHARGE THEIR WEAPONS BEFORE ENTERING THIS ESTABLISHMENT. The doorperson was a puce-lipped brunette with a Louise Brooks haircut.

"Have you lads been here before?"

Michael turned to Wilfred. "Have we?"

"Once," said the kid. "Don't worry. We're bent."

The doorperson smiled at him. "Just checking. Have a good time, now."

The room was smoky and low-ceilinged, with a row of couches along one wall. Four or five lesbian couples were slow-dancing to Anne Murray beneath a jerky mirror ball. Most of the women were stylishly dressed, and some of them were astonishingly beautiful. Michael sat down on one of the couches and motioned Wilfred to join him.

"This is really a long shot," he said.

The kid shrugged. "Can't hurt."

"It's not really her kind of place. It's so . . . unpolitical."

"Yeah."

"Of course . . . her looks have changed completely. I guess the rest could've changed too."

176

"Have you thought about ringing her?"

"That address, you mean? I tried that three days ago. There isn't a listing for Roughton in Easley-on-Hill."

A cocktail waitress stopped at the sofa. "Something to drink, gentlemen?"

"No, thanks," said Michael. He glanced at Wilfred. "How about you?"

The kid declined.

Michael looked back at the waitress. "You wouldn't happen to know an American woman named Mona Ramsey?"

The waitress thought for a moment, then shook her head.

"She's in her late thirties. Wears her hair like Princess Diana. Swears like a sailor."

"Sorry, love. I don't catch the names usually." She smiled apologetically and moved to the next customer.

"How much longer have you got?" asked Wilfred.

"Till what?"

"Till you go."

"Oh." He thought for a moment. "Six days, I guess. I leave on Tuesday."

Wilfred nodded.

"Why?" asked Michael.

"Well . . . we could go there."

"Where?"

"You know . . . Easley-on-Hill."

"Oh."

"We could go there for Easter, couldn't we? It's lovely country, Gloucestershire. We could take the train. I've some money put away. And . . . if we don't find her, there's no harm done, is there?"

The kid's earnestness frightened him. "Actually," he replied gently, "I think I may do that."

Wilfred blinked at him. "Without me, you mean?"

Michael hesitated.

"I understand," said Wilfred. "Forget I said that."

"It isn't you," said Michael.

"Doesn't matter."

"Yes, it does. I don't want you to think . . . that I don't like you."

"I know you like me."

"I just think . . . it would be easier with . . . just me. I mean, if I come crashing in on her scene, whatever *that* is. Do you see what I mean, Wilfred?" He found the kid's hand and squeezed it.

Wilfred nodded.

"Do you dance?"

The kid glanced around. "Here?"

"Sure."

Wilfred shrugged, then stood up. Michael took him in his arms and led as they danced to "You Needed Me." "Cripes," murmured Wilfred, his head against Michael's chest. "If me mates saw me, I'd be so bleedin' humiliated."

Michael chuckled. "Same here." He was actually remembering a time when he and Jon had necked around the pool table at Peg's Place in San Francisco. A dyke bar was the best place in the world for man-to-man romance; the management was always sympathetic, and there were no distractions. He wondered if lesbians felt the same way about gay men's bars.

"When will you leave?" asked Wilfred. "For Gloucestershire, I mean."

"Oh. Friday, I guess."

"Will I see you after that?"

"Sure. I'll be back for a day or so before I . . . go home."

"Right."

"Don't get gloomy on me, Wilfred."

"Right."

It was almost midnight when they returned to Colville Crescent. Wilfred's father was lumbering about upstairs, obviously drunk. Michael opened the door of his apartment, then turned to the kid: "Why don't you come in for a while? Until he passes out, at least."

Wilfred nodded and followed him into the room just as the phone rang. Michael reached for it and flopped on the sofa.

"It's Miss Treves," said the voice at the other end.

"Oh, hi."

"Listen, love . . . have you had any trouble?"

"Trouble?"

"Oh . . . prowlers . . . that sort of thing."

"No. Not that I know of. What is this?" Her ominously vague warnings were beginning to get on his nerves.

"Oh . . . well, there may be a bit of . . . I doubt if it's serious, but I thought it best to let you know . . . just in case. There's been a misunderstanding, and the silly ass is drunk, so . . ."

"Miss Treves . . ."

"Just stay there, love. I'll be round shortly. I'll explain everything."

"OK, but . . ."

"Lock the doors, love. Don't let anyone in. Check the windows too. I'll be there in five minutes."

She hung up.

Michael rose, a little dazed.

"Who was it?" asked Wilfred.

"Miss Treves."

"Who? Oh . . . the midget?"

"She said to lock the doors and windows."

"Why?" asked the kid.

"Good question. Somebody's drunk. It doesn't make any sense. She's coming over to explain it . . ." His words trailed off as he remembered the door that opened onto the garden from the kitchen. He hurried to lock it.

Wilfred trailed after him like an anxious puppy. "Maybe it's that fat bloke I saw."

"What fat bloke?"

"You know. When that bitch was here."

"Oh."

As he secured the back door, he peered out into the dark garden, but all he could make out was the grim filigree of the rusty bedspring propped against the fence. The sky glowed luridly, pinkish-orange, reflecting the lights of the city. There was no movement anywhere.

He went to the kitchen window and tugged on the sash. "This god-damn thing won't close all the way."

Wilfred nodded soberly. "We've got one to match upstairs. Look, mate . . . what's happening? Is someone coming?"

"I don't know. She seemed to think so."

"Then why don't we leave?"

"We can't. Miss Treves is coming over."

The kid was silent for a moment, then said: "You forgot the window in the bedroom."

"God, you're right!" He dashed into the bedroom, with Wilfred at his heels. The window was already shut, so they returned to the living room where Michael waited nervously at the window facing the street.

"What if he gets here before she does?" asked Wilfred.

"Don't make it worse," said Michael. A car rumbled past the elephantine silhouette of the cement mixer on the sidewalk. He watched until it rounded the corner and passed out of sight. Did Miss Treves drive? he wondered.

Moments later, the little manicurist arrived on foot, bustling along the sidewalk like a Munchkin bringing word of the Wicked Witch. Michael admitted her before she had a chance to reach for the buzzer.

"I'm sorry love," she said in an earnest whisper as she hurried into the apartment and locked the door behind her. "You really shouldn't be involved in this."

"There's two of us, actually. This is my friend, Wilfred. He lives upstairs."

She nodded a brisk hello to the kid, then turned back to Michael. "It may be nothing, actually. I just wanted to be here in case . . . it got ugly."

Great, thought Michael.

Miss Treves turned and looked out the window.

"Look," said Michael, "could you at least tell us who we're expecting?"

The little woman hesitated, then said: "Bunny Benbow."

"Who?"

"Hush, love." She hoisted herself onto her favorite chair. "Close the curtains, please. Quickly!"

As Michael did so, he heard footsteps. It was a drunk's gait, heavy and faltering. The man muttered to himself as he passed the house, but his words were too slurred to be understood. Holding his breath, Michael glanced at Wilfred, then at Miss Treves, perched motionlessly on the edge of her chair with a forefinger pressed to her lips.

The footsteps stopped.

For a moment there was no sound at all except for the angry screeching of tires several blocks away. Then the man bellowed out a single word—*Simon!*—and overturned a trash can in the yard. Seconds later, the squawk of the door buzzer made the three listeners go rigid in unison, like victims of a joint electrocution.

Michael and Wilfred looked to Miss Treves for guidance. She shook her head slowly, once more using her finger to call for silence.

The buzzer sounded again, followed by the thud of the man's fists against the front door. *"Simon, you bloody little bastard, I know you're in there!"*

Still, Miss Treves insisted they remain quiet.

"Simon, lad . . . c'mon now . . . It's your old man . . . I won't hurt you." The man paused for a moment, waiting for a reply, then continued his plea in a more reasonable tone of voice. "Simon, lad . . . she lies about me . . . she's a bloody liar, son . . . C'mon now, open up, eh? Your old man needs your help, lad."

He got nothing for his efforts.

"Simon!" he bellowed again.

"Hey," came another voice, just as angry. *"Sod off!"*

Michael locked eyes with Wilfred, who pointed to the ceiling to indicate the identity of the other shouter.

"Who said that?" yelled the man at the door.

"Up here, you bleedin' fool!"

Another garbage can clattered to the ground as the caller apparently staggered back into the yard. *"Call me a fool, you goddamn black bastard. Come down here and call me that, you woolly-headed wog!"*

The man returned to the door and began pounding again, a racket that was presently accompanied by the menacing thud of Wilfred's father's footsteps on the stairs. "C'mon, lad . . . doncha even wanna see what your old dad looks like? I know what *you* look like. Tell you what, lad . . . talk to me for just a bit and I'll leave you be. Eh? That's the least you . . ." His words were cut off by a bone-chilling howl from the aborigine and the bang of the door as it was thrown open. "*I told you to sod off, didn't I?*"

Michael turned to Wilfred, whispering though it was no longer necessary. "This is insane. We can't just sit here."

"Says who?" the kid replied. "I'm not going out there."

Miss Treves slipped out of her chair and inched toward the door. "Dear God," she murmured. "This is dreadful. Isn't there something we can do?"

The noise in the corridor was horrendous, a mixture of animal grunts and maniacal wheezing. Someone slammed against the wall so hard that a tin engraving fell off the wall in Simon's living room. After almost a minute of desperate battle, there was nothing left but the sound of one man's heavy breathing. Then someone opened the front door, closed it, and ran away from the house.

The corridor was still again.

Michael made his way toward the door.

"Wait!" said Wilfred.

"We have to see," answered Michael.

Miss Treves said nothing, hands aflutter at her throat.

Pressing his ear against the door, Michael listened for a moment. Nothing. He eased the door open, to reveal a large white man lying on his back in the corridor. He knelt by the form and watched for breathing, then laid his ear against the wet polyester above the man's heart.

"It's the fat bloke," said Wilfred.

Miss Treves waddled glumly into the corridor. "He's just . . . unconscious, isn't he?"

Michael looked up and shook his head.

"He's dead?" asked Wilfred.

Miss Treves whimpered softly and fainted, falling against the hillock of the corpse's belly.

Michael looked at Wilfred, then down again at the macabre tableau at his feet. His mind flashed perversely on the last scene of *Romeo and Juliet*.

Wilfred said the first sensible thing. "Have you any smelling salts?"

Michael shook his head. *Did* anyone have smelling salts? "Wait," he said, suddenly remembering. "I've got something that might work." He rushed to the bathroom and returned with the little bottle of concentrated liquid deodorant he had bought at Boots.

Wilfred frowned. "I don't know, mate. Poppers?"

"It's not poppers." Michael knelt next to Miss Treves and scooped her into his arms. He uncapped the bottle and waved the pungent stuff under her nose. Nothing happened. He set the bottle down. "There's not enough ammonia, I guess. This is like spraying her with Glade."

"I'll get something wet," offered Wilfred, dashing out of the room. He came back with a sea sponge from the bathroom and dabbed delicately at the midget's features.

Miss Treves's nose was the first thing to move. Then her left eye twitched. Then a little convulsion shook her whole body awake. "Thank God," murmured Michael. He carried her back to the living room and laid her carefully on the sofa. It took a moment for her to realize where she was. Then the terror returned to her face. "Are you sure he's dead?" she asked.

"Uh-huh," nodded Michael.

"Who was that? Who did it?"

"Wilf . . . uh, the man upstairs."

"Me dad," put in Wilfred. He gave Michael a quick glance to show that he didn't need to be protected.

"They were both drunk," said Michael. "It was just a . . . freak thing."

Miss Treves nodded wearily. "Bunny has a bad heart." She glanced toward the corpse in the hallway. "The bally fool . . . the stupid, bally fool. I told him to leave well enough alone, but he was always . . ." Her voice trailed off in despair.

"Are you all right now?" asked Michael.

She nodded.

"I don't know what this is all about, Miss Treves, but I'll have to call the police."

"No! Not yet . . . please, love, not yet."

"Why?"

Her hands flopped about like injured sparrows. "It's best that we talk first. For Simon's sake. There's nothing to be gained by destroying everything he's ever . . ."

"Is that Simon's father?" Michael jerked his head toward the corpse.

Miss Treves swallowed once, then looked away.

"Is it?" asked Michael.

She nodded.

"And he thought I was Simon?"

Another nod. "I told the bally fool you weren't. He read that vile piece in the *Mirror* and saw you leaving one day and convinced himself that Simon had come home from California."

Michael was totally lost. "He didn't know what his own son looked like?"

"Uh . . . mate." Wilfred was tugging on his arm. "There's a body out there. This is no time for a bleedin' chat."

"He's right," said Miss Treves. "Perhaps we should bring it in."

"Now wait a minute . . ."

"Just for a bit, love. We can put it back."

"But the police will know that something . . ."

"No they won't, love. Just be careful about fingerprints. The lad will help you. Won't you, love?" She gave Wilfred a surprisingly winning little smile.

The kid shrugged at Michael. "They can't arrest us for movin' him, can they?"

So Michael gave in. He and Wilfred each took a leg and dragged the man-mountain into the apartment. Miss Treves showed her gratitude with another smile and said: "Would you mind covering him, love? Just for now?" Michael hesitated, then fetched Simon's duvet from the bedroom and draped it over the body.

"OK," he said crisply, turning back to Miss Treves. "What is it you want me to do?"

She looked down at her hands. "Nothing, really. Except . . . you mustn't mention what he said about . . . being Simon's father."

Michael studied her face. "Simon doesn't know that, I take it."

"No. And he mustn't. Ever."

"This guy . . ." He gestured toward the quilted mound. "He got Simon's mother pregnant?"

"No," replied the nanny. "Well . . . yes. Technically."

Wilfred giggled.

Michael ignored him. "And this man's name was . . . ?"

"Benbow. Bunny Benbow. He was the head of the revue I used to sing with. We met the Bardills at a hotel where we were playing in Malta. Nineteen fifty-six. They were on holiday, an extended trip around the world. Mrs. Bardill took a fancy to Bunny . . . which was only natural, since we were all in show business. Mrs. Bardill was much more famous, of course, but . . ." She glanced almost sorrowfully at the corpse. "Bunny was a dashing figure in those days."

"So he came here tonight . . . ?"

"To see his son, in part. He was hopelessly sentimental, for all his faults. He knew that the Bardills were dead . . . and he thought there might be a chance of . . . being a father to Simon again."

"Again?" Michael frowned. "It doesn't sound as if he ever was."

Miss Treves fidgeted. "He also wanted money. That piece in the *Mirror* made it sound as if Simon was very rich."

"So this guy comes waltzing back after . . . what? . . . twenty-eight years, and expects Simon to buy that? To give him money, just because he got Simon's mother pregnant?"

The nanny looked away. Her lower lip had began to tremble.

"Miss Treves . . ."

"He was in prison for most of that time. He robbed a hotel in Brighton. That's why the revue broke up. That's why I came back to London and found the Bardills and asked for the job as Simon's nanny."

Michael simply stared at her.

"He tried to reach Simon," she continued. "He wrote letters from prison, but I intercepted them. He had no right to spoil their lives. To spoil Simon's life. We were all so very happy, and he had no . . ."

"Wait a minute. How could he have known for certain?"

"Known what?"

"That he was Simon's father."

She looked at him balefully.

"I need the truth, Miss Treves."

"Love . . . I'm telling you the truth."

He reached out and took her child-size hand. "All of it?"

She heaved a world-weary sigh. "Mr. Bardill was sterile."

He nodded to encourage her.

"The Bardills wanted a baby very badly. *Very* badly." She brought her fingertips to her temple and made a circular motion, as if to expel a private demon. "I'm sorry, love. There's some brandy on the shelf above the fridge. Would you mind awfully?"

"I'll get it," chirped Wilfred, bounding to his feet and dodging Bunny Benbow on his way to the kitchen.

"You must be my friend," Miss Treves said to Michael.

"I am your friend." He gave her hand a squeeze. "You did my nails, didn't you?"

She mustered a wan smile for him as Wilfred returned with a tumbler of brandy. She downed it in two efficient gulps and gave the glass back to the kid. "Thank you, love."

"My pleasure," replied Wilfred, sinking to the floor again. He propped his chin on his fist and gazed at the two of them as if they were a television set about to flicker into action. "Don't mind me."

Michael turned to Miss Treves. "So . . . ?"

"Yes. Well . . . Mr. Bardill was sterile, as I said . . . and it was a source of great anguish for both of them. When we met them at the Selmun, I knew there was . . ."

"The what?"

"The Selmun Palace Hotel. Where we were performing."

"Oh."

"It was a lovely old place, miles away from Valletta . . . up on a hill, overlooking the sea. One of the Knights of Malta lived there long ago. The people who stayed there were all lovely people, and the Bardills were the loveliest of the lot. She was a famous actress, but she wasn't a bit stuck-up. They bought bicycles in Valletta, which they rode all over the island, and she wore these lovely long scarves that trailed along in the breeze like . . ."

"Miss Treves." The brandy had been a terrible idea. "Time is of the essence."

She nodded. "I just want you to know that I didn't think of them as strangers, the Bardills. I felt as if I'd known them all my life."

"All right."

"I knew that I could trust them."

He nodded.

"At any rate . . . one night Mrs. Bardill took a long stroll with Bunny and told him about . . . Mr. Bardill's condition. Bunny offered to make arrangements for them . . . to obtain a child."

"To adopt one, you mean?"

"No," she replied dimly. "To buy one."

Wilfred drew in breath audibly. Michael shot a quick glance at him, then turned back to Miss Treves. "But you said he was . . . It was *his* baby, you mean? He sold Simon to the Bardills because they wanted . . . ?"

"Yes," she answered, before he could finish.

"He *sold* his own baby?"

"Our own baby."

He blinked at her.

"Simon is my son."

A car swooshed through a puddle out in Colville Crescent. Wilfred's eyes were porcelain saucers. Michael's failure to respond immediately prompted Miss Treves to add defensively: "It can skip a generation, you know."

"I'm sorry," he gulped. "I didn't mean to . . ."

"Don't be a silly-billy. It's not what one would expect, is it now?"

"No . . . I guess not."

"Bunny and I weren't married. We weren't even lovers in the conventional sense. We were professional partners mostly. Simon was simply the result of . . . a night of foolishness. It was a stupid mistake, but we salvaged it rather well. Until now."

Michael hesitated, then asked: "You . . . didn't want a baby?"

"No, love." She smiled at him sweetly. "I wanted a career."

He nodded.

"I wanted to be a star, if the truth be known, but that wasn't in the cards. Bunny robbed that hotel in Brighton, and the whole bally world fell apart. If the Bardills hadn't taken me on as Simon's nanny . . ."

"They took you in, knowing that you were Simon's . . . ?"

"Oh, no! Bunny told them that Simon was the son of a girl in Valletta. He was simply acting as . . . broker. I imagine they suspected he was the father, but they never said as much. All they really cared about was having a beautiful son to care for."

"Does Simon think he's their natural son, then?"

"Everyone does. The Bardills were away from England for almost three years. They told their friends he was born in a Maltese hospital while they were on holiday . . . which was quite true. Mr. Bardill even had a birth certificate made, I'm not sure how. He was a barrister, you know."

"But what if Simon . . . ?"

". . . had grown up to be little? Well, he didn't, now, did he?"

"No."

"It was naughty of us—I admit that—but it solved everyone's problem at the time."

Michael looked back at the problem under the duvet. "And . . . this guy came here to spill the beans . . . and he expected Simon to give him money for that?"

"Not exactly. He wanted money, yes . . . but he thought Simon already knew about him."

"You told him that?"

She nodded. "I thought it would discourage him from seeking out Simon. I'm afraid I was wrong about that. It only sent him into a fury." She cast a scolding glance at the father of her son. "He has such a temper, that one."

If there was something appropriate to say under the circumstances, Michael couldn't think of it. Miss Treves sensed his discomfort and smiled sympathetically. "It's a bit much, isn't it?"

He waited a moment longer before asking: "What do you want me to tell the police, then?"

"Everything," she replied. "Except the reason he came here." She turned to Wilfred. "That won't make matters any worse for your father, love. They were both drunk—obviously—and they got into a senseless fracas. Bunny was wandering by on the pavement and . . . made too much noise, which . . . distressed your father . . . and they began to fight. They'll see that he died of a heart attack, I'm sure."

Michael wasn't so sure. "But couldn't they trace him to Simon?"

"How? I haven't seen him myself for over twenty years. They have no reason whatsoever to link him with me if . . ."

"What if Wilfred's father comes back?"

The kid shook his head. "He won't, mate."

Miss Treves gave him a pitying look. "He might, love. I doubt if the police would hold him completely responsible for . . ."

"Doesn't matter. I don't care."

"Of course you care. Don't be silly."

Wilfred smiled and shook his head.

Miss Treves raised herself to a sitting position, then sought the floor with her tiny feet. She wobbled a little standing up—because of the brandy, no doubt—but her resolve seemed firm as she strode toward the corpse.

"What are you doing?" Michael asked.

She knelt next to the body. "Looking for something."

As she searched Bunny Benbow's pockets, Michael grew increasingly nervous. "I don't think you should do that. They might be able to tell if . . ."

"We were looking for identification," she said curtly. "That's perfectly understandable. Here!" She had found what she wanted: Benbow's ragged clipping of the *Mirror* story—ROYAL RADIOMAN ON FRISCO PLEASURE BINGE. She handed it to Michael. "Burn it, will you, love?"

Michael stuffed it into his pocket. "Is there anything else on him?"

Her frisking produced only a few coins and a St. Christopher medallion. She brushed off her hands and stood up. "Well, now . . . are we clear on everything?"

"I think so," said Michael.

She turned to Wilfred. "How about you, love?"

The kid nodded.

"Good. Then I'll just slip back to . . ."

"Wait a minute," blurted Michael. "Where should the body be when the police arrive?"

"My, yes . . . well . . . I suppose we should put him back in the hallway, don't you? That way you can say he burst in when . . . the lad's father opened the door. Of course, you could very well have brought him in here . . . no, I think the hallway's best. Would you mind awfully?"

So Michael and Wilfred dragged Bunny Benbow back to the site of his untimely demise.

"Splendid." Miss Treves beamed as she supervised the arrangement of the corpse. "That looks quite natural, I think." She headed toward the door. "I'll just toddle on home. Would you ring me, love, when the police have gone?"

"Wait . . ."

"The number's on the fridge under 'Nanny.'"

"Oh . . . OK."

"I'm just around the corner. Chepstow Villas." She gave him a supportive smile. "Keep your pecker up, love. It'll all be over soon."

She reached for the doorknob—reached *up*—then froze and turned around again, gazing wistfully at the body as she spoke: "Goodbye, Bunny. Safe journey home." Her eyes glimmered wetly as she glanced back at Michael. "Such a child, that one. Such a big, overgrown child."

All She Gets

Mary Ann was slicing kiwi fruit when Michael called. "You sound so close," she said. "Are you sure you're in London?"

"I'm sure." His tone seemed tinged with irony.

"Is something the matter?"

"No . . . I'm fine. What time is it there?"

"Oh . . . suppertime."

"Is Simon there?"

"No. Why would he be here?"

"I meant . . . around."

"Oh." She must have sounded far too defensive. "He and Brian are out running, actually. We're having Simon to dinner tonight. Wait a minute . . . what time is it *there?*"

"Late. Or early, rather. I just saw a bobby to the door."

"A *bobby?*" She giggled. "Sounds like you're doing all right."

"Not that way."

"Oh."

"A man had a heart attack in our hallway. He was in a fight, and he died right outside my door."

"Oh, Mouse . . . how awful."

"Yeah."

"Are you OK?"

"Sure."

"You don't sound OK."

"Well . . . I'm rattled, I guess. I'm not used to being interrogated."

"What did they want to know?"

"You know . . . just what I heard."

"What did you hear?"

"Not much, really. Just a couple of drunks yelling."

"Was it anybody you knew?"

"No. Well . . . the other guy lived upstairs. He ran away when . . . the guy had the heart attack. It's over now, anyway. How are *you*, Babycakes?"

"Fine. Well . . . OK. Nothing to speak of, one way or the other."

"Is Simon enjoying himself?"

"Oh, yes. As far as I know."

"I've got a message for him. Tell him Fabia Dane stopped by. She used to be Fabia . . . uh . . . Pumphrey, but she got married and she wants him to . . ."

"Hang on. I'd better write this down." She scrambled for a pencil. "What were those names again?"

He spelled them for her. "She's having a summer party at her new country place. She's sending him an invitation later. Her new husband makes potato chips. And she's a cunt."

"Is that part of the message?"

"That's a footnote. I think he knows it already."

"OK. Anything else?"

"That's it. She looked to me like a jilted girlfriend."

"Oh, really?"

"Uh-huh."

"What was she like?"

"Uh . . . cunt wasn't enough?"

"Well . . ."

"An upper-class cunt. How's that?"

"Great." She giggled, pleased with this elaboration. She needed all the reinforcement she could get. "When will we see you again?"

"Tuesday night, I guess. Tell Simon I'll leave the keys with his nanny."

"His *nanny*?"

He laughed. "That's a whole different story. She's his former nanny, actually. If you try to reach me after tomorrow, I won't be here. I'm going to the country for Easter."

"How elegant."

"Maybe. I'm not exactly sure where I'm going. I mean . . . I know where I'm going, but I don't know what I'm going to find."

"That makes sense."

"No. Get this: I think Mona's there."

"Mona? *Our* Mona?"

"I think so, but there's no way of knowing for sure. She won't talk to me."

"You've seen her?"

"Just briefly. From a distance. Her hair is blonde now, and she cuts it like Princess Di."

"I can't believe it."

"It's macabre, isn't it?"

"How do you know she's in this country place?"

"I don't. It's kind of a long shot. I don't know . . . at least I'll see the countryside."

"Are you going alone?"

"I don't know."

"C'mon, Mouse . . ."

"I might go with a friend."

She heard someone whoop in the background. "Uh, Mouse . . . who was that?"

"Who do you think? The friend."

"He just found out he's going?"

"Right."

"He sounded pleased." He sounded delirious, in fact; the whooping hadn't stopped. "How old is he?"

"Eleven, at the moment. Wilfred, get down from there."

"Wilfred, huh? How English can you get? He isn't really eleven, is he?"

"No."

She waited for him to elaborate, then said: "Is that all I get?"

"That's all you get. Until I'm home."

"Is there good dish?" she asked.

"Some. Plenty, actually. I'm not sure you'll believe it."

193

"Like what?"

"When I get home, Babycakes."

"You're no fun," she pouted.

Outfoxed

Good Friday came, gray and drizzly. Michael stood on a platform at Paddington Station, mesmerized by the soot-streaked silver trains as they thundered into the great glass cavern. The depot was swarming with haggard Londoners, all intent upon an Easter somewhere else.

He checked the time. Eleven fifty-six. The train to Oxford would leave in seventeen minutes. He set his suitcase down and perused the other passengers queuing at Platform 4. Wilfred was plainly not among them.

They had agreed to meet at eleven-thirty, just to be safe, so the kid was almost half an hour overdue. If they missed this train, Michael realized, they would miss their connecting train in Oxford. He chided himself for trusting the kid to run off on his "last-minute errand," whatever it was.

He wouldn't get in a snit about it. He hauled his suitcase to the newsstand and lost himself in the screaming headlines of the tabloids. One said: RANDY ANDY'S ROYAL DIP. It featured a disappointing telephoto shot of Prince Andrew in a bathing suit. Another pictured the prince's porn star girlfriend and said: KOO D'ETAT.

He bought an apple and checked the time again. Ten minutes till departure. What the hell was going on? Had Wilfred changed his mind? Or misunderstood his instructions? What if Wilfred's father had come home?

The last thought was too creepy to pursue. He returned to the platform and saw that the train had arrived, so he paced alongside it, growing antsier by the second. *It better be serious*, he told himself, *but not too serious*. He couldn't leave without knowing what had happened. He would just have to cancel the trip.

He approached a conductor. "Excuse me. I'm trying to get to Moreton-in-Marsh."

"Right you are. This is the one. Change at Oxford."

"I know, but if I miss this train . . . ?"

"Then you'll miss Moreton-in-Marsh, sir. Till tomorrow, that is."

"Shit."

"Expecting someone, are you?"

"Yeah. I was. Thanks." He skulked away, supremely disappointed, then stopped in his tracks as he caught sight of Wilfred's bronze-brown ringlets bobbing through the crowd. "*There* you are."

The kid's expression was appropriately sheepish. "Sorry, mate." He was wearing jeans and a bright yellow sleeveless sweater with a matching bow tie. He carried a canvas satchel under one arm and a large cardboard box under the other.

Michael ditched his lecture and grinned at him. "We're not emigrating, you know."

Without answering, Wilfred boarded the train and strode through the carriages until he found one that was sparsely populated. "How's this?" he asked

"Fine."

The kid took the seat by the window and stowed the satchel beneath him. He kept the cardboard box in his lap. "It took longer than I thought," he said.

"For what?"

A cryptic smile. Then Wilfred tapped the side of the box.

Michael looked down at it. It was wrapped in masking tape, and there were four or five little holes in the top. The light dawned. "Jesus, Wilfred . . . *if that's what I . . .*"

"Keep it down, mate."

"They'll throw us off."

"No they won't."

"It's gotta be . . . against the law or something."

The kid shrugged. "You're good with cops."

Michael stared at him incredulously, then looked down again. "Are you sure he can't get out of there?"

The kid nodded.

"But couldn't he bite his way . . . ?"

"He doesn't want to, mate. He's stoned."

"What?"

"I put a bit of hash in his meat."

The train lurched into motion just as a conductor entered the carriage. Wilfred leaned forward, folding his arms across the top of the box. Then he remembered his ticket, retrieved it from his jeans, and handed it to Michael. Hastily, he hunched over the box again.

The conductor loomed above them. "Where to, gents?"

"Moreton-in-Marsh," answered Michael, handing him the tickets.

"Lovely village, that. Heart of England."

"Yes. So we hear." His smile was forced and must have looked it. "We're going near there, actually. Easley-on-Hill."

The conductor's eyes darted to Wilfred, then fixed on Michael again. "Easter holiday, eh?"

"Right." Another insipid smile.

"Have a good one, then."

"Thanks," they replied in unison.

The conductor shambled to the next carriage.

Michael focused on Wilfred again. "Are you out of your mind?"

"Not a bit."

"What are we going to do with him?"

The kid shrugged. "Just turn him loose."

"Where?"

"I don't know. Gloucestershire. Anywhere."

"Great," muttered Michael. "*Born Free.*"

"What?" The kid's nose wrinkled.

"A movie. Before your time. Stop making me feel old. Look, what happens if ol' Bingo here . . . ?"

"Dingo."

"Dingo. What happens if his dope wears off before we make it to the wilds?"

Wilfred gave him a brief, impatient glance. "Well, there's nothing we can do about that *now*, is there?"

He had no answer for that.

"Just settle back, mate. Look . . . look out there. There's our green and pleasant land. You're on holiday, remember?"

Michael bugged his eyes at the kid, then sank back in the seat. He flopped his head toward the window as an endless caravan of suburban back gardens flickered past in the rain. They gave way eventually to grimy Art Deco factories, random junkyards, mock-Tudor gas stations squatting grimly beneath flannel-gray skies.

"It's clearing up," said Wilfred.

Michael blinked at him, then looked out the window again. "When does it start getting quaint?"

The kid snorted. "You Americans and your bleedin' quaint." He paused a moment before asking: "Where will we stay in Gloucestershire?"

"Oh . . . I guess a bed-and-breakfast place. We'll have to play it by ear." Somehow, he liked the idea of that very much. He looked at Wilfred and smiled. "Got any ideas?"

The kid shook his head. "Never been there."

"We may have to rent a car. It all depends on what that address means."

"Right."

"What about your father?" Michael asked.

"What about him?"

"Well . . . if he doesn't come back, what will you do?"

Wilfred tossed it off with a brittle laugh. "Same as before, mate."

The landscape grew greener, more undulating. The train stopped at four or five little gingerbread stations before they reached Oxford, where they disembarked and waited for the train to Moreton-in-Marsh. They had coffee and sweet rolls in the station snack bar while a noisy downpour brutalized the neatly tended flowerbed adjacent to the platform.

On the next leg of the journey, they sat in silence for a long time as the train rumbled across the rain-blurred countryside. Dingo had begun to stir slightly, but not enough to attract attention. Wilfred cooed to him occasionally and stuffed pieces of ham sandwich into the air holes. The fox made grateful gulping sounds.

"What did your lover do?" the kid asked eventually.

Michael looked up from a guidebook on the Cotswolds. "For a living, you mean?"

Wilfred nodded.

"He was a doctor. On an ocean liner." He smiled faintly. "He was a gynecologist when I met him."

"Really?"

Michael nodded. "I've heard all the jokes."

The kid smiled. "How long was he your lover?"

"That's hard to say. I knew him for about seven years."

"He didn't live with you?"

"Some of the time. Not in the beginning, then we did, then we broke up. When we finally got back together, he had the job on the ship, so he wasn't at home part of the time. That's when we were happiest, I think. For ten days or three weeks or whatever, I would save up things to tell him when he got home."

"What sort of things?"

"You know . . . dumb stuff. Items in the paper, things we both liked . . . or disagreed on. I hate Barbra Streisand but he loved her, so I became responsible for any Barbra trivia he might have missed when he was on the high seas. It was a terrible curse, but I did it." He smiled. "I *still* do it."

"Did you date other blokes when he was away?"

"Oh, sure. So did he. We didn't sleep together anymore."

"Why not?"

Michael shrugged. "The sex wore off. We were too much like brothers. It felt . . . incestuous."

The kid frowned. "That's too bad."

"I don't know. I think it freed us to love each other. We didn't ask so much of each other anymore. We just got closer and closer. We had great sex with other people and great companionship with each other. It wasn't what I had planned on, but it seemed to work better than anything else."

Wilfred's brow furrowed. "But . . . that's not really a lover."

"Oh, I know. And we made sure our boyfriends knew that, too. We'd say: 'Jon's just a friend . . . Michael's just my roommate . . . We used to be lovers, but now we're just friends.' If you've ever been the third party in a situation like that, you know that the difference doesn't mean diddlyshit. Those guys are *married* . . . and they're always the last to know."

"But *you* knew," said Wilfred.

Michael nodded, "Toward the end. Yeah."

"Then . . . that's better than nothing."

Michael smiled at him. "That's better than everything."

"Does your family know you're bent?"

"Sure," said Michael. "Jon and I went to visit them in Florida a few months before he got sick." He grinned at the memory. "They liked him a lot—I knew they would—but God knows *what* they were envisioning between the two of us. That's funny, isn't it? They didn't have a damn thing to worry about. I spent five years getting them used to the idea of me sleeping with men . . . only to bring them one I didn't sleep with anymore."

"Where did you meet him?" asked Wilfred.

"At a roller rink. We collided."

"Really?"

"I got a nosebleed. He was so fucking gallant I couldn't believe it." He gazed out the window at two mouse-gray villages crouching in a green vale. "We went home to my place. Mona brought us breakfast in bed the next morning."

"You mean . . . the one at Harrods."

"Right. We were roommates at the time." Several ragged scraps of blue had appeared above the distant hills. He felt a perverse little surge of optimism. "I hope you get to meet her. She's not really . . . what was it you called her?"

"A twitzy-twee bitch?"

"Yeah. She's not like that. She's just a good, basic dyke."

Wilfred looked skeptical.

"You'll see," said Michael. "I hope you will, anyway."

When they arrived in Moreton-in-Marsh, the stationmaster directed them to the village center, a former Roman road called Fosse Way. It was lined with buildings made of grayish-orange Cotswold limestone, tourist facilities mostly—china shops, map stores, tea-rooms. The one at the end, closest to the town hall, was a pub called the Black Bear. They found two empty seats in the corner of the smoky room.

"See a barmaid?" asked Michael.

"I think Doll is it."

"Who?"

"Behind the bar, mate. The one with the eyeliner."

"How do you know her name?"

Wilfred smiled smugly and pointed to a sign above the bar: YOUR PROPRIETORS—DOLL AND FRED. "Any more questions?"

"Yeah. What about . . . our little friend?" He pointed to Dingo's box.

"Right. In a bit. How 'bout a cider?"

"Perfect."

While Wilfred was at the bar, Michael combed the titles on the jukebox and found Duran Duran and the Boystown Gang, San Francisco's own gay-themed rock group. The global village was shrinking by the second. He returned to his seat and took refuge in a reverie about ancient inns and craggy wayfarers and Something Queer Afoot.

"Success." Wilfred beamed, setting the ciders down.

"How so?"

"I asked ol' Doll about Roughton in Easley-on-Hill."

"And?"

"Well . . . Roughton is Lord Roughton, for one thing."

Michael whistled.

"For another, the house is very grand . . . one of the grandest in the Cotswolds."

Michael thought for a moment. "We can't just walk up and ring the doorbell, I guess."

The kid grinned mysteriously. "Not exactly."

"Wilfred . . . don't be coy."

"I'm not. There's a tour."

"You mean . . . of the house?"

Wilfred nodded. "Take us right there."

"Then we could . . ."

"I've booked us on it. Tomorrow morning."

It was almost too good to be true. Michael shook his head in amazement.

"Was that wrong?" asked Wilfred.

"Are you kidding? It's perfect. Did she say if there's a place to stay?"

"Upstairs. They have rooms. The bus leaves here at ten o'clock tomorrow morning. Ten pounds for the two of us. That's the tour, rather. The room is another eight pounds."

Michael rose, feeling for his wallet. "I'd better . . ."

"It's done, mate."

"Now, Wilfred . . ."

"You can pay for dinner. Sit down. Drink your cider."

Michael obeyed, acknowledging the kid's coup by lifting his mug.

Wilfred returned his salute, but remained deadpan. "I'm going to make someone a lovely husband."

The skies had cleared completely by dusk. They walked to the edge of the village until they found a meadow bordered by a dense thicket of beech trees. Wilfred set Dingo's box down with ceremonious dignity and untaped one end.

The fox emerged, looking slightly dazed, and stood perfectly still observing his captor.

"Go on," said Wilfred. "Get out of here."

The fox scampered several feet, wobbling somewhat. Then he stopped again.

"He doesn't want to go," said the kid.

"Yes, he does. It's just new to him."

Dingo waited a moment longer, considered his options again, and bounded toward the shadowy freedom of the trees.

The Rock Widow Awaits

Brian was sure the weekend would be fattening, so he made a point of running two extra miles on Saturday morning. On the way home, he stopped by the Russian Hill fire station and picked up one of the red-and-silver "Tot Finder" stickers he had seen in windows all over North Beach.

The sticker was designed to show firemen which window to break in order to rescue your child. There was a fireman on it, stalwart beyond belief, and he was holding a little girl in his arms.

Corny, maybe, but practical.

And not nearly so corny as the bumper sticker that Chip Hardesty had slapped on his Saab: HAVE YOU HUGGED YOUR CHILD TODAY? That one drove him crazy every time he passed Hardesty's house.

When he reached the courtyard, Mrs. Madrigal was scrubbing the mossy slime off the steps leading to the house. "It's getting so slippery," she explained, looking up. "I was afraid someone might have a nasty spill."

"I wouldn't worry about it," he said.

She stood up, wiping her hands on her apron. "I've got to worry about *something*. It's so quiet around here. Doesn't anyone have any problems?"

He grinned at her. "If you're really pressed, I'm sure we could cook up a disaster or two."

"That's quite all right." She eyed the "Tot Finder" decal. "What have we here?"

"Oh." He could already feel his face burning. "It's just . . . kind of a joke, really."

"Look at you," she teased, recognizing his embarrassment. "What's the matter? Did I catch you counting chickens?"

There was nothing he could do but laugh. "Do you have to ask?"

"No," she answered, fussing with her hair. "You're quite right. *Well . . .*" She put on a chipper face as she changed the subject. "You'll be up bright and early in the morning."

He wasn't sure what she meant.

"For the sunrise service," she added.

"Oh . . . no, that's Mary Ann. I'm going to Hillsborough for the weekend."

"Ah." Despite her tone of voice, she still looked vaguely confused.

He began to wonder if he'd gotten his wires crossed. "You mean . . . she told you I was going?"

"No . . . no."

"Then how did you . . . ?"

"Well, Simon mentioned the service, actually . . . and I just assumed that the three of you . . ." She tapped her forehead and looked annoyed with herself. "Don't mind the old lady. She's getting senile. What's happening in Hillsborough?"

"Uh . . . what?" He lost his train of thought for a moment, then recovered it. "Oh . . . a house party. Theresa Cross. Remember her? From the Cadillac?"

"Very well." Her expression said it all.

"You don't approve?"

"Well . . . I don't really know her."

"I'm going for the pool, really."

The landlady ducked her eyes.

"I'm a big boy, you know."

"Oh, my dear . . . I *know*." She gave him a playful look, then signaled the end of their conversation by searching for her scrub brush.

When he reached the apartment, he could hear Mary Ann inside, so he stuffed the "Tot Finder" into the pocket of his Canterbury shorts. He didn't want her to regard it as a pressure tactic. Her moods were too variable these days.

"Don't get near me," she said, seeing his coating of sweat.

He pretended to be hurt. "I thought you *liked* me pitted out."

"At certain moments, my love. This isn't one of them. Shouldn't you be packing?"

"Packing what? I'll be back tomorrow afternoon."

"Well . . . a bathing suit, at least."

He shrugged. "I'll wear one under my jeans."

She thought for a moment. "The Speedos, huh?"

He nodded. "The others are too baggy. Why?"

"Just curious."

She was worried about Theresa again; he liked that.

"Go shower," she said.

He went to the bedroom and shed his shoes and shorts and jock-strap. As he sat on the edge of the bed, collecting his thoughts, Mary Ann came to the door. It was almost as if she had heard him thinking.

He looked up at her. "You didn't tell me Simon was going."

"Where . . . oh, the Mount Davidson thing?"

He nodded.

She went to her vanity and began rearranging cosmetics. "Well, it was kind of a last-minute thing, more or less. The poor guy obviously didn't have any place to go for Easter, so . . . I thought it would be nice for him."

He didn't respond to that.

She turned around. "Don't do this, Brian."

"Do what?"

"Work yourself up again. I thought we'd put that behind us."

"Did I say anything? I just wondered why you hadn't mentioned it to me . . . that's all."

She shrugged. "It didn't occur to me. It's no big deal. It's just an assignment."

"At five o'clock in the morning."

She uttered a derisive little snort. "And we all know what a *lustful* creature I am at that time of day."

She got the smile she wanted. "OK," he said, "OK."

Sitting next to him, she leaned down and licked a drop of sweat off his breastbone. "You big, smelly jerk. Just relax. OK?" She pulled back and looked at him. "How did you hear Simon was going?"

"Mrs. Madrigal mentioned it." He felt stupid about it already. "Let's drop it, OK?"

"Gladly." She nuzzled his armpit. "Whew! That is *potent.* Don't let Dragon Lady catch a whiff of that." She kissed his neck and rose. "I vacuumed the car this morning."

"Great. Thanks."

"It's up on Union next to the Bel-Air. I think there's enough gas."

He got up. "Look, I'm sorry if . . ."

"Hey," she interrupted. "No apologies. Everything is fine."

A long, hot shower did wonders for his spirits. Afterwards, he put on his bathrobe and returned to the bedroom. Mary Ann was still sitting on the bed. When he approached the mirror on the closet door, he found the "Tot Finder" taped there. He turned around and looked at her.

She was waiting with a cautious smile. "I thought we should put it up, at least. Until we decide on where to put the nursery." Her face was full of gentleness and resolution. He knelt next to her, resting his head on her lap. She smoothed the hair above his ear. "I want one too," she murmured.

It was almost three o'clock when he arrived at Theresa Cross's rambling ranch house in Hillsborough. There was plenty of room to park in the rock widow's oversized driveway, so he slipped the Le Car between a Rolls and a Mercedes, shamed by his embarrassment. Here, of all places, such things shouldn't matter. Bix Cross was the very man who had taught him to be suspicious of materialism.

After asking directions from a uniformed Latin American maid, he made his way through the pearl-gray living room until he came to a knot of people drinking furiously by the pool. They had all the single-mindedness of an ant colony trying to move something large and dead across a room.

Someone fell out of the circle of chatter, as if thrown by centrifugal force. He was somewhere in his early forties, and his face was bland but tanned. "Hello there," he said, extending his hand. "I'm Arch Gidde, Theresa's realtor-slant-escort."

"Hi. I'm Brian Hawkins."

"You're looking for her, I suppose."

"Well . . . eventually. This is the party, I guess." A dumb thing to say, but he felt so unannounced.

Arch Gidde smirked. "This is it." He cast a sideways glance at a lavish buffet, largely uneaten. "I hate to think how many salmon have died in vain."

"Uh . . . she was expecting more?"

Another smirk. "Do you see Grace Slick? Do you see Boz Scaggs? Do you see Ann Getty, for that matter?"

How the hell did you answer that one? "Is there . . . uh . . . a specific reason or something?"

"Oh, God. You haven't heard, have you? And I'll bet you're one of Theresa's rock-and-roll buddies. *Quelle* bummer. You missed the big one." He sighed histrionically. "We *all* missed the big one." He leaned forward and lowered his voice to a furtive mutter. "Yoko Ono is throwing a little do in her suite at the Clift."

"Uh . . . now, you mean?"

The realtor nodded grimly. "As we speak."

"No shit." It was all he could muster.

"And madame is pissed. Madame is extremely pissed. Her guests have been bailing out all afternoon."

"I see." *Jesus God. Yoko Ono in San Francisco.*

"So," continued Arch Gidde, "she has retired to her chambers to compose herself." He tapped the side of his nose with his forefinger, then narrowed his eyes at Brian. "You look awfully familiar, for some reason."

Brian shrugged. He had waited on plenty of jerks like this during his career. "I don't think we know each other."

"Maybe. But I can't help thinking . . ."

"What's the party for?"

"This one? Or that one?"

"That one. I mean . . . why is Yoko Ono in town?"

"Oh, God." The realtor splayed his fingers across his face. "That's the part Mother Theresa hasn't heard yet. Mrs. Lennon is looking for a house."

"You mean . . . to live here?"

His informant nodded. "She thinks it's a good place to raise . . . little whatshisname."

"Sean," said Brian.

"Imagine what this is going to mean to Theresa. Two rock widows in the same town. Two Mrs. Norman Maines."

He didn't know who that was, and he didn't want to ask. Seeking escape, he let his eyes wander until he spotted his hostess as she emerged from her seclusion. She was wearing a black-and-pink bikini in a leopard-skin pattern. Her hair seemed larger than ever.

She stopped at the edge of the terrace, resting her weight on one hip, then clapped her hands together smartly. "All right, people! Into the pool! You know where to change. I want to see *bare flesh*." She strode toward Brian, pointing her finger at him. "Especially *yours*."

He tried to stay cool. "Hi," he said.

"Hi." She came to a halt, once again settling her weight on one hip. "Where's Mary Ann?"

"Oh . . . I thought she told you. She had to work. She was really sorry she couldn't make it." For some reason, that sounded phoney as hell, so he added: "I'm here to tell her what she missed."

"Good," replied Theresa, arching an eyebrow, "but don't tell her everything." There was something about her leer that rendered it harmless. What she seemed to offer was not so much lust as a genial caricature of it, an eighties update of a Betty Boop cartoon. She was accustomed to scaring off men, he decided; she counted on it.

Her body surprised him somewhat. Her breasts weighed in at just above average, but her big peasant nipples dented her bikini top like a pair of macadamia nuts. Her ass was large and heart-shaped, really a lot firmer than he had expected. All in all, a package that suggested a number of interesting possibilities.

"So get naked," she said. "We won't have the sun much longer."

Some of the other guests were already changing, so he doffed his shirt, shoes, and jeans and stashed them behind the cabana. Theresa, meanwhile, eased her way into the deep end of the pool, taking care not to damage her mammoth gypsy mane.

Brian gave his Speedo a quick plumping and ambled toward the pool. The rock widow's hair bobbed above the water like a densely vegetated atoll. "You wet me," she said, "and it's your ass."

He grinned at her, then dove in effortlessly, without splashing at all. It was one of his specialties. When he surfaced, Theresa was dog-paddling in his direction. "Have you eaten?" she asked, sotto voce, as if it were an intimate question.

He shook his head, tossing water off his brow. "It looks great."

"Better do it now. You won't feel like it later."

He didn't know what she meant until she aped Arch Gidde's gesture and tapped the side of her nose. "Right," he said. "Sounds good to me."

She made good half an hour later when she led him into her flannel-paneled screening room and began chopping cocaine on a mirrored tray. "Take that one," she said, pointing to the fattest line of all. "It looks about your size." She handed him a rolled bill.

He took it in one snort, then made the obligatory face to show that it was good stuff. "Thanks, Theresa."

"Terry," she murmured.

"No shit? I never heard that."

A heavy-lidded smile. "Now you have."

He nodded.

"Only the real people get to use it." She powdered her forefinger with the remains of the coke and rubbed it across her gums. "I don't waste it on the phoneys. You know what I mean?"

He nodded again. "Thanks, then."

"Terry's what Bix always called me."

This offhand brush with immortality seemed to put more bite in the cocaine. He was pretty sure she knew that.

"I wish they'd leave," she said.

"Who?"

"Them. Those others."

"They aren't your friends?"

"I never do this," she said, without answering his question. "I loathe people who sneak the stuff. But they'll never leave if I offer them some. I know how they are."

"Yeah."

She grabbed his hand suddenly. "Did I show you Bix's panties?"

It wounded him slightly to see that she had forgotten. "Yeah. Last time. During the auction."

"Oh. Right." She smiled penitently. "Brain damage."

"That's OK."

"I don't show them to just anybody. Only the real people." He nodded.

"You're a good guy, Brian."

"Thanks, Theresa."

"Terry," she said.

"Terry," he echoed.

Phantom of the Manor

There were eleven passengers in all, six of whom were Americans. The driver doubled as guide, providing commentary as the bus left the village behind and plunged into the engulfing green of the countryside.

"Today, ladies and gentlemen, we shall be visiting Easley House, the focal point of the village of Easley-on-Hill. Easley House is an outstanding example of an English Jacobethan manor house." He chuckled mechanically in the manner of every bad tour guide on earth. "That's right. You heard me correctly. *Jacobethan*. That's a cross, don't you see, between Jacobean and Elizabethan. The house was built between fifteen eighty-seven and sixteen thirty-five by the Ashendens of Easley-on-Hill, a Gloucestershire gentry family which had owned property in the county since before the Conquest."

Wilfred made a not-so-subtle yawning gesture.

Michael smiled at him. "It was your idea," he whispered.

"She's your friend," said the kid.

"I wouldn't count on that," answered Michael, gazing out the window at a meadow full of sheep. "I'm not counting on anything."

The bus slowed down as it entered Easley-on-Hill, a picture-perfect village built entirely of crumbling umber limestone. They bounced along a sunken lane for a minute or two, then crossed another sheep-dotted meadow until the manor house came into view.

Wilfred's voice assumed a near-reverential softness. "Look at *that*, mate."

"I'm looking," Michael murmured. "Jesus."

Easley House shone with the same burnished glow as the village, a looming conglomerate of gables and chimneys and tall mullioned windows winking in the sunshine. It was bigger than he had pictured, much bigger.

"She's running drugs," said Wilfred.

The guide pulled into a parking lot (he called it a car park) several hundred yards from the house. Michael and Wilfred shuffled out with the other passengers, reassembling in a passive clump like raw recruits awaiting orders. The guide, in fact, made a passable drill sergeant, with his blustery delivery and time-worn anecdotes and his disconcerting Roquefort cheese smile.

"We shall proceed from this point on foot. Easley House is the private residence of Lord Edward Roughton, son of Clarence Pirwin, fourteenth earl of Alma, so I trust we shall all remember that and conduct ourselves accordingly at all times."

Wilfred made a farting noise.

"Now," continued the guide, oblivious of Wilfred's punctuation, "the first building you will notice on your left is the tennis pavilion, a thatched structure erected in the nineteen twenties. The building across the road there is the tithe barn of the village, built in the late fourteenth century by the abbots of Easley to store the produce tithed to them by their parishioners. The slit windows in the gables were put there to admit fresh air and . . . what else?" He looked around, flashing more Roquefort cheese, and waited for an answer; none came. "No guesses? Well . . . that's a private entrance for the owls. They needed them, don't you see, to control the vermin."

Four or five of the other passengers made sounds of recognition. "See, Walter," piped one of the Americans, tugging on her husband's arm, "see the little slits for the owls?" Her spouse nodded dully. "I see it, Phyllis. I have eyes. I see the slits."

Michael and Wilfred brought up the rear as the group was led through an ornate gatehouse built of the ubiquitous golden limestone. A small church lay to their left, encrusted with moss and whittled away at the edges by five hundred Gloucestershire winters. Its tombstones bore an uncanny resemblance to the guide's teeth.

"Now," he was saying, "we are passing the brewhouse, which was last used before the Great War when a brewing woman would come each autumn on a bicycle to brew the year's barley crop. We shall enter the house through the archway just ahead, passing first through the old kitchen . . ."

"In other words," whispered Wilfred, "the servants' entrance."

"Just behave yourself," said Michael.

A rusted lawn roller was parked by the door. Next to it lay a hinged, V-shaped sign, apparently still in seasonal storage. Its flaking letters said: EASLEY HOUSE—OPEN FOR TEA. Michael visualized the arthritic old butler who would drag it down to the public road when summer began.

"You will note," intoned the guide, as they entered the house and filed through a narrow passage, "these unusual-looking steel bars along the walls. This corridor was used as a larder some years back, and joints of meat were hung along these bars."

"See?" said Phyllis.

"I see," muttered Walter.

They were led into an empty paneled space which the guide identified as the dining room. The label seemed honorary at best; it obviously hadn't been used for years. Then came the butler's pantry and the lamp room, "where paraffin lamps were cleaned prior to the electrification of the house in nineteen thirteen."

"This next room is the audit room," the guide continued. "Lord Roughton is justifiably proud of the fact that he has not sold off the cottages of the estate. He has made every effort to preserve the visual charm of the entire village. His lordship collects the quarterly rents in person, using a special rent table—that's it in the center there— and that table was made especially for Easley House in seventeen eighty. His lordship informs us that this practice not only saves postage but facilitates complaints about leaking roofs and the like."

By the time they reached the great hall, Michael had been lulled into lethargy by the steady drone of the guide. He was hardly prepared for the dimensions he encountered, the heavenward leap of the high mullioned windows facing the chapel, the echo of their footsteps on the rough plank floor.

He was certainly not prepared for Mona.

Watching from a balcony.

Standing there, cool and blond, looking down on them.

Catching his eye.

Frowning.

Disappearing.

He touched the small of Wilfred's back. "I saw her."

"Where?"

"Up there." He led the kid with his eyes. "That little balcony at the end of the room."

With uncanny timing, the guide directed their attention to the same spot. "Above us, ladies and gentlemen, is all that's left of the original minstrels' gallery—the place where musicians would gather to perform for the gentry gathered in the great hall. The gallery was converted to a bedroom in the late eighteen forties, at which time the oak posts supporting the gallery were sheathed with the present stucco Doric columns."

"Are you sure?" whispered Wilfred.

"Uh-huh."

"What now, then?"

"Nothing. We can't. Not yet."

The kid glanced impishly around the room.

"I don't know what you're thinking," murmured Michael, "but *don't*."

"Over there," the guide rattled on, "next to the bay window, you will see a very rare Chippendale exercising chair. Bouncing on that rather odd contraption was believed to be beneficial to one's health." He grinned stupidly at the one named Walter. "How about you, sir? Would you care to try it?"

"No, thanks," was the sullen reply.

"Oh, Walter, don't be such a fuddy-duddy." His wife gave him a little shove.

"Phyllis . . ."

The guide coaxed his victim with a big hammy hand. "C'mon, sir. There's a good sport. Let's have a hand for the gentleman, shall we, everybody?"

Even Michael became engrossed in the man's humiliation, joining in the applause as the hapless Walter sat down in the suspended chair and began to bounce. The laughter that followed was all the diversion Wilfred had needed. When Michael turned around again, the kid was gone.

His absence wasn't noticed as the group was led up a short flight of stairs into the drawing room. Nor was he missed as they explored the library and the sitting room. "The sitting room," the guide explained, "is something known as the *boudoir*. Does anyone know what *boudoir* means in French?"

No one did.

"Well, *boudoir* is the French word for 'to sulk,' so this room was the place where the ladies of Easley House came to sulk about the wretched behavior of their husbands." He chuckled manfully. "I expect many of you ladies know a thing or two about that, eh?"

A chorus of giggles. Michael glanced anxiously down the corridor, but Wilfred was nowhere to be seen. He was ready to murder the kid.

The group was herded into an open space behind the house, where the guide pointed out the stables, a formal topiary garden, and a pyramidal folly capping the hill above the estate. "Please feel free to wander a bit," he told them, "but do not go back into the house. We shall reassemble in the car park in thirty minutes. I trust you will all be prompt. Thank you very much."

Michael loitered in the topiary garden, keeping a close eye on the house. He began devising emergency plans to minimize the embarrassment in the event that Wilfred never showed up. The least troublesome scheme was set into motion in the parking lot, five minutes before departure time.

"I won't need a ride back to Moreton-in-Marsh," he told the guide. "I'll be staying in Easley-on-Hill tonight."

"What about your chum?"

Shit. He had noticed. "Oh . . . he walked into the village about twenty minutes ago. He wasn't feeling well . . . thought he'd catch a nap at the inn."

"I see. Then you'll be riding with us as far as the village?"

"Well . . . it's just across the meadow. I'm sure I'd enjoy the . . ."

"Just the same, sir . . ."

"Right. Great. That would be fine. Sure. Thanks."

So he took the bus back to the village.

"There," he said, pointing at the first believable-looking inn. "That's the one. That's where we're staying. Just let me out at the corner."

The driver grunted and brought the bus to a stop.

Michael could feel their eyes on him as he climbed down from the bus and marched purposefully into the pub adjoining the inn. Once inside, he embraced the absurdity of his plight and bellied up to the bar for a cider.

Fifteen minutes later, feeling much better, he left the pub and looked both ways down the road. The bus had gone. The only vehicle in sight was a green Toyota parked next to the inn. It was late afternoon now, and a cider-colored haze had settled on the distant meadows. A row of plane trees cast long purple shadows at the edge of the village. He felt quiet and peaceful and alone for the first time all day.

He set off toward the manor house, whistling with the Michael Jackson song wafting from the pub. *She says I am the one, but the kid is not my son . . .*

The lane lost its mossy walls and climbed into the meadow. He stopped for a moment and said idiotic things to a sheep, enjoying himself thoroughly. His view of the house was obscured by a clump of oaks, so he pressed on until the woods had given way to meadow again.

The windows of Easley were ablaze with the sunset, and the ancient limestone blushed magnificently. He had always loved that color, that pinkish orange which seemed to change with every shift of the light. Once upon a time, he and Jon had painted a bedroom that shade.

There was clearly no way to sneak up on the house. His approach could be observed from dozens of windows, not to mention the crenellated parapet which ran the length of the building. He would confront the place as any legitimate guest would, striding confidently.

You bet. And tell them what? *Pardon me. I seem to have misplaced a small, gay aborigine.*

Them? Who was in charge there? There had been some signs of life in the house—current magazines, postcards in mirrors—but much of the place had seemed uninhabited. Was Lord Roughton alone except for Mona? Did he even live there?

And what if—just what if—that wasn't Mona?

He decided to declare his legitimacy by presenting himself at the front door. He realized the absurdity of that when he tried to lift the knocker, a rusted iron ring almost the size of a horse collar. The door had been nailed shut; no one had used it for years.

He retraced his steps and passed under the archway linking the manor house to the brewhouse. He approached the kitchen door and rapped on it. In a matter of seconds, he heard someone stirring inside.

The woman with the Princess Di haircut opened the door and glowered at him.

"You're an asshole," she said. "I hope you know that."

Ethelmertz

When Mary Ann returned from her aerobics class at St. Peter & Paul's, she found Simon stretched out in the sunshine of the courtyard. "Well," she said, "I see you've discovered Barbary Beach."

"Oh . . . hello." He raised himself on his elbows, squinting into the sun. "Is that what it's called?"

She nodded. "Michael named it that."

"Ah."

"Don't get too much now. You look a little pink already."

He pressed the flesh on his forearm. "Well . . . it's proof, at least."

"Of what?"

He gave her a gentle, bemused smile. "My defection to sunny California."

"Oh . . . right. Sorry it hasn't been nicer for you."

"Quite all right."

"It's been just as bad in London, according to Michael."

"So I hear."

She sat down on the courtyard bench, several feet away from him. "I can't believe you're leaving in two days. It seems like just yesterday. Olive Oil's, I mean."

He looked puzzled.

"The bar where we met," she explained.

"Oh . . . yes, it does."

"What will you do . . . when you go back?"

He shrugged. "Something civilian, I daresay. Publishing, perhaps. I rather fancy the idea of that. My uncle Alec works at William Collins. I expect he'll put in a word."

"That's a publisher?"

"Mmm. They do the Bible. Among other things."

"I see." She smiled at the thought. "That sounds a little . . . dignified."

He smiled back at her. "I *am* a little dignified."

She giggled. "I guess you are."

He was quiet for a moment, his dark eyes boring into her. Then he said: "Your friend . . . uh . . . Connie stopped by earlier today."

"When?" Was there no shaking that woman?

"When you were exercising. She seemed disappointed to have missed you."

"Oh . . . well . . ." She didn't really give a damn, and she didn't care if it showed.

He smiled. "I take it *you* aren't disappointed?"

"Well, she's kind of a pest, actually."

He nodded.

"She's one of those childhood friends who won't go away. She's all right, I guess, but we don't have very much in common. Did she . . . uh . . . want anything in particular?"

"No."

"Is she still pregnant?"

"Very." He smiled.

She rose. "Well . . . I'll leave you in peace. Are we still on for tonight?"

"Dinner?"

"Right."

"Lovely," he said.

She headed toward the house, then stopped. "Watch that sun now."

Three hours later, as they sat at a table overlooking Washington Square, she remarked on how easily he tanned.

"Yes," he replied. "It's rather odd, I must say. Both my parents were quite fair."

"It's very becoming," she said.

He looked out the window, seeming faintly ill-at-ease. "I like this place. You come here often, do you?"

She nodded. "Usually for breakfast. It feels almost like home."

"Well . . . the name helps, I suppose. Mama's."

"Yeah. Only my mother wasn't much of a cook."

He smiled at her. "Nor was mine. And no one had the heart to tell her. We lived for the times when Nanny would cook."

She remembered suddenly. "Shit."

"What's the matter?" he asked.

"I forgot to give you your messages."

He didn't seem particularly distressed.

"Michael said to tell you he's leaving the keys with your nanny."

"I know," he said. "I talked to her yesterday."

"Oh."

"Anything else?"

"Yeah. Somebody named Fabia stopped by. She's gotten married, and she wants you to come to a party this summer."

His lip flickered sardonically. "Did he say who she married?"

"Uh . . . a guy named Dane who makes potato chips." Another flicker.

"You know him?"

He nodded. "Poor bastard." He seemed to acclimate himself to the idea as he sipped his wine. "Well . . . he has the money she's after, if not the breeding."

She hesitated, then asked: "Was she after you?"

"She was after everyone. She all but went into mourning when Prince Charles announced his engagement."

"Well," she teased, "Michael got the impression you had broken her heart."

"Fabia? No one has ever mistaken that for a heart."

She laughed.

He smiled warmly at her. "I know about hearts," he said.

She felt herself reddening. What did he mean by *that*? She scrambled to change the subject. "You . . . uh . . . have a nanny, huh? I mean had."

"Have, actually. She's still very much around."

"I guess that's pretty common in England. I mean . . . not *common*, but . . ."

He chuckled. "Widespread."

"Thank you."

"It's not, actually. It's gotten frightfully expensive."

"It's a nice tradition," she said.

His dark eyes squinted as he summoned something. Then he began to recite: "'When the world was but a cradle, Nanny Marks, when our jelly faces called within the dark, it was you that made us happy—shook the rattle, pinned the nappy. It was you we really cared for, Nanny Marks.'"

"How sweet! Who said that?"

"Uh . . . Lord Weymouth, I think."

"Do you feel that way about your nanny?"

He nodded. "She didn't pin any nappies, mind you. I was a little boy when she came to us. She still treats me like one. She fusses over me dreadfully."

"Good," she told him. "I'm glad you have someone who fusses over you."

He studied her for a moment, saying nothing.

Abandoning subtlety, she reached across the table and squeezed his hand. "I hate this," she said.

"What?"

"Your going."

"Do you?" He hadn't squeezed back yet.

She nodded, trying not to panic. "I think we're . . . a lot closer than we allow ourselves to be."

His eyebrow jumped ever so slightly.

"If it's not mutual, I won't be hurt, Simon. I just had to say it."

"Well, I . . ."

"Is it, Simon?"

"What?"

"Mutual."

Finally, he returned her squeeze. "It's not as simple as that."

"Why?"

"Because . . . you have a husband. And he's my friend."

She regarded him soulfully. "Do you think I would hurt him?"

"No. I don't."

"Then . . . what?"

219

"I'm leaving in two days," he said.

"And Brian is gone until tomorrow afternoon."

He peered out at the square. Chinese children were sailing Frisbees in the gathering gloom. His eyes became glazed, unreadable. He turned back to her. "Would one night make that much difference?"

"It would to me," she answered softly.

He hesitated, looking down at his plate.

"We're both grownups," she said. "We know what we're doing."

"Do we?"

"Yes. *I* do. I know what I want."

He regarded her for a long time, then glanced down at the remains of her hamburger. "Is that why you told them to hold the onions?"

She laughed nervously.

He reached for the check, giving her a vague, ironic smile. "C'mon," he said.

They walked home beneath a royal purple sky. She was relieved when they reached the steep slope of Russian Hill, since the ascent made conversation difficult, and she was hardly equipped with small talk for the occasion. Simon seemed to feel the same way.

As luck would have it, Mrs. Madrigal was smoking her evening joint in the courtyard. Her outfit was anything but motherly— paisley tunic over purple slacks, dangly Peter Macchiarini earrings, celadon eye shadow—but Mary Ann felt oddly like a wayward teenager caught in the act by a watchful parent.

"Lovely evening," said the landlady.

"Isn't it?" Simon replied.

"Beautiful," said Mary Ann.

Mrs. Madrigal took a toke off her joint, then waved it in their direction. "Would anyone care . . . ?"

They both declined.

She smiled at them. "Early to bed, eh?"

Mary Ann felt her cheeks catching fire.

Simon salvaged the moment. "Can you believe it? Five o'clock in the morning! It wasn't this bad in Her Majesty's Navy!"

"You won't be sorry," said the landlady. "It's a lovely service. More pagan than Christian, really." The mischief surfaced in her huge blue eyes. "I guess that's why I enjoyed it. Well . . . I won't keep you, children. Run along. Have a good one."

Inside, as they climbed the stairs, Simon asked: "Am I just paranoid, or does that woman read minds?"

"I've been wondering that for years," said Mary Ann.

Simon stopped at the second-floor landing. "Forgive me for this, but . . . my place or yours?"

She was ready for that. "Yours, if you don't mind."

He nodded. "Fine."

As he slipped the key into the lock, she reminded herself that this was really Michael's place, but she must never, ever tell him about tonight. The thought of that made her just a little melancholy. She had no secrets from Mouse.

Simon headed for the brandy as soon as the door was locked behind them. "How about you?" he asked, holding up the bottle. "A small one."

"Oh . . . sure. Thanks. I'm gonna use your bathroom, OK?" Under the circumstances, the request sounded awkward, overly formal.

Simon saw that. "My house is your house," he said.

She found what she was looking for in the bathroom: that familiar sticky discharge, the telltale tears of her *mittelschmerz*. She fixed her face hastily, checked for food in her teeth, and returned to the living room.

Now wearing only his brown corduroy trousers, Simon handed her a glass of brandy.

"Thanks," she said. She downed half of it in one gulp, pausing until the burn subsided.

"Take your medicine," Simon said. And there was something faintly resentful about his tone.

"Are you all right?" she asked.

"I'm fine."

"Good. So am I." She polished off the brandy and set down the glass. "Could we . . . uh . . . go to the bedroom?"

He shrugged. "What's wrong with here?"

"I don't know." She cast a quick glance at the chrome-framed poster across the room. "Bette Midler is watching."

Simon nodded at her. "Christopher Isherwood is watching in the bedroom."

She grinned. "You've had this discussion before."

"A few times." His eyes were half-lidded and playful.

"I'll just bet."

He looked at her a moment longer, then took her by the hand and led her into the bedroom. When they were naked on the bed and Simon was upon her, she cupped her hands against the small marble mounds of his ass and tried like hell to think of Brian. It seemed the very least she could do.

Mo

As usual, the kitchen was cold as a tomb, so Mona lit the butane heater and rolled it over to the corner nearest the sink. She could see blue sky through the diamond-shaped panes above the draining board, but the unexpected sunshine was no match for the marrow-chilling damp of Easley House.

She found two chipped bowls amongst Teddy's motley collection of china and filled them with cereal. Opening the refrigerator, she came face to face with a bowl of greenish kidneys growing fuzz. She winced and dumped them into the trash, then doused the cereal with milk and arranged four pieces of toast in Teddy's tarnished silver toast rack. She shifted everything onto a Chinese lacquer tray—along with marmalade, teacups and a pot of tea—and climbed the stairs to the second floor.

Finding the right door, she set down the tray and knocked three times.

"It's not locked," was the petulant response.

She opened the door, picked up the tray and went in. Mouse was propped up in bed like a pasha awaiting his concubine. Seeing his surly expression, she did her best to keep her own anger under control. "Happy Easter," she mumbled, laying the tray on the chest at the foot of his bed.

"Thanks," he answered blandly.

She walked to the window. "It's a nice one. At least the rain has stopped."

All she got was a grunt.

"Look, Mouse." She turned around and faced him. "I'm sorry I yelled at you last night."

He wouldn't look at her. "If I'd known you would take it like this . . ."

"But you didn't," she said as calmly as possible. "You didn't know anything and . . . you thought it would be a lark to come here. I understand that."

He fiddled with a loose thread on his quilt.

"What I'm trying to make you understand is . . . I'm a guest here too. Not even that, really. I'm here on business. I'm flying back to Seattle day after tomorrow. I can't have friends just . . . showing up. Defecting from a tour, for Christ's sake."

He shrugged. "We could have left last night."

"Mouse . . . there's one cab in the whole fucking county."

"What about that car?"

"*What* car?"

"That yellow Honda in the courtyard."

She jerked her head toward the window. He was right. Teddy was back from London. "That's . . . uh . . . that came in during the night."

"Oh, really?" he said archly. "Was anybody driving it?"

She gave him a dirty look. "I'll see if I can make arrangements to drive you to Moreton-in-Marsh. The trains to London are fairly regular."

"Is that Lord Roughton?"

She weighed that one for a moment, then nodded.

"And he's your client?"

She headed for the door. "I'll pick up the tray later. Don't bother to bring it down."

"Am I allowed to leave my room?"

"If you want to. That food is for Wilfred too."

"He's out exploring," said Michael.

That made her nervous. "Uh . . . what is he, by the way?"

"What do you mean, what is he?"

"C'mon, Mouse . . . his ethnic origin."

"Aborigine," he answered, seeming rather pleased with himself. "With a little Dutch and English thrown in."

"He seems very nice," she said.

"He *is* nice."

"Are you shtupping him?"

He shot daggers at her.

"OK, OK. I'll see about the car."

She returned to the kitchen. It had warmed up considerably, so she sat there for a while, sipping her tea and collecting her thoughts. The raisin bread had moved from the top of the refrigerator to the counter next to the sink. Teddy, obviously, had fixed a quick breakfast and returned to his room.

She heard whistling in the topiary gardens, so she stood up and peered through the diamond panes. It was Wilfred, prancing along in the sunshine, enjoying his solitude the way a puppy would. She smiled involuntarily and went to the door.

"There's breakfast in Michael's room," she yelled.

He stopped and hollered back: "Thanks, Mo."

Mo? Where had he picked *that* up?

She walked toward him. "The weather's nice, huh?"

"Super!" His sleeveless sweater was exactly the color of the daffodils along the path. He tilted his nose toward the sky and breathed deeply. "It smells . . . spicy."

"It's the box hedges," she explained. "The sun does that to them."

"Fancy that."

She hesitated, then asked: "Why did you call me Mo just now?"

He shrugged. "Dunno."

"Did Mouse call me that?"

"Mouse?"

"Michael," she amended.

"Oh . . . no. Mo's me own idea."

She couldn't help smiling. "You've known me half a day."

He cocked his head at her. "So? I make up me own names for everything."

"Oh." It touched her to know that she already occupied a niche in this kid's version of the universe. "Feel like a walk around the grounds?"

"Sure."

"Great." She pointed toward the stables. "Let's head in that direction. Oh . . . I forgot. Your breakfast."

"Doesn't matter," he said.

"I'll make you some later. How about that?"

"Super."

They strolled side by side through the pungent corridors of the topiary gardens. Finally, she asked: "Did Michael tell you anything about me?"

"A bit," he replied.

"Like what?"

"Well . . . he said I would like you."

That stung a little. She'd been anything but likable, she felt. "I'm usually better than this," she said.

The kid nodded. "That's what he said."

She turned and looked at him.

"He said your hair isn't usually that color and that you're really just a good basic dyke."

She broke stride, then came to a halt. "He said that?"

"Uh-huh."

"Well . . ." She began to walk again. "I haven't been quite so basic lately."

"You mean . . . sleeping with men?"

"God, no. I mean . . . you know . . . not so political."

He blinked at her.

"You *don't* know, do you?"

He shook his head.

"Lucky little sonofabitch."

"Eh?" He seemed to take that the wrong way.

"I just mean . . . you seem to have missed most of the bullshit we have in the States. It's different back there."

"I dunno . . ."

"It is. Trust me. How old are you?"

"Sixteen."

"Jesus."

He made a face. "That's what *he* said. Sixteen's not so bleedin' young."

"OK. If you say so."

"It's *not*."

She picked a leaf off a shrub. "Are you and Michael . . . ?"

He finished the question for her. "Doin' it?"

She chuckled. "Yes."

"He doesn't want to," said Wilfred. "I've done me best, believe me."

She gave him a sympathetic smile. "Sometimes he's hard to figure out."

Wilfred nodded, looking straight ahead. "Yeah."

"Don't take it personally."

"I don't," he said.

She stopped and gazed up at the folly on the hilltop. She could smell hyacinths and wet loam and the warm musk of the hedges. There were swallows making check marks in the cloudless blue sky. "I don't want to leave this," she said.

"When do you go?" he asked.

"Day after tomorrow."

"How long have you been here?"

"Oh . . . almost three weeks. I've been in London off and on."

He nodded. "That's where we saw you."

"You were on the heath that day?"

"No. When you were at Harrods. Buying the pajamas."

She couldn't believe it. "You were *there*?"

He nodded delightedly. "I followed you to Beauchamp Place. Where you bought the dress."

She shook her head in amazement.

His expression was almost devilish. "The dress you needed by Easter."

She paused, then gave him a reproving glance. "You're dangerous."

He laughed.

"And *that's* how you got the address."

He nodded proudly.

"Has Michael told you what he thinks about . . . all this?"

He shrugged. "He doesn't know what you're doing."

"Do you?"

"No. Michael thinks you're ashamed of it, whatever it is."

"It's nothing to be ashamed of," she replied somewhat defensively. "And stop looking at my hair."

"I'm not."

"Yes you were."

"I was just wondering . . . you know . . . what it really looks like."

"Well," she snapped, "right now it really looks like this."

"OK."

"I only dyed it for . . . this job. I wanted a change and this seemed like a good excuse."

He nodded.

"It looks like shit, doesn't it?"

Another nod.

"Your honesty is refreshing," she scowled.

A Theory

It was their third, maybe fourth, trip to the screening room.

"My appetite is shot," said Brian.

Theresa was hunched over the mirror, chopping away. "This is why they invented sushi. Or why they imported it to Beverly Hills. Here. Do that one." A blood-red nail pointed the way to Nirvana.

Brian sucked it up.

"The crowd's getting smaller," she said. "Thank God."

"Is it Easter yet?"

She rolled her eyes. "Two hours ago. Where have you been?"

"Well . . . no one blew a horn or put on a funny hat or anything."

"Right." She took the rolled bill from him.

"How many are spending the night?" he asked.

"Oh . . . five or six, I guess. That's all I want to deal with for brunch. Arch and his new indiscretion. The Stonecyphers. Binky Gruen, maybe. You. I don't know . . . we'll see."

"What about that guy with the beard?"

Theresa snorted a line. "What? Who? Oh . . . Bernie Pastorini?"

"Yeah. I guess so."

"I don't know if he's staying or not. Why?"

"Nothing. I just wondered about him."

"Wondered what?"

"Well . . . he said he wanted to talk to me about something. Maximal something. It didn't make any sense."

"Oh . . . *Maximale.*"

"What's that?"

"His male empowerment group."

"Huh?"

"Well . . . the theory is that some guys have been turned into wimps by feminism and the peace movement, so they . . . you know, teach them to be aggressive again." She pushed the mirror toward him. "Take some more."

"No, thanks."

"C'mon."

He hesitated a moment, then complied. "Is it . . . like . . . a serious thing?"

"At three hundred bucks a pop? You bet it's serious! He's raking it in like Werner Erhard did in the old days."

"Jesus."

She shrugged. "Makes sense to me. I've known plenty of 'em."

"Plenty of what?"

"Soft males. That's what they call 'em."

"What do they do with them?"

"I don't know. Take them on wilderness hikes . . . survival living, that sort of thing. There's also some aikido, I think. And hypnosis."

He was beginning to take this personally. "So this guy thinks I'm a wimp, huh?"

She glanced at him sideways. "Don't get threatened, now. He pitches it to everybody. Besides, it's what *you* think that matters."

"It's really unbelievable."

"No it isn't."

"A seminar for guys who are pussy-whipped."

She threw back her mane and roared. "Now, *there's* an expression I haven't heard for a hundred years or so."

He gave her a rueful look. "I guess it's in fashion again."

"Relax," she said. "I think you'd be wasting your money." She gave him a smoldering glance. "*Now* . . . the late Mr. Cross was another story. He was practically a classic case."

"Of what?"

"Soft male."

"Really?"

She nodded. "He was so-o-o-o in touch with his feelings. Christ. Sometimes it made me wanna puke."

It jarred him to hear his idol defamed. "I admired him for that," he said.

She shrugged. "It made for a pretty song, I guess."

"It made for a nice guy too."

"Listen," she said. "You weren't married to him. I would push and push just to get a rise out of him, and he would cave in every time. There are times when a woman wants . . . you know . . . authority."

"So we march bravely back to the fifties and drag our women by the hair. Is that it?"

"Sometimes," she replied. "Sometimes that's just the ticket."

He thought for a moment. "If men are soft now . . . it's because women want it that way."

She smiled faintly. "I know marriages that have collapsed under that assumption."

He met her eyes, wondering what she meant.

"Of course," she said, "I'm sure yours is different."

Mad for the Place

When Wilfred didn't return, Michael left his room and searched the hallway for a toilet. Most of the rooms he passed were devoid of furniture—musty, mildewed spaces inhabited only by spiders. Suddenly, a man's head emerged from a doorway. "Hallo!"

Michael jumped.

"Sorry," said the man. "You gave me a fright too."

Collecting himself, Michael said: "I'm looking for the bathroom . . . I'm sorry."

"Well, I shouldn't be sorry about that. It's the last room on the right." He thought for a moment. "Unless you mean the loo."

Michael smiled sheepishly. "I do, actually."

"Ah. Just across the way there."

"Thanks so much."

The man extended his hand. "I'm Teddy Roughton. Uh . . . what are you doing here?"

"Oh." Michael flushed, shaking his hand. "I'm Michael Tolliver, a friend of Mona's. I thought she'd told you."

"Well . . . no matter. I expect she will. How splendid. A guest for Easter."

"Guests, actually. There's two of us."

"Even better."

"I hope it isn't an imposition."

"Don't be silly. Look . . . why don't you lurk off to the loo, then come back and join me for elevenses?"

"If you're sure . . ."

"Of course I'm sure."

"Thanks. Then I'll just . . ." He made an ineffectual gesture toward the loo.

"Yes. Go on. I'll be here."

When Michael returned, Lord Roughton was pouring tea at a little table by his bedroom window. He was forty-five or thereabouts, tall and lean, almost gangly, with melancholy gray eyes that bulged slightly. His graying hair was cut very short, and he was wearing the pajamas Mona had bought at Harrods.

"So," he said, looking up. "How is everything in Seattle?"

"Oh . . . I'm not from there."

"Sit down, for heaven's sake."

Michael sat down.

"Where *are* you from?"

"San Francisco."

"*Really?* How extraordinary!"

"How so?"

The gray goldfish eyes popped at Michael. "I'm moving there. Didn't Mona tell you?"

"No. She didn't, actually."

"Well . . . I am. I was there six months ago and went mad for the place. What do you take in your tea?"

"Thanks, I just had . . ."

"Please. I insist. You may be my last houseguest."

Michael smiled at him. "Thanks. Milk is fine."

"Good." He doctored the tea and handed it to Michael. "I must say, this is a pleasant surprise."

Michael sought refuge in his tea, then asked: "When are you moving to San Francisco?"

"Oh . . . a fortnight or so. I have to sell the house first."

Michael hadn't figured on that. "I see. Then this is . . . really permanent."

"Oh, yes."

"And there's no one in your family who can . . ."

"Carry on? I should hope not. I am . . . how shall we put this delicately . . . ?"

"The end of the line?"

"The end of the line," nodded Lord Roughton, whispering as if he'd offered an intimate confession.

Michael smiled at him.

Lord Roughton returned it. "Mummy and Daddy are still alive—as you'll see soon enough—but I'm afraid they're never coming back from the Scillies."

The sillies? They were senile? "You mean . . . ?"

"They live in the Scillies now. To escape the taxes."

Michael nodded.

"Off Lands End, you know. The islands."

"Oh . . . right."

"It's the only way to be an expatriate and still be British about it." He lifted his teacup and stared down his lashes at Michael. "We've driven our aristocrats into the sea."

Michael laughed.

"So," said Lord Roughton, "how long have you lived in San Francisco?"

"Almost . . . nine years."

Lord Roughton sighed, peering out the window at the moss-tufted gatehouse and the fields beyond. "We've lived here nine *hundred*." He rolled his head languidly toward Michael. "That's the family, mind you. I've lived here barely *half* that time."

Michael wouldn't indulge him. "It can't be that bad."

"Well . . . it isn't. Not always. But I've made some decisions about the rest of my life, and Easley isn't part of the picture. Do you know what I do here? I'm a landlord. I sit at that table once a month and take money from the villagers. I live in two rooms—the kitchen mostly, because I can heat it—and sometimes I get money for having tea with people named Gary and Shirley who arrive at my doorstep in charabancs. I spend long, leisurely mornings sweeping the batshit out of the guest bedrooms and picking moss off the stone, because it costs five hundred pounds to replace *one* of those ornamental blocks along the parapet and the moss is eating this place alive."

Michael smiled at him. "I hope this isn't your sales pitch."

That got a chuckle. "I have a buyer already."

"Someone you know?"

He nodded. "A woman I've known for years and her horrid new husband. They've already begun making noises about Returning It To Its Former Glory." He shuddered noticeably.

"I like it like this," offered Michael, "all frayed around the edges."

"Thank you."

"I mean it."

"I can tell you do." His brow furrowed earnestly. "Would you mind awfully if I showed you something?"

"No," Michael replied. "Of course not."

Lord Roughton hesitated, then set down his teacup and unbuttoned his pajama top, holding it open. There were substantial gold tit rings in both his nipples.

"Aha," said Michael, somewhat awkwardly.

"Folsom Street," said Lord Roughton.

"No kidding."

He gazed down at them like a proud sow regarding her piglets. "It took me three Scotches to work up the nerve. The man who did it was a shop assistant in that little emporium above the Ambush. Do you know it?"

"Sure. That's Harrison Street, actually. Same thing."

Lord Roughton let go of his lapels.

"Nice job," Michael added, to be polite.

"I expect it's frightfully old hat to you." He buttoned the buttons.

"No . . . well, I've seen it before, but . . . I think it suits you."
The man was giving up Queen and Country to hang jewelry from his
nipples; the very least you could do was admire it.

Lord Roughton thanked him with a nod. "The pajamas are a
bit of a copout, I'm afraid. I don't usually wear them."

"I was with Mona when she bought them."

"Really?"

Michael nodded. "At Harrods."

"How extraordinary." His jaw slackened for a moment, then
went rigid again. "At any rate . . . I thought it best to keep the gold
out of sight while there are houseguests."

"You mean . . . there are others?"

"Possibly. Mummy and Daddy most certainly. And Mummy
has a perfectly beastly way of bursting into one's bedroom in the
morning. Are you staying for a while, I hope?"

"Well . . . Mona and I haven't actually . . ."

"Oh, you *must* stay. It'll make the whole thing so much more of
an adventure!"

What whole thing? "Well . . . thanks, but . . . my flight to San
Francisco is day after tomorrow."

Lord Roughton drew in breath. "So soon?"

"'Fraid so."

"I don't blame you. If I could snap my fingers and be there . . ."
His eyes wandered wistfully out the window.

Michael smiled at him. "Where will you stay when you get to
San Francisco?"

"With friends," said Lord Roughton. "Two sweet boys who live
in Pine Street." He poured more tea for Michael, then replenished
his own cup. "One's a bartender at the Arena. The other has a line of
homoerotic greeting cards."

"I think I know them," grinned Michael.

"Really?"

"No. I meant . . . generically."

Lord Roughton looked confused.

"I was just joking," Michael said lamely.

234

"Ah."

He seemed faintly hurt and put off. Michael berated himself; you should never make jokes about the Holy Land in the presence of a pilgrim.

"When did you decide to do this?" Michael asked finally.

The fervor returned to Lord Roughton's eyes. "Would you like to know the exact moment?"

"Sure."

"It was . . . just before Halloween, and I was at the Hot House. Do you know the Hot House?"

"Of course."

"I was in the orgy room. Very late. I had smoked a little pipe of sinsemilla, and I was feeling glorious. There were two chaps next to me going down on each other, and another chap was going down on me, and I had my face on someone's bum, and it was easily the most triumphant moment of my entire life."

Michael smiled. "I think I can follow that."

"I think you can too. *Now* . . . what do I hear in the midst of all this but . . . 'Turn Away!' "

"The Bix Cross song?"

"Yes. Exactly. And where do you think it was recorded?"

"Where?"

"Two villages away from here. In Chipping Campden. There's a studio in a converted barn."

Michael nodded. "That's . . . really interesting."

"But you see . . . I was *there*. I was there when he cut the record. And that bloody song had followed me all the way across the world to that room full of gorgeous men. I almost cried. I *did* cry. It was such a simple moment, Michael. I just . . . gave up. *That's it*, I said to myself. *You've got me. I give up.* It was such a relief."

"Yeah," said Michael.

"That doesn't sound idiotic?"

"No. I remember the same moment."

Lord Roughton smiled at him. "One learns a lot in orgy rooms. Camaraderie. Patience. Humor. Being gentle and generous with strangers. It's not at all the depravity it's cracked up to be." He cocked his head in thought. "Just a lot of frightened children being sweet to one another in the dark."

Michael sipped his tea.

"Unfortunately," said Lord Roughton, "we do leather rather poorly here."

Michael looked up. "I've been to the Coleherne."

"*Gawd!*"

"It's not *that* bad," said Michael, trying to be gallant.

"Of course it is! All those . . . Uriah Heeps lurking about!"

"Well . . ."

"Hardly a match for your great San Francisco brutes in their shiny black pickup trucks."

His romanticism amused Michael. "They use them to move ficus trees, you know."

Lord Roughton blinked at him, confused. "Sorry? Oh . . . you're teasing me again. Go right ahead. I've made a very serious study of the whole matter. I know what I'm talking about."

Michael smiled at him. "I'm with you, believe me."

"Are you?"

"Yes. I'm just . . . enjoying your innocence."

Lord Roughton drew back. "I show you my tit rings and you call me innocent. What am I to make of that, sir?"

He laughed. "We're all innocent about something."

"Quite right." His lordship arched an eyebrow. "What are you innocent about?"

Michael thought for a moment. "Country houses, mostly."

His host laughed genially. "Mona's shown you around, I trust?"

"Well, I took the regular tour."

"Oh, dear. We shall have to undo that *immediately*. Where's your chum? Would he like to join us?"

Where was Wilfred, anyway? "I'm sure he would, but . . . look, can I be perfectly frank with you?"

Lord Roughton raised his forefinger. "You can if you call me by name. It's Teddy."

"Fine," Michael smiled. "Teddy."

"Good. Spill your guts."

"Well . . . I have no idea what Mona's doing here."

Teddy frowned, then chortled. "You're joking, surely?"

"No. She hasn't told me yet."

His mouth made goldfish motions. "Why, that silly girl . . . the silly, silly girl."

Unholy Mess

When the alarm went off at 4 A.M., Mary Ann woke to find herself pinned under Simon's left arm. She slipped free as gently as possible and sat on the edge of the bed, rubbing her eyes while Christopher Isherwood watched.

"Where are you going?" whispered Simon.

He startled her. "Upstairs. To change."

"Is it Easter already?"

"'Fraid so." Her voice was croaky and sleep-fuzzed.

He raised himself on his elbow. "Then . . . I'll meet you down in the garden."

She squeezed his knee. "You don't have to go."

He paused. "I thought you wanted company."

"Well . . . I *said* that, but . . ."

"You wanted this."

It was a joke, of course, but it made her uneasy.

"Hey," she whispered, conscious of Mrs. Madrigal's presence in the building. "If you want to march up Calvary with a zombie, the zombie would be glad to have you along." She reached over and gave his cock a friendly yank. "OK?"

"What's the attire?"

"Casual." She stood up. "Give me half an hour and meet me in the courtyard. Crepe soles might be a good idea. If there's any of that dope left, you could roll us a joint. OK?"

"OK. But how are we getting there?"

"My crew is picking us up."

"Of course. Your crew."

"Anything else?"

"Yes. Where are my pants?"

"In the closet. You hung them up. Remember?"

"Right." He climbed out of bed and headed for the bathroom. Was he bent out of shape about something? Even his perfect little butt looked tense.

He kept quiet most of the way to Mount Davidson, so she spent the time talking shop with her cameraman. They parked the truck on Myra Way—as close as they could get to the concrete cross—and finished the journey on foot, climbing a slippery pathway through a eucalyptus grove until they reached the summit.

Several dozen people were already gathered at the base of the mammoth monument. In the pearly predawn light they looked as pale and gray-green as the young eucalyptus leaves. Mary Ann turned and admired the extravagant sweep of the city, the telltale red stain that had begun to seep into the eastern sky above Mount Diablo.

She touched Simon's arm. "Isn't it gorgeous?"

"Gorgeous," he repeated, with little conviction.

She studied his expressionless face. "You're as grumpy as *I* am in the morning."

"If I were you, I wouldn't . . ." He cut himself off.

"You wouldn't what?"

"I wouldn't . . ."

"*Darling . . . you naughty thing. I told you we don't need you.*" Father Paddy had materialized, as usual, out of thin air.

"Oh . . . hi," she blurted back.

"You're so damn *noble*, Mary Ann!" The cleric grabbed Simon's arm. "I have told this dear, sweet girl for weeks now that I'm perfectly capable of handling this gig on my own, but she's *determined* to be a martyr." He bussed her on the cheek. "Aren't you, darling?" His head spun toward Simon again. "I know this stalwart soul. I've seen him on television. You're that runaway lieutenant, aren't you?"

"More or less," was the less than cordial reply.

"Well, you've just taken our little city by storm, haven't you?"

Simon answered with a faint, glacial smile.

Father Paddy turned back to Mary Ann. "There's coffee and doughnuts if you need the rush, and . . . *oh* . . . is Matthew our cameraman today?"

"Yeah."

"Marvelous. Tell him to stay away from my underside, will you?"

"What?"

"Don't let him shoot from *below*, darling. I'm all chins, and it frightens the little children. All right?"

"OK."

"You're an angel," said the priest, merging with his flock again. Mary Ann glanced cautiously at Simon. "I guess I should have warned you about him."

He didn't respond.

"Is something the matter?" she asked.

He pulled a leaf off a bush and fiddled with it. "You set this up, didn't you?"

"Set what up?"

"This morning. You got yourself assigned to this . . . *gig*, as he calls it, so that you and I could be together."

"Well . . . it worked out that way, I guess. But I certainly didn't plan it."

He frowned at her.

"Anyway," she added, "what if I had? Would that be so terrible?"

"How long ago? Two weeks? Three? I've been inked into your little agenda for quite some time now."

As she stared at him, she felt her throat go dry.

"Tell me if I've missed the mark," he added.

"Well, I was certainly . . . pleased . . . when I realized we'd be able to get together . . . if that's what you mean. What's the big deal? I certainly had no way of knowing that Theresa would invite Brian to Hillsborough for the weekend."

"Both of you."

"What?"

"She invited both of you."

"So?"

"So . . . Brian suggested taking me in your place, but you vetoed the idea."

"That isn't so," she said.

He shrugged. "That's what he told me."

"Well . . ." She wanted to throttle Brian. "OK, then . . . I'm a desperate woman. You forced it out of me. I confess. I'll stop at nothing until I've got you in my clutches. C'mon, Simon . . . what is it you want from me?"

"I want you to tell me you planned this."

She threw up her hands. "OK. Fine. Easy enough. I planned this."

"You planned this at least two weeks ago, *knowing* this would be the eve of my departure."

"Simon, what the hell are you getting at?"

"I think you know."

"I don't have the slightest idea what . . ."

"You and Brian are trying to have a baby. I know that already."

That stopped her cold for a moment. "From Brian, I suppose?"

"Yes."

"Well . . . what if we are?" It wasn't much, but it was all she could muster.

"Then . . . that means you're off the pill."

She felt the blood pounding in her temples. The moment took on an ominous quality as a woman in harlequin glasses began to play "He Is Risen" on a portable electric organ behind the cross. Mary Ann scanned the crowd in search of her cameraman, then turned back to Simon. "This is easily the most bizarre conversation I have ever . . ."

"You never said a word about contraception, Mary Ann. Not a word. Don't you think that's a little strange for a woman who's trying . . ."

"I think you don't know *shit* about romance, Simon. That's

what I think. What did you expect me to do? Ask you if you had a rubber or something? I can't believe we're even *discussing* this!"

He gave her a distant, weary smile. "Such indignation. My-my."

"Well, what the hell do you . . . ? Look, I have to find my cameraman."

He caught her arm. "No."

"What?"

"I have something else to tell you."

"What?"

"Your friend Connie . . . the one who was looking for you."

"Yeah?"

"She left a message for you."

Please God, she thought. *Don't let Connie drive the final nail.*

"She said to tell you to be sure to watch Channel Nine yesterday at two o'clock."

She nodded. "So?"

"Well . . . you weren't at home, so I watched it for you, considerate fellow that I am. Any idea what you missed?"

"Simon, the service is starting in exactly . . ."

"C'mon . . . give us a guess."

"Frankly, I really don't care what that asinine woman . . ."

"It was a chat show, Mary Ann. Three housewives discussing their husbands' *sterility*."

The word hovered between them like nerve gas.

"It so happens," she said finally, "that Connie's husband is sterile, and she had artificial insem . . ."

"It so happens that Connie doesn't have a husband."

She looked away from him.

"At least," he added, "that's what *she* said."

She hesitated, then said: "Sounds like you two got along famously."

"As a matter of fact," he said, "I rather liked her. I found her candor refreshing."

"Great. Terrific." She turned and walked away.

Once again, he stopped her. "Is this how you're going to handle this?"

"Handle what? I have a job to do."

"Oh . . . right. This is a working weekend, isn't it?"

"Let go of me, Simon."

"You've been a busy little beaver, haven't you?"

"*Simon . . .*"

"Are you absolutely sure that three times was enough . . . or shall we have another go at it right here?"

She pulled free of his grip and slapped him hard. He reeled slightly but didn't change his stance. She could see the imprint of her fingers on his pale face. His nostrils flared. When he brought his fingers to his cheek, the cynical glint had faded from his eyes and the look that remained made her heartsick.

"I'm sorry," she said.

"Don't be," he replied.

"What do you want me to do?"

He shrugged. "Deny it, I suppose."

She hesitated.

"I thought so," he nodded, turning away from her.

"Simon, look . . . it isn't as black and white as . . . where are you going?"

"Home. Or a reasonable facsimile thereof."

"But . . . the service."

"Thanks awfully, but I know how it turns out."

"No . . . I mean . . . you don't have a ride. I can't leave until . . ."

"Then I'll call a taxi." He was plunging through the undergrowth in search of the path.

"Simon, please don't . . ."

But he was already gone.

Guilt Trip

It was well past noon when Mona returned to the kitchen and found Teddy rinsing his breakfast dishes. "Your friend is quite smashing," he said.

"Which one?" asked Mona, just to be difficult.

"Well . . . the little brown one is cute, but . . ."

"Never mind. Spare me."

"I gave them my little Cook's tour of the grounds. The dog graveyard . . . all that. They seemed quite taken with the place. It was rather sweet, I must say . . . seeing it all through their eyes." He rubbed a damp rag across an egg-encrusted plate. "I think you should talk to your friend, Mona."

"Why? What happened?"

"Well . . ."

"You didn't tell him anything about tonight, did you?"

"Well . . . I'm amazed, really, that *you* haven't told him."

She was working on an answer for that when they both heard the crunch of tires against gravel in the courtyard. Teddy peered through the leaded windows above the sink with a look of bug-eyed horror. "Bloody hell."

"Who is it?"

"The buyers. His wife, rather."

"I thought they weren't expected until . . ."

"They weren't. I expect she's come to take more Polaroids."

"For *what?*"

"I don't know. Her decorator needs them. It's too vile to think about. Look. I'm right. She's brought that fucking camera." He blotted his hands hastily on the damp rag. "Be a lamb, will you? I'll take care of her, but come and rescue me in, say, ten minutes."

After he had gone, she used the stairway closest to the library to creep back to her room for makeup repair. Her auburn roots had become distinctly visible, reminding her that the end was near. If she neglected them for another week or so, she could go for punk and nobody would be the wiser.

She gave Teddy his allotted ten minutes, then strolled down to the great hall with an ill-prepared lie on her lips. "Sorry to bother you, Teddy. Mr. Harris wants to talk to you. On the phone."

Teddy and the buyer's wife were standing next to the huge window facing the chapel. The woman was a broad-beamed blonde in a blue blazer. "Mr. Harris?" said Teddy, turning to Mona with a look of mild confusion.

"You know . . . the gardener."

"Oh. Of course. Mr. Hargis. Right. Well, I expect he wants instructions. Do make yourself at home, Fabia. Oh . . . Fabia, this is Mona. I trust you two will get acquainted." He backed away, then all but broke into a run.

Smirking, the woman watched his exit. Then she turned to Mona: "How very odd."

"Uh . . . what?"

"Did you say Mr. Hargis *rang* Teddy?"

"Right."

"Why didn't *I* hear it, then?"

"Well . . . I guess . . . well, I don't know. That's funny, isn't it?"

"Yes. Very."

"Anyway . . . if I can show you anything."

The woman's eyes widened. "I beg your pardon."

"I mean . . . like . . . around the house."

The woman's laughter was a total surprise, like a tractor trailer honking on a hairpin curve. "My dear Moira . . . I came to Christmas parties in this house when I was eight years old."

"Oh . . . I see."

The woman picked up the Polaroid and aimed it toward the minstrels' gallery. *Click. Whir.* She looked at Mona again. "I've been watching Easley's sad decline for many, many years." Shielding herself with a simpering smile, she removed the print and laid it daintily on the window seat. "He hasn't told you a thing about me, has he?"

"No," Mona replied calmly. "Actually, he hasn't."

"Well . . . that's a pity."

"Is it?"

The flat smile came back. "If nothing else, Moira, it would make your little *charade* so much easier. That's all I meant." She picked up the print and squinted at it. "The light is rather poor, I'm afraid."

"It's Mona," said Mona.

"Mmm?"

"My name is Mona, not Moira."

"Oh. Sorry." She looked down at the print again.

"I take it you don't need me."

"Whatever for?" said the woman, smiling.

Mona marched out of the room. She didn't break stride until she had gone the length of the house and accosted Teddy in the sitting room. "Why the fuck did you do that to me?"

Teddy looked up from his Martin Amis novel with a rueful smile. "Isn't she a delight?"

"You could've told me she knows."

"Well, I . . . she does, does she?"

"Yes. You didn't know that?"

"No . . . well, I might have guessed. She doesn't miss much. I'm sorry, Mona. People talk about me. I've never been able to prevent that, and . . . some of it's bound to rub off on you. Has she left yet?"

"I don't know," she replied, "and I don't care."

"Neither do I." He shoved his book aside. "I have a bit of that lovely hash left. Shall we take a stroll along the parapet and leave her to stalk the halls in peace?"

"Great idea," she said.

She followed him upstairs to the water-spotted bedroom that led to the attic stairway. As they climbed, hunching toward a sliver of light, the roof beams of Easley arched above them like the blackened rib cage of some prehistoric beast. Teddy leaned against the parapet door; they were momentarily blinded by the white April sunshine.

Mona looked toward the western hills and drank in the spring-scented breeze. "This is sort of our place, isn't it?"

Teddy's eyes twinkled. "It is, rather." He poked around in the breast pocket of his salt-and-pepper tweed jacket and produced one of his fat hash-and-tobacco joints. Lighting it with his Bic, he took a toke and handed it to her. "I should warn you about my father," he said.

Eyeing him suspiciously, she took in smoke and held it.

"I don't mean warn you, really. Just . . . an explanation."

She nodded.

"Daddy . . . uh . . . has this mental thing."

She exhaled.

"It's quite harmless, I assure you. The doctor say he's retreated from . . . the usual reality, as it were, and taken refuge in happier times . . . his happiest time, actually. He lives it over and over again. There's a clinical term for it." He took the joint back. "It escapes me at the moment."

"What was his happiest moment?" she asked.

"Well, *apparently*, a fortnight he spent with the Walter Annenbergs."

"The who?"

"Oh . . . I thought they were household words in California. Walter and Lee Annenberg. He was ambassador to the Court of Saint James's when Daddy met him. They hit it off straight away, Daddy and Walter . . . so Mummy and Daddy spent time at the Annenberg's estate in Palm Springs. And Daddy, I'm afraid, never quite got over it."

"You mean . . . ?"

He nodded. "He thinks he's still there."

She smiled at him. "You're kidding, aren't you?"

He shook his head, smiling back.

"He walks around Gloucestershire thinking he's in Palm Springs?"

He shook his head again. "The Scillies."

"What?"

"He walks around the Scillies thinking he's in Palm Springs."

"Oh."

He offered her the hash again.

"No, thanks," she said. "The tobacco makes me dizzy."

"Most of his major symptoms have subsided, thank God. Mummy's broken him of the white shoes, the golf togs, that sort of thing."

"That's good."

"I just thought you should know. It can be bloody embarrassing sometimes."

"Thanks," she said. "I appreciate that."

He heaved a long sigh, then turned and surveyed the landscape.

"Is that really Wales?" she asked.

"No," he replied. "It's not, actually. But you can see it from the folly. The most distant ridge is the Black Mountains. You can see the Malverns too."

She stood a silent vigil with him, then said: "I don't understand it."

"What?"

"How you can just . . . dump all this. Surrender Easley to that lard-assed bitch down there."

He turned away. "I'm not surrendering Easley."

"Well, what would you call it?"

"Mona . . ." He plucked a clump of moss off the parapet. "Easley is just a job. I'm bloody tired of that job. I know what you're saying, believe me . . . but I can't be two people at once."

All but lost in the scenery, a white van bounced along the one-lane road from Easley-on-Hill. "If I'm not mistaken," said Teddy, "that's the caterers."

"Looks like it," she said. It made her a little queasy to realize that other people—lots of them—had been mobilized to act upon a split-second decision she had made one rainy night in Seattle.

Teddy heard the uncertainty in her voice. "Are you all right, Mona?"

"Sure."

"The tobacco, eh?"

"Yeah. I think I could use a nap, actually."

"Of course." He gave her a kindly smile. "Get some rest."

She patted him on the shoulder and climbed into the dark in-
nards of the attic. When she got back to her room, she eased shut the
door to the minstrels' gallery, since she could still hear the ghoulish whirring of that Polaroid in the great hall. Sleep wouldn't come,
however, so she braced herself for conflict and headed down the hallway toward Michael's room.

He was there, propped up in the window seat with an old *Country Life* opened against his knees. Wilfred lay on the bed—stomach
down, knee bent—watching him. When she cleared her throat, Michael gazed toward the door. "What's this?" he asked. "More gruel
already?"

She managed to smile. "I thought we could talk."

"OK," he said blandly.

Wilfred did a somersault on the bed. "And children should
leave." He headed for the door, stopping to give Mona a peck on the
cheek.

"You aren't a child," she said.

"Twenty minutes," Wilfred replied.

She crossed the room and sat in the armchair flanking the
window seat. "He's such a doll," she said.

Michael shrugged. "Looks like it's mutual."

"Well . . . he's got a big crush on you, I can tell that."

He blinked at her, then looked out the window.

"Is that a problem?" she asked.

"I don't know. I worry about him . . . what he'll do when I go
home."

"What about . . . his family?"

"There isn't one. He was living with his father, and his father
ran off. He killed a man."

Mona frowned. "Sounds like Wilfred's better off."

"I don't know. Is nothing better than something?"

She could feel him getting heavy and moved to avert it. "Works
for me," she smiled.

Remaining sober, he turned away from her. He had changed in
lots of little ways, she realized. It was almost as if he had bequeathed

his flippancy to Wilfred. He seemed cold and colorless, drained of his irony.

"Any messages?" he asked at last.

"Uh . . . for who?"

"Barbary Lane. No one's heard from you for years."

"It hasn't been that long," she said.

"A year and a half, then. How's that?"

She could see Wilfred on the hillside, a tiny smudge of yellow and brown climbing toward the folly; he looked like a bumble-bee from this distance. "I've been sorting things out," she told Michael.

"I know," he said. "Since nineteen sixty-seven."

"That isn't fair."

"Then don't use that crummy excuse."

"Mouse . . ."

"You could have dropped a postcard, for Christ's sake! You moved and never gave us your new address. Your phone wasn't listed . . ."

"I didn't have one half the time."

"You could've called us then. Something. What is it, Mona? Are you cutting us off? What the hell is happening? Do you know how much you're hurting Mrs. Madrigal?"

The last one stung a little. "Look," she said, "I didn't wanna check in with you guys until I had my shit together. You knew I wasn't dead or anything. I just wanted to show up on your doorstep one morning out of the blue . . . with some incredible piece of news about myself."

"And this is it?" His eyes narrowed in disbelief.

"What?"

"Marrying . . . ol' Tinseltits."

She felt both mortified and relieved. "No," she replied quietly. "I didn't plan on publicizing this."

"Did you plan on telling *me*?"

"Yes."

"When?"

"Now." She smiled feebly. "A little too late, huh?"

He looked away, fixing his gaze on the hillside. Wilfred had reached the folly and was now just a fleck of yellow beneath the duncecap roof. "In more ways than one," said Michael.

"It doesn't really mean anything," she said.

"What?"

"This marriage. It's just an arrangement to satisfy the immigration people, so Teddy can get a green card . . ."

". . . and wag weenie in San Francisco."

"I didn't ask about that," said Mona.

He stared at her, slack-mouthed. "How did this happen? I mean . . . how long has this been in the works?"

"About three weeks, I guess. Not long."

"You met here or in Seattle?"

"Neither. The arrangements were made through . . . a sort of clearinghouse in Seattle."

"A clearinghouse?" He almost spit out the words. "For *what?* Mail order brides?"

"Yes," she replied flatly. "As a matter of fact."

He gave an ugly little snort. "Does anyone *here* know about this?"

She flashed on that Fabia woman, snapping her way through the house. "Oh, yes," she answered. "It appears to be Easley's worst-kept secret."

"It figures," he said. "I'm always the last to know."

His petulance made her impatient. "You weren't supposed to know at all, Mouse. You weren't supposed to be here."

"When is it happening?"

"Tonight. In the chapel."

"Swell."

"It's just the family. And a few of their friends."

"Don't worry. I'll stay out of the way."

"I didn't mean that." She felt better, just the same; the whole ordeal was embarrassing enough as it was. "It's not like it really means anything," she added. "People get married for immigration purposes all the time. It's just a business proposition."

"How much?"

"What?"

"How much is he paying you?"

"Oh . . . five thousand."

"Not bad."

"Well," she acknowledged somewhat proudly, "it's usually just a thousand or so, but this was a special case, and they thought I could handle it." She couldn't help thinking what a feeble boast that was. "The organization gets ten percent, of course. Like an agent. Anyway . . . it's a fair price for all concerned."

"Sure," he replied. "It's a double ring ceremony."

She didn't get it.

He tweaked one of his nipples.

"Oh." She laughed uneasily, then tried to counter with her own joke; it might be the only way out of this mess. "Yeah," she said. "I told him to hell with Immigration—he'll never make it through the metal detector."

He remained sullen.

She studied his face, then got up and went to the dresser and began arranging his breakfast dishes on the tray. "I'm going back to Seattle in two days," she said. "I've had a nice little vacation . . . made some money. And everyone's better off. I don't need this guilt trip, Mouse."

"That's your doing," he said. "Not mine."

She slammed down the marmalade jar. "When the *fuck* did you get to be such a little prig?"

He didn't answer right away. "You don't know what I am," he said quietly. "You haven't stopped running long enough to find out."

"Mouse . . ."

"What do you want from me, anyway?"

"What do you mean?"

"Why are you telling me this now? What do you want me to say? Congratulations on a lucrative but meaningless marriage?"

She picked up the tray and headed for the door. "I wanted your blessing, I guess. I have no idea why. I have no idea why I'm even talking to you."

251

"If you ever made a real commitment . . ."

"Oh, fuck you, Mouse! Just . . . fuck you. I don't need this. Since when did you get to be an expert on commitment. You and Jon and your half-assed little . . . whatever you call that relationship . . ."

He scorched her with a long, silent glance. "I'll give him your best," he said.

She drew herself up and tried to remain calm. "I'm my own person," she said.

"Fine," he replied. "Go for it."

She looked at him a moment longer and stormed out, marching back to her room with a tray. She threw herself on the bed but avoided a crying jag by rising again and hurling a paperweight at the suit of armor next to the window.

Hearing the noise, Teddy came running. "Good Lord," he murmured. "Are you all right?"

She glared at the pile of metal on the floor. "I hate that fucking militarist drag."

He nodded. "I didn't much fancy it myself."

She slumped into a chair.

"Is it . . . jitters?" he asked.

"We have to talk," she replied.

Undoing the Damage

It was roughly seven-thirty when Mary Ann climbed out of the camera truck at the foot of the Barbary Lane stairway. Without stopping to admire the daffodils sprouting between the garbage cans, she went directly to Simon's apartment and knocked on the door. When he opened it, he was wearing Michael's green robe.

"Yes?"

"I wanted to start over," she said.

"Meaning?"

"I want your forgiveness."

He gave her a thin smile. "Wait a bit, won't you? I haven't for-given myself yet."

"For what?"

"Oh . . . damning the torpedoes."

"What?"

"I knew what you were doing," he said. "I suspected. I could have said no . . . and I didn't."

"That wasn't all I was doing, Simon."

"Don't," he said. "It isn't necessary. There's no point in getting muddled over motives."

"No . . . I want you to be clear on this." She glanced nervously over her shoulder, wondering about Mrs. Madrigal. "Do you mind if I come in?"

He hesitated.

"Please," she whispered. "Just for a little while?"

He nodded and stepped out of her way. She went in and took a seat on the end of the sofa. Simon remained standing, pacing sol-emnly with his arms folded. The damage she had done was evident in his eyes.

"I was going to tell you," she said.

He made a little muttering noise.

"I would never have done this with someone who didn't matter to me."

He stopped pacing and looked at her.

"Can't you take it as a compliment?" she asked.

"I could," he replied, "but I haven't yet."

"Well . . . think about it. It's not like this was a one-night stand or something. I put some thought into it, you know."

He seemed amused by that. "Does Brian know?"

"No, of course not!"

"Well, this is laid-back California. It seemed perfectly reason-able to assume . . ."

"Is that what you think of me, Simon?"

He shrugged.

"Well . . . OK, forget about me. But Brian would never do that."

"Comforting," said Simon.

"He doesn't know anything." She decided to throw herself on his mercy. "He doesn't even know he's sterile. The hell of it is . . . *he's* the one who wants the baby. It's no big deal to me. He doesn't have a job now, and he thinks the baby would be something he could . . ."

"Wait. Stop."

"Yeah?"

"How do you know he's sterile, if he doesn't know it?"

"I just do," she said.

He nodded. "Very well. Proceed."

"Well . . . that's it. I wanted to give him a baby . . . so I came up with this dumb idea."

"And artificial insemination didn't occur to you?"

She nodded. "Connie suggested it. I hated the idea. It isn't . . . personal enough." It sounded so stupid that she smiled apologetically. "I thought I could do it without hurting anybody. I didn't. I fucked up."

He looked directly at her. "Then last night . . . ?" He waved away the thought.

"What? Last night what?"

"Were you really . . . ?"

"Into it?" she asked, finishing his question.

"Yes."

"Simon . . . couldn't you tell?" She caught his hand. "Don't go back to England thinking I'm a monster. I've had such a wonderful time with you."

He stood there, keeping his distance, looking down on her.

"I think you're a gentle, intelligent . . . incredibly sexy man."

"Thank you," he said softly.

"I mean it."

He nodded.

"I'll always remember you. I don't need a baby for that."

"Thank you."

"Stop saying thank you," she said. "Come here. Don't be so insecure."

"I've had a vasectomy," he said.

"What?"

"I've had a vasectomy."

She tried to read his face. "Are you serious?"

"Yes," he replied. "Are you?"

She looked at him a moment longer, then leaned down and took his cock in her mouth.

"Thank you," he said.

This time she didn't bother to reply.

Sack Time

The skylight above Theresa's living room had taken on a creepy, milky translucence—like a giant eyeball with a cataract. Brian stared at it in disbelief. Had they really been up all night?

"You're a lotta fun," said Theresa.

"Oh . . . sorry." Had she asked him a question? What time was it, anyway?

"You're grinding your teeth," she said. She was on the sofa across from him, her feet tucked under the heart-shaped ass. "I think it's sack time."

"Yeah."

"Want some papaya juice?"

"Great."

She rose. "I'll get us a 'lude too."

"That's OK."

"It'll bring us down."

He shook his head. "I don't do 'ludes anymore."

"Well . . . a joint, then."

Three minutes later, she returned with a glass of juice and a joint that was already lit. She held it for him as he toked, pressing her fingers against his lips. "I like the feel of your mouth," she said.

255

"Thanks," he replied.

Her laughter seemed brittle. "You can do better than that."

"Sorry. I'm kinda zonked."

"The joint'll fix you right up."

He would have to be more explicit. "Hey . . . I hate to be a party pooper, but I am really tired. It's been great, really. If you'll show me which bedroom is mine, I'll . . ."

"Jesus Christ." She flung the joint into an ashtray. "What the hell have we been doing all night?"

She had jarred him. "Uh . . . rapping, I thought."

"*Rapping?* How quaint!"

"Look, Terry . . . I'm sorry, OK?"

"Don't be."

"You knew I was married," he said.

She stared at him incredulously. "You're not going to tell me that's the *reason?*"

"Well . . . partially."

"So what's the other part?"

"Well . . . that's the main reason, more or less."

"This is un-fucking-believable."

"Also . . . I'm not real terrific after a lot of coke. That's another reason."

"That's not a reason. I've told you I have 'ludes."

He rose on wobbly legs. "This has been a real experience, believe me."

"Swell."

"If you'd told me last month that I'd spend Easter doing coke with the wife of the man who . . ."

"Shut up about him."

"I didn't mean that you aren't . . ."

"I know what you meant, Brian. I know who you came here for." She retrieved the roach and relit it with trembling hands. "You should've fucked *him* when he was still alive. He might have appreciated it."

256

She smiled at him with surprising tenderness, then handed him the roach. "I think you should go home," she said.

Nanny Knows Best

They formed a big T against the rumpled flannel sheets, Simon from side to side, she with her head against his trampoline-tight stomach.

"I'm curious about something," she said.

"Mmm."

"Why did you get a vasectomy?"

"Oh . . . well, actually, my nanny talked me into it."

"C'mon."

"It's quite true. She gave me a stern little lecture. She said I was a confirmed bachelor and flagrantly irresponsible and it was the only decent thing to do. It was a remarkable speech."

"Was she right?"

"About what? Flagrantly irresponsible?"

"No. Confirmed bachelor."

He hesitated. "More or less, I suppose. Marriage is rough on a true romantic."

"What do you mean?"

"You know what I mean?"

"Maybe," she said.

"A certain spontaneity is lost, isn't it?"

"Not necessarily."

"Then why are we doing this?"

She rolled over on her stomach and kissed his navel. "Because I like you very much. And I like doing this without babies on the brain."

"You're not sorry, are you?"

"No."

"It hasn't utterly devastated your marriage?"

She gave him a little pinch, smiling.

"Just asking," he said.

"Brian isn't everything to me, but . . . he's the only constant."

"You don't have to explain yourself."

"It would take a long time for me to fall out of love with him. It took long enough to love him. He's sort of like . . . a maze I wandered into."

"You're brighter than he is," he said.

"I know. I don't care. He gives me other things." She shifted slightly, kissing him again. "You've given me something too."

"What?"

"Oh . . . a fresh perspective."

"On your husband." He said it without rancor.

"Not just that."

"Then . . . I'm glad."

"I'll think about you," she said.

"I'll think about you," he replied. "Should we be watching the clock?"

"Huh?"

"Brian."

"Oh . . . he's not coming back till afternoon."

He chuckled. "I should have known you'd know that."

Red-handed

The clock in the Le Car said eight twenty-three when Brian parked on Leavenworth and began the trek up the Barbary Lane stairway. There were birds twittering in the eucalyptus trees, and the neighborhood tabby had already staked out a sunning spot on the first landing. He sat down and stroked the old cat's belly.

"How's it goin', Boris? You havin' a good Easter? You didn't know it was Easter? Well . . . wake up and smell the coffee, man!"

Beneath him, on the steep slope of Leavenworth, two pint-sized Chinese kids emerged from a doorway and began fighting over a plush Smurf that was bigger than both of them. He watched them for a while, then shouted through cupped hands: "Hey, guys!"

Their squealing stopped. They looked up at him.

"Easter Bunny bring you that?"

Without answering, they stood and stared at the crazy man on the stairs.

"Be cool," he said.

The kids backed into the doorway, emerging seconds later with their mother.

Brian waved at the three of them. "Happy Easter," he yelled.

The woman waved back halfheartedly, then herded the children into the house.

Brian got up and headed into the leafy canyon of the lane. When he reached the courtyard, he noticed that a row of pink hyacinths had popped up in the soft, dark loam where Jon's ashes had been buried. Mrs. Madrigal's doing, no doubt.

The landlady was probably still sleeping, so he took special care to close the door quietly behind him. Tiptoeing across the foyer, he reached the carpeted stairs and began to climb, avoiding the familiar squeaky spots.

As he reached the second floor, he heard movement in Simon's apartment. The Englishman was already up. He wondered for a moment: *Should I stop and tell him about my all-nighter with the rock widow?*

Why not?

The buzzer was noisy as hell, so he rapped on the door.

There was more activity inside, but no one came to the door.

He knocked again.

Footsteps.

The rattle of the latch chain.

A slice of Simon appeared through the door. "Oh . . . hello there."

Brian kept his voice down. "You weren't asleep, I hope?"

"Well . . . ah . . . no, actually."

"I'm back from the front." Brian grinned.

"What?"

"Theresa's bash."

"Ah."

"We've been doing nose candy all night."

Simon nodded.

"It was wild, man. She was after my ass."

Simon arched an eyebrow. "Indeed?" He was trying to sound impressed, but something was distracting him.

The light dawned.

"Jesus." Brian banged his forehead with his palm. "You've got a lady in there."

Simon blinked, then nodded.

"Sorry," whispered Brian, backing away. "Catch you later." He gave the lieutenant a thumbs-up sign. "Carry on, old man."

He climbed the stairs feeling pretty stupid. The coke had obviously numbed his reasoning powers. It was Sunday morning, the morning after Saturday night; Simon was hardly likely to be alone.

No.

Simon had gone to the sunrise service.

Maybe he had changed his mind, though.

Maybe he had bailed out at the last minute.

Maybe he had picked up someone at the service.

Maybe not.

Maybe he didn't have to.

He reached his door and found it locked. His temples were throbbing angrily as he searched for his keys. *Be cool*, warned the last tattered remnants of his reason. *Be cool.*

He went straight to the bedroom.

The bed was empty.

Maybe Mary Ann was still on the job.

Maybe there had been technical problems.

Maybe she had gone to breakfast afterwards.

He sat down, then got up again and went to the landing. He had been there almost a minute when he heard Simon's door open and close. He ducked back inside and sat there massaging his temples as the crippling green poison flooded his brain.

Someone was climbing the stairs.

A Name for This

She tried to be stately about it, chin up and shoulders back, like Mary Queen of Scots striding toward the ax. If Brian had been doing coke all night, her own levelheadedness was even more important.

She opened the door. He was sitting in the armchair facing her.

"Hi," she said, closing the door behind her.

His face seemed to be a dozen different things at once.

"I'm not going to lie to you," she said.

"Go ahead," he said darkly. "One more time won't make a fucking bit of difference."

"It isn't as bad as it looks, Brian." She skirted his chair, heading for the kitchen.

"*Where are you going?*"

"To get us a drink."

"*No!* Get back here. We're talking."

"OK, but . . ."

"*Get back here, I said.*"

She came back and sat on the sofa. "We shouldn't be doing this now. You've been up all night. Your nerves are raw. There's no way you can rationally . . ."

"Shut the fuck up!"

She folded her hands in her lap.

"Did you spend the night down there?" he asked.

"Yes," she replied.

He stared at her with horror in his eyes.

"Brian . . . it was more . . . friendly than anything else."

"*Friendly?*"

"I just mean . . . it wasn't the beginning of something, it was the end of something."

"Oh, yeah? How long have you two . . . ?"

"No. I didn't mean that. Last night was the only time."

"Goddamn him, *goddamn* him!"

"Please don't blame Simon."

"You forced him, huh?"

"No, but . . . he's your friend."

"Yeah . . . and you're my loving wife. There's a name for this, isn't there?"

"I don't love him," she said, feeling oddly disloyal to Simon.

"You're just a *slut*, huh?"

"Brian . . ."

"Well, what possible reason?"

"Come off it. They don't have sluts anymore. I *like* Simon, that's all. I didn't plan for it to happen, but . . . it happened. It'll only affect us if you *make* it affect us, Brian."

"I get it," he said. "*I'm* the problem here. Me and my quaint ideas about husbands and wives and *sluts*."

He was wielding that word like a switchblade, trying to goad her into a fight. She regarded him in silence, then got up and went to the bedroom door. "I'm taking a shower," she said. "If you want to discuss sluts, I suggest you talk to that woman who's so hot for your ass in Hillsborough."

When she saw his expression, she realized she shouldn't have said it. "Maybe I'll do that," he said. "Maybe I'll just fucking do that!" He sprang to his feet, grabbing his keys off the coffee table.

"Brian . . ."

"Take your goddamn shower. I'm sure you need it."

"Brian, you can't . . ."

"I can't *what?*"

"Drive in that condition. Look at you. Your eyes are bloodshot . . ."

"You think I'd stay here?"

"Please . . . just get some rest first. Do what you want later, but don't get back on that freeway in that . . ."

But he was already out the door.

Nuptials

It was almost dark now and Michael had withdrawn to the folly on the hill above Easley House. From this dunce-capped pavilion he could see the twinkling cottages of three villages and the backlit stained glass of Easley's family chapel. Headlights crisscrossed a field adjacent to the manor house as the guests began to arrive on the road from Easley-on-Hill. An unseen organist struck a few exploratory chords. A woman's shrill laughter reverberated in the courtyard. Here he sat on a hilltop overlooking Wales and somewhere below him—probably cursing her fate—Mona Ramsey was about to be married.

He felt absolutely nothing.

A cog in his emotional mechanism had ceased to function. He didn't care anymore. His heart had been kicked around enough.

He would wait here until it was over. Then he would find Wilfred and they would ask for a ride into Moreton-in-Marsh. They could stay at the Black Bear, catch the first train to London in the morning.

The organ in the chapel plunged into an unidentifiable Anglican hymn. Almost simultaneously, Mona's wholly identifiable voice cut through the encroaching darkness. *"Mouse! Where are you, god-damnit?"*

She was standing in the courtyard, looking from left to right, much as she had done that day on the heath. This time, however, she was decked out in a peach-colored wedding gown. *"I'm not standing for this shit, Mouse!"*

He hesitated a moment longer, then shouted: "I'm up here. At the folly."

She swung around, fixing her gaze on the pyramid, then hiked her gown above her knees and sprinted up the slope. Her curses exploded like cherry bombs as her heels dug into ground that had been booby-trapped by moles. When she finally reached the folly, her chest was heaving violently. "Why the hell didn't you *tell me?*"

He didn't answer.

"Wilfred just told me. I can't believe it! What is the matter with you? *Why the fuck didn't you tell me?*"

"You're getting married," he said. "It's hardly the time to . . ."

"Fuck that shit, Mouse! I had a right to know!"

"You never once asked about . . ."

"All right, then! I'm a self-centered asshole! What do you want me to say? Christ, Mouse . . . you rigged it so I would hurt you! You deliberately . . ." She didn't finish. There were tears streaming down her face. "He can't be dead!" she said in a much weaker voice. "How can that beautiful man be dead?"

He felt himself crumbling. "I don't know," he said, reaching out for her as his own tears came.

They held on to each other for a long time, sobbing.

Finally he said: "We tried to reach you."

"I know."

"He sent you his love. He said to give you that turquoise ring you liked."

"Oh, God, Mouse!"

"I know. It's a bitch. I know."

"Was he in much pain?"

"Some. For a while. Not always. He was wonderful, really. He cracked jokes and did his Tallulah Bankhead impersonation . . . and flirted with the orderlies."

"That tart." She swiped at her cheeks.

"They loved it, of course, since he was a doctor and knew all the inside dish. It wasn't so bad, Mona. Not all the time. We got much closer to him . . . to each other. You don't really know for certain about a family until somebody dies. You don't know anything until that happens."

She pulled away from him. "And you weren't going to tell me."

"Why do you think I've chased you across England?"

"I don't know. To punish me, I guess. To make me feel like shit. Your usual motives."

"You're wrong"—he smiled—"and you're missing your wedding."

"*In a fucking minute.*"

"Yes, *ma'am.*"

"I want to know something."

"What?"

"Do we . . . still love each other?"

"Mona . . . ?"

"Because I love *you*, you little shithead . . . and if you think you can pretend that I don't, you can just go fuck yourself!"

He was touched. He smiled at her.

"OK," she added, "I should've called or something. You're right about that. *Obviously* I should've called. And I shouldn't have run from you that day on the heath . . ."

"Why did you do that, anyway?"

She looked away. "I dunno . . . I was a little uncomfortable about the whole thing . . . and this man from the Home Office was with us . . . and I knew that introductions would be awkward. I figured I could write you about it later."

"It looked like you were looking for somebody."

"I was," she replied. "Teddy."

"I thought you said he was with you."

"Well, he *was* earlier. The three of us had lunch together at this inn on the heath. Teddy just wandered away. You can't take the man near bushes of any kind."

He smiled.

"If you think that's funny, you should've heard me explaining it to the Home Office."

He gave her a hug. "I'm all right. Go get married."

"You haven't answered me," she said.

"What?"

"Do you love me?"

He smiled at her. "I do."

"Will you come to the wedding?"

"I think I'd like to stay here for a while. Do you mind?"

She threw up her hands. "Hey . . . no big deal." She kissed him on the cheek. "Come to the reception, though. I've got a little surprise for you."

"What?"

"Just come, Mouse."

"Well, my clothes aren't exactly . . ."

"Look, the fucking bride has mud on her shoes. You'll look just fine." She left the folly and hoisted her skirts, beginning the perilous descent.

"I don't like surprises," he shouted.

"You'll like this one," she yelled back. "You'd better."

"Where's the reception?"

"In the great hall." She hit another mole hole and cursed again.

"Break a leg," he called.

"*Fuck you,*" she answered.

The glow of her old familiar roar kept him warm. He sat there in the meadow-scented darkness of the folly for another half hour until the final chords of the organ had rolled away down the vale like summer thunder. Then he got up, brushed off the seat of his Levi's, and headed slowly down the slope.

He entered Easley House through the kitchen, making his way toward the sound of the reception. There were several dozen people in the great hall, already nattering away to the music of a string quartet. Champagne was being dispensed at a long table in the alcove next to the window.

"Hey, mate!" Wilfred came wriggling through the crowd.

"Hey, kiddo."

"Where were you?"

"Up at the folly."

"Are you OK?"

"Sure. Great."

"The wedding was super."

"Good. Mona says there's gonna be a surprise."

The kid glanced at him. "You know already?"

"Know what?"

Wilfred giggled. "You won't get it from me, mate."

"Now, just a . . ."

"I'll get us some champagne. Hang on." He darted away again. While he was gone, Michael struck up a conversation with a nice old man who turned out to be the gardener. His name was Hargis, and they talked in earnest about flowers. Michael liked that about England; men were allowed to be earnest about flowers.

When Wilfred returned with the champagne, he looked a little ruffled. "Old sod."

"Who?" He took a glass from the kid.

"Over there . . . ol' baldie by the bar."

"What did he do?"

"He gave me fifty P and told me to fetch his golf bags."

"C'mon."

"That's what he said. 'Fetch me golf bags and tell Bob Hope I'll meet him at the clubhouse.'"

"He must've been joking."

"I told him to stuff it."

Mona appeared. "Hi, guys."

"Hi," said Michael. "Is Bob Hope here?"

"Huh?"

"Somebody told Wilfred that Bob Hope is here." She frowned for a moment, then rolled her eyes in recognition. "That man by the bar, right?"

"That's the one," said Wilfred.

"That's the earl," said Mona. "Teddy's father. We had a nifty chat about Betty Ford. If you're nice to him, he'll introduce you to her."

Michael was dumbfounded. *"Betty Ford is here?"*

"Nobody's here," she replied. "He's a sweet old poop, but he's got one wheel in the sand." She turned to Wilfred. "You haven't seen Teddy yet, have you?"

The kid nodded. "He's breaking the news to Fabia."

"He's too nice to her," said Mona.

"Wait a minute," said Michael. "Fabia who?"

"Fabia *Crisps*," said Wilfred.

Michael could hardly believe it. "She's *here?* That woman who . . ."

"Just button the lip," Mona told Wilfred.

The kid grinned at her and obeyed.

Michael glanced from one to the other, but their bond of silence was unbreakable. Seconds later, Teddy strode into the great hall and joined them. "Oh, Michael . . . lovely. I'm delighted you could join us." He turned and addressed Mona. "I think we've just about tidied everything up."

"How did she take it?" asked Mona.

Teddy made a face. "It wasn't a bit pretty."

"Can she . . . do anything?"

"Not a thing, my love. Nothing's been signed yet." He hoisted himself onto a seventeenth-century shuffleboard table, commandeering it as a speaker's platform. "My friends," he called. "May I have a word with you, please."

The crowd in the great hall muttered its way into silence.

"Lovely," said Lord Roughton. "Now . . . as most of you know, it has been my intention for some time to move to California for the purpose of pursuing my studies in anthropology."

Wilfred mugged at Michael.

"Just keep quiet, you two," Mona whispered, looking more dignified than Michael had ever seen her.

"That," Teddy continued, "compelled me to confront the unhappy prospect of parting with our beloved Easley." A sympathetic murmur passed through the gathering. "Believe me, I have made every effort to see to it that the house would fall into the hands of people who would honor its . . . unselfconscious beauty." Affectionate chuckles erupted here and there as Teddy smiled down at a slight, white-haired woman in a pale green cocktail dress. "That's what my mother wants . . . and that's what my mother assures me my father would have wanted."

"I thought he was here," muttered Michael.

"He *is*," Mona answered.

"Old sod," said Wilfred.

"On my last trip to America," Teddy went on, "I met the exceptional woman who has done me the honor of becoming Lady Roughton." As he extended his arms in Mona's direction, the celebrants turned and applauded politely. Mona gave them an uneasy smile and a half-assed little Elizabethan wave.

Teddy beamed at her with genuine affection. "It was this lovely girl who showed me the error of my ways."

Girl, thought Michael. No one called Mona a girl and lived to tell about it.

Mona saw him smile and reacted silently with a middle finger pressed against her temple.

"To come to the point," said Teddy, "I have reconsidered the entire matter and decided against selling Easley."

Thunderous and prolonged applause swept through the great hall.

Teddy seemed enormously pleased. "Mind you, I will still be spending the next few years in California . . . but my dear wife has gallantly offered to remain here at Easley and run the business of the house . . . preside over the rent table, as it were."

"My God," murmured Michael.

Mona grinned at him and grasped his hand, then gazed up at Teddy again.

"It's a thankless job, in my opinion . . . one for which I seem to have increasingly less talent. So I am very grateful that she's shown such concern not only for the perpetuation of Easley as we know it, but for . . . the furtherment of my education." He stooped down and signaled Wilfred. "May I have your champagne, old man?"

The kid handed him his glass.

Teddy rose, hoisting the glass in Mona's direction. "To the Lady of the Manor!"

His guests echoed the toast: "*To the Lady of the Manor!*"

General applause ensued. Teddy climbed down from the shuffleboard table, still smiling at Mona.

"Thanks for that," she said.

"My pleasure," he replied.

"I can't believe this," said Michael.

"Believe it," Mona beamed. She turned to Teddy. "Do you have any more social duties?"

"That's it. We're done."

"Fabulous. Why don't you help Wilfred pick out his room? Michael and I are gonna take a little stroll."

Wilfred grinned at Michael. "I'm gonna live here, mate! How 'bout that?"

"Pretty good, kiddo." He put his arm around Wilfred's shoulders and shook him, then glanced at Mona. "You're just full of surprises tonight."

"C'mon," she said, "let's promenade on the parapet." She took his arm and led him away, stopping suddenly to shout a final instruction at Wilfred. "And *don't* take the one above the library. That's mine. It's the only one that doesn't leak."

As they headed up the stairs, Michael asked: "How long has *this* been in the works?"

"Since this afternoon."

"You're kidding."

"Nope. Well . . . maybe a little longer than that, but I finally talked to Teddy about it this afternoon. I thought about what you said, you know. I *was* just running away again. I'd sold myself cheap and I knew it. Teddy was never really big on selling the place, you know. He just didn't want the responsibility."

"Yeah," he said, "but what about the money involved?"

"Oh, I waived my fee."

He laughed. "I meant the money he would've gotten for the house."

"Well, he won't get it. We'll still get rent from the villagers, though, and I'll mail him a check every month. It'll work out fine. Wilfred's gonna help me set up a tearoom this summer for the tourists."

"Really?"

"A *real* tearoom, dipshit."

"I know."

"We could use a gardener," she said as they entered one of the bedrooms and stopped at the stairs to the parapet.

He smiled at her invitation. "You have Mr. Hargis."

"You've met him, huh?"

He nodded. "Just now."

"Isn't he dear?"

"Yeah . . . he is."

"His wife is a trip too. They know how everything works . . . or doesn't work, as the case may be. I can do it, Mouse. I know I can. Lady Fucking Roughton. Can you *stand* it? Won't I make a fabulous landlady?"

"I don't know why not," he replied. "Your father does."

Her smile was so warm. "How is she doing?"

"Good. Better, when I tell her about you."

"Let me write her a note or something. I think it should come from me this time." She led him up the narrow stairs in the darkness. "The problem with me and her is . . . we're too much alike. She wants me to be one of her brood, and I want a brood of my own." She opened the parapet door and walked out into the moonlight.

"Yeah," he said, following her, "but the hens can get together from time to time."

There were headlights streaking the dark fields below as some of the celebrants made their way home. "I can picture her here," said Mona. "Can't you? Trooping around in that cloche of hers."

"God," agreed Michael.

"I want you to stay, Mouse."

He turned and looked at her.

"We could have so much fun," she said. "Think what it would be like with the three of us."

"I've thought about it, Mona. Ever since you mentioned gardener."

"Well, think about it some more. A whole new life, Mouse. Away from all that shit back there."

He chuckled.

"What's the matter?" she asked.

"Well . . . I *like* all that shit back there."

"Right."

"I do. I'm not sure how long I could leave it. I'm actually missing it."

She sighed and looked toward the horizon. "Be that way, then."

He remembered something and smiled.

"What?" she asked.

"Those three things . . . what were they? Hot job, hot lover, and . . . ?"

"Hot apartment."

He laughed. "I'd say this qualifies as a hot apartment."

"Also a hot job," she added.

"The lover part may be a little tough out here."

She turned to him indignantly. "Have you seen the postmistress in Chipping Campden?"

"No." He grinned.

"Then don't be so goddamn sure of yourself."

"A hot *postmistress?* C'mon."

"Swear to God. Makes Debra Winger look like dogshit."

He hooted.

She smiled and leaned against him, slipping her arm around his waist. "Oh, Mouse," she murmured.

He knew that she was thinking about Jon again. "I'll send you that ring," he said.

"Thanks."

"And thanks for being so nice to Wilfred."

"Are you kidding? We're made for each other. He says you met that Fabia woman in London."

"Fabia Dane?"

"That's the one."

"How bizarre. She came by the place I'm staying and was rude as shit. She's the one that's buying the house?"

"Was," said Mona.

"Jesus . . . That must mean that their new country place . . ." He laughed, getting the picture. "I invited Simon to a party here this summer."

"Simon?"

"The guy I swapped places with."

"Oh," she said. "Well, tell him he's still invited. He's a nice guy?"

"Very. And handsome."

"How nice for you."

"No, he's straight."

"How nice for *someone*, then."

"Are you off men completely?"

She gave him a languid nod. "And vice versa. I am a simple English country dyke and don't you forget it."

"It suits you." He smiled.

"Does it?"

"It does. It really does."

"You can be funky here. People really are very funky here, Mouse. It's not widely known, but it's true."

He nodded.

"I will *never* be a lipstick lesbian. I hate that shit on my face!"

"This shit."

"What?"

"You've got on makeup *now*, Mona."

"Well, true . . . but it's my fucking wedding. Gimme a break."

Michael laughed. "Your non-fucking wedding."

"My non-fucking wedding. Right." She looked behind her anxiously. "I should go help Teddy say goodbye to the non-fucking guests." She pecked him on the cheek. "Stay here. Take your time. Smoke this." She removed a fat joint from the peach lace of her bodice. "It's one of Teddy's. It has hash in it."

He took it from her. "Thanks, Babycakes." She reminded him so much of Mrs. Madrigal it was almost eerie.

"When you're really loaded," she advised him, "go down and

look at the moon through the window in the great hall. And check out the graffiti in the glass. It's three hundred years old. Teenagers put it there."

"All right," he nodded.

"And come for coffee later in the kitchen. Teddy wants to show you his slides of San Francisco."

He chuckled.

"And watch these goddamn steps on your way down. OK? I love you, Michael Mouse."

"Same to you, fella."

She disappeared into the roof.

He lit the joint and fixed his gaze on the procession of lights winding toward Easley-on-Hill. The night was peppered with laughter and the scuffing of feet against gravel paths. He heard a cuckoo, a real cuckoo. He couldn't recall the last time he had heard one, if at all.

Wilfred joined him on the parapet. "Lady Mo said you were up here."

"Lady Mo, huh?" He laughed.

"It's me own name."

"It's great! Lady Mo!"

Wilfred grinned at him. "Are you fucked up, mate?"

"A little, I guess. Here." He handed the joint to Wilfred, who took a short hit and handed it back. "I picked out me room," said the kid. "Wanna see it?"

"Sure, kiddo. In a little bit."

"Are you all right?"

"I'm great."

"Yeah . . . me too."

"Look at where we are, Wilfred. It's real! There really are places that look like this!" He pried a chunk of moss off the stone and tossed it over the edge.

"What about it, then, mate?"

"What about what?"

"Well," said Wilfred, "you're staying, aren't you?"

The Longest Easter

Simon was leaving, framed in her doorway, suitcase in hand.

"I managed an earlier flight," he said, "but I can certainly hold off until you get some word."

"I'll be all right," she said.

"Are you sure?"

She nodded. "He'll be back. It's only been seven hours or so." It was easily the longest Easter in memory.

"Look," he said, setting his suitcase down, "what if I call Theresa? She doesn't know me, and we could at least find out if he's there."

"No. It's OK. He's run off before."

"Oh . . . I see."

"Not over anything like this, of course."

He grinned at her ruefully. "Of course."

She looked at him for a moment, then flung her arms around his neck. "Oh, Simon, I'll miss you!"

He pecked her on the cheek somewhat formally. "Take care of yourself," he said.

"I will."

"I left Michael's keys with Mrs. Madrigal."

"Fine," she said.

"His toaster wants repairing, I'm afraid. It died on me several days ago."

"I'll tell him," she replied. "That's OK."

They looked at each other helplessly.

"Will you write?" she asked at last.

He reached out and stroked her hair. "I'm not very good about that."

She smiled at him. "Neither am I."

"Give Brian my best," he said. "When the time is right."

"I will."

"Well . . . I'd best be going. My taxi is probably . . ."

"Simon, please don't hate me."

He studied her face for a while before leaning over to kiss her forehead. "Never," he said softly.

And then he walked away.

As night fell, she tried to stay occupied, but she couldn't shake the dread that gripped her. When the phone rang at seven-fifteen, she lunged at it like a madwoman.

"Hello," she answered hoarsely.

"Hi. It's DeDe."

"Oh . . . hi."

"Is this a bad time?"

"No," she lied.

"Good. Well, D'or and I thought you and Brian might like to play tonight. Mother's got the kids, and we're just a couple of good-time gals on the town."

"That's sweet," said Mary Ann.

"But?" replied DeDe.

"Well . . . Brian isn't here right now."

DeDe heard the uncertainty in her voice. "Is . . . uh . . . something the matter?"

"Yeah. More or less."

"Sounds like more," said DeDe.

Mary Ann hesitated. "We had a fight."

"Oh."

"It was major, DeDe. I'm worried. He left here early this morning, and I haven't heard from him since."

"He'll be back."

"It isn't that," said Mary Ann. "He was in no shape to drive. He'd been up all night doing coke, and . . . I don't know. I just feel creepy about it."

DeDe paused, then asked: "Did he give you any idea where he was going?"

"Well . . . sort of."

"Where?"

"Uh . . . Theresa Cross's house."

"Jesus. How did he meet *her?*"

"Through me," Mary Ann answered lamely.

"Big mistake," said DeDe.

"I don't care about that part, really. I can deal with that. I just want to be sure he's not . . . you know."

"Yeah."

"I'd rather know where he is than not know where he is."

"Well," said DeDe, "she lives just half a mile away. I could check out her driveway and see if his car is there."

Mary Ann was flooded with relief. *Of course.* "Oh, DeDe . . . would you mind?"

"Gimme a break. Of course not. Call you back in half an hour."

"It's the Le Car," said Mary Ann, "and please don't let her see you."

It was more like forty-five minutes, but she answered after only one ring.

"Yeah?"

"It's DeDe."

"Yeah?"

"The car isn't there, hon."

"Oh."

"They could've gone out, of course. I mean . . . I wouldn't jump to conclusions. You don't even know for sure that that's where he went."

"No."

"Please don't worry, hon."

"I won't."

"It's early yet," said DeDe. "Maybe he's just visiting a friend."

"Yeah."

"Do you have any Valium?" asked DeDe.

"Yeah."

"Then take one before you go to bed."

Mary Ann did as she was told.

Weirding Out

The funeral was being held in a small shingled chapel with orange and green stained-glass windows. Mouse stood next to her, holding her hand. She was crying more than he was, but she knew he was probably cried out by now. As the organist began to play "Turn Away," she turned toward the window and saw that it wasn't stained glass at all but dozens of orange and green parrots arranged geometrically on perches. One by one, they flew toward the starless sky, and darkness spilled like molten tar into the hole they had left behind . . .

The phone rang.

Her hand, only barely connected to her brain, felt for the receiver in the dark. She croaked something unintelligible.

"Mary Ann?"

It was Michael. "Oh . . . Mouse."

"I know it's early, Babycakes."

"What?"

"Don't be pissed at me. I just wanted to give you a change of . . . oh, God, you're pissed."

"No. It's OK. Gimme a chance to get it together."

"You sound really out of it."

She checked the bedside clock. "It's five fifty-three, Mouse."

"I know. I'm sorry."

"And I took a Valium before I went to bed."

"Uh-oh." He began to hum the theme from *Valley of the Dolls*.

"Lay off," she said. "Where are you?"

"In England," he replied. "Easley-on-Hill."

"Where?"

"I'm staying at Lady Roughton's manor house."

"Right," she said, impatient with his teasing.

"I'll tell you about it later. I just wanted you to know I'll be staying another three days."

Her reply was colorless. "Oh." How long was she going to be alone?

"It's great here," he added. "I guess I should've waited to tell you. I'm sorry. I'll see you on . . ."

"Don't go, Mouse."

"Huh?"

"Stay on the phone. Talk to me. I'm weirding out."

"How many Valiums did you say you . . . ?"

"Brian's gone. We had a fight yesterday, and he walked out, and . . . I think something's happened to him."

"It can't be that bad," he replied.

"It is."

"Sounds to me like he's punishing you. How long has it been?"

"Almost twenty-four hours."

Michael said nothing.

"Should I call the police?" she asked.

"I dunno."

"I mean . . . if he's checked into a motel or something, don't you think he would've called by now?"

"I guess," he replied, "but maybe you oughta give it a few more . . ."

"I had this awful dream, Mouse."

"When?"

"Just now. Before you called. You and I were at a funeral together."

"You're just thinking of Jon," he said.

"No. This was different. It was in a little chapel of some sort. And Brian wasn't with us."

"Babycakes . . ."

"It felt so *real*, Mouse."

"I know. That's natural. You're under a lot of stress. You need sleep, that's all. If I hadn't woken you, you wouldn't have remembered that dream."

This was true, she decided.

"Besides," he added, "I think Brian's just moping."

"You do? Really?"

"Yeah. I do. Get some sleep, OK? It'll all seem better in the sunshine."

"OK."

"And I'll see you on Friday."

"All right. I'm glad you're having a good time, Mouse."

"Thanks. Night-night now."

"Night-night."

She rose just after ten o'clock and called in sick to Larry Kenan. He was relatively pleasant about it, which only reinforced her nagging suspicion that something was seriously off kilter in the universe. She made herself a defiantly big breakfast. If Brian was trying to make her suffer, she had done more than enough suffering already.

She was reading a *Cosmopolitan* in the courtyard when Mrs. Madrigal appeared and sat down next to her in the toasty sunshine.

"Lovely day," said the landlady.

"Mmm."

"Did you have a nice Easter?"

She hesitated. "It was OK."

Mrs. Madrigal smiled tenderly. "I miss him already, don't you?"

For a moment, Mary Ann thought she meant Brian. "Oh . . . sure . . . he was a nice guy."

The landlady nodded but said nothing. Mary Ann looked down at her magazine again.

"And Brian's gone too, isn't he?"

Mary Ann met her eyes. "How did you know?"

"Oh . . . just a feeling."

Mary Ann felt her anxiety rise. If Mrs. Madrigal was having premonitions, maybe that dream really meant something.

"Do you want to talk about it, dear?"

In five minutes, she had told the landlady everything: Brian's sterility, her pregnancy scheme, how Simon's feelings were hurt and how she had tried to apologize, Brian's ill-timed return and angry departure. Mrs. Madrigal took it all in stride, but drew a deep breath when Mary Ann had finished.

"Well, I must say . . . you've outdone yourself this time."

Mary Ann ducked her eyes. "Do you think I was wrong?"

"You know better than that."

"What?"

"I don't do absolutions, dear." She reached for Mary Ann's hand and squeezed it. "But I'm glad you told me."

"He wanted a baby so badly."

"I know. He told me."

"He did? When?"

"Oh . . . back when you were covering the Queen."

"What did he say?"

"Oh . . . just that he wanted one . . . and you were somewhat cool to the idea."

"I would have one for *him*," she replied.

"I can see that," said the landlady.

"I'm just so afraid it's too late. It isn't like him to stay away this long."

Mrs. Madrigal smiled faintly. "Let him concoct a little mystery, dear. It may be his only defense."

"Against what?"

"Against your layers and layers of mystery."

"Wait a minute," said Mary Ann. "I'm not so hard to figure out."

The landlady patted her knee. "You and I know that, child . . . but he doesn't."

"Then . . . ?"

"Don't ask him where he's been, dear. Let him have that for his own." Mrs. Madrigal rose suddenly. "It's time for me to tidy up the basement."

Her abrupt departure puzzled Mary Ann until she looked across the courtyard and saw her husband coming through the lychgate. His gait was leaden, and his face seemed devoid of all emotion as he turned and headed in her direction.

"Hi," he said.

"Hi," she replied.

He sat down on the bench, but kept his distance. "Shouldn't you be at work today?"

"I called in sick."

He nodded, hands dangling between his knees. "Is Simon still . . . ?"

"He's back in England. He left yesterday."

He sat there in silence for a long time. When he finally spoke, he addressed his remarks to the ground. "I wasn't doing a number on you. I needed time to think."

"I know."

"I couldn't do it here. There was too much to . . ."

"I understand completely."

"Stop doing that," he said edgily.

"What?"

"Just let me talk. I'm not looking for explanations. I've worked this out."

She nodded. "OK."

"I think I should go," he said.

"Go?"

"Live somewhere else for a while. Find another job, maybe. I've got no function here."

"Brian, please don't . . ."

"Listen to me, Mary Ann! I'm almost forty and I haven't left a mark on anything. I can't even give my wife everything she wants. I can't even do that."

"But you *do!*"

"I *don't.* What the fuck was that little scene about, huh?"

"It wasn't about that, Brian. It was . . ."

"It doesn't matter. I know how I feel, Mary Ann. It'll only get worse if I stay here."

"Do you know how *I* feel, Brian? What would happen to me if you left?"

"You'd handle it," he said, smiling faintly. "That's one of the things I like about you. You're strong."

"I'm *not* strong."

"You're stronger than I am," he said. "I'm a soft male."

"A *what?*"

"Chip Hardesty's got a vacant studio in his new place. He says I can stay there until . . ."

"Brian, for God's sake!" The tears had begun to stream down her face. "We're in love with each other, aren't we?"

He wouldn't look at her. "There has to be more than that, sweetheart."

"Like what?"

"I dunno. A reason. A purpose."

"We'll find you a job, then."

He shook his head. "*I'll* find me a job."

"Well, sure . . . but you can do that here."

"Uh . . . excuse me." It was a third voice, awkwardly interceding. They both looked toward the lych-gate, where a tall, heavily freckled man was standing. "Mary Ann?"

She rose, wiping her eyes. "Yeah . . . that's me."

The man came forward. He was in his early twenties, but his corn-fed demeanor and prominent ears and the canvas sack slung from his neck instantly suggested the clumsy kid who had been her paperboy fifteen years ago in Cleveland.

Only this time he wasn't delivering the paper.

This time he was delivering a baby.

Familiar Mysteries

The first thing Michael noticed were the hyacinths in the garden, half a dozen pale pink erections smiling in the face of death. He smiled back at them, rejoicing in his family, savoring his return to the family seat.

Mrs. Madrigal spotted him from her kitchen window and hooted a greeting. He set down his suitcase and motioned for her to come outside. She emerged seconds later, almost running, rubbing her hands on her apron. "Dear boy," she crooned, hugging him heartily. "You've been sorely missed."

"Thanks for the hyacinths," he said.

"What? Oh . . . you're welcome. You look *wonderful*, dear. You've put on some weight."

"Don't say that."

"Well . . . oh, don't be such a man. Your beauty is still intact. C'mon. Let's get that bag inside. Mary Ann and Brian will want to see you." She grabbed his suitcase and led the way, charging toward the house.

"Good," said Michael. "He's back, then."

She looked at him as she shouldered her way through the front door. "You knew about that?"

He nodded. "We talked on the phone. She was freaked."

"Well . . . she's fine now."

He reached for the suitcase. "Let me carry . . ."

"No. You've had a long flight. We'll leave this in the foyer for the time being." She dropped the suitcase and flung open the door of her apartment. "And you'll stop in for a very small sherry."

"Great," he replied. "Wait a minute, let me get something." He stooped to open his suitcase, then dug around in a side pocket until he found the envelope. "This is from Mona," he explained, handing it to her.

"Where on earth . . . ?"

"In England." He smiled.

"You can't mean it!"

He nodded. "She's in good shape. She's happy, and she wants you to come visit her."

"*In England?*"

"Just read the note."

Mrs. Madrigal looked dubious as she set the envelope on her

284

telephone stand. Mona was right, he decided. The landlady did act an awful lot like a father when the subject was Mona.

She beckoned him into the apartment, pointing to the sofa. "All right, now . . . sherry." She bustled off to the kitchen, leaving him to absorb the familiar mysteries of this faded velvet cavern where silk tassels hung like stalactites. God, it was good to be back.

When she returned, she handed him a rose-colored wineglass full of sherry. "She's actually living there?"

"No pumping."

"Well, tell me what she's doing, at least."

He sipped his sherry and smiled at her. "Following in her father's footsteps."

"Now, dear, if . . ."

"That's all you get."

The landlady fussed with a wisp of wayward hair. "Well, drink your sherry, then."

He kept smiling as he sipped. Unable to restrain herself, she rose and went to the phone stand. She picked up the envelope, then set it down again and picked up the phone and dialed a number.

"What are you doing?" he asked.

"Alerting the troops." She spoke into the receiver. "Our wandering boy is home. Yes . . . that's right . . . that's right. Fine . . . I'll tell him." She hung up and turned back to Michael. "Your presence is requested in the Hawkins residence in exactly three minutes." She headed toward the kitchen.

"What am I waiting . . . ?"

"Just sit there and finish your sherry, young man."

He chuckled at her revenge. The sherry went down like sun-warmed honey. He sat there in the musty embrace of Mrs. Madrigal's sofa and counted his blessings while she puttered about in the kitchen.

Finally, he rose. "Do you want to come with me?" he yelled.

"No, thanks," came the reply. "I'm involved with a lamb stew at the moment." Her head poked into view, her angular features ruddy from the stove. "We're having dinner here tonight. I hope that's all right."

"Perfect," he said, on his way out the door.

He picked up his suitcase and climbed the stairs, leaving it on the landing before heading up to the third floor. Mary Ann met him outside her door. "Look at you," she squealed. "Chubbette."

"Fuck you very much."

They hugged for a long time before she led him into the apartment.

He looked around. "I thought Brian was here."

"Sit down," she said.

Something was the matter. He felt his sherried security begin to ebb. This was why he usually hated homecomings, this queasy preparation for the news they didn't want to spoil your vacation with. His first thought was: *Who else has died?*

"What's wrong?" he asked.

"Nothing. This just takes some . . . easing into. Sit down."

He sat down.

She perched on a footstool. "Remember my old friend Connie Bradshaw?"

He shook his head. "Sorry."

"You know . . . who I stayed with . . . when I moved out from Cleveland."

"Oh, yeah. With the oil paintings on velvet."

She nodded.

"The tacky stew."

She winced. "She wasn't tacky, Mouse."

"But you always said . . ."

"Never mind that. She was very good to me, and I shouldn't have said that."

"OK."

"She died, Mouse."

"Oh." He was relieved in spite of his better instincts. Thank God, it was no one he knew.

"She died in childbirth. Well . . . not during, but a day or so after. It was something called eclampsia. Her blood didn't clot. She had a stroke."

He frowned. "I'm sorry. That's awful."

She nodded, then gazed at him soulfully. "She left me her baby, Mouse."

"Huh?"

"She wasn't married, and her parents are dead, and her brother's a bachelor in med school and . . . she left me this note before she died and asked me to . . . raise it." She finished with a sheepish little shrug and waited for his reaction.

"You mean . . . is it . . . ?"

She nodded. "In the bedroom. With Brian."

"My God . . . then it's going to be . . ."

"She," she put in. "She's going to be our little girl."

He was flabbergasted. "This is *amazing*, Mary Ann."

"I know."

"Well . . . uh . . . how do you feel about it?"

She hesitated. "Pretty good, I guess."

"Guess?"

"Well . . . I'm still adjusting to it."

"What about Brian?"

She smiled at him. "Come see for yourself."

Rising, she took his arm and led him into the bedroom. Brian was seated in the armchair by the bed, cradling the baby in his arms. A gooseneck lamp on the dresser formed a sort of ersatz halo behind his head. Michael couldn't help wondering if there was a masculine equivalent of *madonna*.

"Welcome home," Brian beamed.

Michael shook his head in amazement. "Look at you."

"No . . . look at this face." He meant the baby.

Moving to his side, Michael peered down into a tiny pink fist of a face. Brian jiggled the baby. "Say hello to your Uncle Michael, Shawna."

"Shawna, huh?"

"Connie named her," Mary Ann put in.

"Shawna Hawkins," mused Michael. "That works." He looked around the room. "A crib and toys and everything. You guys have been busy."

"No," said Mary Ann. "Connie had them already."

"Oh." He sympathized with her confusion. "It happened awfully quick, didn't it?"

"Awfully," she nodded.

"Instant baby," said Brian.

Mary Ann opened a drawer and removed a sheet of pink-and-green stationery. "Here's the note she left." She handed it to Michael. It was scented. *Mary Ann*, it read, *Please take care of my precious angel. Love, Connie.* She had sketched a smile face next to her signature.

"It's just like her," said Mary Ann.

Michael nodded.

"Poor thing," she added.

"Well," he offered, "at least she had the comfort of knowing who the new mother would be."

"I knew her too," said Brian. "I dated her."

"Once or twice," said Mary Ann.

Looking down again, Brian extended his forefinger to Shawna. Five little fingers clamped around his. "We met at the Come Clean Center," he said.

"Pardon me?" Michael frowned.

"The laundromat in the Marina."

"Oh."

Mary Ann glowered at them both. "I don't think little Shawna needs to press that in her book of memories."

"Who's the natural father?" asked Michael.

Mary Ann took the note from him and returned it to the drawer. "It's apparently some guy who took her to the Us Festival. She wasn't really sure. She just wanted a baby."

Michael was sorry he had asked. "It doesn't matter," he said.

"No," agreed Brian, "it doesn't." He smiled at Michael, then turned to his wife. "Does it?"

"Not a bit," she replied.

An awkward silence followed, so Mary Ann added, "I just feel a little dumb, I guess. Our baby just . . . shows up on our doorstep. I feel as if I should've done something to earn it."

"You did something," said Brian.

She gave him a funny look which puzzled Michael.

"I mean that," said Brian, looking down at the baby. "It's the thought that counts."

Mary Ann seemed vaguely unsettled. "Well . . . we just wanted you to meet her."

"She's wonderful," he said, and he meant it.

When he finally trudged downstairs to his apartment, he found a joint taped to the door with a note: *Smoke this and catch 40 winks before supper. AM.* He removed it, smiling, and let himself in.

There were only a few traces of Simon remaining: a half-empty bottle of brandy, several *Rolling Stones*, alien numbers scribbled on the pad by the telephone. The place looked pretty much the same. Nothing special, just home.

A joint and a nap sounded like a great idea. He remembered his suitcase and retrieved it from the landing. Dumping it on the sofa, he snapped it open and felt around for his toothbrush. In the process he discovered a small cardboard box imprinted with the logo of a gift shop in Moreton-in-Marsh. There were holes punched in the side of the box.

He lifted the lid and found a tiny porcelain fox nestled in tissue paper.

With this note: *Find a good home for him. Love, Wilfred.*

Requiem

Connie's memorial service was held in a small funeral chapel in the Avenues. Mary Ann and Michael arrived early and sat in the back, out of earshot of the others. Moments later, a priest emerged from a door near the altar and began organizing index cards on the podium.

"Hey," whispered Michael. "Isn't that Father Paddy?"

She nodded.

"I didn't know Connie was Catholic."

"She wasn't. I asked him to do it. These funeral home services are so . . . you know . . . cold-blooded. I thought it would be nice if she had a real priest."

He nodded.

"I feel so awful, Mouse."

"Why?"

"I don't know. I guess because . . . I don't deserve to have her baby."

"C'mon now."

"I don't. I was so mean to her."

"Look . . . she wouldn't have done it if she didn't think you were a good person."

She didn't answer.

"You know that's true," he said.

"It's not just the baby," she replied.

"What else, then?"

"She saved my marriage, Mouse."

"C'mon."

"She did. He was ready to leave me when that baby showed up."

"He would never have left you."

"I don't know that."

"Well, *I* do. That's bullshit."

Father Paddy spotted Mary Ann and gave her a cheery wave from the podium. She waved back, then turned to Michael again. "I put Brian through hell."

"How?"

"Well . . . I'd rather not say."

"OK, then don't expect me to reinforce your guilt."

She fidgeted with her program.

"Look," he whispered, "whatever it was, Connie didn't die for your sins. She just died."

She nodded.

"This isn't like you, Babycakes." He reached for her hand as her eyes brimmed with tears. "Why are you so freaked?"

A man in rimless glasses took a seat behind the small electric organ and began to play "Turn Away."

Michael was thrown. "Who requested *that*?" he asked.

"She did," wept Mary Ann. "Before she died." She tightened her grip on his hand. "It was her favorite song."

He thought for a moment. "Then that means . . ." She nodded.

"This is your dream!"

Another nod.

"And . . . yeah, of course . . . Brian wasn't in it because he's home taking care of the baby."

She wiped her eyes. "You got it."

"Jesus," he murmured.

Father Paddy cleared his throat and surveyed his flock with a kindly smile. "My friends," he intoned, "we are gathered here today to honor the memory of . . . uh . . . Bonnie Bradshaw."

"Shit," muttered Mary Ann.

In the Pink

"The weather was beastly," she told her manicurist.

"What a shame! All the time?"

"Mmm."

"Ah, well . . . it was beastly here too. I suppose it's been beastly everywhere."

"Mmm."

"Simon says San Francisco was quite lovely when he left."

"Well, he had more time to find out about that, didn't he?"

"The other hand, Your Majesty."

"What?"

"I'm done with this one. See? Don't those cuticles look smashing?"

"Dash the cuticles."

"Sorry."

"We were talking about Simon."

"You're quite right."

"He's been *very* naughty."

"I quite agree."

"Any other officer would have been court-martialed straight away. No questions asked."

"You're so right. Shall we go a shade lighter?"

"What?"

"The nail varnish."

"What about it?"

"Shall we pink it up a bit?"

"No."

"Summer is just around the . . ."

"Miss Treves!"

"Very well."

"If one isn't *feeling* pink, one shouldn't wear it."

"How true."

"Have you scolded Simon?"

"Repeatedly, Your Majesty. And he greatly appreciates your intercession."

"One would hope so."

"He's spoken to a publishing firm. They're going to take him on."

"Charmed his way in, no doubt."

"No doubt."

"He's too bally charming for his own good, that boy."

"I quite agree, Your Majesty."

"What sort of pink?"

"Beg pardon, Your Majesty?"

"The nail varnish. What sort of pink is it?"

"Oh . . . here. This one."

"I see. Well, that's not as drastic as one might imagine."

"No, ma'am."

"What's it called?"

" 'Regency Rose,' Your Majesty."

" 'Regency Rose?' "

"Yes, ma'am."

"Very well. That will do nicely. Carry on, Miss Treves."

THE END

Significant Others

For Terry Anderson,
who took his time getting here

For Jane Stuart Maupin,
who has been there all along

NOTE TO THE READER

The Bohemian Grove is a real place whose rituals I have compressed, though not substantially altered, to suit the time frame of this tale.

Wimminwood is a fictitious entity based on the actual practices of women's music festivals in Michigan, California, Georgia and elsewhere.

I am indebted to my friends in both camps.

—A.M.

If you go down in the woods today
You'd better not go alone.
It's lovely down in the woods today
But safer to stay at home.
For every Bear that ever there was
Will gather there for certain because
Today's the day the Teddy Bears
*   have their picnic.*

—CHILDREN'S SONG, 1907

Descent into Heaven

Brian's internal clock almost always woke him at four fifty-six, giving him four whole minutes to luxuriate in the naked human body next to him. Then the Braun alarm clock on the nightstand would activate his wife with its genteel Nazi tootling, and her morning marathon would begin.

Today, with three minutes to go, he slipped his arm around her waist and eased her closer until her back had once again settled against his chest. It was risky, this part, because sometimes she would jerk awake with a start, as if frightened by a stranger.

He pressed his face against her neck, then traced with his forefinger the shallow swirl of her navel. It was smooth and hard now, miraculously aerobicized into a tiny pink seashell. She stirred slightly, so he flattened his hand to keep from tickling her and made sure their breathing was still in sync.

At the two-minute mark, he eased his knee between her legs and tightened his grip around her waist. She groaned faintly, then cleared her throat, so he let his hand fall slack against her belly. She countered by squeezing his knee with her thighs, telling him not to worry, he wasn't smothering her, she needed this time as much as he did.

The French had it wrong about *le petit mort*. If you asked him, "the little death" was not so much the slump after sex as these few piquant moments of serious cuddling before the demands of Mary Ann's career sent her vaulting over his piss-hardened manhood in the direction of the toilet and the coffee machine.

Another Nazi, that coffee machine. Even now, as he fondled

her navel again, it was grinding its beans in the kitchen. The sound of it caused her to shift slightly and clear her throat again. "Like that?" she asked.

"What?"

"My belly button."

"Mmm."

"Took seven hundred hours," she said. "I figured it out."

He chuckled at the tyranny of numbers that governed her existence. *Everything has a price*, she was telling him. It was her favorite theme these days.

She rolled over in his arms and poked her finger into his navel. "Hey," he muttered, uncertain whether the gesture was one of affection or reprimand. She wiggled her finger. "Watch out," he said. "You fall in there and we'll have to organize a search party."

He waited for a faint cry of protest, but none came. A half-assed "Come off it" would have sufficed, but all she did was remove her finger and prop herself up on one elbow. "Well," she said, "I guess I'm up."

He knew better than to argue with this pronouncement. He would only receive the standard recitation of her crypto-fascist morning regimen. Aerobics at six. A bowl of bran at seven. A meeting with the producer at seven-thirty. Makeup session at eight. A meeting with staff and crew from nine to nine-fifteen, followed by promo shots for the next day's show and a session in the green room with this morning's guest celebrities. Life was a ballbuster for San Francisco's most famous talk show hostess.

"So what's the topic today?" he asked.

"Fat models," she replied.

"Huh?"

"You know. Those porkos who model for the big-and-beautiful fashions."

"Oh."

"It's a huge racket." She laughed. "Pardon the pun." She bounded over him and swung her legs off the bed, yawning noisily. "The book's on the dresser if you wanna take a look at it."

As she headed for the bathroom, he brooded momentarily about the extra ten pounds around his waist, then got up and went to the dresser, returning to bed with the book. He switched on the bedside light and examined the cover. It was called *Larger than Life: Confessions of the World's Most Beautiful Fat Woman*. By Wren Douglas.

A glamorous star-filtered cover photograph seemed to confirm the claim. The woman was big, all right, but her face was the face of a goddess: full red lips, a perfect nose, enormous green eyes fairly brimming with kindness and invitation. Her raven hair framed it all perfectly, cascading across her shoulders toward a cleavage rivaling the San Andreas Fault.

"What is this?" Mary Ann was brandishing the roll of paper towels he had left in the bathroom the night before.

"We ran out of toilet paper," he said, shrugging. He could do without her rhetorical questions at five o'clock in the morning.

The alarm sounded.

"Fuck off," he barked, not to her but to the clock, which deactivated obediently at the sound of his voice.

Mary Ann groaned and lowered the roll of towels, banging it angrily against her leg. "I specifically told Nguyet to make sure we had enough to—"

"I'll tell her," he put in. "She understands me better." She also liked him better, but he wasn't about to say so. He'd shared a special rapport with the Vietnamese maid ever since he'd discovered she couldn't tell the difference between Raid and Pledge. His pact of silence about the incident seemed the very least he could do for a woman whose uncle had been killed in an American bombing run over the Mekong Delta.

"It's just a language problem," he added. "She's getting much better. Really."

Mary Ann sighed and returned to the bathroom.

He raised his voice so she could hear him. "Paper towels won't kill you. Think of it as a learning experience."

"Right," she muttered back.

"Maybe there's a show in it," he offered, trying to sound playful. "A dreaded new medical condition. Like . . . the heartbreak of Bounty butt."

She didn't laugh.

He thought for a moment, then said: "Viva vulva?"

"Go to sleep," she told him. "You're gonna wake up Shawna."

He knew what she was doing in there. She was reading *USA Today*, briefing herself for the show, learning a little about a lot to keep from seeming stupid on the air.

He picked up the book again and studied the face of the world's most beautiful fat woman. Then he switched off the light, burrowed under the comforter, and slipped almost instantly into sleep.

He dreamed about a woman who had tits the size of watermelons.

The next time he woke, his daughter was conducting a Rambo-style maneuver on his exposed left leg, propelling a green plastic tank up his thigh in an apparent effort to gain supremacy of the hillocks that lay beyond. Shawna invariably chose some sort of guerrilla theater over the simple expediency of saying, "Get up, Daddy."

He remained on his stomach and made a cartoon-monster noise into the pillow.

Shawna shrieked delightedly, dropping the tank between his legs. He rolled over and snatched her up with one arm, tumbling her onto the bed. "Is this my little Puppy? Yum-yum. Puppy Monster eats little puppies for breakfast!"

He wasn't sure how this Puppy business had begun, but he and Mary Ann both made use of the nickname. In light of Mary Ann's distaste for the child's given name, maybe it was simply their way of avoiding the issue without being disrespectful to the dead.

Connie, after all, had named the little girl, and Connie had died giving birth to her. They couldn't just choose a new name the way people do when their pets change hands.

Was that what "Puppy" really meant? Something that wasn't theirs? Something they had picked out at the pound? Would the nickname hurt Shawna's feelings when she was old enough to consider its implications?

He seized his daughter's waist and held her aloft, airplane fashion. The little girl spread her arms and squealed.

He rocked forward, causing her to soar for a moment, but his butt made a graceless landing on the toy tank.

"Goddamnit, Puppy. Mommy didn't buy that, did she?"

She managed to keep a poker face, still impersonating an airplane. He lowered her to the bed and reached under him for the offending war machinery. "It's Jeremy's, isn't it? You've been trading again."

The kid wasn't talking.

"I didn't buy it, and Mommy didn't buy it, and I know you don't take things that don't belong to you."

She shook her head, then said: "I'm hungry."

"Don't change the subject, young lady."

Shawna sat on the edge of the bed and let her head dangle in a loose semicircle. The little charlatan was condescending to cute as a last resort.

"What did you trade for it?" he asked.

Her answer was unintelligible.

"What?"

"My *Preemie*," she said.

She slid off the bed, hitting the expensive new carpet with a soft thud. "My Cabbage Patch Preemie." Her tone indicated that this was a matter of simple laissez-faire economics and none of his goddamn business.

He felt a vague responsibility to be angry, but he couldn't help smiling at the inevitable scene in the condo across the hallway: Cap Sorenson, the ultimate Reaganite, returning home after a hard day of software and racketball, only to come upon Daddy's little soldier playing mommy to a premature Cabbage Patch doll.

Shawna tugged on his arm. "Dad-dee . . . c'mon!"

He checked the clock. Seven thirty-seven. "OK, Puppy, go pick

305

out a tape." This was his usual ploy to get her out of the room while he pulled on his bathrobe. It was no big deal to him, but Mary Ann thought it "inadvisable" that he walk around naked in front of Shawna. And Mary Ann should know; she was the one with the talk show.

"No," said Shawna.

"What do you mean, no?"

"No VCR. Go see Anna."

"We'll do that, Puppy, but not yet. Anna's asleep. Go on now . . . pick out a tape. Mommy brought you *Pete the Dragon* and *Popeye*, and I think there's—"

A whine welled up in the child. She pawed the carpet belligerently, cutting a silvery path through the powder-blue plush. He couldn't help wondering if parenting was an age-related skill like warfare—tolerable, even stimulating, at twenty, but inescapably futile at forty.

He looked his daughter in the eye and spoke her name—her given name—to signal his seriousness. "I want you to go pick out a tape before Daddy gets unbelievably mad at you. We'll go see Anna later on."

Shawna's lower lip plumped momentarily, but she obeyed him. When she was gone, he dragged himself to the bathroom and brushed his teeth. The floor was still wet from Mary Ann's frantic ablutions, so he mopped it with a damp towel and tossed the towel into the laundry hamper.

He hesitated before weighing himself, then decided that the ugly truth was a surefire antidote for his late-night jelly doughnut binges. The scales surprised him, however. He had lost four pounds in four days.

This made no sense to him, but he had never been one to argue with serendipity.

Shawna threw her usual tantrum over breakfast. This time her yogurt was the wrong color and there wasn't enough Perrier to make her cranberry juice "go fizzy." Would she ever tire of testing him?

After breakfast, according to custom, he let her pick out her clothes for the day. She chose a green cotton turtleneck with lady-bugs on the arm and a pair of absurdly miniature 501s. He dressed her, then left her in the custody of Robin Williams and the VCR while he changed into his own version of her ensemble.

The clock said eight forty-six when he went to the window and peered down twenty-three stories into the leafy green canyon of Barbary Lane. From this height, Anna Madrigal's courtyard was nothing more than a terracotta postage stamp, but he could still discern a figure moving jauntily along the perimeter.

The landlady was making her morning sweep, brandishing a broom so vigorously that the ritual seemed more akin to exercise than to practical considerations of cleanliness. Later, she would cross the postage stamp diagonally and sit on the bench next to the azalea bed. For all her professed free-spiritedness, she was a creature of blatant predictability.

He lifted his gaze from the courtyard and surveyed their vista, a boundless sweep of city, bay and sky stretching from Mount Diablo to Angel Island and beyond.

There were no chimney pots or eucalyptus branches blocking their vision, no unsightly back stairwells or rocky rises framing some half-assed little chunk of water. What they had at The Summit was a goddamn *view*—as slick and unblemished as a photomural.

And just about as real.

Sometimes, when he stared at the horizon long enough, their teal-and-gray living room lost its identity altogether and became the boardroom of a corporate jet dipping its wings in homage to the Bank of America building.

Today, the sky was cloudless and the air was clear. No hint of the holocaust raging sixty miles south of the city. There, amid the brittle manzanita brush of the Santa Cruz Mountains, a jagged trail of fire seven miles wide had already blackened fifteen thousand acres and driven five thousand people from their homes.

But not here at The Summit. Nature wouldn't stand a chance at The Summit.

He sometimes wondered about that preposition. Should he tell people he lived *at* The Summit, *in* The Summit or *on* The Summit? Usually, when pressed, he admitted to 999 Green and left it at that.

If he was embarrassed, he had every right to be. He'd lived in the shadow of this concrete leviathan for nearly eight years, cursing it continually. Now, at his wife's insistence—and using his wife's money—he'd joined the enemy in a big way.

They had done it for Shawna. And for security. And because they needed a tax shelter. They had also done it because Mary Ann wanted a glossier setting for her "lifestyle" (God help her, she had actually used that word) than could ever be provided by the funky old bear of a building at 28 Barbary Lane.

Mrs. Madrigal had taken it well, but Brian knew she'd been hurt by their departure. At the very least, her sense of family had been violated. Even now, five months after their ascension, their old apartment on the lane remained empty and unrented, as if something had died there.

Maybe something had.

Life was different now; he knew that. The guy who had once waited tables at Perry's bore scant resemblance to this new and improved postmodern version of Brian Hawkins.

The new Brian drove a twenty-thousand-dollar Jeep. He owned three tuxedos and a mink-lined bomber jacket from Wilkes (which he wore only while driving the Jeep). Something of a fixture at Pier 23, he knew how to do lunch with the best of them.

When the new Brian went to parties, he usually ended up making man talk with the mayor's husband or Danielle Steel's husband—and once even with Geraldine Ferraro's husband.

OK. He was a consort.

But even that took skill, didn't it?

And who was to say he didn't rank among the best?

When Shawna grew bored with television, he helped her into a windbreaker and briefed her for the trek to Barbary Lane. His basic requirements were two: Don't scream bloody murder on the elevator, and don't point at the doorman and yell "Mr. T!"

She did as she was told, miraculously enough, and they reached Green Street without a hitch. As they trooped along the crest of Russian Hill, his limbs felt curiously leaden; his temples pulsed a little, threatening a headache.

If this was the flu, he didn't need it. There were four major events in the next week alone.

Shawna insisted on being carried in his arms as they descended the steepest slope of Leavenworth, but she squirmed her way to the ground again as soon as they reached the rickety wooden stairs leading to Barbary Lane.

"Anna steps," she said, already recognizing the boundaries of another duchy. The lane, after all, belonged to Mrs. Madrigal. Even the grownups knew that.

There was a bulletin on the landing that confirmed the landlady's sovereignty: SAVE THE BARBARY STEPS—*Insensitive city officials have plans to replace our beloved wooden steps with hideous concrete ones. Now is the time to speak up. Contact Anna Madrigal, 28 Barbary Lane.*

Damn right, he thought. Give 'em hell, Anna.

Nevertheless, he took Shawna's hand as the beloved rotting planks creaked ominously beneath their tread. At the top, where the ground bristled with a stubble of dry fennel, he let her go and watched as she pranced between the garbage cans into the musky gloom of the eucalyptus trees. She looked like a child heading home.

By the time he'd arrived at the first clump of cottages, she was already playing havoc with Boris.

"Take it easy," he told her. "He's an old kitty. Don't pet him so hard."

She snatched her hand away from the tabby, cackling in her best mad-scientist fashion, then dashed up the lane again. The path at this point was paved with ballast stones, treacherous even for grownups.

"Slow down, Puppy. You're gonna hurt yourself again." He caught up with her and took her hand, leading the way toward the smoother, wider portion of the lane.

"You remember Anna's number?" he asked the kid.

Of course she didn't.

"It's twenty-eight," he said, feeling stupid as soon as he said it. Why the hell should she have to learn *that*?

Because the house at the end of the lane was all he had to give a child.

It was all the lore he knew, his only storybook.

The door to the lych-gate was open.

The landlady stood in the courtyard, hunched over her largest sinsemilla plant. She was plucking its leaves with a tweezer, coaxing the potency into its blossoms. Her face suggested brain surgery in progress, but she was humming a merry little tune.

Shawna bolted into the courtyard, losing herself in the folds of Mrs. Madrigal's pale muslin skirt. The landlady gave a startled yelp, dropping the tweezers, then laughed along with the kid.

"It's the Feds," said Brian, grinning.

Mrs. Madrigal looked down at the creature clamped to her leg and stroked its hair affectionately.

"She's missed you," said Brian. "It's been two whole days."

The landlady's huge blue eyes swung in his direction momentarily. She offered him a dim smile before returning her attention to Shawna. "I've missed her too," she said to the kid.

It was asinine, but he felt a little jealous of Mrs. Madrigal's undivided devotion to Shawna. "I saw your notice," he said, searching for something to please her. "Are those crazy bastards really gonna tear down the steps?"

The landlady nodded soberly. "If we don't put up a fight."

She said *we*, he noticed; that was something. She still considered him part of the lane. "Well . . . if there's anything I can do . . ."

"There is, actually."

"Great."

"I thought perhaps if Mary Ann could say something on her show . . . you know, just a few words about preserving our heritage, that sort of thing." She fussed with a wisp of hair at her temple, waiting for his response.

"Yeah . . . well, sure . . . I could mention it to her. They have an awfully rigid format, though." He was backtracking now, remembering Mary Ann's aversion to what she called "hokey local items." Mrs. Madrigal's crusade would almost certainly fall into that category.

The landlady read him like a book. "I see," she murmured.

"I'll tell her, though. I'm sure she'll be upset about it."

Mrs. Madrigal studied him for a moment, almost wistfully, then began scanning the ground around her feet. "Now where did those damn things go? Shawna dear, look over there in that ivy and see if you can find Anna's tweezers."

He thought briefly of begging her forgiveness, then turned frivolous in his embarrassment. "Hey," he blurted, "you should grow your fingernails long."

Now on her hands and knees, Mrs. Madrigal looked up at him. "Why is that, dear?"

"You know, like those housewives in Humboldt County. Works much better than tweezers, they say."

She handled this clumsy inanity with her usual grace. "Ah, yes. I see what you mean." Falling silent again, she searched until she found the tweezers, then stood up and brushed her hands on her skirt. "I tried that once . . . growing my nails long." She caught her breath and shook her head. "I wasn't man enough for it."

He laughed, hugely relieved. In Mrs. Madrigal's repertoire, a proffered joke was the next best thing to forgiveness. When her eyes locked on his, they were full of their old familiar playfulness. He saw his entry and took it.

"I wonder," he said, "if I could ask a big favor of you."

She looked at him for a moment, then peered down at the child hanging on her skirt. "Tell you what, dear. Go into the house and look on the sofa. There's a nice new friend for you."

Shawna looked skeptical. "A Gobot?"

"You'll see. Be careful of the steps, now. The door is open."

As the child toddled away, Mrs. Madrigal beamed appreciatively. "She's just as smart as she can be."

"What did you get her?" he asked.

"Just a stuffed animal," came the mumbled reply.

It embarrassed him a little that the landlady spent money on Shawna. "You really shouldn't," he said.

She answered with a faint who-gives-a-damn smile, then said: "What sort of favor?"

"Well," he said, "my nephew is coming to town for a few days, and I wondered if . . . if he could stay at our old place."

She blinked at him.

"If it's a problem," he added hastily, "just say so, and I'll . . ."

"How old is he?"

"Uh . . . eighteen, I think. Maybe nineteen."

She nodded. "Well . . . there's no furniture, of course. There's a cot in the basement and maybe a chest of drawers." She tapped her forefinger against her lower lip. Her maternal juices were obviously functioning again. It cheered Brian to know that he could still do this for her.

"His name is Jed," he said. "He's in pre-law at Rice University. That's all I know, except that he's probably straight."

The landlady gave him a sly smile. "That's what he told you? He's probably straight?"

He laughed. "Well, he's currently in love with Bruce Springsteen, so I just assumed he was."

"Now wait a minute."

"It's Michael's theory. Get him to explain it. He says every generation produces one male performer that straight boys are allowed to be queer for. It was Mick Jagger for a long time, and now it's Bruce Springsteen. So I figure the kid's straight."

"You and your featherbrained theories."

"It's not *my* theory. I just—" He cut himself off, realizing she'd addressed her remarks to Michael, who had sauntered into the courtyard from the house.

"What have I done now?" asked Michael.

Brian smiled at him. "I was just explaining your Springsteen theory."

"It's true," said Michael. "Straight boys will go all the way for him."

Mrs. Madrigal turned to Brian. "Is he including you in this sweeping generality?"

"Sure," Michael cut in. "He'd do it for The Boss in a second." He cast an impish glance in Brian's direction. "I mean, if he *asked* you, right?"

Brian actually got off on this. It was Michael's way of socking an arm in friendship. "You're a dipshit," he told him, socking back in his own fashion.

"I think it's great," said Michael. "Springsteen's done wonders for guys named Bruce. There used to be such a stigma attached." He paused for a moment, then added: "I'm late, y'all. I'd love to stick around and hash this out, but . . . Wren Douglas cannot be kept waiting."

It took Brian a moment to place the name. Then her face and chest flickered in his head like a soft-core video. "Oh, yeah. The fat model. You know her?"

"No, but I'm a major fan. Mary Ann got me a ticket for the show today."

Mrs. Madrigal looked confused. "She's . . . uh . . . heavy?"

"Yeah," said Brian, "but kind of hot."

"Kind of?" yelped Michael, with surprising indignation. "How about very?"

Brian gave the landlady a you-and-me glance. "And he should know, right?"

Michael headed for the lych-gate, stopping briefly to sniff a bud of Mrs. Madrigal's sinsemilla. He staged a little mock swoon for her benefit, then said: "Better be careful. They're busting people for this now."

"Well," said the landlady, remaining deadpan, "if Mrs. Reagan should drop by for tea, I trust you'll give me fair warning."

Mrs. Madrigal agreed to keep Shawna for a few hours, so Brian did some shopping at the Searchlight Market (Diet Pepsi, a box of Milky Ways and the new Colgate Pump) before returning to The Summit. Back on the twenty-third floor, he found Nguyet Windexing the kitchen window with what appeared to be the last of the paper towels.

And that reminded him: He had forgotten to buy toilet paper.

So what do you use when the paper towels are gone?

"Uh . . . Nguyet?"

The maid stopped Windexing and looked at him, a nervous smile on her face.

"This afternoon. When you go shopping. Buy toilet paper, OK?"

Her smile faded; he had lost her.

"Toilet paper . . . you know . . ." He considered miming it, then discarded the idea. Finally, he went to the bathroom and returned with the little cardboard tube.

Nguyet's face radiated understanding. "Ah," she said. "Shommin."

"Right," he replied. "Shommin. Buy Shommin this afternoon, OK?"

She nodded energetically and returned to her labors, watching out of the corner of her eye as he searched the pantry and came up with a box of Melitta No. 4 coffee filters.

Paper product in hand, he headed for the john, only to be stopped in his tracks by the monumental Wren Douglas, peering up at him from the bedside table. His cock stirred appreciatively, so he made a quick detour and took the book with him to the john.

Vanessa Williams would just have to wait.

Wren in the Flesh

Rising late in her suite at the Fairmont Hotel, Wren Douglas ordered a hearty breakfast, then ambled into the bathroom to take stock of the cornucopia of miniature creams and shampoos that undoubtedly awaited her.

Hotel rooms were really the best part of a book tour. The bathroom bonuses you could stash away for future use. The king-sized beds with their sheets turned back and peppermint patties on the pillow. The thirsty, sweet-smelling towels and silent-flush toilets and TV sets hidden in armoires, ready to offer the transcontinental consolation of Mary Tyler Moore.

This was her sixteenth city in three weeks. Her fat rap had become a well-worn tape, almost too fragile to survive another playing. She was sick of the sound of her own voice and sicker still of the Ken-and-Barbie anchoroids who habitually asked her the same four questions.

Were you fat as a child? ("I was fat as a *fetus*.")

Do you think American women are being tyrannized by the current fitness craze? ("Not necessarily. Everyone should be as fit as possible, including fat people. The tyranny comes when we're told we should all look the same.")

What are your vital statistics? ("Two hundred and two pounds . . . fifty-two, thirty-seven, fifty-seven . . . five feet eight inches tall.")

What do you think caused you to become an international sex symbol? ("Beats me, honey. Some guys just go for a girl with thighs in two time zones.")

All that glibness had begun to catch in her throat like so many dry cornflakes. She was biding her time now, counting the cities—only Portland and Seattle to go—until the final flight would spirit her back to Chicago, to her loft and her cat and her hot Cuban lover with the permanent stiffie.

Not that she had hurt for attention on the tour. There'd been that body-building cameraman in Miami, brick-shithouse beautiful and full of surprises. And that cute kid in Washington who'd taken her to dinner, entrusted her with his virginity, and driven her to the airport the next morning, whistling all the way. She'd done all right for herself, horizontally speaking.

She mounted the scales in the bathroom, almost afraid to look.

A hundred and ninety-two! Her worst fears confirmed! Thanks to the rigors of the tour, she was losing weight like crazy. If she didn't shape up and soon, the headline writers would lose their two-hundred-pound sex symbol and she—shudder, gasp—would be out on her ever-dwindling ass.

She savored this preposterous dilemma, then washed her face with a violet-scented English soap.

Soon there would be blueberry pancakes to set things right again.

Forty-five minutes later, she waited for her limousine on the curb in front of the Fairmont. She was decked out in her favorite touring ensemble: a low-necked turquoise sweater dress cinched at the waist by a brown leather cummerbund.

The cummerbund and her boots—Victorian-style lace-up numbers—gave her, she felt, the air of a good-natured dominatrix. As her nerves grew increasingly ragged, she needed all the authority she could muster when she faced her interrogators.

Her driver was a welcome surprise: young and dark, with pronounced Italianate influences and a set of lips she could chew on all night. As he whisked her down California Street toward her rendez-vous with today's anchoroid, she asked him what he knew about the show.

"Not a whole helluva lot," he replied. "Just . . . it's called *Mary Ann in the Morning.*"

She let out a faint groan. She could picture the little fluffball already.

"My old lady watches it," said the driver. "It's real popular. She has on . . . you know, stars like yourself . . . Lee Iacocca, Shirley MacLaine, that kid o' Pat Boone's with the barf disease . . ."

"Right," she said.

"I saw you on Carson the other night."

"Oh . . . did you?" She hated it when they left you dangling. What the hell were you supposed to say?

"You were good."

"Thanks."

"We're the same age. I noticed that right off. You're twenty-eight and I'm twenty-eight."

"No shit."

He laughed and peered over his shoulder at her. "My ol' lady's big too, ya know?"

"Yeah?"

"Not as big as you, I mean. Not as big as I'd like her to be."

"I hear you," she said.

"I like 'em really big. Like you . . . if you don't mind my saying."

She found her little egg of Obsession, gave her tits a quick squirt, and lowered her voice an octave. "Not at all," she said.

"I didn't wanna sound like I was . . ."

"What's on our schedule this afternoon?"

"You mean . . . after this show?"

"Yeah."

He thought for a moment. "Just a personal appearance."

"Where?"

"You know . . . one of those Pretty and Plump shops on the peninsula."

She dropped the atomizer into her purse. "And then we're done until tomorrow?"

"Right."

"So . . . we've got time."

She noticed that he swerved the wheel a little, but he recovered instantly and curled those edible lips into a comprehending smile. "Sure," he said. "We got time."

Things went smoothly enough at the television station until the makeup man tried to camouflage her chins with darker makeup. "These babies," she told him sweetly, "are my bread and butter. What will people think if I'm obviously trying to hide them?"

"It won't be obvious, hon. You'll see. It's Light Egyptian, very subtle. Lena Horne uses it all over."

"Sweetie," she said patiently, "my chins and I are not of different races. If we were, I'd call them The Supremes or something, but we're not, OK?" He looked a little wounded, so she added: "Nice Swatch. Is it Keith Haring?"

He glanced down at his watch and answered with a lackluster "Yeah."

"Look," she said, trying another tactic. "You can go for broke when you do my eyes. How 'bout that? Turquoise, gold, whatever. There must be something you've always wanted to try."

As she'd expected, this did the trick. She had offered herself up as a palette, and the artist could not be contained. His eyes grew bright with obsession as he plunged into the depths of his kit. "I think there's an Aztec Gold in here . . . that on the lips, very lightly down the center."

"Super," she said.

"And a little pale purple powder just under the eyes."

"There you go."

Sometimes it seemed there wasn't a man on earth she couldn't handle.

An associate producer led her into the green room, which was peach and cream this time, with loads of hideous seventies Deco. On the walls were huge framed photographs of the fabled Mary Ann: Mary Ann with Raquel Welch, Mary Ann with Dr. Ruth, Mary Ann with Ed Koch, Mary Ann with Michael Landon.

"Make yourself at home," said the associate producer, backing toward the door. "There's coffee there . . . and sweet rolls and whatever. Mary Ann will drop by to say hello in a little while."

"Am I the only guest?" she asked.

He nodded. "Except for Ikey St. Jacques. We're taping him for 'Latchkey Kitchen.'"

"What's that?"

"One of our segments. Fifteen minutes at the end. Famous kids come on and . . . you know, teach latchkey kids how to cook for themselves while their parents are out working."

"Come on," said Wren.

"It's very popular." He sounded a little defensive. "We've had offers to syndicate it."

Wren tried to picture the tiny black star of *What It Is!* whipping up a quick-and-easy tuna casserole. "He's such a baby," she said. "He can't be a day over seven."

"Uh . . . look . . . I'm kind of rushed right now. I hope you don't mind if I leave you on your own for a while."

He was flustered about something, she could tell. "I'll be fine," she said. "Are you kidding? Alone with all this food?"

Laughing uncomfortably, the associate producer backed out the door and closed it. She puzzled over his behavior for a moment, then headed straight for the sweet rolls, remembering her dwindling weight. She had downed one and was repairing her lips with a napkin the next time the door opened.

"Awwriiiight, mama!"

It was Ikey St. Jacques, grinning like a jack-o'-lantern and cute as the devil in his tiny red-and-white workout suit. His hands were outstretched, Jolson-style, and one of them held a lighted cigar.

She tried to stay cool. "Uh . . . hi. You're Ikey . . . right?"

"I knew it," he said with a husky chuckle. "That fool lied to me."

"Who?"

"That candy-ass producer out there. He knows I like big mamas, so he lied to me, the sucker! I knew you was in here." He took a long drag on his cigar and looked her up and down. His head was no higher than her waist. "I saw you on Carson. I said to my agent, that is one foxy lady."

She wasn't buying this at all. "Look, junior . . ." She flailed toward the cigar. "Those things make me sick. The entrance was cute, but the bit is over."

He regarded her dolefully for a moment, then went to the table, reached up and stubbed out the cigar.

"Thank you," she said, extending her hand. "Now . . . I'm Wren Douglas."

He shook her hand. "Sorry 'bout that."

"Hey . . . no biggie."

"I come on strong sometimes. Don't know why."

She was beginning to feel like a bully. "Well, it was just that cigar. You ought not to smoke those, even for a joke. It'll—"

"Stunt my growth?" He laughed raucously. "I'm seventeen years old, lady!"

"Wait a minute. Says who?"

"Says me and my birth certificate. And my mama."

She drew back and studied him. "Nah. Sorry. No way. I'm not buyin' that."

"You think I'm lyin?'"

She shifted her weight to one hip and appraised him coolly. "Yeah. I think you're lyin'."

He glared at her defiantly and shoved his sweat pants down to his knees.

She took stock of the point he was making and responded as calmly as possible. "OK . . . Fine . . . we've established your maturity."

The kid wouldn't budge, arms still folded across his chest. "Say I'm seventeen!"

She glanced anxiously toward the door. "Pull your pants up, Ikey."

"Say I'm seventeen."

"Ikey, if somebody walks in here we could be arrested for . . . I don't know what. All right, big deal. You're seventeen. I'm sorry. I was wrong."

A half-lidded smile bloomed on the kid's face as he returned his sweat pants to their rightful position.

Wren clapped her hand to her chest and heaved a little whinny of relief. "God," she muttered to no one in particular.

Ikey moved to the table and picked up a sweet roll almost as big as his face.

"It seems to me," said Wren, now angered by his nonchalance, "you could find a subtler way to tell people."

The kid licked the edge of the pastry, then shrugged. "Saves talk."

"Don't give me that."

Another shrug.

"You *like* doing it."

He set the roll down and fixed her with the same sweet spaniel gaze he used on his television father. "Lady, if you spent your whole fucking life impersonating a seven-year-old, you'd rip your pants off every now and then, too."

She smiled, realizing his predicament for the first time. "Yeah, I probably would."

"I'm a fan of yours," he added. "I don't wanna fight with you."

She was embarrassed now. "Look . . . everything's cool, Ikey."

"Isaac."

"Isaac," she echoed.

"Can I light my cigar now?"

"No way." She softened this ultimatum with another smile. "I really can't handle 'em, Isaac."

He nodded. "Are you mad 'cause I called you foxy?"

"Not a bit. I appreciate that."

"Well, I appreciate what you're doing for . . . people who don't fit the mold."

In half a dozen words, he had explained the bond that linked them; she was unexpectedly moved. "Hey . . . what the hell. I *like* doing it. I mean, most of the time. This is the end of a tour, so I'm a little antsy, I guess. You know how that can be." She wanted this to sound like a confidence shared with another professional.

He emitted a froggy chuckle. "Yeah."

"I watch your show all the time," she said.

This seemed to please him. "You do?"

"I think you're amazingly believable. Most TV kids are so cloying, you know . . . too cute for words. Plus, I like your scripts."

He gave her a businesslike nod. "They're gettin' better, I think." He hesitated a moment, then said: "Look, can I ask you something?"

"Shoot," she said.

"I don't want you to get pissed off again."

She smiled at him. "I'm over that now. Don't worry." As a matter of fact, she felt completely comfortable around him. He'd done nothing but tell her the truth. "Go ahead," she said. "Ask away."

After another significant pause, he said: "Can I put my hand . . . in there?" He was pointing to her cleavage.

She pursed her lips and scrutinized his face. That spaniel look was doing its number again. "For how long?" she asked.

He shrugged. "Twenty seconds."

"Ten," she counter-offered.

"OK."

"And no jiggling." She bent over to afford him easier access. "Make it quick. We've got a show to do."

Isaac's arm was engulfed to the elbow when the door to the greenroom swung open. The dumbfounded woman who stood there was the woman whose likeness adorned the walls. "Oh . . . excuse me. I . . ."

"Hey," said Wren. "No problem." She removed Isaac's arm with a single movement and straightened up. "I lost an earring." She reached down and gave the kid's shoulder a pat. "Thanks just the same, Ikey. I'll look for it later."

The television hostess became a stalagmite, then cast her stony gaze in Isaac's direction. "The director wants to see you on the kitchen set, Ikey."

The kid said "Yo" and strode toward the door. He gave Wren a high sign as he left.

"Well," said Wren, turning back to the anchoroid, "you must be Mary Ann."

The woman wouldn't melt. "You must be sick," she said.

"Now wait a minute."

"I've done shows on child molestation, but I never thought I would—"

"That child," said Wren, "is seventeen years old!"

"Well, I don't see what . . . Who told you that?"

"He did."

Thrown, the anchoroid thought for a moment, then said: "And I suppose that makes it all right."

"No," Wren replied evenly. "That makes it none of your business."

Member in Good Standing

The show hadn't gone as Michael had expected. Instead of a free-wheeling romp, there'd been stiffness and long silences and palpable tension in the air. The trouble had begun, he suspected, when Mary Ann introduced Wren Douglas to the studio audience as "the woman who's shown America how to make the most of a weight problem."

Whatever the cause, something had soured the interview beyond repair, so he decided against requesting an introduction after the show. Mary Ann had already obliged him with introductions to Huey Lewis, Scott Madsen and Tina Turner. There was nothing to be gained by abusing the privilege.

Besides, it was eleven-fifteen, and he had a nursery to run.

The place had been his since 1984, when his partner, Ned Lockwood, had moved back to LA. The exhilaration of ownership had been a new experience for Michael, prompting him to renovate and expand beyond his wildest imaginings. He had built a new greenhouse for the succulents, then enlarged the office, then changed the name from God's Green Earth to Plant Parenthood.

The only problem with being sole proprietor, he had long ago discovered, was that you couldn't call in sick to yourself. To make matters worse, his three employees at the nursery (two other gay men and a lesbian) knew subtle ways to trigger his guilt whenever he showed up late for work.

Actually, he relished his time at the nursery. The busyness of business helped him to forget how much he missed what had come to be known as "the unsafe exchange of bodily fluids."

If he remained idle too long, his euphoric past could creep up on him like a Frenchman pushing postcards, a portfolio of fading erotica fully capable of breaking his nostalgic heart.

It wasn't just an epidemic anymore; it was a famine, a starvation of the spirit, which sooner or later afflicted everyone. Some people capitulated to the terror, turning inward in their panic, avoiding the gaze of strangers on the street. Others adopted a sort of earnest gay fraternalism, enacting the rituals of safe-sex orgies with all the clinical precision of Young Pioneers dismantling their automatic weapons.

Lots of people found relief on the telephone, mutually Master-charging until Nirvana was achieved. Phone sex, Michael had observed, not only toned the imagination but provided men with an option that had heretofore been unavailable to them: *faking an orgasm.*

Michael himself had once faked an orgasm over the phone. Unable to come, yet mindful of his manners, he had growled out his ecstasy for at least half a minute, pounding on his headboard for added effect. His partner (someone in Teaneck, New Jersey) had been so audibly appreciative of the performance that Michael fell asleep afterwards feeling curiously satiated.

Most of the time, though, he ended up in bed with the latest issue of *Inches* or *Advocate Men*, his genitals cinched in the cord of his terrycloth bathrobe.

He had learned several interesting things about pornography. Namely: (1) it wore out; (2) it reactivated itself if you looked at it upside down; and (3) you could recycle it if you put it away for several months.

Unlike most of his friends, he did not have sex regularly with a VCR. He had done that once or twice, but only at a JO buddy's house, and their timing had been so hopelessly out of sync that his only memory was of lunging through the sheets in search of the fast-forward button.

"What are you doing?" his buddy had asked when the video images accelerated and Al Parker and friends became the Keystone Kops.

Michael had replied: "I'm looking for that cowboy near the end."

And this was what bothered him about owning a VCR. If that cowboy was yours for the taking—yours at the flip of a switch—what was to stop you from abandoning human contact altogether?

He had taken the test in April, and it had come back positive. That is, he was carrying the virus or had already fought it off, one or the other. According to some doctors, this gave him (and a million others) a 10 to 25 percent chance of developing a full-blown case, but other doctors disagreed.

What did doctors know?

All he knew was that his health was fine. No night sweats or sluggishness. No unusual weight loss or mysterious purple blotches. He ate his vegetables and popped his vitamins and kept stress to a minimum. For a man who'd lost twelve friends and a lover in less than three years, he was doing all right.

Just the same, a mild case of the flu or the slightest furriness of the tongue was now capable of filling him with abject terror. The other paramount emotion, grief, became more and more unpredictable as the numbers grew. His tears could elude him completely at the bedside of a dying friend, only to surface weeks later during a late-night Marilyn Monroe movie on TV.

And people talked of nothing else. Who has it. Who thinks he has it. Who's positive. Who couldn't *possibly* be negative. Who will never take the test. Who's almost ready to take the test.

To get away from the tragedy—and the talk—some of his friends had moved to places like Phoenix and Charlottesville, but Michael couldn't see the point of it. The worst of times in San Francisco was still better than the best of times anywhere else.

There was beauty here and conspicuous bravery and civilized straight people who were doing their best to help. It was also his home, when all was said and done. He loved this place with a deep and unreasoning passion; the choice was no longer his.

When he reached the nursery, a renegade Pinto was parked in his usual place out front. He spotted Polly among the arborvitae, clipping a can for a customer, and tapped the horn gently to get her attention. "Someone we know?" he hollered, pointing toward the offending car.

His young employee set her clippers down and wiped her brow with the back of her hand. "David's new squeeze," she yelled back. "I'll get him to move it."

He could see another parking space at the end of the block, so he decided not to make an issue of it. "That's OK," he told her. "Don't break up the lovebirds." It was lunchtime, after all, and David and his new beau were undoubtedly in the greenhouse making goo-goo eyes over Big Macs.

He parked and walked back to the nursery in the toasty sunshine. Polly was on the sidewalk now, hefting the arborvitae into the back of the customer's station wagon. "Sorry about that. Didn't know you'd be back so soon."

"No problem," he said.

Brushing the dirt off her hands, Polly followed him to the office. "How did it go? Did you bring me a lipstick print?"

"Shit," he murmured, remembering his promise.

"You didn't," she said calmly. "That's OK."

"I didn't meet her," he explained. "She and Mary Ann had rotten chemistry, so I decided not to risk it."

Polly shrugged.

"You're disappointed," he said. "I'm really sorry." So far she had cajoled lipstick prints from Linda Evans, Kathleen Turner and Diana Ross.

"Was she gorgeous?" Polly asked, leaning dreamily against the cash register.

"Yeah," he answered. "In a Fellini sort of way." He thought it wise to downplay the thrill of it all.

Polly sighed. "She's welcome in my movie any ol' day."

He amused himself by picturing the confrontation: the voluptuously rotund Wren Douglas putting the moves on pretty Polly Berendt, muscular yet petite in her faded green coveralls. "Well," he said, "she shows every sign of being hopelessly het."

"So?" said Polly. "I'm no separatist."

He laughed. The new lesbian adventurism was a source of endless amusement to him. If gay men could no longer snort and paw the ground in fits of purple passion, it seemed only fitting that gay women could. *Somebody* had to keep the spirit alive.

Polly slipped her hand around his waist and pressed her freckled face against his shoulder. "I want a wife, Michael. I want one bad."

"Yeah, yeah."

"Is it because I'm twenty-two? Is that what it is? Were you this way when you were twenty-two?"

"I was that way when I was thirty-two, but I got over it."

She tilted her face toward him. "My friend Kara went to a psychic last month, and she said that Kara's true love would show up within the month . . . and that she'd be driving a golden chariot."

"Right."

"I swear this is true. Kara met this girl called Weegie last month and they've been inseparable ever since."

"What about the golden chariot?"

"She was driving a Yellow Cab!"

He snorted.

"Kara called a cab from DV8 and Weegie drove up, and that was it. Wedded bliss. Me . . . I look and look and end up with some former battered wife who takes me to see *The Women* at the Castro and hisses at all the sexist parts."

"Why are you telling me this?" he asked.

She hesitated, then said: "Cuz I wanna go to Wimminwood."

"Where?"

"A women's music festival up at the river."

He shrugged. "Go. You've got vacation coming. What's the problem?"

"Well . . . it's next week, when you're on vacation."

He saw her point; that left only David and Robbie to run the nursery.

"I really wanna go, Michael."

"Sure, but . . ."

"I've talked to Kevin," she added. "He says he'll be glad to stand in for me."

"Who's Kevin?"

She jerked her head toward the greenhouse. "David's new squeeze. He's had experience."

"He works at Tower Records, I thought."

"Yeah, but he's off next week . . . and he used to do gardening for an admiral when he was in the navy, and . . . C'mon, Michael, don't make me miss this opportunity."

He smiled at her. "Thousands of half-naked women going berserk in the redwoods."

"No!" she protested. "Some of them are *totally* naked."

He laughed. "You don't sound like somebody looking for a wife."

Actually, she reminded him of himself years ago, relishing the prospect of a weekend of lust at the National Gay Rodeo in Reno.

David's new boyfriend stayed at Plant Parenthood for the rest of the afternoon, making himself useful in the fertilizer shed. He was industrious, cheerful and seemingly honest. Michael saw no reason why he wouldn't serve as an adequate substitute for Polly.

At four twenty-five, Teddy Roughton called. "It's late notice," he said, "but there's a JO party at Joe's tonight. I thought you'd wanna know."

Michael felt faintly embarrassed. "Thanks, Teddy. I think I'll pass."

"Why?"

"I don't know. Those things make me feel . . . self-conscious or something."

Teddy clucked his tongue like a disapproving English matron. "Foolish, foolish boy . . ."

"I know, but . . ."

"He's got brilliant visuals, Michael. That chap from the Muscle System is coming."

Michael thought for a moment. "The one with . . . ?"

"That's riiight. And if that's not enough for you, Joe's rented *One in a Billion*."

"Fine, but . . ."

"Think about it, at least. All right?" He might have been recruiting for a parish bake sale. "Eight o'clock. Joe's house. We'll see you if we see you."

The weather was unnaturally balmy at closing time, so Michael took down the top of his VW for the ride home. Tooling along Clement, he marveled at the warm silkiness of the air against his face. This was nothing less than a true summer evening, and the city smelled of steaks and hibiscus. His loins took note of the tropicality and began to lobby for their rights.

You remember that guy, they said, *that stud from the Muscle System with the beer-can dick and the pecs that won't quit. What would it hurt to sit in the same room with him? OK, to sit there naked with him and two dozen naked guys and beat the old* . . . No, it was too embarrassing.

Think of it as the Explorers, his loins argued. *That camping trip in north Georgia, 1961. Guys around the campfire, weary from the hike. The sunburned necks, the smell of Off, Billy Branson's perfect smile flashing in the firelight, tantalizing beyond belief. The circle jerk that almost happened but didn't.*

Well, now it could happen.

When he arrived at 28 Barbary Lane, Mrs. Madrigal confronted him on the landing. "You'd better hurry," she said. "It starts in less than an hour."

He felt his jaw go slack. If she wasn't a closet clairvoyant, she sure as hell acted like one.

"I heard about it on the radio," she explained, as if that took care of things.

"You heard about what?" he asked.

"The welcome home," she said, "for those gay hostages."

The light dawned. Two of the thirty-nine American tourists held hostage by terrorists in Beirut had proved to be gay San Franciscans—lovers, no less. Upon their return to the States, they had faced the cameras as a couple, beaming proudly, moments before accepting the unconditional gratitude of Ronald and Nancy Reagan.

Michael had thrilled to the sight and had told Mrs. Madrigal as much.

"Where's the ceremony?" he asked.

"Eighteenth and Castro," she said. "They're blocking off the street."

He did some hasty calculation. The JO party was on Noe at Twenty-first, only four blocks up the hill from the rally. If he hurried, the evening might be made to accommodate both the erotic and the patriotic. "Thanks for the tip," he told his landlady.

She bent and picked up a plastic bucket full of cleaning gear. "Well, I thought you'd want to know, dear."

He pointed to the bucket. "Did Boris barf on the stairwell again?"

She chuckled. "Brian's nephew is staying with us for a few days."

"His nephew? Is he . . . grown?" Everything made him feel older these days. At thirty-four, he still had trouble remembering that some of his contemporaries were the parents of teenagers.

"He's nineteen," said Mrs. Madrigal. "I'm fixing up Mary Ann and Brian's old place for him. Perhaps later you could give me a hand with that twin bed in the basement?"

"Sure," he answered. "Yeah . . . sure . . . be glad to."

His antsiness must have been obvious, for the landlady smiled at him. "I won't keep you," she said. "I know you've got a busy, busy evening."

That extra "busy" made him wonder again.

Back at his apartment, he took a quick shower and trimmed his mustache. Tonight especially, he was glad he hadn't shaved his mustache when everyone else had. It suited him, he felt, so to hell with the fashion victims who found him lacking in the new-wave department.

When it came time to dress, he dug to the bottom of his bottom drawer and found his oldest 501s. The denim was chamois smooth and parchment thin, and the very feel of it against his legs filled him with exquisite melancholy.

He left undone the middle button of his fly, just for old times' sake.

When he reached the Castro, he found a parking place on the steep part of Noe, then strode downhill in the direction of the music. On a platform in front of the Hibernia Bank, a gay chorale was already singing "America the Beautiful." Hundreds of people, some of them crying, had gathered in the street.

He wriggled through the crowd until he could catch a glimpse of the hostage/lovers. One was lean and blond and bearded. The other was also bearded, but he was darker and somewhat older, more of a daddy type. Michael could picture them together quite easily. He could see them on that hijacked plane, desperate when death seemed imminent, passing love notes under the murderous gaze of their captors.

Then the gay band broke into the national anthem, and the crowd began to sing. Michael noticed how many couples there were, how many broad backs settled against broad chests as tenor voices filled the warm night. The world was pairing off these days, no doubt about it.

The hostages took turns at the podium. They talked about home and family and the need for expressing love openly. Then they asked for a moment of silence for the sailor who'd been killed on their plane. When it was over, Michael wiped his eyes and checked his watch. He was already half an hour late for the JO party.

He strode briskly at first, then began to run up Castro as the band blared forth with "If My Friends Could See Me Now." At Nineteenth, he cut across Noe and completed his ascent to Joe's apartment. The house, as he'd remembered, was a potentially handsome Victorian that had been hideously eisenhowered with green asbestos shingles.

He caught his breath for a moment, then pressed the buzzer. Joe came to the door wearing nothing but cut-offs. "Oh . . . Michael. You're a little late, fella."

"It's over?"

"No. Just sort of . . . Round Two. C'mon in."

Michael entered the dark foyer and lowered his voice to a whisper. "Sorry," he said. "I was singing the national anthem and the time got away from me."

If his host appreciated the irony, he didn't remark on it. "Take your clothes off out here. Stack your stuff on the stairs." He slapped Michael's butt and slipped behind the bedspread separating the foyer from the parlor.

Michael stripped, piling his T-shirt, jeans and boots next to a dozen similar groupings on the stairs. He faced the hall mirror and checked himself briefly—for *what*? he wondered—before pulling aside the bedspread to greet his public.

The men were slouched on sofas and chairs arranged in a crude crescent in front of the TV set. On the screen, two men in business suits were sucking cock in an elevator. A few heads swiveled in Michael's direction, but most remained fixed on the movie, intent on the business at hand.

He scanned the room for available seating. Nothing was left but the middle section of a sofa on the far side of the room. Heading there, he passed in front of the TV set, and it occurred to him—perversely— that someone might shout "Down in front!" just to embarrass him.

No one did. He sat on the sofa, nodding gravely to his sofa mates, then glanced discreetly around the room at the other participants. This was Round Two, all right. As Teddy might have put it, there were very few members in good standing.

In a La-Z-Boy next to the window sat Teddy himself, cock in hand, smirking ruthlessly at the latecomer. Michael looked away from him, fearful of losing the moment altogether.

After a while, he got into it. There were some hot guys there— including that number from Muscle System—and the porn video suited his tastes perfectly. Once his self-consciousness had passed, he began to savor the sensation he had missed so dearly, the lost tribalism of years gone by. It wasn't the way it used to be, but it stirred a few memories just the same.

He was on the verge of coming when two men next to Teddy's La-Z-Boy rose and left the room. They were followed, moments later, by three others. Presently a small din was emanating from the foyer, where the dressing ceremonies had begun.

The guttural commands and primal grunts of the video were no match at all for the brunch being planned beyond the bedspread. "Don't do pasta salad," someone said quite audibly. "You did that last time and everybody hated it."

The fantasy collapsed like a house of dirty playing cards. As Teddy exited through a sliding door to the dining room, Michael caught his eye with a rueful smile. Teddy leaned over and whispered in his ear: "There's no such thing as being fashionably late for a JO party."

There were two other men left in the room. One of them, the Muscle System hunk, was watching the screen with unblinking singlemindedness; the other, in similar fashion, was watching Michael watch the hunk. It was getting too intimate, Michael decided, so he gave up the effort and left.

He dressed hurriedly, avoiding conversation, then remembered his manners and thanked the host. As he headed down Noe toward his car, he stopped long enough to admire the reddish remnants of a sunset behind Twin Peaks.

He could still hear the music down at Eighteenth and Castro.

A Handsome Offer

Wren Douglas and the limousine driver had watched the sunset from her big bed at the Fairmont. The ripening nectarine sky had been a perfect backdrop for their postcoital cuddling, a pagan benediction of sorts.

"Does it do that often?" she asked.

"Sometimes," he replied. "When the weather's warm like this."

Idly, she massaged his temples with her fingertips, then worked her way up to his scalp. He gave a little faux-Stallone moan and re-positioned his head against her chest, as if he were plumping pillows. His dark, curly hair was pungent with Tenax.

"This would make a fabulous ending," she said. "The credits should be rolling over that sunset. Here endeth the book tour."

"Two more cities," he mumbled.

She gave his cheek a reproving whack. "Don't remind me."

"Portland and Seattle, right?"

"Yeah."

"You don't wanna do it?"

"I wanna do nothing," she said. "I wanna lie around and be a total slug."

The bedside phone rang, mangling her reverie. "That's my publicist," she said. "I'll put money on it." With one hand still buried in the driver's curls, she grabbed the receiver and barked into it. "Yes, Nicholas my love, I'm still alive and I'm still on schedule."

There was no immediate response, no telltale bleat of laugh-ter from the adenoidal Nicholas, so she realized her guess had been wrong. Eventually, the caller said: "I beg your pardon. I'm trying to reach Miss Douglas . . . Miss Wren Douglas?"

"You got her," she replied. "I thought you were somebody else."

"Oh," said the caller.

"What can I do for you?"

"Well . . . I have some business I'd like to discuss with you. My name is Roger Manigault. I'm chairman of the board of Pacific Ex-celsior."

Excelsior? What? The packing material? What could a fat girl do for an excelsior company? "Sorry," she said. "Never heard of it." Using her free forefinger, she traced the fleshy oval of the driver's lips, then popped the finger into his mouth. He sucked on it oblig-ingly.

"We make aluminum honeycomb," explained the caller. "Among other things."

She didn't know what that was and she didn't care. "Oh . . . right. Why don't I give you my agent's number? You can tell her what you've got in mind. This really isn't the best time to discuss . . ."

"I'm in the lobby, Miss Douglas. I know this is irregular, but . . . time is of the essence. If I could have just ten minutes with you."

She looked down at the classic features of the fallen Pompeiian sprawled against her chest. "Look, Mr . . . whatever. Maybe if you call tomorrow . . ."

"There's a handsome fee involved."

She hesitated a moment, remembering her lust for shoes, envisioning how her Chicago loft would look with pink neon tubing around the windows. "Oh, yeah?" she said. "How handsome?"

The driver looked up at her and narrowed his eyes. She smirked and gave his earlobe a wiggle.

"Five thousand dollars," said the caller. "For three or four days of your time."

"Look, Mr. . . ."

"Ten thousand, then."

She muffled the receiver and spoke to the driver. "Find my Filofax, would you, doll? I think it's in the other room."

The driver looked puzzled.

"My appointment book," she explained. "It's in one of the drawers. Just check, OK?"

When he was out of the room, she uncovered the receiver and said: "Look, does this involve sex?"

The caller seemed prepared for that question. "No," he said quietly and almost immediately. "I can explain things better if you'll meet me downstairs. I'm in the Cirque Room."

"What's that?"

"The bar," he replied, "in the lobby."

"Fine. I'll see you there in fifteen minutes. What do you look like?"

"Um . . ." He faltered for a moment. "I'm wearing a gray pin-striped suit . . . and I have white hair and a white mustache."

"I'll find you." She hung up the phone.

The driver appeared in the doorway with her Filofax. "This what you mean?"

"That's it," she said.

He laid the Filofax on the bedside table and hopped under the covers with her. "So what's this shit about handsome?"

"A handsome *offer*," she replied, tweaking his cheek, "not a handsome man. Don't get that pretty Neapolitan nose out of joint."

"What kind of offer?"

"I don't know," she said, climbing out of bed, "but I'm about to find out."

After some indecision, she donned a pale blue sailor dress with puffed sleeves and a dropped waist. It was cute and becoming (without being overtly sexy) and would do nicely for a business meeting.

As she tied the big floppy bow, the driver spoke to her languidly from the bed. "You comin' back?"

"You bet. Wanna stick around?"

He nodded. "How long?"

"Dunno. He's down in the bar. Hour or so, I guess." She patted the bow into place, then turned to face him. "Isn't your wife expecting you?"

He shook his head. "Tonight is PTA."

She slipped into her shoes and headed for the door, picking up her purse on the way. "Keep the bed warm. There's some champagne and Almond Roca in the fridge if you get hungry."

Down in the Cirque Room, she had no trouble spotting her mysterious caller. He sat ramrod straight in a corner banquette, so markedly military in his bearing that she half expected to find epaulets on his business suit. She guessed him to be about seventy.

He shot to his feet when he saw her approaching. This effort at gallantry—or at least *his* idea of gallantry—was far more endearing than she might have imagined. She smiled at him, then knelt by the glass he had knocked off the table, scooping up the scattered ice cubes.

"Please," he said, growing flustered, "don't do that."

She looked up at him. "Why the hell not?"

A waitress approached. "We have a little accident here?"

"I'm such a klutz," said Wren, glancing up at the waitress. "You'd think I could sit down without knocking the gentleman's drink over."

The waitress took the glass from her, then looked at the old man. "What was it, sir? I'll get you another."

"Scotch and water," he told her. "And whatever the lady's having."

Something kick-ass was in order, she decided, slipping into the banquette. "I'll take the same," she said, then turned back to the man. "Your name makes no sense to me."

He didn't understand.

"Pacific Excelsior," she explained. "I thought excelsior was packing straw."

"Oh no. In this instance it's a Latin word meaning 'ever upward.'"

She winked at him. "I knew that." She extended her hand and waited until he shook it. "Wren Douglas," she said. "And your name again is . . . ?"

"Boo . . . Roger Manigault."

"Boo-Roger. Interesting. Never heard that one before."

He smiled for the first time. "Some of my friends call me Booter. That's what I'm used to."

"Booter, huh? Why?"

"I played football," he replied. "Years ago. At Stanford."

"I like it. Can I call you that?"

"If you like."

She laid her hands on the table, palms down, and made a smoothing motion. "So . . . what's this about ten thousand dollars?"

He faltered, then said: "I have . . . well, a very comfortable lodge up in the redwoods. I'd like you to be my guest there for a few days."

She studied him for a while, then gave him a rueful, worldly chuckle.

"I'm on the level," he said, reddening noticeably.

She shook her head slowly. "You lied to me, Booter. You've been a bad boy."

"I wanted you to meet me first. Before you said no."

"Get real," she said, just as the waitress returned with their drinks. She nursed hers for a while, saying nothing, regarding him out of the corner of her eye.

"I've never done anything like this," he said.

"That's a comfort," she replied drily.

"Do you think I would . . . do this, if . . ."

"Where did you see me?" she asked.

He looked confused. "What do you mean?"

"What set this off?" She laughed. "I mean, ten thousand dollars, Booter. That ain't whoremongering, that's . . . Christ, I don't know what it is."

"You're not a whore," he said glumly.

"Answer the question."

He looked down at his drink. "I saw your picture in *Newsweek*. I think you're an extraordinarily lovely woman."

She nodded slowly. "So you read my book and decided: What the hell—maybe I'll have a shot at it."

"No," he said.

"What?"

"I haven't read your book."

She drew back, affronted for the first time all evening.

"I stay busy," he explained apologetically. "There's time for a little Louis L'Amour but not much else."

"Are you married?" she asked.

"Yes."

"Are you really . . . you know . . . chairman of the board and all that?"

338

"You can check me out," he said. "I'm not a lunatic." He looked at her earnestly. "I'm sorry if I insulted you. I'm a rich man, but not a young one. I wanted to make it worth your while."

"Oh, please," she murmured, rolling her eyes.

He stood up to leave. "Let's forget I ever—"

"Sit down," she ordered, seizing his hand. It was large and fleshy, surprisingly strong.

He obeyed her.

"How old are you?" she asked.

"Seventy-one," he replied.

"I've had lovers that old," she said. "You'd know that if you'd read my book."

Generation Gap

Brian's nephew turned out to be a lanky redhead, as soberly and self-consciously devoted to the Wet Look as Brian had once been to the Dry. Jed was an average-looking kid, barely rescued from dorkiness by a rudimentary grasp of current teen fashion. (He affected hightop Reeboks of varying hues and let his shirttails hang out beneath his crew-neck sweaters.)

For some reason, Brian felt a little sorry for him.

"So," he said one night after dinner, "you're a sophomore next year, huh?"

Jed nodded, finishing off the last piece of pizza. They were seated at a card table Mrs. Madrigal had hauled up from the basement. Except for a bookshelf and a battered sofa, this was the only furniture in the candlelit room. Here and there, the landlady had compensated for the austerity by cramming jelly jars with yellow roses from her garden.

"I remember my sophomore year," Brian offered, trying to draw the kid out. "I screwed around the whole time. The ol' freshman terror had gone, and the girls started lookin' good."

No response. Zilch.

He tried again: "Guess things haven't changed all that much, huh?"

"I party some," answered Jed, measuring out his words, "but I have to keep my grades up if I want to be competitive in the job market."

Oh, right, thought Brian. Spoken like a true automaton of the state.

"Cissie and I have worked out a plan."

"Cissie's your girl?"

The kid nodded. "We wanna get married my first year in law school and start a family and all. But that takes money, so I figure I'd better graduate with at least a three point six or I won't get into Harvard Law School. The more prestigious firms never hire out of the . . . you know, minor law schools."

Brian repressed an urge to stick his finger down his throat.

"You gotta plan," added Jed. "Families cost money."

"Right."

"Of course, I don't need to tell *you* that. Look how long you and Mary Ann had to wait."

This observation was not so much malicious as naive, Brian decided. "We didn't have to wait," he said quietly. "It's what we both wanted. We were both in our thirties when we married."

"Wow," said Jed, as if he were digesting an entry from the *Guinness Book of World Records*.

Brian took the offensive, intent upon liberating the kid. "I enjoyed my time as a bachelor. It taught me a helluva lot about myself and the world. I think I'm a better husband because of it."

"Yeah," said Jed, "but wasn't life kind of . . . empty?"

"No. Hell, no." This wasn't entirely true, but he hated the kid's priggish tone. "I was an independent man. Sex helped make me that way."

Confronted with this hopelessly old-fashioned concept, Jed smiled indulgently.

"It's the truth," said Brian. "Didn't you feel more . . . in charge of yourself the first time you got it on with a girl?"

The kid tugged at the cuff of his sweater. "There weren't any girls before Cissie."

"OK, then . . . the first time you got it on with Cissie."

Silence.

Brian studied his nephew's face, where the awful truth was blooming like acne. "Hell, I'm sorry . . . I didn't . . . I mean, lots of guys . . ."

Jed greeted his stammering with another faint smile, more smug than the last. "It's a matter of choice, Brian."

"Oh . . . well . . ."

"We don't believe in premarital sex. Neither one of us."

Premarital sex? He couldn't recall having heard that term since the early sixties, when it ceased to be a racy topic for high-school debate teams. Who was this Cissie bitch, anyway? What gave her the right to pussywhip this innocent kid into a life of marital servitude?

"Jed . . . listen, man . . . maybe it's none of my business, but I think you're making a serious mistake. A little experimentation never hurt anybody. You owe that to yourself, kiddo. How can you be sure about Cissie if . . ."

"I'm sure, Brian. All right?"

Brian shook his head. "There's no way. You're too young. You haven't lived enough."

"I'm not interested in one-night stands," said Jed.

"You're scared," Brian countered, "and that's cool. Everybody's first time is . . ."

"Things are different now, Brian. It's not the way it was with your generation."

Or with your mother's, thought Brian. Sunny had had four lovers and an abortion before she got around to having Jed. How could life have changed so radically in twenty years? "Some things still apply," he told his nephew, hoping to God it was true.

Jed rose and dumped the pizza box into a Hefty bag in the corner. "I've had a long day, Brian." It was clearly a signal for the meddling uncle to leave.

"Yeah," said Brian. "Right." He stood up and went to the

341

door. "I'm up at The Summit if you need a tour guide or anything. Mrs. Madrigal says she'll be glad to answer any questions about the neighborhood."

"Forget that," said Jed. "She's too weird."

Brian didn't bother to reprimand him. Why waste his breath on this tight-assed little bastard?

Ten minutes later, back at The Summit, Mary Ann asked him how dinner had been.

"The pits," he replied.

"Well, I hope you were nice to him."

He gave her a peevish glance. "I was nice to him. He was the one who wasn't nice to me."

"What do you mean?"

"I dunno," he said. "Just rude and uptight." He saw no point in mentioning the virginity part. Mary Ann, no doubt, would find it "sweet."

"He's young," she said, stacking her dishes in the dishwasher.

Her phoney generosity annoyed him. "You want me to invite him over?"

"No," she replied demurely. "Not if you think he's . . . difficult."

"Save your platitudes, then. The kid is an asshole."

She closed the dishwasher and looked at him. "What is your problem, Brian?"

A damn good question. He felt headachy still, and his gut had begun to seize up in a peculiar way. Was this weird fatigue a function of the flu? Or merely a function of being forty-two? Was that what made him so resentful of Jed's unspent youth?

"I'm sorry," he said finally. "My head hurts. I'm getting a bug, I think."

She frowned, then felt his forehead. "There's no fever."

He shrugged and turned away.

"I'll make us some hot chocolate," she said. "Go put your feet up."

342

"No, thanks."

"C'mon," she said. "Don't be so grumpy. It's sugar-free."

A soundless TV was their blazing hearth while she rubbed his feet. "Oh," she said after a long silence, "DeDe called this afternoon. She and D'or want us to come use the pool this Sunday."

He grunted noncommittally. He distrusted his wife's escalating chumminess with the Halcyon-Wilsons, not because they were dykes but because they were rich and social. Mary Ann was simply climbing in this instance, he felt almost certain.

"I thought it would be nice for Shawna," she added, giving his little toe a placatory tug. "I know you aren't crazy about them, but that pool is to die for."

"Whatever," he said.

"C'mon," she cooed. "Don't be like that."

"Fine. We'll go. I might be sick as a dog . . ."

"Oh, poor you." She pressed her thumbs into the arch of his foot. "You'll feel better by then, and—"

A ringing phone silenced her.

Brian reached for it. "Yeah?"

"It's Jed, Brian."

"Oh . . . yeah."

"I just wanted to thank you for bringing the pizza by. And the place and all. You're a real lifesaver."

"Well . . . sure. No sweat."

"You're a terrific uncle. I see why Mom likes you so much."

"Hey . . . no problem. We'll do it again, huh?"

"Sure," said the kid.

"Great. Then we'll—what?—check in with each other tomorrow?"

"You bet."

Brian hung up.

"Jed?" asked Mary Ann.

He nodded.

"He has manners," she said. "You have to admit."

"Yeah," he said absently, retrieving the towel he had thrown in so hastily. The kid, after all, was his own flesh and blood. He deserved a second chance.

Maybe all he really needed was a good piece of ass.

Ladies of the Evening

The Halcyon-Wilsons dined that night at Le Trou, a tiny French restaurant on Guerrero Street.

"It means The Hole," said D'orothea.

DeDe, who was reapplying lipstick, looked up with exaggerated horror. "Ick. What does?"

"The name of the restaurant," said D'orothea. "Stop being misogynistic."

"Misogynous," said DeDe.

"What?"

"The word is 'misogynous,' while you're accusing me. But I fail to see how . . ."

"You were making a hole joke," said D'orothea. "You don't think that's demeaning?"

"Look, *you* brought it up. Besides, you make pussy jokes all the time."

D'orothea stabbed sullenly at her *bijane aux fraises*. "Pussy is friendly. Hole is not."

A woman at the next table looked at them and frowned.

"Tell the world," muttered DeDe. "Better yet, put it on a sampler. 'Pussy is friendly. Hole is not.'"

"All *right*," said D'or.

"You're just mad at me because I don't wanna go to Wimminwood."

"Well . . . I think that's indicative of your larger problem."

"My larger problem?"

"Your total resistance to anything you don't—"

"I told you," said DeDe. "I've already invited Mary Ann and Brian to brunch."

D'or scowled. "That's just an excuse. The fact is . . . you're threatened."

"Oh, right," said DeDe. "By what?"

"By women-only space."

DeDe snorted. "I was in the Junior League, wasn't I?"

D'or's eyes became obsidian. "Don't make fun of this. I won't have it. Wimminwood is very important to me."

"You've never even been there."

"I went to the one in Michigan. I know how it feels, OK? It's part of who I am, and it's . . . something special I want to share with you."

DeDe poked at her dessert. "That's what you told me when we left for Guyana."

Her lover gave her a long, incendiary look. "That was low."

Feeling the reprimand, DeDe looked away.

"You're becoming your mother," D'or added darkly. "Is that what you really want?"

"Talk about *low*," said DeDe.

D'or shrugged. "It's the truth."

"It *is* not. I'm nothing like her."

"Well, you're not a substance abuser." The very phrase was pure lesbianese, epitomizing everything DeDe hated about D'or's reemerging consciousness.

"C'mon, D'or. Can't you just call her a drunk and be done with it?"

This was a bit harsh, DeDe realized. Widowed nine years ago, her mother had struggled valiantly to keep the bottle at bay, never fully capitulating until her remarriage in 1984.

DeDe's stepfather had been their next-door neighbor in Hillsborough for as long as DeDe could remember. (That is, his tennis courts bordered on the apple orchard at Halcyon Hill.) Her mother had married him nine months after the death of his first wife and moved into his rambling postwar ranch house.

That had left the mock-Tudor pile of Halcyon Hill for the sole tenancy of DeDe, D'orothea and the children. Absolutely nobody objected, since her mother and D'or were always at odds, and her mother's new husband had no intention of living under the same roof with his lesbian stepdaughter and her eight-year-old Eurasian twins.

By implicit mutual consent, they got tipsy on white wine spritzers at the Baybrick Inn.

When the floor show began, a sinewy stripper in full police drag made a beeline for their table, bumping and grinding all the way. DeDe giggled uncontrollably as the cop began gesturing lewdly with her nightstick.

"Did you set this up?" she asked her lover.

D'or's eyes were full of mischief. *"Moi?"*

"I'll get you for this. I swear."

"She's waiting. Give her something."

The stripper began to hump the back of DeDe's chair, egged on by the roar of a hundred women.

"Money, you mean?"

"Of course money!"

The cop doffed her helmet and held it out to DeDe, who fumbled frantically in her purse. The crowd was going wild. "D'or . . . how much?"

"The twenty."

"Isn't that a little too . . . ?"

"It's for AIDS. Give it to her."

She placed the bill in the helmet, to the sound of tumultuous applause. To show her gratitude, the cop leaned over and stuck her tongue in DeDe's ear.

"You looked utterly stricken," D'or told her later as they sped home to Hillsborough in their big Bulck station wagon. "I wish I had a picture of it."

DeDe laughed along with her. "Thank God you don't."

346

When the city lights were gone and the highway became a dark ribbon through the hills, they both fell silent for the final stretch, with DeDe stealing occasional glances at the volatile, loving woman behind the wheel.

"D'or?" she said at last.

"Yeah?"

"Could we take the children?"

"Where?"

"Wimminwood."

D'or turned and smiled at her sleepily. "Sure."

"Well . . . maybe you're right, then. Maybe it would do us some good."

"Are you sure?"

"Yeah. I mean . . . I'm willing to give it a shot."

D'or reached over and squeezed her leg. "I figured that stripper would do the trick."

Their baby-sitter was a leggy freshman from Foothill Community College. When they got home, she was watching *Love Letters* on the VCR. Since they'd acquired the movie for the sole purpose of ogling the naked body of Jamie Lee Curtis, DeDe had the uneasy sensation their privacy had been violated.

The sitter, however, seemed totally oblivious of the smoldering eroticism on the screen. "This is so lame," she said without getting up.

D'or grinned wickedly at DeDe, who said: "Well, you two can settle up. I'll go look in on the children."

The kids were dead to the world, sprawled like rag dolls across their respective beds. Their almond-eyed faces seemed smoother and rounder than ever, gleaming like ivory in the bright summer moonlight.

A little healthy exercise in the woods would be good for them, she told herself. There would be other children at Wimminwood, playmates with similar home environments. What better reinforcement could she find for them?

She adjusted Edgar's blanket, then leaned over and kissed him on the forehead. His eyes popped open instantly.

"You weren't asleep," she whispered.

"Did you have a good time?" he asked.

"Yes, darling." She sat on the edge of the bed and brushed the hair off his forehead. "How 'bout you?"

"That sitter is a retard," he said.

"Why?"

"She likes David Lee Roth."

"You didn't give her a hard time, did you?"

He shook his head.

"Go to sleep, then. In the morning I'll tell you about a great trip we're gonna take to the Russian River."

"D'or told me already," he said.

"She did? When?"

"Long time ago."

She wasn't surprised. It was typical of D'or to marshal the forces before mounting the attack.

"I can't go," Edgar added, "cuz I'm a boy."

"Who told you that?"

"D'or."

"Well, she must have been joking, darling."

"I don't think so."

"You misunderstood her, then. We're all going. We would never go anywhere without you." She pulled the blanket up under his chin. "Go to sleep now. Before we wake up Anna."

She descended the staircase to the foyer, her face burning with anger. She could hear the sitter's car spewing gravel in the driveway as she cornered D'or in the kitchen. "Did you tell Edgar he couldn't go to Wimminwood with us?"

D'or opened the refrigerator and took out a half-gallon carton of milk. "No. Of course not."

"He says you did."

"Well, I didn't, damnit. I told him just the opposite, in fact. I said we should all go this year, because he's not ten yet." D'or set a saucepan on the stove and poured milk into it.

"And?" prodded DeDe.

"And . . . little boys don't get to go when they're ten. It's the rule, DeDe. I wanted to be up front about it. Children can understand rules."

"This is what I hate, you know. This is exactly what I hate."

"Oh, c'mon."

"This doctrinaire bullshit, this . . . this . . ."

"You want some cocoa?"

"You hurt Edgar's feelings, D'or. A little boy doesn't understand what's so threatening about his penis."

"I'll talk to him—all right?"

"When?"

D'or opened the cabinet, removed a can of cocoa and handed it to DeDe. "Fix us some and bring it to the bedroom. I'll be there in a little while."

DeDe was still fuming when D'or finally joined her in bed. "Is he OK?" she asked.

"Just fine," said D'or.

"What did you tell him?"

"I told him they made that rule about little boys because ten-year-old boys were almost men, and men were all rapists at heart."

"D'or, goddamnit!"

"All right. Jesus . . . don't hit me."

"Then tell me what you told him."

"I told him I explained things all wrong."

"Is that all?"

"No. I told him it wouldn't be any fun without him along, and that I love him just as much as you do. Then Anna woke up and asked me what smegma was."

"*What?*"

349

"That Atkins kid called her smegma today."

DeDe groaned. "That little brat has the foulest—" The phone rang before she could finish the tirade. D'or reached for the receiver, mumbled hello, and passed it to DeDe. "It's your mother," she said, grinning. "Ask her what smegma is."

DeDe gave her a nasty look, then spoke into the receiver. "Hello, Mother."

"Don't use that tone with me."

"What tone? I just said hello."

"I can tell when you're being snide, darling."

"It's after midnight, Mother."

"Well, I would have called you earlier, but I got busy."

"Busy" sounded more like "bishy."

"Go on, then," said DeDe.

"Were you asleep?"

"No, but we're in bed."

"Don't be vulgar, DeDe."

"Mother . . ."

"All right, I called to ask if you and D'orothea would come for lunch on Sunday. With the children, of course."

"That's sweet, Mother, but we've already made plans. I was giving a lunch myself, but I'm canceling it."

D'or smiled victoriously, then reached over and stroked DeDe's thigh.

Her mother wouldn't give up. "Oh, darling, please say yes. I'm gonna be all alone."

"Why?" asked DeDe. "Where's Booter going?"

"The Grove," said her mother bitterly.

"Oh. It's that time of year again."

"Do you realize," said her mother, "how many times I've been a Grove Widow? I counted it up. Thirty-two times. It isn't fair."

DeDe had heard this sob story all her life. Grove Widows, as they were popularly known, were the wives left behind by Bohemian Club members during their two-week encampment at the Bohemian Grove. The Grove was a sort of summer camp for graying aristocrats, an all-male enclave in the redwoods, whose secret fraternal rituals were almost a century old.

DeDe's father had been an ardent Bohemian, provoking her mother to bouts of acute depression during her annual ordeal of separation. Since her mother's new husband was also a Bohemian, the torment had continued unabated. "You should have married a commoner," DeDe told her.

"That isn't a bit funny."

"Well, what do you want me to say?"

"I want you to come to lunch."

"Mother . . . we're going away."

"Where?"

"Just . . . up north. We're packing the kids in the station wagon and taking off." Wimminwood, in fact, was only a mile or two downriver from the Grove, but to say as much would only heighten her mother's sense of familial desertion.

"I worry about her," she told D'or later. "I can't help it."

D'or pulled her sleep mask into position. "What's the matter this time?"

"Oh . . . Booter's taking off for the Grove."

"Christ," sighed D'or. "The crises of the rich."

"I know."

"This happens every year. Why didn't she plan something?"

"She did plan something. She invited us to lunch." DeDe reached over and turned off the light.

"And now you're feeling guilty as hell."

"No I'm not."

D'or paused. "Of course, we could always bring her along."

DeDe flipped on the light. *"What?"*

"Sure. Gettin' down with her sisters . . . tits to the wind. She'd like that."

DeDe turned off the light again.

D'or kept at it. "Turkey baster study groups, S and M workshops . . ."

"Shut *up*, D'or."

Her lover chuckled throatily and snuggled closer, hooking her leg around DeDe's. "It's gonna be great, hon. I can hardly wait."

DeDe said: "We don't have to go topless, do we?"

Another chuckle.

"Don't laugh. I think we should discuss it."

"OK," said D'or. "Discuss."

"Well . . . whatever we decide, I think we should be consistent."

"Meaning?"

"That we either both do it, or . . . you know . . . both don't do it."

"Maybe," said D'or, "if we both bared one breast . . ."

"Ha ha," said DeDe.

"Well, gimme a break."

DeDe paused. "I just think it would be disorienting for the children, that's all."

"What are you talking about? The kids've seen us naked plenty of times."

"I know, but . . . if one of us goes topless and the other one doesn't . . ."

"What you're saying is . . . you plan to keep your shirt on, and you want me to do the same."

"OK," said DeDe. "Yes."

"Why?"

DeDe hesitated. "We don't . . . well, we don't need to prove anything, that's all."

"Who's proving anything?" said D'or. "It feels good. What's the big deal? You went topless all over the place in Cabo last summer."

"That was different. It was secluded."

"This is secluded."

"Hundreds of people, D'or. That is not secluded."

"Well, they're all *women*, for God's sake."

"Exactly," said DeDe.

"What arc you talking about?" asked D'or.

She was talking about jealousy, of course, but she couldn't bring herself to say it.

Something for Jed

The defloration of his nephew became Brian's pet project. After reviewing half a dozen candidates for the job, he narrowed it down to Jennifer Rabinowitz and Geordie Davies, two Golden Oldies from his personal Top Forty. Jennifer, it turned out, was in Nebraska visiting her brother, so the honor fell by default to Geordie.

Geordie was thirty and lived alone in a garden apartment near the southern gate of the Presidio. They had met one night at Serramonte Mall while buying software for their Macintoshes. Feverish with lust, they had babbled clumsily about Macpaint and Macdraw before beating a hasty retreat to the parking lot. He'd followed her home in his Jeep.

Since that night—two, almost three years ago—he'd visited her cottage less than a dozen times. Neither her lover nor his wife had intruded on their lovemaking, which was refreshingly devoid of romance. Geordie was a true bachelor girl, who liked her life exactly the way it was.

The problem, of course, was how to set it up without scaring Jed off, but Geordie would probably have a few ideas of her own. When he called her cottage in midafternoon, he got her answering machine, which surprised him with its minimalist instruction to "leave your name and number at the tone." Usually her tapes featured barking dogs or old Shirelles tunes or her own unfunny impersonation of a Valley Girl.

His guess was that she was home auditioning callers, so he used his manliest tone of voice when he left his name and number. It didn't work, or she was out. You never knew for sure with Geordie.

By evening, he had decided to make his request in person. The scheme might not seem as cold-blooded if there was eye contact involved. "Do me a favor and fuck my nephew" wouldn't quite cut it on the telephone.

After dinner, he told Mary Ann he was going down to Barbary Lane to visit Jed.

She looked up from her homework, a book about scalp reduction, the subject of tomorrow's show. "Don't let her corner you," she said.

He didn't get it.

"Mrs. Madrigal," she explained. "She's obsessed with those steps. It's sweet, but it's a hopeless cause. Hasn't she told you about it?"

"Oh, yeah . . . she mentioned it."

"Personally," said Mary Ann, "I think she gets off on being colorful."

"I like the steps," he said ineffectually.

"Well, so do I, but they're lethal. And the city isn't about to build brand-new wooden ones." She returned to her book, closing the discussion.

He headed for the door. "I won't be late."

"Say hi to Jed," she said.

It took him twenty-five minutes to reach Geordie's cottage. He parked in the driveway of the house in front and made his way through the fragrant shrubbery to the rear garden. There was a light on in her living room.

He rang her bell, but there was no response. He had never before shown up unannounced, so it was entirely possible that her lover was visiting. She was probably madder than hell.

When she came to the door, however, her pale face seemed drained of all expression.

"I was going to call you," she said.

Escape to Alcatraz

On his first day of vacation, Michael Tolliver took his mail to the Barbary steps and stretched out in the sunshine. According to the paper, there were fires still blazing to the south, and the warm spell showed no sign of imminent departure. His sluggish Southern metabolism had ground almost to a halt.

He plucked a stalk of dried *finocchio* and chewed it ruminatively, Huck Finn style. In the spring, this stuff was lacy and pale green, tasting strongly of licorice, a flavor he had never understood as a kid. It grew anywhere and everywhere, remaining lush and decorative in the face of constant efforts to exterminate it.

Finocchio, he had read somewhere, was also Italian slang for "faggot."

And that made sense somehow.

He set aside the less promising mail and tore into a flimsy blue envelope from England. These short but vivid bulletins from his old friend Mona had become enormously important to him.

Dearest Mouse,

The tourist season is upon us at Easley, and we're up to our ass in Texas millionaires. I'd say to hell with it, if we didn't need the money so badly. I am actually dating the postmistress from Chipping Campden, but I'm not so sure it's a good idea. She uses words like Sapphic when she means dyke. Also, I think she likes the idea of Lady Roughton more than she actually likes me, which is pretty goddamn disconcerting, since I don't feel titled. (Mr. Hargis, the gardener, insists on calling me Your Ladyship when there are tourists around, but I've got him trained to lay off that shit the rest of the time.)

Wilfred got a mohawk for his eighteenth birthday

355

and has taken to lurking in the minstrels' gallery and terrorizing the tourists. He's grown at least three inches since you last saw him. The mohawk looks good, actually, but I haven't told him so, since I'm afraid of what he'll try next. He's signed up for fall classes at a trade school in Cheltenham, but he'll be able to commute from here.

They've finally heard of AIDS in Britain, but it mostly takes the form of fag-baiting headlines in the tabloids. According to Wilfred, their idea of safe sex is not going to bed with Americans. He misses you, by the way, and told me to tell you so. I miss you too, Babycakes.

Mona

PS. Did you know there is still a Greek island called Lesbos? It's supposed to be wonderful. Why don't we meet there next spring?

PPS. If you see Teddy, tell him Mrs. Digby in the village wants to install an automatic garage door. I'm pretty sure this isn't allowed, but I want his support before I say no.

Smiling, Michael put down the letter. Mona's green-card marriage to Teddy Roughton was apparently the best thing she'd ever done for herself. By swapping countries with a disgruntled nobleman, she'd found a perfect setting for her particular brand of eccentricity.

And Teddy, obviously, was enjoying himself here.

Michael had yet to decide on the disposition of his vacation time. Some of it would be spent on reassuring domestic rituals: writing letters, painting the kitchen, helping Mrs. Madrigal with her garden. He had also promised to distribute fliers for her save-the-steps campaign, which had so far met with indifference in the neighborhood.

After lunch, he drove to Dolores Street for a Tupperware party hosted by Charlie Rubin. Charlie had come home after another scary stint at St. Sebastian's and was making up for lost time.

The Tupperware saleslady was a big-boned Armenian woman whose spiel had been written expressly for housewives. A creature of cheerful routine, she apparently saw no reason to alter the scheme of things now. When she proudly displayed the Velveeta cheese dispenser, the thirteen assembled men erupted in gales of laughter.

Mrs. Sarkisian smiled gamely, pretending to understand, but he could tell her feelings had been hurt. He felt so sorry for her that he bought a lettuce crisper immediately thereafter and later spent five minutes telling her in private how much it would change his life.

When the rest of the guests had straggled home with their booty, he joined Charlie on the deck. "Well, that was different," he said.

Charlie stared out at the neighboring gardens, a patchwork of laundry and sunflowers. "I always wondered what one was like," he said. "Didn't you?"

Michael nodded. "And now we know."

They were both quiet for a while. Then Charlie said: "I made a list when I was in the hospital, and that was on the list." He paused, then looked at Michael. "You haven't commented on my new lesion."

What was there to say? It was a dime-sized purple splotch on the tip of Charlie's nose.

Charlie cocked his head and struck a stately Condé Nast pose. "It doesn't suit me, does it? Should I get my money back?"

Managing a feeble laugh, Michael moved closer to him and slid his hand into the back pocket of Charlie's Levi's. "It doesn't look so bad," he said.

"Please," said Charlie. "It makes me look like Pluto."

Michael smiled at him. "C'mon."

"Not even Pluto. He was friendly looking."

"You're friendly looking."

"Who were those guys who were always robbing Uncle Scrooge's money bin?"

"The Beagle Boys," said Michael.

"That's it," said Charlie. "I look like a Beagle Boy."

Michael reproved him with a gentle shake. "What else is on your list? Besides Tupperware."

Charlie thought for a moment. "A balloon ride, a fan letter to Betty White, finding you a husband . . ."

"Well"—Michael chuckled—"two out of three ain't bad."

"Don't be that way. There were some nice guys here today. Didn't you get any phone numbers?"

"No, I did not."

"Why not?"

"Because," said Michael, "I don't pick up men at Tupperware parties."

"You don't pick up men, period. You don't even date. When was your last date?"

"Stop nagging. It won't work. Let's go for a balloon ride."

Charlie inspected his nails. "Too late. Richard and I are going next week. You could join us."

"That's OK," said Michael.

"What about Alcatraz?" asked Charlie. "I've never been to Alcatraz."

"Neither have I," said Michael.

"It could be depressing, I guess."

"Yeah, maybe."

Charlie's fingers traced the grain of the railing. "I heard they gave the view cells to the worst offenders, because that was considered the greatest punishment. To see the city but not be able to go there."

Michael winced. "You think that's true?"

"Probably not," murmured Charlie.

"Let's check it out . . . take the tour."

"You sure you want to? It's awfully Middle American."

"And a Tupperware party isn't?"

Charlie smiled. "Did you absolutely hate it?"

"No. I thought Mrs. Sarkisian was very sweet."

"She was, wasn't she?"

A seagull swooped over the neighbor's laundry, then landed on the fence. "Everything is sweet," said Charlie. "It makes no sense to me at all."

Michael looked at him and thought of *finocchio*, popping up again and again through the cracks of the sidewalk.

Their tour boat was called the *Harbor Princess*, much to Charlie's amusement. The other passengers were a Felliniesque assortment of pantsuited tourist ladies and their husbands, plus a gaggle of Catholic schoolgirls in blue-and-gray plaid skirts.

There was also a singular beauty aboard—a strawberry blond with long, pale lashes and eyes the color of bleached denim. Charlie was sold on him.

"I'm telling you, Michael. He's cruising you like crazy."

Michael lifted his coffee cup and blew on the surface. "Don't make a scene, Charlie."

"Well, do something, damnit. Stop being coy."

"He's not even looking at me."

"Well, he *was*, for God's sake."

"Look at those gulls," said Michael. "It's amazing how long they can drift without flapping their wings."

Charlie heaved a plaintive sigh and peered out to sea. "What am I gonna do with you?"

A thin scrim of fog covered the island as they approached. The cellhouse was still intact, crouching grimly along the crest of the Rock, but many of the outbuildings were skeletal ruins, rubble overgrown with wildflowers.

Above a sign saying FEDERAL PENITENTIARY Michael could barely make out the word INDIANS, painted crudely in red—obviously a relic of the Native American occupation in the late sixties.

They disembarked with the mob, flowing across the dock and past the ranger station into a building that felt curiously like a wine cellar, with clammy walls and low, arched ceilings. There, a ten-minute slide show assured them that inmates at Alcatraz had been the meanest of the mean, incorrigibles who deserved the isolation of the Rock.

Afterwards, they assembled at the rear entrance of the cellhouse to await further instructions. When their ranger arrived, he explained that due to the size of the crowd, visitors would be required to split up and choose among three lecture topics.

"The three topics," he explained soberly, "are Security Measures, Famous Inmates and Discipline."

Charlie leaned forward and whispered "Discipline" in Michael's ear.

Michael grinned at him.

As if reading their minds, the ranger added briskly: "Those of you who've chosen Discipline please follow Guy through the shower room to D Block."

"Oh, Guy," crooned Charlie.

By the time they had all assembled in the shower room, the demography of their tour group had become absurdly evident: Michael, Charlie, the strawberry blond, and at least two dozen girls from the Catholic school.

The ranger led the way into D Block, doing his best to herd the giggling children. "There were a lot of different names given to this area—solitary, segregation, special treatment unit, isolation. Prisoners here spent up to twenty-four hours a day inside their cells. They had their own shower facilities down there at the end of the cellblock, since they were forbidden to shower with the other inmates."

Michael and Charlie exchanged glances.

"Cells nine through fourteen were known by the inmates as the 'dark cells' and were the most severe form of punishment on Alcatraz. The men stayed in total darkness inside these cells, which are steel-lined, and they were given mattresses only at night. They were fed twice a day on what was known as a 'reduced diet'—mashed vegetables in a cup."

"Eeeyew," went the schoolgirls in unison.

"If you'd like to see what it was like to spend time in a 'dark cell,' pick a cell and I'll close the door behind you."

The children squealed with fun-house terror, formed protective clumps, and crowded into the six chambers. Michael was headed for Cell 11 when Charlie grabbed his arm. "Use your head, dummy. Go for twelve."

He glanced toward Cell 12 and saw a splendiferous smile hovering above a sea of schoolgirls.

"Go on," said Charlie.

Michael hesitated, then entered the cell, watching the smile grow broader.

Seconds later, the ranger approached and closed the heavy door with a resounding clang. The tiny room was plunged into instant and total darkness, provoking another shriek from the girls.

Their mock ordeal lasted only a second or two; then the door swung open again, spilling light into the cell. The strawberry blond was no longer smiling, but he seemed a little closer than before. "Pretty creepy," he said.

"Isn't it?" said Michael.

"And we had company," said the man. "What can it be like when you're alone?"

Michael let the tide of children sweep him out of the cell. The man caught up with him and extended his hand. "I'm Thack," he said.

Michael shook his hand. "I'm Michael."

Charlie was watching them, arms folded across his chest, a triumphant gleam in his eye. "How was it?" he asked.

"Um . . . Charlie," Michael fumbled, "this is Thad."

"Thack," said the man, correcting him. "It was great. Didn't you try it?" He met Charlie's gaze without flinching, Michael noticed. A point in his favor.

Charlie shook his head. "I can't handle a crowded cocktail party."

Thack laughed, then turned back to Michael. "You guys from around here?"

"Yeah," Michael replied, avoiding his eyes. They were too easy to drown in.

"Isn't this kind of . . . touristy, for a local?"

Michael shrugged. "We'd never done it, so we thought it was time."

"Like New Yorkers and the Statue of Liberty."

"Right." Charlie nodded. "Is that where you're from?" He was hovering like a Jewish mother interviewing a candidate for son-in-law.

"Charleston," said Thack.

"West Virginia?"

"South Carolina."

"A Southerner!" exclaimed Charlie, far too gleefully. "Michael's a Southerner. You don't sound like one, though. Where's your drawl?"

Michael was squirming. "I think we'd better move it," he said. "There's another tour coming."

The three of them left the cellhouse through the main entrance and stood beneath the lighthouse, watching the fog erase the city. "I almost forgot," said Charlie suddenly. "I wanna take a picture of the shower room."

"You didn't bring your camera," said Michael.

"Didn't I? Damn." He gave Michael a glare that said *Shut up, stupid.* "Maybe they sell postcards or something."

"Right," said Michael.

Charlie turned to Thack. "Keep an eye on him, would you?" As Charlie strode away, Thack asked: "Your guardian angel?"

"He thinks so," said Michael.

"Is that KS?" Thack touched the tip of his nose.

Michael hesitated, then said: "Yeah."

"I've never actually seen it."

Michael nodded. "That's it."

"Is he your lover?"

"No. A friend."

Thack turned back toward the city. "You live over there, huh?"

"Uh-huh. I can see this light from my bedroom."

362

"Must be nice."

"It is," said Michael. He snatched a pebble off the ground and flung it in the direction of the warden's house.

"This is my first time here," said Thack.

"How do you like it?"

"It's OK," said Thack. "The swimming isn't much."

"The ocean's a killer," said Michael, "but the river is nice. You should go up to the Russian River."

"I've heard of that. Where is it?"

"Up north. Not far."

Thack sat down on a low stone wall and yanked a weed from a crack.

"How long will you be here?" asked Michael.

Thack shrugged. "Another week. Give or take a few days."

"Where are you staying?"

"The San Franciscan. On Market Street."

"Well, if you need a tour guide . . . I mean . . . I'm on vacation myself right now."

"Oh . . . yeah. Well, sure."

"I'm in the phone book," said Michael. "Michael Tolliver. Spelled just like it sounds."

Thack nodded. "Great."

"Want me to write it down?"

"No," said Thack. "I'll remember it."

The return voyage to the city was marked by small talk and bi-ographical data. Thack made a living renovating antebellum houses in Charleston. He was thirty-one years old, seldom ate red meat and never watched *Dynasty*. His full name was William Thackeray Sweeney, thanks to a mother in Chattanooga, who still taught high school English.

Charlie pressed Michael for details as soon as Thack had left them at Pier 41. "I want to be matron of honor," he said. "That's all I ask."

"He won't call," said Michael.

363

"Why not?"

Michael shrugged. "He's a tourist. He wants instant gratification. He'll find somebody in a bar or order somebody out of the *Advocate*."

"Don't be such a cynic," said Charlie. "It isn't becoming."

They took a cable car up Hyde Street, parting company at Union, where Michael disembarked and walked home to Barbary Lane. When he reached his apartment, Mrs. Madrigal came gliding up the stairs and called to him.

"Uh . . . Michael dear?"

"Yeah?"

"Brian was by. He asked if you'd give him a jingle."

"Did he say what it was about?"

The landlady shook her head.

"Probably his nephew," said Michael. "He's gay and Brian can't handle it."

She smiled demurely. "I don't think so."

"I hope not. I don't want him on our side."

She cast her eyes upward in the direction of Jed's apartment, then put a finger to her lips. "There are no sides, dear."

He tried to look contrite.

"He's young, that's all. I expect you and Brian can both be of help to him."

He seriously doubted this.

"Call Brian," said Mrs. Madrigal, heading down the stairs. "I think it's important."

The Boy Next Door

Eager for escape, Booter Manigault left work early and drove home to Hillsborough. He found his wife drinking Mai Tais on the terrace, his maid brooding in the kitchen. This was a tiresomely familiar scenario, since Emma was plagued by Frannie's drinking even more than he was.

"OK," he said, setting his briefcase on the kitchen table. "What happened this time?"

The maid was poker stiff with indignation. "I told her she was killin' herself, and she said none o' your business, nigger."

Emma had heard worse, of course. She had been with Frannie so long that she'd arrived as part of her dowry, along with the crystal and the Persian rugs and the John Singer Sargent of Frannie's grandmother.

The Sargent looked like holy hell in Booter's modern low-beamed ranch house, but Emma and the other furnishings had worked out fine. She was old and cantankerous, but her loyalty was indisputable. In his eyes, that made her the last of a breed.

"She didn't mean it," he told the maid quietly. "It's the whiskey talking."

Emma grunted, then rearranged her licorice-stick fingers on the tabletop. "Crazy ol' white woman, that's who was talkin'."

He left her and confronted his wife on the terrace. "Would you go make up with Emma, for God's sake!"

Frannie looked at him with red-rimmed basset eyes, then squared her jaw in a pathetic imitation of resolve. "I'd sooner fry in hell," she said.

"Did you call her a nigger, Frannie?"

She thrust out her lower lip.

"Did you?" he persisted.

"You use that word all the time."

"Not about people I know," he said. "Not to their faces."

"I've known her for forty years." She raised her bejeweled fingers to her head and repositioned her wig. "I can call her anything I want."

"She's a servant, Frannie. It isn't done."

"It's none of your business, Booter. Emma and I understand each other."

In a way, she was right about that. The two women bickered constantly, then drew blood, then made up. Emma and Frannie were more of a couple than he and Frannie would ever be.

"When are you leaving?" she asked.

"This afternoon," he replied.

"For how long?"

He hated this kind of third degree from a woman he still regarded as an old friend's widow. "Four or five days," he muttered.

She heaved a melodramatic sigh.

"Don't give me that. Edgar used to go for the full two weeks."

"It's not just the Grove," she said glumly. "You never take me anywhere."

She had said the same thing the year before when he'd gone to Europe without her for the fortieth anniversary of D-day. As a member of the American Battle Monuments Commission, he'd been entitled to bring her along for the festivities, but he'd known better than to risk the embarrassment.

Emma, as usual, had held down the fort at home, while he trudged about the beaches of Normandy in a drip-dry blazer, only paces away from the President. Traveling alone had been his only option, given Frannie's drunken mood swings and her long-standing feud—dating back to gubernatorial days—with Nancy Reagan.

"We'll do something soon," he said.

She took a sip of her drink and stared forlornly at the distant hills.

"I'm making a speech," he said brightly, trying to pull her out of it.

"Where?"

"The Grove."

She grunted.

"It's a Lakeside Talk."

"Is that an honor or something?"

Damn right, he thought, annoyed by her deliberate indifference. Edgar, after all, had never been asked to make one.

"What's it about?" she asked.

"The SDI," he replied.

"The what?"

"Frannie . . . the Strategic Defense Initiative."

"Oh. Star Wars."

He winced. "We don't call it that."

"Well, I do. I don't care what that horrid old actor calls it."

He glowered at her, then turned away, catching sight of a diminutive figure as it dashed across the tennis court and up the lawn. It was little Edgar, Frannie's half-breed grandson, intruding once more on his peace and quiet.

"Damn it to hell," he muttered.

"Don't be mean to him," said Frannie.

"I'm not mean to him. When have I been mean to him?"

"Well, you aren't very nice. He's your grandson, for heaven's sake."

"Oh, no," said Booter. "He's *your* grandson, not mine."

"Well, you could at least show a little concern."

"Look. Just because DeDe had no more sense than to get knocked up by a chink grocery boy—"

"Booter!"

"At least that was normal," he added. "It beats the hell out of this unnatural—"

"Edgar darling," Frannie called. "Come say hello to Gangie and Booter." She gave Booter a venomous look and polished off her drink just as the boy arrived breathless on the terrace. Booter couldn't help wondering what Edgar Halcyon would have made of this slant-eyed namesake.

"Mom sent me," said the boy.

"That's nice," said Frannie. "You want Gangie's cherry?" She held out her glass to the boy.

Little Edgar shook his head. "D'or won't let me."

"Don't be silly, darling. Just the cherry."

"It has red dye," said the boy. "It's poison."

Frannie looked confused, then faintly indignant, setting the glass down. Served her right, thought Booter. What did she expect from a couple of bulldaggers raising a child?

Little Edgar said: "Mom wants to know if you guys still have that two-person tent."

"I am not a guy," said Frannie, bristling.

The boy studied his grandmother for a moment, then turned to Booter. "It's the one Anna and me set up in the orchard last summer."

Booter nodded. "It's in the potting shed. On the shelf."

"Can we use it?"

"*May* we use it," said Frannie.

Booter ignored her. "C'mon, I'll help you get it down."

They walked together to the potting shed. "So," said Booter. "Your mother's going camping?"

"We're all going," said the boy.

"Well, you'll need more than one tent."

"I know," said Edgar. "We've got a pup tent for me and Anna."

Booter pictured this unwholesome arrangement and got a bitter taste in his mouth. "Where are you going?" he asked.

The boy gave him a guarded look, then shrugged. "Just camping."

When they reached the shed, he found the tent, telling Edgar: "I think those plastic rods are all present and accounted for. You'd better get your mother to check."

The boy hefted the bundle and said: "I can check."

"Good," said Booter. He reached behind a row of flowerpots and retrieved the plastic dinosaur he had found there two days earlier. "This is yours, I think."

The boy nodded, taking the toy. "Thanks," he said. "This one's my favorite."

"It is, huh? You know the name?"

"Protoceratops."

Booter steered the boy toward the door. "They were big fellas," he said.

"No," said Edgar. "This one wasn't."

"Well, maybe not that one . . ."

"They were only six feet long and three feet high. Their eggs were only six inches long."

"I see."

"I've got some of the big ones too. Wanna see 'em?"

"Not today, son."

"I could bring 'em over here. You wouldn't hafta come to our house."

"I'm busy, Edgar."

"Why?"

"Well, I'm going on a trip this afternoon. Just like you."

"Oh."

They walked across the lawn in silence. He was afraid Edgar might follow him back to the house, but the boy blazed his own trail when they reached the tennis court, squeezing through a hole in the privet before crossing the orchard to Halcyon Hill.

Call Waiting

Charlie didn't bother to identify himself. "Well, has he called?"

"How could he," Michael answered, "when you keep calling to find out if he's called?"

"Bullshit. You've got Call Waiting."

"Well . . . he hasn't. OK?"

"He will. What are you gonna tell him?"

That was the burning question, all right. What would he say? *I like you, Thack. I'm attracted to you, and I think we could have something here. But I think I should tell you before we go any further that I'm antibody positive.*

Yeah, boy. That was the stuff of romance, all right. Who wouldn't be turned on by a line like that?

"I'll play it by ear," he told Charlie.

"What about the river?"

"What about it?"

"Why don't you take him there? You said he's never been."

"I can't afford it, Charlie."

"Ah, but I have a place."

"Since when?"

"Since my Shanti volunteer went to Boca Raton to inseminate a lesbian."

Michael laughed. "Great. Thanks for clearing *that* up."

"Well, it's a big compliment, actually. Who's asked for *your* semen lately?"

"Charlie, what the hell are you talking about?"

"OK. Arturo—my Shanti buddy—has this great place in Cazadero. Only he can't use it now, since he's gonna be a sperm donor."

"Right."

"He took the test two weeks ago, and it came back negative, so the girls went into a huddle and sent him a plane ticket. Which leaves this great cabin completely empty. And I can't use it, since I'm going ballooning."

"Well, that's really nice, but . . ."

"Just remember it, that's all. When Thack calls."

"*If*, Charlie."

Michael's Call Waiting beeped.

"There," said Charlie. "Right on cue."

"Hang up," said Michael.

"No way. I want a report."

Michael sighed and tapped the button on his receiver. "Hello."

"Hi, it's Brian."

Against all reason, Michael's heart sank a little. "Oh, hi. Mrs. Madrigal said you came by."

"Yeah. I kinda wanted to talk."

"Oh . . . well, sure."

"Is this a good time?"

"Now? On the phone?"

"No. Could I come down?" Brian's solemn tone suggested urgency. Another fight with Mary Ann, no doubt.

"Uh . . . sure. Come on down." The phrase sounded faintly ridiculous, like an instruction to game-show contestants, but he'd used it a lot since his friends had moved to The Summit.

"Thanks," said Brian.

Michael hit the button again. "It wasn't him," he told Charlie.

"Damn."

"I've gotta go now."

"Keep me posted," said Charlie.

Brian's smoky green eyes darted about the room, never lighting anywhere for long. His crow's feet seemed more plentiful than ever (McCartney's syndrome, Michael had once dubbed it), though they hardly detracted from his amazing chestnut curls and the twin-mounded rise of his sandpaper chin.

"How 'bout some coffee or something?" Michael asked.

Brian took a seat on the sofa. "No, thanks."

"I have decaffeinated . . . and Red Zinger."

"Michael . . . I'm in big trouble."

Michael pulled up his mission oak footstool and straddled it in front of Brian's chair. "What's the matter?"

Brian hesitated. "Remember Geordie Davies?"

Michael shook his head.

"The woman I met at the Serramonte Mall?"

"Oh, yeah."

"She's got AIDS."

"What?"

"She's got AIDS, man. I saw her yesterday. She's really sick."

Michael was dumbfounded. "How did she get it?"

"I dunno. Her lover's a junkie or something."

"Oh . . ."

"What the fuck am I gonna tell Mary Ann?"

Michael thought for a moment. "How often did you . . . see her?"

Brian shrugged. "Six or seven times. Eight, tops."

"I thought you told me . . ."

"OK. I saw her more than once. It was no big deal. Neither one of us wanted a big deal." He chewed on a knuckle. "What am I gonna tell her?"

"Geordie?"

"Mary Ann, for Christ's sake!"

"Don't yell," said Michael calmly.

"We did anal stuff. Does that . . . you know . . . ?"

"You and Mary Ann?"

"No!" Brian's eyes blazed indignantly. "Me and Geordie."

"You mean . . . you fucked her?"

"No."

Michael drew back a little. "She fucked you?"

"Really funny, man! Really goddamn funny!"

"Well, I don't get it."

"She had these beads, OK?"

"Oh."

Brian paused, looking down at his feet. "They weren't very . . . big or anything."

Michael did his damnedest not to smile. "Brian . . . it's not that easy for a woman to give it to a man."

"It's not?"

"No. We'll get you tested. I know a guy at the clinic in the Castro. I'll make an appointment for you."

"You can't give them my name," said Brian.

"It's just a number. Don't worry."

"What sort of number?"

"Just a number you make up." He reached across and shook Brian's knee. "You've felt OK, haven't you?"

"Yeah. Mostly. I felt kind of funky a few days ago, but it seemed like the flu."

"Then it probably was."

Brian nodded.

"You're gonna be all right."

"I've never been so damn scared . . ."

"I know. I've been through this, remember?"

"Yeah, but . . . this is different."

"Why?"

"Michael, there are innocents involved here."

"What?"

"Mary Ann . . . Shawna, for Christ's sake."

"Innocents, huh? Not like me. Not like Jon. Not like the fags."

"I didn't mean that."

"Well, lay off that innocent shit. It's a virus. Everybody is innocent." He tried to collect himself. "I'll call the clinic."

"I'm sorry if I . . ."

"Forget it."

"I didn't know who else to talk to."

"You'll be all right," said Michael.

Brian looked him squarely in the eye. "I loved Jon too, you know."

"I know," said Michael.

These Friendly Trees

Like Booter, most Bohemians arrived at the Grove by car from the city. The press in its endless fascination with money and power grossly exaggerated the number of Lear and Lockheed jets that landed at the Santa Rosa airport during the encampment. Many of the members—well, some of them, anyway—were uncomplicated fellows with ordinary, workaday jobs in the city.

They came to the Grove for release from their lives, not to plan mergers, plot takeovers or wage war. So what if the A-bomb had been brainstormed there back in 1942? That, Booter knew for a fact, had been in mid-September, almost two months after the encampment had shut down.

The real function of the Grove was escape, pure and simple. It provided a secret haven where captains of industry and pillars of government could let down their guard and indulge in the luxury of first-name-only camaraderie.

Escape was certainly what Booter had in mind as he sped north on the freeway, away from Frannie and the city and the cruel vagaries of a career in aluminum honeycomb.

After an hour's drive, he left the freeway and headed west on the road to Guerneville, where sunlit vineyards and gnarly orchards alternated abruptly with tunnels of green gloom. When the river appeared, glinting cool and golden through the trees, so too did the ragtag resort cabins, the rusting trailers, the neon cocktail glasses beckoning luridly from the roadside.

He drove straight through Guerneville, doing his best to ignore the pimply teenagers and blatant homosexuals who prowled the tawdry main street. He had liked this town better in the fifties, before its resurgence, when it was still essentially a ruin from the thirties.

In Monte Rio he turned left, crossing the river on the old steel bridge. Another left took him along a winding road past junked cars and blackberry thickets and poison oak pushing to the very edge of the asphalt.

At the end of this road lay the big wooden gates to the Grove and the vine-entangled sign that invariably caused his heart to beat faster:

PRIVATE PROPERTY. MEMBERS AND GUESTS ONLY. TRESPASSERS WILL BE PROSECUTED.

He drove through the gates and past the gray-frame commissary buildings, coming to a stop in front of the luggage dock and check-in station. Climbing out of the car, he adjusted his tie, brushed the wrinkles out of his suit, and inhaled the resinous incense of the great woodland cathedral that awaited him.

The familiar cast of characters was already assembled: the jubilant new arrivals, the blue-jeaned college boys who did the valet parking, the leathery rent-a-cops with their cowboy hats and huge bellies and belt buckles the size of license plates.

Sweating a little, he opened the trunk and hauled his two suitcases to the luggage dock marked "River Road." He was filled with inexplicable glee as he grabbed a stubby golf pencil and inscribed two old-fashioned steamer trunk labels with the words *Manigault* and *Hillbillies.* Why did this feel so much like coming home?

After relinquishing his BMW to a valet parker, he spotted Farley Stuart and Jimmy Chappell and sauntered up behind them. "Damn," he said, "we're in trouble now!"

Both men hooted jovially, clapping him on the back. Jimmy looked a little withered after his bypass operation, but his spirit seemed as spunky as ever. Farley, heading for the shuttle bus, turned and aimed a finger at Booter. "Come for fizzes tomorrow morning. Up at Aviary."

Aviary was the chorus camp. Farley was a valued baritone, an "associate" member whose talent alone had qualified him for a bunk in Bohemia. He wasn't an aristocrat by any stretch of the imagination, but he was a nice fellow just the same.

Booter pointed back at him and said: "You got a deal."

He knew already that he wouldn't go (he expected an invitation to fizzes up at Mandalay), but his burgeoning spirit of brotherhood made saying no a virtual impossibility.

He was amused, as always, when the guard at the check-in station punched him in, using a conventional industrial time clock. This, he'd been told, had largely to do with billing for food, as members were charged for any meals that occurred during their time at the Grove, regardless of whether or not they chose to eat.

The guard was one he liked, which comforted him, since this was the fellow who would know the most about his comings and goings.

When he was done, he found Jimmy and Farley holding the shuttle bus for him. He decided to walk, flagging them on—a joint decision, really, between a vain old man proud of his endurance and a wide-eyed boy ready to explore.

Somewhere up ahead, someone was playing a banjo.

The ceremonial gates, the ones meant to welcome rather than re-pulse, were a boy's own daydream, a rustic Tom Swiftian portal built

375

of oversized Lincoln Logs. As Booter passed through them, a blue jay swept low over his shoulder, cackling furiously, and his welcome seemed complete.

He strode briskly, following the road into a forest so thoroughly primeval that some of it had been here when Genghis Khan began his march across Asia. Something indescribable always happened at this point, some soothing realignment of boundaries which contracted his world and made it manageable for the first time all year.

Sky and trees and river notwithstanding, the Grove was not the great outdoors at all; it was a room away from things, a cavernous temple of brotherhood, locked to the rest of humanity. There was order here, and a palpable absence of anarchy. No wonder it made him so happy.

He whistled as he passed the post office, the grocery store, the barbershop, the museum, the telegraph office, the phone bank, the hospital, the fire station. Other members, already anonymous in comfortable old clothes, moved past him in jocular clumps, brandishing whiskey in plastic glasses, calling his name from time to time.

At the height of the encampment, over two thousand men would be assembled at the Grove in one hundred twenty-six different camps. As Booter understood it, this made for a population density greater than that of Chinatown in San Francisco.

As he approached the Campfire Circle, he stopped to read the posters tacked to the trees—each a work of art, really—heralding gala nights and concerts, costume dramas and Lakeside Talks. His own address was somewhat drably listed as: *Roger Manigault: Aluminum Honeycomb and the Future of the Strategic Nuclear Defense Initiative.*

Another shuttle bus—this one labeled "The Old Guard"— bumped past him as he skirted the lake. Henry McKittrick was seated in the back, red-faced and solemn in his sweaty seersuckers. Booter gave him a thumbs-up sign, but Henry merely nodded, obviously still sore about the contract with Consolidated.

He headed down the River Road toward Hillbillies, immersing

376

himself in the sights and sounds of the frontier community coming to life beneath the giant trees. The very name of the camps triggered half a lifetime of memories: Dog House, Toyland, Pig 'n' Whistle, Sons of Toil . . .

Someone was playing a piano—"These Foolish Things"—on the ridge to the left. To the right was a Dixieland band and a chorus practicing a classical number he didn't recognize. Their voices trailed heavenward, hovering like woodsmoke in the slanting afternoon light.

As night fell, he assembled with the others at the Owl Shrine for the Cremation of Care. The already drunken crowd fell silent as the lakeside organist began to play the dirge and the High Priest summoned his acolytes. Then the barge materialized, poled silently across the lake, bearing the palled figure of Care.

When the barge reached the shrine, two acolytes removed the pall, revealing the macabre effigy with its papier-mâché mask. The effigy was dutifully placed upon the pyre, but its incineration was halted, as always, by sinister, electronically enhanced laughter from the hillside

All eyes turned toward the ridge as a puff of smoke and a flash of light revealed the presence of the ghostly white Tree of Care. From deep inside the tree thundered the voice of Care itself:

"Fools, fools, fools, when will ye learn that me ye cannot slay? Year after year ye burn me in this Grove, lifting your silly shouts of triumph to the pitying stars. But when ye turn your feet again to the marketplace, am I not waiting for you as of old? Fools, fools, to dream you conquer Care!"

The High Priest answered:

"Year after year, within this happy Grove, our fellowship has damned thee for a space, and thy malevolence that would pursue us has lost its power beneath these friendly trees. So shall we burn thee once again this night, and in the flames that eat thine effigy we'll read the sign that, once again, midsummer sets us free."

Then, after lighting their torches at the gas-jet altar fire, the acolytes descended upon the pyre and set Care aflame, piercing the night with shouts of ecstasy. The band broke into "Hot Time in the Old Town Tonight."

Booter smiled, feeling the old magic, then withdrew into the darkness as fireworks burst in the trees above the lake. When he reached the phone bank, he was relieved to see that no one else was there. He placed a local call.

"Yello," said Wren Douglas.

"It's me," he said. "Just making sure you're comfortable."

"Sittin' pretty," she said.

"Good. I'll be up there tonight."

"No problem," she replied.

Mary Ann's Good News

The clinic was an L-shaped concrete-block building on Seventeenth Street between Noe and Sanchez. Behind a row of ragged palms lay two distinct entrances: one for people taking the test, the other for people getting their results. Inside, while Michael waited in the car, Brian was shown a videotape about T-cells and helper cells and the true meaning of HTLV-III.

Then they drew his blood, and sent him on his way.

"Damn," he said to Michael, climbing into the VW. "You didn't tell me it took ten days."

"I thought you knew."

"Why would I know that?"

"Well, *I* took it, remember?"

"Oh . . ." Brian gazed absently out the window, weighing his options. He'd counted on coming home with a clean bill of health, a note from his doctor to soften the blow when he told Mary Ann about Geordie. But now . . .

"It's the lab procedure," said Michael. "Apparently it takes that long."

"Ten fucking days."

Michael smiled at him wanly, turning on the engine. "Ten non-fucking days."

"It won't work," said Brian.

"What do you mean?"

"Well, she'll know something's up." He gave Michael an admonitory look. "Don't make a pun out of that."

"You've never gone for ten days without doing it?"

"No."

"Well, I'm impressed."

Brian didn't laugh. Michael's flip tone was beginning to get on his nerves.

"What about rubbers?" asked Michael.

"We never use them," said Brian.

"Well, start. Tell her you think they're a safer form of birth control."

"Michael," he said, faintly annoyed. "I'm sterile, remember?"

"Oh, yeah. Sorry." Michael seemed to ponder this for a while before slipping into a reasonable facsimile of Dr. Ruth's Teutonic twitter. "Well . . . what about something in a nice decorative model . . . with whirligigs on the end?"

Brian laughed in spite of himself. "You bastard."

"Tell her," said Michael.

"No. Not yet."

"Sooner or later you're gonna have to. Sooner is always better than later."

"No it isn't. Why should she suffer for the next ten days?"

"Because you're suffering. And she's your wife."

Michael's logic annoyed him. "And I've been a great husband, haven't I?"

"Look, Brian . . . if you don't tell her now . . ."

"Forget it, all right? I have to do this my way."

"Fine," said Michael.

● ● ●

Twenty minutes later, Michael dropped him off in front of The Summit. The doorman fired off a friendly "Yo," but Brian scarcely heard him as he made his wooden way to the elevator.

Could he fake it for ten days? Carry on his life as if nothing were wrong?

Making his ascent, he stood stock still and tried to read his body's signals. There was a heaviness in his limbs which may or may not have been there earlier. Some of the soreness seemed localized, a dim ember of pain lodged in a corner of his gut.

This could be anything, of course. Indigestion or a flare-up of his old gastritis. Hell, maybe it *was* the flu, after all. His headache seemed to have gone away.

The elevator opened at the twenty-third floor. He stepped out into the foyer to confront the insufferable Cap Sorenson, his face plastered with a shit-eating grin. "How's it hanging, Hawkins?"

"Pretty good," he said, adopting a similar hail-fellow tone. "Pretty good."

They changed places, Cap holding the door to get in the final word. "I closed that deal I told you about."

"Great."

"Forget great," said Cap. "We're talking megabucks this time."

Brian nodded. The elevator had its own way at last, obliterating Cap's idiot smirk.

He let himself into the apartment, moving to the window like someone walking underwater. The sun had swooped in low from the west, turning white buildings to gold: shimmering ingots against the blue. Far beneath him, the tangled foliage of Barbary Lane cast dusty purple shadows across the bricks of Mrs. Madrigal's courtyard.

Mary Ann emerged from the bathroom. "I wondered where you were."

What was she doing here? Hadn't she planned on working late tonight? "Oh," he said. "Michael and I drove out to the beach. Where's Nguyet? She was here when I . . ."

"I let her go home. I thought she could use an afternoon off."

"Oh."

She added: "I took off early myself. Just said to hell with it. Feels good." She rocked on her heels several times, a curious light in her eyes. "Guess what."

"What?"

"You're never gonna believe this."

He looked around, unsettled, distracted. "Where's Puppy?"

She frowned at him. "Will you let me tell this? She's riding her Tuff Trike at the Sorensons'."

He tried to look apologetic. "What's up?"

"Well . . . here's a hint." She paused, then sang: "Dah-dah-dah-dah-dah-*dah* . . . dah-dah-dah-dah-dah-*dah*."

It made no sense to him whatsoever.

"C'mon," she prodded. "I know you know it. It's theme music."

He shrugged.

"Oh, Brian." She sang again: *"En-ter-tain-ment To-niiight . . . En-ter-tain-ment To-niiight."*

"Right," he said. "What about it?"

She beamed at him. "I'm gonna be on it, Brian."

"On the show?"

"Yes! They're doing a series about . . . you know, the best local talk shows. And they want me! Isn't that fabulous?"

He nodded, doing his best to echo her excitement. "That's really great."

"They wanna tape us here for part of it."

"Me, you mean?"

"Sure, you." She did a sort of Loretta Young twirl around the room. "You and me and Puppy and our drop-dead apartment high atop the city." She burst into triumphant giggles, flinging her arms around him.

He patted her shoulder and said again: "That's really great."

"I've been mentally decorating all day." She broke away from him and began to pace. "I think we need *lots* more flowers. Orchids, maybe . . . in those planters made out of twigs and moss."

He scarcely heard her.

She stopped pacing and scolded him with a little smile. "Somebody looks out of it. What's the matter?"

"Nothing," he said.

"Are you still having those headaches?"

"No. I'm fine now."

"Good." She surveyed the room, obviously checking camera angles. "I want everyone back in Cleveland to be eating their crummy little hearts out. Oh . . . Jed stopped by this afternoon."

He grunted. He'd completely forgotten about the kid.

"Hey," she said gently. "I thought you were gonna give him a second chance."

"He's not worth it," he said.

"Well, he's leaving tomorrow afternoon. If you're gonna talk to him at all . . ."

"Look," he snapped. "I'll go see him—all right?"

She recoiled a little, shaking her hand as if she'd scorched it on a stove. "Somebody needs supper and a back rub," she said. "I'll fix us a drink."

The back rub meant what he thought it would mean. When he felt the pressure of her knees, the cool rivulet of cedarwood lotion against his back, he knew she intended this as a prelude to sex.

"Guess what my show is about tomorrow?" She smoothed the lotion across his shoulder blades, then swept downward toward his ass.

"What?"

"Foreskin reconstruction. Is that gross or what?"

He laughed into the pillow.

"I have a book I'm supposed to read, but to hell with it." He grunted.

"I'd rather play, wouldn't you?" She leaned down and kissed the left cheek of his ass.

He smiled at her and petted her head and looked at her as lovingly as he knew how. "I'm not up to it, babe. I'm sorry."

"That's OK," she said brightly, nuzzling his neck. "I like it up here too."

"Mmm. So do I."

"You're the best company, Brian."

"Thanks."

"We have the best time." She tightened her grip on him and sighed. "I can't believe it, really. All this and *Entertainment Tonight*."

They lay there for a while, drifting off together. Then Mary Ann retreated to the armchair with her circumcision book, peering around it from time to time to catch his eye sympathetically.

He slept fitfully, waking all the way when she turned off the light and climbed into bed next to him.

"What time is it?" he asked.

"Almost midnight," she replied. "Go to sleep, baby."

It felt later for some reason. It should have been morning. He turned over several times, trying to find a position in which his muscles wouldn't ache.

"Are you all right?" she asked, snuggling against his back.

"Just . . . kinda warm."

"You're burning up."

"If you could just . . . move over a little."

She did so. "I'm gonna take your temperature."

"No. Forget it. I'm OK."

"But if—"

"I want to sleep, Mary Ann!"

A wounded silence followed. Finally, she patted his butt and rolled over. "Feel better," she said.

He slept straight through until her alarm went off. She silenced it by saying "OK," then sat bolt upright in bed. "Brian, these sheets are soaking wet!"

He felt the covers. She was right.

She pressed his forehead, reading his temperature. "I think your fever's gone."

He felt much better, he realized. Maybe the worst was over.

She climbed over him and got out of bed. "You lucked out," she said. "It was one of those twenty-four-hour things."

"I guess so," he said.

She reached the bathroom and stopped, adding: "Change the sheets and get back into bed. You don't wanna push it."

"You're right, though. I feel fine."

"Never mind. Go to sleep. Nguyet can feed Puppy. I'll leave a note for her."

He drifted off in the damp sheets, sleeping for another three or four hours. When he woke, he heard Nguyet singing to Shawna in Vietnamese. Mary Ann's foreskin forum was blaring away full tilt on the set in the kitchen.

He eased the Princess out of its cradle and punched Michael's number. He answered with a breezy hello on the first ring.

"Let's go somewhere," he said, without identifying himself.

"Where?" asked Michael.

"Anywhere. I gotta get outa here, man."

"Are you watching her show?"

"The maid is watching it," said Brian.

"It's too fabulous. A new low. I love it."

"Michael . . ."

"You didn't tell her, did you?"

"No."

"You're going to, aren't you?"

"Yes. Soon. I gotta sort it all out first. Look, if we could just haul ass for a few days . . . go to Big Sur, the Mother Lode, whatever . . ."

"Just you and me?"

"Yeah."

"Brian . . ."

"I won't spend the whole time talking about it. I swear. I just need some company . . . some laughs."

"Ten days, Brian."

"Four, OK? Five. How's that?"

"Are you feeling OK?"

"Sure. Fine. Never better."

Michael paused, then asked: "How do you feel about the Russian River?"

"Great. What's up? You know a place?"

"I think so," said Michael. "A cabin in Cazadero. A friend said I could use it."

"Yeah? And you wouldn't mind . . . you know . . . ?"

"Putting up with a dork like you?"

Brian laughed. "We've talked about doing this."

"You're right."

"So let's do it."

"OK," said Michael. "You got a deal."

The Road to Wimminwood

They were heading north at last, D'orothea at the helm of the station wagon, DeDe in the navigator's seat. The children were in back, burrowed in a warren built of camping gear, arguing bitterly over ownership of the Nerds.

"Mom bought them for me," Edgar declared.

"She bought them for both of us," said Anna. "Didn't you, Mom?"

DeDe had heard enough of this. "Lay off me, you guys. I'm about to crack some heads back there."

"Ooooh," mugged Anna. "I'm really scared."

"I mean it, Anna."

"Well, Edgar ate all the Nerds, and you bought them for me."

"I bought them for both of you."

"Well, he ate all of them."

"You bought them Nerds?" asked D'or.

"I told her she could have some," said Edgar.

"You did not!" said Anna.

"What's a Nerd?" asked D'or.

DeDe knew what was coming next. "Never mind," she said. "Let's see the box."

"D'or . . . don't read to me, please. I know they're disgusting."

"'Sucrose, dextrose, malic acid and/or citric acid . . . '"

"All *right*, D'or."

"'Artificial and natural flavors, yellow dye number five, and carnauba wax.' Yum-yum . . . carnauba wax . . . one of my personal faves."

DeDe let it go. There was no point in arguing with D'or when she was soapboxing about nutrition. DeDe addressed the children instead: "Can't you guys just cool it? We're almost there."

"How much further?" asked Anna, always the stickler for details.

"Not much."

"How much?"

"I don't know, Anna. Less than an hour."

"If we hate it, can we come home?"

"You won't hate it," D'or put in. "They've got a special duck pond just for kids."

"Big deal," said Anna.

"What's blue and creamy?" asked Edgar.

"Shut up," said Anna.

"And," D'or added, still on her sales pitch, "we get to sleep out under the stars, and eat our meals in the open air, and meet lots of—"

"What's blue and creamy?" repeated Edgar.

"Edgurr," whined Anna. "Shut your big trap."

"It's a riddle," said Edgar, leaning over the seat to confront D'or. "Give up?"

"Sit down," ordered DeDe. "You're gonna make D'or drive off the road."

"OK," said D'or, "what's blue and creamy?"

"Smurf sperm!" said Edgar, laughing triumphantly.

DeDe stared at him in horror. "Where did you hear that?"

The boy hesitated, then said: "Anna told me."

"I did not," said Anna.

"Yes you did."

"Liar!"

"All right, both of you! Let's keep it down back there!" This was D'or, raising her voice above the din. There was just enough menace in her tone to command the silence of the twins. DeDe both admired and resented D'or's flair for authority. Why couldn't mothers invoke such terror?

As they drove through Montc Rio, D'or turned to DeDe and said: "I guess ol' Booter's around here somewhere."

DeDe nodded. "Across that bridge and to the left."

"To the left, huh. Must be tough for the old fascist."

DeDe shot her a nasty look meaning *Not in front of the children.*

D'or persisted. "That's fair enough, I think. He laid a wreath on a Nazi grave."

"It was a reconciliation ceremony. You know that."

"Sure."

"And it was part of his official duties."

"Mmm."

"It was also a peacemaking gesture," said DeDe tartly. "Aren't you supposed to be in favor of that?"

D'or shrugged. "I don't notice him making peace with the Russians."

DeDe frowned at her lover, then turned and gazed out the window. She was hardly Booter's biggest defender, but she hated it when D'or used him to pick a fight. What was going on, anyway? Why was D'or looking for trouble?

"Mom?" said Edgar.

"Yes, darling?"

"How much longer?"

"Oh, two or three miles at the most. Do me a favor, will you?"

"What?"

"Don't tell that joke when we get there."

After Monte Rio, the landscape opened up to the blazing blue sky. The river wound lazily toward the Pacific, flanked by summerhumming thickets and shiny white thumbnails of sand. They crossed the bridge at Duncans Mills (groaning at the self-conscious Old Westernness of the storefronts), then turned left on the river road.

"'Moscow Road,'" said D'or, reading the sign. "Now, here's a road worth turning left on."

DeDe smiled, feeling mellower now. She reached over and squeezed D'or's leg. "What an adventure," she said.

They followed the road into a small stand of willows, which obscured their view of the river. Next came an imposing hedge of evergreens and an equally imposing redwood fence. "The security looks good," said D'or.

It reminded DeDe vaguely of the approach to the Golden Door, her favorite fat farm of yesteryear, but she decided not to say so. She turned to the kids instead.

"So," she said, hoping her newfound enthusiasm was contagious. "You guys are gonna have your very own tent."

The twins said "Yay!" in unison, their Nerd dispute all but forgotten.

"Look," chimed D'or. "Here we are."

A young black woman stood by the roadside, flagging them into the entrance. D'or slowed down, turned left, and spoke to the woman. "Registration?"

"All the way down," said the woman. "Park first and unload your gear. There's a shuttle to the land."

"The land of what?" asked DeDe.

The woman laughed and leaned into the car. "The land of Looney Tunes, if you ask me." She stuck out her hand to D'or. "I'm Teejay," she said. "Welcome to Wimminwood."

"Thanks. I'm D'orothea. These are DeDe, Edgar and Anna."

Teejay smiled and raised a pink palm in the window. "Hi, guys." Turning to D'or, she pointed at DeDe. "Tell her about the land," she said.

D'or gave her a high sign and drove on.

"Well," said DeDe. "Tell me about the land."

D'or smiled. "It's just a term for the encampment. It fosters a sense of community."

Maybe to you, thought DeDe.

D'or parked in a dusty clearing that was already chockablock with cars. Several dozen other arrivals were in the process of disembarking, hooting hellos, hoisting their bedrolls to their shoulders.

"We just leave the car here?" DeDe asked.

"You got it," said D'or. She turned to the kids. "OK, gang, here's the deal. Everybody grab a handful of stuff. Mom and I will get the tents and the heavy things. You get the bedrolls and whatever's left."

The twins tackled this chore with uncharacteristic vigor. DeDe cast an optimistic glance in D'or's direction, then threw herself into the team effort.

Judging from the other new arrivals, their own paraphernalia was quite Spartan indeed. Some of these women were weighed down like pack animals, toting coolers and lawn chairs, Coleman lanterns, fishing gear and guitars. They converged, along with the Halcyon-Wilson household, on a central loading dock, then stood in line for registration.

"Pick a duty," said D'or, when their turn came.

"What?"

"What work duty do you wanna do?"

"Wait a minute," said DeDe. "Nobody mentioned any work duty."

"It's in the brochure, Deirdre. Don't be such a damn debutante."

DeDe would have put up a fight then and there, but the children were watching, and she didn't want to inaugurate their stay by setting a bad example. "What are the choices?" she asked icily.

D'or read from a list posted at the registration table. "Kitchen, Security, Garbage Patrol, and Health Care."

"Which one are you picking?"

"Garbage Patrol."

DeDe grimaced, but the choice made perfect sense for D'or. The woman loved to clean more than practically anything. "What's Security?" DeDe asked.

389

D'or shrugged. "Patrolling, mostly. Keeping an eye on things."

That sounded tame enough. Better than Kitchen, certainly, and a lot less icky than Health Care. "Put me down for that," said DeDe.

They were issued orange wristbands—plastic hospital bracelets, actually—which indicated they were festivalgoers rather than performers or technical people. This smacked of concentration camp to DeDe, and she couldn't help saying so.

"I know," said D'or, "but there's a reason for everything. All of this has evolved from past experience."

After registering, they walked back to their gear and waited with the other women for the shuttle. It arrived ten minutes later in the form of a flatbed truck—much to the delight of the children, who invariably applauded any form of transportation that promised to place their lives in jeopardy.

As they bounced along a rutted dirt road into the wilderness, DeDe shouted instructions above the engine noise. "Hold on to something heavy, Edgar. Anna, stop that . . . Sit down this minute."

D'or threw back her head and laughed, a strange primal glint in her eyes.

Ten minutes later, the truck lurched to a stop in a clearing near the river. DeDe hopped down first, grateful for release, then gave the children a hand. Readjusting the belt around their double sleeping bag, D'or said: "Now we're on our own. Where you wanna camp?"

DeDe shrugged. "Someplace pretty."

D'or scanned the map she had picked up at registration before pointing downriver to a clump of trees. "The party-hearty girls are over there. The S and M group is half a mile behind us."

"Swell," said DeDe drily. "What else?"

"Mom," chirped Anna. "Let's go down there. It's pretty next to the river."

DeDe draped her arm across her daughter's shoulders. "Sounds good to me. What about you, Edgar?"

"I like the river," said her son.

DeDe turned to D'or. "How's it look on your map? Anything we should know about down there?"

Her lover caught the irony in her tone and reprimanded her with a frown. Then she said: "The Womb is up at the next cove, but that's fairly far away."

"The Womb," echoed DeDe, deadpanning. "I'm almost afraid to ask."

D'or lifted the bundled tent and began to stride toward the river. "If you're going to be snide about everything, I'd rather not hear it."

DeDe let it go. Turning back to the twins, she checked for dangling or abandoned gear, then said: "Now stick close, you guys. This is uncharted territory we're heading into."

"Oh, sure," said Anna, rolling her eyes.

DeDe helped Edgar rearrange the weight on his backpack, then hurried to catch up with D'or. "OK," she said. "Tell me about the Womb."

"Don't patronize me."

"I'm interested, OK?"

D'or hesitated, then said: "It's a place women can go when they need emotional support. This is a big festival . . . people can get hurt."

DeDe visualized a tent full of wailing women, all boring the Birkenstocks off the poor dyke who'd pulled Womb duty. But she now knew better than to say so. "It sounds very supportive," she told D'or.

When the time came to pitch their tents, they chose a stretch of riverfront property separated from the other campers by a stand of madrone trees. No one, not even D'or, had the slightest idea as to which plastic rods went where, but the process of finding out drew the family together in a way that warmed DeDe's heart.

Afterwards, flushed with their achievement, the four of them crammed into the larger tent and sat staring out at the light dancing on the water. They had been there only a matter of minutes when someone approached through the madrone trees.

The head that appeared through the tent flap had been shaved just short of bald. The remaining hair had been etched with a female symbol, with the circle part of the crown and the cross coming down to the forehead.

"Hello there," said the woman, smiling at them.

"Hi," they chorused.

She extended her hand to D'or. "I'm Rose Dvorak."

"I'm D'orothea Wilson. This is my lover, DeDe Halcyon . . . and our kids, Edgar and Anna."

The woman looked at Edgar for a moment longer than necessary, then addressed D'or. "I saw you come in. Just wanted to welcome you."

"Oh," said D'or. "Are you . . . uh . . . with the Wimminwood staff?"

Rose smiled in a way that was meant to convey both mystery and authority. "I'm pretty much all over."

Great, thought DeDe. Thanks for sharing that. "Do you know the way to the dining area?" she asked.

"Sure," said Rose. "If you come out, I can show you."

DeDe left the tent and followed Rose to the other side of the madrone trees. "Look," said Rose, when they were out of earshot. "That boy can't stay here."

"What do you mean?"

"Don't play dumb. This is women-only space."

"But he's not ten yet. He's only eight."

"Ten is the cutoff date for attendance. He still can't camp on women-only space. That's made perfectly clear in the regulations."

"Well, Jesus . . . what are we supposed to do with him? Float him on a raft in the river?"

The woman gave her a long, steely stare. "Have you read the regulations? Maybe that would help."

"Well, I've—"

"There's a separate compound for boys under ten. It's over next to the—"

"A compound?" said DeDe. "Give me a break. A compound?"

"It's called Brother Sun," said Rose.

"So . . . my daughter can stay with me, but my son has to be . . . deported?"

"I never used that word," said Rose.

DeDe was livid. This was Sophie's Choice without the choice. "Well, this is truly sick. This is really the dumbest thing I've ever . . ."

"They should have told you at the gate," said Rose. "I don't know why they didn't."

"Yeah. Must have been an oversight on the part of a *human being.*"

Rose's eyes narrowed noticeably. "I have an obligation to report the boy. My job is to ensure that this remains women-only space. If you're not willing to comply with the rules, you're free to leave at any time."

DeDe faltered, then turned, hearing D'or approach. "What's the matter?" D'or asked Rose.

"It's Edgar," said DeDe. "His wee-wee is a major threat."

D'or met the remark with a scowl and spoke to Rose. "He's not ten, you know."

"Ten has nothing to do with it," said DeDe.

This time D'or gave her a look which said: *Shut up and let me talk to the woman.*

"We have a separate camp for the boys," Rose explained, sounding far more placatory than she had with DeDe. "It's a courtesy we provide for women who can't leave their kids at home. If you'd like to see the facility . . ."

"But we came here as a family," said D'or. "Surely you can bend the rules enough to . . ."

Rose shook her head, a maddening smirk on her face. "You know where that would lead." She turned and swaggered away, yelling her final edict over her shoulder. "The person to see is Laurie at Brother Sun. I'll check with her later to see if he's situated."

"Let's go home," said DeDe.

"Now wait a minute."

"I won't stand for this, D'or. That woman will not tell me what to . . ."

"I know, I know." D'or slipped her arm around DeDe's waist. "She's a bitch. I'll grant you that."

DeDe felt a sudden urge to cry. At this rate, she'd be down at the Womb before she knew it. "D'or . . . why didn't you tell me about this compound business?"

"I didn't know, hon. Honest."

"Well, I think we should just leave. I couldn't possibly tell Edgar . . ."

"Hang on, now. We don't know what it's like. It could be very nice."

"Forget it."

"He'd be with other boys his own age. Haven't we talked about that? It would be like summer camp . . . only we'd be just a few hundred yards away. And we could visit him all the time."

"But he couldn't visit us. He'd feel excluded."

"How do you know, hon? He doesn't wanna go to the concerts. He told us so himself."

This was true enough, DeDe decided. Or were they just rationalizing their way out of a difficult situation? What if Edgar didn't understand? What if this marred him for life?

"Tell you what," said D'or. "Let's you and me go see this Laurie person at the boys' camp. If the place is the pits, we'll scrap the whole thing . . . pack our gear and find a good public campground somewhere in the area."

DeDe nodded tentatively. D'or was at her very best when building bridges over troubled waters.

Brother Sun turned out to be far nicer than DeDe had imagined. There were at least a dozen boys, and most of them were Edgar's age. Wasn't this what she had always wanted for her son? Edgar, after all, was the sole male in a household of women. For the time being, at least, an all-boy environment would probably do him a world of good.

Laurie, the boys' overseer, was fiftyish and warmhearted, with an apparent devotion to her mission at Wimminwood. She referred to her charges as "the little hellions," but it was obvious that the boys liked her. The camp itself was a semicircle of redwood lean-tos, only yards away from a boys-only swimming hole.

In the end the decision was left up to Edgar. He took to the idea almost instantly, banishing any vestige of guilt DeDe might have felt. Only Anna put up a mild protest, faintly envious of this "special place for boys," but D'or assured her that there was plenty here for girls to do too.

Leaving Edgar at the compound, they set out across the land to get their bearings. They found women laughing around camp-fires and perched in trees along the river, women playing bridge and chopping wood and drinking beer with other women.

When they reached the central stage, a square dance was in progress. A hundred sun-flushed women, clad only in boots and bandannas, were do-si-doing to the music of a string band. Amused yet riveted by the sight, DeDe turned and caught her lover's eye.

"Well?" said D'or. "It's something, huh?"

DeDe nodded. It was something, all right.

Historical Interest

At 28 Barbary Lane, Michael was packing his suitcase when the phone rang.

"Michael?" said the voice on the other end.

"Yeah."

"It's Thack Sweeney. The guy you met in solitary."

"Oh, hi." Didn't it figure? Didn't it just figure he would call now?

"I told you I'd call."

"Yeah, you did."

"Listen, what's your schedule like tomorrow?"

Shitfuckpiss, thought Michael. "Well, actually, I'm going to the river with a friend."

"Oh, yeah? Sounds like fun." If he was devastated, he didn't show it.

"What did you have in mind?" asked Michael.

"Oh . . . nothing much. Just hanging out."

Hanging out had never sounded so good. "This trip is kind of set," said Michael. "Otherwise . . ."

"I understand," said Thack.

Michael wavered, then asked: "What are you doing tonight?"

Thack laughed. "Lurking outside your door at the local mom-and-pop."

"Huh?"

"Well, not technically, but pretty close. The grocer says you're a block or two away. I was walking up Union Street and just decided to call. It's the wildest coincidence."

Michael wanted more than coincidence. "You're at the Search-light?"

"That's the one."

"You . . . uh . . . want to come over?"

"Well . . . you must be packing."

"No. I mean, I'm finished. Come on over, if you want."

"How do I get there?"

"Uh . . . walk over the crest of Union, take a left on Leaven-worth. Barbary Lane is on the left, halfway down the hill. There's a stairway you can see from the street."

"Got it," said Thack.

Michael hung up, sat down, smiled uncontrollably, stood up again and did a little jig around the room. Then he finished washing the dishes, gave the bathroom a quick once-over, and plucked the dead blossoms off his potted azalea.

When Thack arrived, ten minutes later, his cheeks had been pinched pink by the fog. "Boy," he said, coming into the apartment. "You didn't warn me about those steps."

"Oh, no," said Michael. "Did one break?"

Thack nodded. "I bailed out just in time."

"Where was it?"

"Up near the top . . . just before you reach the part with the killer stones. Get many lawsuits?"

Michael smiled at him. "The lane dwellers are used to it."

Thack looked around him, like a dog sniffing out his bedding, then went directly to the window and peered out to the bay. "The lane dwellers, huh? Sounds almost anthropological."

"Well, it is . . . kinda."

"Like an Amazonian tribe or something. Well, there it is, all right."

"What?"

"The Alcatraz lighthouse. You said you could see it from here."

"Oh . . . yeah. That's it. Look, if you don't mind making yourself at home, I should go fix that step."

"Now?"

"It's kind of . . . an agreement we all have. There are planks in the basement already cut to fit. It shouldn't take that long."

"This I gotta see," said Thack.

"If you'd rather wait here . . ."

"No. Go on, lead the way."

So Michael went to the basement, with Thack on his heels. He took a plank from a stack of ten (marked *SOS—Save Our Steps* by Mrs. Madrigal) and found a hammer and the appropriate nails.

"The steps are in jeopardy," he explained, as they crossed the courtyard into the pungent darkness of the lane.

"As are the steppers," said Thack.

"If the city gets another complaint, they'll tear them down, no questions asked. They've already got plans to replace them with reinforced concrete."

"Can't have that," said Thack, a little too deadpan about it.

Michael looked at him, then continued: "We're buying time right now, trying to get public support." He gave up the pitch, wary of Thack's irreverence.

When they reached the steps, the broken one was immediately apparent, white as a dinosaur bone under the Barbary Lane street-light. Michael pulled the fragments free and removed the rusty nails with his hammer.

Thack squatted next to him. "The support beam is almost as rotten."

"I know."

"Hardly seems worth it."

Michael looked up at him. "I thought you said you were a preservationist."

Thack shrugged. "Antebellum stuff. These steps don't have any historical interest."

Michael lifted the plank into place. "Maybe not to you."

Thack watched him hammer for a while, then said: "Gimme that."

"What?"

"Do it right, if you're gonna do it. Gimme the hammer."

Michael blinked indignantly.

"You hammer funny," said Thack.

Michael considered several retorts, then handed him the hammer. "I'm a nurseryman, all right?"

Thack made the nail disappear in three deft strokes. In spite of his mild humiliation, Michael actually enjoyed the moment, his eyes fixed on the set of Thack's jaw, the corded white flesh of his neck. When he had finished, Thack sat on the mended step and patted the spot next to him. "Try it out," he said.

Michael took a seat. "I guess this seems kinda dumb to you."

"What?"

"Caring so much about these steps."

"I dunno," said Thack.

"I've been here almost ten years, so this place is kind of in my blood."

"Yeah. I'm that way about Charleston. I'd have a hard time leaving it."

"Well," said Michael, "then you understand."

Thack drummed his fingers against the railing.

"How long will you stay?" asked Michael.

"Oh . . . four or five more days."

Michael nodded, mad at himself for capitulating to Brian's panic. It was high time he started catering to his own needs again. "You know," he began, "if you'd like to join us at the river . . ."

"Thanks," said Thack. "I wouldn't horn in on your date."

"Oh," said Michael. "He's just an old friend."

"Oh."

"He's straight," Michael added. "I'm sure he wouldn't mind. I mean, I was the one who asked him. It's no big deal." He felt a little traitorous saying this, but Brian would just have to deal with it.

"Well," said Thack. "It does sound like fun."

"You bet."

"Three buddies in the boondocks."

"Right," said Michael a little uneasily. What sort of compromise was he accepting? "You'll like Brian, I think. He's a great guy."

They stayed there on the steps, bantering jovially under a lemon-drop moon. Half an hour later, having established a late morning rendezvous, Thack bid Michael a hearty farewell and set off to catch the cable car at Union and Hyde.

Elated but a little confused, Michael called Brian and broke the news to him. He took it well, all things considered.

"No problem, man. It's your cabin."

"Well, it's our trip, though. I didn't wanna . . . you know . . . impose my . . ." He didn't finish, since it would have been an outright lie. He had done what he'd wanted to do. Why pretend to be considerate now?

"It's OK," said Brian. "I just wanna get away. You didn't tell him about . . . Geordie and all?"

"No," said Michael. "Nothing."

"Good. That's strictly between us, Michael."

"I know," said Michael.

Settling In

Wren's nest, as she had come to think of it, was an oversized redwood bungalow with porches on three sides and a huge central fireplace built of smooth stones. It was perched on the ridge above Monte Rio, the last house on the road. From her porches she could look down on a squadron of turkey vultures, circling endlessly above a sleepy river.

There was a washer and a dryer, a black-and-white TV set, an assortment of comfy old chairs and couches. The refrigerator had been extravagantly stocked with wines and exotic deli food. The linen closet would have been ample for a family of six.

After several days in this cleansing environment, her end-of-tour tension had all but disappeared. She had lost track of time again, and the sensation was pure bliss. Life was a random pastiche of reading, eating, sleeping, sunning, wandering, and eating some more.

Sometimes, she would drive down to the Cazadero General Store in the white Plymouth Horizon Booter had rented for her use. She would loiter there with a dripping Dove bar, marveling at the time-warpy blend of tourist kitsch, organic grains and tie-dyed T-shirts. Most of all she adored the bulletin board, with its folksy index cards about belly-dance classes and "fixer-uppers" and solar panels for sale.

Her only other foray into the outside world had been to see *Some Like It Hot* at the movie house in Monte Rio. The Rio Theater was an entertainment in itself, a riverside Quonset hut with a Deco façade, noble in its failure to be grand. After the show, a chubby teenager had recognized the world's most beautiful fat woman and requested an autograph.

Comforted to learn that her fame was still intact, Wren had written "Think Big" on the kid's popcorn box.

Her agent had been pissed, of course. Not to mention her PR man, to whom fell the sorry task of canceling her Portland and Seattle engagements. Neither one of them believed her cock-and-bull story about this impromptu getaway, and her now-delayed return to Chicago had alternately wounded and enraged her lover, Rolando.

She didn't give a damn, really. She was more content now than she'd been in ages, and she was being paid handsomely for it. Her bed time with Booter had totaled less than two hours so far, and his requirements had been reasonable and few.

Besides, she liked the old buzzard.

"Where is it?" she asked him when he arrived for his third visit. It was late afternoon and they were standing on the porch.

"Where's what?"

"You know. This mystical scout camp of yours. Point it out to me."

He gestured vaguely off to the left. "You can't really see it from here. It's a sort of bowl. You can only see it from Bohemian property. That's the beauty of it."

She gave him a teasing look. "When you're plotting world domination."

He smiled thinly and shook his head.

"Don't you swim in the river?" she asked.

"Sure. That part down there with the platform. We call it the swimming pool."

She followed his finger to a gray pier, a row of tented changing rooms. "Those teeny little people . . . they're Bohemians?"

He nodded.

"They don't look very Bohemian from here."

He chuckled. "And even less so close up."

She laughed. "And there are no girls allowed?"

"Not during the encampment."

"I bet I could get in." This made him flinch a little, so she added: "Not that I would, of course."

"The gate guards are pretty smart," he said.

"I'd swim the river," she said. "I'd wait until it got dark and I'd swim the river naked, with my clothes in a plastic bag. Then I'd—"

"I hope you're not serious."

She shook her head, smiling. "I like making you nervous, Boo-Roger."

His relief was evident. "I don't know you that well," he said. "I don't know when you're joking."

"I was right, though, wasn't I?"

"About what?"

"Getting in. That beach is your weak flank."

He shrugged. "You'd still be a woman. You couldn't do much about that. You'd be spotted the first time you showed your face."

She smiled as cryptically as possible.

"How about a drink?" said Booter.

"You're on," said Wren.

She left him there in the dwindling light and went to the kitchen, returning minutes later with a couple of Scotch and waters.

"Thank you," said Booter.

She clinked her glass against his. "I'm a helluva gal."

He smiled faintly, then turned his gaze back to the river. "So it's . . . back to Chicago after this?"

"Yep."

"You like it there?"

"I adore it," she said.

"What about San Francisco?"

"What about it?"

"Did you like it?"

She shrugged. "It was OK."

"Just OK?"

She laughed. "Good God!"

"What?"

"You're all alike here."

"How so?" he asked.

"You demand adoration for the place. You're not happy until *everybody* swears undying love for every nook and cranny of every precious damn—"

"Whoa, missy."

"Well, it's true. Can't you just worship it on your own? Do I have to sign an affidavit?"

He chuckled. "We're that bad, are we?"

"You bet your ass you are."

He swirled the ice in his glass, then took a gulp and set the glass down on the porch railing. "You have a . . . uh . . . beau back in Chicago?"

"Sure," she replied.

"Nice fellow?"

She smiled at him. "Don't know any other kind."

He nodded. "Good." The light in his eyes seemed almost paternal.

"He's Cuban," she added, just to catch his response. It showed in the set of his mouth, a brief involuntary twitch of the mustache. "Thought so," she said, smiling slightly.

"What?"

"You're a bigot."

His jaw became rigid.

"It's OK," she said, wiggling his fleshy old earlobe. "It's your generation, that's all. Tell me what your wife is like."

He was thrown off balance for a moment.

"Do you *like* her?" she asked.

"She's a fine lady," he said finally. "She drinks a little too much, but she's . . . very nice."

"I'm glad."

"That she drinks?"

She made a goofy face at him. "That you like her. That she likes you."

"Oh, we're friends," he said. "Most of the time."

"Amazing. After . . . how many years of marriage?"

He smiled. "Almost two."

She laughed. "C'mon."

"We were next-door neighbors for thirty years," he explained. "We were married to other people, but . . . they died. So it made sense."

"Were you in love when you were still married to the other people?"

403

"We aren't in love now," he said.

She nodded. "But she's still your significant other."

He gave her a blank look.

"Your spouse and/or lover and/or best buddy."

"Somewhere in there," he said.

They laughed in unison, creating a momentary intimacy which seemed to unsettle him as much as it did her. "Actually," he said, shaking his drink, "I was closer to her husband."

"Oh?" She arched an eyebrow at him.

"Nothing like that," he said.

She aped his expression, looking stern and jowly. "No, of course not."

"He was in my camp," said Booter, "down at the Grove."

Wren gazed down at the distant swimming platform, conjuring up the happy couple, genial and spider-browed, stretched out platonically on the gray wood.

"He was a good man," Booter added.

Wren nodded.

"He died about ten years ago. He brought a mistress here himself. He told me so."

"I'm not your mistress," said Wren.

"No," said Booter. "I meant . . ."

"That her first husband fucked around too."

"Yes," he said meekly.

"Does she know?"

He shook his head.

"Did your first wife know?"

"No." He looked decidedly uncomfortable. "This hasn't been a regular thing."

"Uh-huh."

"It's just that . . . when I saw you—"

"I know," she said, cutting him off, "and I'm the kinda gal who takes that as a compliment."

He gave her a hapless look.

"Lighten up," she said. "We understand each other."

Up a Creek

Honey-blond meadows flew past them in a blur as the VW left the freeway and headed west toward the river. Michael and Brian were in the front seat; Thack was in the back. This unromantic arrangement had been Thack's doing, since he had climbed in first, but Michael had chosen not to take it personally.

"Well," said Brian, out of the blue. "Mary Ann wasn't exactly thrilled."

"About what?" asked Michael, playing it safe. As agreed, he'd said nothing to Thack about Geordie.

"This trip," said Brian. "I didn't give her much notice."

"Oh."

"I'm gonna miss *Entertainment Tonight*."

Michael didn't get it. "Can't you tape it?"

"No, I mean . . . I'm gonna miss being on it."

Thack leaned forward. "You were gonna be on *Entertainment Tonight?*"

"You didn't tell me that," said Michael, even more impressed than Thack.

Brian shrugged. "She was gonna be on it. I was just gonna be there. Part of her goddamn persona."

"Hey," said Michael. "Ease up."

"That's what she said. *Persona* is exactly the word she used."

"Well . . ."

"Your wife is in show business?" asked Thack.

"She's got her own talk show," Michael explained.

"That's great," said Thack, turning to Brian. "What sort?"

"The regular sort," said Brian. His tone was colorless, bordering on hostile.

"She's good," said Michael, trying to keep it light. "She got some major dish out of Bette Midler . . ."

"What about here?" Thack pointed to the side of the road.

405

"What?" asked Michael.

"We're off the freeway. Let's put the top down."

"Oh . . . right. Good idea." Michael swung off the road into the dusty parking lot of a fruit stand.

"I could use something cold," said Thack. "How 'bout you guys?"

"Sure," said Michael. "Apple juice or something."

"Yeah." Brian nodded. "Fine."

"I'll get 'em," said Thack. "You get the top." He slid out from behind Michael's seat and strode toward the fruit stand.

Michael turned and looked at Brian. "You OK?"

"Yeah."

"This was a rotten idea, huh?"

"No."

"Well, you don't seem to be having a good time."

"Would you be?" Brian wouldn't look at him. "This was gonna be our time, man. I mean, this guy is perfectly nice, don't get me wrong . . ."

"I'm really sorry," said Michael.

"Don't be. I can handle it."

It didn't look that way to Michael. "I thought this would work out great. He likes you, Brian . . . I mean, he seems to. And you seem to like him."

"C'mon. He likes you a helluva lot more than he likes me." He threw up his hand in a gesture of resignation. "That's cool. I'm a fag hag. I can handle it."

Michael laughed. "Stop it."

Brian offered him a game smile. "I just don't wanna be in the way."

"C'mon."

"Well, you guys are an item."

"Says who?" asked Michael, nursing the faint hope that Thack had told Brian as much when he, Michael, had run back to the house for his sunglasses.

"Well . . . I just assumed."

"We don't *all* go to bed with each other, Brian."

Brian shrugged. "This one looks like he might."

"How can you tell?"

Another shrug. "I can tell with you guys."

"Oh, yeah?" It amused him that Brian considered himself an expert on fags—prided himself on it, in fact. "Wrong again, Kemo Sabe."

"We'll see."

"This is strictly brotherly."

"OK."

"Maybe even sisterly, for all I know." There hadn't, after all, been so much as a peck on the cheek the night before.

Thack returned with the juice. "Nice job," he said, handing them the bottles.

"Of what?" asked Michael.

"Taking the top down."

Michael grimaced. "Oh, fuck." He set down his juice and reached for the chrome clamps at the top of the windshield. "We started talking and . . ." Standing up, he pushed back the accordion roof until it fell into place of its own weight.

"Sunshine," said Thack, vaulting into the back seat.

"Hey," Brian said to him, "why don't you let me get back there?"

"I'm fine," came the reply.

"You sure? It's kinda cramped, isn't it?"

"No. Really. It's great. I can stretch out and look up at the red-woods."

"It's not much further," said Michael, disassociating himself from Brian's effort to remedy things.

When they reached Guerneville, Michael announced: "Here it is, boys—our humble tribute to Fire Island."

Thack, who'd been recumbent in the back seat, sat up with telling suddenness and scanned the men along the main drag. Seeing this in the mirror, Michael felt some distant cousin of jealousy, nasty but manageable, like a paper cut on the finger.

"I came up here once," said Brian, "to the jazz festival."

Michael turned and smiled at him. Sterile or not, this man was breeder through and through. "Best of Breeder," he had called him once. Surely there were gay men somewhere who revered jazz, but Michael didn't know any.

"Do they get good people?" asked Thack.

"Brubeck," said Brian. "I saw Brubeck here."

"No shit," said Thack.

Brian said: "Tell Michael how good he is. Michael hates him."

"I don't *hate* him," said Michael.

"He hates him," said Brian.

"I like tunes," said Michael. "Call me crazy, but that's the way I am."

Thack kept his eyes on the sidewalk. "This is a nice town."

"It's too much like Castro Street," said Michael, mouthing the stock criticism. It wasn't really true, but he resented the place for consuming so much of Thack's attention. "I'm glad we're gonna be out a ways."

"Where is Casanova?" asked Thack.

"Cazadero," said Michael. "We follow this road along the river until we get a few miles past Monte Rio. Then we hang a right and follow Austin Creek for a few more miles. We're at the mercy of Charlie's map."

"We'll find it," said Thack.

What they found was a smallish, newly built structure in the redwoods along Austin Creek. Its siding was plywood, the front door was aluminum, and the main room was paneled with the sort of pre-grooved faux walnut used in rumpus rooms the world over.

Michael's heart sank. The yawning stone fireplace he'd envisioned had been usurped by a hooded atrocity built of shiny orange metal. There was a comfortable sofa (herringbone corduroy, obvi-

ously late seventies) and a decent bathroom, but the place was nowhere near the stuff of fantasy.

And nowhere near big enough.

"Where's the bedroom?" asked Brian.

"Let's see," said Michael, his depression mounting.

"You're lookin' at it," said Thack. "That sofa converts, I think,
and there are two studio couches."

Brian gave Michael an accusatory glance. "Did you ask Charlie
whether . . ."

"Yeah," said Michael, "of course. He said he was sure it had at
least three rooms."

"Uh-huh," said Thack. "This room, the kitchen and the bathroom."

"Shit," said Michael.

Brian looked around. "We can put a studio couch in the
kitchen."

"Oh, sure," said Michael.

"This'll be fine," said Thack. "There's plenty of room for all of
us." He peered out the aluminum-frame window. "There's a great
view of the creek."

Michael looked over Brian's shoulder. "Yeah. It's really . . .
close." Even closer were a rusting pink trailer and another prefab
cabin, slightly more soulless than theirs. "I fucked up, guys. I'm
sorry."

"Hey," said Brian.

Thack just shrugged it off. "We've got a fire," he said brightly.
"A place to swim. Big trees. Good company. I'm happy."

They unloaded the car in silence. Then Brian stretched out on the
sofa while Michael and Thack made an exploratory trek to the edge
of the creek. When they returned, their roommate was fast asleep
and snoring.

"Hey," whispered Thack. "Let's take some beers to the creek."

"What beers?" asked Michael, increasingly disturbed by
Thack's chatty-fratty demeanor.

"Check the fridge," said Thack.

Michael did; there were two six-packs of Oly inside. A minor consolation, but a welcome one.

Back at the creek, Thack said: "Hunkering."

"What?"

"That's what this is called in the South."

"They still call it that, huh?"

"Oh, yeah." Thack kicked off his loafers and rolled up the cuffs of his khakis. "I know lots of gay boys who are hunkering fools."

Michael followed Thack's example, doffing his Adidas, finding a flat place on a sunny rock, sliding his pale feet into water which was surprisingly warm.

Thack handed him a cold Oly. "It isn't officially hunkering until the beer is in the hand."

"Right," said Michael.

From neighboring rocks, they lifted their bottles in unison. "To the woods," said Thack.

"To the woods," said Michael.

The beer and blazing sunshine lulled them like a finger on the belly of a lizard. After a long silence, Thack said: "How did you two meet?"

"Me and Brian?"

"Yeah."

"Well . . . he used to live in my building. Him and his wife both. I've known them since they were Swinging Singles."

Thack smiled. "What's she like?"

Michael thought for a moment. "Perky. Sweet. Ambitious. Too serious about the eighties."

"Oh."

"It doesn't bother me. She was just as serious about the seventies."

"Are you friends with her?"

"Oh, sure," said Michael. "Not as much as I used to be, but . . . well, I see her off and on." He trailed his fingers in the water.

Thack skinned off his T-shirt. His chest was white-skinned

and pink-nippled, distractingly defined. Michael caught the briefest whiff of his sweat as the T-shirt went over his head.

"Something's bothering Brian," said Thack.

"Why?"

"Well . . . I think I must rub him the wrong way."

"No, you don't. He likes you. He told me so."

"He did?"

"Yes."

Thack took a sip of his Oly. "I like him too, actually. I wish there were more straight guys like him."

"He's fighting with Mary Ann," said Michael, telling a medium-sized white lie. "He gets a little weird when they fight." That was certainly true enough. "He's a great guy most of the time. Funny, generous . . ."

"Hot," said Thack.

Michael felt the sting of that paper cut again. "Yeah, I guess so."

"You guess so?"

"Well, I've known him such a long time. We're more like brothers or something. I know he's good-looking, but I really don't think of him that way."

He was jealous, he realized suddenly. He was actually jealous of Brian.

Campfire Tales

Drifting back into consciousness, Brian stirred on the sofa. The corduroy gave off a faint aroma of mildew, which tingled in his nostrils. He could hear a noisy bird behind the house and Michael's laughter down by the creek.

He wasn't sure whether he'd been there for thirty minutes or three hours. The headache that had nagged him on the road had subsided somewhat, but the spot in his gut was still burning. He was hot all over, in fact, and his mouth tasted foul.

His tongue made its usual rounds, searching for raw spots that hadn't been there earlier. Finding nothing, he propped himself up on his elbows and gazed out toward the creek. Michael and Thack were still sunning on the rocks.

Brian found his shaving kit and dragged himself into the bathroom. He splashed water on his face, then brushed his teeth, then examined his face in the mirror. His grinding fatigue had made itself known in charcoal smudges under his eyes.

He left the house and walked down to the creek. The guys didn't see him approaching, so he hollered: "How 'bout some grub, men?"

"We gotta go shopping," Michael answered.

"That's what I meant. I'll do it. Tell me what you want."

Thack sat up. "Great."

"Take the car," said Michael.

"Nah," said Brian. "I need the exercise. Whatcha want?"

"Hot dogs," Thack replied, "and baked beans and nachos . . . and stuff for a salad."

"And Diet Pepsi," Michael added. "You know where the store is?"

"Yeah," said Brian.

"We'll get a fire going," said Thack. "We thought we should cook out."

"Good," said Brian.

He left them and headed toward the Cazadero road. It was late afternoon now. Dusty shards of sunlight pierced the redwoods along the creek. As he walked, a family of quail scurried to avoid him. A blue-bellied lizard flickered like a gas flame, then dove into a mossy woodpile, extinguishing itself.

With a mission in mind, he felt better already, picking up his pace as he passed the little green-and-white frame church that marked the edge of the village. By the time he'd reached the Cazadero General Store, he was calmer than he'd been in days.

After assembling the food they needed (plus a Sara Lee lemon cake for dessert), he waited in a short line at the cash register. The woman in front of him—huge breasts, huge hips, startling green eyes—turned and smiled warmly.

"Dinner?"

He looked down at the contents of his red plastic shopping basket. "Yeah. We're gonna cook out."

Her emerald eyes widened. "We?"

"My buddies and me."

"Ah." Without actually smiling, her full mouth registered amusement at some private joke. Something about her seemed familiar, but he was positive they'd never met. He would have remembered for sure.

He looked around the store. "This place is handy. It's got a little bit of everything."

"Yes," she replied. "Doesn't it?"

There was flirtation in her tone, but he pretended not to notice. What was left of his libido had been beaten into cowering submission. He had never gone for such a long time without being horny.

The woman paid for her purchases and left. As the clerk tallied his bill, Brian peered out the doorway in time to see her cop another glance in his direction.

Grinning, she fluttered her long pink fingernails at him, then climbed into a white sedan and drove away.

Thack had found firewood under a plastic sheet behind the house, but there wasn't enough for a big fire, so Michael foraged for flotsam along the creek.

When he returned to the cabin, Thack was hunched over his fire, blowing on a stack of crisscrossed twigs. The sky was still indigo, but here beneath the trees, darkness had come early. The light of the fire cast a coppery glow on Thack's pale features.

Michael laid the wood down. "Your faggots, milord."

"Aye, and fine faggots they are." He smiled. "This isn't illegal, is it?"

"What?"

"Building a fire."

Michael shrugged. "Someone's obviously done it here before."

"Right," said Thack, feeding a dry branch to the flames. "Good

413

enough for me." He looked up at Michael and smiled again—fire builder to wood gatherer—and Michael smiled back. It was a moment of prehistoric domesticity. Words would probably have ruined it.

A nearly full moon looked down on them as Michael finished off his salad. "We should've done baked potatoes," he said. "You know . . . in mud."

Brian said: "When did you ever bake a potato in mud?"

"When I was a scout."

"You were a scout?" asked Thack, sounding a little too amazed.

"I was an Eagle," he replied. "Thank you very much."

"So was I," said Thack.

"Really?"

Thack nodded.

"I never made it past Tenderfoot," said Brian. "I hated it."

"Why?" asked Michael.

"Well, it was fascist, for one thing. We had a belt line at my troop. You know, where we all took off our belts and whipped this other guy's butt while he ran past us."

"That's not fascist," Thack said drily. "That's all-American."

Michael threw another log on the fire. "I hated it too. I did it, but I hated it. My father had been an Eagle, so damned if I wasn't gonna be one too."

"I liked camping trips," said Brian. "I liked that part."

Thack nodded. "Same here."

"I went to Philmont," said Michael. "You know . . . that Explorer camp in New Mexico?"

Both Thack and Brian shook their heads.

"Well . . . anyway, it was a big deal. Guys went there from all over. It was a big deal for me, anyway. I found out about love."

"Oh, God," groaned Brian.

Thack chuckled.

"I was fourteen," Michael said, "and my Explorer troop went on this two-week trip to Philmont. We went by bus, and we stayed at army bases along the way . . ."

"What did I tell ya?" said Brian. "Fascist."

Thack laughed, then turned back to Michael, waiting for him to continue.

"They fed us army food, and we bunked in barracks buildings, and went to movies at base theaters, and . . . God, I'll never forget those soldiers as long as I live. Most of them were just four or five years older than I was, but . . . *vive la différence.*"

Thack said: *"Vive la similarité."*

Brian laughed.

"It was total fantasy," Michael continued. "I wouldn't have had the slightest idea what to do. But . . . it got my engines going. I was hornier than a two-peckered goat by the time I got to Philmont."

"Isn't he quaint?" said Brian, turning to Thack.

"One night," said Michael, ignoring them, "we were camped in this canyon, and there was this hellacious hailstorm, which knocked down our tents and got everything wet, so we were more or less adopted by this group of older scouts—"

"Wait a minute," said Thack, grinning. "Didn't I read this in *First Hand?*"

"First what?" said Brian.

Michael ignored them. "So . . . we went over to the other camp, and dried off in front of the fire, and this older scout shared his poncho with me. He put his arm across my shoulders, and I sort of . . . leaned against him." He stared into the firelight, remembering this.

"And?" said Brian.

"And . . . I just leaned against him. It was the most comfortable, wonderful, amazing thing . . ."

"That's it?" said Thack, joining in the torment.

Brian looked at Thack. "Pretty scorching stuff."

Michael scowled at them both. "You had to be there." He picked up a stick and used it to rearrange the embers. "That's all anybody wants, isn't it? That feeling of being safe with somebody." Hideously embarrassed, he looked at Brian, then at Thack, and dropped the stick into the fire.

Later, back at the house, the three of them went about their separate rituals of ablution, passing each other like salesmen in a boarding-house, toothbrushes in hand, unnaturally formal. Brian went to bed first, falling asleep almost instantly on one of the studio couches. Thack stripped to his underwear and took the other couch, leaving Michael with the convertible sofa, which he didn't bother to convert.

He slept fitfully, awaking just before dawn. Thack was still asleep under his blanket, breathing heavily. Brian stood across the room in his boxer shorts, awkward and disoriented as a wounded bear.

"You OK?" Michael whispered.

Brian held up a corner of his sheet. "Look at this," he said. It was drenched with sweat.

"There's fresh linen in that cedar chest," said Michael. "I'll just get—"

"What the fuck's happening, man?"

Michael took a sheet from the chest and flung it over the studio couch. "Lie down," he said.

"Look, Michael . . ."

"Go on. Lie down."

Brian lay on his stomach. Michael blotted his back with the wet sheet, then kneaded the knotty muscles above his shoulder blades. There was a moment of deceptive quiet before Brian began to sob into the cushions.

"Hush," whispered Michael. "It's OK . . . It's OK."

Dede's Duty

Day broke at Wimminwood. DeDe was the first in her family to stir, rubbing her eyes until they focused on the smooth green ribbon of river, the shimmering willows along the shore. She slipped free from the comfy entanglement of D'or's arms and eased herself out of the sleeping bag.

She sat there naked for a while, hugging her knees, listening to the wrens in the madrone trees. As much as she treasured D'or and the kids, she couldn't help savoring a moment when the world was all hers.

Things had gone beautifully, so far. Edgar had acclimated instantly to Brother Sun, displaying a knack for communal living which had dazzled even Laurie, his overseer. When his NCQ (Non-Competitive Quotient) was measured, he had beaten the socks off all the other kids in the compound.

DeDe, D'orothea and Anna had sampled most of the wonders of Wimminwood. They had played New Games, learned to face-paint, and splashed in the river like overheated ponies. The night before, with a thousand other women, they had sprawled on their backs under the stars while Hunter Davis sang to them:

You're the perfect match/for the imperfect me/coming on when I hold back/holding back when I come on/and darling I love you.

Hearing those lyrics, DeDe had turned and gazed at the miraculous planes of her lover's face, the bottomless black eyes tilted toward the moon.

Then, almost instinctively, she had reached for her daughter's hand, so small and silky-cool in the evening air.

She was happy, she realized. She had everything she wanted. D'or had been right about Wimminwood.

They ate breakfast, as usual, in the open-air vegetarian "chow hall." Food servers clad only in aprons and boots, all four cheeks ruddy from the grills, plopped mounds of steaming oatmeal onto their plates, ordering stragglers to "move it, please, *move it.*"

They found a place at a picnic table with three other people. "Listen," said D'or, digging into her oatmeal. "Anna and me thought we'd go visit Edgar, then maybe check out the Crafts Tent."

DeDe looked at her daughter. "Shopping again, huh?"

"D'or said it's OK."

"We have a limited need for stoneware, you know."

Anna made her grumpy face.

"The same goes for tattoos, temporary or otherwise."

The little girl shot D'or an accusatory glance. "Did you tell her?"

D'or acted as negotiator with DeDe. "Maybe just a little one, huh? Femme. Something in Laura Ashley."

DeDe laughed in spite of herself. "Well, you're the culprit if it doesn't wash off."

"Yay!" crowed Anna. The child was a chronic shopaholic, DeDe realized. Like her grandmother. Like DeDe herself back in her post-debutante, pre-People's Temple days. Was it something in the genes?

"Aren't you coming with us?" asked D'or.

"No," said DeDe. "My work duty is this afternoon, so I'm gonna goof off for a while."

"Go to a workshop," said D'or.

"I might," said DeDe.

"There's one just made for you in Area Five."

"What?"

D'or's lip curled mischievously. "Check it out. Ten o'clock. Area Five."

Alone again, DeDe stood at the bulletin board and considered her options:

9:00–10:00   CRYSTAL WORKSHOP: Cleaning and caring for quartz crystals. How to use different crystals for healing, dreaming and meditation. Mariposa Weintraub, facilitator. Area 8.

9:00–10:00   BODY AND FACIAL HAIR: In slides, stories and song. Bonnie Moran, facilitator. Area 3.

9:30–11:00   YOUR DIET COLA IS OPPRESSING ME: How the patriarchy kills fat wimmin through dieting and harassment. Sandra Takeshita, facilitator. Area 4.

418

10:00–11:00   DOWRY DYKES SUPPORT GROUP: A chance for
               wimmin with money to share with each other
               their feelings about the personal and political
               issues connected with inherited wealth. Leticia
               Reynolds, facilitator. Area 5.

Dowry Dyke, huh? So *that's* what she was. Finally, she had an identity.

She was still smiling at D'or's little joke when a woman next to
her made a snorting noise. "What do you do if you're not hairy, fat or
rich?" She herself was young, lean and tomboyish.

DeDe smiled at her sympathetically. "Something with crystals,
I guess."

"Yeah." The tomboy scuffed the ground with the toe of her
loafers.

"Have you been to one yet?" DeDe asked.

"What? A workshop?"

"Yeah."

"Well, I went to the pottery one yesterday."

"How was it?" asked DeDe.

"Disgustingly PC. It's called 'The Herstory of Pots.'"

"Forget it," said DeDe.

"Our facilitator kept talking about the Hispanic influence on
pottery, and finally I said, Don't you mean 'Herspanic?' and she
looked at me like I'd just pissed in the punchbowl."

DeDe laughed.

"I told her, Pardon me but I gotta go . . . I'm late for my herst-
erectomy."

DeDe giggled. "Did you really?"

"No." She ducked her head in the most beguiling way. "I
thought of that later."

"Esprit de l'escalier," said DeDe.

"What?"

"It's just an expression. For thinking of things later."

"Oh."

They looked at each other sheepishly, both at a loss for words.

"Have you been to many of the concerts?" the young woman asked at last.

"Hunter Davis," said DeDe. "Kate Clinton."

"Wasn't Kate Clinton a riot? Your little girl is gorgeous, by the way."

DeDe was confused.

"I saw you there with her," the woman explained.

"Oh . . . I see."

"I'm Polly Berendt." She extended her hand.

DeDe shook it. "DeDe Halcyon."

"Is that . . . uh . . . swarthy woman your lover?"

DeDe nodded, wondering how closely they'd been watched. "This is our first festival," she said, moving artfully from the specific to the general. "How 'bout you?"

"First one," said Polly, toeing the ground again. "Got off work for it, even."

"What do you do?"

"I work in a nursery. Plant Parenthood."

"Oh," said DeDe. "Michael Tolliver's place."

"You know him?"

"Well, he's sort of a friend of a friend. His lover delivered my kids."

"Jon?"

DeDe nodded. "Sweet guy. Did you know him?"

"No," said Polly. "He was . . . before my time." She paused. "You don't shop there, though. I would've remembered."

DeDe wondered if she was blushing. Even before this strategic compliment, she'd been mildly distracted by Polly's freckled cheeks and white teeth, the sun-gilded down on her forearms. "Actually," she said, "we don't live in the city. We're down on the Peninsula. In Hillsborough."

Polly nodded slowly, taking it in. "That's pretty swanky, isn't it?"

"Well . . . parts of it."

"Are you a Dowry Dyke?"

DeDe laughed. "Not if I don't go to that workshop."

Polly smiled at her. "Wanna go for a walk instead?"

Their hour-long odyssey took them through most of the subdivisions at Wimminwood, through the chemical-free and chemical-tolerant communities, through the zone for the loud-and-rowdy, the zone for the differently abled, the zone for sober support. "God," said Polly when they reached the riverbank, "it's a wonder they don't issue us fuckin' visas or something."

"I suppose it makes things easier," said DeDe, paying lip service to D'or's argument. She wasn't used to dealing with someone so unapologetically incorrect.

Polly's brown eyes wandered to the end of the beach, where a woman was sunning in the nude. "You ever take your shirt off?" she asked.

"No," said DeDe. "Not really. No."

"Why not?"

DeDe shrugged. "My lover and I discussed it. We just don't think it's necessary. We don't need to prove anything to anybody."

Polly looked at her sideways, then skipped a flat stone on the water. "Chicken," she said.

Having lost track of the time, DeDe left Polly in haste just before noon. She ran the last hundred yards to her appointed duty post, a large open-sided tent near the entrance to Wimminwood. It was crawling with efficient women in black T-shirts.

She approached the one she recognized, the cheerful black woman who had greeted them at the gate. "Excuse me, please."

The woman swung around. "I know you. Uh . . . big Buick full of brats."

DeDe laughed. "Don't rub it in."

"I'm Teejay, and you're . . . ?"

"DeDe."

"Right. What can I do for you?"

"I'm looking for the security chief."

Teejay looked around. "I think she's gone out for . . . No, there she is . . . over there, next to the butt cans."

"I'm sorry . . . the what?"

"Butt cans, precious. You know . . ." She made a cryptic motion, encircling her waist with her hands. "Her name is Rose. The one with the haircut."

DeDe felt her face drain. Rose with the haircut. The hateful Rose. The monster who'd deported Edgar to the boys' compound.

Unmistakably the chief, she was leaning against a tent post in loose green fatigue pants. Her breasts, which were bared today, had turned Spam-pink in the broiling sun.

DeDe approached warily, berating herself for not choosing Garbage Patrol, or even Health Care, for heaven's sake. Rose looked at her and said: "We meet again."

"Looks like it," said DeDe.

"You the noon relief?"

"Uh-huh."

"You're not in uniform, then." Rose reached into a box on the ground and produced one of the black T-shirts, handing it to DeDe. "I need you at the gate," she said. "I usually handle it myself, but there's been some trouble over in chem-free."

DeDe nodded. "Will somebody show me . . . uh . . . what I'm supposed to . . ."

"Right. That's my job." Rose winked at her almost amiably, and DeDe felt a little surge of relief. If all the woman wanted was to be in charge, DeDe was more than willing to oblige.

Leading her out to the gate, Rose explained the intricacies of the job. "Mostly you answer questions. Stuff about the various zones, where they should park. *Don't* let any cars onto the land unless they've got a pass."

DeDe was still a little uneasy. "The zones. I don't really know where . . ."

"Here's a map," said Rose, handing her a dog-eared pamphlet. "It's all there."

"Good."

"Oh, yeah. You'll probably have to deal with the Porto-Jane men."

"I'm sorry . . . the what?"

"We call the toilets Porto-Janes," said Rose.

Wouldn't you just? thought DeDe. "Then . . . I let these guys come onto the land?"

"Yeah," said Rose. "They're the only men we allow onto the land. They clean out the Porto-Janes and leave. It takes about an hour total. They've got a truck and ID badges, so ask to see 'em."

"Gotcha," said DeDe.

"There's a walkie-talkie at the gate. You can always call for re-inforcements if there's anything you can't handle on your own. It's been quiet so far."

"Thank God," said DeDe.

"Don't you mean Goddess?" said Rose.

The shift turned out to be far less threatening than DeDe had imag-ined. She spent most of her time chatting with friendly women in overloaded cars. When they groused about the parking regulations, they did it with good humor, and one or two of them had even sent wolf whistles in her direction.

Twenty minutes before the end of her shift, an enormous white limousine pulled up at the gate. The windows were the one-way kind, so she couldn't see a soul until the front window hummed open.

A redheaded woman in a chauffeur's cap leaned out and asked: "Which way to the stage?"

"Well," said DeDe, "it's down this road and to the right, but I'm afraid you can't drive there."

"Why not?"

"It's the policy. No cars on the land. You can park in this lot, if you like. There's a shuttle to the land every fifteen minutes."

The chauffeur looked peeved. "We were told to go to the stage."

"Well, if you're a scheduled performer . . . I mean, if whoever . . ."

"Nothing is scheduled. My customer is a friend of the festival organizer."

"Do you have a pass?" DeDe asked.

"No. We were told we wouldn't need one."

"Gosh, I'm really sorry. My instructions are to make sure that no one—"

"I'll speak to her!" This was a voice from the back seat, raspy but resonant. It was followed by the whir of another shiny black Darth Vader window as it descended into the door. The face revealed was pale and without makeup, framed by a shock of black hair with a white skunk stripe down the middle.

DeDe felt her heart catch in her throat. It was Sabra Landauer, the legendary feminist poet-playwright, whose one-woman show, *Me Only More So*, had been the rage of the last two seasons on Broadway.

"Oh . . . Miss Landauer," said DeDe. "Welcome to Wimminwood."

"Thank you. Is there a problem here?"

"Well, a bit. If they'd told me you were performing . . ."

"I'm not performing. I'm visiting my friend Barbara Farrar, the *founder* of this festival."

"Ah . . . well . . . of course." Her resolve crumbled. When it came to catching hell from Rose or catching hell from Sabra Landauer, there was no contest. "So anyway, the stage is down this road, then off to the left. It's the only big clearing. Anybody with a blue wristband can help you."

"Thanks," said the chauffeur.

"And Ms. Landauer," DeDe added hastily, touching the limo to make it wait, "I have to tell you . . . *Medusa at the Prom* is my favorite book of poems *ever*."

Sabra Landauer made a pistol barrel out of her forefinger and fired it rakishly at DeDe. "Read my latest," she said. "There's something in it just for you."

Before DeDe could respond, the dark window ascended. The limousine sped off down the road in the proverbial cloud of dust. Left standing in it, DeDe felt mildly disgusted with herself.

Why on earth had she said that? She had never even read *Medusa at the Prom*. Why had the mere sight of a famous woman made her lose it completely?

Muddled, she flagged on two other cars, only to be jolted back into reality by the sight of two rough-hewn men in a pickup truck. Remembering their mission, she stepped forward crisply and said: "Porto-Janes?"

"Yo," said the driver, showing a snaggletooth smile. Poor guy, she thought. To have such a job!

She flagged him on, giving him a thumbs-up sign by way of moral support. The pickup moved on, slowly at first; then it scratched off amidst a barrage of maniacal laughter. Both men reached out the window to flip her the bird.

"Dumb-ass lezzie!" one of them shouted.

She stood there for a moment, paralyzed by shock, her head ringing with Rose's admonition to ask for an ID badge. Stupid, stupid, stupid! Those weren't the Porto-Jane people at all!

She lunged for her walkie-talkie, but couldn't remember what people always said in the movies. All she could think of was "Roger," and that, she felt certain, was patently sexist.

"Hello, Security," she said at last, all but shouting into the walkie-talkie. "Security, this is DeDe . . . Come in, please . . . This is an emergency."

No reply.

She checked the talk button to see if it was set correctly. Who knew? She tried again: "Emergency, emergency . . . This is DeDe at the gate. Men on the land! Men on the land!"

Still no answer. She shook the machine vehemently, then threw it into the ditch in a fit of pique.

Coming to rest in a blackberry patch, it startled her by talking back: "Security to gate, Security to gate . . . Come in *immediately* . . ."

She climbed into the ditch and made her way gingerly through the treacherous tendrils, holding them at arm's length like dirty diapers. As she reached for the walkie-talkie, a bramble sprang out of nowhere and pricked her hand. "Damn!" she muttered.

"DeDe, this is Security . . . Come in."

She fidgeted with the button again. "Men on the land, Rose! Men on the land!"

"Tell me!" Rose replied, just as the renegade pickup roared out of Wimminwood, occupants still cackling, spewing a cloud of reddish dust over everything.

Numb with terror, she stared at the departing marauders, then turned back to the walkie-talkie. "Is everybody OK down there?"

A damning silence followed. Finally, Rose said: "Wait there, DeDe. *Do you read me?* Wait there!"

The wait was almost half an hour, reducing DeDe to a nervous wreck. When Rose appeared at last, her jaw was rigid, her eyes chillingly devoid of emotion. A thin white icing of sunscreen now covered her breasts. "OK," she said. "What happened?"

DeDe spoke evenly. "I thought they were the Porto-Jane men."

"Did you ask to see their IDs?"

"No. I asked them if they were the Porto-Jane men, and they were driving a pickup like you said."

"I didn't say pickup. It's a big truck, DeDe. It sucks up the shit."

"Well, how was I supposed to know?"

The security chief shook her head slowly. "You are something else. You reeeally are."

"OK. I made a boo-boo. I apologize."

"Made a boo-boo?"

"Fucked up, then."

"Do you have any idea what those assholes just did?"

DeDe caught her breath. *Please God, don't make it gross.* She shook her head warily.

"They drove past the Aura Cleansing Workshop, screaming 'Fucking dykes' at the top of their lungs—"

"I realize I—"

"Wait a minute. Shut up. On their way out, they knocked over a Port-Jane."

"God."

"With somebody in it, DeDe."

DeDe pressed her fingers to her lips as her stomach began to churn. "Was she . . . hurt?"

An excruciating pause followed. "She was severely traumatized," Rose said at last. "We had to hose her down at the Womb."

Racked with nausea, DeDe looked away from her accuser. "If I'd had any idea . . ."

"You didn't follow instructions," said Rose. "It's as simple as that."

DeDe nodded. "You're right . . . you're right." She couldn't help wondering, though, what would have happened if she'd refused entry to the marauders. Would they have obeyed her? Her children certainly never did.

"I'd think you'd want to prove yourself," said Rose. "Considering your background."

"My *background*?" said DeDe.

"You know what I mean."

"No, I don't. Please tell me."

"I know about your father, OK?"

"You know *what*? My father is dead."

"Your stepfather, then. Whatever. I've known all about his fascist Reagan connections."

DeDe's face burned. "So what does that make me, then?"

Rose shrugged. "You tell me."

Hesitating a moment, she considered several retorts, then handed Rose the walkie-talkie. "It's past two," she said. "My shift is over."

She walked back to her tent in a daze, tormented by an issue far more troublesome than a toppled Porto-Jane: How could Rose—or anyone else—have known about Booter, unless D'or had said something?

And why would D'or do that? Why?

Broken Date

Booter's Lakeside Talk had been a resounding success. So far, at least a dozen Bohemians had pulled him aside to congratulate him, comparing him favorably to Chuck Percy and Bill Ruckelshaus, who had also addressed the multitudes that week. Sure, he had scrambled his notes once or twice, but no one seemed to notice, and the ovation afterwards had verged on thunderous.

He was walking now to burn off energy, filling his lungs with the pungent afternoon air. On the road above Green Mask, he passed a shirtless young man in his late twenties. His age and musculature suggested that he was an employee, so Booter felt duty bound to say something.

"Hot one, isn't it?"

The young man made a sort of whinnying noise to indicate that it was.

"You work here?" Booter asked, doing his best to sound pleasant about it.

"Yessir."

"Well, there's a rule about shirts, you know."

The young man looked at him blankly.

"You have to wear them," said Booter.

"Oh." He reached for his shirt, dangling from the back pocket of his khakis.

"It's fine by me," said Booter. "But . . . somebody else might give you trouble about it."

The young man slipped on the shirt, buttoned it up.

"I'd say the same thing to a member," Booter added, not wishing to seem a despot. "It's just the rule."

"Right."

"It's a hot one, though, isn't it?"

"Yeah."

Booter smiled at him and continued on his way back to the river road.

Order. Mutual respect. This was why the Grove was his favorite place on earth.

He found Jimmy Chappell in his tepee at Medicine Lodge. "There he is," piped Jimmy. "The William Jennings Bryan of the SDI."

Humility was in order, so Booter grunted disparagingly and sat down on the cot next to him.

"You want a drink?" asked Jimmy.

"Nah."

Jimmy poured cognac into a plastic cup, downing it with a satisfied smack. "Low Jinks sounds good," he said.

Christ almighty. Was that tonight?

"It's called 'I, Gluteus,'" Jimmy added, picking up a Grove program to read: "'Bohemians and guests will thrill to love duets by Erotica and Testicus, shiver at the plot hatched by Castrata against Fornicatio, giggle at the airy antics of Flatus, and feel tension mount between Nefario and Intactica, leader of the Restive Virgins.'"

"Fart jokes," said Booter. "Can't we do better than that?"

"Well . . . you laughed your ass off at that song I did for . . . What the hell are you talking about? You helped me write it."

"I was drunk," said Booter.

Jimmy snorted.

"I can't go tonight, Jimmy."

"Why not?"

"I'm . . . going into town."

"Town?" said Jimmy.

"Yeah."

"Monte Rio?"

Booter nodded.

"Why the hell would you leave the Grove on the night of the Low Jinks?"

"You're not gonna be in it," said Booter.

"Well, I know, but . . . what the hell, forget it."

"I'll be at the Grove Play, Jimmy. Wouldn't miss it."

"Yeah, yeah."

Booter felt the weight of his guilt. He and Jimmy hadn't missed a Low Jinks together for at least a decade. Jimmy was a born annotator, a bantamweight Boswell who loved nothing so much as the act of explaining. Without a listener, he was lost.

"Look," said Booter. "If you keep your trap shut, I'll tell you the real reason."

Jimmy's scowl slackened. He scratched himself under his arm. "Go on," he said.

"It's George," said Booter. "He's coming in tonight."

Jimmy blinked at him.

"The Vice-President."

"Yeah. So what? I knew that." He scratched again and frowned. "What does that have to do with Monte Rio?"

"Nothing," Booter replied. "Forget I said that. There's gonna be a reception up at Mandalay." This was a much safer lie, since Jimmy had never been invited to Mandalay.

"A reception?" Jimmy said quietly. "During Low Jinks?"

The truth, Booter decided, might have been preferable to this tangled web. "It's very small," he said at last. "They don't wanna make a big noise."

Jimmy nodded slowly, taking it in.

"You know I wouldn't miss the Jinks with you if there wasn't a good reason."

Jimmy ran his fingers through his wispy hair. "Yeah, well, that's a reason, all right."

Booter could tell he was hurt.

Jimmy looked up dolefully. "Tell him I said hello, will ya?"

Betrayed

Stinging from the incident at the gate, DeDe returned to her campsite, to find it empty. D'or and Anna were gone, apparently still on their shopping spree at the Crafts Tent. In her current state, she found solitude unendurable, so she doubled back to the boys' compound and asked for Edgar.

He arrived dripping wet, fresh from the swimming hole, already the color of a new catcher's mitt. "What's up, Mom?"

"Oh . . . nothing in particular. Just thought I'd stop by and say hi."

He nodded. "I'm OK, Mom."

"I know that."

Gesturing behind him, he said: "There's this really major water fight . . ."

"Go for it," she said, smiling at him. He smiled back, then vanished into the undergrowth.

She headed inland toward the Day Stage. The walk and the music would be just the thing for her blues. She was here to have a good time, wasn't she? Why let somebody like Rose Dvorak ruin her day?

Once out of the woods, she rejoiced in the feel of the sun against her skin. Linda Tillery was on stage singing "Special Kind of Love." An endless line of women snaked jubilantly across the clearing, drunk on the music.

She had been there less than five minutes when she saw Sabra Landauer.

The first thing she noticed was the skunk stripe. The second thing was the tall, bare-breasted woman who stood at Sabra's side, deep in animated conversation with the poet-playwright.

It was D'or.

Her throat went dry. Her skin grew prickly with dread.

431

Before she could retreat, D'or spotted her and waved. "Come join us."

As if in a nightmare, she moved across the field.

"I want you two to meet," said D'or. "Sabra . . . this is DeDe Halcyon."

Not "DeDe Halcyon, my lover," just plain old "DeDe Halcyon," thank you very much. Sabra, of course, didn't need a last name.

"Hello," said DeDe, shaking the large, bony hand of the poet-playwright. She was certain she wouldn't be remembered, and she wasn't. She turned back to D'or and asked: "Where's Anna?"

The accusation in the question wasn't lost on her lover, but she remained breezy. "Over in Day Care, bless her heart. She wanted to show off her treasures to the other kids."

She's not the only one, thought DeDe.

"This is Sabra's first time at Wimminwood," D'or added. "I'm giving her the grand tour."

Sabra smiled obligingly. "It's truly wonderful," she said.

"Isn't it?" said DeDe.

"Can you join us?" asked D'or.

"Not really."

"Oh . . . OK." D'or's insistent smile finally faded. "See you back at the homestead, then."

"That's up to you," said DeDe.

Twenty minutes later, when D'or returned to the tent, DeDe was waiting for her. "One of us should go get Anna," she said coldly.

"She's meeting us at the chow hall," D'or said, kicking off her boots. She turned and gazed at DeDe. "I wouldn't have believed it."

"What?"

"You are actually jealous."

"I'm embarrassed, D'or. I'm embarrassed for you."

"Oh, really?"

"Yes."

"Do you mind if I ask why?"

432

"C'mon. Look at you. Flashing your tits all over the place as soon as a famous woman—"

"Now, wait just a goddamn minute."

"It's unworthy of you," said DeDe. "That's all."

"It was hot today."

"I noticed," said DeDe.

D'or drew back. "Oh, boy . . . ohboyohboyohboy."

"I also don't appreciate your blabbing it all over camp about Booter working for Reagan. If you can't respect our privacy—"

"Wait a fucking minute."

"Well, did you or did you not tell Rose?"

"Who?"

"The one who deported our son."

D'or looked totally dumbfounded. "I haven't even seen her since—"

"Well, you told *somebody!*"

D'or's brow wrinkled. "I may have *mentioned* it to Feather at the Salvadoran workshop."

"And Feather told that runty, big-mouthed lover of hers . . ."

"DeDe . . ."

"OK, forget runty . . . Vertically challenged. How's that?"

D'or shook her head slowly. "It was just a lighthearted remark. I can't imagine how . . ."

DeDe rose. "I'm sure you get plenty of mileage out of it. Why don't you try it on Cruella de Vil?"

Slack-mouthed, D'or observed her, then broke into raucous laughter.

"Keep laughing," said DeDe as she charged out of the tent.

She was heading for the loud-and-rowdy zone.

Adoring Fan

As night fell, Wren Douglas found herself on the deck at Fife's, a gay resort on the outskirts of Guerneville. The evening was so balmy that several dozen people were still gathered outside. Shaking the rocks in her Scotch and water, she stood at the rail and watched as a blond man in parrot-green shorts swam laps in the pool.

She felt crisp and glamorous tonight in serious makeup and a turquoise-and-white sailor suit, fresh from a country Martinizing. She'd expected to be recognized—hoped for it, in fact—and she was.

"Excuse me," he said. "You're Wren Douglas." He was brown-haired and brown-eyed, mustachioed. The mischief and sweetness in his expression would have betrayed him as gay at a PTA meeting in Lynchburg, Virginia.

"Yes," she replied.

He stuck out his hand. "I'm Michael Tolliver. I was in the audience when you did *Mary Ann in the Morning*. You were fabulous. You're always fabulous."

She smiled and squeezed his hand. She was used to this kind of homo hyperbole, but it never failed to please her. "You didn't see me on *Donahue*," she said with a rueful expression.

"No. What happened?"

She shrugged. "Some large lady from Queens called me . . . let's see . . . 'an insult to *decent* fat people everywhere.'"

"Oh, no."

"It was a big breakthrough for me, I'm tellin' ya. I wasn't just fat anymore . . . I was a *fat slut*. What a revelation! A minority within a minority, and getting more specialized all the time."

He laughed, but it sounded a little lame, carrying the weight of dutiful fandom. She wondered if he'd heard her tell the same story on the Carson show.

"What . . . uh . . . brings you here?"

"Where? This place?"

"Well . . . the river."

"I'm staying over in Monte Rio," she explained. "A friend of mine rented a house there."

"Same here," he said. "We're in Cazadero. Know where that is?"

"Mmm. Love their general store."

"Well, we're not very far from there."

"And 'we' means . . . ?"

He pointed down to the pool. "The guy who's swimming laps, and . . . over there, under the trees . . . the one in the plaid shirt."

"Well . . ." She raised an eyebrow artfully. "How nice for you."

He laughed. "The one in plaid is straight."

She nodded soberly. "Gay guys haven't worn plaid for years."

Another laugh. "As a matter of fact, he's married to Mary Ann Singleton."

"Who?" she asked.

"The woman who interviewed you."

"Oh, God, yes. Miss Terminally Perky. Poor guy. He's *married* to her?"

He looked a little upset. "She's OK once you get to know her."

"I'm sure."

"She just hasn't . . . responded well to being famous."

Right, thought Wren. World famous in San Francisco. She glanced over at the man in the plaid shirt and admired his dimpled chin with a sudden twinge of déjà vu. "Oh, *him*," she exclaimed. "We've met. I tried to pick him up at the general store."

He laughed. "Seriously?"

"You bet. I *seriously* tried. He didn't mention me?" She made a hurt face. "I'm crushed."

"Well, he's been kind of under the weather lately."

I could cure him, she thought.

"This is such an honor," said Michael.

She cocked her head at him. "Thanks."

"Would you . . . uh . . . possibly care to have dinner with us?"

"Thanks, but . . ." She checked her watch. "I'm meeting my friend back at the house."

"Oh."

Her eyes perused the man in plaid again before returning to Michael. "He's leaving about ten o'clock, though. You could come up for a nightcap."

"Really?" He seemed genuinely elated. "Are you sure?"

"Sure I'm sure."

435

"All of us?"

"By all means," she replied.

Trouble in Chem-Free

Darkness had come early to the loud-and-rowdy zone, a loose configuration of tents and RVs near the gate at Wimminwood. After less
than half an hour there, DeDe had come to feel curiously comfortable, like a child who'd been kidnapped by gypsies and had grown to
like it. Or maybe like Patty Hearst; she wasn't sure.

"Pour that girlie another drink!" This was Mabel, apparent
high priestess of the Party Animals. "She's lookin' all mopey again."

"No," said DeDe, covering her tin cup with her hand. "I'm
fine, really."

"Pour her a damn drink. Ginnie, get some more rum out o' the
tent. Get your ass in gear and fix this sweet thing a drink."

Ginnie, who'd been absorbed by her own bongo music, stopped
playing and looked at DeDe.

"Well," said DeDe, "maybe a little one." She'd been holding
back out of some sense of obligation to the kids, but it seemed silly
at this point. Edgar had his own life now, and Anna was at the chow
hall with D'orothea.

Oh, God. Was Sabra with them?

"Smile," barked Mabel.

DeDe smiled.

Mabel winked at her. "Attagirl." She was reclining on an air
mattress in front of her Winnebago. With her short gray hair and
lumpy gray sweatsuit, she bore an uncanny resemblance to a plate of
mashed potatoes.

"I know that bitch," said Mabel. "Her and me go waaay back."

For a moment, DeDe thought she meant Sabra. Then she remembered her other nemesis, the one she'd told them about. "You
mean Rose?"

436

Mabel grunted. "She confiscated my crossbow at the Michigan festival. Fuck her."

DeDe tried to look sympathetic, but had a hard time of it. Mabel with a crossbow? Mabel *drunk* with a crossbow in the midst of a thousand people? Please.

"All that shit about Goddess this and Goddess that. I told her: 'I'm gonna get you back, I swear to God.' And she said: 'Anybody who swears to God is only bowing to the patriarchy.' And I said: 'I'm gonna patriarchy your butt all the way to East Lansing, if you don't get the hell out o' my Winnebago.'"

One of the other rowdies let out a whoop. "Go get her, Mabel."

"I've been beatin' men at their own game for sixty years. You think I need some sorry-ass little drill sergeant tellin' me how to talk like a dyke? Tellin' me I'm a threat to the general welfare because of a harmless little crossbow?"

DeDe watched as the bongo player swapped smirks with a lanky woman seated on an ice chest next to Mabel's air mattress. Mabel and her trusty crossbow had obviously become a central motif in their shared familial lore.

"And now," Mabel added, "she's treatin' you like dirt too. Small damn world, huh?"

"I guess so," DeDe said.

"Somebody should have a talk with that girlie."

"Oh, no," said Ginnie wearily. "Here we go again."

Puffing a little, Mabel hefted her weight onto her feet. "Somebody should just go tell her it's time to stop pushing my friends around."

DeDe glanced nervously at Ginnie. This wasn't for real, was it?

"You should be flattered," said Ginnie, smiling sardonically. "Your honor is about to be defended."

DeDe turned back to Mabel. "Mabel, really, I appreciate your concern, but I don't . . ."

Mabel lumbered past her toward the Winnebago. "Yessirree-bob," she said as she climbed inside.

Panic-stricken, DeDe turned to Ginnie and asked: "The crossbow?"

Ginnie laughed. "It's back in Tacoma. Don't worry."

Thank God, she thought.

"She gets like this," offered the woman on the ice chest. "She was with the Post Office for thirty-seven years."

Mabel emerged from the Winnebago, gave DeDe a rakish salute, and began marching down the road toward the chem-free zone.

"You don't even know where she is," yelled Ginnie.

Mabel maintained a determined gait. "The hell I don't."

"She's doing this for you," said the woman on the ice chest, addressing DeDe. "She's showing off."

DeDe felt utterly helpless. "What's she gonna do?"

Ginnie shrugged. "Kick butt."

"Look," said DeDe, "the last thing I want is some horrible fight over . . . Can't somebody stop her?"

"She's not gonna do anything," said the woman on the ice chest. "She's blowin' smoke."

"Don't be so sure," said Ginnie. She turned to DeDe with a look of gentle concern. "Maybe you'd better go after her, huh?"

"Me? I don't even know her. Why should I be the—?" She cut herself off, suddenly envisioning Mabel and Rose locked in woman-to-woman combat. She leapt to her feet and bounded down the road after Mabel.

She caught up with her as they approached the border of the chem-free zone. "Mabel, listen . . ."

"Comin' along for the fun?"

"No! If you're doing this for me . . ."

"I'm doin' this for *me*, girlie."

DeDe strode alongside her, breathing heavily but keeping pace. "But if she thinks that I sent you down there to . . ."

"Who the hell cares?"

"*I* care, Mabel. I'm here with my lover and kids, and . . . I'm just trying to have a good time."

Mabel slowed down a little and smiled at her. "How's it been so far?"

"Shitty," said DeDe.

"Well, see there? It's time we had us some fun."

"Mabel, a rumble with the security chief is not my idea of a good—"

"Shhh," Mabel ordered, whipping a forefinger to her lips. "There it is."

"What?" DeDe whispered.

"Her lair." She seized DeDe's arm with a grip of iron, pulled her into a thicket of madrone trees, let go suddenly, and flung herself to the ground like an advancing infantryman.

Rose's tent was beneath them, at the bottom of a gentle slope. A lantern burned inside, making it glow like the belly of a lightning bug.

"Mabel, I want no part—"

"Get down!"

DeDe dropped to the ground, her heart pounding furiously. Mabel gave her a roguish wink and made another silencing gesture with her finger. There were sounds coming from Rose's tent. Not voices exactly, but sounds.

First there was a kind of whimpering, followed by heavy breathing followed by: "Yes, oh yes, uh-huh, you got it, all right, OK, *there* . . . yes ma'am, yes ma'am . . ."

DeDe tugged on Mabel's sweatshirt, making a desperate let's-get-out-of-here gesture. Mabel used her palm to stifle a snicker, then peered down the slope again, obviously enthralled by the drama of the moment.

The sounds continued: "Uh-huh, oh yeah, oh yeah, mmmmmm, oh God, oh God please . . . oh Gawwwddd . . ."

Mabel shot a triumphant glance at DeDe, then sprang to her feet, cupped her hands around her mouth and shouted, *"Don't you mean Goddess?"*

All sounds ceased in the tent.

DeDe tried to shimmy away on her belly, but the underbrush

enfolded her. She lurched to her feet and stumbled frantically away from the scene of the crime. Behind her, Mabel was cackling victoriously, thoroughly pleased with herself.

"Come *on!*" DeDe called, suddenly worried about Mabel's safety.

Mabel savored the scene a moment longer before effecting her own escape. She crashed through the madrones, puffing noisily but still cackling. "Was that *perfect*, girlie? Was that the best damn—"

She tripped and fell with a sickening thud.

"Are you OK?" DeDe called. "Mabel? . . . Mabel?"

Mabel wasn't moving at all.

Sick with fear, DeDe made her way back to the grounded figure, knelt, touched the side of her face. "Please don't do this to me. Please don't."

Mabel's nose wiggled.

"Thank God," said DeDe.

The old woman emitted a sporty growl and hoisted herself to her knees. DeDe was pulling her the rest of the way when Rose emerged from the tent and peered up at the two invaders.

She locked eyes with DeDe for an excruciating eternity, then went back into the tent. Mabel shrugged and flopped her arm across DeDe for support. "You think she was alone?" she asked.

"I'm done for," said DeDe as they made their way back to the Winnebago.

"No you're not."

"I am. You don't know. She hated me already. Now . . ."

"I'll protect you," said Mabel.

"Right," said DeDe.

They passed a group of tents near the edge of chem-free. She distinctly heard someone say the words "Junior League," followed by a chorus of harsh laughter.

They knew, they all knew. Her debacle at the gate had entered into the lore.

It was time she got out of there.

Making Up

Jimmy looked moody and drunk when Booter returned to his tepee. "How was the Jinks?" Booter asked.

No answer.

"Bad huh?"

"I didn't go."

"Why not?"

Jimmy shrugged. "How was the Vice-President?"

"Fine," said Booter. "Optimistic."

"About what?"

Booter was thrown for a moment. "Well . . . economic indicators . . . the Contras. That sort of thing."

"Oh." Jimmy nodded, then looked down at the empty plastic glass in his hand.

"You should've gone to the Jinks," said Booter.

"Why?"

"I dunno. To give me a report. I was kinda curious."

Jimmy grunted.

"Sounded like your kinda show." Why was Jimmy acting this way? Because Booter hadn't gone to the Jinks? Because Booter hadn't invited Jimmy to meet the Vice-President? Because Jimmy turned maudlin after three drinks?

Applause came clattering through the woods like lumber spilling from a truck.

"There's the end of it," said Booter.

"Of what?" asked Jimmy.

"The Jinks."

"Oh."

Booter hated it when he got like this. "I thought I'd wander down to Sons of Toil . . . have a drink with Lester and Artie."

Another grunt.

"You wanna come along?"

441

"You go ahead," said Jimmy.

Booter frowned and sat down on the cot next to him. "Jimmy, ol' man . . ."

Jimmy rose, fumbling in his shirt pocket for a cigarette.

"You don't need that," said Booter.

"Hell with it." Jimmy lit the cigarette and tossed the match out into the night. He took a drag, then expelled smoke slowly, forming a contemplative wreath over his head.

"I wasn't up at Mandalay," Booter said at last.

"Oh, yeah?" said Jimmy. "Where'd you meet him?"

"I didn't."

"You didn't have drinks with George Bush?"

"No."

"Then what the hell . . . ?"

"I was with a woman, Jimmy."

Jimmy cocked his head slightly, like an old retriever inquiring about the prey.

"I rented a house in Monte Rio," Booter added. "She's been . . . staying there for a few days."

Jimmy looked dumbstruck for a moment, then started to laugh. As usual, his laughter deteriorated into a coughing jag. Booter clapped him on the back several times.

When Jimmy had collected himself, he said: "Why didn't you tell me it was just a woman?"

Booter shrugged. "You're a thespian. You've got a big mouth."

"Then . . . you didn't see Bush at all?"

"No."

Jimmy smiled and shook his head in amazement. No, in relief. "A woman," he said.

Booter gave Jimmy's leg a shake. "C'mon. Let's go see Lester and Artie."

"Is she . . . uh . . . long-term?"

"No," said Booter.

"You buy one of those whores down at the Northwood Lodge?"

442

"No."

Jimmy's eyes grew cloudy with reminiscence. "I bought a whore once. Nothing spectacular. Just this . . . nice little gal from Boulder during the war. Her name was . . . damn, what was it?" He sucked in smoke, then expelled it slowly. "Funny name . . . not like a whore's name at all."

"Let's go," said Booter.

"I always figured there'd be more just like her . . . or better. I had time for everything. Hell, five or six of everything." He was mired in memory again.

Booter found Jimmy's jacket and handed it to him. "We gotta hurry," he said. "Lester wants to play his saw for us."

Jimmy struggled into his jacket. "She have big titties, your girl-friend?"

Booter chuckled. "You ol' whorehound."

"I'm not as old as you," said Jimmy. "God damn, where do you get the energy?"

Booter shrugged and smiled.

"The only big titties I ever see are around this place." Jimmy sighed elaborately. "Old men and their big titties. It's so depressing. Where the hell is my hat? Some of those fellows out there could use a brassiere, Booter. Ever notice that?"

Booter found Jimmy's hat, a model he'd worn since the fifties, when he'd seen a similar one on Rex Harrison in *My Fair Lady*. He handed it to Jimmy and said: "You look as young as I've seen you in a long time."

In point of fact, Jimmy's bypass had whipped at least thirty pounds off him, imparting a sort of crazed boyishness to his face. "What is it that happens, Booter? Why do we all start looking like old women? What the hell is it? Revenge?"

Booter preceded him out of the tepee, merging with the tide of returning Jinks-goers. A screech owl heralded their exit. Jimmy caught up with him and said: "My wife's Aunt Louise had a full mustache by the time she was seventy."

Booter kept walking.

"There's a message there," said Jimmy, sighing again. "There's a terrible message there."

Midnight Quartet

The road above Monte Rio was rutted and unlit, deadly after dark.

"Are you sure this is right?" asked Thack.

He thinks I'm a flake, thought Michael. Useless with a hammer and useless in a car. "Well," he said evenly, "she said it was the very last house on the road."

"Yeah," said Brian, "but is this the road?"

"That's what I was wondering," said Thack.

Now they were ganging up on him. "What other road could it be?" he asked.

"That last turnoff," said Thack.

"Yeah," said Brian.

"But it was heading down, wasn't it?"

"Hard to tell," said Thack.

There was nothing to be gained by capitulating now. "I'm gonna keep on," said Michael.

"Whose place is this, anyway?" This was Brian again.

"I dunno," said Michael. "Some friend of hers rented it."

"Male, female, what?"

Michael chuckled. "Male, probably. Didn't you read her book?"

"I looked at the pictures," said Brian.

"I can't believe you didn't recognize her."

"She looked different."

"I wouldn't have recognized her," said Thack.

"She's a big star," said Michael, irked with them both for not understanding the honor they'd been afforded. "And she's so accessible."

"I noticed," said Brian drily.

Thack laughed.

444

"You're both pigs," said Michael.

The crumbling road became a driveway, which led them up the steepest incline yet.

"This is crazy," said Thack.

"Yeah," said Michael, "but I think this is it." Ahead of them, caught in the headlights, lay an enormous moss-flecked chalet.

"Jesus," said Thack. "It looks like a Maybeck."

"A what?" asked Brian.

"He was an architect," Michael explained. "Early twentieth century."

"You know his work?" asked Thack.

"Very well," said Michael. Take that, Mr. Butch-with-a-Hammer.

He parked next to a white sedan behind the chalet. There were broad stairs leading to the second floor, where the living quarters seemed to be. The ground floor was shingled-over storage space.

The three of them climbed the stairs as a phalanx. Halfway up, Brian turned to Michael and said: "Let's don't make this long, OK?"

"OK," Michael whispered.

As they reached the top, Wren flung open the door. "Hi, boys."

"Hi," said Michael.

"Your timing is perfect," she said.

"Really?"

"Really. I'm ready to party." She sailed ahead of them like a galleon, listing here and there to turn on a lamp. When they reached a big stone fireplace, she stopped and stuck her hand out to Thack. "I'm Wren," she said.

"Thack Sweeney."

"You're quite a swimmer," she said.

"Thanks."

"Are you another San Franciscan?"

"No," said Thack. "Charlestonian. South Carolina."

"Ah." She turned to Brian. "And we've met."

"Yeah," said Brian sheepishly. "I guess so. I'm Brian Hawkins."

"Charmed." She dipped coyly, smiling at Brian. Michael thought she looked fabulous tonight in her pale pink sweatsuit. A satin ribbon of the same shade secured her sleek dark hair behind her head.

"Michael, my love, how 'bout a hand?"

"Sure," he said instantly, seduced by the way she'd made them sound like old friends. He followed her into a dimly lit kitchen with an industrial sink, a sloping wooden floor, and a pair of cobwebby antlers over the stove. She gathered glasses and dumped ice into a bucket. "Glad you could come," she said.

"Glad to be here," he replied stupidly. "Has your . . . uh . . . friend gone?"

"Oh, yes." She opened the liquor cabinet. "There's some grass in the bedroom. The cigar box on the dresser. Roll us a couple, would you?"

"Sure." He made his way down a redwood-paneled hallway to a cozy bedroom. There, he sat on a rumpled bed and rolled joints while an owl hooted outside the window and Thack and Wren laughed over something in the living room.

When he returned, Wren was seated in an armchair next to the fireplace. Thack and Brian were on the sofa.

"There's drinks on that tray," said Wren, as he handed her the joints.

"Thanks," said Michael. "I'm fine." He sat on a tapestry cushion next to the hearth.

"In that case . . ." Wren struck a safety match against the fireplace and lit a joint. She took several dainty tokes before offering it to Michael.

"No, thanks," he said.

"C'mon."

"I'm on the wagon for a while. Cleaning out my system."

She made a face at him, then offered the joint to Brian.

He shook his head, smiling dimly.

"I'll take some," said Thack.

"Thank God." She leaned over and handed Thack the joint. "These Frisco boys are a lot of fun, aren't they?"

Thack laughed.

"So," said Wren, turning to Michael. "What's there to do in this neck of the woods?"

"Well . . . we've been walking a lot, swimming in the creek."

"Swell."

Michael shrugged. "You came to the wrong place if you wanted action. There are one or two discos . . ."

"Forget it."

"I agree," said Thack, returning the joint to Wren.

"What about your friend?" said Michael.

"What about him?" She took another hit off the joint.

So, thought Michael, we've established the gender. "Well, hasn't he shown you around?"

"No, not really. He's gone most of the time." She gave him a crooked, faintly knowing smile, telling him to mind his own business. Was she being kept? Was it somebody famous—like half the men in her memoirs?

"Michael says you're gonna make a movie with Sydney Pollack." This was Thack, jumping in.

"Well . . . Michael knows more than I do."

"I read it somewhere," said Michael defensively.

" 'Inquiring minds want to know,' " said Wren.

"No," said Michael, grinning at her. "It was . . . maybe I saw it on *Entertainment Tonight*."

Wren gave him a teasing smile. "Oh, well, then . . . it must be true."

"C'mon," he said.

"We're just in the talking stage," she told him. "I don't wanna jinx it."

"It's such a fabulous idea," said Michael.

"Brian's wife is gonna be on *Entertainment Tonight*." This was Thack.

"Is that right?" said Wren, turning to Brian with the dimmest of smiles. Michael braced himself.

Brian nodded. "They're taping this weekend, as a matter of fact."

"My," said Wren, "that's quite a coup for . . . you know, some-one local."

There was a definite edge to this remark, but Michael found it forgivable. Mary Ann, after all, had bad-mouthed Wren on the air.

"She's pleased about it," said Brian.

"You should be there," said Wren. "Can't they use a husband?"

"She wanted me there," he replied.

"What's the matter? Afraid of the camera?"

"I dunno."

"Shouldn't be," she said. "That chin would look great on camera." She turned to Michael for a second opinion. "Doesn't he have a great chin?"

"Great," said Michael, deadpanning.

Thack laughed and exchanged glances with Brian, whose em-barrassment was evident.

"It's like a little tushie," she said. "Two perky little hills." She squeezed her own chin in an effort to create the same effect. "A plas-tic surgeon could make a fortune."

They all laughed.

Wren winked at Brian, granting him clemency, then turned to Thack. "So . . . are you two . . . you know?"

Thack looked puzzled. "What . . . me and Michael?"

"Yes."

Thack hesitated so long that Michael took over. "We're bud-dies," he said.

"Yeah," said Thack. "We just met."

"I see," said Wren, nodding slowly. "You guys are worse off than I am."

They drove back to Cazadero an hour later. Their arrival was heralded by a sally of yaps from a neighbor's toy poodle. The people in the pink trailer had built a fire, from which sparks ascended like fireflies into the blue-black velvet sky. There seemed to be more stars than ever.

"I'm gonna take a walk," said Thack, as they climbed out of the VW.

"Oh," said Michael. "OK."

He and Brian entered the cabin, flipping on lights, kicking off their shoes. Brian went to the kitchen sink and began washing the dishes from lunch.

"I'll get that," said Michael.

"No problem," said Brian.

Michael sat down at the kitchen table and watched Brian for a moment. "You feel OK?"

"Fine."

"All day?"

"Yeah. I feel much better, actually."

"Good," said Michael. "Must've been a bug."

"Yeah."

"Wren's nice, isn't she?"

"Yeah," said Brian. "She is."

"Is there more of that lemon cake in the fridge?"

"I think so."

Michael went to the refrigerator and found the ravaged Sara Lee tin. "She likes you," he said, plunging a fork into the cake.

"I know," said Brian.

When Thack returned to the cabin, Brian was fast asleep; Michael was pretending to be. Through half-lidded eyes, he watched as Thack shucked his clothes and shimmied under the covers on his studio couch.

Thack rolled over once or twice, then threw back the covers and got up again, crossing the room to Michael's bed. He knelt and brushed his lips softly across Michael's cheek.

"Good night, buddy," he said.

Michael opened his eyes and smiled at him. "Good night," he said.

A piney zephyr passed through the room. Down by the creekbank, a frog was making music with a rubber band.

Red Alert

Feeling achy and cotton-mouthed, DeDe awoke at first light, to find D'or sitting by the river's edge.

"There's coffee if you want it," said D'or, barely looking up.

"Is Anna awake?" asked DeDe.

"No."

DeDe sat down next to D'or in the sand.

High above them, a huge black bird was circling Wimminwood in a sinister fashion. She had seen these birds before, but this one struck her as an omen, a harbinger of horrors to come.

"I wanna go home," she said.

"Why?"

"I just do, D'or. I don't like what it's doing to us."

D'or hesitated, then said: "You're overreacting."

"I am not."

"You're letting that . . . business at the gate get to you."

DeDe looked at her and frowned. "Who told you about that?"

D'or shrugged.

"It's all over Wimminwood, isn't it?"

D'or looked away.

"Why are they blaming *me*? That's what I wanna know."

"Nobody's blaming you. It's over, hon. Put it behind you."

"OK, fine," said DeDe. "It's behind me. Let's go home."

D'or heaved a forbearing sigh. "Hon, I promised the kids we'd stay a few more days."

"Why did you do that?"

"Because they *like* it here, OK?"

"When did they tell you that?"

"Last night, DeDe. When you were out getting drunk."

"I didn't get drunk."

"Whatever."

"I drank. There's a big difference. Why were you getting the kids on your side?"

"What?"

"You never ask their opinion unless you want their support. What's the big deal about staying here?"

D'or dug a little trench in the sand, then patted the sides methodically. "There's lots we haven't done."

"Like what?"

D'or shrugged. "The Holly Near concert. Sabra's doing a poetry workshop this afternoon."

"A poetry workshop," echoed DeDe.

"Yes."

"Since when have you been interested in poetry?"

She felt the whip sting of D'or's eyes. "Since when have you asked?"

"Oh, c'mon."

Using her palm, D'or smoothed over the little trench. "If you wanna take the car, go ahead. The kids and I are staying."

DeDe and Anna were still sunning when D'or returned from Sabra's workshop. It was almost four o'clock, and the willows were awash with gold.

"Don't burn yourself, hon." D'or sat down on the sand next to Anna.

Anna held up her Bain de Soleil bottle. "I'm wearing number eight," she said.

"Yeah, but you've had enough."

Anna turned to DeDe. "Mom," she intoned, elongating the word until it sounded like a foghorn. "Do I hafta?"

"I think so, precious. Go on. Hit the showers. I'll be up in a little while."

As the child scampered away, DeDe turned to D'or. "So," she said. "How was it?"

"Interesting," said D'or. "You should've come."

DeDe shrugged. "I know what she's all about."

"Oh, you do, huh?"

"Or *not* about, as the case may be."

D'or shifted irritably. "Meaning?"

"Well, she's not talking about being a lesbian is she?"

"She talked about it plenty."

"Sure. *Here.* Just not on *The Today Show.*"

"She's a feminist," said D'or. "She'd lose her effectiveness if people knew she was gay. Get real."

"You're the one who's not being real."

D'or picked up a pebble and flung it into the river. "Since when did you get to be such a radical?"

"Is that radical?" DeDe asked. "To expect people to tell the truth?"

"When didn't she tell the truth?"

"All the time. OK . . . When she was on Merv Griffin. She kept talking about the kind of man she likes."

"Well . . . a lesbian can like men."

"But she doesn't say that, does she? She deludes people, D'or. It's the same as lying. She's a tired old closet case."

"She's a great poet," said D'or.

"Well," said DeDe. "Did you learn anything?"

"Do you really care?"

"You must've written something," said DeDe.

"No."

"You just listened?"

"If you must know, I assisted her during the reading."

"Assisted her?" said DeDe, gaping. "Turned the pages? What?"

"Very funny."

"Well, tell me."

D'or raked her fingers through her hair. "One of the pieces required . . . interpretive body work."

DeDe blinked at her. "Dancing?"

"Yes."

"You danced while she read?"

"Yes."

"Oh, swell," said DeDe.

"I considered it an honor."

"Who wouldn't?" said DeDe.

D'or rose, dusting off the seat of her pants. "I don't need this."

DeDe followed her back to the tent. "You see what she's up to, don't you?"

"She enjoys my company," said D'or.

"She enjoys your tits," said DeDe.

D'or's eyes flashed again. "She relates to my energy. She thinks we knew each other in a past life."

"Oh, please."

"Back off, DeDe, OK?"

"Fine."

"I like talking to her. She likes talking to me. It's as simple as that."

DeDe snorted. "You think she wants you for *conversation?*"

D'or spun around. "Is that so hard to believe?"

"Oh, for God's sake, stop acting like such a . . . ex-model. Wake up and smell the hormones, D'or. The woman is in heat."

D'or crawled into the tent. "I'll keep that in mind." She grabbed her knapsack and crawled out again. "I'll certainly keep that in mind."

"Where are you going?"

"Use your imagination," said D'or.

Night fell, and D'or did not return. Anna and DeDe ate dinner together at the chow hall, then went to visit Edgar at Brother Sun. He showed them a wallet he'd stitched and a knee wound he'd incurred during a wrestling match. He seemed happy enough, DeDe decided; her escalating misery would find no company at the boys' compound.

On their way back to the campsite, they passed a large tent where two women in mime makeup were entertaining kids with "a festival of non-violent, non-sexist cartoons." Recognizing two of her playmates inside, Anna asked if she could join them, so DeDe left her there and continued the trek on her own.

She was taking a shortcut across the hearing-impaired zone when she saw her tomboy friend from the bulletin board. Polly Something.

"Hey there," said Polly, waving merrily. "How's it been goin'?"

DeDe rolled her eyes. "Don't ask."

Polly smiled. "That was you on the gate, wasn't it? When the men got in."

Jesus. Had there been a press release?

"I remembered you were heading for your work duty," Polly explained, "so I just figured . . ."

"Well, it's over now," said DeDe, maintaining her stride.

Polly walked alongside, swinging her arms, bouncing on the balls of her feet. "I thought I might see you at that emergency meeting. That's the only reason I went."

"What emergency meeting?"

"You know . . . the one ol' baldie called."

"Rose Dvorak?"

"Yeah."

"She called a meeting?"

"A major one," said Polly.

DeDe's stomach constricted. She wondered if they'd discussed her—her ineptitude, her Neanderthal stepfather, her dubious loyalty to Womankind.

"They've beefed up security something fierce," said Polly. "Rose thinks it's gonna happen again."

"Bullshit," said DeDe.

Polly shrugged. "Seemed pretty random to me."

"It *was* random," said DeDe.

"They're getting off on it. That's what I think. Rose just creams at the thought of declaring martial law. Slow *down*, DeDe."

"Sorry."

"Why are you so wound up?"

"I don't know." She stopped suddenly and looked at Polly. "Yes I do. My lover is messing around with Sabra Landauer."

Polly blinked, then emitted a long, low whistle. "You *know* that?"

"I suspect it."

"Well, that's different."

"She'd like to," said DeDe. "I can tell you that."

"Who wouldn't? Sabra gets more offers than Rita Mae Brown."

DeDe glowered at her. "If you think you're being comforting, Polly . . ."

"All I know is, this wife swapping isn't fair. If you're gonna have an affair, have it with a single girl. That's what we're here for."

DeDe thought for a moment. "Does Sabra have a lover?"

"She did," said Polly. "She dumped her last month."

"Great," said DeDe numbly.

They began walking again. When they passed a stern sentry brandishing a walkie-talkie and a nightstick, Polly tugged on DeDe's arm. "See what I mean?" she whispered. "The troops are on Red Alert."

Jimmy's Big Entrance

This year, Jimmy Chappell was to play a Sister of Mercy in the Grove Play, an epic called "Solferino," about the founding of the Red Cross. Another adventure in tedium, no doubt, but Booter showed up anyway, to keep peace with his old friend. Ten minutes before curtain time, he scaled the slope of the great outdoor stage and found Jimmy waiting in "the wings"—a bark-covered screen disguised as a redwood tree.

"Christ," said Booter. "I hope you look better from down there." Jimmy's wig and nurse's cap, a single macabre unit, were hanging next to him on a nail. His few strands of real hair were matted and sweaty, and his white uniform was already streaked with makeup. "It's all illusion," said Jimmy.

"It better be," said Booter. "What's your first scene?"

"Well . . . I call for more tourniquets."

"Is that all?"

Jimmy looked annoyed. "It's a speech, Booter. It's an important moment."

"I'm sure it is."

Jimmy plucked a cigarette from the pocket of his uniform and lit it with his lighter. He took a long drag, then said: "It gets more substantive later on."

"What happens then?"

Jimmy smiled a little and tapped his cigarette. "I call for more plasma."

Booter chuckled.

"It's not my finest role," said Jimmy.

"What the hell," said Booter.

"I don't care. It's theater." Jimmy gazed down on his fellow Bohemians, filing in to the log benches. "God, I love it." He cast a pensive glance in Booter's direction. "What the hell am I doing in real estate?"

"Making a damn good living," said Booter.

"Yeah, I guess."

A stage manager rushed past them with an armful of prop rifles. "Places, Jimmy. Two minutes."

"OK," said Jimmy.

"I'd better hightail it," said Booter.

"Where are you sitting?"

"Toward the back. With Buck Vickers and the rest of that gang."

"Well . . . stay if you want."

"Here?"

"Sure. Keep me company. I sit right here most of the time."

"Won't they throw me out?"

Jimmy made a stern face. "I'll raise hell if they do. I might not be the star of this extravaganza . . ."

Booter laughed. "You get a pretty good view up here." He

456

peered through a fist-sized hole in the bark screen. Below, a lilliputian stagehand scurried across the main stage, scattering bloodied bandages in preparation for battle. The audience in the redwood amphitheater spoke with a single voice, whiskey-charged and jovial.

The lights dimmed suddenly. The audience fell silent as the orchestra plunged into the overture.

"Too late now," said Jimmy. "You're stuck with me."

"What the hell," said Booter. As a matter of fact, he rather liked the idea of staying here in Jimmy's lair—like a couple of schoolboys playing hooky in a secret tree house.

Jimmy snatched his nurse wig off the nail and plopped it onto his head. Squatting a little, he faced a triangle of broken mirror and made final adjustments. His face exuded the humorless concentration of a man devoted to his craft. He gave Booter a thumbs-up sign, then marched into the public eye, his jaw set with the now-or-never determination of a paratrooper.

A blue spotlight followed him as he descended the long switchback trail to the main stage. A fifty-voice chorus sang about the rigors of war, the nobility of dying. After two or three minutes of this, Jimmy confronted Hubert Watkins (who was dressed as a general) and recited a list of casualties, making a desperate but eloquent plea for sterile dressings.

He returned five minutes later, breathless from the climb. He leaned against the bark wall and slid to a sitting position. "Whew," he said.

"Brilliant as usual," said Booter.

"You're not just saying that?"

"No. It was very moving."

"Nobody laughed, at least."

"No," said Booter. "You could've heard a pin drop."

Jimmy took off the wig and mopped his brow with a Kleenex. "Stupid ol' Lonnie Muchmore missed two light cues."

"Didn't show," said Booter.

"It didn't?" Jimmy glanced up hopefully.

"Looked fine from here. The audience liked you."

"Yeah," said Jimmy, grinning. "They did, didn't they?" Jimmy's plasma scene went without a hitch. Back in the wings again, he unwound with Booter. "I forgot to tell you," he said. "I met George Bush."

"Oh, yeah?"

The bewigged face smiled. "I guess you could say I met him. I peed on a tree next to him."

Booter nodded soberly. "Congratulations."

Jimmy laughed. "When I joined this outfit fifteen years ago, all I ever heard was: So-and-so peed on a tree next to Art Linkletter or John Mitchell . . ."

"Henry McKittrick peed on a tree next to J. Edgar Hoover."

"There you go," said Jimmy.

"You're not really a Bohemian until you've peed on a tree next to somebody."

"So there I was, answering the call of nature." Jimmy spun his yarn with histrionic relish. "And I look over, and who's standing there not five feet away but ol' Number Two himself."

"Doing number one," said Booter.

Jimmy ignored this witticism. "Right, and I look at him big as life and say: 'What's the matter? Don't they have toilets up at Mandalay?'" He laughed at his own joke, then began coughing violently.

"Take it easy," said Booter. "You OK?"

Jimmy nodded, gasping. "Never better." He hoisted himself to his feet. "I gotta change for the finale."

"Another costume?"

"Well, there's a different sash, at least. I put this red cross on the front of . . ." For a moment, it seemed he was considering something, then he fell back against the wall, clutching his chest.

"Jimmy, for God's sake . . ." Booter lunged for him, but Jimmy collapsed into a heap on the floor, thrashing his legs about like an injured thoroughbred. "Jimmy, is there medicine? Where the hell is your . . . ?"

Jimmy's eyes looked up at him, blinking. Then he registered another jolt, groaning between clenched teeth, clamping his palm against the pain. In another instant, his body went slack again and there was no movement of any kind.

Booter knelt next to him. "Jimmy, damnit . . . don't do this, ol' man." He checked Jimmy's heart, his pulse. Nothing. "You're gonna miss the big number, fella . . ."

Down below, the orchestra was piling strings upon trumpets upon drums, thundering toward the finale. Roman candles burst above the hillside in a festive facsimile of warfare. The chorus was singing angelically about the formation of the Geneva Convention.

The stage manager rushed up, out of breath. "Wake him up, will you? He's missing his entrance."

"No he's not," said Booter.

The stage manager looked exasperated and left, issuing orders to other nurses behind other trees. The music soared, the sky burned with pink phosphorescence, the forest reverberated with applause.

When it was over, Booter removed Jimmy's wig and hung it back on its nail. Then he took a Kleenex and—slowly, meticulously—removed Jimmy's lipstick. It wouldn't do for him to look like this when they came to take him away.

Goodbye and Hello

Wren woke at eight thirty-eight with a vague sense of being behind schedule. Her limousine from the city was due to arrive at ten, which left—what?—three hours or so before the departure of American Airlines flight 220 to Chicago. Her head was already cluttered with numbers again. The wilderness had lost its hold on her.

She ate a farewell breakfast on the porch, gazing down on the cruising vultures, the ancient forest, the diamond-bright landscape of bluest blues and greenest greens. She would miss it, she decided. She would miss the exquisite *texture* of being alone in such a place.

Rolando would be waiting for her at O'Hare—seven-fifteen Chicago time—overflowing with candy and wilted carnations, looking dear and out of it in a suit. She had welcomed this respite from his boundless energy, his excruciating attentiveness, the ardor which bordered on priapism. Now she couldn't wait to be back. Her heart tap-danced at the thought of him.

After breakfast, she did the dishes for the last time, then dragged out her suitcases. She decided against packing a bird's nest she had found in the woods, picturing how forlorn it would look amidst the chrome and whitewash of her loft. Vacations, she had learned, hardly ever survived transplanting.

As she gathered her loose receipts and paperbacks, she looked at Booter's check and smiled. He had originally made it out for ten thousand, but she'd insisted that he change it. Five thousand, after all, had been his first offer, and there was no point in being greedy.

The phone rang. What now? Was her driver lost?

"Wren Douglas," she purred, reassuming the mantle of an incorporated woman.

"It's me," came a weak voice. It was Booter, but he didn't sound like himself.

"Oh, hi."

"I have to see you again."

"Are you OK?" she asked. "You sound like a truck just hit you."

"Something has happened," he said quietly, his voice drained of color. "I have to see you."

"Booter, my flight is at one o'clock."

"Cancel it. Please."

"I can't. There's a driver coming from the city."

"He can stay here overnight. I'll pay for it."

"Look," she said, "if I flake out on my boyfriend one more time . . . What's the problem, anyway? Tell me about it."

"No," he said quietly. "Not now."

"Well, then, if . . ."

"I'll pay you more, of course."

That made her mad. "Damnit, Booter . . ."

"Well, what do I have to do?"

"Nothing," she said wearily, resigning herself to another shouting match with Rolando. "If it's really important . . ."

"You can catch the same flight tomorrow. Tell your driver he can stay at the Sonoma Mission Inn. It's very nice. I have an account there. I'll call ahead and arrange everything."

"Well . . . OK."

"I'll be there this afternoon."

"When?"

"No later than three," he said.

His Own Mischance

When someone died at the Grove, the news of it rumbled through the encampment like the drums of the Navajo. Jimmy's death had been no different from the rest, electrifying Bohemia for a few uncertain hours until banality came along to put the horror in its place. Discussing it over breakfast fizzes the next morning, Jimmy's campmates had spoken with a single voice: "He loved performing more than anything. He died a happy man."

Booter knew better. He had been there. He had seen the look on Jimmy's face. These fond farewells were too damn facile, if you asked him. When *he* went west, by God, he wanted serious mourning. If not weeping and wailing, at least a little gnashing of teeth.

Most of this occurred to him during Jimmy's impromptu memorial service at Medicine Lodge, Father Paddy Starr officiating. Booter knew the priest only slightly (he was a member of Pig n' Whistle), but the fellow struck him as a little too swish for his own good.

"He was one of the greats," Father Paddy told him afterwards.

"Yes," said Booter.

"I loved him in that Egyptian thing."

Booter nodded.

"I suppose his wife has been notified."

"His wife is dead," said Booter.

"Oh." The cleric clucked sympathetically. "What about children?"

"I dunno," said Booter, walking away. "I think there's a son in the East."

He downed two Scotches at the Medicine Lodge bar and walked back to Hillbillies by himself. On the way, he passed one of the Grove's infamous "heart-attack phones." Housed in their own miniature chalets, these infirmary hot lines had been installed for the sole purpose of saving lives.

Sometimes they did the job; sometimes they didn't.

Bohemians made grim jokes about the phones, the worst of which Booter had heard from Jimmy.

Poor bastard, he thought, as he stumbled into the compound at Hillbillies. I know damn well you weren't ready.

He had two more drinks at Hillbillies, but left shortly thereafter, finding the camaraderie oppressive. He walked down the river road past the Club House, then decided to forsake this eternal gloom for the sunshine of the riverbank.

The sentry at the guardhouse gave him a funny look. The old codger had always struck him as slightly impertinent.

"Havin' a good mornin'?" he asked.

"Not particularly," said Booter.

"Well . . . hope it gets better."

Booter grunted at him and kept walking. He wondered where they had kept Jimmy overnight. Was there a morgue in the infirmary? The funeral people had arrived from the city this morning, so Jimmy must've stayed somewhere in the Grove, away from his brothers, alone in the dark . . .

He crossed the footbridge above the gorge leading down to the beach. Laughter drifted up from the water, but it sounded callous to him, disrespectful of the dead. Didn't they know what had happened to Jimmy? Didn't all of Bohemia know?

Descending the slope to the river, he checked out a canoe at the dock and padded it with one of the thin cotton mattresses they issued for sunbathing. Snug in this waterborne nest, he paddled away from the cruel mirth of the swimmers, intent upon solitude.

When he was fifty yards or so downriver, he pulled in his paddle and leaned back against the mattress. There was virtually no current, and the sun felt good against his skin. He thought of Wren for a moment, welcoming the comfort she could offer in only a matter of hours.

He took his flask from his hip pocket and wet his whistle. Where did that come from—wet your whistle? He had heard it all his life without actually stopping to think about it. Jimmy would know, damn him. Why wasn't he here?

Jimmy would like this a lot. Jimmy was a real kid in a canoe. Naming all the birds, spinning yarns. He could tell his story about the narrow-gauge railway that ran along the river road in the 1890s . . . how the old-timers had come to the Grove using public transportation, starting with the Sausalito ferry, then taking the old Northwestern Pacific . . .

A huge, hungry-looking creature was patrolling the sky above the canoe. *Nothing dead down here, fella. Beat it.* It was a predatory bird of some sort, probably an osprey. Or was it a turkey vulture? Jimmy would know . . .

But Jimmy wasn't there, was he? He had marked out his life in encampments, summer to summer, and now he was gone, rocketing down the freeway, stiff as a board, robbed of his finale.

Just like that, Jimmy, just like that.

He closed his eyes and let his fingers trail in the water. For some reason, this pose struck him as vaguely Pre-Raphaelite, like that painting of the Lady of Shalott, supine in her boat, drifting off to her death.

Tennyson. How did it go?

"And down the river's dim expanse,/ Like some bold seer in a trance,/ Seeing all his own mischance,—/ With a glassy countenance/ Did she look to Camelot . . ."

It was his mother's favorite poem. He had memorized it four or five years after she died, for an English lit project at Deerfield.

"And at the closing of the day / She loosed the chain, and down she lay:/ The broad stream bore her far away,/ The Lady of Shalott."

He opened his eyes. The great bird of prey was a dark smudge against the sun. The brightness was too much for him. His eyelids caved in under the weight.

"And as the boat-head wound along, / The willowy hills and fields among, / They heard her singing her last song, / The Lady of Shalott."

Her last song . . . Mother's last song . . . Jimmy's last song . . .

The canoe found the current and swung around as he melted into the mattress and entered a realm of sweet release. His progress down the river was marked only by the vulture, who made several lazy loops in the air and returned to her nest in the forest.

The Honeymoon Period

Michael and Thack had driven out to the ocean that afternoon. From Cazadero they had followed a crumbly one-lane road which snaked through the dark green twilight of the redwoods before climbing to a mountain meadow the color of bleached hair. There were gnarly oaks here and there, and Wyeth-gray fences staggering down to the sea.

"Look," said Michael, pointing to the roadside. "Naked Ladies."

Thack blinked his pale lashes once or twice.

"Those lilies," Michael explained. "Pink, see? And no leaves. Naked Ladies."

"Oh," said Thack.

"You don't have 'em in Charleston?"

Thack shrugged. "We might. I'm not good on flowers."

"Just houses, huh?"

"Yep." He smiled faintly and returned his hand to Michael's denimed thigh. It had been there for most of the drive, pleasantly warm and already familiar.

"This was nice of Brian," Thack said.

"What?"

"Giving us time to ourselves."

"Oh . . . well, actually he wanted some time alone himself."
This was true enough, even though it *had* been Michael who'd broached the subject to Brian. "He's a good guy," he added, feeling vaguely guilty again.

"I like your friends," said Thack. "Was that Charlie who called this morning?"

"Yeah."

"Just . . . checking in?"

"Yeah," said Michael. "Wondering how the cabin was." This was a bald-faced lie.

"Has he been sick long?" asked Thack.

"A year or so," said Michael. "He came down with pneumocystis last month."

Thack made a little whistling sound.

"He's OK now," said Michael.

"He seems to be. I mean, aside from the lesion."

"It usually gets better," said Michael, "before it comes back. They call it the honeymoon period."

"Oh."

Michael gave him a rueful glance. "Isn't that a terrible expression?"

They passed a parched field, the carcass of a barn. The sea burned blue below them.

"Do you know anyone with AIDS?" Michael asked.

"A few."

"In Charleston?"

"No. New York, mostly."

"You have them in Charleston."

"I know," said Thack.

"Sometimes I think we're all gonna die."

Thack paused. "Have you thought about taking the test?"

"I've taken it," said Michael.

Thack looked at him.

Michael managed a rueful smile. "I was not amused."

Thack hesitated. "It doesn't really mean anything, you know."

465

"Promise?" said Michael.

Thack returned his smile, then faced the blinding blue of the Pacific. "I haven't taken it," he said.

Michael nodded.

"Are you sorry you took it?" Thack asked.

"No," said Michael. "I hate surprises."

They spent an hour or so roaming through the old Russian settlement at Fort Ross, then found a niche at the foot of a cliff where they leaned against each other and watched the waves. "Sometimes," said Michael, "I feel like Hermione Gingold."

Thack chuckled.

"You know . . . in *A Little Night Music*. What was the name of that song?"

" 'Liaisons,' " said Thack.

"Exactly." He gave Thack a teasing nudge. "Fags are so handy."

Thack smiled at him. "Why do you feel like Hermione Gingold?"

"Oh . . . everything seems like such a long time ago."

"Like what?"

"Just . . . the good ol' days. There used to be this beach up at Wohler Creek. Still is, I guess. It was a nude beach, only it was divided up into straight, gay and hippie. The hippies were a sort of buffer zone between the straight part and the gay part."

"That makes sense," said Thack.

"Somebody told me once that it belonged to Fred MacMurray."

"What? The beach?"

"Well, the land, I guess. People just showed up there by the hundreds, and he was nice about it. He just owned it, apparently. He was never there."

"Oh."

"The gay part was amazing. Dozens of naked guys, all stretched out on the beach, and *everybody* had a raft. You could lie on the beach and look out across the water, and it was nothing but a sea of beautiful butts." He smiled. "They called it the San Francisco Navy."

Thack laughed.

Michael looked out to sea. "That was nineteen eighty-one . . . the last time I went."

"Four years," said Thack.

"It seems like forty," said Michael. He turned and looked at Thack. "Does it bother you that I'm positive?"

Thack returned his gaze, then gave him a gentle, leisurely kiss on the mouth.

"Is that an answer?" said Michael.

"Well . . . it's the best I can do right now."

Thack pulled him closer and kissed him again. Beneath the burnished ribs of his old corduroy shirt, his back felt like warm marble. His lips were incredibly soft, tasting faintly of apple juice.

"That's more like it," said Thack.

"Uh-huh," said Michael.

Thack smoothed the hair over Michael's ears. "You know what?"

"What?"

"Our sleeping arrangement is fucked."

Michael smiled. "I know. I'm sorry."

"Stop being sorry," said Thack, kissing him again.

Shortly after four, they followed the wiggly road back to Cazadero. When they parked in front of the cabin, Michael spotted Brian in a lawn chair by the creek and gave him a wave. "Yo," Brian hollered.

"See you inside," Michael told Thack. "I'm gonna go talk to him."

He walked down to the creekbank in the slanting afternoon light. Brian looked healthier, more relaxed, with color in his face. "How was it?" he asked.

"Great," said Michael.

"Good. I'm glad."

"That drive is incredible."

"Maybe I'll take it," said Brian. "You guys need the car to-night?"

"Tonight?" asked Michael.

"Well . . . for the next three or four hours."

"I guess not."

"I thought I'd go look at the sunset, maybe eat dinner at that place in Jenner."

"By yourself?" asked Michael.

"Sure."

"Brian, listen . . ."

"I want to, Michael. I like being alone. I've had fun today."

"Are you sure?"

Brian nodded.

"Well . . ."

"So . . ." Brian rose, picked up his copy of *Jitterbug Perfume*, folded the lawn chair. "The drive was nice, huh?"

"Wonderful," said Michael.

"Great."

They walked back to the cabin together, Brian's arm across Michael's shoulder.

"Oh," said Brian, "I put fresh sheets on the sofa bed."

Michael looked at him and smiled.

"Just thought I'd mention it," said Brian.

He left in the VW twenty minutes later.

Thack turned to Michael and said: "Beer?"

"Hug," said Michael.

Thack obliged him, kneading the knots in Michael's back. "Shall we eat before or after?"

Michael laughed. "Anything but during."

"Right." Thack let go of him and headed for the bathroom. "I'm gonna shower."

"OK."

Thack called from the bathroom. "Is it too warm for a fire?"

"Not for me," said Michael.

"Great. Why don't you build us one?"

Michael gazed at the freestanding fireplace—hooded, orange

and hideous—and decided that it was easily the finest fireplace in the Western world.

His kindling had just begun to crackle when the phone rang. If this was Charlie again . . .

"Hello."

"Uh . . . Michael." The voice was velvet-gloved and unmistakable.

"Wren? I thought you'd gone."

"Well . . . that's sorta the problem. Something kinda weird has happened."

"What?"

"My friend has disappeared."

"Your friend. You mean . . . ?"

"Yeah, him."

"What do you mean, disappeared?"

"Well . . . it takes some explaining. Could you come up here?"

No way, he thought. "Gosh, I'm really sorry. Brian took the car, so Thack and I . . ."

"I could come get you."

"Now?"

"Yeah."

"Wren . . . this is really not a good time."

"Oh." She knew what he meant immediately. "I'm sorry."

"I hope you understand."

"Well," she said, "you told me to call if I needed anything."

This was true, and he kicked himself for it. "Can't I help over the phone?"

"No," she replied. "I have to show you."

The bathroom door opened. Thack emerged towel-wrapped, on a cloud of steam. "What's the matter?" he asked, seeing Michael's grim expression.

"Wren's friend is missing."

"What?"

469

"Tell me where you are," said Wren. "I'll come get you."

Michael heaved a sigh and told her. He couldn't help wondering if she always got what she wanted.

The three of them stood on her deck above the river. "That's where he's supposed to be," said Wren, pointing to a distant chunk of water. She was wearing voluminous white Bermuda shorts and a pink cotton blouse with the collar turned up.

"What's down there?" asked Thack.

"The Bohemian Grove. Ever heard of it?"

Thack shook his head.

"It's a club," said Michael. "For society people."

"Not people," said Wren. "Men."

"Right," said Michael.

"When did you last talk to him?" asked Thack.

"This morning. I canceled my flight for him. He called and said he wanted to see me. He sounded really out of it and desperate."

Thack's brow furrowed. "In what way?"

"I dunno. He made me cancel my flight, for one thing."

"Made you?" asked Michael. He was still a little angry with her.

"Asked me. He sounded desperate, so I did it. He said he'd be here no later than three, and I know Booter well enough to know that he would never—"

"Booter?" said Michael. "His name is Booter?"

"No jokes, all right?"

"No . . . I think I know him."

"Oh, God."

"Booter Manigault?"

"Jesus," said Wren. "How small is that town, anyway?"

"Small," said Michael. "Microscopic."

Thack turned to Michael. "He's a friend of yours?"

"No," said Michael, "but I know who he is. My lover delivered his . . ." He thought for a moment. "Step-grandchildren."

"Oh, well," said Wren drily, looking at Thack. "Clears it right up, doesn't it?"

470

"Why don't you just go down there and ask?" said Michael.

"Where? The Grove? I did, darling. It's strictly Tubby's playhouse. No Girls Allowed."

"Couldn't you leave a message?" asked Thack.

"I did. They said they'd write it on the chalkboard at the Civic Center . . . whatever *that* means."

Michael chuckled. "I picture them walking around in togas or something."

"The thing is," said Wren, "the whole damn place is designed to protect them from women. If you haven't got a pecker, they don't wanna hear from you."

"I still don't get it," said Michael. "Why don't you just take off? If he didn't show, he didn't show. What's the big deal?"

"Because," said Wren, "I feel an obligation."

"How long have you known him?" asked Michael.

"Not very."

"How long is that?"

"A week, ten days."

"Well, maybe this is the kind of stunt he pulls."

"No," she said. "I don't think so."

"OK," said Michael. "Then maybe he got called home on an emergency or something. You could call his house in Hillsborough."

"No way," she replied.

"I'll do it," he said.

After at least eight rings, an ancient-sounding maid answered the phone. He asked to speak to Mr. Manigault, deciding that he could either hang up or make a landscape-gardening pitch if Manigault should be at home. The maid, however, reported that he was "up at the Grove" and that Mrs. Manigault had "gone to a fashion show in the city."

Michael thanked her and hung up. "He's still here, apparently."

Wren looked troubled. "Something's the matter, guys. There's no way I can fly home without knowing . . ."

"We could go down there," said Thack.

"Would you?" asked Wren.

Michael frowned. There went their evening at home.

"Maybe," said Thack, obviously getting into it, "we could talk to the guard, tell him we're friends of Booter."

"No," said Wren. "The gate's no good, if they don't have your name on a list."

"Then what?" asked Thack.

"Well . . . there's another way in." She turned to Michael and asked: "Are you as good a swimmer as Thack?"

Foreign Shores

Booter awoke to find himself staring at the stars. They were bright tonight, brighter than ever, pulsing like the light bulbs in the cellars of his childhood. He felt oddly peaceful in his mattress-lined cocoon, even though it was night and he was sunburned and the canoe had beached itself on the shores of God-knows-where.

How long had he slept? Three hours? Four? And how far had he drifted?

He gazed up the moonlit river for some reassuring point of reference—the Monte Rio bridge, a neon-trimmed roadhouse, an A-frame bathed in the blue light of television.

But there was nothing.

Only bone-pale sand and gray shrubbery and black trees pricking the blue-black sky.

And drums. And the song of sirens.

It was a dream. That was his first thought.

He remembered the whiskey (tasted it, in fact) and remembered his sleeplessness after Jimmy's death. He had needed sleep and it had come to him, so he was still asleep, that's all. And whiskey invariably made him dream.

The breeze, though, seemed real enough as he climbed out of the canoe. So, too, did the ache in his limbs and the rodent squeak of aluminum against sand as he pulled his craft ashore and tried to get his bearings again.

So why were the drums still beating, the sirens still singing?

The voices were female, certainly. And lots of them.

He moved in their direction, shaking the stiffness out of his joints. There were Christian retreats in the area, he remembered. Baptist Bible camps. These girls could easily be part of such a place.

He headed into the underbrush somewhat warily, fearful of frightening them. Beet red and rumpled, he knew he must look like a wild man, but he had no choice but to ask for their assistance.

They could lead him to a phone, and he could call the Grove. Someone would send a car for him. He'd be back in time for the Campfire Circle, no worse for wear and no one the wiser. Hell, he might even tell them about it, make it into a story. The way Jimmy would have done.

Following the music, he threaded his way through a dense thicket of madrone trees. There was a campfire up ahead—quite a large one—and he caught glimpses of swaying figures and faces made golden by the fire.

The drums stopped abruptly as he approached. Spurred by this primeval sign of danger (or the memory, perhaps, of Tarzan movies), he ducked behind a redwood, then chuckled at the absurdity of his reaction.

He emerged again, to see something extraordinary:

A tall, full-breasted woman, naked but for slashes of blue and green body paint, lifting her arms toward the heavens.

He hid himself again, collecting his wits as the woman began to chant:

"We invoke you, Great One . . . in the memory of nine million women executed on charges of witchcraft . . ."

What on earth . . . ?

"We invoke the name of the Great Goddess, the Mother of all living things . . ."

Peering incredulously around the tree, he saw that the other

473

women were naked too. Some held bowls of fruit or bunches of flowers. Others were draped with amulets or holding amethyst geodes in
their cupped hands.

"We invoke you, Great One . . . you whose names have been
sung from time beyond time. You who are Inanni, Isis, Ishtar, Anat,
Ashtoreth, Amaterasu, Neith, Selket . . ."

There was nothing to do but retreat. As quickly and quietly as
possible. He would find help elsewhere, but not here, for God's sake,
not here.

". . . Turquoise Woman, White Shell Woman, Cihuacoatl,
Tonantzin, Demeter, Artemis, Earthquake Mother, Kali . . ."

He crept away from the tribal fire, but Nature took note of
him and acted accordingly. Dry branches crackled underfoot, young
tendrils caught hold of his limbs, night birds screamed warnings to
anyone who'd listen . . .

And something large and terrible leapt from the shadows to
strike a blow to the back of his head.

Night Crossing

Setting their scheme in motion, Michael and Thack took Wren's car
and drove to the Guerneville Safeway, where they bought a box of
heavy-duty Hefty bags. When they returned to the hilltop lodge,
Wren was smoking a joint on the deck, her eyes on the dark river
below.

"Any word?" asked Michael.

She shook her head. "He's not gonna call. I've got this gut feeling."

Michael wasn't so sure about her gut feelings, but he kept his
mouth shut. "What do you want us to do?" he asked. "Once we get
there."

"Just find out where his camp is. Hillbillies, it's called. Ask
around for him. If he's there, or somebody at least knows where he
is, then I can go home."

"If we find him," said Thack, "what do you want us to tell him?"

Wren rolled her eyes. "Tell him to call my ass."

"He'll wonder how we got in, won't he?"

She shrugged. "Tell him. He won't report you. I can promise you that."

"And if he's not there?" asked Michael.

"Then," said Wren, "we figure out something else."

"How do we get back?"

"Through the gate. You'll be OK on the way out. It's a mile or so down to Monte Rio. Call me from that greasy spoon at the bridge and I'll come get you."

"Got it," said Thack.

"I'm glad *you* do," said Michael.

Ten minutes later, she drove them to the river's edge, parking in a neighborhood that seemed disturbingly suburban. Why, Michael asked himself, do people move to the redwoods to build mock-Tudor split-levels with basketball hoops over the garage?

The nearest house was dark, so the three of them scurried burglar-like across the side yard until they found a sandy path leading down to the water.

"See?" whispered Wren, pointing across the river. "There it is."

The Bohemian swimming platform and dressing rooms were a dark jumble of geometry in the distance. Michael estimated the swim to be no more than fifty yards. Easy enough, assuming the absence of crocodiles or unfriendly natives with blowguns.

"According to Booter," said Wren, "there's a bridge above that ravine and a guardhouse a few yards beyond that. You can probably avoid both of them if you follow the ravine up from the beach."

"Are you sure?" asked Michael.

She shook her head with a wry little smile.

"Great," he said.

"They won't shoot at you," she said. "It's just a club. If worst comes to worst, you can use Booter's name, and they'll send for him."

"They're gonna know we're not members," said Thack.

"Nah," she replied. "There's a thousand men in there. Nobody knows everybody."

Thack sat down on the sand and began to strip, stuffing his clothes into a Hefty bag. "If you want," he said to Michael, "put your things in here with mine. No, forget it. It'll be too heavy with the shoes."

Michael sat next to him and began to stuff his own bag. Thack had stripped all the way, so he did the same, willing away the last vestiges of his Protestant self-consciousness.

Pale as moonlight, Thack waded into the river with his bag of clothes. When he was knee-deep, he turned and spoke to Wren. "Wish us luck."

"More like a bon voyage." She laughed. "Shall I break some champagne across your bow?"

Michael followed Thack into the water, which was warmer than he expected, but his skin pebbled anyway. The silt of the river bottom oozed up between his toes. "If we're not back by sunup," he said, "send in the Mounties."

"Ha!" said Wren. "Think I'd trust you with a Mountie?"

"Keep your voices down," said Thack.

Wren clamped her hand to her mouth, then came to the water's edge and whispered: "I'll be waiting for your call. You have the number, don't you?"

"No," Michael replied.

"I do," said Thack.

Michael looked at him and said: "God, you're organized. I bet you alphabetize your albums."

"Wait," said Wren. "I forgot." She poked through the high grass until she found the terry-cloth towels she'd brought, then handed them to Michael, who stuffed them into his Hefty bag.

"You're such a doll to do this," she said.

He shrugged. "Life's been boring lately."

"It's Hillbillies," she said. "Don't forget."

"I won't." He waded out to join Thack again. They commenced a sort of tortured sidestroke, dragging their bags beside them.

When they reached midriver, puffing like steamboats, they looked at each other and burst into laughter.

Wren was still watching from the shore, a dead giveaway in her white Bermudas.

A Debutante Reason

Reclining topless on her cot, Polly Berendt folded her hands behind her head and said: "Something weird is happening down in chem-free."

Also topless, but sitting on the ground, DeDe asked: "What do you mean?"

"Well, when I went out to pee, I saw this huge huddle of those black-shirt girls. I mean, more than I've ever seen in one place. They clammed up when I walked by, like I'd just walked in on a cabinet meeting or something."

"I don't even wanna know," said DeDe. She was finished with Security and their nasty little intrigues.

Polly chuckled. "They probably found somebody with a Stevie Wonder tape."

DeDe didn't get it. "What's the matter with Stevie Wonder?"

"What else?" said Polly. "He's male."

"C'mon."

"Sure. It's a violation of women-only space. No records with male singers. Read your regulations." Polly rolled over, propping her head on her elbow. "You know what I want?"

"What?"

"A burger. With lots of cheese and pickles and blood pouring out of it . . ."

"Yuck," said DeDe.

"Well, it beats the hell outa this place," said Polly. "Did you try that phoney meat tonight?"

DeDe smiled grimly. "Sloppy Josephines."

"When are these girls gonna drag their asses out of the sixties? That's what I wanna know."

DeDe turned and gave her a big-sisterly smile. A lucky combination of sunshine and lantern light had turned Polly's taut little tummy the color of the rivets on her 501s. DeDe observed this effect with appreciation but without passion, like an art-conscious matron perusing a Rembrandt.

And she *was* a matron, compared to this kid.

"You don't remember Kennedy, do you?"

Polly rolled her eyes. "They always, always ask that."

"Well, *excuse* me."

"Why was he such a big deal, anyway? He made it with Marilyn Monroe. Big deal. Ask me if I remember the first moon landing."

"OK . . . Do you?"

"No."

DeDe groaned and threw a sweat sock at her. "You little turd."

Polly cackled triumphantly. She reminded DeDe of Edgar somehow. After he'd dropped a worm down Anna's back.

"The thing about the sixties," said DeDe, feeling older by the minute, "is that it wasn't so much a time as it was . . . a transformational experience. Some people did it then. Others waited until later."

"Like, wow," said Polly, mugging shamelessly. "Heavy."

"Fuck you," said DeDe.

Polly smiled at her. "So when did you transform?"

DeDe thought about it, then said: "The spring of nineteen seventy-seven."

"So specific?"

"I joined the People's Temple. In Guyana."

Polly looked stunned. "Jesus," she said.

"We got out, of course . . . before . . . all that."

"You and your lover?"

"Mmm. And the kids."

"They must've been babies," said Polly.

"They were. They don't remember anything."

There was a long silence. Then Polly said: "Why did you go?"

"I don't know." DeDe gave her a rueful glance. "It was D'or's idea."

Polly digested that, then said: "Like this, huh?"

DeDe nodded vaguely. "I guess so. I have a mind of my own, believe it or not."

"I believe you."

"She's strong, so I let her be strong. I like it that way. Most of the time."

Mischief flickered in Polly's eyes. "Is she the one who lights the charcoal and grills the steaks?"

DeDe wasn't sure how to take that, but she laughed, anyway. "The tuna," she said, correcting her.

"Oh. Right. No red meat. I forgot." Polly nodded solemnly. "And she's the one the kids obey?"

"What is this?" asked DeDe.

"I'm just curious."

"Yes, you are."

"Well, we're friends, aren't we? I just wanna . . . share." Polly smiled. "Like in the sixties."

DeDe popped the top on a Diet 7-Up. "You're incorrigible."

"Don't say that," said Polly.

"Why not?"

"It sounds like my seventh-grade English teacher."

DeDe took a sip. "You hated her?"

"No," said Polly. "She turned me on."

"Don't make me self-conscious, OK?"

Polly stared at her for a moment, then shook her head slowly and said, "Boy!"

"What?" asked DeDe.

"DeDe the Debutante."

This irked her. Why did everybody get to fire off this potshot? Debutantes—no, *reformed* debutantes—were probably the last oppressed minority on earth. "Look," she said, "I took off my shirt, didn't I?"

"You did," said Polly quietly, "and breast fans everywhere are grateful."

DeDe groaned at her.

"*But,*" said Polly, "you took it off for a debutante reason, not because you're really comfortable that way."

"C'mon. What the hell does that mean—a debutante reason?"

Polly shrugged. "You took it off because D'or took hers off, and you're afraid that Sabra's gonna take hers off pretty soon. So you beat her to it."

"Oh, please," said DeDe.

"It's so obvious," said Polly. "It's the Pillsbury Boob-Off."

"Will you stop? In the first place, Sabra Landauer would never take hers off in a million years."

"OK . . . So you took yours off to prove that you're better than Sabra."

"I did not."

Polly picked up an apple, polishing it against the leg of her 501s. "So where is she now?"

"Who?"

"D'or."

"At the Holly Near concert."

"Is she with Sabra?"

"Probably," said DeDe.

"You think they've been doing it?"

DeDe thought exactly that, but she refused to give shape to her fears.

Polly took a bite of the apple, chewed and swallowed. "You know what?"

"What?"

"You should fake her out, pretend to be fucking around yourself."

DeDe gave her a doubtful look. "With you, I suppose."

"Sure. I could be real convincing."

"I'll bet."

Polly turned and grinned at her.

"I could never be that pretty," said DeDe.

"Force yourself," said Polly. "There are big stakes here. Sabra's wrecked a few marriages in her time."

DeDe didn't want to hear this. "She's not all that good-looking," she said.

"Yeah, but she's rich."

"I'm rich," said DeDe.

"She's rich and famous," said Polly. "And she gets to do everything. Broadway openings, limos all over the place, personal friends with Lily and Jane . . ."

"Thanks," said DeDe. "Thanks a lot."

Polly studied her a moment, then sat up and pulled on a celadon sweatshirt.

"Where are you going?" asked DeDe.

"I'm outa here," said Polly. "There's a burger out there with my name on it."

DeDe felt deserted again. What would she do? Go back to her tent and wait for Anna to return from her quilting class? Should she be there, looking useless and alone, when D'or returned?

And what if D'or *didn't* return?

Polly hopped to her feet and began searching the tent for her socks. "Come with me," she said. "I won't be gone that long."

"Well . . ."

She handed DeDe her shirt. "C'mon, Mama. Let's get dressed and go to town."

Name-Dropper

According to Jimmy, the most imposing spiders were female, and this one certainly fit the bill. Fat, furry and crimson-bellied, she dangled from a fragile trapeze, weaving her macramé only inches from Booter's sunburned face.

He was in a tent; he could tell that much. His mouth tasted foul, and his head was throbbing. His feet were bound together, and his hands were tied behind his back. He was lying on his side, facing the spider.

His first thought was: "Weaving spiders come not here."

That was the Bohemian motto, but he drew no comfort from it now. At the Grove, the phrase meant dealmaking was prohibited, no business on the premises.

Here, it meant nothing.

Here, that spider could weave where she wanted.

He'd been conscious for almost five minutes when he heard a woman's voice outside the tent.

"Where is he?" she asked.

Someone hissed for quiet.

"We have to call the police."

"Sure. Turn him over to men."

"I don't care, Rose. We have to."

He heard boots scuffing against earth, then saw the tent flap move, revealing a woman in a black T-shirt. She held a walkie-talkie in one hand, and her head was shaved to varying degrees, forming a sort of topiary garden on her scalp. She squatted on her haunches to examine him.

"Listen," he said, "whatever you think I did—"

"I don't think. I saw."

"I was in a canoe," he said.

"I know that."

"I fell asleep. I must have drifted."

"Did you enjoy the show?" she asked.

So they had seen him watching.

"Answer the question," she said.

"It was an accident," he said. "I didn't know where I was. I went up there to ask directions."

"You're lying," she said.

"Don't tell me I'm lying!" How dare she talk to him like that? Who, after all, had clobbered whom?

"What's your name?" she asked.

He hesitated. What if she called the police? He could clear himself, of course, but what sort of indignities would he be forced to endure? "I don't have to tell you that," he said at last.

She appraised him coolly for several seconds before dropping the tent flap and walking away. He hollered, "Wait!" but got no response.

She came back about fifteen minutes later.

"Thirsty?" she asked.

He was and said so.

"I'll have some water sent by for you."

"Wait a minute," he said. "Don't go."

"What?"

"You're making a very big mistake, young lady."

"Yeah?"

"I know how it may have looked to you, but I'm no Peeping Tom."

"OK. Then who are you?"

"I'm a member of the Bohemian Club. We're up the river a bit. I don't want to make trouble for you, but   "

"I asked your name."

"Manigault," he muttered.

"What?"

"Manigault. Roger Manigault."

"Sure."

"Well . . . I don't have my wallet with me."

"As in Pacific Excelsior?"

"Yes!" He literally sighed with relief. Thank God she knew about business! "That's me!"

"That's you?"

"Yes! I'm not the sort of man who—"

She cut him off with a wild bray of laughter. "Booter. They call you Booter?"

"Yes. Now will you please untie—"

"Reagan's friend?"

"Well . . . I know him . . . I wouldn't exactly say—"

She dropped the tent flap and went howling into the night.

A Dream Come True

Thanks to Booter, dinner hadn't happened tonight, so Wren postponed her journey home, stopping off at the greasy spoon near the Monte Rio bridge. Michael and Thack wouldn't call for at least an hour, so why not settle her nerves with a basket of fries and a chicken-fried steak?

The greasy spoon was a "family restaurant," replete with squawling brats, cracked plastic menus and redwood room deodorizers for sale next to the cash register. She was debating dessert when a teenaged girl approached, wearing an expression of tentative fandom. "OK," she told Wren. "If you're not, you might as well be."

Wren put her fork down and stuck out her hand. "I guess I am, then. What's your name?"

The teenager, on closer inspection, seemed more like a young woman. She was short and wiry, with freckles and a sparkling pink-gummed smile. "Polly Berendt," she replied. "I really can't believe this."

"What?" said Wren. "That you found me eating?"

Polly laughed. "You look just like you look on TV. Better. This is the most amazing thing. This is so great."

"Sit down." Wren winked at her and patted the place mat across from her. "We're frightening the nuclear families."

Polly cast a glance over her shoulder, then sank into the chair. "Sorry," she said. "I get loud."

"Yeah," said Wren. "Me too." She popped open her compact mirror and began to repair her lipstick. "You on vacation or something?"

Polly didn't answer for a while, lost in her amazement. "What?" she said at last.

"You on vacation?"

484

"Oh . . . yeah. I'm down at Wimminwood. Know what that is?"

"Uh . . . well, a women's music festival, right?" She'd read about it on the bulletin board at the Cazadero General Store. She'd figured the kid for a lesbian.

"Yeah, that's right."

"So what are you doing here? Playing hooky?"

Polly chuckled. "Yeah, more or less."

"All by yourself?" OK, she was flirting a little, but what harm could it do?

"No. I'm here with a friend. I mean, here at the restaurant. That blonde lady over there."

Wren dropped her lipstick into her purse and gazed across the room. Caught in the act of watching them, the blonde looked decidedly uncomfortable. Wren gave her a little smile, which induced even more embarrassment.

"She's against this," said Polly.

"Against what?"

"Me coming over here."

"Why?"

Polly shrugged. "She says it's tacky."

"Nah," said Wren. "I think she's jealous."

Polly cast a quick glance at the blonde, then looked back at Wren. "No shit?"

Wren gave her one of her Mona Lisa smiles.

"That would be wonderful," said Polly.

"What?"

"If she would be jealous. I don't think she likes me that much."

"Well . . ."

"Could I get a lipstick print from you?"

Wren blinked at her.

"I collect them," said Polly. "It's a hobby. I already have Diana Ross and Linda Evans and Kathleen Turner."

"Sure. Fine. What do I do?"

Polly beamed at her. "I can't believe this."

"What do I do?" Wren asked again. "Blot on a napkin?" Her

eyes wandered across the room. The blonde woman was staring straight down into the remains of her hamburger. She was obviously mortified.

"Or," Wren added, "I could pucker up and really smooch on it." She looked back at Polly and grinned conspiratorially. "Your friend would like that."

Polly giggled.

Wren picked up a napkin and settled on something between a blot and a smooch, giving the results to Polly. "Happy summer," she said.

"Same to you," said Polly, shaking Wren's hand briskly. "Same to you."

Into the Grove

Michael and Thack had crossed the river without a hitch, drying off and dressing in a dockside room erected for just that purpose. They'd followed the ravine up the forested hillside until they found the footbridge Wren had told them about. It loomed above them, huge and skeletal, like an abandoned railway trestle.

"What now?" whispered Michael.

"We go under it," Thack replied. "Up that hill."

"Wait!"

"What?"

"I heard something."

Thack cocked his head. There were rustling sounds, then the resonant thump of footsteps on the bridge. Michael flattened himself against a support post, pulling Thack back into the shadows. The moon was traitorously bright.

A voice called: "Who goes down there?"

Michael held his breath, glancing at Thack. Wren's words reverberated in his head. *They won't shoot at you . . . It's just a club . . . They won't shoot at you . . .*

Thack pressed his finger to his lips, clearly intent upon going through with this madness.

The footsteps commenced again, then stopped at midbridge. A flashlight beam probed the underbrush only yards away from their hiding place. Michael hugged the post and prayed for release. Or at least leniency.

"Who goes?" yelled the guard.

Michael looked at Thack. Enough was enough.

Thack shook his head emphatically.

The guard stood there for half a minute, then began to walk again. Away from them. Off the bridge and up the hillside.

Thack's eyes flashed triumphantly. Michael expelled air and whispered: "Let's get the fuck outa here."

"What? Swim back?"

"Sure."

"C'mon. The worst is over."

"How do you know?" asked Michael. "What if he comes back?"

"Well, we've come this far. Don't be such a pussy."

"I'm being practical," said Michael.

Thack gave him a friendly goose. "Then don't be so practical, Maude."

They waited another five minutes, then continued up the hillside until the lights of a road led them into the Grove. Men passed them in boozy clumps, singing and jostling, hooting hello as if they, Michael and Thack, had been there all along, making merry under the redwoods.

Manhood, it seemed, had been their only requirement, their only badge of identity.

"This is so unreal," said Michael. "It's like a hologram or something."

"*Pinocchio,*" said Thack.

"What?"

"You know. Those wicked boys on Pleasure Island."

They were walking through a gorge, apparently, with ferny forests climbing the slopes on either side. The redwoods along the road were as fat around as Fotomats, clustered so tightly in some places that they became walls for outdoor rooms, foyers for the camps that lay behind them.

The camps were wonders to behold. Giant tepees and moss-covered lodges and open-air fireplaces built for the gods. Strings of lanterns meandered up the canyon wall to camps so loftly that they seemed like tree houses.

And everywhere there was music. They heard Brahms for a while, then Cole Porter. Then an unseen pianist began tinkling his way through "Yesterday."

Thack asked: "There are no women at all?"

"Nope," said Michael. "They've been to court over it."

"How do they defend it?"

Michael shrugged. "Women make 'em nervous. They can't be themselves."

Thack chuckled and slipped his arms across Michael's shoulder.

"I wouldn't do that," said Michael.

"What?"

"This is the straightest place on earth, Thack."

"Oh." Thack removed his arm, looking vaguely wounded. "Plenty of *them* are doing it."

"Yeah, but . . . you know . . . it's different." Michael knew how gutless this sounded, but he was still feeling incredibly paranoid.

A hawk-faced old man was catching his breath against a tree. Thack approached him, somewhat to Michael's alarm.

"Excuse me, sir. We're kinda lost."

The old man chortled. "New here, eh?"

"Yeah."

"Where ya wanna go, podnah?"

"Well . . . Hillbillies, we were told. Booter Manigault's camp."

"Ah." He nodded slowly. "You guests of Booter?"

488

Thack hesitated ever so slightly, so Michael said: "Right."

"Good fella, Booter."

"Yeah, he is," said Thack.

"The best," Michael added, perhaps a little too eagerly.

"I tell you what you do," said the old man. "You keep on down the river road . . . this road right here . . ."

"OK," said Thack.

"It's a few camps down, on the left. You'll see the sign."

"Thanks a lot."

The old man said: "What'd ya do? Pass it and double back?"

"Uh . . . yeah, I guess we did."

"Well, you just keep on down this way. You're on the right track now."

"Great," said Michael.

"On the left," added the old man. "You can't miss it."

"Terrific."

"Sign's over the entrance. Big bronze one."

As they withdrew, both nodding their thanks, Michael wondered why old men take such a long time to give directions. Was it senility or a yearning for company?

Or just the unexpected exhilaration of feeling useful again?

The Hillbillies plaque depicted Pan with his pipes and a naked female spirit rising from the steam of a caldron. "Would you look at that?" said Thack, standing back to admire it. "Pure Art Nouveau."

Michael, who still felt like an impostor, refrained from a telltale display of aesthetic appreciation.

Thack led the way into an enclosed compound dominated by a two-story redwood chalet. Half a dozen men of varying ages were gathered around a fireplace in the courtyard. One of them stared hard at the newcomers, then sailed in their direction at great speed, wearing a phosphorescent smile.

"Michael, my child!"

It was Father Paddy Starr, the television priest who presided over religious affairs at Mary Ann's station.

"Oh, hi," Michael said feebly, panicked at the sight of a familiar face.

"What a lovely surprise!" Father Paddy clamped his chubby hands together. "Have you been here the whole time?"

It was probably an innocent question, but Michael got flustered, anyway. "Well . . . uh . . . no, actually. We just got here. We're guests of Booter Manigault."

Father Paddy's brow wrinkled. He began to cluck his tongue and shake his head. "The poor old dear," he said.

Thack shot Michael a quick glance.

"Has something happened to him?" Michael asked.

"Well," the cleric replied. "I expect you heard about Jimmy Chappell?"

"No . . . uh . . . not really."

"Oh. Well, Jimmy died last night."

"I'm sorry. I don't think I know who . . ."

"No, of course not. How silly of me. He was one of Booter's oldest chums."

"Oh," said Michael.

Father Paddy heaved a sigh. "I think it's been hard on him, poor dear."

"You haven't seen him, have you?"

"No. I expect he's gone home."

"No," said Thack. "We were supposed to meet him here."

"Ah . . . well, then he must be up at Lost Angels. He has friends up there."

"Lost Angels?"

"C'mon," said Father Paddy. "I'll show you." He turned to Thack and extended his hand, palm down, as if to be kissed. "I'm Father Paddy . . . since Michael's forgotten his manners."

Thack shook the cleric's hand. "Thack Sweeney," he said.

"An Irishman! I might have known."

Thack pointed to the Hillbillies plaque. "What can you tell me about the artist?"

"Not a blessed thing," said Father Paddy, "but isn't it adorable?" As the priest sashayed out, leading the way, Thack spoke to Michael under his breath. "So," he said. "The straightest place on earth."

The Escape Plan

Booter heard footsteps again. The tent flap opened, to reveal a Negro girl wearing gym shorts and a bright blue T-shirt. "Hi," she said, with surprising cheerfulness. "I'm Teejay."

He wasn't about to swap nicknames with her.

"The water girl," she added, holding up a canteen.

"You know," he said, "you can all be arrested for this."

Kneeling in front of him, she lifted him to a sitting position. "Are your wrists uncomfortable?" she asked.

"What do you think?" he replied.

She examined his bonds for a moment. "I can't loosen it without taking the whole thing off."

"Then do it," he said.

"Sure." She smiled at him. "And let you bop me on the head." She lifted the canteen to his lips, tilting it slowly, wiping away the overflow with a blue kerchief.

When she was done, Booter said: "I don't bop people on the head."

She tightened the top of the canteen. "Rose says you make instruments of war."

"I make aluminum honeycomb," he said.

"She says you went to Bitburg and laid wreaths on Nazi graves."

"That was a *reconciliation* gesture. Look . . . what's going on here? You can't just hold me indefinitely. I didn't do anything."

The girl used her fingers to comb the hair off his forehead. "We've had . . . some harassment. Rose thinks you're part of it. She wants to hold a tribunal."

"A tribunal? What? Here?"

She nodded.

"She's crazy," said Booter. "She's a complete lunatic. If she thinks she can humiliate me . . ." He collected himself and tried to sound as reasonable as possible. "Look . . . I don't have anything against you or anybody here. I'm a man of my word. If you let me go, I promise I won't lay a finger on you."

"No," she said. "You have to."

"What?"

"We have to make it look that way."

"Like what?"

"Like you overpowered me. Otherwise I'll catch hell."

He grasped her meaning with a rush of relief. "OK. Fine. However you want to do it."

Leaning closer, she said: "The best way out is the way you came. Your canoe is still there."

"Are you sure?"

"I've already checked," she said.

"Are we near the river?"

"Oh, God," she said. "You don't know where you are?"

"No. How could I? That . . . whatshername—"

"OK," she cut in. "There's a dirt road just outside the tent here. Down a little and to the right. Follow it until you reach the river. Then . . ." She fell silent suddenly and cast an uneasy glance over her shoulder.

"What's the matter?" he whispered.

"Nothing," she said. "I thought I heard something." She listened a moment longer, then continued: "The canoe is up the river about fifty yards from the point where the road meets the river. Got that?"

"I think so, but . . ."

"What?"

"Well, I can't paddle back to . . . my place. The current's against me."

She pondered the problem, then said: "There's a Baptist camp about a mile downstream. You'll be safe there." She knelt behind him and began to tug at the ropes around his wrists. "Just make it damn quick and don't look at anybody on your way out. This is women-only space."

"If they see me, though . . . ?"

"You'll be all right," she said soothingly. "We're not all like Rose."

"Is that right?" came a voice outside the tent.

There was no mistaking it, and no mistaking the sculptured scalp which burst into view through the tent flap.

The girl let go of the ropes and spun around to face her superior. "Rose . . ."

"This'll go on my report," said Rose.

"I was just loosening them," said the girl.

"I heard what you were doing."

"Rose, he's an old man."

"So was Mengele," said Rose.

Booter had heard enough. "Listen here, young lady—"

"Don't you call me that!"

"I'll call you anything I want!"

"Rose, we can't legally—"

"Get out, Teejay!"

The girl stood there a moment longer, saying nothing, then muttered under her breath and left.

"Please," Booter told her, "call the police . . ."

The shaved woman began rummaging noisily through a pile of gear in the corner of the tent. Booter watched as she ripped open a cardboard box, then tore off lengths of masking tape. She leaned over him and clamped something white and gauzy against his mouth, binding it in place with the tape.

His eyes had begun to water a bit, but he could still discern the label on the box: *New Freedom Maxi-pads.*

Mrs. Madrigal's Lament

It was almost nine o'clock when Brian returned to the cabin on Austin Creek. All he had done was drive, following the coastal highway as far as Elk, then swinging south again in time for dinner in Jenner at the River's End Restaurant. Having spoken to no one except a waitress and an Exxon attendant, he welcomed the prospect of company.

But Michael and Thack were gone. They weren't in the cabin and they weren't by the campfire, and they didn't have a car. Had they walked into Cazadero for dinner?

He lit a fire and tried to get back into *Jitterbug Perfume*, but his mind began to wander. On an impulse, he picked up the phone and called Mrs. Madrigal.

"Madrigal here."

"Hi. It's Brian."

"Oh . . . yes, dear. Are you home?"

"No. We're still here. Just thought I'd check on things."

"Oh . . . well . . . good."

"Has Puppy been a problem?"

"Don't be silly. As a matter of fact . . . Puppy dear, come say hello to Daddy. Go on. That's right, it's Daddy. Say 'Hello, Daddy.' "

"Hello, Daddy," came a small, familiar voice.

"Hi, Puppy. Have you been good?"

"Yes."

"I miss you a lot."

Silence.

"Do you miss Daddy?"

Silence.

"Puppy?"

Mrs. Madrigal came back on the line. "The telephone throws her. She thinks you should be on TV."

"What do you mean?"

494

The landlady chuckled. "When Mommy's away, Mommy's on TV. So when Daddy's away . . . well, it makes sense, doesn't it?"

"I suppose."

"She misses you, dear. Take my word for it."

"Is Mary Ann OK?"

"Fine," she said evenly. "I haven't seen her that much, but she's been so busy lately. Did you try to reach her at The Summit?"

"No."

"Well, she's at some big gala tonight, but she should be home by ten."

"OK."

"She was lovely on that Hollywood show. Did you get a chance to watch?"

"No," he said.

"Well, she was . . . very poised. What's the name of that show?"

"Entertainment Tonight," he said.

"Yes. She was just splendid. I'm sure she taped it. You can watch it when you get home."

He couldn't think of anything to say.

"Dear, are you all right?"

"Yeah. Fine."

"No you're not."

"I'm just a little tired tonight."

"Well, put your feet up. Have some chamomile."

"OK."

"When are you coming home?" she asked.

"Tomorrow."

"Good." She paused. "We lost our appeal, by the way."

"Oh . . . the steps, you mean?"

"Yes."

"What does that mean exactly?"

"Well . . . they tear them down on Monday."

"So soon?" said Brian. "How will we get up to the lane?"

The landlady sighed. "Apparently on some horrid temporary

thing. Aluminum. Until the concrete sets." She was quiet for a moment, then added: "It's too awful to contemplate."

He murmured in agreement.

"Am I being silly?"

"No. Not at all."

"You know . . . I sit there with my tea in the morning. The wood gets warm in the sun. The very *feel* of it under my fingers . . ." She sounded like someone remembering a love affair.

He asked: "Couldn't they build a new one in redwood or something?"

"That's exactly what I proposed. They can't be bothered. *Maintenance*, they said."

"Those assholes," said Brian.

"All of life is maintenance, for heaven's sake. That's the *pleasant* part. Taking care of things."

He thought about that for a moment. "Have you spoken to Mary Ann?"

"Yes, but . . . you were right. It's not really suited for her show."

"Maybe so, but she could . . . I dunno . . . talk to the people in News, at least."

"Well, I mentioned that to her, but she said they would need . . . a hook, I believe she called it."

"A hook!" All of a sudden he was mad. "They're tearing down the steps! There's the hook!"

"I know, but . . . she's the professional."

"That's for goddamn sure! What does she want you to do? Chain yourself to the steps?"

"Dear . . . calm down."

"Well, she pisses me off sometimes."

Mrs. Madrigal paused. "Why are you so cross with her?"

"I'm not cross with her," he said.

He was back on the sofa, buried in his book, when the phone rang. "Yeah?"

"Brian?"

"Yeah."

"It's Wren Douglas."

"Oh, yeah."

"If you're wondering about your roomies," she said, "I made off with them."

"Oh. That explains it."

"They asked me to call you. They've gone on a little mission for me."

"They're not there, you mean?"

"No. I'm gonna meet 'em down in Monte Rio in an hour or so. I'm just here, waiting for their call. I thought you might wanna join me."

After a moment's hesitation, he said: "Uh . . . sure. Great."

"We can hang out . . . talk. Whatever."

"Terrific."

"You remember the way?"

"How could I forget?" he said.

Friends Are One Thing

Their stomachs aglow with forbidden food, DeDe and Polly returned to the Halcyon-Wilson campsite, to find Anna reading comic books in her pup tent.

"Hey," said DeDe, "did you cut your quilting class?"

Her daughter shook her head. "We got out early."

"You've been here all alone?"

DeDe felt a twinge of guilt. "Have you been OK?"

"Mom."

"Polly and I just . . . took a walk." She wasn't quite sure why she lied about this, why her trip to the greasy spoon had felt so much like going AWOL. Polly was just as puzzled, apparently, giving DeDe a funny sideways look.

"This lady was looking for you," said Anna, turning back to the ThunderCats.

"When?" asked DeDe.

"Little while ago."

"What sort of lady, Anna?"

The child shrugged, but didn't look up. "A black lady."

"Did she tell you her name?"

"No . . . yeah. Two letters."

"Two letters?" DeDe gave her daughter the evil eye. "Put that down and look at me."

Anna did so begrudgingly. "What?"

"What do you mean, two letters? Was it Teejay?"

"Yeah. Teejay."

"Did she say what she wanted?"

Anna screwed up her face. "She said . . . meet her behind the Womb as soon as possible."

Polly snickered.

DeDe glared at her and turned back to her daughter. "Why, Anna? Did she say?"

"There's gonna be a tri-something."

"A tri-something?"

"A triathlon," said Polly.

"Shut up," DeDe muttered. "A tri*bunal*, Anna?"

"Yeah. That's it."

"I'm supposed to meet her?"

"Yeah. Behind the Womb."

"Dear God."

"What is it?" asked Polly.

"Nothing," said DeDe, her heart rising to her throat.

She left Anna's tent and walked back to her own, Polly nipping at her heels. "C'mon, DeDe, what is it?"

"They're gonna nail me," she said. "They're gonna burn me at the stake."

"*Who?*"

"Rose Dvorak . . . and the rest of 'em."

"I don't get it."

"Teejay *works* for Rose."

"Oh." Polly wrinkled her nose. "So what are they gonna do?"

"I dunno. Whatever they do at tribunals."

"C'mon. They're gonna *try* you? What for? Letting those red-necks in? That was a mistake."

"It isn't just that," said DeDe.

Polly looked at her, slack-mouthed. "What else have you done?"

"It wasn't me. It was this woman named Mabel. I was with her when . . ." She ducked into her tent and collapsed on the sleeping bag.

Polly sat across from her. "When what?"

"It doesn't matter," said DeDe.

"Aren't you gonna see her?"

"Who?"

"This Teejay person."

"No. Hell, no. I'm gettin' outa here first thing in the morning."

"What about . . . you know . . . D'or?"

"What about her?" asked DeDe.

"What if she doesn't wanna leave?"

DeDe shrugged. "She can stay. The kids and I are going."

Polly looked at her wistfully. "What if *I* don't want you to leave?"

"You're sweet," said DeDe. "You're really nice."

Polly slid closer on her denimed butt, then leaned down and gave DeDe a clumsy peck on the mouth. "D'orothea is nuts," she said, her voice turning husky. "I'd be with you all the time."

"Polly . . ."

"All the time."

DeDe backed off a little. "It's not that way when you've been together for a while. Not for anybody."

"I dunno."

"Well, I do."

Polly gave her a crooked grin. "Whatever you say, Deirdre."

This rattled her. "Where did you hear my real name?"

"Anna told me yesterday. When you were swimming."

For some reason, this struck her as vaguely conspiratorial. "She just . . . volunteered that?"

"No. I asked her. I wanna know all there is to know about you." DeDe fidgeted with the zipper on the sleeping bag.

"I'm really gonna miss you," said Polly.

"And I you." She hated people who said that, but it just tumbled out in her embarrassment.

"Will you come visit me at the nursery sometime?"

"Well . . . D'or does most of the gardening."

"I can call you, can't I?"

DeDe avoided her gaze.

"OK, forget it."

"Polly . . ." DeDe took her hand. "Friends are one thing. What you want—"

"You don't know what I want."

DeDe chose her words carefully. "Maybe not, but . . . c'mon, I'm a stuffy old married lady."

"I don't care," said Polly.

DeDe drew back. "You're supposed to say I'm not stuffy, I'm not old."

"I like 'em old," said Polly.

DeDe groaned and lobbed a sneaker at her. Polly deflected it, grinning impishly. "OK," she said. "I'm outa here."

"No," said DeDe. "Stay and play Pictionary."

"We need three people for that."

"Well . . . practice with me, then."

"Your lover might come back," said Polly.

"So what?" said DeDe. D'or could certainly use a dose of her own medicine. Besides, Rose was on the rampage, and DeDe hated the thought of being alone.

Divine Intervention

Father Paddy led them into the wilderness, chattering incessantly.

"By the way," he said as he charged up a winding trail. "I'm aware the dress is a bit much."

He meant his cassock, obviously, but Michael refrained from comment.

"I wore it for poor Jimmy's memorial service, and I haven't had a *moment* to change. Please don't think me ostentatious."

"No," said Michael.

"Usually," added the cleric, addressing Thack, "I'm content with a simple turtleneck and crucifix—especially at the Grove—but the deceased was a theatrical sort, so I felt a little pageantry was in order."

Michael detected a puckish gleam in the priest's eye. He was testing Thack, apparently, trying out his time-proven shtick on an unwitting neophyte.

"How did he die?" asked Thack.

"Oh, you know . . . the ticker. Happens fairly often here."

"I can imagine," said Thack, drier than usual for Michael's benefit.

Now well above the floor of the gorge, Father Paddy turned off the main trail and led them across an elevated boardwalk spanning a dry creekbed. At the end of it lay a tented pavilion, vibrant with lights and laughter. Three or four similar camps were visible beneath them, clinging to the side of the hill.

"Lost Angels," said the priest, gesturing toward the pavilion. "Booter's bound to be here."

"Why do they call it that?" asked Thack.

"Well . . ." Father Paddy leaned closer and spoke from behind his palm, as if imparting a shameful secret. "Some of them are from Los Angeles." He approached a fortyish man near the end of the boardwalk. "Evening, Ollie."

"Evening, padre."

"Haven't seen Booter, have you?"

The man shook his head. "Not since the funeral."

Scanning the revelers in the pavilion, the priest said: "I thought perhaps . . ."

"Look around," said the man. "Help yourself to some chow while you're at it." He turned to Michael and Thack. "You fellows look like you could use a drink."

Michael glanced at Thack.

"Go ahead," urged Father Paddy. "Belly up. That's what it's there for."

"I'll get 'em," said Thack, addressing Michael. "What do you want?"

Michael pondered. "Uh . . . gin and tonic."

Thack turned to the priest. "Father?"

"Oh, thanks, no. I only drink on duty."

Thack grinned and headed for the bar. When he was gone, Father Paddy pulled Michael aside and said: "He is absolutely adorable."

"I know," said Michael.

"Are you two . . . together?"

"Not really."

The priest looked stern. "Don't be coy, my child."

"Well," said Michael, "it hasn't been that long. He's just visiting from South Carolina."

"Oh."

Uncomfortable, Michael glanced around and tried to change the subject. "Do you think maybe Booter . . . ?"

"You look just perfect together."

Michael shrugged.

"Just for the record, I have a marvelous little solemnization ceremony."

"What?"

"It's not a marriage, mind you. The Holy Father will have none of that. But it's a blessing of sorts, and it's very sweet."

"Father."

"All right. I'll shut up. Forget I mentioned it."

"It's a deal," said Michael.

"I've never done one, and I've always wanted to. *But . . .*" His hand made several wistful loops in the air.

"He's going back to Charleston," said Michael.

"Very well."

"And we're both very independent."

"Mmm."

"Plus, you forget . . . I'm not even Catholic."

"Oh, really," said Father Paddy. "Picky, picky!"

Later, when they'd retreated to a bench above Lost Angels, Thack asked: "What do we do now? He's obviously not here."

"It's impossible to tell," said Michael. "There are so many camps."

"Yeah, but we could spend all night looking."

"I guess we should call Wren."

"You think something's happened to him?" Thack asked. "I mean, like . . . foul play?"

"Not really."

"I don't, either."

"I think Wren's overreacting."

"Yeah," said Thack.

They were quiet for a moment, then Thack asked. "What were those eye signals all about?"

"What eye signals?"

"You know. Down there. Between you and Sister Bertrille."

"Oh." Michael rolled his eyes. "You're not gonna believe this."

"Try me."

"He's matchmaking."

Thack gave him a blank look.

"He offered to marry us." Michael widened his eyes to emphasize the frivolous nature of the idea.

"What?"

"To perform the ceremony," said Michael. "Cute, huh?"

Thack frowned a little. "Where did he get that idea?"

"Beats me. He just liked the way we looked together."

Silence.

"I told him we were buddies. That you didn't even live here."

"Here" wasn't right somehow, considering their location. Softened by woodsmoke, the tiny tent villages beneath them seemed more dreamlike than ever. It was hard to imagine *anyone* living here.

"Fuck him," said Thack. "Who needs the church for that?"

His vehemence was a little surprising. "Are you Catholic?" Michael asked.

"Ex. I belonged to Dignity for a while, but I quit."

"Why?"

Thack shrugged. "Why should I keep kissing the Pope's ass when he doesn't even *approve* of mine? I don't call that dignity. I call it masochism." He smiled suddenly. "I've got a great idea."

"What?"

"Wait here." He shook Michael's leg and ran off down the trail, darting into the undergrowth near the lights of Lost Angels. He returned five minutes later, dragging a twin-sized mattress behind him.

"Where did you get that?"

"One of the cabins," said Thack.

Michael frowned.

"An empty one. We'll return it."

"Yeah, but what if . . . ?"

"C'mon," said Thack.

Michael followed him up a slope through a tangle of pesky undergrowth. When they reached a ledge about twenty feet above the path, Thack dropped the mattress.

"I wonder if we should be paranoid?" said Michael.

"That's easy," said Thack. "We shouldn't."

"Yeah, but we don't really know how private . . ."

"Look, we can see the path from here. They're too old and

drunk to make it up this far." He sat down on the mattress and dug into his shirt pocket, removing a joint and a matchbook.

"Where did you get that?" Michael asked, sitting next to him.

Thack lit the joint. "Wren. Our reward." He toked a couple of times and offered it to Michael.

"No, thanks . . . Oh, to hell with it." He took the joint and filled his lungs with the stuff. He'd been careful all year. Tonight, his immune system could just go fuck itself.

"Listen," said Thack. " 'The Trail of the Lonesome Pine.' "

"How wonderful." Michael tilted his head to hear pianos and banjos rambling through the old tune.

"That was Gertrude Stein's favorite song," said Thack.

"It was?"

"I think so."

Michael returned the joint. "Where'd you hear that?"

"I don't remember, really."

"It's a great song," said Michael.

Thack stretched out, arching his ivory neck. "Look at that fucking moon. Is that beautiful or what?"

It was full and fluorescent, a real troublemaker. Michael stretched out next to Thack, leaned back on his elbows. There was something supremely sexy about a man who planned ahead like this, who wore his options like a tool belt, ready for any emergency.

Thack took another toke, then stubbed out the joint. He rolled his head over lazily and gazed at Michael. "I thought this would never happen."

Michael smiled at him.

"You're a great guy," said Thack.

"You too." Michael turned on his side and flicked open the pearly snaps on Thack's denim shirt.

His mouth went straight for the left nipple, pink and proud as a tiny cock.

Afterwards, they lay there motionless, listening to the music. A snail's trail of semen still glimmered on Thack's stomach. He kept his hand cupped gently around Michael's cock, as if it were a wounded bird trying to escape.

Michael said: "Where's a priest when you really need one?"

Thack chuckled and nuzzled Michael's shoulder.

"Was that really Gertrude Stein's favorite song? Did you make that up?"

"Why would I do that?" asked Thack.

"I dunno. To get me in the mood."

"Gertrude Stein is a turn-on?"

"Well . . . it worked for Alice."

"You were already in the mood," said Thack.

"This is true," said Michael.

Further down the gorge, another piano began to play. Joyful male voices floated toward them on the breeze. For some reason, Michael thought of a faded daguerreotype he had seen in an antique shop on Union Street: a dozen lumberjacks with huge mustaches and vintage Levi's, straddling a fallen redwood tree.

"Brian would have loved this," he said.

"Think so?" said Thack.

"Yeah. He's a big kid."

"Like you."

"Yeah. I guess so."

Thack snuggled closer and slid his hand up to Michael's belly. "You're kind of a couple, aren't you?"

"Who?"

"You and Brian."

"Well . . . yeah . . . in some ways."

"How long have you known him?"

Michael thought about it. "Nine years, almost ten."

"Have you always been friends?"

"Not at first," said Michael. "But we . . . you know, swapped stories."

"About what?"

"Oh . . . getting laid."

Thack chuckled.

"He'd come bounding down the stairs after breakfast—he lived on the roof then, so he could see anybody who crossed the courtyard. He'd say something like: 'Michael, my man, how dark was it when you dragged that one home?'"

"Nice guy."

"Oh, I'd get him back. You know . . . tease him about the dog he took to bed. It was just a game."

"Yeah, but . . ."

"OK, objectifying other people. But it brought us closer, and we never hurt anybody. I loved dishing with him. He loved sex as much as I did."

"Did?" Thack nipped at his ear.

"Do," said Michael, smiling.

"That's better."

"He was a big romantic, really. Mary Ann wouldn't date him for years, because she thought he was such a pig. When he finally fell in love with her, he courted her like crazy. He spilled his guts to me whenever the slightest thing went wrong. Meanwhile, I was having this on-again-off-again thing with my lover, and lots of other people. So Brian and I just kept on coming back to each other."

"I see," said Thack.

"It's funny," said Michael. "When I look back, he was the only constant."

"Mmm."

"He was there in the room with me when my lover died. Holding my hand." Tears welled up in his eyes, blurring the moon. He wiped them away with two efficient strokes of his fingertips.

"Was it AIDS?" asked Thack.

"Yeah. When Jon got sick, I was so angry, because nobody really gave a fuck. They pretended to be concerned, but these were just faggots dying. They were sick to begin with. I remember thinking . . ." He couldn't find the right words for this.

"What?" asked Thack, stroking his arm.

"Just . . . that nothing would ever happen, no one would ever care until straight people started getting it."

"I know the feeling."

"But I prayed for it. I actually prayed for it."

"You didn't mean it."

"Does that make a difference?" asked Michael.

Nothing Romantic

Wren appeared at the top of the stairs when Brian parked the VW behind her hilltop chalet. "Bring a few logs," she hollered. "We're almost out."

He looked around him in the dark.

"To the left," she said, pointing. "Next to that bench. There's a woodpile."

He found it and loaded his arms with redwood logs. Most were green enough to be oozing sap, and their weight surprised him, causing him to stagger a little. His clumsiness embarrassed him. He was grateful for the cover of darkness.

When he reached the top of the stairs, he was out of breath. Holding the door for him, Wren said: "Dirty trick, huh? Didn't know you'd have to work."

"No problem," he said, making his way to the fireplace.

"They're so gunky," she said, following him. "I hate getting them, but I adore having a fire."

He dumped the logs on the big stone hearth. "They're awfully green."

"They do OK," she said, "once it gets hot enough." She picked up several of the smaller logs and tossed them onto the flames. "Now," she said, brushing off her hands. "A drink, a joint . . . what?"

"I'm fine," he said.

"Sure?"

"Yeah."

She gestured toward an armchair. "Sit down."

He did so, as she curled up on the sofa. She was wearing a pink blouse and white shorts. Her big friendly knees were as pale and round as a couple of honeydew melons. She cocked her head and smiled at him. "I saw your wife on *Entertainment Tonight*."

"Oh . . . yeah."

"Did you watch it?"

"No."

"She was all right."

"So I heard. My landlady told me. My ex-landlady."

"Did you watch her show the morning I was on?"

No, he thought perversely, but I jerked off to the book. "Actually, I didn't," he said.

"She didn't like me," said Wren.

He nodded. "Sometimes she does that. Just to get a rise out of people."

Wren snorted. "She got one."

He smiled at her. "Good."

She studied him for a while, then rose and plucked a joint from a box on the mantelpiece. She lit it with a kitchen match and returned to the sofa, where she took a toke and held it, observing him again.

"If this is tacky," she said, "tell me."

He shrugged. "Go ahead."

"Do you usually take vacations without your wife?"

He laughed uneasily. "You mean with gay guys?"

"No," she said. "I mean without your wife."

He felt his head jerk reflexively. "I think we both . . . needed a little breather."

"I know just what you mean," she replied.

"You're married?"

"No, but I have a lover."

"Well," he said. "I guess he couldn't exactly go on a book tour with you . . ."

"The tour was over last week."

"Oh."

"I needed time alone." She smiled mysteriously. "Well, mostly alone."

There was her "friend" again.

"But now," she added, "I really miss Rolando." She took a puff on the joint and held it for a while. "I even miss his snoring."

He chuckled. "You *do* miss him."

"Are you a snorer?"

"Mary Ann," he said. "She's the worst."

"She snores? I love it."

"She'd kill me if she knew I told you."

Wren made a zipping motion across her lips. "And you don't blab to Rolando."

"What could I tell him?"

"Well . . . he thinks I'm still on tour, for starters."

"A-ha." He felt much more at ease now that their conversation involved four people instead of three.

"He'll be all right," she said. "Once I'm home."

He looked at her for a moment, then said: "I wish I could say the same thing."

"She's . . . uh . . . on your case?"

He shook his head. "It isn't her."

"Oh," she said.

"I was seeing this girl. Nothing romantic. Just . . . friends who had sex from time to time."

She smiled sleepily. "I can relate to that."

"She has AIDS," he said.

Wren blinked at him.

"I saw her last week. She looked like someone else."

"Christ." She put the joint down.

"I took the test, but the results won't be back for another week."

"And your wife . . . ?"

"Doesn't know. I couldn't tell her until . . ." He made a lame gesture, unable to finish.

She jumped into the breach. "You're OK, though. You look just fine."

He shrugged. "My stomach kinda burns. My energy is gone."

"That could be lots of things."

"That's what the doctor said."

"Well, there you go."

An awkward silence followed. Then she asked: "Are you scared?"

He nodded.

"Don't be," she said.

He shrugged again, afraid of crying.

"You're too nice a guy to be hurting."

He couldn't look at her. "Does a nice guy do this to his wife?"

"Hey," she said gently.

"If I've . . . passed it on . . ."

"You haven't. You don't know that."

"If I have, I deserve it."

"Stop that. Shut up. You shouldn't worry about that until . . . God, Brian, worry about yourself. That's who I'm worried about."

He felt himself unraveling. "Look . . . I'm really sorry. I should go."

"Oh, no," she said. "No way. That's hit and run, buster."

"I'm sorry if . . ."

"Come here," she said.

"What?"

"C'mon. Haul that cute ass over here." She patted the cushion next to her on the sofa.

He hesitated, then obeyed her.

She put her arm around him, easing him down until his head reached the expansive softness of her chest. "There," she said, stroking his hair. "Now just shut up for a minute."

When his tears surfaced, she began to rock him gently, humming a tune he couldn't quite place.

D'or Confesses

Pictionary practice had occupied DeDe and Polly for almost an hour. DeDe had performed like a champ until Polly sketched a standing figure, with another figure stretched out on a table. DeDe had tried "doctor," "mortician," and "masseuse," to no avail.

"C'mon," said Polly.

"What else is there?" asked DeDe.

Polly groaned and drew a huge penis on the standing figure.

"Masseur!" DeDe shouted.

"Yes!"

They shrieked in unison.

DeDe said: "Call Kate and Trudy. I'm ready for the play-offs!"

They were still giggling maniacally when DeDe heard footsteps advancing through the madrone trees. The gait was unmistakably D'or's.

DeDe made herself wait for a count of ten, then turned and said, "Oh, hi," as casually as possible.

"Hi," echoed D'or. Her voice was flat as day-old Diet Pepsi.

"You've met Polly Berendt, haven't you?"

D'or shook her head. "Not officially." She nodded in Polly's direction but didn't extend her hand.

"I was just leaving," said Polly.

"No," said DeDe. "Stay. We'll make some cocoa." She turned back to D'or. "How was the Holly Near concert?"

"I didn't go," said D'or, stonier than ever.

Polly rose and slapped the seat of her jeans, knocking off the sand. "Past my bedtime," she said.

This time DeDe didn't bother to protest. "Thanks for the evening," she said feebly.

"No sweat," Polly replied, heading off into the dark.

D'or sat down on the sand, but didn't speak until Polly's footsteps had died out. "Sorry," she said grimly, "if I interrupted something."

"You're one to talk," said DeDe.

D'or stared out at the water for a while. Then she said: "I stopped off and saw Edgar."

"How was he?"

"Fine. He really likes it there."

"I know," said DeDe.

"He told me I couldn't come in. Said it was men-only space." D'or smiled at this, obviously trying to break the ice.

DeDe refused to thaw.

"They have their own hierarchy already. Little lieutenants running around. It's really funny."

DeDe grunted.

D'or turned and looked at her. "You wanna leave tomorrow?"

"I'm planning to."

"Good. I think it's time." She looked around. "Where's Anna?"

"Asleep," said DeDe.

D'or untied the laces on one of her sneakers, tightened and retied them. "Why are you doing this?"

"Doing what?"

"You know."

DeDe resisted a sudden urge to slap her. Why was she, DeDe, always the one whose behavior required explanation?

D'or added: "She's gone. If that's what's bothering you."

"She?" asked DeDe. There was no point in making it easy for her.

"Sabra."

DeDe muttered.

"You were right about her. She's a big phoney."

It took some effort to conceal her relief. "How did you come to *this* brilliant conclusion?"

"I just saw," said D'or.

"Oh, yeah?"

"She was looking to get laid."

"Well . . . did she?"

D'or hesitated, then nodded.

"I see," said DeDe. "And then she left?"

Another nod.

"Just . . . wham bam thank you, ma'am."

D'or played with the sand under her legs. "Laugh all you want. I deserve it."

DeDe kept quiet.

Her lover looked truly pathetic. "For what it's worth, I really did think it was my mind she admired. I thought she respected my input."

Two minutes earlier, DeDe could have fired off a pithy rejoinder to that one. "Well," she said instead. "Maybe she really did."

D'or shook her head. "It was like . . . shut-up-and-lie-down time."

DeDe abandoned the role of hurt child and assumed the mantle of mother confessor. "I knew she was a shitheel," she said.

"I couldn't believe it," said D'or. "We'd just come back from a Holocaust workshop."

DeDe felt a smile flicker at the corner of her mouth.

"I was so mortified I just went through with it. I don't know why. I really don't know why." She paused a moment, throwing a pebble into the river. "I guess I wanted to show her there was . . . something I could do better than her."

Than *she*, thought DeDe.

"She was so *cold* afterwards. Like she'd been humoring me all along."

DeDe thanked God for making Sabra Landauer such a callous, manipulative and thoroughly undependable person.

D'or patted the sand between her legs. "I wish I'd finished college."

DeDe slipped her arm around D'or's waist. "C'mon . . ."

"I do. I feel so dumb sometimes."

"D'or . . . you made several hundred thousand dollars before you were twenty-five. You traveled, you met people . . ."

"Yeah, but I don't know anything. I'm really illiterate."

"Come off it. Just because Sabra was so tacky as to . . . Listen, have you actually ever read *Medusa at the Prom?*"

"No."

"Well, I have," she said, telling D'or the same lie she'd told Sabra. "It's just plain awful. It's trite and . . . lugubrious."

"See?" said D'or. "I don't even know what that means."

"Ohhh." DeDe gave her a little shove.

D'or shoved her back, pinning her against the sand. "I love you so much," she said.

"You're a mess," said DeDe.

"Maybe."

"Definitely."

"OK." She leaned down and gave DeDe a kiss. "I'm sorry. I'm really sorry."

"Can we get out of here tomorrow?"

"First thing," said D'or. "Do you forgive me?"

"Ask me tomorrow," said DeDe.

"Where did you go tonight?"

"Into town," said DeDe, "where I consumed mass quantities of animal flesh."

"Oh."

"And I don't want any grief."

"You won't get any from me," said D'or.

In a burst of hideous insight, DeDe realized the depth of her commitment to this marriage.

She had just traded adultery for a cheeseburger and an order of french fries.

The Littlest Pallbearers

Somewhere out there in the darkness, a creature was skittering through the underbrush. It sounded larger than a rabbit or raccoon, but it seemed to move in fits and starts, as if pausing for reconnaissance. It was joined, eventually, by an identical sound on the other side of the tent.

What now? thought Booter. Should he attract attention or not? He could thrash about, maybe, make the tent move, create some sort of sound in his throat. What if it was just the bulldagger again? She could make things even worse for him.

"Cuckoo," came a call from the darkness.

"Cuckoo," came the reply.

Not a bird sound, but a human one.

Children?

He tilted his head to listen.

"Wait there," whispered one of them.

"Where?" asked the other.

"You know . . . where I said."

"Well, how come you get . . . ?"

"Just shuddup. I told you I'm Platoon Leader. What did you get?"

There was a rustling of paper.

"Big deal. Another granola bar. Gag me."

"Look, she almost saw me."

"Well . . . so? You volunteered for this duty."

"Yeah, but I don't—"

"Just shuddup . . . and keep your head down. I'll meet you back here in three minutes."

Moments later, he heard someone ease open the big zipper on the tent. A thin electric beam searched the space, splashing light on the orange polyester walls. He arched his neck and came face to face with a boy of eight or nine, fat-cheeked and ginger-haired.

Booter groaned at him and made a thrashing motion. The boy's jaw went slack. For a moment, before he dropped the flashlight, his startled face became a levitating jack-o'-lantern, comic yet terrible in its intensity.

Then he ran away.

Booter kept groaning through the gag.

He heard the boy go yelping through the underbrush like a scalded pup. Then the silence closed in again, and he was left panting and sore, indignant in defeat. What the hell was the matter with the stupid brat?

Then the voices came back.

"If you're lying, Philo . . ."

"I'm not. I swear. His face was like . . . the Mummy or somethin'."

"Oh, sure."

"I swear."

"Which tent?"

"That one."

"You better not be lying. I'll report you to the Brigadier." Only slightly less terrified than Philo, the tough one seemed to be stalling for time.

Booter awaited them in silence. Moaning and twisting would only scare them off again.

The tent flap opened. Another beam, this one brighter than the last, found its way to Booter's tape-wrapped head.

He decided to wiggle a little, just to show them he was alive.

"See?" said the redheaded boy. He was standing next to the flashlight-wielder, his eyes big as quarters, his jaw even slacker than before. "Maybe they're holdin' him captive, huh?"

"Who?"

"I dunno. The chem-frees or somebody."

The boy with the flashlight steadied the beam on Booter's face, blinding him momentarily.

The redhead added: "He could be really dangerous."

There was no reply from the other boy. He knelt and leaned forward slowly to examine Booter's features.

Booter blinked several times, then beheld the familiar face of a handsome half-breed child. When their eyes met, the boy made an expression like a clenched fist and leaned even closer. "Booter?" he said.

Just as amazed, Booter uttered a grunt and nodded.

The boy turned to his henchman. "It's Booter," he said.

"Who?"

"He's married to Gangie. My mom's mom."

"He's your granddad?"

"No, booger-brain. He's married to my mom's mom. That doesn't make him my—"

Groaning indignantly, Booter cut him off.

"You better do somethin'," said the redhead.

Edgar tugged a piece of tape off Booter's cheek. It stung like hell. He made a sound to say so.

"Be careful," said the redhead.

Seizing another piece of tape, Edgar tugged more gently this time, until the whole sticky webbing, gag included, came away from his face. He gulped air and licked his parched lips.

"You OK?" asked Edgar.

He nodded, still filling his lungs. Then he said: "Where's your mother?"

"At her camp," the boy replied.

"Where's that?"

"Down by the river."

"Get her for me."

Edgar shook his head gravely.

"Why not?"

"It's women-only space."

"What?" It was a madhouse, this place, pure and simple. "What the hell are you talking about?"

"I can't go," the boy said earnestly. "They won't let me."

"Untie me, then. Help me, you little idiot! Don't just stand there!"

The redhead frowned and peered at Edgar for the final word. Edgar, in turn, gnawed on his fingernail and pondered. "Did you do something bad?" he asked.

"No," thundered Booter. "Of course not!"

"We better go," the redhead told Edgar. "Somebody's gonna come back and—"

"No," Booter blurted. "Don't go. Just untie my hands."

Wrinkling his brow again, Edgar began to pick ineffectually at the knot.

"Hurry up," said Booter.

"I can't. It won't untie."

"Find a knife, then."

The redheaded accomplice tugged on Edgar's sleeve. "I'm gettin' outa here."

Edgar kept his eyes on Booter. "If you didn't do anything wrong, how come they tied you up?"

"I fell asleep in a canoe, Edgar. It drifted ashore. They tied me up because I'm a man."

The boy bit his lower lip.

For emphasis, Booter added: "I swear."

Edgar studied his step-grandfather a moment longer, then grabbed the redhead's arm as he tried to leave. "Philo," he barked, "get Jackson and Berkowitz and the two Zacks. Tell 'em I need 'em here. On the double."

"Hey, Edgar, I'm not—"

"On the double!"

"Isn't there a knife?" asked Booter.

Edgar shook his head. "We'll get you outa here. Don't worry."

As the other boy scrambled into the night, Edgar squatted on his haunches next to Booter's head. "You wanna sit up?" he asked.

"Yes, son. Please."

The boy helped him into a sitting position, propping bedrolls behind his back. When he was done, he searched his blue quilted jacket until he found a chocolate bar. Breaking off a piece, he said: "Want some?"

"Please," said Booter, opening his mouth for the proffered chunk. Its dark sweetness tasted sacramental on his tongue. When it was gone, he said: "When will they be back?"

"Not long. Few minutes."

"Those women could come back at any time."

"I know." Edgar patted his shoulder. "Don't worry, OK?" He looked at Booter gravely, then plopped down next to him against the bedrolls. "Hey," said the boy, brightening. "What's blue and creamy?"

Booter looked at him, utterly confused.

"It's a riddle," said the boy. "Guess."

"Edgar, this is no time—"

"C'mon," urged Edgar. "What's blue and creamy?"

"I told you . . . no!"

Edgar looked crestfallen for a moment, then broke off another chunk of chocolate. "Want some more?" he asked.

"Yes," said Booter evenly. Like taking candy from a baby, he thought bitterly.

Edgar fed it to him in small pieces this time, licking his fingers when he was through. "Is your canoe still down there?" he asked.

"I don't know," said Booter.

"Where did you come from?"

Booter thought for a moment, then said: "The Bohemian Grove. Has your mother told you about that?"

"I don't think so," said Edgar.

"It's sort of a camp. Your grandfather Halcyon used to belong."

"I was named for him," said Edgar.

"Yes . . . exactly." The boy was quick, at least.

"What do you guys do?"

"Where?" asked Booter.

"At your camp."

Booter wet his parched lips. "Well . . . we talk a lot. We go to plays, concerts. Read books."

Edgar screwed up his face. "It's a camp?"

Booter nodded. "More or less. Look . . . are you sure your friends are coming back?"

"Positive. Was my grandfather your best friend?"

"Yes, he was."

"Who's your best friend now?"

Booter took the easy way out. "Well, of course, your grand-mother and I . . . Gangie . . ."

"No," said Edgar. "Girls don't count."

Booter hesitated. "I guess I don't have a best friend right now."

The boy looked concerned. "Why not?"

Booter felt an unexpected little stab of pain. "What are you doing here, anyway? Pinching candy?"

Edgar's eyes narrowed.

"I won't tell them," said Booter.

"It's just a game."

"I know. Don't worry, son. We're on the same side."

Philo returned breathless, with four other boys in tow.

"Who brought the knife?" asked Edgar.

No one had.

"Goddamnit," Booter muttered.

"OK," said Edgar, "here's the deal. We carry him back to the compound."

"Sure," said one of them.

"It's easy," said Edgar. "We spread out this sleeping bag, and we put him on it, and we each grab some of it . . . three to a side."

Booter didn't like it. "Wait a minute . . ."

"We gotta," said Edgar, checking his watch. "The concert's almost over."

"What concert?"

"C'mon, Zack . . . gimme a hand. You other guys wait outside."

Edgar and Zack seized Booter under the arms and pulled him over to the sleeping bag. Then they dragged the bag out into the open air, where the other boys were already in position, ready for the hoist.

"Hey, Edgar," said Philo, "what if he hops instead?"

Edgar groaned. "He's an old guy, numbnuts. He can't hop."

Booter didn't argue. He was an old guy, all right. Hopping was out of the question.

Edgar surveyed his henchmen. "Jackson, swap places with Zack Two. He's stronger."

"He is not," said Jackson.

"Just shuddup," said Edgar. "OK . . . Lift when I say so. One . . . two . . . three . . . *lift*."

As he ascended, Booter gazed up at six intent little faces and thought of them suddenly as his pallbearers.

"Where are we going?" he asked Edgar.

"Back to Brother Sun."

"Where?"

"The boys' compound. Brother Sun."

The boys began to walk, carrying him perilously close to the ground. The darkness was almost total; the terrain seemed strewn with obstacles. There were rocks and spongy spots, impenetrable thickets, prickly branches that swooped down without warning, thrashing the boys like vindictive schoolmarms.

"Is it far?" asked Booter.

"No," said Edgar.

One of the boys broke stride, then stumbled.

"Philo!" barked Edgar. "Stop spazzing out."

"I heard something," said Philo.

"Big homo," said someone else.

"I did. Hold up, you guys."

Amidst groans of protest, the boys came to a halt, still holding Booter aloft. He could see the moon through the trees and not much else, but he didn't move for fear of upsetting the balance of their cargo.

The woods seemed quiet enough. An owl or two. Guitars and voices in the distance, dim and harmless.

"It's nothing," said Edgar. "What did you think it was? The boogey-woman?"

The other boys shared a laugh at poor Philo's expense as Booter's magic-carpet ride began anew, faster this time. They seemed to be going down a slight incline, and the foliage had grown more sparse.

"How much further?" asked Booter.

"Not far," said Edgar, puffing a little.

"What is this place, anyway?"

"What place?"

"Here. This camp. These . . . ladies."

"Wimminwood," said Philo, obviously eager to redeem himself.

"Aren't there any men here?"

Philo said: "You're lookin at 'em."

Philo's tormentor snorted derisively. "Big homo."

"Zack, shut up," said Edgar, slowing their pace a little. "I think I heard something."

"Now he hears it," muttered Philo.

"What the hell?" came a voice from the darkness. It was growly and female.

The boys shot panicked glances at one another and began to trot. Booter winced as the sleeping bag banged against a protruding stump.

"Stop right there," bellowed the voice.

"We'd better stop," whispered Zack.

"No way," said Edgar, picking up speed.

From Booter's viewpoint, the moon was caroming crazily off the treetops. Vertigo overwhelmed him, so he shut his eyes and set his jaw and waited for the worst. Their nemesis was so close he could hear her lumbering Sasquatch gait, the sound of her labored breathing.

One of the middle boys deserted his post, hightailing it into the woods.

"Hey," called Edgar, his reedy voice full of anger and despair.

The boy next to Edgar stumbled, dropping Booter's legs. The whole flimsy mechanism jerked rudely to a halt and Booter was deposited on the ground, his fall somewhat softened by the sleeping bag.

Another boy fled. Then another. Only Edgar was left, staring down into his step-grandfather's stunned face. "Get outa here," said Booter, giving the boy the absolution he sought. "You did your best."

Edgar regarded him gravely for a moment, then darted off into

523

the forest. The same faint scampering sounds that had marked the arrival of this band now betrayed its departure. Booter swallowed hard and tried to right himself.

The growly voice said: "What the hell?"

Turning his head, he saw a short, heavyset woman emerge from the underbrush. She approached him warily, raking her fingers through the short gray hair over her ears. Even from here, he could tell she was drunk.

"Please," Booter began, "can you help me?"

She inched forward and regarded him in a pitcher's squat, legs spread, hands clamped on her knees. Her mouth hung slack for a moment before she said: "Well . . . if that don't beat all!"

"I won't hurt you," he said.

"Hurt me?" She threw back her head and hooted. Her voice was raspy with nicotine and whiskey. "Oh, yeah . . . please don't do that." Laughing again, she was seized by a sudden coughing jag, which threw her off balance and sent her tumbling ingloriously to the ground.

She rose slowly, but only to a sitting position. "Damn," she said.

He licked his lips and swallowed. "If you help me, I'll pay you anything . . ."

"Who the hell are you?"

He remembered what had happened the last time he used his name. "I came down the river," he told her. "By canoe. I fell asleep, and I—"

"Who did this?"

He hesitated. "I don't know. She hit me on the head first. Look, I haven't done anything . . ."

"She just tied you up and left your ass?"

"Yes."

"You see her? What'd she look like?"

He decided to risk the truth. "Her head was shaved. In patterns."

"Oh, hell." Catching her breath, she rose falteringly to her feet. "OK. Ol' Mabel better get her ass in gear . . ."

"No," he said, "please don't go."

"Sit tight," she answered, hulking away into the night.

Passions

In the kitchen at Wren's lodge, Brian was pouring juice into Flint-stones glasses. He bounced around jauntily, with self-conscious aplomb, like a television chef confronting his first national audience. Why, Wren wondered, do men always retreat a little after sex or confession?

"You think the guys got lost in there?" he asked. She had told him about Booter's disappearance, about their shack-up arrangement, even about the check Booter had left for her. One confession had seemed to merit another.

"Maybe it's a black hole," she said, leaning against the doorway.

"Yeah. Sort of a Bohemian Triangle." He handed her a glass of juice.

"You and Michael are pretty close, aren't you?"

"Yeah."

"I thought so."

"Why?"

"Well . . . he told me to call you, for one thing."

"When? Tonight?"

"When else?" Seeing his expression, she added: "I would've done it anyway."

"Did he tell you about . . . ?"

"No. Nothing." She looked him squarely in the eye to assure him that his revelation had, in fact, been a revelation.

The phone rang. "There they are," she said, setting her glass on the counter, heading into the living room.

"This better be you," she said.

"It is," said Michael. "Are we that late?"

"No. Never mind. Did you find him?"

"No. Not a sign."

She heaved a sigh. "Did they say if he'd gone home?"

"We asked at the gate," said Michael. "He hasn't checked out yet."

"He must be there, then."

"I guess so, but the place is like a small city."

She nibbled on a nail. "It just doesn't make sense. Why wouldn't he call me?"

"You got me," said Michael. "I don't know the man."

But I do, she thought, and something is horribly wrong. She imagined him lying dead somewhere in the dark, victim of a heart attack. Or suicide. His last phone call, after all, had been inexplicably forlorn, tinged with desperation.

"You tried his camp?" she asked.

"Yeah. And a bunch of the others. Nobody's seen him since this morning, when he went to a memorial service."

"Somebody died?"

"A friend of his," said Michael. "You think that's got something to do with it?"

"God . . . I dunno."

He waited, then said: "What do you want us to do?"

"Are you at the greasy spoon?"

"No. We're still in the Grove."

"Are you swimming back?" She was teasing, of course.

"Oh, please. Nothing but the gate this time. We're practically members."

"They like you, huh?"

Michael chuckled. "Thack got cruised by a priest."

She heard Thack laughing in the background. "I'll bet he did," she said.

"People keep pouring us drinks, inviting us in. It's amazing what just having a dick can do for you."

"Tell me," she said. "I haven't had one lately."

Another chuckle. "Poor thing."

"Never mind. I can cope."

"You'll be home to Rolando in no time."

That threw her. "How do you know about him?"

"You talked about him," he answered. "On the air. Mary Ann's show."

"Oh, yeah. A girl's got no secrets."

He laughed. "Not when the girl sells them."

"Fuck you," she said. "I'll meet you in half an hour at the greasy spoon."

"Fine," he said. "Is Brian with you?"

"None of your business," she replied, and hung up.

"Who died?" asked Brian.

"Died? Oh . . . a friend of Booter's."

He frowned, taking it personally.

"I'm not gonna worry about it," she said. "I've worried enough."

On the way into Monte Rio, Brian said: "You're flying out tomorrow?"

She nodded, pulling on the wheel. They were rounding a treacherous curve, drastically eroded on one side, obscured on the other by an almost perpendicular slope of dusty ferns. She knew it well, this curve. She had been here long enough for it to seem grimly familiar.

"I'm leaving," she said. "Come hell or high water."

He stared out the window for a moment, then asked: "Would you like company tonight?"

She turned and smiled at him.

"Just to cuddle," he said. "I really don't feel like . . ."

"I know. Shut up. Give me credit for a little versatility."

His eyes turned back to the road. "What about . . . you know . . . Booter?"

"What about him?" she asked.

"Well . . . if he comes back tonight."

She chuckled. "He doesn't *sleep* with me, sweetie."

"Oh."

"I'm just his afternoon delight. He sleeps with his buddies. Back at the Grove."

"I see."

"I'm just pleasure. The Grove is his passion." The road became asphalt finally, and there were random yellow porch lights to lead the way. "What about you?" she asked. "What are your passions?"

He seemed to think it was a trick question.

"What do you do?" she asked. "I know what your wife does, of course . . ."

He looked more stricken than before.

"Sorry," she said. "That was grossly un-Californian of me."

"No," he said finally, "it's OK. I take care of our daughter. I manage the house."

"Well, that's a lot." It sounded patronizing, she realized, and it was. The man thinks he's dying, so she reminds him he has no purpose in life.

"It's not a lot," he said quietly.

"Raising a child? Are you kidding?"

"It's not enough." He gazed out at the lights of Monte Rio. "It's not . . . a manhood thing with me. It just isn't enough. It used to be all I ever wanted . . . having a kid, being a husband." He turned and looked at her. "I was a lawyer once. Does that count?"

She laughed, determined to keep it light. "What I meant was . . . what are your hobbies?"

He didn't seem to hear her. "The person I really envy is Michael."

"Why?"

He shrugged. "He loves his job. He's outdoors a lot, not shuffling paper. He makes stuff grow." Another shrug. "Seems like a good life."

"You have a good life," she said.

"Do I?" he asked.

The Wayward RV

Brandishing a huge serrated hunting knife, the gray-haired woman had returned. She knelt by Booter's inert body and began sawing at the ropes around his wrists. "Dvorak did a job on this," she said, breathing heavily.

"Yes," was all he could manage.

He rubbed his wrists and swung his arms while she went to work on his legs. "I brought my Winnebago around," she said, "but we gotta haul ass. It ain't s'posed to be here."

When she'd pulled free the last bit of rope, he tried to stand up. His knees were exceptionally weak, but they did the job. He sucked in air and stretched his arms. The next signal he received was from his bladder.

"I'm sorry," he said. "Would you mind . . . I haven't been able . . ."

"Go over there," she said, getting the message. "I won't look. You think I wanna see that ol' thing?"

When he was done, she led the way through a thicket to a narrow dirt road where a green RV was parked. He climbed into the front seat, sinking gratefully into the embrace of its cracked green vinyl.

"Get in back," said the woman.

"What?"

"We're gonna pass the gate. Get in back and keep your head down."

He did as he was told.

"If there's trouble," she added, "I can handle it. I'm packin' heat."

She pointed to an unmade bunk and laughed. There, amidst the zebra-patterned sheets, lay a gleaming steel crossbow.

"Hold on," he said.

"Joke," she said, starting the engine. She gazed at him over her shoulder and winked. "You're gullible, aren't you? What's your name?"

"Uh . . . Roger."

"Mine's Mabel," she said, handing him a pint of Jack Daniel's. "Be my guest, Roger."

He accepted without protest. The whiskey stung his throat like iodine, then seeped into his aching limbs, warming them. He wiped off the bottle on the sleeve of his Viyella shirt and handed it back to her.

"Take another," she said.

"No, thank you."

"Go on. If Dvorak didn't kill you, a little Jack Daniel's sure as hell won't."

It reassured him to learn that his captor had such a reputation for heinousness. His subjugation had been the work of a mastermind, at least, not just some random woman. He returned the bottle to his cracked lips and took another swig.

"Who is she?" he asked, handing back the bottle.

"Security chief," she said. "They're all alike."

His knowledge of female security chiefs was woefully deficient.

"I believe in law and order," she added. "I voted for Reagan. But Dvorak is something else." She swatted the air in his direction, her eyes still fixed on the road.

"What?" he asked.

"Get down!" she ordered darkly. "The gate."

He flattened out on the shag-carpeted floor. There were cigarette butts amidst the shag. Dust balls the size of gophers. A Debbie Reynolds album. His heart beat wildly.

Someone outside the RV said: "You checking out?"

Mabel said: "Nah. Takin' her for a spin."

"It's a little late, isn't it?"

"Listen, girlie," said Mabel. "Don't mess with me."

Somewhat more meekly, the guard said: "Well, it's not like it's a car."

"You through?" asked Mabel.

"Go ahead," said the guard.

The RV lurched when Mabel hit the gas. "Stupid spic," she muttered.

Booter pressed against the yarny carpet to keep his equilibrium. They had reached asphalt and were barreling along at a disarming speed.

"C'mon up," called Mabel. "It's over."

Grabbing the side of the bunk, he hoisted himself to a sitting position. "You're going awfully fast," he said.

"Nah," she said. "Jus' seems that way from back there."

He rose on uncertain legs and hunched his way to the front, collapsing into the seat. The scrubby moonlit landscape flew past them like a painting on a freight train. It was freedom, he supposed, but a shaky one at best.

"Where to?" asked Mabel.

How, he wondered suddenly, would he explain this vehicle to the gatekeeper at the Grove? "Uh . . . Monte Rio," he told her, resigning himself to another half mile on foot.

"You got it," she said, unscrewing the top on the whiskey.

They thundered down the deserted road in silence, civil strangers sharing only a time and a place. He did his damnedest not to notice their speed, which was considerable, or Mabel's expression, which was just this side of maniacal.

"You voted for Reagan?" he asked eventually.

"Damn straight."

"Then . . . you're a conservative?"

"Always have been. Hate welfare, hate communism, hate all that stuff."

It made no sense to him. "But . . . that place?"

"What?" she asked. "Wimminwood?"

"Yes. It's . . . leftist, isn't it?"

She shrugged. "Mostly."

"Why do you go?"

Mabel gave a little snort. "That's easy. Pussy."

He was almost certain he had heard wrong until she began to guffaw exuberantly, slapping the dashboard with her flattened palm. When she turned to see his reaction, she lost control of the wheel, and he heard the sickening clatter of gravel as the RV slipped onto the shoulder.

"Watch out!" he hollered.

Her reaction wasn't nearly quick enough. The RV leapt a

narrow ditch, then ripped through a curtain of brambles, plummeting willy-nilly into the darkness.

His hands shot to the dashboard. He gritted his teeth as she slammed on the brakes and the RV skidded to a stop in the underbrush.

"Good God," he murmured.

"Holy shit," said Mabel.

The RV was tilting dramatically, its two right wheels lower than the left.

"You OK?" she asked.

"Yes . . . I'm OK." If she had been his wife, he would have yelled at her, but she was his rescuer, and a man doesn't yell at his rescuer.

She climbed down from the RV and inspected the damage. "It's gonna take Three-A," she said, returning. "Sonofabitch." She shook her head slowly, obviously annoyed with herself. "That's what I get for thinking about pussy."

He took the whiskey from the dashboard and offered it to her. Mabel accepted with a weary grunt, unscrewing the cap. "Ever have one of those days?" she asked.

"Yes," he answered dryly, feebly. "Yes, I have."

She blinked at him with red-rimmed eyes and began to chuckle. "Yeah, I guess so," she said, and took a swig of the whiskey, smacking appreciatively. Then she gave it back to him.

This time he tipped the bottle like a seasoned wino. "You on vacation?" she asked.

He nodded. "Supposedly."

"Yeah. Me too."

"Where are you from?" he asked.

"Tacoma," she said.

"Ah." There wasn't much he could say about Tacoma. He'd never even been there.

Mabel filled the silence by taking another nip from the bottle. When she had finished, she said: "Well, better get our tails in gear.

There's a phone down at Duncans Mills. It's not all that far. You can wait here." She slapped the dashboard. "Keep an eye on the ol' girl."

Booter heard her, but just barely. His glazed eyes drifted toward the moon, which was dangling like an off-kilter ornament in the broken branches above the windshield. The night was uncannily still. He couldn't remember when he'd last felt so alone with someone.

"You OK?" she asked.

"Yes," he answered quietly.

She regarded him for a moment, then said: "That's Venus. The big, shiny one under the moon. The Greeks called it Lucifer in the daytime and Hesperus at night."

This odd footnote, imparted tersely and without provocation, reminded him instantly of someone else. Even the light in her eyes was right, the half-mad, tutorial glint which awaited his response like a child who had just told a favorite joke.

"You know much about that stuff?" he asked.

She squared her jaw in an eerily familiar fashion. "Nah. I watch that guy . . . whatshisname . . . the billions-and-billions man."

He nodded. "I know who you mean."

"Why the hell are you doin' that?"

"What?"

"Lookin' at me funny."

"I'm sorry," he said. "You reminded me of somebody. Just briefly."

"Who?"

"It's ridiculous. Somebody who knows a lot about . . . outdoor things. Knew, that is." He was embarrassed now; she was bound to take it the wrong way. "It's not a physical resemblance. He just enjoyed . . . explaining things."

Her brow wrinkled. "He's dead now?"

"Yes," he answered vacantly, feeling oddly relieved to be able to say it. "Last night."

She scratched her arm, staring at him.

"He was my best friend," said Booter, realizing how curious it sounded to him. He had never told Jimmy as much. Why was he telling her?

Mabel looked puzzled. "He was traveling with you?"

"No. We're members of the same . . . camp." He was wary of explaining Bohemia to a woman, even to one who'd befriended him. So far it had brought him nothing but trouble.

"Here?" she asked.

"Yes."

"He died at camp?"

He nodded. "During a play."

Sympathizing, Mabel shook her head dolefully. "Just sittin' there, huh?"

"No. He was performing in the play."

"What was it about?"

"Uh . . . the Red Cross, actually."

"I remind you of him?"

"Well . . . his spirit."

"What was he like?"

He thought for a moment, discarding any adjectives that might be loaded. "Well . . . interested in nature. Adventurous."

"Wild-ass," she said.

"Yeah." He smiled a little. "That too."

"So you got drunk, huh? And you passed out in that canoe."

He nodded in resignation.

"Then your poor ol' white ass just drifted on down into Lez-zieland."

What was this woman's story?

"You get drunk much?" she asked, plucking a pack of Trues from the dashboard.

"No," he said.

"I do. I like it." She poked a cigarette into her mouth, then flicked her Bic. Her red-veined face flared up in the darkness. "So," she asked, holding in smoke, "how did you like them dykes?"

He looked out the window to compose an answer. "It wasn't

534

what I felt," he said at last. "What I felt had nothing to do with anything."

She nodded gravely. "I know what you mean." Holding the cigarette with her thumb and forefinger, she offered it to him.

"No, thanks," he said.

"Did you and your buddy live together?"

"No," he replied. "He lived in Denver."

"Huh?"

"It wasn't like that," he said. "I have a wife."

She narrowed her eyes a little, then asked: "Where do you live?"

"Hillsborough," he said.

"If he was your best friend"—smoke curled out of her and hovered overhead like a question mark—"when the hell did you see him?"

"Here," he said impatiently. "At the camp."

"How often?"

"Once a year."

"For how long?"

He thought about it. "Four or five days, usually. For twenty-seven years."

How many days did that make in all? As many as six months' worth? No, not even that many.

Mabel seemed to be doing the same arithmetic. "Was it mutual?" she asked.

"What do you mean?"

"Were you his best friend?"

He didn't look at her. "No. Probably not."

She nodded. "Never told him, huh?"

"No."

Another nod. Another drag off her cigarette. "Doesn't matter," she said.

"No. I guess not."

"It's just words," she said. "Doesn't matter." She stubbed out the cigarette in a beanbag ashtray. "What kinda candy bars you like?"

"What?"

"There's a machine up in Duncans Mills."

"Oh . . . nothing, thanks."

"I'll be back in half an hour." She gave his knee a jovial shake. "Doesn't matter," she said.

She climbed out and made her way up to the highway, puffing noisily, cursing every villainous branch that got in her way.

Rearrangements

Still on foot, Michael and Thack crossed the graceless iron bridge at Monte Rio and made their way to the greasy spoon. Ten minutes earlier, the midnight audience at the Rio Theater had been released from *Giant*. Now the movie-goers stood in circles, jabbering, like patrons at a cockfight.

When they entered the restaurant, Wren waggled her nails to get their attention. Brian was with her, looking a little sheepish.

"You're back in one piece," Brian said.

To confirm this, Michael held out his hands in a beatific pose. "How was your drive?" he asked.

"Great," said Brian.

"Sit down," said Wren.

Thack slipped into the booth next to Wren, leaving the spot next to Brian for Michael.

"What was the Grove like?" asked Brian.

"Beautiful," said Michael, "but weird."

"Too straight for you?"

"Too white," said Thack, frowning at a menu. "You guys eaten yet?"

"I ate here earlier," said Wren. "And I wouldn't recommend it."

"I'm starving, for some reason." Thack gave Michael a devilish sideways glance.

It wasn't lost on Wren, Michael noticed. "Go ahead," she said. "Eat. You've earned it."

"We ate at the Grove," said Michael. "We noshed our way through the place."

"You're right," said Thack, abandoning the menu.

"The coffee's OK," said Wren.

"Actually," said Michael, "we just wanna crash. If you could drive us back to the cabin . . ."

"Fine," said Wren. "Your car is at my place, so we'll just all go back there."

"Oh . . . right," said Michael.

There was room here for a cheap shot, but the look in Wren's eyes told him not to take it.

In the car, she said: "I have a limo coming tomorrow, guys. I'd love company."

Thack said: "I thought you were going to the airport."

"Yeah, but we have to go through the city, anyway."

The prospect seduced Michael for a second or two, until he remembered. "What are we gonna do with the VW?"

"Oh, yeah," said Wren. "That's right."

"I could drive it," said Brian.

Wren gave him a funny look.

"No way," said Michael. "That's really nice, but . . ."

"Really," said Brian. "I like driving alone. I'd be glad to." He shrugged. "I've been in a limo. You seen one, you seen 'em all."

Thack chuckled. "Isn't that what Reagan said about redwoods?"

"It's no problem," said Brian.

Wren reached over and patted his cheek. "This man is such a doll."

"I could do it," said Thack.

Shut up, thought Michael. Leave well enough alone.

"I'm a troublemaker," said Wren. "I forgot all about the other car."

"I really don't mind," said Brian. "I prefer it."

"To our company?" asked Wren, pretending to be hurt. She

turned to Michael and said: "Does he mean this or is he just being nice?"

"I think he means it," said Michael.

They made the bumpy ascent to the lodge in virtual silence. When they were all out of the car, Wren planted kisses on Michael and Thack. "You were so sweet to do this," she said.

"Hey," said Michael.

"Would you like . . . a nightcap or something?"

"No, thanks," said Thack. "It's late."

Good answer, thought Michael.

Wren turned to Brian and said: "Give the man his keys."

"Oh." Brian fumbled in his pocket and handed the keys to Michael. Even in the dark he looked embarrassed.

"The driver's coming at ten," Wren told Michael. "We'll swing by sometime after that."

"Fine," said Michael. He gave Brian an awkward little salute and climbed into the VW with Thack.

"Well, well," said Thack as they drove off down the hill.

One with Nature

A peculiar thing happened to Booter as he languished there in the darkness, a virtual prisoner of Mabel's Winnebago: He found that he liked it. It was soothing, somehow, to be stranded this way, so thoroughly a victim of chance and circumstance that all decisions were moot, all responsibilities void.

Only twice during his forty-minute wait did a car whiz past on the narrow road, and the woods were seductively silent, except for owls and an occasional murmur from the leaves.

Briefly, but with startling drama, a raccoon had mounted a branch outside the window and studied him dispassionately through the glass. Booter had remained still, confronting the little bandit creature-to-creature, holding his breath like a child playing hide-and-seek.

When the raccoon padded away, curiosity sated, Booter made an appreciative sound in the back of his throat. An outsider might have mistaken it for a giggle.

One with Nature, he thought, tilting the bottle again. That was the expression, wasn't it?

Presently Mabel came loping through the broken branches. He couldn't help thinking of one of those amiable, rumpled bears out of Uncle Remus.

"Half an hour," she said, climbing into the RV. "The tow truck's comin' from Guerneville." Wheezing a little, she caught her breath, then reached into her shirt pocket. "They only had Butterfingers," she said, handing him a candy bar.

He thought of the chocolate Edgar had given him, remembered the curious expectant light in his eyes. What did the boy want from him?

"I said no, thanks," he told Mabel.

"Well, I don't listen to what men say." She prodded him with the Butterfinger, like a new father proffering a cigar. "Take it, Roger."

He accepted.

"What are you grinnin' about?" she asked.

"Nothing."

"Well, eat your damn candy, then."

He peeled back the yolk-yellow wrapper. "We had these when I was a boy."

"Yeah," she said, working on her own wrapper. "Same here."

"They were bigger." He looked at the dark bar, then bit off a chunk.

She did the same. "How old are you?" she asked, crunching away.

"Seventy-one," he replied.

As if to match his fearlessness, she said: "I'm sixty-seven."

He nodded and hoisted his Butterfinger in a sort of salute.

"I don't look sixty-seven," she added.

"No," he agreed, "you don't."

In another gulp, she finished off the candy, wadding the wrapper. "So tell me about this camp of yours."

"Like what?"

She shrugged. "What do you do?"

He thought for a moment. "I made a speech a few days ago."

"Yeah? What on?"

"Well . . . the Strategic Defense Initiative."

She nodded with judicial dignity. "Good thing."

"Well, I certainly did my best to—"

"Damn good thing. If the Russians don't beat us to it."

"Well," he said, "there's certainly a danger of that."

"You can't trust them bastards."

"No, you can't. You're right."

They both fell silent. Mabel drummed her stubby red fingers on the dashboard. The night sounds grew louder, making talk seem alien.

"You wanna get out and stretch?" she asked eventually.

"No. Thank you."

"I'm sorry about your friend," she said.

"Thank you."

"You miss him?"

He nodded.

She heaved a noisy sigh and looked out the window for a moment. Then she said: "I got another bottle in back."

He turned and smiled at her. "Get it."

Pajamas without Feet

Back at the cabin, Michael lay on the sofa bed, his head against Thack's chest. "What a night," he said.

"A-men, brother." Thack toyed idly with Michael's earlobe, like someone working dough. "Don't you feel a little guilty?"

"For what?" asked Michael with mild amazement. "Crashing the Grove?"

"No. Being an accomplice to adultery."

Michael hesitated. "I don't think that's adultery."

"You don't?"

"No."

"What would you call it, then?"

"I think it's more like . . . company."

"C'mon."

"I'm pretty sure of it," said Michael.

"You don't think they're up there banging each other's eyes out?"

"No."

"You're a rotten judge of lust."

"Maybe."

Michael lay there for a while, listening to the thump of Thack's heart. Outside, there were froggy choruses in the high grass along the creek. Someone in the pink trailer was playing Buddy Holly's "True Love Ways."

"I love that song," said Michael.

"Yeah."

They listened for a while, Thack humming along shamelessly.

"You're a corny guy," said Michael. He almost said "romantic," but the word struck him as dangerous.

"Well," said Thack. "We seem to get music every time we do this."

Michael chuckled. "That's true."

Thack traced Michael's shoulder with his finger, then laid his warm palm to rest on Michael's back.

"I'm corny too," said Michael. "It's not a bad thing."

"No, it's not."

"I mean . . . not if it's balanced. If both people are corny . . . then it's OK."

Silence.

"You wanna know something funny?" asked Michael.

"What?"

"When I first met you, I tried to picture how you'd look in a jockstrap."

Thack smiled.

"Now," said Michael, "I wanna see you in pajamas."

"Pajamas?"

"Yeah. Flannel ones. Baby blue."

"Not the kind with feet in them?"

Michael laughed. "No. Just . . . the regular."

Thack stroked Michael's hair. "Maybe next time, huh?"

"Yeah, maybe so." He ran his hand across Thack's flat stomach. "When do you think that might be?"

"I dunno," said Thack. "Hard to say. Do you get back East much?"

"No, not really."

"I'd like to come back," said Thack.

"Would you?"

"Sure."

"We could work on this a little more."

"This?" asked Thack.

"Us," said Michael.

Thack said nothing, stroking Michael's hair.

Michael was pretty sure he had gone too far.

A Woman Scorned

Up at the lodge, Wren attended to Brian, who lay with his head against her chest.

"Will you call me?" she asked.

"When?"

"Oh . . . when the moon comes over the mountain. When the swallows come back to Capistrano." She gave his cheek a gentle whack. "When do you think, dummy?"

"OK," he said.

"Promise?"

"Yeah."

"Just yes or no will do."

"OK."

"If you don't," she said, "I'll call your house and embarrass the shit out of you."

He smiled.

Her fingers explored his springy chestnut curls. "You were sweet to let the boys take the limo."

"It's no big deal," he said. "What's gonna happen to your car?"

She began to fret again. "Well, Booter said to leave it here."

"Oh."

"I've done what I can do," she said. "I'm not his wife."

"Right."

Why the hell was she still issuing disclaimers? "I'll call his house when I get to Chicago. Somebody'll know something by then." She heaved a mother's sigh before adding glumly: "I hate being a whore. There are too many responsibilities."

"Don't talk like that," he said.

She smiled and slid her fingers through the swirly hair of his chest. "Thanks for the indignation, but I'm not ashamed of it. I wanted the experience, and I wanted the money. And Booter got his money's worth."

The bedside phone rang.

"Yell-o," she piped in her best receptionese.

"Wren," said the caller, "iss me."

"Booter?"

"Yeah, iss me."

If he wasn't shitfaced, he sure sounded like it. "Where are you, Booter?"

"Uh . . . Guerneville."

"Are you all right?"

"Yeah. I'm . . . I'm OK."

"You could have called, for Christ's sake. Why didn't you call?"

"I couldn't . . . Was in a canoe."

"What?" She heard a woman mutter something in the background. "Booter . . . who's with you?"

A pause and then: "Nobody."

"Oh, right." Now she was boiling mad.

"Iss juss somebody who—"

"You have one helluva lot of nerve, Booter." She turned to Brian and said: "He's ripped to the tits and he's got some woman with him."

"No," said Booter.

"What do you mean, no? I can hear her."

"Iss not like that."

"I'm leaving tomorrow, Booter. That check better be good."

"Iss good."

She could hear the woman cackling in the background. "I'm hanging up, Booter."

"Gobblesshew," he said.

"Right," she said, and slammed the receiver down.

She fumed in silence. Then Brian said: "I'm sorry you worried so much."

"I wasn't worried," she said.

"Well . . . still."

"Fuck him," she said. "I should've charged him the full ten thousand."

She went to sleep angry and woke up that way, rising before Brian to finish her packing. He made french toast for them both, then took out her last bag of garbage. When the limousine arrived at nine forty-five, they were waiting for it on the back steps. The driver was a new one (not, thank God, the one she had slept with), and he was openly curious as to why he'd been treated to a night at the Sonoma Mission Inn.

She let him wonder, determined to put the fiasco behind her.

They drove in silence to Cazadero, where Michael and Thack swapped places with Brian amidst coos of approval for the limousine. She gave Brian a quick hug at the door of his little cabin. "Call me," she whispered.

"OK," he answered.

She waved goodbye to him from the back window of the limo, but wasn't sure he had seen her.

• • •

Back in the city, at Michael's insistence, she told the driver to climb Russian Hill on its steepest slope. This turned out to be a street called Jones, a near-sheer cliff of a street which taxed the limo to the fullest and had them all whooping like idiots.

"Is this legal?" she gasped, clapping her hand to her chest.

Michael laughed. "It's even better going down."

"You're twisted," she said.

"I've never done this in a limo," he said.

She snorted. "There are better things to do."

"I'll bet," said Thack.

"Christ," she gasped. "Is that a stop sign up ahead?" She leaned forward and tapped the driver's shoulder. "Don't stop, OK? My system can't take it."

Another laugh from Michael. "Can it take a speeding Muni bus?"

The driver stopped where he was supposed to stop, then turned right and kept climbing, though far less precipitously this time. Taking another right, he inched his way down another nauseating drop-off. The bay lay beneath them in the distance, ridiculously blue.

"All right," she said, turning to Michael. "Enough with the Space Mountain."

"This is it," he said, wide-eyed. "Really."

"This is really what?" She was pressing her fingertips against the back of the front seat, as if this would prevent her from tumbling forward, out the window, down the hill and into the bay.

"Where I live," he replied. "That stairway beneath us. The wooden one."

"Sure."

"It is!" he said, beaming proudly. "You can park on the right there," he told the driver. "The rest is on foot." He turned back to her and added: "That big high-rise above us is where Brian lives."

"I can't look up," she muttered. "Or down. I'll blow lunch."

The driver parked on the right, using the emergency brake.

Michael and Thack hastily assembled their stuff. Then Thack began collecting empty juice bottles in a paper bag. "Leave it," she told him. "That's part of the fun."

"He's compulsive," said Michael.

Thack gave them both a hooded glance and continued to gather trash.

"Just what you need," Wren told Michael.

This minimal shot at matchmaking seemed to embarrass Michael, so she thrust her hand into his and added: "It's been great."

"Same here," he said. "I can't believe I met you."

"Brian has my number," she said, wondering if he'd guess the reason.

Michael nodded.

"Take care of him," she said.

"I will," he replied, without meeting her eyes.

She turned and took Thack's hand. "Give my love to Charleston."

"OK," said Thack. "Thanks for the joyride." He climbed out and waited on the curb.

Michael regarded her for a moment, then gave her a quick peck on the cheek and bounded out of the limo. She watched as he and Thack crossed the street and began to ascend the ramshackle wooden stairway he had indicated. In the dry grass next to its base stood an off-kilter street sign bearing the word BARBARY.

"Is that safe?" she hollered, when they reached the first landing.

He cupped his hands and yelled back at her: "What the hell is?"

She was still smiling when he vanished into the dusty trees at the top of the stairs.

Her driver turned and said: "The airport, Miss Douglas?"

"Yeah," she replied. "Time to go home."

Prisoner of Love

When they reached the courtyard at Number 28, Michael found Mrs. Madrigal watering her parched garden. The rigors of the heat wave had forced her into an old gingham sundress, which seemed far too Miss Marpleish for her particular brand of rawboned grace.

"How was it?" she called, as they came through the lych-gate.

"Terrific," said Thack.

She shut off the spray, dropped the hose, and tended to the stray wisps at her temples. "It's been dreadful here, absolutely murderous. In the eighties every day."

"You're spoiled," said Thack.

She gave him a surprisingly coquettish glance and patted her hair again. "Nevertheless," she said.

"The garden looks gorgeous," Michael told her.

"It's getting there. Did Brian come back with you?" There was a purposeful glint in her eye which belied her breezy delivery.

"No," said Michael. "We bummed a ride with somebody else. He came home in my car."

"I see," said the landlady.

"Why?"

"Oh . . . well . . . Mary Ann asked."

Michael wondered how much Mrs. Madrigal knew. "He should be home soon," he said as blandly as possible.

She fixed her huge Wedgwood eyes on him. "He hasn't called her," she said. "He's been very naughty."

He made a helpless gesture. "What can I tell you?"

She looked at him a moment longer, then swooped down to pick up her gardening gloves. When she was upright again, she turned her attention to Thack. "Michael's showing you the sights, is he?"

"Oh, yes," answered Thack.

"Do you like it here?"

"Very much."

"I'm so glad. How much longer will we have the pleasure of your company?"

"Well," said Thack, "till tonight, I guess. My flight's tonight."

This was news to Michael, but he didn't look at Thack for fear of betraying his emotions. Mrs. Madrigal, he imagined, already saw the distress in his face, sensed the enormity of the cloud settling over him.

Up in his bedroom, after they had both showered and changed into clean sweats, Michael said: "What time is your flight?"

"Six-fifteen," Thack replied.

Michael went to the window and looked out. "I thought it was tomorrow, for some reason." His eyes fixed vacantly on Alcatraz, the cause of this pain, the scene of the crime. "I had sort of pictured us sleeping here."

Thack hesitated, then said: "It's a nice thought."

"But?" he asked, pushing the issue in spite of his better instincts.

Thack came up behind him, enfolding him in his arms. "They're expecting me at Middleton Plantation bright and early Tuesday morning."

"What for?" asked Michael, alienated by such an exotic excuse.

"To make a speech," said Thack, "to some Yankee preservationists."

"What about?" asked Michael.

Thack kissed him on the ear. "Funding, mostly. Boring stuff." He rocked Michael back and forth. "Sooner or later, real life comes crashing back in, doesn't it?"

This was much too glib, Michael felt, a ready-made coda to a shipboard romance. He lived here, didn't he? This was his ship. What hadn't been real-life about it?

"C'mon," said Thack, leading him to the bed. "Let's cuddle."

As they lay there, Thack's back against Michael's chest, Michael said: "I hate this. It seems like a Sunday afternoon."

"It *is* Sunday afternoon," said Thack.

"I know, but . . . I mean, like when you were a kid, when you knew that Monday was coming, and the clock was ticking away. Saturdays were perfect, because there was Sunday, which was sort of a buffer. But Sundays just got worse and worse."

Thack took Michael's hand and kissed it. "Hang on to the moment," he said.

To hell with that, thought Michael. "You know," he said quietly, "you're much more of a Californian than I'll ever be."

The late sun, slashing through the Levolors, turned them into prisoners again, striped by shadows. Michael slept for a while, waking when the stripes were gone. Thack was still asleep.

The clock said four forty-seven. For a six-fifteen flight, they should leave the house no later than five-thirty. If they overslept—and who was to say they couldn't?—the next flight might not be until God-knows-when . . .

His deviousness under pressure was truly amazing. To repent for it, he slipped his hand around Thack's biceps and squeezed gently. Thack woke up smiling. How could he look so happy? For that matter, how could he sleep so soundly when the time—no, their time—was slipping away?

"You should pack," said Michael.

"Already am," said Thack.

Michael rubbed his eyes. "I'll drive you, of course."

" 'Fraid not."

"What?"

"Not unless Brian's back."

"Damn. You're right. Well . . . he must be." He grabbed the bedside phone and dialed The Summit. After three rings, Mary Ann answered with a glacial hello.

"It's Michael," he said. "Is Brian back yet?"

"I thought he was with you."

"No . . . I mean, he was, but we came home in separate cars."

"Why did you do that?"

"No special reason," he said, wary of mentioning Wren. "We met a friend there, and Brian said he'd enjoy being on his own."

"How long have you been home?" she asked.

"A few hours. Maybe he took the ocean road home."

"Yeah," she said distantly. "Maybe. I have no way of knowing. You saw him last."

This was clearly an attempt to assign guilt, and Michael would have none of it. "He said he was coming home," he countered tartly. "I'm calling because I need the car for an airport run. Just ask him to call me, OK? When he gets in."

She was silent for a while, then said: "Are you mad at me, Mouse?"

The nickname was as old as their friendship. She was using it, he realized, to signal her earnestness.

"No . . . I'm not."

"You sound furious. What have I done?"

"Nothing."

"I looked for you after the show the other day. You just took off."

"Sorry," he said, "if it looked that way. I had work to do, that's all."

"You said you wanted to meet Wren Douglas." A certain wounded tremolo, perfected in Cleveland, had come back into her voice. Michael hadn't heard it for a while, but it never failed to work on him.

"I didn't much care for her," he lied. "I changed my mind about meeting her after I saw the show."

"Oh."

"She wasn't that great," he added, somehow feeling traitorous to two women at the same time. "It had nothing to do with you, I promise."

"OK. I just wondered."

"We'll talk later, all right? My friend'll miss his flight if I don't call a cab."

"I love you, Mouse."

"Same here, Babycakes. Bye-bye."

He hung up, racked with guilt, then called Veterans and ordered a cab for the foot of the Barbary steps. "We should go," he told Thack afterwards. "It won't take them long."

Thack's luggage in hand, they navigated the wobbly ballast stones along the lane. "I could go with you," Michael said suddenly.

Thack looked confused.

"To the airport," Michael added.

"Oh . . . well, you'd just have to pay the fare coming back."

Michael didn't argue with him. He pictured himself alone in that cab, and it seemed even worse than this.

"Besides," said Thack, "I like the idea of saying goodbye at the steps. I like the symmetry of it, a clean break."

It sounded like carpentry to Michael, precise and a little cold-blooded.

"Oh," Thack added. "Tell Mrs. Madrigal I'm sorry."

"For what?"

"Aren't they tearing down the steps tomorrow?"

"Oh, yeah." He hadn't thought about that for days. "I'll tell her."

Reaching the steps, Thack set his suitcase down. Michael did the same with the carry-on. Thack said: "It's been really great. Some great memories."

"Same here," said Michael.

Sadistically early, the cab appeared on the street beneath them. Thack waved authoritatively, then put his arms around Michael. "Gimme a kiss. We'll make him squirm."

"I don't think so," said Michael, seeing who the driver was. "Hello, Teddy," he hollered down.

"Hello, Michael," came the melodious reply.

"He's a friend of mine," he explained. "He must've recognized the address."

"Oh."

"He's a lord."

"Of what?"

"Of England," said Michael. "Lord Roughton. He married this lesbian friend of mine. Get him to tell you about it."

"All right," said Thack, smiling. "I'll do that." He kissed Michael lightly on the mouth. Twice. "Stay well," he said softly.

"I plan to," said Michael.

Thack grabbed his bags and headed down the steps, stopping only to reexamine his earlier handiwork. When he saw Michael watching him, he grinned sheepishly. "Our plank," he said.

"I know," said Michael.

There was nothing even close to comfort food in the house, so Michael ran down to the Searchlight and bought a quart of milk and a package of Oreos. He was tearing into them when the phone rang.

"Yeah," he answered flatly, faking civility for no one, least of all Brian, who should have called hours ago, if he was going to be this late.

But it was Charlie. "Well, how did it go?"

"It was fine," he said.

"Fine? What does that mean? What's that noise?"

"I'm eating," said Michael.

"Not cookies? Oreos?"

"Yes."

"Oh, shit. It's bad. Is he still there?"

"No. He left."

"There was a fight?"

"No, Charlie, no fight. He just went home."

"Well . . . you knew he was gonna do that."

"This is true," said Michael. "Now change the subject."

"Swell," said Charlie. "How 'bout going to a wake with me?"

Michael felt his skin prickle. "Whose?"

"You don't know him. Philip Presley. He worked on the Peninsula, I think."

"You think? Don't you know him?"

"Well, not exactly. His Shanti volunteer helped me out with Lou Pirelli's memorial service, so I kind of owe him one. Please, Michael, his parents are snake-handlers or something. I can't deal with Bible-thumpers without a little moral support."

"I'm running out of outfits," said Michael.

"Do the blazer," said Charlie. "The blazer is you."

"When is it?"

"Tomorrow."

"I should be at work, actually."

"It's during lunch hour. I'll pick you up. It won't take long. It's potluck, but I'll make my pecan pie, and it can be from both of us."

Michael capitulated with a weary laugh. "What time?" he asked.

"Noon," said Charlie. "You're a prince."

"See you then," said Michael.

"Bye-bye," said Charlie.

Michael hung up and continued ravaging the Oreos. He ate half a dozen of them and took the rest to the bathroom, where he soaked in the tub and waited for Brian to call.

Homesick at Home

For DeDe, this was the very landscape of peace: the apple orchard, the swimming pool, the familiar line of bee-bristling lavender marching into the yellow hills. If Wimminwood had been D'oro-thea's Oz, here lay her own beloved Kansas, her eternal consolation, her Halcyon-only space.

Smiling, she sat up on her towel and watched as the sun sank like a hot penny into the buttery distance. A soft umber dust covered over the orchard, motes dancing in the light, rendering the scene in sepia tones.

She called to her daughter, frolicking solo in the pool.

"What?" came the put-upon reply.

"Time to get out."

"Awww . . ."

"No lip, Anna. You'll shrivel up."

"No I won't. I gotta catch up. I've been pool-deprived."

DeDe mugged at her. "You poor little thing. You had a wonderful river right there in your front yard."

"A wonderful, yucky river," said Anna, climbing out of the pool.

To a certain extent, DeDe agreed with her, but she wouldn't think of saying so. Anna ran to her, squealing, then did a little on-the-spot warpath dance, waiting to be dried. True luxury, DeDe decided, was only bestowed upon children.

"Where's Edgar?" she asked, toweling Anna's legs.

"In our room," said Anna.

Something about her daughter's tone made her suspicious. "You two aren't fighting again?"

"No," said Anna. "He says he feels crummy."

"He's sick?"

"No. He's homesick."

"Homesick?"

"For Brother Sun."

DeDe blotted Anna's face, then wrapped the towel around her like a sarong. "Well, I bet if you challenged him to a game of Parcheesi . . ."

Anna shook her head slowly. "He won't," she said.

DeDe scooped up her sunning stuff and strode across the terrace to the sun porch, where D'or was kitchen-knifing her way through the bills. "Your mother called," she said, looking up. "She wants us for brunch tomorrow."

"How did she sound?" DeDe asked.

"Good, actually. Cheerful. Not herself."

"Did you accept?"

"I did," said D'or. "Even more cheerfully."

DeDe smirked. "Look who's not herself."

Dropping her stuff in the kitchen, she swept through the house and up the stairs, then stopped outside the children's door, which was slightly ajar. He sat Indian-style in the window seat, his diary in his lap.

"Hi," she said.

He looked up gravely. "Hi," he replied.

"Lots to write about, huh?"

He shrugged.

"Sure," she said, sitting next to him. "You made lots of new friends, learned how to make wallets . . . lots of good stuff."

He nodded.

"It's all right to miss your friends, you know."

"I know," he said.

"I liked that one boy a lot. Philo? Was that his name?"

Another nod.

"Did you write about Brother Sun?" she asked.

"Yeah."

"Maybe if you read it to me . . ."

He shook his head.

"Why not?" she asked.

"It's just for boys," he replied.

"Oh . . . I see."

"No offense," said Edgar.

"I understand." She put her hand on his little knee, gave it a shake and got up. "D'or is grilling tuna tonight. Your favorite."

"With peanut butter sauce?"

"I think so," she said.

"Yum."

Stopping at the door, she looked back, to find him absorbed in his diary again. She felt an unmistakable pang of jealousy.

Geordie

On a sand dune at Point Reyes, Brian watched until the sun had been extinguished by the coastal fog. Then he trudged back to the car, past the secret inland sea called Abbott's Lagoon. He loved this spot—had loved it for years—for its desolation and drama, its pristine white knolls and sparkling water, a storybook Sahara rolling down to a Biblical shore.

The threat of death, apparently, was a last-minute eye-opener for some people, but not for him. He had known already how special this place was. He had said so a thousand times. On the proverbial path of life, there weren't many goddamn roses he hadn't already stopped and smelled.

Shouldn't that count for something?

He drove back to the city by way of the dizzying Stinson Beach road, then sat in traffic at the bridge while a wounded Saab was hauled away. It was after dark when he finally arrived at the doorstep of Geordie's cottage.

She checked him out through the little hatch, then opened the door. "Forget something?" she asked blandly. She looked less haggard than before. Rested, at least.

"I'm sorry," he said.

She shrugged.

"I shouldn't have run off like that."

"A week ago," she said, smiling wearily. "I've already forgotten about it."

"Can I come in?"

She shrugged again, then made a frivolous welcoming gesture. He stepped past her awkwardly into the low-ceilinged room. A half-eaten TV dinner, still steaming, sat on the coffee table.

"I'm interrupting supper," he said.

"So what else is new? Sit down." She raked newspapers off the sofa to make a place for him. "Want me to heat you one? It's Lean Cuisine."

"No," he said. "Thanks."

She could tell what he was thinking, and smiled. "It's not denial," she said. "I'm not dieting. I just haven't shopped since the diagnosis."

"Looks good," he said lamely.

"Did you take the test?"

"Yeah."

"When do you get your results?"

"Five days," he said.

She cut a piece of turkey with her fork and chewed it vigorously. "You're gonna be all right."

He didn't know what to say. It seemed selfish somehow to wish for something she had already been denied.

"How 'bout a beer?" she asked.

"No, thanks."

"You're a blast," she said, deadpanning.

He smiled back at her, then sat there tongue-tied, hands dangling between his legs. "How's your friend?" he asked at last.

"Not good," she replied. "Tubes . . . all that. He doesn't recognize me."

"I'm sorry." He looked down again, composing his thoughts. "Look . . . I could shop. I'm a good shopper."

"For who?" She drew back a little.

"For you . . . whenever."

"Hey," she said. "So they found a lesion. I can still get around, Brian."

"You should eat better," he said. "Greens. Healthy stuff. Shiitake mushrooms."

"I loathe mushrooms," she said.

"Yeah, but these are great for the immune system. It comes in a powder. You put it in V-8 and it tastes just like pizza." He remembered Jon, sitting up in bed with a glass of the stuff, smacking his lips and saying: "What? No pepperoni?"

"That is dis-gusting," said Geordie.

He laughed. "Liquid pizza. Works for me."

"Thanks, but no thanks."

"You're gonna need somebody," he said.

She turned and stared at him.

"I have all sorts of free time," he added.

"You have a wife and a child."

"And a maid," he said. "Who does most of the work."

She studied his face a moment longer, then said: "My sister said she'd help."

557

"Good," he answered. "Then that makes two of us."

She cut off another piece of turkey, then asked: "Will your wife know where you're going?"

Tonight of all nights, he found a parking space at the very foot of the Barbary steps. When he reached the courtyard, he looked up at Michael's window, a bar of burnished gold embedded in the dark ivy of the second floor. Seeing a shadow pass, he almost called out, but changed his mind and pushed the buzzer instead.

Michael looked angry when he opened his door on the landing.

"I'm late," Brian said quietly. "And you needed the car."

Michael's face remained stony. "Thack wanted a ride to the airport," he said.

So that was it. He had robbed them of a decent send-off, a prolonged farewell. "Sorry," he said, as contritely as possible. "I didn't know he was leaving tonight."

"No big deal."

"I figured everybody would just . . . kick back."

Michael gave him a twisted little smile. "He's kicking back on a 747."

"Can I come in?"

"Sure," said Michael. He stood aside, then closed the door. "It's not your fault. I didn't know he was leaving, either."

Brian headed for the armchair and collapsed into it.

"I think he just freaked out," said Michael, sitting down on the sofa.

"About what?"

Michael plumped the pillow next to him. "My being positive."

"You told him that?"

"Yeah."

"When?"

"A couple of days ago," said Michael. "Before we went to bed."

Something didn't compute. "Wouldn't he have said something earlier, then?"

"Oh, he was cool about it," said Michael, "and we were safe and all. Unless you count French kissing, which I don't."

"Then why would he all of a sudden . . . ?"

"I think it just ruled out any . . . long-term considerations."

"But that wouldn't make him leave early."

Michael ran his palm along the arm of the sofa. "I dunno. I may have been *looking* long-term." He gave Brian a wistful smile. "You know me."

Now it made sense.

"I don't blame him," said Michael. "Who wants to start something with somebody who . . . you know." He chewed on his lower lip. "He was a nice guy. Some guys won't even *date* outside their own antibody type."

Before Brian could react, Michael added: "You got some sun."

"Did I?"

"Where did you go?"

Brian shrugged. "Down the coast. Point Reyes. Then I went to visit Geordie."

"Who?"

"My . . . friend."

"Oh. How is she?"

"OK, I guess. Better than I was, actually."

Michael nodded. "I know what you mean."

"How can she do it?" Brian asked.

"What?"

"Act so normal. I'd be throwing things, tearing the house apart."

"She may have done that," said Michael.

"I'd keep doing it," said Brian. "I'd be crazy."

Michael gave him a dim smile. "Sooner or later, it's a question of how you want to spend your time."

"I'm sorry," said Brian. "That's too pat."

Michael regarded him for a moment, then said: "My mother gave me a new address book last Christmas. I haven't written in it yet, because I can't make myself leave out the people who are dead. I can't even cross out their names."

Brian nodded.

"How pat is that? There's one on every page. All of the *H*'s are gone except you."

It felt a lot like a punch in the gut. "Thanks for telling me," he said.

"Oh, right," said Michael, rolling his eyes impatiently. "Homosexuals, Haitians, hemophiliacs and people whose name begins with *H*."

"Look, if you're gonna . . ."

"It's OK to be afraid, Brian."

"I know that."

"It's also exhausting, and I'm tired of it. So I don't do it anymore. It's probably that way with your friend. There's nothing particularly noble about it. It just happens."

"So that's it, huh? Just don't be afraid. That's your advice."

"You can do what you want to do," said Michael.

He didn't need this. "Great," he said, getting up to leave.

"Sit down," said Michael.

"Just forget it, man."

"Sit down, OK? I'm sorry. I'm just being crabby about Thack."

Brian sat down but didn't look at him.

"It just gets old, you know? Talking about it."

Brian nodded.

"If you really want some advice . . . get your shit together with Mary Ann."

"I know," he said.

"You're gonna be all right. I know it. You're feeling guilty right now and that makes it worse."

"Maybe."

"That's most of it, Brian. I can tell."

"What about . . . you know, the night sweats?"

"It only happened once," said Michael.

"Twice."

"OK, twice. Your mind can cook up all sorts of ugly stuff."

"You think my mind did that?"

"It could have."

"I dunno."

"Your headaches are gone, aren't they? Your sluggishness."

They were, he had to admit.

"You're not gonna die," said Michael. "Somebody's gotta take care of me."

"Hey." Brian looked across at him. "Shut the fuck up."

"OK, OK . . . So nobody's gonna die."

Brian saw the elfin glimmer in his eyes and smiled back at him. "I love you, Michael."

Michael plumped the pillow again. "So marry me."

Brian laughed.

"I mean it," said Michael. "I need a partner."

"A partner?"

"At the nursery, you dildo."

"Since when have you wanted a partner?"

Michael shrugged. "I've thought about it ever since Ned left."

"You talked to Wren," said Brian.

Michael frowned. "What's Wren got to do with it?"

"Everything, I'm sure."

"Oh, don't be such an asshole. I've thought about this for at *least* a year."

"But you still talked to Wren."

"Well, she may have mentioned that you'd expressed an interest . . . Look, if you hate the idea . . ."

"I don't hate the idea," said Brian.

"I wanna buy that lot next door, expand the greenhouse. I need an investor, and I miss having a partner. You're strong enough, we get along, there'd be no rude surprises." Michael smiled. "'You hold no mystery for me, Amanda.'"

Brian smiled back. *"Private Lives."*

"See? A breeder who knows Coward. What more could I want?"

Brian hesitated. "It could work, I guess."

"*Work?* It'll be the best fun we ever had." Michael reminded him of a kid coaxing his buddy into a tree house. "C'mon. Say yes."

"I'll have to talk to Mary Ann," he said.

Walking home to The Summit, he warded off the specter of dread that dogged him across the moon-bright hill. The doorman made a lame joke about the fires still smoldering in the Santa Cruz Mountains. Whole neighborhoods had been incinerated, it seemed, and he hadn't thought about it for days.

On the twenty-third floor, Mary Ann greeted him in Levi's and a pink button-down. There were more candles than usual, and the synthesizer music they used for sex was playing in the background. He wondered if she'd had the tape on all evening, awaiting his return.

"Well," she said softly, once more in his arms.

"I'm sorry," he replied.

"It's OK."

"I drove out to Abbott's Lagoon. Lost track of the time."

"Have you eaten?" she asked, heading into the living room.

"I'm not hungry," he replied, realizing it wasn't exactly true; he just hadn't envisioned food in this scenario.

"There's some great fruit salad. Everything fresh."

"No," he said.

She slipped her arm around his waist. "You've lost weight," she said. "It looks good."

He avoided her gaze.

"Cheekbones," she said, touching the side of his face.

He sat on the sofa and kicked his shoes off. She curled up next to him and said: "I taped *Entertainment Tonight*. It looks pretty good."

"So I heard."

"Who told you?"

"Well . . . Mrs. Madrigal, actually. Michael talked to her." He couldn't very well admit to calling the landlady, not when Mary Ann hadn't heard from him.

"I thought *you* did," she said. "Shawna said you did."

"Oh, well . . . yeah, that time. This was another time." Seizing upon his daughter as an evasion tactic, he added: "How's she been?"

"Fine. She sprayed the Sorensons' cat with mousse this morning."

He smiled a little.

"The hair kind," said Mary Ann. "Not the chocolate."

He chuckled.

"She missed you," she said.

"I missed you both."

She looked at him with tenderness, but obliquely, cautiously. "Did it help?" she asked.

"What?"

"Getting away."

What could he say to that? He put his arm around her, pulled her closer. "I wasn't trying to get away from you."

"It's OK," she said, her cheek against his chest. "People get sick of each other." She giggled and patted him. "I get sick of you sometimes. You just beat me to it this time."

This stung a little. He had never really been sick of Mary Ann. Even when he'd been with Geordie, it hadn't been because he was sick of Mary Ann.

When he didn't reply, she asked: "What's the matter?"

"We have to talk," he said.

It was terse enough—and dire enough—to make her sit up, blinking at him. "OK," she said quietly.

"I have this friend who has AIDS," he began, delivering the line as rehearsed.

Her brow furrowed. Her fingertips came to her chin and lighted, gently as a butterfly. "Brian . . . don't tell me Michael is . . . ?"

"No," he said forcefully. "No, he's fine."

"God, you scared me!" Her hand slid to her chest in relief. "Who is he?" she asked.

"It's a woman," he replied.

Man and Boy

It was late morning when Booter finally emerged from his bedroom in Hillsborough, enticed by the camplike aroma of sausage frying. He had slept for over fourteen hours, and his system seemed to have recuperated admirably. The aches in his limbs were nothing more than the aches of being seventy-one. He could live with that, as always.

In the kitchen, he found Emma laying out paper towels on the countertop. "That smells wonderful," he said, hovering over the big iron skillet.

"Don't snitch none," she said. "It's for company."

He gave her a teasing glance. "Aren't I company? I'm invited, aren't I?"

"Ask Miss Frannie," said the maid. "You been gone so long, I don't reckon she remembers who you are."

"Oh . . . now." He smiled at her, largely in recognition of her dauntless loyalty. When Frannie pouted, Emma pouted right along with her. It had been that way as long as he could remember. "Where is she?" he asked.

Emma laid some links out to drain. "The patio, I reckon. She's fixin' flowers for the table."

He found Frannie doing just that, up to her elbows in blowsy pink roses. Seeing him, she seemed to brighten a little, so the maid's grumpiness had probably been residual, a lingering ceremonial gesture.

Frannie said: "Aren't these lovely?"

He nodded and smiled at her, his old friend. "There are some nice ferns down behind the tennis court."

She fluttered her eyelids, faintly befuddled. Her face took on a plump-cheeked childishness which always tickled him.

"To go with the roses," he explained.

"Oh, well . . . yes . . . fine."

"Where are the shears?"

564

She rummaged in her garden things, handed him the shears and said, "Thank you," with a look of mild amazement.

From the border next to the tennis court he clipped five or six large maidenhair fronds, returning to his wife as she adjusted the little linen tepees on the glass-topped table. "Those are perfect." She took the fronds, beaming.

"Who's for breakfast?" he asked.

"Oh . . . just family today. You look much more rested, Booter."

"I am," he assured her. "What family?"

"DeDe and D'orothea."

"And the children?" he asked.

"Mmm," she replied. "Emma's setting up a card table on the lawn. They won't be trouble."

He wasn't so sure about that.

As it turned out, the children were remarkably subdued, keeping to themselves at the other table, showing no interest whatsoever in the grownups. Booter relaxed a little, soothed by the sunshine and the soporific tones of the talking women.

"So," Frannie was saying, "where did you end up going?"

DeDe, he noticed, shot a quick glance at her friend before replying: "Eureka, ultimately. But we drove around a lot. Just . . . taking it easy."

"Did you stay in motels?" Frannie grimaced a little when she said the word.

"No," said D'orothea, with almost as much hauteur. "Bed-and-breakfast places."

"Some of them are very nice," DeDe added defensively. "Carpeting and everything."

D'orothea rolled her eyes.

"I'm sure you're right," Frannie said pleasantly, clearly intent on avoiding trouble. "I'm sure they're very nice."

"What about you, Mother? What have you been up to?" DeDe shifted the spotlight rather deftly, he thought.

"Oh . . . you know me. A little gardening, a few tiresome

lunches. Lots of TV. I saw that woman, by the way, the one you like so much. This morning. On Mary Ann's show."

"What woman?"

"You know, that poetess who was on Broadway."

"Poet," said D'orothea. "Sabra Landauer."

"Yes," said Frannie. "That's the one."

DeDe frowned. "She was on Mary Ann's show?"

Frannie nodded. "The whole time. Except for the last fifteen minutes, when they had a dog psychic."

Booter couldn't let that pass. "A dog psychic?"

"She's quite extraordinary." His wife reproved him with a look. "Don't mock what you don't understand."

DeDe kept her eyes down as she spaded her grapefruit. "Did the psychic say what was on Sabra's mind?"

Booter chuckled. DeDe fired off a good one every now and then.

His wife turned to DeDe, looking puzzled. "I thought you admired her. For being a feminist."

"She's all right," said DeDe, as Emma arrived with a parsley-strewn platter of scrambled eggs and sausages. Booter detected another hurried visual exchange between DeDe and D'orothea.

Frannie took the platter from the maid and said: "Well, she was much prettier than I expected."

DeDe grunted. "Did she read her poetry, or what?"

"No," replied Frannie. "She talked, mostly."

"About what?" asked D'orothea.

"Oh . . . her fiancé, for one thing."

"*Her fiancé?*" This came from both young women at once.

"He's an actor," said Frannie.

"He would be," said DeDe.

Frannie added: "He was on *St. Elsewhere* last week. What do you mean, he would be?"

"It's a career move," said DeDe.

"I don't understand."

"She's gay, Mother."

566

D'orothea began to chuckle.

Frannie was lost. "Then, why would she . . . ?"

"To throw people off the track."

"You mean she would . . . ?"

"She's a star, Mother. Stars aren't supposed to be gay."

"Well, I know, but . . . that poor man!"

"Mother, he's probably gay himself."

"He is?"

"Yes. Now they're both covered."

D'orothea's laughter gathered steam. Pushing away from the table, she threw back her head and gasped for air.

Frannie was plainly offended. "Well, just because I don't know what her—"

"No," DeDe cut in, "she's not laughing at you, Mother." Frannie stuck out her chest like a pouter pigeon. "I mean . . . *really!*"

"I'm sorry," said D'orothea, rubbing her eyes, recovering control. "When are they getting married?"

Frannie continued brooding.

"Mother," said DeDe, "when?"

"Tomorrow, I think. That's what she came here for."

D'orothea looked at DeDe and shrugged. "I must've been her bachelor party."

After breakfast, Booter withdrew from the women and strolled through the garden, savoring the pleasant predictability of home. Out on the lawn, the children were engaged in a raucous croquet match, which he watched from afar, enjoying their enthusiasm.

When the boy came toward him in search of the ball, Booter seized the moment. "Son," he said quietly. "Could I have a word with you?"

Edgar approached almost guiltily. Good God, thought Booter, am I really that terrifying?

"I wanted to thank you," he said. "For your help the other night."

The boy said nothing, shrugging a little.

"You were very brave, and I appreciate it."

Edgar scratched the side of his neck. "How did you get away?"

Booter decided not to elaborate. "Someone else came along," he said.

Anna yelled to the boy from the lawn. "Edgurr . . . hurry up." Booter looked at the little girl, then asked: "Did you tell her about it?"

"No," said Edgar.

"Your mother?"

"No."

"Why not?" asked Booter.

"They're girls," said Edgar.

Booter smiled at him and tousled his dark corn-silk hair. "Attaboy."

"Edgurr," screamed Anna.

"I gotta go," said the boy.

"I thought," said Booter, "maybe we could do something next weekend. Just the two of us. Go to the museum . . . look for dinosaurs?"

The boy hesitated.

"We men gotta stick together, right?"

"I guess so," said Edgar.

"Edgurr, I am leaving right this very minute!"

"Better run," said Booter, smiling.

"She's a pain," said Edgar.

"Well, hang in there. Oh . . . tell me the answer."

"What answer?"

"You know. What's blue and creamy?"

"Tell you later," said Edgar, running back to his sister.

Forgotten Lady

The wake was to happen in a house somewhere in the Richmond district. They drove there in Charlie's Fairlane, so Michael kept his eyes peeled for parking places as soon as they crossed Park Presidio.

"There's one!" he called when they were still three or four blocks away.

"Fuck that," said Charlie.

"We're not gonna get any better," said Michael.

Charlie tapped the dashboard, indicating a card imprinted with a wheelchair. "Handicap parking," he said.

"Hey," said Michael. "Perks of the eighties."

"Right," said Charlie. "Win a parking place and die."

Most of the other celebrants had come directly from the inurnment at the Neptune Society Columbarium. Michael couldn't help feeling a little fraudulent, like a bum on the sidewalk talking Chekhov with an intermission audience.

"I don't know a soul," he whispered, as they circled the dessert table.

"No one's eating my pie," said Charlie, frowning.

"Here." Michael held out his paper plate. "I'll take a slice."

"No. Not unless you mean it."

Michael laughed. "Give me a goddamn slice."

Charlie gave him one. "That Key lime pie is half gone, and look at the color of it. It's practically Day-Glo."

"Well," said Michael, "it's sort of a postmodern crowd." He took a mouthful of Charlie's gooey-rich pecan pie, enjoying its slow descent. "I never know how to act at these things," he said.

"What do you mean?"

"You know. Whether to laugh or not."

Charlie shrugged. "It's a celebration. That's what they called it."

"I know, but some of these people feel awful right now."

"You'd better laugh at mine," said Charlie.

"Right."

"I've fixed it so you will, actually. I drew up the plans while you were gone. I won't spoil it for you, but it involves several hundred yards of mock leopardskin and an Ann-Margret impersonator."

Michael licked the sweetness off his fingers. "Why not just plain Ann-Margret?"

569

"Well, she's optional, of course. Use your discretion."

"Who's optional?" It was Teddy Roughton, funereally attired in black jeans, white shirt, and black leather bow tie. He slipped his arm around Michael's waist and surveyed the raspberry tarts.

"It's a long story," said Michael. "Teddy, this is Charlie. Charlie, Teddy."

"We've met," said Teddy, extending his hand. "At the Ringold Alley AIDS do."

"Oh, yes . . . of course." Charlie's tone became ingratiating, Michael noticed, as soon as he remembered that Teddy was three parts *Vanity Fair* to one part *Drummer.* Charlie was impressed by titles.

"Meanwhile," said Teddy, rolling his eyes as he drew out the word, "our laddie here has broken the heart of another unsuspecting tourist."

"What laddie?" asked Charlie, confused.

"This one," said Teddy, giving Michael a shake.

"Me?" said Michael. "What did he say?"

Charlie frowned. "What did *who* say?"

"He was bereft," said Teddy, oblivious of Charlie's question. "Said he was mad for you, but you weren't mad for him."

"Come off it," said Michael, convinced of a hoax.

"Is this Thack?" asked Charlie.

"Teddy drove him to the airport," Michael explained.

"Poor boy," purred Teddy. He was playing it for all it was worth.

"You see?" said Charlie, looking Michael in the eye. "You see?"

"What did he say?" Michael asked Teddy.

"I told you. That he fancied you. And it wasn't mutual."

Michael felt a sudden urge to whoop, right there in the middle of the wake. "Wasn't mutual?"

"Well, those are *my* words, of course . . ."

"He was the one who was standoffish," said Michael. "He left early, he . . . Is this the truth, Teddy?"

Teddy leaned over the table, examining the tarts at closer range. "Oh, yes," he said vaguely.

"Try the pecan pie," said Charlie, exuding graciousness. "It's extraordinary." Then he turned and scolded Michael. "Didn't I tell you?"

After the wake, Michael was too distracted to work, so he asked Charlie to drive him home. When they reached the Barbary steps, Charlie said: "Don't look now, but your landlady has finally flipped her beanie."

Michael turned, to find Mrs. Madrigal chained to the landing of the steps. Her bonds were of the modest hardware-store variety, faintly ridiculous in this context. She was wearing her semiformal getup, a loose skirt and a tweed jacket over a high-necked white blouse. She was obviously giving it all she had.

"It's a protest," Michael told him.

"Oh, right." Charlie rolled his eyes. "You Russian Hill people are so weird."

Michael smiled and pecked him on the cheek. "I'll call you tonight."

"Not until you've called Thack."

"All right."

"I mean it, Michael. Don't fuck this up."

Michael laughed and bounded across the street. Charlie beeped twice and drove away down Leavenworth. Mrs. Madrigal offered him a cheery wave from the steps, then called down to Michael: "I hope I didn't scare him away."

"No," said Michael. "Not at all." He climbed the steps to the landing where the landlady sat in dignified splendor, fussing idly with the neck of her blouse, the drape of her chain.

"I'm waiting for Mary Ann," she said, "in case you're wondering."

"She's gonna tape this?" He hardly knew what to say.

She nodded demurely. "I'm afraid she's a bit late."

"What time was she supposed to be here?"

"I'm sure she'll get here soon," said the landlady. The look in her eyes told him not to be so indignant on her behalf. She knew what she was doing, it said.

He asked: "Are there . . . uh . . . demolition people coming?"

"We don't know," she said grimly.

"Doesn't Mary Ann know?"

"No," said the landlady. "She says she doesn't. She needs this for human interest." She threw up her hands and gave him a crooked little smile. "If this is what it takes, then this is what it takes."

He wondered for a moment if Mary Ann's absence was a function of Brian's homecoming. If he had told her, and she had freaked out . . .

"When did you last talk to her?" he asked.

"Oh . . . late yesterday afternoon. She told me I should be . . . uh . . . chained up from noon on. She couldn't be here when I did it, or it would look like we're in cahoots."

"You haven't talked to her this morning?"

"No." Her brow furrowed. "Is something the matter?"

"No," he replied calmly. "I just wondered. Look, I'll call the station for you."

"That would be very kind." She saw his expression. "Don't be cross with her, dear."

He continued up the steps, then stopped. "Oh," he said, "what did you think of Thack?"

"He seems very sweet," she said. "Just right for you."

"He does, doesn't he?"

"Has he gone yet?" she asked.

"Last night."

"Oh, dear."

"It doesn't matter," he said. "I mean, not yet. Right now I'm just enjoying the feeling. You know what I mean?"

"I know what you mean," she said.

He smiled at her.

"Bring me a caramel, dear, when you come back. They're in that crystal dish on my piano."

He climbed the remaining steps in seven-league boots, basking in the glow of her benediction.

● ● ●

When he phoned the station, a peevish associate producer told him Mary Ann had left immediately after the morning taping, and he personally knew nothing about a crew being sent to the Barbary steps.

He tried The Summit. Brian answered with a lackluster hello.

"It's Michael," he said. "Is Mary Ann there, by any chance?"

"Well . . . yeah. She's not really taking any calls right now."

So, thought Michael, he did tell her. "I know it's a bad time," he said. "It's just that Mrs. Madrigal is down here chained to the steps."

"What?"

"Tell Mary Ann. She'll know what it means."

Brian left the phone. Twenty seconds later, Mary Ann came on. "God, Mouse."

He tried to be gentle about it. "It's not too late."

"I'll call the station," she said. "I'll get a crew."

"Good."

"I completely forgot, Mouse! I'm so sorry. Please tell her I didn't mean . . ."

"I'll take care of it," he said. "What time do the wreckers come?"

"Uh . . . three o'clock."

"Good," he said. "If you hurry, you can   Are you two all right?"

"Mouse . . ."

"Just yes or no."

"More or less," she replied.

"I love you," he said.

She was silent for a moment, then said, "You guys," with weary resignation, as if she meant every man on earth.

Michael said: "Ask Brian to bring that big butch chain of his."

"What?"

"That chrome job he uses on the Jeep. It'll beat what we've got now, believe me. If I'm gonna be filmed in bondage, I want it to look real."

"Mouse, we don't need two."

"C'mon," he said. "Let's make this fun."

She groaned.

"We'll make those steps look like a fucking charm bracelet."

"All right," she said. "Whatever. We'll see you down there. And listen, Mouse . . ."

"Yeah?"

"If she's smoking grass when the crew shows up . . ."

"Don't worry. I'll tell her. Bye-bye." He hung up, flew to the bedroom, flung off his clothes and showered like a madman. Four minutes later, when he shut off his blow-dryer, he discovered that the phone had been ringing.

He lunged for it. "Yes . . . hello."

"Bad time?" asked Thack.

"Well . . . there's a camera crew coming. We're saving the steps."

"Oh, yeah. I forgot."

"So did we. Almost."

"I miss you," said Thack.

"Do you really?"

"Damn right."

Michael laughed. "That is so great. I miss you too."

"What are we gonna do about it?"

"Well," said Michael, "for starters, I'm gonna write you a long, gooey letter, embarrassing the hell out of myself."

"Mine's finished," said Thack. "In the mail."

"Hey," said Michael, laughing again.

"You're in a hurry. I won't keep you."

Keep me, thought Michael. "I'll call you tonight. OK?"

"Great. I'll be here."

Michael hung up and rushed to the closet, where he agonized momentarily over the proper attire for a televised chain-in. He settled finally on a sort of architectonic look: corduroy trousers, plaid shirt, knit tie, Top-siders.

Halfway into the courtyard, he remembered Mrs. Madrigal's caramels and doubled back, scooping up a generous handful from the dish on the piano.

They would need enough for the duration.

Five Days Later

Now this, thought Wren, is more like it.

It was almost midnight, and she and Rolando were sprawled across her bed, basking in the blush of her 1939 (all-tango) Empress jukebox.

She had paid for the Empress with Booter's check—Booter's *new* check: ten thousand dollars exactly. That pleased her somehow, knowing her memories of Monte Rio would always be embodied in this tango-lover's wet dream.

He had been so sweet to send the money, and she had accepted it readily, knowing how much it meant to him. He wasn't such a bad old shithead, when you got right down to it. At least, he was a gentleman in bed.

The Chicago night was deliciously balmy. A lake-sent breeze meandered through the loft, tickling the lace on the big industrial windows. She moaned contentedly and nestled into Rolando's warm, bay-rummy flesh.

The phone rang.

"Oh, hell," said Rolando.

"I'll get it," she said.

"Leave it."

"No," she said, sensing something. "I'll be right back." She slid out of bed and made her way naked to the phone in her work cubicle.

"Hello."

"Wren, it's Brian."

"Oh, yeah. How are you, sweetie?" For once, she realized, that question really meant something.

"I'm fine," he said.

"Really?"

"Yeah. It came back negative."

"Thank God," she said, sinking into a chair.

"Really," he replied.

She heard a woman's voice, then the unmistakable sound of Michael's laughter. "Are you having a party to celebrate?"

He laughed. "Well, yeah . . . but not that. We just won a battle with the city."

"Are you at home?" she asked.

"My landlady's house."

This made no sense to her. That high-rise condo had a land-lady?

"Is your wife there?"

"Yeah. Not in the room, but . . ."

"Is she OK?"

"Yeah," he said. "Pretty much."

"Good . . . Does she know about us?"

"No."

The laughter swelled again. "Is Michael loaded?" she asked.

Brian chuckled. "Just in love, I think."

"Anybody we know?"

"I believe so. They're getting mushy by mail."

"Oh, God."

"I'm gonna be his partner at the nursery. Isn't that great?"

"That is," she said.

He paused before asking: "How's Rolando doing?"

He had remembered; how sweet. "He's fine, actually. As usual."

"He's a lucky man."

"Thanks."

"Well, I just wanted to—Puppy, wait a minute . . . All right . . . Daddy's talking."

"Your offspring?" asked Wren.

"Yeah. They want me back at the party . . . It's kind of hectic. I'm sorry."

"Well, thanks for calling. This Rock Hudson thing had me so worried . . ."

"Rock Hudson? What about him? Puppy, let Daddy talk."

"Turn on your TV set," she said. The little girl began to yell. "Look, I'll let you go."

576

"Guess I'd better," he said.

"Have a wonderful life, sweetie."

"Same to you," he said. "And thanks."

"Anytime," she replied.

She hung up and returned to the bed, where Rolando lay sprawled on his stomach, snoring. In the light of the Empress, his magnificent rump looked like two scoops of tangerine sherbet. The effect was too perfect to spoil, so she slipped under the sheets without a word and sat there remembering, waiting for the tango to end.

THE END

Sure of You

For Ian McKellen

Piglet sidled up to Pooh from behind.
"Pooh!" he whispered.
"Yes, Piglet?"
"Nothing," said Piglet, taking Pooh's paw.
"I just wanted to be sure of you."

—A. A. MILNE
The House at Pooh Corner

Pretty Is

There was something different about his wife's face, Brian Hawkins had decided. Something around the mouth, maybe. It was there at the corners, where her real mood always showed, even at a moment like this, when she certainly couldn't want it to show. He tilted his head until his eyes were even with hers, then withdrew a little, like someone appraising a portrait.

God, she was pretty! She gave depth to pretty, investing it with seriousness and intent. But something was eating at her, nibbling away from inside, while she sat there smiling, nodding, speaking softly of pet bereavement.

"And Fluffy is . . . ?"

"A Pomeranian," replied this morning's guest, a big, blowsy matron straight out of Laurel and Hardy.

"And when did she . . . pass away?"

The pause was masterful, he thought. Mary Ann's gentle little search for the euphemism was either admirably kind or savagely funny, depending on the sophistication of the viewer.

"Three months ago," said the matron. "Almost four."

Poor old cow, he thought. Headed straight for the slaughter-house.

"So you decided to have her . . . ?"

"Freeze-dried," said the woman.

"Freeze-dried," said Mary Ann.

There was nervous tittering in the studio audience. Nervous because Mary Ann had yet to abandon her respectful, funereal face. Be nice to this lady, it said. She's a human being like anyone else.

583

As usual, it was hugely effective. Mary Ann was never caught with blood on her hands.

His partner, Michael, walked into the nursery office, dropped his work gloves on the counter, draped an arm across Brian's shoulders. "Who's she got today?"

"Watch," said Brian, turning up the sound. The woman was opening a wooden carrying case, shaped like a doghouse. "She's my child," she was saying, "my precious little baby. She's never been just a dog to me."

Michael frowned at the set. "Whatthefuck."

The camera moved in for a tight shot as Mary Ann silenced the gigglers with another glance. The woman plunged her chubby hands into the box and produced her precious Fluffy, fluffy as ever.

"It's not moving," said Michael.

"It's dead," Brian told him. "Freeze-dried."

While Michael hooted, the woman arranged the rigid beast on her lap, patting its snowy fur into place. To Brian she seemed horribly vulnerable. Her lip trembled noticeably as her eyes darted back and forth between the audience and her inquisitor.

"There are some people," said Mary Ann, even more gently than before, "who might find this . . . unusual."

"Yes." The woman nodded. "But she keeps me company. I can always pet her." She demonstrated this feature halfheartedly, then gave Mary Ann a look of excruciating innocence. "Would you like to try it?"

Mary Ann shot the quickest of takes to the audience. The camera, as usual, was ready for her. As the studio reverberated with laughter, Brian reached out and slapped the set off with his palm.

"Hey," said Michael. "That was good stuff."

"She was set up," said Brian.

"C'mon. You don't go on TV with a freeze-dried dog and not expect a little teasing."

"Did you see her face, man? She wasn't expecting that."

"Hey, fellas," said a customer in the doorway.

"Oh," blurted Michael. "Find what you need?"

584

"Yeah. If someone could help me load them . . ."

Brian jumped to his feet. "Hey . . . fix you right up."

The woman strode—no, slinked—through several aisles of shrubbery, making her selections. Brian followed her, feeling a boner growing in his overalls, then lugged the cans back to the office, where he
tallied her bill and clipped the cans.

"Will that be all?"

She handed him her Visa card. "That'll do it." Her hair was
brick red and sleek as sealskin. Something watching from behind her
molten eyes made him think she might be shopping for more than
shrubbery.

Fumbling, he ran her card through the machine.

"You been here long?" she asked.

"Uh . . . me or the nursery?"

Her mouth flickered. "You."

"I've been here three years, I guess."

She tapped her long fingers on the countertop. "I used to come
here when it was called something else."

"God's Green Earth."

"Oh, yeah." She smiled. "I like Plant Parenthood better."

"Yeah, so do I."

He removed the slip and handed it to her with a pen. She signed
it with a flourish, then ripped the carbons into neat little squares,
smirking at him all the while. "Not that I don't trust that face," she
said.

He felt himself reddening. *You fucking dork. How long has it
been, anyway?*

"Think I could tax those muscles?"

"What? Oh . . . sure."

"My car's down the street."

He gestured toward the cans. "Is this all?" Of course this is all,
asshole. You just rang up the purchase, didn't you?

"That's it." She wet her lips with a cat's precision, touching
only the corners with the tip of her tongue.

585

He had grabbed two of the cans when Polly came bolting into the office. "Need a hand with those?"

"That's OK," he said.

"You sure?"

"Yeah."

His employee sauntered around the shrubs as if to size up the situation for herself. "You can't do three."

"Says who?"

Polly gave him a half-lidded smile and a courtly little sweep of the hand, as if to say: She's all yours, greedy. Polly was young enough to be his daughter, but she could be pretty damn intuitive when it came to sex.

The woman looked at Brian, then at Polly, then at Brian again.

"OK," he told Polly. "Gimme a hand."

Flashing a freckled grin, Polly hefted two of the cans and strode out of the office. "Where to?"

"Over there," the woman told her. "The Land Rover."

Polly led the way down the sidewalk, her tank top wet at the breastbone, her silky biceps made wooden by her cargo. Behind her strode the redhead, pale and cool as marble, her ass looking awesome in a knee-length white sweater. Brian brought up the rear, lugging his lone plant and feeling, against his better instincts, less a man for it.

"This is nice of you," said the woman.

"No problem," said Polly.

"You bet," Brian put in idiotically. "Part of the service."

They stuffed the cans into the back of the Land Rover, Polly pondering the placement a lot longer than usual. "That oughta hold you," she said at last, whacking one of the cans.

"Thanks." The redhead smiled at Polly, then slipped behind the wheel and pulled the door shut.

"Remember," Brian said, dropping his voice conspiratorially. "Keep 'em real wet. I know we've got a drought on, but they'll die if you don't."

"I'll do it at night," she said, looking at both of them, "when the neighbors aren't looking."

He laughed. "There you go."

"Thanks again." She turned on the ignition.

"Nice car," said Polly.

The redhead nodded. "She's all right." She pulled away from the curb, flashing her palm in a sort of parting salute. Brian and Polly watched until the car had disappeared around the corner.

"She's been here before," Polly told him as they walked back to the nursery.

"Oh, yeah?"

She nodded, scratching a fleck of dirt off her cheek. "I'd have those panty hose off so fast . . ."

Brian smirked at her sideways.

"You would too," she said.

"Nah."

"C'mon."

"In a pinch, maybe."

Polly chuckled.

"You think she likes girls?" he asked.

She shrugged. "Maybe. Maybe not."

"I thought she might be one of yours."

"Why?"

He thought about this for a moment. "She called her car 'she,' for one thing."

"Huh?" Polly screwed up her face.

"Her car. She referred to it as a she."

"And you think that's some kinda . . . what? Secret lesbo code?"

He shrugged.

"I call my car Dwayne," she said.

He smiled, picturing Polly behind the wheel of her vintage Mustang.

"You're something," she said. "You check 'em all out, don't you?"

"Look who's talking," he said. "I thought you found your main woman last month."

"Who?"

"Whoever. That one you met at Rawhide II."

Polly rolled her eyes.

"Done with her, huh?"

No answer.

Brian chuckled.

"What?"

"How long did that last, anyway?"

With her ragged haircut and guilty grin, Polly looked like something out of Norman Rockwell: a truant schoolkid, maybe, caught red-handed at the fishing hole.

"You know," he told her, "you're worse than any man I know."

"That's because"—she moved alongside him and bumped him with her lean little butt—"I'm *better* than any man you know."

Polly's teasing aside, he was hardly the rogue he used to be. He hadn't strayed from home for over three years now, ever since Geordie Davies got sick. Diagnosed several weeks before Rock Hudson's announcement, Geordie had lasted almost two years longer than the movie star, finally succumbing offstage, at her sister's house, somewhere in Oklahoma.

He had offered to care for her himself—with Mary Ann's knowledge—but she had dismissed the idea with a laugh. They had been playmates, not lovers, she'd told him. "Don't make us into something we weren't. We had a good time, pilgrim. Your services are no longer required."

When his test came back negative, his relief had been so profound that he embarked on a regime of feverish domesticity. Now he rented movies and baked brownies and stayed at home with his daughter, even on the nights when Mary Ann had "important" parties to attend. He had lost his stomach altogether for the sycophants and socialites who revolved around his famous wife.

If something had been lost between him and Mary Ann, it was nothing dramatic, nothing he could pinpoint with certainty. Their sex life still flourished (though it slacked off dramatically during ratings periods), and over the years they had grown increasingly adept at avoiding arguments.

Sometimes, though, he wondered if they weren't *too* careful in each other's presence, too formal and solicitous and artificially jolly. As if their domestic arrangement were no more than that: an arrangement, which demanded courtesy in the absence of the real thing.

Or maybe, as she often suggested, he was just overanalyzing again.

He was back in the office, updating the work schedule on the computer, when Michael's beeper sounded. He tracked the shrill plastic disk to the pocket of his partner's cardigan, clicked it off, and took it out into the greenhouse, where he found Michael on his knees, potting succulents.

"Oh, thanks," he said, pocketing the pillbox. "Sorry 'bout that."

"Hey." Brian shrugged, embarrassed by the apology. He had long ago accepted the beeper as a fixture in both their lives, but it was Michael for whom it really tolled. Every four hours. "You need some water?" he asked.

Michael had already returned to his potting. "I'll take 'em in a minute."

As a rule, he realized, Michael refused to jump to the beeper's commands. It was his way of keeping the poisonous drug in its place.

"So," asked Michael, "which one of you got her?"

Brian pretended not to know what he meant.

"You know." Michael jerked his head toward the door. "Jessica Rabbit out there."

"Who said there was a contest?"

"That's funny. I could have sworn I smelled testosterone."

"Must've been Polly," said Brian.

Michael laughed and plunged the trowel into the soil. "I'll tell her you said that."

Brian turned and headed for the door. "Take your pills," he said.

"Yes, Mother."

Chuckling, he headed out into the sunshine.

Her Day

Back in the dressing room, a vein pounding brutally in her temple, Mary Ann Singleton stretched out on the sofa and kicked off her shoes with a sigh. No sooner had she done so than someone rapped tentatively on the door.

"Yes?" she called colorlessly, already certain it was Raymond, the squirrely new assistant they'd assigned her while Bonnie, her regular, was off houseboating in the Delta with her boyfriend.

Just what she needed right now. Another greenhorn who didn't know squat about television.

"Mary Ann?"

"Yeah, Raymond, come in."

The door eased open and Raymond eased in. He was wearing a thigh-length black Yamamoto shirt that was meant to be stylish but only served to exaggerate his dorkiness. "If this is a bad time . . ."

"No," she said, managing a thin smile. "Sit down, it's fine."

He took the stool in front of the makeup table and fidgeted with the notes on his clipboard. "Interesting show."

She groaned.

"Where did they find her?"

"Are you kidding? They find *us*. Have you seen the lineup this week? It looks like talent night at Napa."

He nodded solemnly, obviously not getting it.

"It's a mental hospital," she explained. "Up north."

"Oh."

"You're not from here, are you?"

"Well . . . I am now, but I'm originally from the Midwest."

After a moment's consideration, she decided not to tell him she was from Cleveland. This was a professional relationship, after all, and she didn't want things to get too chummy. Why give him something he could use against her later?

"So," she said, "what have you got for me?"

Gravely and with great deliberation, Raymond perused his clipboard. It might have contained a list of fatalities from an airlines disaster. "First off," he said, "Channel Two wants you for the Jerry Lewis telethon next year."

"Meaning what? That I have to go to Oakland for it?"

He shrugged. "I guess."

"OK, tell 'em I'll do it, but I don't wanna be paired off with that imbecile cohost they gave me this year. Or anybody else, for that matter. And make sure it's at a decent hour, like not after midnight or something."

"Gotcha." He was scribbling furiously.

"Did you know they actually like him in France?"

"Who?"

"Jerry Lewis."

"Oh. Yeah. I'd heard."

"That is the sickest thing," she said. "Isn't it?"

Raymond merely widened his eyes and shrugged.

"Don't tell me you like him," she said.

"Well . . . I know he's been sort of a joke for a long time, but there's an increasing number of American cineastes who find his early work . . . well, at least comparable to, say, Tati."

She didn't know what that was and didn't care. "He uses too much Brylcreem, Raymond. Give me a big break."

His tiny eyes locked on the clipboard again. Apparently he found her uncool for not knowing that Jerry Lewis was cool again— among film nerds, at any rate. If she'd told him she was from Cleveland, he'd be using that against her now. You just couldn't be too careful.

"What else?" she asked.

He didn't look up. "Some professor at City College wants you to address his television class."

"Sorry. Can't do it."

"OK."

"When is it? Never mind, can't do it. What else?"

"Uh . . . one of your studio regulars wants you to autograph a picture."

"Talk to Julie. We have a whole stack of them, presigned."

"I know, but he wants something personal." He handed her the clipboard with a glossy. "I brought you an unsigned one. He said anything personal would do."

"Some people," she said, grabbing a felt-tip. "What's his name?"

"Cliff. He says he's watched you for years."

After a moment's consideration, she wrote: *Cliff—Thanks for the Memories—Mary Ann.* "If he wants more than that," she told Raymond, returning the clipboard, "he's shit outa luck. Is that it?"

"That's it." He turned up his hands.

"Great. Fabulous. Get lost." She gave him a lame smile to show that she was kidding. "I'm about to do our PMS show a week ahead of schedule."

"Oh . . ." It took him a while to get it. "Can I get you a Nuprin or something?"

"No, thanks, Raymond. That's OK."

He edged toward the door, then stopped. "Oh, sorry—there was a phone call during the show. A guy named Andrews from New York."

"Andrews?"

He retrieved a pink phone memo slip from the pocket of his Yamamoto. "Burke Andrews," he read.

"Oh, *Andrew.* Burke Andrew."

"Yeah. I guess so. Sorry." He set the slip on the makeup table. "I'll leave it here."

A thousand possibilities whirred past her like a Rolodex. "Is it a New York number?"

Raymond shook his head. "Local," he said, sliding out the door. "Looks like a hotel."

Had it really been eleven years?

He'd moved to New York in 1977 after the Cathedral Cannibals fuss, and she hadn't heard from him since, unless you counted the Kodak Christmas card, circa 1983, of him, his grinny, overdressed wife, and their two little jennifer-jasons—strawberry blonds like their father—hanging cedar garlands somewhere in Connecticut. It had stung a little, that card, even though, or maybe even because, she was already married to Brian.

She had met Burke on the Love Boat, as irony would have it, drawn instantly to his affable collie face, his courtliness, his incredible thighs. Michael Tolliver, who'd been there at the time, maintained later that it was Burke's amnesia she'd fallen for: the tempting clean slate of his mind. His memory had returned, however, in a matter of months, and he'd moved to New York almost immediately. He'd asked her to come with him, of course, but she'd been too enraptured with her new life in San Francisco to seriously consider leaving.

From then on her interest in him had been strictly professional. She had followed his increasingly prestigious byline through a succession of glamorous magazines—*New York*, where he'd started out, *Esquire*, a media column in *Manhattan, inc.*—and through television, where he'd recently been making waves on the production end of the business.

She had often wondered why he'd never made an effort to get in touch with her. Their brief romance aside, they had a certain media visibility in common, if nothing else. True, she wasn't a national figure in the purest sense, but she'd been profiled on *Entertainment Tonight*, and no visitor to San Francisco could have failed to notice her face on television or, for that matter, on billboards on the sides of buses.

Oh, well. She had a funny feeling he was about to make up for it.

He was staying at the Stanford Court, it turned out. The operator put her through to his room.

"Yeah," he said briskly, answering immediately.

"Burke?"

"Yeah."

"It's Mary Ann. Singleton."

"Well, hello! Hey, sorry—I thought you were room service. They keep botching my order and calling back. How are you? Boy, it's great to hear your voice!"

"Well," she said lamely, "same here."

"It's been a long time."

"Sure has."

A conspicuous silence and then: "I . . . uh . . . I've got kind of a problem. I was wondering if you might be able to help me."

Her first thought, which she promptly discarded, was that his amnesia had come back. "Sure," she said earnestly. "I'll do what I can." It was nice knowing that she could still be of use to him.

"I have this monkey," he said.

"Excuse me?"

"I have this monkey. Actually, she was more like a friend than a monkey. And she died this morning, and I was wondering if you could arrange to have her freeze-dried for me."

Catching on at last, she collected herself and said: "You shit-head."

He chortled like a fifth grader who'd just dropped a salamander down her dress.

"God," she said. "I was actually picturing you with a dead monkey."

He laughed again. "I've done worse."

"I know," she said ruefully. "I remember."

She was embarrassed now, but for reasons more troubling than his dumb joke. Of all the shows he might have seen, why did it have to be today's? If he'd come a week earlier he might have caught her interview with Kitty Dukakis or, barring that, her top-rated show on crib death. What was he laughing at, anyway? Freeze-dried dogs or the way that she had made her name on television?

"How the hell are you?" he asked.

"Terrific. What brings you to town?"

"Well . . ." He seemed to hesitate. "Business mostly."

"A story or something?" She hoped like hell it wasn't AIDS. She'd grown weary of explaining the plague to visiting newsmen, most of whom came here expecting to find the smoldering ruins of Sodom.

"It's kind of complicated," he told her.

"OK," she replied, meaning: Forget I asked.

"I'd like to tell you about it, though. Are you free for lunch tomorrow?"

"Uh . . . hang on a sec, would you?" She put him on hold and waited for a good half minute before speaking to him again. "Yeah, Burke, tomorrow's fine."

"Great."

"Where do you wanna meet?"

"Well," he said, "you pick the spot, and we'll put it on my gold card."

"Only if you can deduct it."

"Of course," he said.

She thought for a moment. "There's a new place downtown. Sort of a tenderloin dive that's been upscaled."

"OK." He sounded skeptical.

"It's kind of hot right now. Lots of media people."

"Let's do it. I think I can trust you."

She wasn't quite sure how to take that, so she let it go. "It's called D'orothea's," she said. "It's on Jones at Sutter."

"Got it. Jones and Sutter. D'orothea's. What time?"

"One o'clock?"

"Great. Can't wait."

"Me too," she said. "Bye-bye."

She hung up, then stretched out on her chaise again, discovering to her amazement that her headache was gone.

The rest of the afternoon was consumed by staff conferences and a typically silly birthday party for one of the station's veteran cameramen. Just before three, somewhat later than usual, she left the building hurriedly and drove to her daughter's school in Pacific Heights.

595

Presidio Hill was a pricey "alternative" institution, which placed special emphasis on creative development and one-on-one guidance. At five, Shawna was the youngest kid in Ann's Class (that was what they called it, never kindergarten), and her classmates included, among others, the daughter of a famous rock star and the son of a celebrity interviewer for *Playboy* magazine.

The adults were "strongly urged" to participate in school functions, so the rock star's girlfriend could be found at Presidio Hill on alternate Wednesdays making pigs-in-a-blanket for the children. Mary Ann herself had been drafted once or twice for these duties, though she deeply resented the intimidation involved. For five grand a year they could damn well hire their own wienie roasters.

When she arrived at the rustic redwood building, the usual afterschool mayhem was in progress. Voyagers, Audis, and latter-day hippie vans were double, even triple, parked on Washington Street, while clumps of grownups gossiped among themselves and clucked over the artwork of their offspring.

She scanned the crowd for Shawna. This was never a simple task, since Brian dressed and delivered the kid, and you never knew what she might be wearing. Lately, egged on by the school's policy of creative dressing, Shawna had delivered one lurid fashion statement after another. Like yesterday, when she came home wearing high-top Reeboks with a tutu and tights.

"Mom," called a reedy voice among many. It was Shawna, bounding toward the car in her flouncy red dress with the big Minnie Mouse polka dots. Mary Ann approved of that one, so she relaxed a little until she caught sight of the rest: the pearls, the lipstick, the turquoise eye shadow.

"Hi, Puppy," she yelled back, wondering whether Brian, a teacher, or Shawna herself was responsible for this latest atrocity. She flung open the car door and watched nervously as her daughter left the curb. Next to her, against the sidewalk, a Yellow Cab was parked, driver at the wheel. A little girl was climbing into the passenger side. Somehow this smacked of parental neglect, and Mary Ann watched the scene with something approaching indignation.

"That's her dad," said Shawna, hopping onto the seat.

"Who?"

"Duh! That guy right there! The cabdriver." The child was getting more smartass by the day. Mary Ann gave her a menacing look. When she glanced at the cabbie again, he beamed back at her knowingly, parent to parent, and she couldn't help being impressed. How many airport runs would it take, anyway, to pay for this glorified baby-sitting service?

"His name is George," said Shawna.

"How'd you know that?"

"Solange told me."

"Solange calls him George? Instead of Daddy, you mean?"

Shawna rolled her eyes. "Lots of kids do that."

"Well, not this one. Fasten your seat belt, Puppy." Her daughter complied, making a breathless production of it. Then she said: "I call you Mary Ann."

This was clearly a gauntlet flung at her feet; she opted to kick it aside. "Right," she said, pulling out into the street.

"I do."

"Mmm."

"I called you that today at circle time."

Mary Ann shot her a glance. "You talked about me at circle time?" Why should this make her feel so uncomfortable? Did she really think Shawna was going to bad-mouth her in front of the other kids?

"We talked about TV," the child explained.

"Oh, you did?" Now she felt foolish. Shawna must have told the other kids about her famous mom.

"Nicolas says TV is bad for you."

"Well, too much TV, maybe. Puppy, did you talk about Mommy during . . . ?"

"Put on a tape," said Shawna.

"Shawna . . ."

"Well, I wanna listen to something."

"You can in a minute. Don't be so impatient."

The child cocked her head goofily and did her impression of Pee-wee Herman. "I know you are, but what am I?"

"Nice. Very funny."

Another tilt of the head. "I know you are, but what am I?"

Mary Ann glowered at her. "I got it the first time, OK?"

After a moody pause, Shawna said: "Guess what?"

"What?"

"We had quesadillas today."

"Oh, yeah? I like those, don't you?"

"Yeah. Nicolas's father made them, and Nicolas had cheddar cheese, and I had modern jack."

Modern jack. She would save that one for Brian. He loved it when Shawna said "aminal" for "animal" or otherwise flubbed a word charmingly.

"Sounds yummy," she told the child, reaching across to pop open the glove compartment. "Find a tape you like. I think there's some Phil Collins in there."

"Yuck!"

"OK, Miss Picky."

Shawna gave her an indignant look. "I'm not Miss Piggy."

"I said *picky*, silly." She smiled. "Go on. Find what you want."

After foraging for a while, Shawna settled on Billy Joel. This was one taste they shared, so they sang along together at the top of their lungs, thoroughly pleased with themselves.

> ALL YOUR LIFE IS *TIME* MAGAZINE
>   I READ IT, TOO. WHAT DOES IT MEAN?

"I like that part," said Shawna, shouting over the music.

"Me too."

> BUT HERE YOU ARE WITH YOUR FAITH AND
>   YOUR PETER PAN ADVICE
> YOU HAVE NO SCARS ON YOUR FACE AND YOU
>   CANNOT HANDLE PRESSURE PRESSURE

. . . PRESSURE . . . ONE—TWO—THREE— FOUR PRESSURE

Mary Ann gazed over at the child's animated face, the tiny hands rapping rhythmically on the dashboard. Ordinarily she welcomed this little sing-along, since it strengthened her tenuous bond with Shawna, but today, because of that damned makeup, something entirely different was happening. All she could think of was Connie Bradshaw.

She'd noticed the resemblance before, of course, but this time it was overwhelming, almost creepy, like a drag queen doing Marilyn just a little too well. She turned the volume down and spoke to Shawna calmly. "Puppy, did you have dress-up at circle time today?"

Shawna seemed to falter before saying: "No."

"Then, why did . . . ?"

"Turn it back up. This is the best part."

"In a minute."

I'M SURE YOU'LL HAVE SOME COSMIC RASH-SHUHNAL . . .

"Puppy!"

"That's my name, don't wear it out."

Mary Ann switched off the tape player. "Young lady!" It was time to play mother now—that is, to impersonate her own mother thirty years earlier. "I want you to listen when I'm talking to you."

Shawna folded her arms and waited.

"Is that my makeup you're wearing?"

"No."

"Where did you get it, then?"

"It's mine," said Shawna. "Daddy bought it for me."

"It's for kids," Brian told her calmly after dinner that evening. Shawna was in the bedroom, out of earshot, watching television.

"You've got to be kidding."

He shook his head, smiling dopily.

"Brian, that is just the sickest!"

"I know, but she's a big fan of Jem, and I figured it couldn't hurt just this once."

"Jim?"

"Jem. This rock star in a cartoon. Saturday morning."

"Oh."

"They make a whole line of cosmetics and stuff." He wasn't in the least disturbed, she realized. "It's just dress-up."

"Yeah, but if she makes a habit of it . . ."

"We won't let her."

"It just looks so tarty."

He chuckled. "OK. No more makeup."

His cavalier tone annoyed her. "I just don't want her running around looking like some kiddie-porn centerfold." Projecting morbidly, she imagined Shawna's daylight abduction, then envisioned her photograph—lipstick, eye shadow, and all—emblazoned on milk cartons across the country.

Brian rose from the table, taking their plates with him. "To tell you the truth," he said, "I thought she kinda looked like Connie."

She thought it best not to comment.

"Didn't you? With all that makeup?"

"That isn't very nice," she said.

"Why not?" said Brian. "She was her mother."

He seemed to be goading her for some reason, so she made a point of staying calm. "Maybe so," she said, "but I don't think we're trying for the total look."

"You noticed it, though?"

"A little, maybe."

"A lot," he said, "I thought."

She followed him into the kitchen and told him about Shawna and her modern jack. When they had both finished laughing, she said: "Guess who I heard from today?" She'd already decided it was best to be breezy about it. Any other approach might freight it with too much importance.

"Who?"

"Burke Andrew."

He opened the dishwasher. "No kidding?"

"Yeah. He called this morning after the show."

"Well. Long time no hear."

She tried to read his face, but he turned away and busied himself with the loading of the dishes. "He's in town, apparently," she said.

"Apparently?"

"Well, I mean, he is. We're having lunch tomorrow at D'orothea's."

It shouldn't have made her feel funny to say this, but it did. There was no reason on earth she should have included Brian in the lunch. He and Burke, after all, had never been friends, even though they'd lived for a while under the same roof. Brian had been too busy trolling for stewardesses to waste any excess energy on male bonding.

"Great," he said. "Say hello for me." She monitored this instruction for irony and couldn't find a trace. Burke might not be an issue at all, though she never could tell for sure with Brian. He had a maddening way of being hip one moment and rampantly jealous the next.

"He's here on business, I think. Sounds like he wants to dish a little television dirt."

"Ah." He closed the dishwasher door. "Should be good."

"We'll see." She didn't want to come off as too enthusiastic.

Fiddling with the dishwasher controls, Brian said: "Does he know you're famous?"

She couldn't tell if he was being snide, so she took the question straight. "He's seen the show, apparently."

He seemed to ponder something for a moment, then asked: "The one today?"

She had no intention of resurrecting those furry little bodies again. "I don't know," she lied. "He didn't say."

Brian nodded.

"Why?" she asked.

He shrugged. "Just wondered."

She started to ask if he'd watched the show, but a well-oiled defense mechanism told her to leave it alone. He'd seen it, all right, and he hadn't approved. Why give him another chance to tell her so?

Life with Harry

When Charlie Rubin died in early 1987, Michael Tolliver and Thack Sweeney had inherited his dog. They had known Harry a good deal longer than that, of course, caring for him intermittently during Charlie's third bout with pneumocystis and later boarding him at their house when it became apparent that Charlie wouldn't leave the hospital again. While Charlie was still alive, Harry had been addressed as K-Y, but Michael had found it more and more humiliating to walk through the Castro calling out the name of a well-known lubricant.

The name change, however, was only partially effective, since he couldn't go to the bank or mail a package at P.O. Plus without discovering someone who had known Harry in his former life. With no warning at all, the dog would pounce ecstatically on a perfect stranger—strange to Michael, at any rate—and this person would invariably exclaim "K-Y!" in a voice that could be heard halfway to Daly City.

Michael and Thack doted on the dog to a degree that was almost embarrassing. Neither one of them had ever planned on owning a poodle—they regarded themselves as golden retriever types—but Harry had banished their prejudices (poodlephobia, to use Thack's term) on his first visit to the house. For one thing, Charlie had always avoided those stupid poodle haircuts, keeping the dog's coat raggedly natural. With his round brown face and button nose, Harry seemed more like a living teddy bear than like a classic Fifi dog.

Or so they assured themselves.

They had lived on the hill above the Castro for over two years now. Michael's decade-long residency at 28 Barbary Lane had come to an end when he and Thack recognized their coupledom and decided to buy a place of their own. Thack, who'd been a preservationist back in Charleston, was far more keen on their home-to-be than Michael, who on first sighting the For Sale sign had regarded the place as a hopeless eyesore.

Faced with green asbestos shingles and walled with concrete block, the house had seemed nothing more than a hideous jumble of boxes, like three tiny houses nailed together at odd angles. Thack, however, had seen something quite different, hurdling the wall in a frenzy of discovery to pry away a couple of loose shingles near the foundation.

Moments later, flushed with excitement, he had announced his findings: underneath all that eisenhowering lay three original "earthquake shacks," refugee housing built for the victims of the great disaster of 1906. There had been thousands of them in the parks, he said, all rowed up like barracks; afterward people had hauled them off on drays for use as private homes.

In negotiation with the realtor, of course, they kept quiet about the house's architectural significance (much in the way the realtor had about the bum plumbing and the army ants bivouacking below the deck). They moved in on Memorial Day, 1986, christening the place with a Chinese meal, a Duraflame log, and impromptu sex in their Jockey shorts.

For the next two years they had set about obliterating the details that offended them most. Much of this was accomplished with white paint and Michael's creative planting, though Thack made good on his promise to bare the ancient wood in both the kitchen and the bedroom. When, after a season or two of rain, their new cedar shingles took on the obligatory patina of old pewter, the householders glowed with parental appreciation.

Yet to come were a new bathroom and wood-frame windows to replace the aluminum, but Michael and Thack were pressed for money at the moment and had decided to wait. Still, when roaming flea markets and garage sales, they thought nothing of splurging on an Indian blanket or a Fiesta pitcher or a mica-shaded floor lamp for the bedroom. Without ever stating it, they both seemed to realize the same thing:

If there was nesting to be done, it had better be done now.

A record hot spell had finally broken. Beyond their deck (which faced west into the sunset), the long-awaited fog tumbled into the valley like white lava. Michael stood at the rail and watched as it erased the spindly red television tower, until only its three topmost masts were left, sailing above Twin Peaks like the Flying Dutchman. He filled his lungs, held it, let it go, and breathed in again.

His potted succulents were looking parched, so he uncoiled the hose and gave them a thorough drenching, taking as always a certain vicarious pleasure in their relief. When he was through, he aimed the cooling stream into a neighbor's yard, where the scorched and curling fronds of a tree fern testified to its need. The fern, in fact, was the last patch of green in sight down there; even the luxuriant weeds of the past spring had turned to straw in the drought.

"Hey," said Thack, coming onto the deck from the kitchen. "We're rationing, remember?"

"I know." Michael turned the nozzle to mist and gave the fern a final, guilty shower to wash away the dust.

"They're gonna fine us."

He turned off the water and began to coil the hose. "I didn't take a shower this morning."

"So what?"

"So the tree fern gets my water. It evens out."

His lover turned and headed back to the kitchen. "Since it's not even *our* tree fern . . ."

"I know. OK." He followed him through the sliding glass door.

Thack opened the oven and knelt to study a bubbling casserole, pungent with shrimp and herbs. "Mrs. Bandoni says the new owners are gonna level the place."

"Figures," said Michael, sitting at the kitchen table. He could see the tree fern from here, see the empty house with its streaky windows and cardboard boxes, the fading beefcake pinup taped to the refrigerator door. The sight of the place always made him shiver a little, like a deserted hamster cage with the straw still in it.

"The foundation's bad," said Thack. "Whoever bought it will have to start from scratch."

The previous owner had been an architect or draftsman of some sort. A wiry little guy with a silvery crew cut and a fondness for jeans and sweatshirts. In the months before his death, Michael could see him at his table, hunched over his blueprints, removing his glasses, rubbing his rabbity eyes. Since his house fronted on another street, they had hardly ever spoken, except to yell neighborly things about the weather or the state of their respective gardens.

He'd been a bachelor, Michael knew, but one who seemed comfortable in his solitude. His illness only became apparent, in fact, when visitors started showing up at his house. There were older folks mostly, people who might have been relatives, arriving with fresh linens and covered dishes, sometimes in groups of three or four. Once, when the man's primroses were still in bloom, Michael looked down to see a uniformed nurse sneaking a cigarette in the garden.

"I hope," said Thack, "it's not some hideous stucco-on-plywood job."

Michael frowned at him, lost for a moment.

"The new house," said Thack.

"Oh. Oh, yeah. Who knows? Probably."

Thack closed the oven door. "Go ahead and water the damn thing, if it bothers you that much."

"No," said Michael. "You're right."

His lover stood up, wiping his hands on his Levi's. "Your mother called, by the way. She left a message on the machine."

Michael grunted. "About the weather, right?"

"C'mon."

"Well, that's usually what she says, isn't it? 'How's the weather out there?'"

"That's because she's afraid of you."

"*Afraid* of me?"

"Yeah, as a matter of fact." Thack took two Fiesta platters from the cupboard and set them on the counter. "You treat her like shit, Michael."

"*I* treat *her* like shit? When have you ever heard me say anything that could . . . ?"

"It's not what you say, it's how. The color just drains out of your voice. I can always tell when she's on the other end. You don't talk that way to anybody else."

He wondered what had brought this on. "Have you been talking to her or something?"

"No." Thack sounded faintly defensive. "Not lately."

"You talked to her at work. You told me so."

"Last week," Thack answered, searching in a drawer. "Are the napkins in the wash?"

Michael thought for a moment. "Yeah."

His lover tore off two sections of paper towel and folded them lengthwise.

"She never calls me at work," said Michael.

"Well, maybe she would, if you wouldn't be so hard on the old gal. She's trying her damnedest to hook up, Michael. She really is."

He didn't want to discuss this. If the "old gal" had made overtures of reconciliation, they hadn't come until last year, when his father had died suddenly of a heart attack. Like most country women in the South, she required a man's guidance at any cost, even if that meant making up with her hell-bound gay son in California.

"She misses you," said Thack. "I can tell you that."

"Right. That's why she calls you."

Thack dumped a handful of butter lettuce into the salad spinner. Slowly, maddeningly, a smile surfaced on his face. "Sounds to me like you're jealous."

"Oh, please!"

In point of fact, Thack and his mother had become cloyingly chummy in recent months, swapping homilies and weather reports like a pair of Baptist housewives in a sewing circle. This from the woman who had never spoken to his first lover—not even when she knew he was dying.

It was her grief, after all, that had finally made the difference, her loss that had sent her to the telephone, desperate for company. If he was jealous, he was jealous for Jon, who had asked for her blessing and never received it. But how could he ever say that to Thack?

"She's against everything you stand for," Michael said finally. "You have nothing in common at all."

Thack began to spin the lettuce. "Except you," he said.

At dinner they talked about Thack's day. He'd worked at the Heritage Foundation for almost a year now, organizing tours of historic houses. Lately, more to his taste, he'd been testifying before the Board of Permit Appeals, pleading the case of endangered buildings.

"They're dragging their asses again. It really pisses me off."

"What is it this time?" Michael asked.

"Oh . . . an Italianate villa off Clement. Fuck off, Harry. I'm not through."

The dog sat at Thack's feet, head cocked for maximum effect, licking his little brown lips.

"It's the shrimp," said Michael.

"Well, he can wait."

Michael gave the dog a stern look. "You heard him, didn't you?"

Harry skulked off, but only as far as the doorway, where he waited stoically, rigid as a temple lion.

"We're gonna lose it," said Thack. "I can tell already."

"Oh . . . the villa. That's too bad."

"It's near the nursery, you know. I stopped by around noon to see if you wanted to have lunch."

Michael nodded. "Brian told me. I was out delivering Mrs. Stonecypher's bamboo."

"Delivering?" Thack frowned. "I thought you had employees for that."

"I do, but . . . she likes me and she spends a lot of money. I make an exception in her case."

"I see." Thack nodded. "You were whoring."

Michael smiled at him. Rich people were beyond redemption in

607

Thack's view of the world—just another corrupt facet of the white, male, sexist, homophobic, corporate power structure. Even poor old Mrs. Stonecypher, with her bad hats and wobbly teeth.

"Sorry I missed you," he said. "You should call first next time."

Thack shrugged. "I didn't know. It's no big deal. I had lunch with Brian."

Michael shuddered to think what his partner and his lover found to talk about when he wasn't there. "Where'd you eat?"

"Some new place downtown. Sort of Mexican nouvelle."

"The Corona," said Michael. "We went there last week."

"It's nice."

"What did you have?"

"The grilled seafood salad."

"Oh, yeah," said Michael. "Brian had that last time."

Thack poked at his shrimp for a moment, then said: "I feel so sorry for that poor bastard."

"Brian? Why?"

"Oh . . . just the way she treats him."

Michael looked at him for a moment. "What did he tell you?"

"Not much, but it's easy enough to deduce."

"Well, stop deducing. You have no way of knowing what goes on between them."

Thack smiled at him slyly. "There in the strange twilight world of the heterosexual."

"That's not what I meant."

Thack chuckled.

"Have they had a fight or something?"

"I don't think they're together enough for that. She's always out somewhere."

"She's a public figure," said Michael, resenting the way Thack always sided with Brian. "She can't help it if people want her to do things."

"But she loves it."

"Well, what if she does? She should enjoy it. She's worked hard enough for it."

"I'm just telling what he said."

"He can be a real slug, you know. He's a helluva sweet guy, but . . ."

"What does that mean—slug?"

"He gets stuck in ruts. He likes ruts. That's why he likes the nursery so much. It doesn't challenge him any more than he wants it to. He can just coast along . . ."

"I thought you said . . ."

"I don't mean he isn't doing a good job. I just meant he isn't as ambitious as she is. I can see how it might be kind of a drag for her."

"I thought you guys got along great."

"We do. Stop changing the subject."

"Which is?"

"The fact that . . ." He stopped, not really sure what the subject was.

Realizing this, Thack smiled. "Did you see her show today? Dead dogs."

"Yes."

"Was that lower than Geraldo or what?"

"I thought it was funny, actually. Besides, she can't help what her producers decide . . ."

"I know. She can't help anything."

Michael gave him a sullen look and let the subject drop. In the long run, Thack was too much of a newcomer to fully grasp the nature of Mary Ann's personality. You had to have known her years ago to understand the way she was today.

Somehow, in spite of the immense changes in their lives, Michael continued to see them all as perennial singles—he and Brian and Mary Ann—still chasing their overblown dreams, still licking their wounds back at Barbary Lane.

But he had been gone for two years; Mary Ann and Brian, even longer. His employee, Polly Berendt, occupied his old digs on the second floor, and the rest of the house was inhabited by people whose names he hardly knew. Except for Mrs. Madrigal, of course, who seemed constant as the ivy.

He had seen the landlady just that morning, poking among the fruit stands at a sidewalk market in Chinatown. She had hugged him exuberantly and invited him and Thack to dinner the next day. He had felt a twinge of guilt, realizing how long he'd neglected her.

He mentioned this to Thack, who shared his concern.

"We'll take her some sherry," he said.

Now they lay on the sofa—Michael's back against Thack's chest, Harry at their feet—watching *Kramer vs. Kramer* after dinner. It was a network broadcast, and the censors had doctored the scene in which Dustin Hoffman and his young son are heard, one after the other, taking their morning pee.

"Can you believe that?" Thack fumed. "They cut out the sound of the pee! Those fuckers!"

Michael smiled sleepily. "Must not be in keeping with Family Values."

"Damn, that pisses me off!"

He chuckled. "So to speak."

"Well, dammit, that was a sweet scene. You can't even tell what's happening now. It's not funny anymore."

"You're right," said Michael.

"Fuckin' Reagan."

"Well . . . he's almost gone."

"Yeah, and his asshole buddy will be running things."

"Maybe not."

"You watch. Things are gonna get worse before they get better. Thack gestured toward the TV. "You wanna watch this?"

"Nah."

"Where's the clicker?"

Michael ran his hand between the corduroy cushions until he found the remote control, one of three at their command. (He had no idea what the other ones did.) Poking it, he watched the screen crackle into black, then turned over and laid his head against Thack's chest. He sighed at the fit they made, the sheer inevitability of this moment in their day.

Thack stroked Michael's hair and said: "I picked up more vacuum cleaner bags."

"Good." He patted Thack's leg.

"I'm not sure they're the *right* ones. I got confused about our model."

"Fuck it."

Thack chuckled. "You know what I've been thinking?"

"What?"

"We should just go to an ACT-UP meeting. I mean, just stop by to see what it's like."

Somehow, Michael had been expecting this. Thack's advocacy had been bubbling like a broth all week, close to overflowing. If it hadn't taken this form, it would have almost certainly taken another. An irate letter to the *Chronicle*, maybe, or a shouting match with a Muni driver.

When Michael didn't react, Thack added: "Don't you feel like kicking some butt?"

He tried to keep it light. "Can't we just hug it for a while?"

Thack was not amused. "I have to do something," he said.

"About what?"

"Everything. AZT, for one thing. How much do we pay for that shit? And Jesse Fucking Helms is gonna fix it so poor people can't even get it. And you know what those sorry bastards think? Serves 'em right, anyway. Shouldn't've been butt-fucking in the first place."

"I know," said Michael, patting Thack's leg.

"I can't believe how cold-blooded people have gotten."

Michael agreed with him, but he found his lover's anger exhausting. Now, more than ever, he needed time for the other emotions as well. So what if the world was fucked? There were ways to get around that, if you didn't make yourself a total slave to rage.

"Thack . . ."

"What?"

"Well . . . I don't understand why you're mad all the time."

His lover paused, then pecked Michael on the temple. "I don't understand why you're not."

Harry heard the kiss and scrambled frantically over their intertwined legs, whimpering like a spurned lover. "Uh-oh," said Thack. "Kiss Patrol."

They parted enough to admit the dog, then scratched him in tandem, Thack attacking the lower back, Michael attending to his head. Harry invariably left the room when they were having sex, but simple affection was too much for him to miss.

"This jealousy isn't healthy," said Michael.

"He's all right." Thack kissed the dog's neck. "Aren't you?"

Harry gave a breathy har-har in reply.

"He smells gross," said Michael.

"Is that right, Harry? Do you smell gross?"

"I'll wash him tomorrow."

Thack leaned closer to the dog's ear. "Hear that, Harry? Better head for the hills."

Soon enough, Harry did retire to the bedroom, leaving his masters to snooze on the sofa. Michael drifted off to a rising chorus of foghorns and the occasional screech of tires down in the Castro. At eleven o'clock he was jolted awake by his beeper, prickly as a needle in the darkness.

A Practicing New Yorker

For several years now the Tenderloin had been on a surprising upswing. Where formerly had been wino dives and inflatable plastic lady shops now bloomed chocolatiers and restaurants with arugula on the menu. Easily the most stylish of the new eateries was D'orothea's Grille, a postmodern fantasia with trompe l'oeil marble walls and booth dividers that looked like giant Tinker Toys.

As Mary Ann entered, her eyes made a clandestine dash to the wall behind the maître d's stand. There a row of caricatures alerted newcomers to the restaurant's more illustrious customers. Her face was still there, of course—why had she worried that it wasn't?—

sandwiched comfortably as ever between the renderings of Danielle Steel and Ambassador Shirley Temple Black.

The maître d' looked up and smiled. "There you are."

"Hi, Mickey. I'm expecting a guy . . ."

"He's already here."

"Ah. Great."

The maître d' leaned forward conspiratorially. "I put him at the banquette in the back. There's a table available in the front room, but Prue's there with Father Paddy, and I thought"—and here he winked—"it might be a little quieter back in Siberia."

She rewarded him with a rakish chuckle. "You're way ahead of me, Mickey."

"We try," he said, and smiled wickedly.

Grateful for this promise of privacy, she fled to the back, while Prue and the priest yammered away obliviously. When she reached the furthermost banquette, Burke Andrew leapt to his feet and hugged her awkwardly across the table.

"Hey," he said. "You look great."

"Thanks. Look who's talking."

He let his head wobble bashfully. She caught a glimpse of the troubled youth who had left her for a career in New York. Most of that person was gone now, with only the broad shoulders and great hair (strawberry blond and receding heroically) remaining to trigger her memories. His earnest collie face, once such a blank slate, had developed crags in becoming places.

He sank to the banquette and studied her for a moment, shaking his head slowly. "Ten years. Damn."

"Eleven," she said, sitting down.

"Shit."

She laughed.

"And you're a star now," he said. "They've got your picture on the wall and everything."

She thought it best not to know what he meant. "Huh?"

"Over there. Next to Shirley Temple."

A quick, dismissive glance at the caricature. "Oh, yeah."

"Don't you like it?"

She shrugged. "It's OK, I guess." After a beat, she added: "Shirley hates hers."

One of his gingery eyebrows leapt noticeably. "She's a friend?"

She nodded. "She lives here, you know."

OK, maybe "friend" was stretching it, but Shirley had been on the show once, and Mary Ann had chatted with her extensively at the French Impressionist exhibit at the De Young. Anyway, she was certain the ambassador wouldn't approve of that pouty-faced portrait with the dashiki and the cigarette. Mary Ann had told D'or as much when they hung the damned thing.

Burke's eyes roamed the room. "I like this."

She nodded. "It's kind of a media joint."

"Yeah. So you said."

At the moment, she realized, the wattage of the lunching luminaries was embarrassingly dim, so she made do with the material at hand. "That showy blonde," she muttered, nodding toward the front room, "is Prue Giroux."

He had obviously never heard of her.

"She was in *Us* last month. She took some orphans to Beijing on a peace mission."

Still no reaction.

"She's a socialite, actually. Kind of a publicity hound."

He nodded. "How 'bout the priest?"

"Father Paddy Starr. He has a show at my station. *Honest to God.*"

"Honest to God, he has a show? Or that's the name of it?"

"That's the name of it."

He smirked.

She smirked back, feeling a little queasy about it. She hated how rubey all this sounded. Burke, after all, was a practicing New Yorker, and the breed had a nasty way of regarding San Francisco as one giant bed-and-breakfast inn—cute but really of no consequence. She made herself a curt mental note not to gossip about the locals.

"How's Betsy?" she asked, changing the subject.

"Brenda."

"Oh. Sorry. I knew it was B." She mugged and rolled her head from side to side. "Burke and Brenda, B and B."

"She's doing fine. Got her hands full with the kids, of course."

Wouldn't she just, thought Mary Ann.

"She wanted to come with me this time, but Burke junior came down with flu, and Brenda didn't trust the housekeeper to manage without her."

"God, I know what you mean!" She seized his wrist lightly. "We have this Vietnamese woman. She's really dear, but she can't, for the life of her, tell the difference between Raid and Pledge!"

His laughter seemed a little strained, and she worried that the remark had come off as racist.

"Of course," she added, releasing his wrist, "I can only speak one language myself, so . . . anyway, her family had a rough time over there, so we figured it was worth a little extra trouble."

"You have a kid or two of your own, don't you?"

"One. How'd you know?"

His smirk came back to life. "I saw you with her on *Entertainment Tonight*."

"Oh . . . you saw that?" It was good to know, anyway, that he'd seen her on national TV. At least now she knew he didn't think of her as completely local. Even if that *ET* segment had been about local talk-show hosts.

"She's a cute little girl," he said.

For an unsettling instant she flashed on Shawna's tarty makeup of the day before. "Well, she's a lot bigger now, of course. That was over three years ago."

"Really?"

"Yeah."

"I bet she looks more like you than ever."

She smiled at him benignly, hoping he wouldn't make a big deal out of this. "She's not my biological daughter, actually. We adopted her."

"Oh. Yeah." He did his bashful wobble again. "I guess I knew that."

"I don't see how you could, really."

"Well, maybe not."

"Her mother was a friend of mine. Or someone I knew, anyway. She died a few days after Shawna was born. She left a note asking me and Brian to take care of her."

"How wonderful."

"Yeah."

"That's a great story. She's a lucky little girl."

She shrugged. "Brian was a little more crazy about the idea than I was."

This unraveled him noticeably. "Still . . . you must . . . I mean, I'm sure it took some getting used to, but . . ."

She smiled to put him out of his misery. "I'm learning," she said. "It's not terrible. It's OK, actually. Most of the time."

"How old is she?"

"Oh . . . five or six."

It took him forever to realize she was joking. "C'mon," he said finally.

"She'll be six next April."

"OK. There." He nodded to fill the dead air. "And . . . Brian?"

"He's forty-four," she answered, though she found the question a little weird.

"No." He laughed. "I meant, who is he?"

"Oh, I thought you knew. Brian Hawkins."

It didn't register.

"He was upstairs at Mrs. Madrigal's."

Now he was nodding, slowly. "The guy who lived on the roof?"

"Right. That's him."

"Well, I'll be damned!"

His apparent amazement unsettled her. "You remember him, huh?"

"I remember how much you hated him."

"Excuse me?" She gave him the sourest look she could muster.

"Sorry," he said. "I mean . . . you know, disapproved of him . . ."

She was about to take him on, when the waiter appeared. "You folks had a chance to look at the menu yet?"

"I'll take the grilled tuna," Mary Ann told him crisply. "And some orange-flavored Calistoga."

Burke cast a cursory glance at the menu, then flapped it shut. "Sounds great."

"Same thing?" asked the waiter.

"Same thing."

"You got it." The waiter spun on his heels and left.

"OK," said Burke. "Let me start over, if I can."

"Let's just leave it."

"No. That sounded terrible."

"I knew what you meant, though. He was a real womanizer then."

"I liked him, though. I thought he was nice."

She realigned her silverware against the salmon tablecloth. "He is nice. He puts up with a lot, believe me."

He smiled gently. "C'mon."

She shrugged. "He does. It isn't easy being married to Mary Ann Singleton."

He blinked at her for a moment, then asked: "When did you start seeing him?"

"Oh . . . a year or so after you left." Make that a week, she told herself. No, make it four days. She remembered all too well the weepy night she had headed up to Brian's room with a joint of Maui Wowie and a bottle of rotgut Chianti. He'd been dating Mona Ramsey at the time, but he'd been ready and willing to offer consolation.

How odd it was to sit here now with the man who had caused her all that pain and feel nothing but a sort of pleasant sense of shared history. She could scarcely remember their passion, much less reconstitute it for a moment's titillation.

"How's Mrs. Madrigal?" he asked.

"She's OK, I guess. I saw her down at Molinari's a month or

617

so ago." She smiled and shook her head. "Just as dear and loony as ever."

Burke smiled back.

"Brian and I moved out of the house after we got Shawna. It had a certain funky charm, I guess, but it wasn't much of a place to raise a kid."

"What about Michael and . . . Jon, was it?"

She nodded solemnly. "Jon died of AIDS in '82."

"Damn."

"I know."

"Is Michael OK?"

Another nod. "He's got the virus, but so far he's been fine."

"Good. Thank God."

"He has a new boyfriend," she told him. "They bought a house in the Castro."

"What does Michael do now?"

"He runs a nursery out on Clement."

"No kidding?"

"Yeah. He and Brian run it together, actually."

He seemed to like this idea. "All in the family, huh?"

"Yeah."

He nodded slowly, absorbing their lost decade with a look of sanguine acceptance. "You look great," he said finally.

Fine, she thought, but isn't this where we came in?

This particular waiter knew she didn't like a chatty presentation, so their tuna arrived without fanfare. Burke took a few bites and said: "I'm producing now. For Teleplex. Did you know that?"

"Sure," she said. "Doesn't everybody?"

He chuckled. "No way."

"Well, I do."

He focused on his plate as he composed his words. "I'm developing a new morning talk show. Out of New York. We think there's a real market for something more home-oriented and . . . more intelligent than what's currently being offered."

"You got that right. People have had it with this tabloid shit. There's bound to be a backlash."

"I think so," he said, still addressing his tuna. "I think we can *make* it happen, in fact. We've got the backing, frankly, and some very real interest from the networks. What we need now is the right host. Someone who knows how to chat with, say, Gore Vidal and yet still be lively in a kitchen segment."

Mary Ann's fork froze in mid-descent. *Don't*, she warned herself, jump to any hasty conclusions. Maybe he just wants your advice. Maybe he . . .

"What do you think?" His eyes met hers at last.

"About what?"

"Doing it."

She set the fork down and waited for a count of three. "Me?"

"Yes."

"As host?"

"Yes."

It took all the discipline at her command to conceal her excitement. "Burke . . . I'm tremendously flattered . . ."

"But?"

"Well, for starters, I have my own show."

"Right. Local."

Stung, she composed herself, then said coolly: "This is one of the most sought-after markets in the country."

He gave her a patient smile. "I know you know the difference."

"Well, maybe so, but . . ."

"And I think you'll find the money is a whole lot better."

"That isn't the point," she said calmly.

"Well, what is? Tell me what I have to do?"

He was practically begging. God, how she loved this. "I have a home here, Burke, a family."

"And they wouldn't want to move?"

"That's part of it, yes."

"OK." He made a little gesture of concession with his hands. "What's the other part?"

619

"When have you even seen me, anyway? I mean, the show."

"Lots of times. On my way through the city. I've never seen you when you weren't brilliant." He gave her an engaging little smile. "We can even keep the name, if you want. I like the sound of 'Mary Ann in the Morning.'"

She was thinking more along the lines of just plain "Mary Ann."

"Look," he added, "if it's gonna be no, fine. But I want to make damn sure you know exactly what's being offered here."

"I think I do," she said.

"Then what can I tell you?"

"Well . . . what you think I can offer, for one thing."

He gave her a disbelieving look. "C'mon."

"I mean it."

"OK." He thought for a moment. "You're not an automaton. You listen to people. You react. You laugh when you feel like laughing, and you say what's on your mind. And you've got this great . . . Cleveland thing going."

She drew back as if he'd hit her with a mackerel. *"Cleveland thing?"*

He grinned maddeningly. "Maybe that was the wrong way to put it . . ."

"I've spent *years* making sure Cleveland was gone forever."

He shook his head. "Didn't work."

"Well, thanks a helluva lot."

"And you're lucky it didn't. That naïveté is the best thing you've got going for you. Look, c'mon . . . where would Carson be without Nebraska?"

With a private shiver, she realized that she could be on Carson in a matter of months, chatting chummily about her meteoric rise to fame.

"So how was it?" asked a throaty female voice, taking Mary Ann by surprise.

"D'or . . . hi. Yummy, as usual. Burke, this is our hostess, D'orothea Wilson." She looked especially elegant today, Mary Ann thought, in a mauve silk blouse and gabardine slacks.

"This is great," said Burke, indicating the remains of his tuna. "Especially the peanut butter sauce."

D'or nodded. "I've been making that one at home for years." She looked at Mary Ann and smiled wryly. "DeDe and the kids are sorta pissed that I went public with it."

"Is she here today?"

D'or shook her head. "Not till two."

"Well, tell her I said hi, OK? It's been a while since we've talked."

"You bet," said D'or, and she sailed off to the front room on her proprietorial rounds.

"She's a beauty," said Burke.

"Yeah. She used to be a model. She and her lover escaped from Jonestown just before everybody . . . you know, drank the Kool-Aid. They hid out in Cuba for three years."

"My God."

She enjoyed his amazement. "Yeah. I broke the story, actually."

"On your show?"

"No. Earlier. When I was still hosting the afternoon movie. Back in '81. It's how I got my start."

"They made you a reporter so you could break it?"

"No."

"Then . . . ?"

She shrugged and gave him an enigmatic smile. "I just broke it during the afternoon movie."

"Uh-huh" was all he could manage.

"It was just a local thing. I doubt if you would've heard about it in New York."

He caught the irony and narrowed his eyes at her. "When did you get to be so dangerous?"

"Who, me?" she replied. "Little ol' me from Cleveland?"

Some Rather Exciting News

The velvety fog which arrived that evening had sketched a halo around the streetlight at the foot of the Barbary steps. Thack stopped beneath it and muttered, "Shit."

"What?" said Michael.

"We forgot to get sherry."

Michael's guilt flared up again. After several months' absence, he hated showing up at Mrs. Madrigal's house without some reassuring talisman of his affection. Gazing up the impossible slope of Leavenworth, he mused aloud. "There's a mom and pop up at the top there."

"Forget it," said his lover. "We can send her some flowers tomorrow."

"Will you help me remember?"

"Of course," said Thack.

When they reached the eucalyptus grove at the top of the steps, a cat shot past them on the path, flashing its tail like a broadsword. Michael called to it seductively, but the creature merely spat at them and bounded off into the mist.

"Carpetbagger," he yelled after it.

Thack gave him a funny look.

"He's from there," Michael explained, gesturing toward the new condo complex at the head of the lane. It was pale green and postmodern, with security gates and sunken garbage cans and buzzers you could hear for miles. Most of the eucalyptus grove had been sacrificed to make room for it.

Beyond the complex, where the path narrowed and the shrubbery grew wild, lay the real Barbary Lane, a dwindling Bohemia of shingled lodges and garbage cans that weren't ashamed to stand up and be counted. As they opened the lych-gate at Number 28, the smell of pot roast wafted across the courtyard from the landlady's kitchen window.

When she buzzed them into her inner sanctum, the place reassured Michael with its constancy—that familiar, immutable hodge-podge of dusty books and dustier velvet. She greeted them effusively in a plum-colored kimono, a pair of ivory chopsticks thrust into the silvery tangle of her hair.

"Are you smoking?" she asked Michael.

He pretended to examine his extremities. "I dunno, am I?"

"Now you mustn't make fun of my only sacrament." She thrust a plate of joints into Thack's hands. "Here, dear. *You* corrupt him. My biscuits are burning." She spun on her heels and sailed back to the kitchen, all fluttering silk.

Thack smiled at the histrionic exit, then offered the plate to Michael.

Michael relented after only a moment's hesitation. This was a special occasion, after all.

When the landlady returned, he and Thack were both thoroughly buzzed, deep in the embrace of her worn-shiny damask sofa.

"Well," she said, taking the armchair, "I have some rather exciting news."

"Really?" said Thack.

She beamed at them both, one at a time, heightening the suspense. "I'm going away," she said.

Michael felt an unexpected stab of anxiety. *Going away? Moving away?*

His distress must have been evident, for she made a hasty amendment. "Just for a month or so."

"A vacation, you mean?" Thack looked just as amazed.

She answered with a wide-eyed nod, her hands clasping her knees. Apparently she was amazed too. Up to now she'd been the world's most committed homebody.

"Well," said Michael, "congratulations."

"Mona wants me to meet her in Greece. And since I never get time with my darling daughter, I thought . . ."

"Greece?"

"Yes, dear."

"Lesbos?"

The landlady's eyes widened. "She's told you about it?"

"Well, not lately, but she's been talking about it for years."

"Well, she's going this time. She's rented a villa, and she's invited her doddering old parent."

"That's great," said Thack.

Michael was already imagining the scenario. Ol' frizzy-haired Mona, sullen and horny in some smoky taverna. Mrs. Madrigal holding court in her oatmeal linen caftan, doing that Zorba dance as the spirit moved her.

"I can hardly take it in." The landlady sighed contentedly. "The land of Sappho."

Michael snorted. "And about a zillion women who go there looking for Sappho. I don't suppose she mentioned that?"

"She did," said Mrs. Madrigal.

"It's practically a pilgrimage."

"Yes."

"She said there are so many dykes there at the height of the season that it looks like the Dinah Shore Open."

Mrs. Madrigal gave him a look. "I think you've made your point, dear."

"Of course, I'm sure they've got men too."

"Yes," came the dry reply. "I'm sure they do."

"When do you leave?" asked Thack.

"Oh . . . early next week."

Michael wasn't expecting this. Nor was he expecting the mild anxiety that swept over him. Why on earth should this bother him? It was only a vacation. "Not much time to pack," he said lamely.

She seemed to be searching his face for clues.

"Of course, you won't need much," he added.

"I'm not sure I know *how* to pack. I haven't been off Russian Hill for years."

"All the more reason you should go," said Thack.

Michael asked: "Isn't it hot there?"

"Warm," she replied.

"But you hate the heat."

"Well, it's dry heat, at least."

"They won't have dope," he reminded her.

"Hey," said Thack, looking at Michael. "Stop being such a wet blanket."

Michael shrugged. "I just thought she should know."

At dinner their talk drifted to Mary Ann and Brian, who apparently hadn't visited the landlady since Christmas.

"They've both been really busy," Michael assured her, provoking a skeptical sneer from Thack, who was always prepared to believe the worst about Mary Ann.

Mrs. Madrigal fussed with a wisp of hair at her temple. "I'd be delighted to take Shawna for them. Brian hasn't asked me to sit for ages."

"Well," said Michael, feeling uncomfortable, "she's in kindergarten now, of course. That takes care of a lot of it."

"Yeah," said Thack.

The landlady bit her lip and nodded. "More potatoes, dear?"

Thack shook his head and patted his stomach. "I'm stuffed."

"There's lots more pot roast in the kitchen."

"I'm fine. Really."

"Michael?"

"Well . . ."

"Ah, he who hesitates . . ."

He smiled at her, abandoning the pretense of this week's diet.

"Come with me," she said, beckoning him toward the kitchen. And then to Thack: "Excuse us, will you, dear?"

In the kitchen she hovered a little too cheerily over the roast. "Still like the crispy part?"

"Sure. Whatever."

As she carved, her eyes remained fixed on her labors. "Should I be doing this, dear?"

"What?"

"Leaving."

"Of course," he said. "Why not?"

"Well . . . if everything's not all right with you . . ."

"Everything is fine," he said. "Don't you think I'd tell you?"

"Well, I'd certainly hope . . ."

He rolled his eyes. "I'll come yelling. Trust me."

She took her time arranging the slab on his plate. "I'll be gone for a whole month."

"Will you stop it!"

She set down the serving fork and wiped her hands on a dish towel. "Forgive me."

"Don't apologize."

"I know it's irrational, but it's all I've thought about ever since . . ."

"Don't I look all right?"

She cupped her hand against his cheek. "You look wonderful. As usual."

The intensity of her gaze embarrassed him, so he looked away. "Mona says it's a beautiful island. They've only had an airport for five years or something."

"Mmm." Her hand slid away, and she busied herself with dishes in the sink.

"Leave those," he said. "I'll get them later."

"You could come with us," she said, spinning around.

"Huh?"

"To Lesbos. I know Mona would love that."

He smiled at her indulgently. "I've got a business to run. And a house to pay for."

Thack appeared in the doorway, holding his plate. "Is it too late to change my mind?"

"Of course not," said the landlady.

Michael stood aside while she heaped meat on Thack's plate. She seemed just as relieved as he that Thack had come along to put an end to their awkwardness.

● ● ●

They were washing dishes, the three of them, when someone rapped on the front door. Before the landlady could finish drying her hands, Polly Berendt had loped into the kitchen. "Oh, hi," she said, seeing Michael and Thack. Then she turned to Mrs. Madrigal: "I was on my way out, and I thought you could use this." She unzipped a pocket on her black leather jacket and produced a check, obviously for the rent. "Sorry it's late."

The landlady tucked this offering into the sleeve of her kimono. "No trouble at all, dear."

Awkwardly, Polly rubbed a palm against a denimed thigh. "Well, I didn't mean to interrupt or anything."

"You aren't interrupting. We've finished our dinner. Come sit with us."

"Thanks. I can't." She looked at Michael. "I'm meeting some friends at Francine's."

"Oh," chirped the landlady. "Do I know her?"

"It's a bar," Polly explained.

Michael couldn't resist. "Guess where Mrs. Madrigal's going."

Polly looked faintly suspicious. "Where?"

"Lesbos."

"Uh . . . you mean . . . ?"

"The island," Thack put in. "Where Sappho's from."

Polly nodded vaguely.

"Don't tell me you haven't heard of her," said Michael.

"Well, of course I've *heard* of her. I'm just not up on my mythology."

"Sappho wasn't mythological."

"Hey," Thack told him, "lay off."

"Yeah," said Polly.

Mrs. Madrigal was frowning now. "If you children are going to quarrel . . ."

Michael shook his head reproachfully at Polly. "How can you call yourself a dyke?"

His employee heaved a sigh and shifted her weight to her other

627

hip. "I don't call myself one. I *am* one. I didn't have to take a course in it, you know."

"And that," said Michael, keeping a straight face, "is what's wrong with the young people of today."

Polly groaned. Thack slid his arm along Michael's shoulder and gave him a vigorous shake. "Such an old poop."

"Indeed," said Mrs. Madrigal. "And such a short memory."

"What do you mean?"

"Well . . . if I'm not mistaken, dear, I had to explain Ronald Firbank to you."

Michael frowned at her. "You did?"

She nodded.

"You couldn't have."

"I think so."

"Well . . . Firbank is much more obscure than Sappho."

"Now," said the landlady, dispensing with the subject as she turned her attention to Polly, "will you be all right while I'm gone?"

Polly shrugged. "Sure."

"I doubt you'll need heat, but if you do and it goes on the fritz, there's a knob on the furnace you can jiggle."

Polly nodded. "I remember."

"I'm leaving the extra keys with the Gottfrieds on the third floor, so you can buzz them if you lose yours."

"OK. Thanks."

"Oh . . . if you could keep an eye out for Rupert. I think he's eating with the Treachers these days, but I keep some kitty food for him just in case. It's in the cupboard here. I'll give you a key before I leave."

Hearing all this, Michael felt old and faintly alienated, like some decrepit alumnus who returns to his campus to find that undergraduate life has gone on without him. Who were these people, anyway—these Gottfrieds and Treachers who were privy now to the age-old mysteries of the lane?

He realized, too, that he was slightly jealous of Polly in her newfound role as junior lieutenant at 28 Barbary Lane. This was irrational, of course—it was he, after all, who had chosen to move away—but the feeling gnawed at him just the same.

When he and Thack left that evening, Mrs. Madrigal took their arms like a dowager duchess and walked them down the foggy lane to the top of the steps. The very smell of this ferny place, pungent with earth and eucalyptus, released a torrent of memories, and Michael felt perilously capable of tears.

"Now listen," said the landlady, as she released them for their descent. "Let's do something fun before I leave."

"You bet," said Thack.

Mrs. Madrigal tugged on Michael's sleeve. "How about you, young man?"

"Sure." Michael avoided her gaze.

"Make him call," she told Thack. "He'll forget."

"I won't forget," said Michael, and he hurried down the steps before she could see his face.

Well Enough Alone

So far, Brian realized, a whole day had passed without a peep out of Mary Ann about her lunch date with Burke Andrew. He had almost brought it up himself the night before, but something about her skittery, overpolite demeanor told him to leave well enough alone. If there was still something left between her and Burke, he didn't want to know about it.

This was paranoia, of course, but what could you do?

It was a clear blue evening, and he was heading home in his Jeep. The ivory towers of Russian Hill had gone golden in the sunset. All things considered, he had plenty to feel golden about himself, so this nagging insecurity would have to stop.

If anything, he decided, he should feel reassured by her be-havior. The reunion had obviously been so uneventful that she had simply forgotten to mention it. What's more, if something *had* clicked between the two of them, she would have known better than to draw attention to the situation by keeping quiet; she would have mentioned it casually and let the subject drop.

He had put the matter behind him when he arrived at the twenty-third floor of The Summit.

"Yo," he hollered, coming into the living room. The slanting sun cast a sherry-colored light on the carpet, where several dozen of Shawna's dolls were arrayed face-down in pristine rows. "I'm home, people."

His daughter emerged from the bedroom and stood scratching her butt. "Hi, Daddy." In her other hand she held the left foot of another doll.

"Hi, Puppy. What's this?"

"I'm giving them away."

"You are?"

"Yes." She knelt and placed the doll next to the others, solemnly arranging its limbs. "To the homeless."

"Was that your idea?" He was impressed.

"Mostly. Mostly mine and partly Mary Ann's."

"Well, that's wonderful. Only not all of 'em, OK?"

"Don't worry." She patted the doll's dress into place. "I'm only giving away the ugly ones."

He nodded. "Good thinking." Then he touched the tip of her nose. "You're a regular Mother Teresa."

In the kitchen his wife was shelling peas, looking raw-boned and Sally Fieldish in her Laura Ashley apron. When he kissed the nape of her neck, he caught a whiff of her ripe six o'clock smell and felt totally, stupidly, in love with her.

"Would you please tell me," he said, "what our daughter is doing?"

"I know." She gave him a rueful look over her shoulder. "It looks like Jonestown out there."

He popped one of the raw peas into his mouth and munched on it as he leaned against the counter. "You sure it's a good idea?"

She shrugged. "Why not?"

"I dunno. What if she misses one? Remember how she was when we threw out her banky?"

"She wants to do this, Brian. It's a rite of passage. She's getting off on it."

"I know, but if she . . ."

"If we'd listened to you, she'd still be sucking on that damn banky."

"OK. You're right."

"She's keeping her nice dolls, anyway."

"Fine."

"Whatcha want for potatoes?" she asked. "Sweet or new?"

"Uh . . . sweet."

"With baby marshmallows?"

He gave her a skeptical glance. "Since when have you bought baby marshmallows?"

She shrugged. "If you don't want 'em . . ."

"Oh, I want 'em. I just thought you said they were gross and Middle American."

She gave him a feisty glance and continued shelling. "Want me to help with that?" he asked.

"No, thanks. I like having something to do with my hands. It soothes me."

He moved behind her and nuzzled her neck again. "Do you need soothing?"

"No," she said. "I just meant . . . it gives me something manual to do."

"Mmm." He nipped at her flesh. "I know something manual you can do."

She giggled. "Go set the table."

"Let's eat in front of the set."

"OK. Nothing's on, though."

"Sure there is. *Cheers.* Two shows in a row."

"What else?"

"Well . . . Michael loaned us *The Singing Detective.*"

"No, thank you."

"It's Dennis Potter."

"Brian, I don't wanna watch some old guy having psoriasis while I'm having dinner."

"You did a show on it last month."

"All the more reason."

"You're hard, woman," he said, and pinched her butt.

She gave him a push toward the door. "Go play with Shawna. Maybe after she's in bed . . ."

"Well, not if you don't . . ."

"Scoot. I've got shrimp to stuff."

"You do?"

"Hey," she said, mugging at his amazement. "I'm a Total Woman."

She hadn't stuffed shrimp for years.

In the living room he sat on the floor and listened as Shawna recited—a little too cheerfully, perhaps—the deficiencies of her soon-to-be-homeless dolls.

"This one doesn't talk anymore."

"Oh, yeah?"

"And this one has dumb hair. And this one I hate."

"You don't hate it, Puppy."

"Yes I do. And this one has a really funny smell."

Brian frowned, then sniffed the doll. The odor nipped his nostrils like tiny fangs.

"Pedro peed on her," Shawna explained.

"Who?"

"The Sorensens' iguana."

"Great." He returned the doll to its resting place.

"Can we get a iguana?"

"No way."

"I'd take care of him."

"Yeah. Right."

"I would."

He thought for a moment, then picked up the reeking doll. "I think we'd better retire this one, OK?"

"What do you mean?"

"Throw it out."

"Why?"

"Because, Puppy, if it smells bad to us, it'll smell just as bad to some other little girl."

"Uh-uh." Shawna, miraculously, shook her head and scratched her butt at the same time. "Not if she's homeless."

"Yes it would. Trust me on this, Puppy."

His daughter gave him a blank look. "Whatever."

"C'mon," he said, taking her hand. "Let's go help Mommy set the table."

The first time he'd seen *The Singing Detective*, Mary Ann had been off networking at a cocktail party.

"It's amazing," he told her now, back in the kitchen. "This ugly ol' guy is in bed in the hospital, with like crooked teeth and this craggy-ass face, and he opens his mouth to sing and out comes 'It Might As Well Be Spring.' Only with like a crooner's voice—you know, whoever sang it originally—and with all the orchestration and everything."

"I don't get it," said Mary Ann.

"Me either," said Shawna.

"You will when you see it," he told his wife.

She wasn't convinced. "Not if it takes six hours."

"Well . . . we can watch it a little bit at a time."

"Forget it," said Shawna.

He turned to his daughter and tickled her under the arms. "You're not watching it, anyway."

The child squirmed, giggling. "Yes I am."

"Nope. You're watching *Cosby* in your room."

"Says who?"

"Says me. And Freddy!" He stiffed his fingers into a claw and clamped it on the back of her head, getting a squeal out of her.

Mary Ann frowned at him. "Brian . . ."

"What?"

"That isn't funny."

"Oh . . . OK." He let the claw wilt, then winked at Shawna. "Mommy's making us sweet potatoes with teeny marshmallows."

"Yummy," said Shawna.

"Why do you think she did that?"

Shawna shrugged.

"He's a child-molester, you know," his wife said.

He glanced at her. "Who?"

"Freddy. In that movie."

"Yeah. OK." He turned back to Shawna. "You think it was because we were good all week?"

"They've made a total hero of him. He's got his own posters, even. It's disgusting."

"I guess it is," he said.

"We're doing a show on it, actually."

He nodded, having guessed as much already.

"I like him," said Shawna.

Mary Ann frowned at her. "Who?"

"Freddy."

"No you don't," she said. "You do not like him."

"Yes I do."

"Shawna." Mary Ann shot him a rueful look. "See?" she said.

"I think he's funny," said Shawna.

Brian gave his wife a glance that said: Lighten up. "She thinks he's funny."

"Right." Mary Ann dumped a handful of peas into a saucepan. "A child-molester."

"You want wine with the meal?" he asked.

"Sure. Whatever."

He went to the refrigerator and removed a bottle of sauvignon blanc, transferring it to the freezer so it would chill the way they liked it. Seeing Shawna wander off again, he sat down on the stool at the butcher-block island. "I meant to ask you," he said as nonchalantly as possible. "How was your lunch with Burke yesterday?"

"Oh." It took her a moment. "Fine."

He nodded. "Get all caught up?"

"Mmm. More or less."

"He still . . . married and all?"

She studied him a moment, then gave him a slow, honeyed smirk. "You're a silly man."

On its own, his eyebrow did something suggestive of Jack Nicholson in *The Shining*. "Oh, yeah?"

Her eyes returned to the sweet potato she was slicing. "I knew you were gonna get like this."

"Hey," he said, shrugging. "What way have I gotten? It was a simple question."

"OK, then . . . Yes, he is still married. Yes, he still has two kids."

"How does he look?"

"What do you want me to say?" she said. "Something really disparaging so you won't be insecure?"

"That would be good."

She smiled. "You're such a mess."

"C'mon. Give it a shot. Has his ass gone froggy on him?"

She hooted, so he sidled up behind her and wrapped his arms around her waist. "You used to like him a lot."

"How do you know?"

"Hey," he said, "I was there, remember? I saw you guys together all the time."

She rotated in his arms and raked the hair above his ears with her fingertips. "Did Michael make a big deal about this lunch or something?"

"I didn't tell him," he said. "Did you?"

"No. Why would I do that?"

He shrugged.

"And what could possibly make you think that after eleven years I would even . . . ?"

"Nothing," he said. "You're right. I'm a silly man."

Her eyes surveyed his with optometrical attention to detail. She gave him a dismissive rap on the butt and turned back to her sweet potatoes.

"If you wanna know the truth," she said, chopping away, "he's gotten kind of prosaic."

"How so?"

"I dunno. Too serious and dedicated. Wrapped up in his career."

"Which is?"

"Television," she replied. "Producing."

"Small world."

"He's nice, though. He was really concerned when I told him Michael was positive." She paused. "Actually, we spent most of the time talking about that."

"They were close, huh?"

"Well, fairly. He asked if we could all get together sometime this week."

"Oh, yeah? With Michael, you mean?"

She nodded. "If you don't want to, of course . . ."

"No. That's fine."

"I think you'd get along with him great."

"I thought you said he was prosaic."

She rolled her eyes. "I meant . . . about his work. Is Wednesday a good night?"

"I dunno," he said. "I haven't checked the book lately." By this he meant *their* book, of course, as opposed to his or hers. For years now, at her instigation, they had maintained three appointment books at home. It had saved them a world of trouble.

"We're free," she said. "Nguyet's available too." Moments later she added: "Probably."

Hauling in the maid sounded a little too grand to him. "We can do it without her, can't we?"

"We could," she said. "But it's five for dinner . . . six counting Puppy . . . and somebody's gotta dish it out. I just thought it would be more convenient."

"I'll cook, then. I'll make my paella."

"That's sweet, but . . ."

"Hey," he said. "It was a big hit last time."

"I know that, but I want us all to be together. What's the point in doing this if you're holed up in the kitchen with the clams?"

"OK," he said.

"You wanna ask Michael, or shall I?"

"Why don't you?" he said. "He sees me all day. I think it would mean more. He hasn't heard from you for a while."

She nodded and lifted the receiver of the wall phone.

His paranoia raged away in silence.

Dance with Me

Michael hung up the phone and went to the bathroom, where Thack sat naked in the empty tub, shampooing Harry. Sleek as a sewer rat in his coat of lather, Harry crooned softly in protest as Thack turned on the hand spray and rinsed the poodle's rump.

"Yes," said Michael, talking to Harry. "You're a good boy. What a good boy you are!"

"You should see the fleas," said Thack.

"I bet."

"We'll have to bomb the house, I'm afraid."

Michael had expected this. As much as he pretended otherwise, Thack loved nothing better than "bombing the house." This adamant antimilitarist turned into Rambo incarnate when there were fleas to be annihilated.

"Who was that on the phone?"

"Mary Ann."

Predictably, Thack winced.

Michael lowered the toilet seat cover and sat down. "We're invited to dinner on Wednesday."

Thack lifted Harry's head and sprayed around his neck. "What brought this on?"

The implication was that Mary Ann had been keeping her distance lately. Fearing the truth of this, Michael didn't bother to argue. "An old boyfriend's back in town. I think she thinks it might get heavy if it was just the three of them."

"Which old boyfriend is this?"

"The one she met on the *Pacific Princess*. Who broke the story about the cannibal cult at Grace Cathedral."

"Oh, yeah."

"He's OK, actually. I mean, he was ten years ago."

"He'd have to be," said Thack. "He got the hell away from her."

Michael was tired of this kind of sniping. "He didn't get away from her. He got a job offer in New York. He asked her to come with him, but she didn't want to leave San Francisco."

Thack nodded. "Too busy conquering it, no doubt."

Michael stood up. "I'll call her and cancel."

"No."

"If there's gonna be a scene . . ."

Thack flicked water at him. "Sit down. Don't be such a prima donna."

Michael sat down.

"Can't I just piss and moan a little?"

"If you pick a fight . . ."

"Who says I'm gonna pick a fight? Brian'll be there. I like him."

Harry made a scramble for the side of the tub, his nails clicking frantically against the porcelain. Thack scooped him up and resumed rinsing.

"He doesn't like it too warm," said Michael.

"I know."

"And don't hit his balls with the spray. He hates that."

Thack laughed. "Yes, Alice."

Michael gave him a dirty look.

"Well, you sounded like her," said his lover. "Just for a minute there."

"Great."

"Everybody's gotta sound like somebody."

"Well, tell me what I'm doing, so I can fix it."

638

Thack smiled. "That wouldn't be the worst thing in the world."

The hell it wouldn't. Homebody or not, he was damned if he was going to turn into his mother.

"Hand me Harry's towel," said Thack.

This was a frayed blue beach towel bearing the logo of All-Australian Boy, a sentimental relic of Michael's tanning days at Barbary Beach. When his heart had still been hungry, he could spend an entire afternoon just getting his body ready for the night.

He snatched the towel off the shelf above the toilet and gave it to Thack. "Let's go somewhere," he said.

"When?"

"Tonight."

"Like where?"

"I dunno. The Rawhide II?"

"Fine by me." Thack wrapped the towel around Harry, then set him down on the floor and gave him a brisk rubdown under the terry cloth. "What brought this on?"

"Nothing," said Michael. "I just thought it might be fun."

"Oh."

"We hardly ever go out."

Thack peered up at him wryly. "That's what I get for calling you Alice."

They'd been talking about going for ages. Charlie Rubin had been there several times in the month before his death and had sent back glowing reports. Michael and Thack had planned on going with Polly and Lucy, but Polly had dumped Lucy—only hours before the date, in fact—for the first runner-up in the Ms. International Leather competition. The new girlfriend preferred S & M to C & W, so Polly renounced the faith, and the boys were left dateless for the hoedown. To Michael's unending glee, Polly had spent the next three weeks being plied with jewelry for her clitoris.

When they arrived at the Rawhide II, a dance class was in progress. The participants were in street clothes, pleasant looking but unextraordinary, as if the commuters on a BART train had acted

639

on a sudden urge to waltz with one another. Fat and skinny, short and tall, couples of every configuration swirled around the room in a counterclockwise tide to the music of Randy Travis.

I'm gonna love you forever—
Forever and ever, Amen:
As long as old men live to talk about the weather—
As long as old women live to talk about old men.

Grinning uncontrollably, Michael found a stool at the bar and sat down. "What do you want?" he asked, since Thack was undoubtedly headed for the john. He peed about as often as a dog in a palm grove.

"Beer," said Thack. "Miller's, I guess."

"OK."

"Do you see it?" He meant the men's room.

"It's the one marked Studs." Michael rolled his eyes. "As opposed to Fillies."

"How sexist," said Thack.

When he had gone, Michael ordered the drinks. As providence would have it, his beeper went off just as his Calistoga arrived. The bartender smiled at him. "Another bionic man."

Michael mugged ruefully. "It usually goes off on a coatrack somewhere." He dug out his pillbox and popped two, chasing them with the Calistoga. When he was done, the man on the stool next to him gave him a knowing look, then tapped the pocket of his Pendleton.

"I'm set to go off any second."

Michael smiled. "Last night at *Big Business*, there were enough to start a symphony."

The man had dark, expressive eyes and the sweet ETish quality Michael had come to associate with guys who'd been sick for a long time.

"Do you take the middle-of-the-night dose?" Michael asked.

The man shook his head.

"Me either. Double doses at seven and eleven?"

"Yeah."

"How's it going?"

The man shrugged. "I've got six T-cells."

Michael nodded and counted his own blessings in silence. The last time he checked, he had three hundred and ten.

"I'm feeling real possessive about them," said the man. "I may start giving them names."

Michael chuckled. "You've said that before."

"Not tonight," said the man.

Thack returned and leaned against Michael's stool, beer in hand. They watched the dance floor in silence as couple after couple revolved into view. This time the song was called "Memories to Burn."

"Look at her," said Thack. "Get a load of her."

The object of his amazement was pantsuited, plump, and seventy-something. A tiny, pink-sequined sombrero was affixed to the side of her lilac hair, and she seemed to be enjoying herself no end. Her partner was a man about forty years her junior.

"She's a stitch," said Michael.

"She's all yours," said the man with six T-cells.

Michael turned and smiled at him. "You know her?"

"I guess so. She's my mother."

"Well . . ." Michael reddened. "She's sure having a good time."

"Isn't she?"

Thack laughed. "She looks like a regular."

The man grunted. "A regular *what*, we won't say."

"Does she live here?" Michael asked.

"She does now. She came out here five years ago from Havasu City. When I got sick."

"Oh, yeah."

"I guess she thought I didn't have too long, but . . . surprise, surprise."

"She lives with you, then?" asked Thack.

"Oh, Lord, no. She lives with a friend of hers from Havasu City. The friend has a son here too."

641

"Oh."

"The two of 'em are real party animals." He smiled dimly. "She knows more queers than I do."

Thack laughed. The old lady twirled into view for a moment, waggled her fingers at her son, and twirled off again.

"She's subdued tonight," he said. "She's got a whole outfit that goes with that hat."

"You know . . ." Michael's brow furrowed. "I think I've seen her before."

The man looked at him. "You play bingo at Holy Redeemer?"

"No."

"How 'bout the Bare Chest Contest at the Eagle?"

Michael laughed. "She goes to that?"

"Never misses one," said the man.

"It must've been somewhere else," said Michael.

The music ended, and the dance floor cleared. The old lady made a beeline for her son, dragging her partner by the hand.

"Ooowee," she declared, patting her lilac wisps.

"How 'bout a Bud?" asked her son.

"Don't mind if I do. George, this is Larry. Larry, George."

"Hi. Uh . . . this is . . ." The man turned to Michael and Thack, looking apologetic. "We didn't actually get each other's names."

"Michael." He raised his hand in a sort of generalized greeting to all and sundry. "This is Thack."

Nods and murmurs.

The old lady cocked her head. "Either of you boys feel like a go at it?"

"Oh, Lord," said her son. "She's worn out one and workin' on another."

"You hush up," said the old lady.

"You don't have to," the man told Michael.

"I'd like to," said Michael.

"You see, Larry," said the old lady.

"I'm not sure I know *how*," said Michael, seeing Thack's amusement out of the corner of his eye.

"Nothing to it." The old lady took his hand and led him toward the floor.

"I thought you wanted a Bud," yelled her son.

"Hang on to it," she called back. "Was it Michael, did you say?"

"Right."

"Well, I'm Eula."

"Hi," he said.

Another song had already begun, so they waited for a space to open, then merged with the stream of waltzers. Custom seemed to demand holding your partner at arms' length, which worked out fine, really, since Eula's immense polyester-ruffled bosom had a few demands of its own.

"You're doin' good," she said.

He chuckled. "It's sorta the old, basic box step, isn't it?"

"That's it." She nodded. "Watch those girls ahead of us. They've got the knack of it."

The "girls" were a pair of fiftyish dykes in Forty-Niners jackets. They were good, all right, so Michael caught the rhythm of their movement and copied it.

"There you go," said Eula. "You got it."

"Well, you're a good dancer," Michael told her. And it was true, amazingly enough. She was remarkably light on her feet.

"First time here?" she asked.

"Uh-huh . . . well, no. I came here once in the early eighties, when it was called something else."

"What was it called then?"

"I don't remember, actually." This was a lie, pure and simple. It had been called the Cave, and the walls had been painted black. Its specialties had been nude wrestling and slave auctions. Why he was hiding this from a woman who frequented the Eagle's Bare Chest Contest, Michael did not know.

"That's my son you were talking to."

"I know," he said. "He told me."

"He don't like to go out much, but every now and then I make him."

He didn't know what to say.

"Ronnie—that's his lover—he's even worse. All them boys wanna do is rent movies and stay home."

"I know how they feel," he said.

"Oh, now," she said. "You're more fun than that."

The coquettish glint in her eye made him register finally on where he had seen her. "You were at the Castro Theatre, weren't you? The Bow-Wow Beauty Pageant?"

"That was me," she said.

"You had the Chihuahua, right? Dressed as Marie Antoinette?"

"Carmen Miranda."

"Yeah. That was great."

"Larry made the little hat," she said proudly. "He found all them little plastic bananas down at the Flower Mart, and he sewed 'em on a doll's bonnet."

"Pretty clever."

"He's good with a needle," she said. "He's been working on the AIDS Quilt."

Michael nodded.

"He's already made ten panels for his friends."

"That's nice," he replied.

Five minutes later, at Eula's insistence, Michael led Thack onto the dance floor.

"Just once," he said. "Then we'll go home."

His lover gave him a grumpy look but went along with it, faking a waltz step admirably.

"Look happy," said Michael. "She's watching."

"She's not your mother."

"I'll say."

"And you wouldn't like it if she was."

"I dunno," said Michael. In his mind's eye, his mother was perpetually lunching at some mall in Orlando, telling anyone who

644

insisted on knowing that her son lived "in California"—never in San Francisco, because San Francisco was such a dead giveaway.

Thack said: "You'd hate it if your mother was a fag hag."

"Eula's not a fag hag."

"That's her name? Eula?"

Michael smiled. "She's just enjoying herself. Look, she's dancing with a dyke now."

"OK," said Thack. "A dyke hag."

"Be quiet. They're coming this way."

Eula and her new partner waltzed alongside them. "Lookin' good," said Eula.

"Thanks," said Michael. "You too."

Eula's partner was as short as Eula, only wiry and fortyish, with a delicate blue flower tattooed on her left biceps.

"Jesus," said Michael, when they had danced out of sight. "If Havasu City could see her now."

Relieved to be done with nightlife for a while, they drove home to Noe Hill well before eleven. Harry greeted them deliriously at the door, toe-dancing like a carnival dog at the realization that they hadn't deserted him.

"Has he been walked?" Michael asked.

"Not by me."

"I'll take him in a minute."

While Thack shed his clothes, Michael sealed off the garbage with a twist tie and dragged it from its niche beneath the sink. Harry recognized this as a sign of impending departure and yelped indignantly for his walk.

"All right," said Michael. "I hear you."

With the dog straining at the leash, he headed out into the darkness again and dropped the garbage into the curbside can. Thack had recently built a little weathered wood house for it, which looked homey and Martha's Vineyard–ish in the moonlight. Michael stopped and admired it long enough to receive another reprimand from Harry.

Dolores Park, Harry's daytime stomping grounds, was bristling with crack dealers and fag-bashers at night, so Michael opted for the safer circle route along Cumberland, Sanchez, and Twentieth streets. He freed the dog at the base of the Cumberland steps and watched as he rocketed through the oversized cacti to the softer, more welcoming green patch at the top. Before he could catch up with him, Harry was yapping in a way that could only mean he'd confronted an unidentifiable human.

"Harry!" he yelled, wary of being branded a noise polluter by the neighbors. "Just shut up. Behave yourself."

At the top of the steps, leaning against the rail, stood a chatty old geezer with a cane, who often "took his constitutional" there.

"Little Harry," said the man, as if that explained everything.

"He's a nuisance," said Michael. "I'm sorry."

"That's just Harry. He's just announcing you."

Harry circled the man, yapping obnoxiously.

"Harry!" Michael clapped his hands authoritatively. "Get your fuzzy butt up the street!"

When the dog was gone, he gave the old man an apologetic smile and continued walking. It was odd to think that Harry had some sort of relationship, however abrasive, with at least half the people on this street. They all knew him by name, while Michael was regarded merely as Harry's owner. When he walked there by himself, the first thing they asked was: "Where's Harry?"

He liked that, and he liked the talk that usually followed: good basic village chat about the drought or the wind, the graffiti problem, the roses in bloom, the ugly new house that looked like a Ramada Inn. What he had with the people on this block was an unspoken agreement to exchange pleasantries without exchanging names. It wasn't so different from the thing he'd enjoyed at the baths, the cordial anonymity that made strangers into equals.

Tagging after Harry, he passed the white picket fences of Cumberland, then turned right on Sanchez and climbed another set of stairs to Twentieth Street. Harry knew the route by heart, so since there was no traffic at night, Michael gave him freedom to explore at will. If the dog got too far ahead, he would wait patiently in the green darkness until Michael trudged into view.

When he reached Twentieth, a woman peeped from behind the curtains of her picture window. Recognizing him—or, more likely, Harry—she gave a chipper little wave. He waved back, realizing she was one of the Golden Girls, Thack's name for a group of Lithuanian ladies who played gin al fresco at a house down on Sanchez.

The moon hung fat and lemony over Twin Peaks when he reached the stairs leading down to Noe. He gazed at it contentedly, Harry by his side, until the beeper jolted him out of his reverie. Turning it off, he clipped the leash on Harry again and headed down the stairs toward home.

"You know what?" said Thack.

They were both—no, all three—in bed now, Thack snuggled against Michael's back, Harry burrowed under the new Macy's comforter, next to Michael's left calf.

"What?" asked Michael.

"I've got a great idea for a trellis."

"OK."

"We build it," said Thack, "in the shape of a triangle. And we grow pink flowers on it."

"Cute."

"I like it."

"You would," said Michael.

"Really," said Thack. "We wanted a trellis, and it would . . . you know, deliver a political message."

"Do you think our neighbors really need the message?"

"Sure. Some of them. Anyway, it's celebratory."

"Can't we just get a gay flag, like everybody else?"

"We could," said Thack. "Like everybody else."

It really wasn't worth debating. "OK, fine."

"What? A flag or a pink triangle?"

"The pink triangle. Or both, for that matter. Go crazy."

Thack chuckled wickedly. "Be careful. My first idea was to write 'Queer and Present Danger' above the door."

He meant this, probably, so Michael kept his mouth shut.

"That would piss off ol' Loomis, wouldn't it?"

"Who's ol' Loomis?" asked Michael.

"You know. The guy who bitched about our Douche Larouche sign."

"Oh, yeah."

"Where the fuck does he think he's living, anyway? Homophobic old asshole!"

Michael chuckled and reached behind him to pat Thack's leg. "You're such a Shiite."

"Well," said his lover, "somebody's gotta do it."

The Designer Bride

Smoldering, Mary Ann left the set and headed straight to her dressing room, barely acknowledging the associate producer who stumbled along beside her, pleading his case. "Ilsa and I both talked to her last week," he said, "and she was a regular Chatty Cathy."

"Swell," she replied curtly. She had all but withered and died out there, and somebody was going to pay for it.

"If we'd had any *idea* . . ."

"That's your job, isn't it? To have some idea? The woman couldn't utter a complete sentence, Al. Forget sentence. I was lucky if I got 'yes' or 'no' out of her."

"I know . . ."

"This is not television, Al. I don't know what it is, but it's not television."

"Well, at least the audience could empathize."

"What do you mean?"

"Just that . . . it was understandable."

"Oh, really? How so?"

"Well, I mean . . . the traumatic aspect."

"Al." She sighed heavily, stopping at the door of her dressing room. "It doesn't help much to know *why*, if she's not communicating with us."

"I understand that."

"Surely *somewhere* out there there's a woman who's been sodomized by her father and is capable of composing a few coherent sentences on the subject."

"But she *did* when . . ."

"I know. When you and Ilsa talked to her. Terrific. Too bad nobody else got to hear it." She opened the door, then turned and looked at him. "I thought you said she was on Oprah."

"She was."

"Did she do that to Oprah?"

He shook his head.

"So what are you saying? It's my fault?"

"I'm not saying anything."

"Good answer," she said, and closed the door on him.

She was removing her makeup with broad, angry swipes when the phone rang. She hesitated a moment, then picked it up, thinking it might be Burke. She hoped to God he hadn't seen the show. It was never too late for him to change his mind.

"Yes?"

"Mary Ann?" It was a woman's voice, fluty and frivolous.

"Who is this, please?"

"It's Prue, Mary Ann. Prue Giroux."

She winced. "Oh, yes."

"They wouldn't put me through until I told them we were friends." Prue giggled. "You have marvelous watchdogs!"

Not marvelous enough, obviously. She'd done her damnedest for years to stay clear of this notorious climber. Prue's appetite for celebrities was such that she regarded Mary Ann as nothing less than a vital link in the food chain. Mary Ann, after all, got first crack at the biggies.

"What's up, Prue?"

"Well, I know it's late notice, but I'm having a little impromptu session of the Forum this afternoon, and I'd love for you to come."

The Forum was Prue's pretentious name for the celebrity brunches she'd been throwing at her house for the past decade or so. They were almost always tedious affairs, populated by dubious local "personalities" and people who hoped to meet them.

"Oh, gosh," she said, unintentionally mimicking Prue's gushy, little-girlish delivery. "That's so sweet of you, but I'm up to my neck in work right now. We've got sweeps month coming up, you know."

"You have to eat, don't you?"

How typical of this star-fucker not to take no for an answer. "Prue," she said evenly, "I'd love to, but I'm afraid it's impossible."

"That's such a shame. I just know you'd adore the Rands."

What Rands? Certainly not *those* Rands.

"Russell just called up out of the blue last night and said that he and Chloe were in town."

The very ones. How in the world . . . ?

Prue giggled. "I told Russell he was naughty not to give me more warning, but . . . what can you do with creative people?"

"You're so right," she replied. "How long are they here for?" She had wanted to interview the designer for ages. The Forum might not be the ideal auspices under which to meet Russell Rand and his new bride, *but* . . .

"Just till Thursday," said Prue. "They're on their way to an AIDS benefit in LA."

"Ah," she replied, wondering why the hell none of her producers had heard about this. She might have been spared the indignity of dealing with Prue Giroux. "Maybe, if I jiggle my schedule a little . . ."

"We aren't convening until two," said Prue. "You'll still have time to change." There was a note of sly triumph in her voice; Mary Ann wanted to kill her. "I've decided to wear the oldest Rand in my closet. Just to give him a giggle."

"Well . . . sounds like lots of fun."

"Doesn't it?" said Prue, thoroughly pleased with herself.

Mary Ann made a point of arriving late at Prue's Nob Hill town house. The usual crowd was assembled in the fussy Diana Phipps living room, converging on the famous couple like flies on carrion. Keeping her distance from this sorry spectacle, she headed for the canapés and waited for her hostess to track her down.

"Well," came a voice from behind. "Look who's here."

It was Father Paddy Starr—red-faced, beaming, and resplendent in a raspberry shirt with a clerical collar.

"Hi, Father."

"I saw you yesterday at D'orothea's, but I don't think you saw me."

"No. I guess not."

"Prue and I were in the front room. You were in the back with a gentleman."

She fussed over the canapés, feigning disinterest. Father Paddy was too much of a fixture at the station to be entrusted with even the sketchiest information about Burke. The situation was ticklish enough as it was.

"Have you met them yet?" he asked

She selected the palest cube of cheese she could find and popped it into her mouth. "Who?"

He rolled his eyes impatiently. "Dwight and Mamie Eisenhower."

"If you mean them," said Mary Ann, nodding toward the corner where the Rands were being eaten alive, "I think they could use a little breather, don't you?"

Father Paddy selected an almond from a bowl of mixed nuts. "They're used to it."

"Maybe so, but it makes us look like hicks. So desperate and overeager."

"Not me," said the priest. "I'm waiting my turn like a gentleman."

"I didn't mean you." She gave him a conciliatory look. "It just makes me embarrassed for the city, that's all."

This produced a sleepy, avuncular smile. "Don't you worry about the city, darling."

She recoiled privately at the "darling" part, since it presumed the sort of cloying chumminess Father Paddy shared with Prue Giroux. Mary Ann simply didn't trust him enough to get campy with him.

The crowd parted a little, permitting a brief, dramatic glimpse of Chloe Rand. A pin spot intended for Prue's Hockney struck her face and rendered it classic: silky auburn hair, very short, and an elegant Castilian nose, which seemed to begin its descent in the middle of her forehead. Mary Ann was impressed.

"Isn't she stunning?" said Father Paddy.

"Very striking, yes."

"Did you see the spread in *Vanity Fair*?"

"Yeah."

"She's wearing a Rand Band," said the priest. "According to Prue."

"A what?"

"That's what he calls his new line of wedding rings. Rand Bands."

"Cute," said Mary Ann. "I thought they were supposed to be affordable."

"They are."

"And you think that's her real wedding ring?"

Father Paddy smirked. "What a naughty girl you are."

The crowd shifted again, and Russell Rand's famous profile came knifing into view. Scrubbed and tan, athletically lean, he looked uncannily like his wife, which lent a distinctly incestuous appeal to the intimacy they expressed so freely—and so frequently—in the presence of others.

"He bought her a Phantom jet for her birthday," said Father Paddy.

"Really?"

The priest nodded, widening his eyes. "Not a shabby little giftie, eh?"

"No," she replied, almost mesmerized by the miraculous synchronism of those two shining faces. What must it be like to present such a picture of unity to the world? To share with someone else a life in which work and play are so artfully interwoven?

Why had she ever settled for less than that? Didn't she deserve the same thing? How had this happened to her?

"Let's go say hello," said Father Paddy. "It looks like there's an opening."

"I think I'll wait." The last thing she wanted was to face the Couple of the Year in the company of this gossipy old auntie. "You go ahead."

"Suit yourself," he said, smiling. Then he clasped his hands across his stomach and glided off majestically, eyes on the horizon, like a wise man in search of a star.

She watched from several different places in the room as the priest bent their ear—and it did seem like one ear. Among the excited throng she spotted Lia Belli, several Aliotos, and the clownishly made up Frannie Halcyon Manigault, pushing seventy from the other side. She had half expected to see DeDe and D'orothea there—hadn't D'or once modeled for Russell Rand?—but the couple was nowhere in sight.

When the Rands were finally free of Father Paddy, she waited a moment before moving into their line of sight. As luck would have it, Chloe locked eyes with her almost immediately and gave her a sisterly smile.

"Hi," said Mary Ann, extending her hand. "I'm Mary Ann Singleton."

Chloe took her hand cordially. "Chloe Rand. And this is Russell." Looking to her husband, she saw that he'd been set upon by someone else, so she gave Mary Ann a wide-eyed shrug and said: "I think we lost him." It came off as pleasant and schoolchummy.

"You must be exhausted," said Mary Ann.

Chloe smiled without showing her teeth. "It's been busy."

"I'll bet."

653

"Have we met before?"

Mary Ann shook her head and smiled.

"You look really familiar somehow. I guess I should know you, huh?"

"Not really. I know how many faces you see."

"I know, but . . ."

"I host the morning talk show here."

Chloe nodded. "Right. Of course. We watched you on our last trip here."

"Really?" She tried to sound pleased without getting gushy about it. Behave like a peer and they'll treat you like one. This was the first law of survival.

"It's a great show," said Chloe.

She ducked her head graciously. "Thanks."

"Russell," said Chloe, taking her husband's arm in such a way as to effect his escape. "I hate to pull you away, but this is Mary Ann Singletary."

"Singleton," said Mary Ann.

"Oh, hell." Chloe buried her elegant nose in her palm.

"It's OK," she replied, shaking the designer's hand, reassuring Chloe with a look.

Russell Rand gave her a world-weary smile. "It's been one of those days, if you know what I mean." Like Chloe, he was making a gallant effort to draw her into their circle of intimacy.

Mary Ann wanted him to know that she sympathized, that she had a public every bit as demanding as his. "I know exactly what you mean," she said.

"Mary Ann has a talk show," said Chloe. "*People Are Talking*, right?"

"No, actually. That's the other one."

"We've seen you, though," said Russell Rand. "I remember your face."

"Which one are you?" asked Chloe.

"Mary Ann in the Morning."

"Of course. How stupid."

"You've got a partner," said the designer, nodding. "Ross something."

Mary Ann wished he would just drop it. "That's *People Are Talking.*"

"Right, right. Your partner's name is . . . ?"

"I work alone."

"Sure. Of course." He nodded authoritatively, as if he'd known that all along.

"I remember the show, though," said Chloe. "It was Cheryl Thingy . . . you know, Lana Turner's daughter."

"Cheryl Crane," said Mary Ann.

"Was that you?"

"That was me." It wasn't, it was *People Are Talking*, but why not spare everybody the embarrassment? "How long are you here for?" she asked, turning to the designer.

"Just a day or so, I'm afraid. We're doing an AIDS benefit in LA."

"It's sort of spur-of-the-moment," said Chloe, "but Elizabeth asked us."

Elizabeth. Just plain Elizabeth. As if Chloe and Mary Ann both knew the woman much too well to bother with her last name. Mary Ann felt worldly beyond belief. "She's doing great work," she said.

"She's the best," said Russell Rand.

"I don't suppose," said Mary Ann carefully, "you're doing any press while you're here."

"Not really." Chloe looked sweetly apologetic.

"Well, I certainly understand."

"I'm sure you do," said Russell knowingly.

"If you wanna get away . . . I mean, just for some quiet time . . . we have a place at The Summit, and I cook a mean rack of lamb."

"Isn't that nice?" said Chloe. "I'm afraid we haven't got a single free moment."

"Well, I understand, of course." She felt herself blushing hideously. Why had she even tried? They could have gone on talking about Elizabeth. All that was left for her now was a graceful retreat.

"Next time, for sure," said Chloe, "when our schedule's less hectic."

"Great," said Mary Ann.

"It was lovely meeting you," said Russell.

"Same here," said Mary Ann, backing away into the pressing throng.

As she had feared, Prue cornered her before she could make it out the door.

"Did you meet them?" asked the hostess, looking preposterous in her "oldest Russell Rand"—a navy wool suit with a huge kelly-green bow across the bosom.

"Oh, yes."

"Aren't they dear?" bubbled Prue.

"Very."

"And so real."

"Mmm."

"They met at Betty Ford, you know. She was a counselor or therapist or something, and she just turned his life around. It's really the most romantic story."

Mary Ann edged toward the door before Prue could regurgitate the entire *Vanity Fair* article. "I'm afraid I've gotta dash," she said. "My little girl's waiting to be picked up at Presidio Hill."

"Well, I'm glad you could make it."

"Me too," said Mary Ann.

"I didn't want you to miss out," said Prue, making damn sure she got credit for the coup.

On her way out the door, Mary Ann caught a final glimpse of the famous couple as they exchanged another look of excruciating intimacy. Their love was like an aura that surrounded them, protecting them from the crush of the crowd. *This is possible*, they seemed to be telling her. *You can have what we have if you refuse to settle for less.*

She knew in that instant what she would have to do.

A Picnic

At noon the next day Brian and Thack took a bag lunch to the top of Strawberry Hill, the island in the middle of Stow Lake. (Typically, a hassle with the nursery suppliers in Half Moon Bay had caused Michael to drop out at the last minute.) As Brian looked out over the dusty greenery of the park, Thack ripped open the Velcro closure of his wallet and produced a joint.

"Hey," said Brian. "My man."

Huddling under his Levi's jacket against the wind, Thack lit the joint, took a drag, and handed it over.

"Boy," said Brian. "It's been a while."

"Has it?"

"Yeah. Mary Ann doesn't do this anymore."

Thack shrugged. "Why should that stop you?"

"Well, it gets in the furniture, she says. People can smell it."

Thack nodded dourly, his wheat-straw hair whipping in the wind, his gaze fixed on a distant flotilla of pedal boats as they rounded the bend into view.

Brian knew what Thack was thinking. "She's got a point," he added, trying to explain himself. "She's kind of a public figure."

No reaction.

Brian found a flat rock and sat on it. Thack joined him, handing him the joint. He took another toke and said: "She's not as bad as you think. You don't see the side of her I do."

"Hey . . ." Thack held up his hands as if to say: Leave me out of it.

"I know how you feel about her, though."

Thack said: "I really don't have an opinion one way or the other."

"Bullshit."

"I don't. How could I? We don't see her that much."

To Brian this sounded a lot like an accusation. "Yeah. I guess so."

"I didn't mean we expect you to . . ."

"She gets wrapped up in things. I don't see her that much myself."

"I know."

"She's missed you both. She told me so last night. That's why tonight is so important to her."

Thack seemed puzzled.

"Dinner at our house."

"Oh, yeah. Sorry." A sheepish smile.

"That's OK. I don't remember that kinda shit either."

"What's the story on this guy?"

"Oh . . ." He took another toke. "Mary Ann used to date him."

"Date?"

"OK, fuck . . . if you wanna get technical."

Thack chuckled.

"He lives in New York now. He's in town doing research on an AIDS story."

"Oh, yeah? As a reporter?"

"Producer," said Brian. "TV."

Thack nodded.

"I've been your basic basket case, of course."

"Why?"

He shrugged.

"When did she last see him?"

"Eleven years ago."

Thack smiled. "Nothing is the same after eleven years."

"I guess not. Plus he's got a wife and two kids and a little dick . . ."

"Whoa," said Thack. "Who told you that?"

"Mary Ann."

"When?"

"Last night."

He laughed. "You asked her . . . ?"

"She volunteered it, OK?"

"Just out of the blue, huh?"

Brian saw Thack's lip flicker slightly. "You think she said that just to make me feel better?"

"Threw you a bone, so to speak?"

Brian laughed.

"I think you're being paranoid."

"Yeah. I guess so. As usual, huh?"

Thack smiled, then twisted off the tops of the ciders and unwrapped the sandwiches. "This is the one with mustard," he said, handing Brian a sandwich. "If you want more, there are some packets in that bag there."

"This looks fine."

"We can fight over who gets Michael's Yoplait."

"We're not gonna fight over his sandwich?"

"Nope. All yours." Thack munched away for a moment, then said: "I wouldn't worry about it."

"I'm not," said Brian.

They left the park at one-thirty and took a bus up Twenty-fifth Avenue to the nursery. Thack would walk from there to a house off Geary he was assessing for the preservation people. When the bus stopped at Balboa, a pair of teenagers boarded with noisy ceremony. Some gut instinct told Brian to brace himself for trouble.

"Better not be," he heard one of them say.

"Yeah," said his much shorter sidekick. They were both overacting for their captive audience.

Brian glanced at Thack, who sat stock-still, cocking his head like a forest creature listening for alien footfall.

The tall teenager dumped his fare into the slot. "Better not be . . . cuz I ain't gettin' AIDS."

"Shit, no," said the short one.

"You catch AIDS and die like a fuckin' dog." He was moving toward the back now, brandishing the acronym like a switchblade. "Whatcha think? Any *faggots* on this bus?"

There was a moment of excruciating silence before Thack did the predictable and piped up. "Yeah," he said, "over here." He was raising his hand with the kind of bored assurance a schoolkid gives off when he knows he's got the right answer.

Brian looked back at the teenagers, who stood slack-mouthed and silent, clearly at a loss for what to do next.

"There's one over here too." This from a stout young black woman across the aisle.

"There you go," said Thack, addressing the boys.

"Back here." Two older guys in the back of the bus raised their hands.

"Yo," called someone else.

Then came laughter, uncertain at first but growing to volcanic dimensions, rumbling from one end of the bus to the other. The short kid was the first to feel the heat, taking cover in the first available seat. The tall one muttered a half-assed "Shit" and scanned the crowd desperately for allies. He seemed on the verge of rebuttal when his buddy grabbed his belt and yanked him down into a seat.

Grinning, Brian turned back to Thack. "You're a crazy man."

"Don't try it in New Jersey," said Thack.

"New Jersey, hell. You could get killed doing that."

"That's what Michael says." Thack turned and looked out the window as the bus lurched down the avenue. "Fuck it. I'm tired of this shit."

Parlor Games

Archibald Anson Gidde, a prominent San Francisco realtor and social leader, died Tuesday at his home in Sea Cliff after a bout with liver cancer. He was 42.

Mr. Gidde was a witty and flamboyant figure who distinguished himself by spearheading some of the City's most notable real estate transactions, among them the recent $10 million sale of the Stonecypher mansion to the Sultan of Adar.

660

A member of the Bohemian Club, he was active on the boards of the San Francisco Ballet, the San Francisco Opera, and the American Conservatory Theatre.

Mr. Gidde is survived by his parents, Eleanor and Clinton Gidde of Ross and La Jolla, and a sister, Charlotte Reinhart, of Aspen, Colo.

"Well, I'll be damned." Michael looked up from the *Examiner* just as his lover emerged from the bathroom.

"You knew him?" asked Thack, reading over Michael's shoulder.

"Not exactly. He bought some things at the nursery once or twice. Jon knew him. He was one of the big A-Gays."

"Figures."

"What do you mean?"

"Liver cancer," explained his lover, scowling. "How tired is that?"

For the past few years Thack had made a parlor game out of spotting the secret AIDS deaths in the obituary columns. Given the age of the deceased, the absence of a spouse, and certain telltale occupational data, he would draw his own conclusions and fly into a towering rage.

"Notice how they called him flamboyant? How's that for a code word?"

Michael was tired of this.

"Fuck him," Thack continued. "How dare he act ashamed? Who does he think he's fooling, anyway? He can sell his pissy houses in hell!"

"C'mon."

"What do you mean, c'mon?"

"The guy is dead, Thack."

"So what? He was a worm in life, and he's a worm in death. This is why people don't give a shit about AIDS! Because cowardly pricks like this make it seem like it's not really happening!"

Michael paused, then said: "We've gotta move it, sweetie. We're gonna be late as it is."

Thack shot daggers at him and left the room.

"Wear the green sweater," Michael yelled after him. "You look great in that."

Mary Ann and Brian's condo-in-the-sky was not Michael's idea of a dream house. From twenty-three stories the city looked like a plaster-of-Paris model of itself, hardly the real thing at all. Lately Mary Ann had made an effort at jazzing up the chilly modern interiors with a lot of Southwestern stuff—painted furniture, steer skulls, and the like—but the effect was not so much Santa Fe as Santa Fe Savings and Loan. Maybe it just wasn't fixable.

The Vietnamese maid took their coats and led them into the living room, a place of too little texture and too much teal. Brian was ensconced behind the wet bar, looking unnaturally cheerful in a pink button-down. Mary Ann and Burke were at opposite ends of the big crescent-shaped couch.

"Michael," said Burke, smiling as he rose.

"Hey, Burke." Michael wondered if a hug was appropriate. It had been eleven years, after all, and the guy was straight.

He played it safe and stuck out his hand.

Burke shook it warmly, using both his hands in the process, suggesting that a hug might have been in order, after all. "You look great," said Burke.

"Thanks. You too." Mary Ann's old flame seemed lean as ever in a blazer and gray flannel slacks. His fine, pale hair—very much the same color as Thack's—had receded significantly, but Michael thought it suited his air of quiet intelligence. True, the yup-yellow tie was a little off-putting, but you had to make allowances for New Yorkers.

Thack stepped forward, touching the small of Michael's back. "Burke," said Michael, "this is my lover, Thack."

Burke pumped Thack's arm energetically. "Good to meet you."

"Same here," said Thack.

Mary Ann hugged Michael and pecked him chastely on the cheek. "We were just talking about you," she said. He was almost positive her scent was Elizabeth Taylor's Passion. When on earth had she started doing that?

He returned the peck. "You want me to go out again, so you can finish?"

She giggled. "No. Hi, Thack." She hugged Thack, who made a passable show of hugging back. You would have thought they did it all the time. "You guys both look *wonderful!*"

It was a little too gushy. Michael hated it when she overcompensated like this. What state of deterioration had she expected to find him in, anyway?

"What'll it be?" Brian asked from behind the bar. "A couple of Calistogas?"

"Great," said Michael.

"I'll take a bourbon, actually," said Thack.

Michael shot his lover a glance. Thack rarely touched the hard stuff. Was he that uncomfortable about the evening ahead?

"Awriight," crowed Brian. "A serious drink."

Burke grinned at this interchange, then addressed Brian: "You used to be a real bartender, didn't you? Down at Benny's."

"Perry's," said Brian.

"That's right."

"I was a waiter, though."

"Oh."

"He was a lawyer before that," Mary Ann put in, "but he took on so many liberal causes that he sort of burned out."

Michael saw Brian's expression and knew what he was thinking: Why does she always have to say that? Wouldn't a waiter have been enough?

Brian locked eyes with his wife, plastered a sickly smile on his face, and returned his attention to Thack's bourbon.

"And now you guys are nurserymen." Still a little over-jovial, Burke looked first at Michael, then at Brian.

"Right," Michael answered.

"You need water . . . soda?" Brian was talking to Thack now.

"On the rocks is fine."

"You got it," said Brian.

"We've been partners for three years," Michael told Burke.

"That's great."

"Here you go, sport." Brian handed Michael a Calistoga on the rocks. Michael and Thack went to the big curving couch and sat down in the space between Mary Ann and Burke.

Mary Ann reached over and gave Michael's knee a shake. "I can't get over how good you look."

Michael smiled and nodded and said: "I feel good."

"Hey," said Burke. "You know who I was thinking about today?"

"Who?" Mary Ann turned, letting go of Michael's knee.

"Our old landlady. Mrs. Thingamabob."

"Madrigal," said Michael. "Shit!"

Mary Ann frowned. "What?"

Flooded with guilt, Michael looked at Thack. "We were gonna call her. You were gonna remind me."

"Oh, hell," said his lover.

Brian settled into the big white leather chair across from the sofa. "You can use the phone in the bedroom if . . ."

"No," said Michael. "It's too late."

"She went to Lesbos," Thack explained.

Burke laughed. "Sounds like her."

"*Damn* it," muttered Michael.

Mary Ann looked lost. "Why on earth did she go to Lesbos?"

"Because it's there," said Burke, laughing.

"She's meeting Mona there," said Michael. "Her daughter."

"Damn," said Burke. "I remember her. Frizzy red hair, right?"

"That's her," said Michael.

"Didn't you use to go out with her?" Burke was addressing Brian now.

"Once or twice," said Brian.

"She became a lesbian," said Mary Ann.

There was an awkward silence before Brian told Burke: "The two events were not related."

This got an awkward chuckle.

Michael felt compelled to speak up on Mona's behalf. "She was a lesbian long before she met Brian."

"Thank you," said Brian.

Mary Ann looked at her husband. "I wasn't impugning your prowess, for God's sake."

"Sorry." Burke laughed, obviously thinking he had opened a touchy subject.

"No," said Mary Ann, laughing to reassure him. "Really."

"Where is she now?" asked Burke.

"In England," said Mary Ann. "She married a lord and lives in this huge house in the Cotswolds."

"Does the lord know she's a lesbian?"

"Oh, sure," Michael told him. "He's gay himself. They don't live together. He lives here. He drives a cab for Veterans."

"Well," said Burke. "Thanks for clearing that up."

As everyone laughed, Michael marveled at the apparent ease with which the four old housemates had reunited. Then in a fleeting moment of self-torment, he pictured poor Mrs. Madrigal sitting alone amid her carpetbags in some fly-specked Grecian airport without benefit of his bon voyage.

They were seated at the big green glass dining table when Michael realized who was missing.

"Hey, where's Shawna?"

"In her room," said Mary Ann.

Brian glanced at his wife, then spoke to Michael: "She's playing with her new Nintendo game."

"Ah." Michael nodded.

"She's not very good around new grownups," said Mary Ann.

"She was fine," said Burke. "Really."

Brian looked faintly apologetic. "Sometimes it takes her a while," he told Burke.

"No problem," said Burke. "Really."

Michael and Thack communicated briefly with their eyes. Had

Shawna been antisocial? Had she thrown a tantrum and been banished to her room?

When the maid appeared with a tray of mint-wrapped fish, Mary Ann jumped at the chance to change the subject. "Nguyet," she said, beaming up at the girl, "those spring rolls were absolutely your best ever."

Burke murmured in agreement, his mouth still full of the food under discussion.

The maid giggled. "You like?"

"Very much," said Thack, joining in the praise. "Absolutely delicious."

Nguyet ducked her eyes, then set down the tray and fled the room.

"She's shy," said Mary Ann.

"But sweet," said Burke.

"Isn't she?" Mary Ann waited until the girl was out of earshot. "Her family had a horrible time getting out of Saigon."

"She was a baby. She doesn't even remember that," said Brian.

"Well, I know, but . . . you can't help but feel for her."

Burke nodded, eyes fixed on the door to the kitchen.

"They live in some awful tenement in the Tenderloin, but they're the nicest, most industrious people." Mary Ann handed the tray of fish to Burke. "They're also incredibly clean. They're much cleaner than . . . almost anybody."

Than who? thought Michael. Cleaner than who? Across the table he saw a homicidal glint come into Thack's eyes. Please, he telegraphed, just leave it alone.

There was one of those moments of total silence—a "mind fart," as Mona used to say—before Thack turned to Burke and announced: "I just realized something."

"What's that?"

"I saw you on CNN last month."

"Oh, yeah?"

"It was some sort of panel discussion about television."

"Oh, right."

"You're producing something, aren't you? Some new show?"

"Well . . ." Burke looked vaguely uncomfortable. Or maybe it was modesty. "There's a new project in the works, but it's not very far along yet."

Mary Ann jumped in. "Burke did that special on Martin Luther King last year."

"I saw that," said Michael. "It was wonderful."

"Thanks," said Burke.

"I actually went to Selma," said Brian. "I mean, I participated."

"Really?" Burke's response seemed a little patronizing, though he undoubtedly hadn't intended it that way. Michael found it touching that Brian had offered up this ancient credential for his guest's approval.

"What's this new show about?" asked Thack.

"Oh . . . just a general magazine format." Looking distracted, Burke turned back to Brian. "You were part of the civil disobedience and all that?"

"Oh, yeah."

"That's when he was a lawyer," said Mary Ann.

"No," said Brian. "That was earlier. I didn't pass the bar until 1969."

"Right," said Mary Ann. "Of course."

"I wish I'd been there," said Burke.

"You were too young," said Mary Ann.

Burke shrugged. "Not by much, really. Anyway, it was a great time. Things happened. People cared enough to make them happen. I mean, look at the seventies. What a great big blank that was."

Michael saw the cloud pass over his lover's face and realized with certainty what was about to happen. "I don't know about that," Thack said.

Burke offered him a sporting smile. "OK. What happened?"

"Well," said Thack, "gay liberation for one thing."

"How so?"

"What do you mean—how so?"

"In what form? Discos and bathhouses?"

667

"Yeah," answered Thack, clearly beginning to bristle. "Among other things."

Burke, thankfully, was still smiling. "For instance?"

"For instance . . . marches and political action, a new literature, marching bands, choruses . . . a whole new culture. You guys didn't cover it, of course, but that doesn't mean it didn't happen."

"We guys?"

"The press," said Thack. "The people who decided that black pride was heroic but gay pride was just hedonism."

"Hey, sport," said Brian. "I don't think he said that."

"He means the press in general," said Michael.

"Well, then don't blame me for . . ."

"I'm not," said Thack, more pleasantly than before. "I just think you should know that something happened in the seventies. It may not have been part of your experience, but something happened."

Burke nodded. "Fair enough."

"The seventies were our sixties, so to speak." Michael contributed this inanity and regretted it as soon as it tumbled out of his mouth. "This decade talk is ridiculous. Everybody's experience is different."

"Maybe so," said Thack, still addressing Burke, "but you should know something about the gay movement if you're doing a story on AIDS."

Burke looked confused.

"Did I get that wrong?" Thack turned to Brian. "Didn't you say he was . . . ?"

Brian shrugged and gestured toward his wife. "That's what she said."

"Oh." Mary Ann looked flustered for a moment, then addressed Burke. "I explained that that's why you're here. To do a story on AIDS."

"Oh," said Burke. "Right. Of course. I drifted there for a moment."

Mary Ann seized a bottle of wine and held it out. "Who needs a little freshener?"

Almost everyone did.

After dinner, while the group was resettling in the living room, Michael headed off to take a leak. On his way back he passed Shawna's room and found the little girl wielding a crayon at her child-sized drafting table.

He spoke to her from the doorway. "Hi, Shawna."

She looked over her shoulder for a moment, then continued drawing. "Hi, Michael."

"Whatcha drawing?"

No answer.

"Just . . . art, huh?"

"Uh-huh."

"Can I come in?"

"May I," said Shawna.

He grinned. "May I?"

"Yes."

He stood behind her and studied her work, a jumble of brown rectangles scribbled over with green. In the corner, inscribed on a much smaller rectangle, was the number 28.

"I know what that is," he said.

The child shook her head. "Huh-uh. It's a secret."

"Well, it looks to me like Anna's house."

She gazed up at him, blinking once or twice, apparently surprised at his cleverness.

"That's one of my favorite houses," he said.

She hesitated a moment, then said: "I like it 'cause it's a on-the-ground house."

He chuckled.

"What's funny?"

"Nothing. I agree with you." He touched her shoulder lightly. She was wearing a white ruffled blouse and a midi-length blue velvet skirt, obviously meant for company. Yet here she sat, stately and alone at her easel, like some miniature version of Georgia O'Keeffe.

He went to the window and peered down on the silvery plain of the bay. A freighter slid toward the ocean, lit up like a power station yet tiny as a toy from this height. Directly beneath him—how many hundred feet?—the house in Shawna's drawing slept unseen in the neighboring greenery.

He turned back to the child. "Anna's gone to Greece on vacation. Did she tell you that?"

Shawna shook her head. "I don't go see her anymore."

"Why not?"

Silence.

"Why not, Shawna?"

"Mary Ann doesn't want me to."

This threw him, but he didn't respond. The kid could make up some pretty off-the-wall stuff. Especially when it came to Mary Ann. It was bound to be more complicated than that.

Shawna asked: "Are you gonna make that noise tonight?"

"What noise?"

"You know. Beep, beep."

He smiled at her. "Not for a few hours."

"Can I see it? I mean, may I?"

"Well, you could, but it's in my overcoat, and that's on the bed in . . ."

"Is she giving you a hard time?"

Michael turned to see Brian standing in the doorway. "No way," he said.

"How's it going, Puppy?"

"OK."

"She's done some beautiful work," said Michael.

Brian looked at the picture and ruffled his daughter's hair. "Hey . . . not bad. What do you call it?"

"Art," said Shawna.

Brian laughed. "Well, OK. Makes sense to me. Did you tell Michael what you're gonna be?"

Shawna gave him a blank look.

"For Halloween," Brian added.

"Oh . . . Michelangelo."

Michael was impressed. "The painter, eh?"

"No," said Shawna. "The Teenage Mutant Ninja Turtle."

Michael looked to Brian for translation.

"You don't wanna know," said Brian. "It's an actual thing. She's not making it up."

"Teenage Mutant . . . ?"

"Ninja Turtle," said Shawna.

"We're going for Turtle mostly, with just a *hint* of Ninja. Wanna come along? It's Halloween morning. Mary Ann'll be at the station."

"What is it?" he asked.

"Just a thing at the school. A parade or something."

"Well . . ."

"We'd be back by eleven, tops." Brian winked at him.

"OK, then. Great."

"Yay," crowed Shawna.

"See," said Brian. "I told you he'd do it."

The child looked at her father. "Can Michael be a Teenage Mutant Ninja Turtle?"

"Well, he *could* . . ."

"It's either that," said Michael, "or Ann Miller."

Brian laughed. "I think your Ann Miller days are over."

"Why?" Michael grinned back at him. "Ann Miller's aren't."

Shawna looked at them both. "Who's Ann Miller?"

"Oh, God," said Michael, laughing. "Don't ask."

"Yeah," said Brian, letting his eyes dart toward Shawna as a signal to Michael. "Certain undersized personages know too much about lipstick as it is."

Michael chuckled, remembering the incident—or at least Brian's version of Mary Ann's version of the incident. "Is she still upset about that?"

"Who's Ann Miller?" Shawna persisted.

"She wasn't really upset," said Brian.

The child, Michael was thinking, must have looked uncannily like her natural mother once a stiff coat of makeup had been applied. No wonder Mary Ann had freaked. Tacky ol' Connie Bradshaw, the bane of Mary Ann's existence, back from the grave to do her embarrassing number all over again.

"Who's Ann Miller?"

"She's a lady who dances," said Brian. "A woman."

"A lady," said Michael.

Brian laughed and touched his daughter's shoulder. "You wanna hit the sack, Puppy?"

"Yeah."

"Kiss Michael good night, then."

Shawna gave Michael a peck on the cheek.

"That's a cool dress," said Michael.

"Thanks," she replied solemnly.

"She got that special for tonight," said Brian.

"Well, it's just right," he told her. "It brings out the blue in your eyes."

Shawna basked in the attention for a moment, then looked at her father. "Are you gonna tuck me in?"

"And anyway," Mary Ann was saying when Michael returned, "it's not exactly a state secret. Raquel Welch is absolutely notorious for being difficult . . ."

Burke chuckled. "To put it mildly."

Thack laughed, apparently enjoying himself. Seeing Michael, he asked: "Have you heard this story?"

"Oh, God," said Mary Ann. "Too many times, I'm sure."

"A few," he said. "It's a good one."

"Well, it's over," she said, laughing, "so you're safe. Where's Brian?"

"Putting Shawna to bed."

"Oh."

The phone rang in the guest bedroom. Since Michael was nearest to it, he said: "Shall I?"

672

"Leave it," said Mary Ann. "The machine's on."

"Actually," said Burke, "I'm halfway expecting a call from some friends. I left your number. I hope that's all right."

"Of course." Mary Ann hurried toward the ring.

Burke offered the rest of his explanation to Thack and Michael. "They're just here for a little while, and they wanted to meet for drinks later. I thought, if no one minded . . ."

"Whatever," said Michael.

"Yeah," said Thack.

Mary Ann reappeared in the doorway. "It's for you," she told Burke quietly, almost reverently. "It's Chloe Rand."

Desperadoes

She couldn't help noticing how placidly Burke received this information. He smiled faintly and nodded, but his face betrayed nothing, not the slightest degree of amazement. She might just as well have told him his wife was on the phone.

When he was out of the room, she turned to find Michael gaping at her. "Not *the* Chloe Rand?"

Thack gave Michael a cranky look. "How many Chloe Rands can there be?"

"They're in town, you mean?" His expression was truly gratifying.

"Yeah." She resolved to remain as nonchalant about this as Burke. "Just for a day or so. They're doing an AIDS benefit in LA."

This provoked a grunt from Thack, but nothing else. She wasn't about to ask him what he meant. He was forever grinding his axes in public, and she'd been singed by the sparks once too often.

Michael gave Thack a peevish glance and seemed on the verge of saying something, when Burke reappeared. "Look," he told her sheepishly, "my friends have asked us to join them for drinks at Stars. If that's not OK . . ."

"No," she said. "It's fine."

673

"It's Russell and Chloe Rand. I think you'd like them."

"Fine. Whatever."

"Guys?" Burke turned to Michael and Thack.

"Great," answered Michael, apparently speaking for both of them. She couldn't tell *what* Thack was thinking. When he brooded, his face became an infuriating blank. She was halfway hoping he would make a fuss, or at least talk Michael into bowing out graciously. Four tagalongs was a bit much. The Rands were already getting more than they had bargained for.

Burke gave her another doggy look. "I would've mentioned it earlier, but . . ."

"Look," she said, getting a brainstorm. "Why don't you invite them here?"

"Well . . ."

"They can just . . . kick back and relax."

"That's nice of you," said Burke, "but I think they're kind of . . . entrenched."

"Right," she said evenly. But she was thinking: He hates the house. He thinks it's not chic enough for them.

"Shall I check with Brian?" Burke asked.

"No," she said. "He'll go."

"Great," said Burke, and he went back to the phone.

Where had she screwed up, anyway? The Indian blankets, the saguaro skeleton, the painted steer skulls . . . ?

The tiny, clear voice of her fashion sense told her that was impossible.

She had copied that stuff from a Russell Rand ad.

It was agreed that they'd arrive at the restaurant in two cars: Mary Ann, Brian, and Burke in Mary Ann's Mercedes; Michael and Thack in their VW. There was also the minor matter of a baby-sitter, and Nguyet, as usual, required nothing less than a bald-faced bribe before consenting to stay at the house past midnight. Brian, typically, knew next to nothing about the Rands, so while Burke was in the bathroom, Mary Ann dug into her stash of *Interview*s and gave her husband a hasty briefing.

On the way there, while Brian and Burke gabbed away in the front seat about Joe Montana's vertebrae, she filled her nostrils with the sweet scent of her gray leather interiors and took stock of herself. Had she known the evening would end with the Russell Rands, she might not have worn this uneventful little Calvin Klein cocktail dress.

Still, it showed she cared about such things. It seemed a bit much, anyway, to wear a Russell Rand outfit in the actual presence of Russell Rand. She conducted a hasty mental inventory of the women she'd seen with him in photographs. Had Liza worn his clothes when she went out with him? Had Elizabeth? Maybe only desperadoes like Prue Giroux did that.

For that matter, what about the Passion she had on? Was it gauche to wear Elizabeth Taylor's perfume around people who knew Elizabeth Taylor? People who knew what she actually smelled like? Maybe her real friends found the stuff laughable and pretentious. Certainly Cher's must. How could they not?

She would not dwell on it. The stuff wasn't cheap, after all, and Taylor had done so much for AIDS. Mary Ann had worn it mostly to please Michael, to show her support. She would say that, if the subject came up. It was the truth, anyway.

"And over there," Brian was telling Burke with great authority, "is the Hard Rock. It's OK, but it's kind of a kid's joint."

"Brian," she said, "I think they've got one in New York."

"I know that. I was just telling him about this one."

"They're all the same," she told him.

"The one in London is decent," Burke put in. "It was the first, I think."

"Yes," she said. "It was."

"Look at that fog," said Brian. "Look what it does to the neon. Isn't that great?"

Burke made an appreciative noise, obviously just being polite.

She shot Brian a quick look. "Not everyone likes fog, you know?"

"Go on," he replied with mock disbelief.

"Well, it's true."

Brian looked at Burke. "You like it, don't you?"

An easy grin and a shrug. "Sure."

"You gotta admit it beats the shit outa that stuff in New York. That stuff you have to scrape off your face." Brian laughed, apparently to keep this from sounding hostile, but it didn't work. "I mean . . . *c'mon.*"

Burke was gallant about it. "Yeah . . . well, you're right about that."

"He's such a San Francisco chauvinist," she told Burke.

"And you're not?" Brian mugged at her.

"I like it," she said calmly. "I don't think it's the be-all and the end-all. And I don't think it's particularly nice to bad-mouth our guest's city."

"C'mon," said Brian, smiling to cover his tracks. "He didn't take it that way." He gave Burke a buddy-buddy wink. "Anyway, I like New York. I wouldn't wanna *live* there . . . et cetera, et cetera."

She clutched for a moment. Was that remark just coincidental, or was he onto her? Either way, she vowed to ignore it.

"How do you know the Rands?" she asked Burke pleasantly.

"Oh, you know," he replied. "Through friends."

She started to tell him about meeting them at Prue's, but changed her mind in fear that they wouldn't remember her. If they *did* remember her and remarked on it, her silence at this point would simply come off as self-effacing. It was better to keep her mouth shut.

As Brian swung the Mercedes into Redwood Alley, she gazed out the window at a gaggle of operagoers heading up the sidewalk toward the restaurant. Who among her associates, she wondered, might see her there tonight with the Rands?

It was almost too delicious to imagine.

The cavernous elegance of Stars never failed to seduce her. To enter this room full of feverish chatter and French poster art was to feel at one with a living tableau, something from the twenties, maybe, and certainly not from here. If you squinted your eyes just so, the illusion was more than enough to transport you.

As she had already envisioned, the Rands were imperially positioned on the platform at the end of the room. Chloe was in red leather tonight, her shoulders pale as milk under the stained-glass chandeliers. Russell looked wonderfully Duke of Windsorish in a herringbone Norfolk jacket. Where had they been, anyway? The opera? Another party?

Chloe saw them first. She wiggled her fingers at Burke, then tilted her cheek to be kissed when he reached the table. "You're so sweet to do this," she said.

Burke kissed her, then clapped Russell amiably on the shoulder. Russell smiled at him for a moment, then turned his gaze toward Mary Ann. "Did we sabotage your dinner?" he asked, as if they had known each other forever.

"Oh, no," she replied, "not at all."

"Are you sure?"

"Yes. Really."

"Aren't there some more?" asked Chloe.

"They're coming later," she said, "in another car."

"This is Mary Ann Singleton," said Burke.

"Yes, I know," said Russell. "I think we've met."

"You have?" asked Burke.

"Russell, Chloe . . ." Secure in her identity again, Mary Ann felt a warming rush of self-assurance. "This is my husband, Brian."

Brian and Russell shook hands. Then Brian and Chloe. "Please," said Russell cordially, "sit down, everybody."

"When did you guys meet?" Burke asked her, taking the chair next to Chloe.

"At Prue Giroux's."

"What's that?"

Chloe smirked. "I don't think you wanna know."

Russell gave his wife a brief, admonishing glance.

So, thought Mary Ann, she hates her too. Things were looking better all the time.

677

"She's kind of a local party girl," Brian told Burke.

"Yeah," Mary Ann said drily. "Kind of." This was just enough, she felt, to let Chloe know she concurred without causing Russell further distress. Prue, after all, had been buying his dresses for years. She could see why Russell wouldn't want to appear disloyal. He had no way of knowing, really, which of these people might blab to Prue.

"I'm a real idiot," Russell told Burke. "When you told me about her, I just didn't make the connection."

At first Mary Ann thought he meant Prue. Then it occurred to her that Burke must have briefed the Rands about the local talk-show hostess he wanted for his new venture. In a moment of abject panic, she realized that Russell was dangerously close to spilling the beans.

"OK," said Chloe. "Who needs a drink? Let's see if we can rustle up a waiter for these people."

"Uh . . . right," said Russell. "Of course."

He had the unmistakable look of someone who had just been given a swift kick under the table.

Half an hour later, in the john, Chloe said: "Look, I'm sorry about ol' dummy out there. Burke told him not to bring up the talk-show stuff."

"It's no problem," said Mary Ann. "Really."

"Have you told him yet?"

"Not yet."

Chloe fixed her lips in front of the mirror. "It's a fabulous opportunity."

"Yeah. I know."

"Burke is so smart. He really is. I don't think you can go wrong with him." She blotted her lips together once or twice, then turned and cocked her head apologetically. "Sorry. I know it's none of my business."

"No," said Mary Ann. "That's OK."

"It's scary to move, isn't it? Gets you right in the gut. I felt that way exactly when Russell asked me to marry him. I mean, I knew what a life it could be, but all I could think of was how *foreign* everything would be. It's so stupid, isn't it?"

"You seem so collected," Mary Ann remarked. "I can't imagine that."

"Sure," said Chloe. "*Now*. Three years ago . . . forget it."

"Actually," said Mary Ann, warming to her, "I'm pretty good about kicking over the traces. I did it when I moved here. I came here on vacation, and just . . . you know, had a few Irish coffees . . ."

Chloe giggled. "And didn't go back?"

"Nope."

"Damn. I'm impressed. Where was home?"

"Ohio," said Mary Ann. "Cleveland."

"Well, no wonder!"

Mary Ann laughed uneasily. "Really."

Chloe stuck out her hand. "Akron."

"You're kidding!"

"Nope."

"But you seem so . . . so . . ."

"Like I said, it takes a while. It didn't hurt to know Russell, of course. I was Geek City before I met him. Stringy hair, awful skin . . . and this honker on top of it."

Mary Ann felt a mild protest was in order. "C'mon. You have a beautiful nose. Like a Spanish aristocrat."

"Try Lebanese."

Thrown and a little embarrassed, Mary Ann changed the subject. "And you really met him at Betty Ford?"

"Yep."

"That's such a romantic story." And what a movie it could be, she thought. She makes him clean and sober. He makes her beautiful and rich.

"It was just an administrative position. I wasn't a therapist or anything."

"Still," she said. "You befriended him in his hour of need."

"Yeah, I guess so. So what's the deal with your husband? He hates New York, huh?"

She nodded grimly. "More or less."

"Well, it's not like you wouldn't have contacts and everything.

679

Burke and Brenda know practically everybody, and if you need help—you know, finding a co-op or something—Russell and I would be glad to help."

Perhaps for the very first time the package she was being offered became vividly clear to her, and it was almost too much to take. Real fame, bright new friends, a home that would be her salon. She could see the place already: big pine cupboards, an antique harp, paper-thin Persian carpets against bleached floors. Something in SoHo, maybe, or just down the hall from Yoko at the Dakota . . .

"That's so sweet of you," she told Chloe.

"Not at all." Gazing into the mirror, Chloe swiped at the corner of her eye with her little finger. "We could use some new faces."

"That's great to know. That dress is genius, by the way."

"Oh, thanks." Chloe turned and smiled at her. "I can't wear it at home. Ivana Trump has one just like it."

"Bad luck," said Mary Ann. She was dying to ask what Ivana Trump was really like, but thought it might sound too hungry, too much like a desperado.

When they returned to the table, Mary Ann found Brian regaling the men—Michael now among them—with his current pet opinion. "I mean, give me a break, man. I'm no Republican, but the woman is being ragged about not dyeing her hair. In the old days, dyeing it was the scandal! What the fuck is going on here?"

Russell Rand, she noticed, made a valiant effort at laughing. Brian had a way of demanding too much from his audience when his turn came for center stage. It put people on the defensive, embarrassed them. He had no way of knowing this, of course, and she had never thought of a nice way to tell him.

That was her problem now, wasn't it? *A nice way to tell him.*

"Where's Thack?" she asked Michael as she slid into her chair.

It was Brian who answered. "He pooped out on us."

"His stomach's bothering him," Michael added.

"I'm sorry," she said. "Hope it wasn't the spring rolls."

"No."

"He dropped you off?"

"Yeah."

They've had a fight, she thought. It was just as well. Thack would only have made trouble.

"You haven't met Chloe," she said. And she touched Chloe's shoulder lightly, just to prove to Michael she could do it. "Chloe Rand, Michael Tolliver."

They greeted each other across the table. Michael was clearly captivated.

"Anyway," said Brian, blundering on, "Barbara Bush is a whole shitload better than that bitch we've got in the White House now. All she ever does is have her hair done and con free dresses out of designers."

Dead silence all around.

Brian looked from face to face for reinforcement.

How typical of him, she thought. If he'd thought for half a second before shooting off his mouth . . .

"Oh," said Brian, looking at Russell Rand. "I guess this means you . . . ?"

The designer managed a thin smile. "It wasn't a con, really."

"Well . . . it's good advertising, at least. I mean, the people who like her are probably the ones who . . . anyway, it doesn't imply a personal endorsement on your part."

"I'm very fond of Mrs. Reagan, actually."

Brian nodded. "Well, I don't know the lady."

Mary Ann gave him a look that said: No, you don't, so shut up.

Russell Rand remained gracious. "She's gotten kind of a bum rap, you know. She's not at all the person she's perceived to be."

"Yeah, well, I guess, since I can only go by things generally available to the common man . . ."

"I don't blame you for thinking that way. I really don't."

Brian nodded and said nothing. Michael sat perfectly still, staring at his Calistoga and looking mortified.

Somebody had to lighten things up, so Mary Ann said: "Can't take him anywhere."

"Not at all," said Russell Rand. "We're all entitled to our opinion."

"Thank you," said Brian, speaking to the designer but casting a quick, sullen glance in her direction.

A Bad Dream

The dream was still vivid as life when Michael stumbled out to greet the dawn. A thick coat of dew covered the deck, and he was reminded of how Charlie Rubin once referred to this phenomenon as "night sweats." Below, in the neighboring gardens, the wetness on the broad, green leaves suggested deceitfully that the drought had passed. Only the garden of his dead neighbor told the truth, its ravaged tree fern blunt as a crucifix in the amber light of morning.

He lifted his eyes until they jumped the fence and fled into the valley below, where a thousand Levolored windows were ablaze with sunrise. Sometimes, though not at the moment, he could see other men on other decks, watching the valley like him from their own little plywood widow's walks.

What he loved most about this view was the trees: the wizened cypresses, the backyard banana trees, the poplars that marched along the nearest ridge like Deco exclamation marks. There were some, of course, the cypresses in particular, that could only be appreciated through binoculars, but he knew where they were just the same.

Suddenly, a flock of parrots—forty strong, at least—landed in the fruitless fig tree of the house next door. While they screeched and fussed with their feathers, he stood stock-still and debated waking Thack for the event. He had never seen them this close to the house.

"Wow," came a voice behind him.

Thack stood in the kitchen doorway. Clad only in Jockey shorts, his smooth body looked heroic in the morning light, but his thinning, sleep-bent hair muddled the effect, lending it a comical, babyfied air.

"Should I come out?"

"Yeah," said Michael, "but make it graceful." He couldn't help but feel vindicated. He'd been raving about these creatures for almost a year now, without so much as a flyover to prove to his lover that he hadn't been hallucinating.

Thack joined him at the rail. "Noisy little fuckers."

"Yeah, but look how beautiful."

"Not bad."

"They used to be pets," Michael told him.

"That's what you said."

"See those little ones? Those are the parakeet groupies."

In the midst of this appreciation Harry scampered onto the deck, causing the birds to ascend in a whirling flurry of green.

"Well, good morning," said Michael as he scratched the poodle's rump.

Thack knelt and joined him, studying Michael's face before he spoke. "Don't be mad at me," he said.

"I'm not mad."

"Yeah, you are."

"Go back to bed," said Michael. "It's too early for you."

"Nah," said Thack. "I'm up now. I'll make us breakfast."

It was oat bran, Sweeney style, black with raisins. They ate it at the kitchen table, while Harry watched them.

"Well, how was it?" asked Thack.

"Fine. They were nice. She's really an extraordinary-looking woman."

"I'm sure."

This could have been snide, but Michael decided that it wasn't.

Thack poked at his cereal for a while, then asked: "Did he drop any hairpins?"

"What do you mean?"

"C'mon. You know what that means."

"I know, but . . . in this case . . ."

Thack sighed impatiently. "Did he just assume that everyone knew he was gay, or did he spend the whole evening playing breeder?"

"It wasn't really one way or the other."

683

"Did you tell him you were gay?"

"No."

"Why not?"

"Because, Thack, it didn't come up. Besides, I'm your basic generic homo. Who needs to be told?"

"He does. He needs to be surrounded by fags and told what a fucking hypocrite he is."

"I thought we were done with this," said Michael. "Is there more milk?"

"In the refrigerator."

Michael brought the carton to the table and splashed milk on his cereal.

"The thing is," said Thack, "he was famous for being gay."

"Not to me he wasn't."

"Oh, c'mon. I heard about it down in Charleston. Everybody in New York knew about him. He fucked every porn star in town."

"So?"

"So now he's out selling wedding rings and singing the praises of heterosexual love."

"It's his profession, sweetie."

"OK, but it doesn't say shit about his character."

Michael was beginning to get irked again. "You don't know him," he said. "Maybe he really loves her."

"Right. And maybe she's got a dick."

"Thack . . . people get married for all sorts of reasons."

"Sure. Money and image, to name two."

Michael rolled his eyes. "He's got much more money than she does."

"And he plans to keep it too. Can't have America knowing he's a pervert."

"They're doing an AIDS benefit in LA," Michael reminded him.

"Uh-huh. Welded at the hip, no doubt. A nice liberal married couple helping out the poor sick gay boys. Only you can be damn sure they won't be mentioning the G-word."

684

"Why are we arguing?" Michael asked. "You know I agree with you. Basically."

"Why'd you go, then?"

"Look, it was a question of not busting up the party. Mary Ann obviously wanted to go."

"No, that's a cop-out. You wanted to go too. This shit matters to you."

"OK," said Michael. "Maybe it does."

Thack sulked for a moment. "Well, at least you admit it."

"Admit what? That I was curious? Big deal. Thack, I can't go through life being some sort of Hare Krishna for homos. I just can't. I'd rather find out what I have in common with people and go from there."

"Fine. But what you have in common with Russell Rand you could never talk about in public. Not if you wanted to be his friend."

"Who said I wanted to be his friend?"

After a long, brooding silence, Thack said: "She should never have bullied us into going. She invited us to her house for dinner, and then she just let Burke take over. It was fucking rude."

"I agree with you," Michael said calmly. "It could have been handled better."

This seemed to placate him. Eventually, Thack began to smile.

"What is it?" asked Michael.

"She told Brian that Burke has a little dick."

"Brian told you that? When?"

"Yesterday at lunch."

"It's not true," said Michael.

Thack gave him a sly look. "How would you know?"

"We double-dated to the mud baths in Calistoga. Him and Mary Ann and me and Jon. They have a girls' side and a boys' side, so we ended up in . . . you know, adjoining vats." He shrugged. "It was kind of glopped with mud, but it looked fine to me."

"Figures," said Thack.

"What do you mean?"

"Brian thinks she said that to make him feel better."

685

"About what?" asked Michael.

Thack shrugged. "Them still having a thing going."

"Burke and Mary Ann? Please."

"Well, you saw them last night."

"Saw what?"

"Those looks she kept giving Burke." Thack looked peevish. "She kept catching his eye all night long. Didn't you see it?"

"No."

"Well, something's going on."

"So why were we invited to witness it? That makes a helluva lot of sense."

"Maybe she wants your blessing," said Thack. "She usually does."

"Oh, right. Why are you so down on her all the time? Does she always have to have an ulterior motive?"

"No, but . . ."

"Just save it, OK? I'm sick of arguing with you!"

This flare-up came so suddenly that Thack frowned. "What brought this on?" he asked.

"Nothing. I'm sorry. It's not you. I had a bad dream."

"About what?"

"Oh, it's stupid. You and I went to Greece, looking for Mrs. Madrigal."

Thack smiled. "What's so bad about that?"

"Well . . . she was hiding from us. She was afraid we were gonna take her back. She had this little lean-to sort of thing on a cliff . . . with lots of her stuff from home. When we finally found her, she invited us in for sherry, and I told her how much we missed her, and she said: 'Life is change, dear.' It was really horrible."

Thack reached across the table and stroked Michael's hand. "You're just feeling guilty about not calling her."

"I know."

"Do you have a number for her?"

"No."

"Well, maybe . . ."

"I just have the creepiest feeling about this trip. There's no real reason for it . . . I just do." Michael knew how neurotic this sounded, but there was no point in denying his dread. Its roots apparently reached far deeper than that ridiculous dream.

Thack observed him for a moment. "You know," he said gently, "you didn't betray her when you moved out."

"I know that."

"Do you?"

"Well . . . if you wanna get technical, I didn't give her that much notice. I lived there for ten years . . ."

"OK, here we go."

"That's not it, though. It really isn't."

Thack gave him a dubious look.

"She wanted this to happen," he said. "She wanted me to fall in love. For Christ's sake, how can you betray your landlady?"

"Exactly." Thack smiled victoriously and took another bite of his oat bran.

The call came when Michael was rescuing an English muffin from the jaws of their recently acquired antique Deco toaster. Mary Ann's voice was subdued enough to suggest that Brian was still in bed. "Is this too early?" she asked without announcing herself.

"Not at all," he told her.

Thack cast a curious glance at him.

"We loved having you last night," she said.

"Thanks. It was fun. We really enjoyed ourselves."

His lover rolled his eyes.

"Aren't the Rands nice?"

"Very." He was keeping it cryptic now to avoid further commentary from Thack.

"Look, I wondered what you were doing tomorrow. I thought we could go down to the Marina Green or something, take one of our walks."

One of our walks. As if they did this all the time. As if they'd never stopped taking them.

"I could pick you up," she added.

He hesitated only because Thack had reserved Saturday for building his pink triangle trellis. "God," he said, "I've got so many chores . . ."

"I could have you back by early afternoon. Please, Mouse, I really need to talk to you."

He marveled at the potency of an old nickname. "OK. Fine. What time?"

"Ten o'clock?"

"Great. Shall I bring anything?"

"Just your sweet self," she said. "Bye."

"Bye."

When he hung up, Thack said: "Mary Ann?"

He nodded. "We're getting together tomorrow morning. The two of us."

Thack said "Fine" and left it at that, but Michael knew what he was thinking.

He was thinking the same thing himself.

Lesbian Sauce

Taking her usual shortcut through the churchyard, Mona Ramsey headed into the high street of Molivos, where a pack of German tourists had already set forth on a predinner prowl through the gift shops. The street, which was barely wide enough for a car, was roofed at this point by a mat of ancient wisteria, so that to enter it was to find herself in a tunnel—cool, dim, and cobbled—descending to the village center.

The tailor shop lay near the upper end of the tunnel, across from a pharmacy where a dough-faced old lady made proud display of condoms with names like Dolly, Squirrel, and Kamikaze. Dick-worship, Mona had found, was as rampant in Lesbos as it was everywhere else in Greece. You couldn't buy a pack of breath mints at the local newsstand without running into a shelf or two of those plaster-pricked Pans.

The patriarchy was out in full force when she entered the tailor shop. The proprietor, who also functioned as vice-mayor of the village, was gabbing away to half a dozen of his male constituents. Seeing her, he rose behind his antique sewing machine and gave a little birdlike bob. His cronies receded noticeably, realizing she was a customer.

Hoping it would speak for itself, she held up the skirt that Anna had torn on her hike to Eftalou. Two days earlier, upon greeting the baker on her morning raisin bread run, Mona had made a stab at "*kalimera*," but it had come out sounding a lot like "*kalamari*." This had provoked gales of laughter from the other customers, who must have thought she had come to the wrong store. Who else but a stupid tourist would ask for squid at a bakery?

"Ahhh," said the tailor, recognizing the skirt. "Kiria Madrigal."

Thank God for that. Another fan of Anna's. "Just . . . you know . . ." She held up the tear, laid her palm across it like a patch, and looked up at him hopefully.

"Yes, yes," said the tailor, nodding. The other men nodded with him, reassuring her. He understands, they seemed to be saying. Now let us get back to our gossip.

She headed out into the high street, glad to be rid of this daughterly duty. An army truck came rattling up the viny tunnel, probably bound for the bakery, so she retreated into a gift shop to let it pass. The island was bristling with soldiers—the dreaded Turks being only six miles away—but the troops were too fuzzy-cheeked and funky to invoke her anti-militarist indignation.

She had been in the shop only a moment or two when she noticed a pair of English girls—one heavy, one slim—both with the same sculpted black-and-blond haircut. They were bent over a calendar called *Aphrodite 89*, obviously ogling the nudes. When the heavy one realized she was being watched, she tittered idiotically and pressed her fingers to her lips.

Mona reassured them with a worldly smile. "Not bad, eh?"

The skinny one made a fanning motion, pretending to cool herself off.

The three of them laughed together, reveling in this shared lechery. Mona couldn't help but notice how good it felt to be a dyke among dykes again. There weren't nearly enough of them in Gloucestershire.

The Mermaid was on the water, down where the esplanade became a sort of cobbled off-ramp to the little harbor. When she arrived, there were already three or four people staking claim to tables along the wall. On the wall itself, almost at eye level with the diners, stood a phalanx of alley cats, oblivious to the sunset, waiting for leftovers.

She tested a couple of tables and chose the less wobbly, then did the same with chairs. The sky was a ludicrous peach color, so she turned her chair to face it while it did its number. She wondered if the gushy couple next to her would burst into applause when it was over.

Costa, the proprietor, swept past her table with a bottle of retsina. "Your lovely mother," he said. "Where is she?"

"She's coming," Mona told him, trying not to sound crabby about answering this question for the fourth time today. "She's meeting me here."

Costa set the retsina down at the next table, then swung past her again on his way to the kitchen. "We have very good swordfish tonight."

"Great. You're onto me." She watched as he continued his progress into the restaurant, nodding to his customers like a priest dispensing absolution. Then he seized a sheet of fresh plastic and returned to her table, whipping it into place with a flourish. As custom seemed to demand, she helped him tuck the edges under the elastic band.

"Well," he said, giving the tablecloth a final whack, "you got some sun today."

"Did I?" She poked doubtfully at her forearm. "Think I should try for one big freckle?"

"It looks good," he insisted.

"Right."

"Would you like wine now?"

"No, thanks. I'll wait till she gets here."

"Very good," said Costa, and he was gone.

Out on the water, a blue-and-green fishing boat was putt-putting back to the harbor. In this orange explosion of evening it looked oddly triumphant, like something about to be hoisted into a mother ship. She wondered if its captain felt heroic, knowing that all eyes were upon him. Or did he just feel tired, ready for his dinner and a good night's sleep?

She looked up the esplanade, to see a pair of strollers stopped at the wall: the mousy little straight couple from Manchester who had bored her so thoroughly two nights before at Melinda's. Next to them, but farther along, stood the sixtyish German dykes she had already dubbed Liz and Iris, after a similar pair she knew at home.

Two by fucking two. The whole damn town was paired off.

Where in the name of Sappho did the single girls go?

The sign in Costa's window said: TRY MY LESBIAN SAUCE ON FISH/LOBSTER. She had laughed at that on their first night in town, pointing it out to Anna, and they had both been charmed by its naïveté. Naïveté, hell. Costa had served plenty of lowercase lesbians—plenty of city people in general—who must have registered amusement over the years. Certainly he had wised up by now, leaving it there only to get a rise out of tourists on the esplanade.

Like, for instance, those babes with the two-tone haircuts. They had stopped in front of the restaurant, lured by that absurd sign, to smirk the way they had smirked in the gift shop. The little one tried to take a picture of it, but her black-hosieried friend glanced at the nearby diners and shook her head disapprovingly.

Go ahead, girl, thought Mona. Don't be such a wimp.

"Ah . . . Mona?"

Startled by this voice, she turned to confront the handsome old codger who had shown Anna the sights this week, while Mona held down her post in a high-street taverna, watching the lovesick librarians go by. "Stratos," she said.

Short and dapper, he was wearing a blue sharkskin suit and smelling faintly of some piny aftershave. In the sunset his oversized white mustache had turned to pink cotton candy. "May I join you?" he asked.

"Of course." She waved toward a seat.

"I thought perhaps . . ." He lowered his compact frame into the flimsy little chair. "I hoped we could dine together tonight. You and your mother and I. But perhaps she has made plans already."

"No. Not really. I mean . . . she's joining me here any moment."

"Oh, yes?"

"You're welcome to join us."

"But perhaps your mother may . . ."

"I'm sure it's no problem, Stratos."

He looked pleased. "Then I insist that you both be my guests."

"Whatever."

"Good, good." He clamped his leathery little hands on his knees. "We must have wine, then. Retsina, yes? Or do you still think it tastes like mouthwash?"

She smiled at him. "I can handle it."

He flagged down the twelve-year-old who was busing tables and placed his order in Greek, patting the boy's shoulder when he was through. "So," he said, turning back to Mona, "have you been enjoying Molivos?"

"It's beautiful," she said, avoiding a direct answer. "Bored shitless" might lose something in the translation.

He murmured in agreement, then gazed out to sea with an air of doggy wistfulness. "The season is over," he said. "The people are leaving. The shops are closing. You can feel a difference in the streets already."

"Fine by me. The sooner that disco closes, the better."

He seemed to know what she meant, giving her a look that was almost sorrowful. "It is a great shame," he said.

"It gets louder and louder after midnight. And it's no good closing your shutters, because it just gets hot and stuffy, and you can still hear the damn thing, anyway."

He nodded gravely. "Many people feel the way you do."

"Why doesn't somebody do something, then? Pass a noise ordinance or something."

"There is such an ordinance," said Stratos. He seemed on the verge of explaining this, when the busboy arrived with the retsina and three glasses. The old man dismissed him, then filled two of the glasses. "There is such an ordinance, but the police have refused to enforce it."

"Fire the damn police."

Stratos smiled warmly, showing a gold tooth. "The police are the national police. They are right-wing."

This made no sense to her. "The right wing hates rock-and-roll."

"Yes, but the police hate the mayor. The mayor is communist, and they have no wish to help him in any way. The mayor has appealed to the police, but they are indifferent. This is not their regime, so . . ." He shrugged to finish it off.

"But this is their village. Everybody's gonna suffer in the end. People come here for peace and quiet, not for Bruce Fucking Springsteen. They'll stop coming."

"Yes." Stratos remained placid in the face of her outburst. "And the mayor will be blamed, you see. The communist regime will be blamed."

Mona groaned. "Disco Wars in the Aegean."

"Ah," said Stratos, raising eyebrows that looked like albino caterpillars. "Here is your mother."

Mona looked over her shoulder to see Anna striding down the esplanade, tanned and majestic in her linen caftan. It was gathered at the waist with a lavender scarf—a recent purchase, apparently—and her hair was up and spiked with her favorite chopsticks. There was even purple eye shadow to match the new scarf.

"Stratos," said Anna, extending her hand. "What a pleasant surprise."

For a split second, Mona thought he was going to kiss it, but he simply bowed and said: "It's a very small village."

"Yes," said Anna, smiling demurely. "I suppose so." She descended gracefully into a chair and folded one hand across the other on the table. Such a femme, thought Mona. "Will you join us for dinner, Stratos? I'm sure we'd both be delighted if you would."

"He asked us," Mona told her. "I said we would already."

"Oh." Anna seemed to redden slightly. "How nice."

Stratos gestured toward the retsina. "I took the liberty. I hope you don't . . ."

"Wonderful," said Anna, holding out the empty glass.

Stratos poured rather elegantly. "Mona has been telling me about your unpleasantness with the disco."

"Oh, yes," said Anna. "Can you hear it where you live?"

He shook his head. "Not much. My house is protected by the hillside."

"Lucky you," said Anna. "We're just above it. The sound bounces off the water and heads straight for our place. There's a sort of amphitheater effect, I suppose."

"It will end soon," he said.

Mona was irked by his typical Greek complacency. "I'm gonna cut the wires one night."

Anna gave her an indulgent little smile, then turned to Stratos and said: "My daughter is an anarchist, in case you haven't noticed."

"She thinks I'm kidding," said Mona.

Stratos chuckled and raised his glass in Mona's direction. "Perhaps I will join you. We will be guerrilla patriots."

Mona clicked her glass against his. "Death to disco," she said.

During dinner, four or five cats climbed down from the wall and did a weird little gavotte around Anna's legs. "This one reminds me of Boris," she said, tossing a scrap of fish to an ancient tabby. "Do you remember him?"

Mona nodded. "Is he still alive?"

"No." Anna looked wistful. "No, he's gone. I have Rupert now."

694

Stratos filled their glasses again. "Did you tell Mona about Pelopi?"

"No," came Anna's soft reply. "Not yet."

Was she blushing, Mona wondered, or was that just the sunset? "What's Pelopi?"

"It's a village in the mountains. Stratos has kindly offered to . . . show it to me."

"Oh."

Stratos said: "It is the birthplace of the father of Michael Dukakis."

"Oh . . . right."

How could she have forgotten about Pelopi? The taverns of Molivos were abuzz with media pilgrims on their way to the sacred birthsite. Several local farm trucks even sported Dukakis bumper stickers. The mayor of Molivos, it was said, had already made plans to ship a traditional Lesbian dance troupe to the White House in the event of a Democratic victory.

She wasn't holding her breath.

"Stratos says it's lovely," Anna put in, giving Mona a meaningful look. "His cousin has a house there."

"That's nice. Another day trip, then?"

"Well . . . no. We thought we'd stay over."

Nodding slowly, Mona saw the light.

Of course. They were fucking. Or at least wanted to be very soon. How could she have been so thick?

Anna regarded her peacefully with a slight, beatific smile, which said: Don't make me spell it out.

"It is much smaller than here," said Stratos. "Very beautiful."

Mona nodded. "Is your cousin away or something?"

"Mona, dear . . ."

She flashed her parent a crooked smile, acknowledging the conquest. That it was Anna, and not her dyke daughter, who was about to be laid on the Sapphic isle was an irony lost on neither one of them.

Oh, well. This was what you got for believing in brand names.

"So," Stratos jumped in, "you will have the villa to yourself for a few days."

"Fine." She smiled at them both. "No problem. Have a good time." After thinking for a moment, she added: "But don't leave on my account."

"We're not, dear."

"Because I can always take a room . . ."

"I'm leaving on my own account," said Anna, cutting her off with a vengeance. "I'm eager to see Pelopi."

"Mmm. Well, I can see why."

Her parent gave her a hooded look.

"That's pretty awe-inspiring. The birthplace of Dukakis's father." Mona shook her head in mock amazement, enjoying herself to the fullest.

Anna avoided this gentle harassment by staring at the big greasy clock on the wall of the Mermaid. Eventually she asked: "What time is it in San Francisco?"

Mona did some quick arithmetic. "Uh . . . nine o'clock in the morning."

"Oh, good." Anna rose suddenly and gave Stratos an apologetic look. "Would you be a dear and keep my daughter company for about ten minutes?"

"With pleasure." Stratos's smile turned cloudy after a moment. "Nothing is wrong, I hope?"

"No, no. Not a thing. I just want to call the children." Anna turned back to Mona. "I'll just dash up to the phone lady and be back in three shakes. We'll all go someplace for dessert."

She gave them both a final glance and hurried off into the gathering dark.

The waiter appeared, distressed about Anna's departure. Mona assured him she would return, then ordered a Sprite-and-ouzo.

"What about you?" she asked Stratos.

He shook his head.

The waiter left.

696

"You have brothers and sisters?" Stratos asked.

Mona smiled at him and shook her head. "She calls her tenants her children."

The old man absorbed this without changing his expression.

"She runs an apartment house," Mona explained. "I guess she told you that already?"

He nodded. "Yes."

There was a long, uncomfortable silence before Stratos said: "I have an idea for you."

"What's that?"

"Perhaps . . . if the disco noise is too much for you at the villa . . . you should go to Skala Eressou."

Mona blinked at him, wondering if Anna's sudden trip to the phone lady had been a setup. Were they trying to get rid of her, after all?

"There is a beach there," he added.

"Like this one?" This sounded harsher than she'd intended, but the local strip was a horror—narrow, rocky, and strewn with garbage.

"No," he replied. "With beautiful sand. It is a simple place, but I think you might like it."

She decided that he was just being nice. Still, she wanted to stay put at the villa. It was paid for, after all, and this "simple place" might be even less exciting than here. "Thanks," she told him, "but I'm OK."

"It is the birthplace of Sappho, and there are many tents on the beach."

"Tents?" she asked.

"Yes."

"What sort of tents?"

"Many women . . . feminists . . . from everywhere. Many more than here."

She studied the face, but it betrayed nothing.

"Perhaps you would like it," he said.

She gave him a slow–blooming smile. "Perhaps I would."

The Wave Organ

Beneath the blue porcelain dome of Noe Valley a lone kite chased its rainbow tail. Mary Ann watched it for a moment, admiring its reckless indecision, then swung the Mercedes into Michael's driveway. October's false springtime gave her an unexpected surge of optimism. The task ahead of her might not be as terrible as she'd once imagined.

Thack called from the garden. "He'll be right out." He was on a ladder, nailing planks to the side of the house.

"Thanks."

"You've got a nice day for it, looks like."

"Yeah," she said. "It does." It occurred to her that he could be very pleasant when he wanted to. "What's that you're building?"

"Just a trellis."

"It looks interesting."

"Well . . . it will. I hope."

Michael hollered at her from the doorway. "Do I need a jacket?"

"No way."

Seconds later, he bounded out of the house in cords and an ancient pale-green Madras shirt, that yappy little poodle toe-dancing around his heels. "No, Harry. You're staying here, poopie. Stay. Here. Understand?"

"Has he been walked?" Thack asked, gazing down from the ladder.

"This morning. To the p-a-r-k." Michael grinned at Mary Ann as he climbed into the car. "We have to spell around him, or he gets unnecessarily excited."

"I know exactly what you mean."

He laughed. "Only, Shawna can spell, remember?"

"Yeah. We're thinking of having that fixed."

She joined in his laughter as they pulled out of the driveway. He always made her feel so reckless.

Down at the marina, they parked in the lot next to the yacht club. The bay was anemic with sails, the volleyballers so jammed onto the west end of the green that they seemed to be playing a single, riotous game. Michael suggested they walk out the seawall to the Wave Organ, which suited her fine, since there were less people out there and she needed all the privacy she could get.

She had done a short feature on the Wave Organ once, but she had never actually seen it. It was basically a series of plastic pipes that ran underwater and surfaced at a stone terrace at the end of the seawall. By pressing an ear against one of several openings on the terrace, you could hear the "music" of the organ, the very harmonies of the sea itself, if you believed the press releases.

Michael knelt by one of the openings.

"How is it?" she asked.

"Well . . . interesting."

"Does it sound like music?"

"I wouldn't go that far."

She found a neighboring outlet, sort of a stone periscope, and listened for herself. All she heard was a hollow hiss, overlaid with a lapping noise. Not exactly a symphony of Neptune.

"Maybe it's better when the tide changes." As usual, Michael refused to abandon his fantasies.

"What is it now? High or low?"

"Who knows?" He looked around, assessing the structure. "The design is nice, though. It's kind of neoclassical post-modern. I like those carved stones."

"They're from cemeteries," she told him.

"They are?"

"That's what I heard."

He sat down in an alcove and caressed the contours of the stones. Joining him, she gazed out at the billowing sails, the gulls swooping low over the water. After a silence, she said: "I'm sorry we've lost touch lately."

"That's OK."

"My schedule gets the best of me sometimes."

"I know."

"Brian fills me in on you, so . . . I feel connected somehow."

"Yeah." He nodded. "He does that for me too."

"I don't want us to drift apart, Mouse. I count on you for too much."

He studied her for a moment. "Was that what you wanted to tell me?"

She shook her head.

"What is it, then?"

"Burke has offered me a job."

"A job?"

"In New York. As host of a syndicated talk show."

He took a while to absorb this, but he seemed more amazed than horrified. "You're kidding."

"No."

"Like . . . national?"

"Yes."

"Hot damn!"

"Isn't it incredible?"

"Are you taking it?" he asked.

"Looks like it. Burke doesn't know that yet, but I've pretty much decided."

"What does Brian think?"

"I haven't told him yet. I wanted to sort things out first."

A couple approached, checking out the Wave Organ. "How is it?" asked the woman.

"Iffy," Michael told her.

The man pressed his head against one of the stone periscopes. He was wearing enough polyester to have been a member of Mary Ann's studio audience. "What are you supposed to hear?" he asked.

"We're not sure," said Mary Ann.

The man listened for a while, then grunted and walked away. This was apparently enough for his wife, who didn't bother to listen.

As they left, she stopped abruptly in front of Mary Ann. "I have to tell you," she said. "I loved your show on phone sex."

Mary Ann did her best to be gracious. "That's very sweet of you."

The woman fled, her message delivered, joining her husband as he left the seawall.

Michael turned and grinned at her. "Are you sure you want to be bigger than this?"

She pressed her finger to her temple and pretended to ponder the issue.

"OK," he said. "Stupid question."

This was what she loved about him. He could wriggle in closer to her real self than anyone she had ever known. He could stay there longer too, snuggled up against her burning ambition like a cat against a coal stove.

"Will you be . . . like the main host?"

She nodded. "They're gonna keep the name. *Mary Ann in the Morning.*"

"Perfect. How star-making."

"Isn't it?"

"So what's the problem?" he asked. "Are you afraid that Brian won't want to go?"

"No," she answered. "I'm afraid that he will."

His face remained composed, but he obviously understood.

"I don't love him anymore, Mouse. I haven't loved him for a long time."

Looking away, he said "Shit" so softly that it sounded like a prayer.

"I know how this must seem to you. We haven't exactly talked about . . ."

"What about Shawna?"

She paused to measure out her words. "I wouldn't take her away from him. She belongs here as much as he does."

He nodded.

"Even if I did still . . . feel something, it wouldn't be fair to make him leave. The nursery means more to him than anything he's ever done. He wouldn't be happy in New York. It's a whole different world. You saw him the other night with the Rands."

"What was wrong with him?"

"Nothing was *wrong*. He just wasn't . . . comfortable. It's not his game; it never has been. He says so himself, all the time." She searched Michael's long-lashed brown eyes for a response. "You know that's true. It would kill him to be reduced to being my escort again."

"Yeah," he replied, somewhat absently.

"There was a time when we had something, but it just isn't there anymore."

He kept his eyes on the water. "Are you still in love with Burke?"

She had expected this, of course. "No. Not a bit."

"Is he in love with you?"

She gave him a small, ironic smile. "I'm not sure he even *likes* me. This is business, Mouse. I swear. Nothing else."

Michael watched a gull as it trooped solemnly along the edge of the seawall. "How long has it been like this?"

"I don't know."

"You must."

"No," she said. "It sort of crept up on me. It was a lot of little things that just added up. It's not like I've been thinking about it for a long time."

"But the talk-show thing forced the issue?"

"Well, it made things clearer. I saw how long I've been settling for less than the whole package. I need a partner, Mouse. Someone who dreams about the same things." Suddenly, she felt hot tears welling behind her eyes. "Sometimes I look at Connie Chung and Maury Povich and get so *jealous*."

"Do you want a divorce?"

"I don't know. Not for a while. It might just complicate things. This would be more like Dolly Parton."

He obviously didn't understand.

"You know. She has a husband back in Tennessee, doesn't she? Who digs ditches or something?"

"Paves driveways."

"Whatever," she said.

"So . . . a separation?"

"I want whatever's easiest on everybody, that's all."

"Maybe you should wait, then. See how this job turns out."

"No. How fair would that be? It's over, Mouse. He has to know that. There's just no other way out." She began to sob, mangling her words. "I'm not a monster. I just can't . . . make him give up his life here for . . . something that isn't working anymore."

"I understand."

She dug a Kleenex from her purse and blew her nose. "Do you? Really?"

"Yes."

"I was so afraid that you wouldn't. That you'd hate me for this. I can't stand the thought of losing you."

"When have you ever lost me?"

"I don't want to now," she said. "Especially not now."

He slipped his arm gently around her waist. "When are you gonna tell him?"

"I don't know. Soon."

"He won't be ready, you know."

She blotted her eyes with the wadded Kleenex, feeling a twinge of anxiety. "You won't tell him, will you?"

"Of course not, but . . . he loves you a lot, Babycakes."

"No," she said. "It's a habit. It's something that just happened to us because we didn't have anywhere else to go. He knows that himself. Deep down."

"C'mon."

"I mean it. It's the truth."

"You and I just happened," he said.

"No we didn't. We've always chosen each other, Mouse. From

the very beginning." She looked at him but didn't touch him, knowing it would be too much. "We're gonna be friends when we're both in rockers at the old folks' home."

A tear slicked his cheek. He swiped at it with the back of his palm, then smiled at her. "Did you pick this spot on purpose?"

"What do you mean?"

"Where we met. The Marina Safeway."

"Oh, yeah." It was down at the end of the green. She hadn't been there in years, she realized. How like him to think that she had brought him here for commemorative purposes.

"Remember Robert?" he asked. "The guy I was with that day?"

"Do I! He was the one I was trying to pick up!"

"Well, thanks a lot."

She smiled. "What about him?"

"I saw him the other day," he explained. "I couldn't believe how boring he was."

"Of course."

"All I could think was: What if he hadn't dumped me? I'd be living in some tract home in Foster City. And I never would've met Thack."

She didn't know exactly what to say to that, so she gazed out at the water. Angel Island squatted in the distance like a dusty shrub in the midst of a wide blue prairie. She and Michael used to picnic there, years ago. They would spread a blanket on one of the old gun emplacements and talk about men for hours on end.

"I want you to come visit me," she told him.

"OK."

"Promise?"

"Of course."

"If you do," she said, "I'll introduce you to everybody in the world."

"It's a deal. And you'll call me every week?"

"With dish like you won't believe!"

When he laughed, she knew that the worst was over. Ten minutes later they strolled to the Marina Safeway in quest of lunch. Out on the seawall, another bewildered couple knelt in homage to the Wave Organ, listening for the music that wasn't there.

Interrogations

On Monday morning, in the greenhouse at Plant Parenthood, Brian turned to Michael and said: "Mary Ann says you guys had a good time catching up."

Michael was thrown, but he tried not to show it. She had been right, of course, to tell him about their outing at the marina. Why harbor any more secrets than absolutely necessary? "Oh, yeah," he replied as breezily as possible. "It was nice. We bought pasta salad at the Marina Safeway."

His partner's sandpaper cheeks dented in a smile. "Is that place as cruisy as it used to be?"

"Got me. I was too busy lusting over the pasta."

"I hear that."

Polly burst into the greenhouse, looking less collected than usual. "It's for you, Michael. The cops."

"What?"

"On the phone. Sounds important."

Shit. His parking tickets. How many were there, anyway?

"He says he knows you."

Brian chuckled. "An old boyfriend, probably."

"What's his name?" Michael asked.

"Rivera, it sounded like."

Michael looked at Brian. "He *is* an old boyfriend."

"What did I tell you?" Brian looked pleased with himself. "I know you better than you do."

He took the call in the office. "Bill. How's it going?"

"You remember, huh?"

"Of course. Good to hear your voice." How long had it been, anyway? Six years? Seven?

705

"Same here."

"What's up?" He half wondered if he was about to be asked for a date. For all Bill knew, Michael was still single, still looking for somebody to play with.

"I'm down at Northern Station. We've got a friend of yours. At least, he gave us your name. He's not making much sense, I'm afraid."

"What's his name?"

"Joe something. He won't tell us anything else."

He thought for a moment. Joe Webster. The guy Ramon Landes was looking after. The one with dementia.

"He's got no ID on him, but I didn't wanna turn him over to a hospital unless . . ."

"Real tall and skinny? About thirty, with brown hair?"

"That's him," said Bill. "You know him, then?"

"Not very well. I took an AIDS workshop with him. We have some friends in common. I'm surprised he even remembered my name."

"Do you know where he belongs?"

"Well, I know his Shanti buddy . . ."

"Could you call him, tell him to come pick him up?"

"Sure. Did he . . . uh . . . do anything wrong?"

"Well," said Bill, "he kind of . . . accosted someone. It was nothing serious. We haven't charged him with anything."

"I see."

"We just need to get him home safely."

"OK. Thanks a lot, Bill. I'll take care of it."

As luck would have it, Ramon wasn't at home, so he left a terse message on his machine and took off for Northern Station on his own. When he announced himself, the sergeant at the desk hollered "Rivera" over his shoulder and buried his beefy face in the pages of *Iacocca*.

Bill was there in a matter of seconds. "Hey . . . long time, buddy."

Resisting the urge to hug him, Michael shook the cop's hand with exaggerated heartiness. "Hey, kiddo. You're lookin' great." Bill had thickened a little around the waist, but he wore it well in his uniform. His civilian clothes of yesteryear—Qiana shirts and over-stitched designer jeans—had never done justice to his sex appeal.

"You still over there . . . what's it called?"

"Barbary Lane."

"Yeah, that's it. Damn." He shook his head, seemingly lost in memory. "I haven't been there for a long time."

"Actually, I moved away a few years ago. I'm over in Noe Valley now."

"Take a load off," said Bill, pointing toward a row of plastic chairs. "I'll get him."

"Wait." Michael grabbed his arm.

"Yeah?"

"What exactly did he do?"

"Oh . . . well, he kind of . . . harassed some Jehovah's Witnesses."

Michael repressed the first comment that came to mind. At the moment his job was to look responsible. "He assaulted them, you mean?"

"Not really." Bill made a notation on his clipboard. "Just waved something around for a while."

"What?" Michael scanned the room guiltily, as if there were Jehovah's Witnesses present, or grownups who might overhear them. "You mean his . . . ?"

The cop shook his head with a dry smile. "Somebody else's." Reaching below the desk, he retrieved a plastic shopping bag and handed it to Michael. "Check it out."

Inside the bag was a box bearing a glossy likeness of Jeff Stryker, the porn star.

"What the hell?"

"Read it," said the cop.

The label said: *The Realistic Jeff Stryker Cock and Balls. Incredibly awesome in size! Molded directly from Jeff's erect cock! Looks and feels amazingly realistic!*

He opened the end of the box, to reveal a velvet bag with a drawstring.

"I wouldn't take it out," said Bill.

"Right."

"The balls are squeezable."

"You're kidding."

"Nope."

"What's the world coming to?" said Michael.

Bill chuckled, but it was a dry, professional chuckle. "Got an address for him?"

"I'm sorry. I don't."

"Think you could phone it in later? For my report."

"Sure," said Michael. "No problem."

"So." The cop looked up from the clipboard. "How have you been?"

"Pretty good. I'm alive."

"Yeah. Really. Are you still . . . on your own?"

"No. I've got a lover now."

"Hey. All right. Where'd you meet him?"

"Alcatraz, actually."

This got a smile. "A tourist or a ranger?"

"Tourist."

"And then he moved here?"

Michael nodded. "About three years ago."

"Well, good for you." If Bill was racked with heartbreak, his police training had taught him to conceal it pretty well.

"How 'bout you?" asked Michael.

"Same as always. Bachelor Number Three."

"Well . . . it suits you."

"You got that right. What would I do with a lover at Pigs in Paradise?"

Michael drew a blank.

"You know, the big party. Gay and lesbian law enforcement. I took you to one, didn't I?"

"Nope."

"You sure?"

Michael rolled his eyes. "I would've remembered, Bill. Trust me."

"Come to the next one, then. Bring your lover."

"Thanks. Maybe we'll do that."

"I'll go get him," said Bill.

He gave Michael's shoulder a brotherly shake and ducked into the back room.

Joe Webster emerged looking gaunt and exhausted, his rangy frame slumped into a sullen pterodactyl stance. When his eyes met Michael's they registered no recognition whatsoever.

"Here's your friend," the officer told him.

"He's not my friend."

"This is Michael Tolliver. You said to call Michael Tolliver, didn't you?"

No answer.

Bill smiled indulgently and looked at Michael. "Is this the guy?"

Michael nodded. "He's right, though. We're not really friends."

Bill shrugged. "Well . . ."

"The bastards wouldn't give me a room," said Joe, scowling. "And they're outa fuckin' towels."

"Did you reach his Shanti buddy?"

"Not yet." Michael turned to Joe and tried to appear as benign as possible. "Why don't we go see Ramon? OK?"

"Where is he? Where's Ramon?"

"He's at home. Or he will be soon." He hoped to hell this was so. "I'm gonna take you there, OK?"

"No fuckin' towels. What the fuck do they think I'm doing? I paid, didn't I? Didn't I pay?"

"What's he talking about?" asked Michael.

"Got me. What're you gonna do if you can't find his buddy?"

"I dunno."

"You have a work number for him?"

"He works out of his house. He must be out shopping or something."

"No fuckin' towels, no fuckin' rooms . . ."

"Maybe you should call again," said Bill.

・ ・ ・

This time Ramon was home. Michael told him what had happened and offered to drive Joe to Ramon's house in Bernal Heights. Ramon thanked him profusely and was waiting on his front steps when they arrived half an hour later.

"Sorry about this."

"No problem," said Michael.

Joe unfolded his lanky frame from the VW and headed up the steps without a word. "Hey," Ramon called after him. "Say thank you to Michael."

Joe stopped and looked down at them. "Why?"

"Because I asked you to."

Michael felt uncomfortable. "That's OK. Really."

Ramon lowered his voice. "He's been losing it a lot lately. Last week he set fire to a trash can at a Louise Hay seminar."

"I see."

"He must really like you, or he wouldn't have given them your name."

"It doesn't matter," said Michael.

"He gets these periods when he's just a different person."

Michael nodded. "He kept talking about towels at the police station."

"He does that at the hospital too. The post office, for that matter. He thinks he's at the baths." Ramon shrugged. "It must be the little window or something."

Joe was watching them from the top of the steps. "You know," he yelled down, "you don't get points for this. Nobody's keeping score in heaven. If you get it, you get it."

Michael ignored him as he handed Ramon the bag with the rubber cock. "I'd keep an eye on this."

Ramon winked at him. "I owe you one."

"That's OK."

"*Did you hear me?*"

"I better go," said Michael.

Ramon nodded. "Yeah."

"It's time to get mad, Michael. Niceness doesn't count for shit!"

"Believe it or not," said Ramon, "he has moments when he's really clear."

Michael had the creepy feeling that this was one of them.

A Blind Item

"So anyway," Polly was telling Brian in the greenhouse, "Madonna and Sandra Bernhard are there on Letterman, their arms totally *draped* around each other. And they're like giggling and making jokes about the Hole, which is the Cubby Hole, this famous dyke bar in New York, and the whole damn thing is going straight over Letterman's head . . . the stupid pig."

Brian didn't buy this at all. "You're not gonna tell me Madonna . . ."

"Why not? Get real." She was scraping out plastic pots, stacking them in the corner. "Just because you can't stand the thought of it . . ."

He chuckled.

"What?"

"I like the thought of it."

"Yeah. Well, OK. That figures, doesn't it?"

He looked at her sideways. "Which am I supposed to do? Like it or not like it?"

"Hand me that pot, please."

He complied, grinning.

"The real question is: What the fuck does Madonna see in Sandra Bernhard? If I were Madonna, I'd be going for the serious stuff. Jamie Lee Curtis, at the very least." She stood up and dusted off her hands. "Shouldn't Michael be back by now?"

"Seems like it, doesn't it?"

"How long does it take to bail somebody out?"

"He didn't need bail," Brian said.

"Oh, yeah."

"I guess he could've had trouble finding the Shanti volunteer."

"Was that Mary Ann in the paper this morning?"

The change of subject threw him. "What do you mean? Where?"

"In Herb Caen's column."

"She was there? What did it say?"

"It might not have been her," said Polly. "It was a . . . you know. What do they call it when they don't use the name?"

"A blind item," said Brian, feeling queasy already. What the hell were they saying about her now? "Is there a paper in the office?"

"Yeah," she said, and followed him out of the greenhouse.

Five minutes later, when Polly had left the office, he collected himself and called Mary Ann at the station.

"Was that you?" he asked without announcing himself.

No answer.

"Was it?"

"Brian." Her voice assumed its most businesslike armor. "This is as much a surprise to me . . ."

"I didn't figure there could be *that* many perky morning girls being wooed by New York producers."

"It wasn't even supposed to be there."

"Oh. Well, then."

"I want to talk to you about this," she said, "but I don't want to do it on the phone."

"Shall I plant an item somewhere?"

She sighed. "Don't be like that."

"Like what?"

"All wounded and alienated. I was going to tell you about it."

"When?"

"Tonight."

"Wrong. We're talking now. Right this minute."

"No," she said quietly. "Not on the phone."

"Then meet me somewhere."

"I can't."

"Why? Do you have to be wooed some more?"

She made him pay for this with a long silence. Finally, she asked: "Where do you want to meet?"

"You name it."

"OK, then. Home."

He gathered from this that she was afraid of risking a public scene.

When he arrived, she was standing by the window, dressed in her traditional garb of apology—jeans and the pink-and-blue flannel shirt he liked so much. It was an obvious gesture, but it soothed him just the same. He was already beginning to feel as if he'd overreacted.

"I sent Nguyet home," she said.

"Good." He sat on the sofa.

"I'm really sorry about this, Brian. I don't know how it got to Herb Caen."

He didn't look at her. "Is it for real?"

"Yes."

"Do you wanna do it?"

"Very much."

"How long have you known about it?"

"A while."

"Since that lunch, right?"

She nodded.

"And what did you think? That I would be so jealous of some old burned-out boyfriend . . . ?"

"No. Never. You know there's nothing there."

"Well, OK. Then what?"

"What do you mean, what?"

"Why wouldn't you tell me? This is what you've been working toward. Didn't you think I'd be happy for you?"

"Brian . . ."

"Am I that much of a self-centered bastard?"

"Of course not."

"Did you think I'd be so attached to the nursery that I'd try to stand in your way?"

"Well . . ."

"You did, didn't you? That's exactly what you thought."

"I know how much you love it," she replied somewhat feebly.

"I love *you*, sweetheart. Your victories are my victories. That's always been enough for me. What do I have to do to convince you of that?"

She left the window and sat down on the chair across from him, tucking her legs neatly under her butt. "I don't think bad things of you, Brian. I really don't. I know how much you have to put up with."

She said this with such tenderness that he felt the last vestiges of his anger melt away. He gave her a chipper smile to let her know. "So what's he offering?"

"Just a show."

"Just? Syndicated, right?"

"Yeah."

"Out of New York?"

"Uh-huh."

"You don't seem very excited," he said.

"I am. There's just . . . a lot to think about."

"What have you told him?"

She shrugged. "That I'd have to talk to you."

This was suddenly making sense to him. "Is that why you brought him here for dinner? So I could see how unthreatening he was before you told me about it?"

She made a sheepish face.

"I don't have a problem with it. Really." He saw that doubts still lingered. "Your ship has come in, sweetheart. We should be celebrating." He gazed at her for a while, then patted the sofa cushion next to him. She left her chair and joined him, leaning her head against his shoulder.

"Call Burke," he said. "Tell him we'll do it."

"No."

"Why not?"

"He's in LA. I don't know how to reach him. He's gonna call me."

"Oh." He thought for a moment. "Did you tell Michael about this?"

"No. Of course not."

"Should I tell him?"

"No," she replied, almost fiercely. "Just leave it alone for a while."

"He's gonna ask. He must've seen the item."

"Oh, yeah." She frowned, deep in thought, obviously concerned about hurting her old friend.

"He'll understand," he told her, squeezing her shoulder. "It's not like he didn't run the place on his own before I came along."

When he got back to the nursery, Michael sauntered toward him in the slanting afternoon light.

"How did it go?" asked Brian, remembering the call from the cop.

"OK. They didn't book him or anything."

"What did he do?"

"Nothing. Waved a dildo at some Jehovah's Witnesses."

Brian laughed. "You sure he's sick?"

Michael's smile was forced. He seemed unusually subdued.

"I'm sorry," said Brian. "It's not funny, I know."

"No. It is. You're right."

"Are you OK, man?"

"Yeah. Fine."

"We were worried when we didn't hear from you."

"Oh, well . . ."

"I guess it took a while with the cops."

"Not really," said Michael. "I drove out to the beach. I needed some air."

"Don't blame you a bit."

"I should've called, I guess."

"No. Not at all." Poor guy, thought Brian. It must've really gotten to him.

"Polly said you had to leave. I hope it didn't make things tight."

"Nah." He wondered if Michael was hinting around about the blind item. At any rate, there was no point in avoiding the subject. "Did you see Herb Caen's column this morning?"

Michael nodded. "Polly showed me."

"It's Mary Ann."

"Oh, yeah?"

"She's gonna do it, I think."

Michael seemed to avoid his gaze. "Well, it's . . . definitely an opportunity."

"Yeah, it is." He hesitated a moment. "We may have to work something out, Michael."

"What do you mean?"

"About the partnership."

Michael blinked at him, uncomprehending.

"If I leave," he explained.

"Oh."

He hoped a smile would soften the blow a little. "If it helps any, this is pretty much of a surprise to me too."

"Well . . . that's OK."

"I'll work it out so you aren't strapped for help. I promise you that. If you want me to remain an absentee owner, fine . . . or whatever you want."

Michael nodded, looking faintly distracted.

"I know this is sudden. I'm really sorry."

"Hey."

"It's not like I love New York, you know."

"No."

"But I'd be a real shit to oppose her on this. It's really a great . . ."

"Maybe we should talk about this later, huh?"

It was obvious that Michael was hurt. "Well . . . OK."

"It seems a little premature at the moment."

"OK . . . Sure. I just didn't wanna hide anything. I wanted you to be in on it."

"I appreciate that," said Michael as he headed off toward the office.

• • •

Mary Ann was already in bed when Brian got out of the shower that night. As he came into the bedroom she was hanging up the phone.

"Who was that?" he asked, sitting on the edge of the bed.

"Michael."

"What did he want?"

"He says to bring the laptop with you when you come in to-morrow."

"Oh . . . OK." He turned and looked at his wife. "Did he say anything about New York?"

She shrugged. "He congratulated me. Not much else."

"I think he's kind of freaked out about it."

"Why?"

"You know. Busting up the partnership."

"Oh."

"To tell you the truth," he said, "I was too."

"Was what?"

"Freaked out."

"Oh."

"I'm over it." He reached across and stroked her thigh beneath the bedcovers. "We've got a real adventure ahead of us. It was all I could do to keep from telling Shawna."

She seemed to stiffen. "You didn't, did you?"

"No. But I don't see what harm . . ."

"It's completely premature, Brian."

"Why?"

"Well . . . it's not a deal yet. She'll blab it all over school."

"Oh, yeah."

"I'm having a hard enough time as it is. Kenan called me into his office today over that fucking item."

"Oh, Christ." He pictured the indignation of the station man-ager, his piggish panic at losing this lone jewel in his crown. "Is he onto you?"

"Oh, yeah."

"You denied it, though?"

"Of course."

"Attagirl." He turned off the light and climbed into bed, snuggling up to her.

"He's such an asshole," she said.

"Absolutely."

"I can't wait to watch him twisting in the wind."

For a moment, for the hell of it, he imagined them lying like this in another city, another season. There was fresh snow on the windowsill, and a streetlight outside, and Shawna was asleep in a wallpapered bedroom down the hall. "You know what?" he said.

"What?" she answered drowsily.

"If we got a place on the ground this time . . . with a garden, I mean . . ."

"Go to sleep," she said sweetly.

She beat him to it several seconds later, purring rhythmically against his back. She was dreaming of the future, no doubt, a land of riches and proper recognition and assholes twisting in the wind.

The Third Whale

Their villa, like most of the houses around it, was a two-story stone building with a red-tile roof and big pine shutters that could be battened against the noonday sun. There was a kitchen (which they never used), a terrace dripping with dusty wisteria, and a pair of huge, high-ceilinged bedrooms overlooking the Aegean. When Mona awoke in hers, it usually took her a while to determine whether it was morning or late afternoon, since she hardly ever missed a siesta.

At the moment, it was morning. She knew because she could hear roosters and the tinny radio in the taverna on the hillside below. (There were entirely different sounds in the afternoon—church bells and asthmatic donkeys and the piratical shouts of children as they clattered down the streets to freedom.)

A frisky zephyr had found its way through the crack in her shutters and was teasing the long, filmy curtains. Out on the landing between the bedrooms she heard her parent's graceful footfall and the unmistakable piglet squeal of the refrigerator door.

The double doors creaked open, and Anna stood there in her caftan, backlit by the morning, holding a bottle of mineral water.

"Are you awake, dear?"

Errant beams bounced off the shimmering blue plastic like rays from a holy scepter. Our Lady of the Liter, Mona thought, rubbing her eyes. "Yeah, I guess so. What time is it?"

"Eight o'clock. I thought you might like an early start, so you don't have to travel in the heat of the day."

Oh, yes. Her long-awaited pilgrimage to Sappho's birthplace. That was today, wasn't it?

"I bought some lovely raisin buns at the bakery. Shall I bring you one with some tea?"

Mona swung her legs off the bed. "No, thanks. I'll come down."

"Stratos says he can find a driver for you, if you like."

"That's OK. I'll just get one on the esplanade."

"Oh . . ." Anna reached into the pocket of her caftan. "I thought perhaps you could do with these." She dropped a handful of joints on Mona's dresser and smiled beatifically. "I'd hate for you to miss anything."

Mona smiled back at her. "Thanks."

"Its name is Sigourney."

The grass, which Mona had already sampled, was from the garden at Barbary Lane. Anna—who named all her dope after her favorite people—had mailed it to herself before leaving home. Despite the buffer of several boxes and four or five layers of shrink wrap, the package had reeked to high heaven when they picked it up in the tiny post office next to the Molivos police station.

No one had said a word, however. Anna could get away with anything.

An hour later Anna and Stratos left for the Dukakis natal site in a beat-up Impala convertible that, to hear Stratos tell it, was all but legendary in Lesbos. Trim and tanned, gold tooth glinting in the sun, the old guy looked almost rakish behind the wheel. Arranging herself next to him, Anna set about doing picturesque things with scarves. "If you can," she told Mona as the car bumped away down the cobblestones, "find something Sapphic for Michael."

"OK." She trotted alongside the car. "If you don't like Pelopi," she said, "feel free to come back and use the house."

Anna gave her an enigmatic smile.

"I'll be gone for a few days . . . is what I mean."

"Yes, dear. Thank you."

As the car pulled away from her, Stratos yelled: "Sappho the Russian." It sounded like that, anyway.

"What?"

"It's a hotel. Remember."

She yelled after the Impala. "Sappho the what?"

His answer was drowned out by a chorus of barking dogs.

She finished up the breakfast dishes, then packed a change of clothes, locked up the villa, and hired a cab on the esplanade. The cabs here were all Mercedeses, beige and battered, with lurid and elaborate shrines to the Virgin obstructing every dashboard. This was Mary's island, really, not Sappho's, and they never let you forget it.

The trip across the island took several hours along winding mountain roads. For most of the journey her driver plied her with cassettes of bouzouki music, so there was blessedly little call for conversation. Beyond the olive groves the landscape became barren and blasted, made vivid here and there by roadside memorials to people who'd gazed too devoutly at the virgin and missed a hairpin turn. She was thoroughly nauseated by the time they descended into the green farming outskirts of Skala Eressou.

It was a beach town, basically: two-story concrete buildings with tile roofs, a row of thatched tavernas forming a sort of boardwalk along the littered gray sand. At the edge of town, where she got out, a jumble of homemade signs offered various services for tourists. Among them, almost as crudely lettered, was one that purported to be official:

WELCOME TO SKALA ERESSOU
Please respect our customs and traditions.
Be discreet in manner and dress.
Happy holidays.

How fucking dare they? How many odes to discretion had Sappho ever written? She wondered if busloads of visiting dykes had become too demonstrative in the lap of the motherland and somehow horrified the Mary-worshippers. It made her want to rip off her shirt and grab the nearest woman.

She walked along the seafront tavernas to get the lay of the land. Most of the other tourists were Greek or German. The British voices were North of England, people on package tours, pale as larvae, buying sunshine on a budget. She spotted several pairs of lowercase lesbians along the way, but hardly enough to qualify the town for mecca status.

Thirsty and still a little queasy, she stopped at the nearest taverna and ordered a Sprite-and-ouzo, the drink she'd learned to tolerate in Molivos. She sipped it slowly, watching the beach. A bare-breasted fräulein with huge mahogany thighs was sprawled towelless on the coarse sand, reading a German tabloid. Her hair was bleached so white that she looked like a negative of herself. Mona made a mental note to pick up some sun block.

The beach curved down to a big gray mountain crumbling into the sea. There were wind surfers in the sparkling water and, just beyond the next taverna, a queue of bathers waiting for an outdoor shower. Despite obvious civic efforts at making the place look like a resort, there was an irrepressible seediness to Skala Eressou, which she found completely endearing.

But what of Sappho? Was there a marker somewhere commemorating her birth? Something noble and weatherworn, bearing a fragment of her work? Maybe she could buy a volume of the verses and read it while she strolled on the beach.

She tried three different gift shops and found not so much as a pamphlet on the poet's life. The guidebooks she checked devoted a paragraph or two to the subject, but the details, at best, were sketchy and embarrassed: The poet had been born in 612 B.C. in Skala Eressou. She had run a "school for young girls." Her passionate odes to the beauty of women had often been "misinterpreted."

Fuming, Mona stalked a statuary shop, where she passed row after row of plaster penises before pouncing on the only female figurine in sight. "Sappho?" she asked the clerk, pronouncing it "Sappo," the way the Lesbians did.

The clerk frowned at her, uncomprehending.

"Is this Sappho? The poet?"

"Yes," he replied, though it sounded suspiciously like a question.

"Forget it," said an American voice behind her. "It's Aphrodite."

Mona turned to see a woman her own age, handsome and lanky, with a big Carly Simon mouth. "They don't do Sappho. Not as a statue, anyway. Somebody told me there's an ouzo bottle shaped like her, but I haven't been able to find it."

Mona returned the figurine to the shelf. "Thanks," she told the American.

"You'd do better in Mitilini. They've got a statue of her down by the harbor." The wide mouth flickered. "It's ugly as shit, but what can you do?"

Mona chuckled. "I can't even find a book of her poetry."

"Well, there's not much left, you know."

"Oh, yeah?"

"The church burned it."

Mona grunted. "Figures."

"You might try the gift shop on the square. They've got some fairly decent Sappho key rings."

"Thanks," said Mona. "I'll do that."

The woman went back to her browsing.

In the shop on the square Mona found the key rings—a crude profile on an enameled chrome medallion. They weren't much, but they did say SAPPHO, so she bought a green one for Michael, thinking that it looked vaguely horticultural. Then she set off in search of a hotel that sounded like Sappho the Russian.

She found it on the boardwalk after a five-minute search. Sappho the Eressian. The room she rented there was spare and clean—blond wood, a single bed with white sheets, a lone lamp. She showered off the grit of the road, then anointed herself with sun block and changed into a crinkly cotton caftan she'd bought in Athens. She was much more comfortable when she returned to the beach and felt her wet hair kinking in the warm breeze.

She headed toward the big gray bluff, since the beach seemed less crowded at that end. The bathers grew sparser—and nuder—the longer she walked. When everyone in sight was naked, she skinned off her caftan and rolled it into a tight little ball, stuffing it in her tote bag. She spread a towel on the sand and lay on it, stomach down, feeling a warmth that seemed to rise from the earth's core.

The nearest sunbathers were a dozen yards away on either side. She raked her fingers through the coarse sand and felt it roll away magically, like tiny gray ball bearings. There was a breeze off the water, and the sun lay on her big white bottom like a friendly hand.

This was all right.

The last time she'd done this had been in San Francisco in the mid-seventies. She and Michael had gone to the nude beach at Devil's Slide. She had shed her clothes with great reluctance, feeling white and blobby even then. Michael, of course, had wussed out at the last minute, supposedly to preserve his tan line.

She missed him a lot.

She had wanted him to explore Lesbos with her, but the little fool had fallen in love on her and never found the time.

He wasn't sick, Anna had insisted. He might have the virus, but he wasn't sick.

But he could be. No, he would be. That was what they said now, wasn't it?

Unless they discovered a drug or something. Unless some scientist wanted the Nobel Prize bad enough to make it happen. Unless one of the Bush kids, or Marilyn Quayle, maybe, came down with the goddamned thing . . .

She laid her cheek against the warm sand and closed her eyes.

Later, in the heat of the day, she strode out into the sea. When she was thigh-deep, she turned and surveyed the broad beach, the prosaic little town and distant dung-colored hills. She didn't know a soul for miles. Anna and Stratos were on the other side of the island, napping by now, no doubt, or making love behind closed shutters, stoned to the tits.

She smiled at the thought of them and splashed water on her pebbling flesh. This has been a good idea, she decided, taking a holiday from her holiday. She felt wonderfully remote and unreachable, even a little mythical, standing here in the cradle of the ancients, naked as the day she was born.

On an impulse, she tilted her chin toward the sky and had a few words with the Goddess.

"You can't have him yet," she yelled.

She was pink by nightfall, but not painfully so. In her monastic room at Sappho the Eressian, she smoked one of Anna's joints and watched as the lights of the tavernas came on, string by string. When she was pleasantly buzzed, she glided down to the pristine little lobby and asked the desk clerk, just for the sound of it, where she could find a good Lesbian pizza.

By the strangest coincidence, they sold just such an item at the hotel taverna. It was a truly awful thing, dotted with bitter-tasting little sausages. She polished it off with gusto, then she began to speculate about the quality of Lesbian ice cream.

"Hello," crooned a familiar voice. "Find those key rings?" It was the woman with the Carly Simon mouth, a good deal browner than before. She was still in her walking shorts, but her crisp white shirt was a more recent addition.

"Yeah, I did," said Mona. "Thanks."

"What did you think?"

"Well . . . I bought one."

The woman smiled. "It's all there is, believe me."

"It's so stupid," said Mona. "You'd think they'd notice there was . . . some interest."

The woman chuckled. There was a comfortable silence between them before Mona gestured to a chair. "Sit down," she said. "If you want."

The woman hesitated a moment, then shrugged. "Sure."

"If you're about to eat, I don't recommend the pizza."

Wincing, the woman sat down. "You didn't eat the *pizza?*"

"I can't help it," said Mona. "I'm sick of Greek food." She held out her hand. "Mona Ramsey."

"Susan Futterman." Her grip was firm and friendly, devoid of sexual suggestion. Mona's current contentment was such that she didn't care one way or the other. It was just nice to have a little civilized company.

Susan Futterman lived in Oakland and had taught classics at Berkeley for fifteen years.

"I'm surprised it isn't Futterwoman," Mona told her.

"It was, actually."

"C'mon!"

"Just for a little while."

"Oh, shit," said Mona, laughing.

Susan laughed along. "I know, I know . . ."

"I had a lover once from Oakland."

"Really?"

Mona nodded. "She runs a restaurant in San Francisco now. D'orothea's."

"Oh, yeah."

"You know her?"

"Well, I know the restaurant." Susan paused. "Do you live in San Francisco?"

"No. England."

She looked surprised. "For good?"

"I hope so."

"What do you do?"

Mona thought it best to be vague. She hadn't been Lady Roughton for almost a month and was beginning to enjoy the anonymity. "I manage properties," she said.

Susan blinked. "Real estate?"

"More or less." She gazed out at the strollers along the boardwalk. "There really are a lot of women here."

"Oh, yeah."

"It's funny how just a *name* can do that much."

"Isn't it? Have you been down to the tents yet?"

"I don't think so," said Mona.

"You'd know," said Susan.

Susan was a seasoned Grecophile and tossed back several glasses of retsina without flinching. Mona stuck with her Sprite-and-ouzo and was feeling no pain by the time they set off in quest of the famous tents.

They were down at the end of town, some yards back from the beach in a dusty thicket. Most of them weren't tents at all but "benders," like the ones the antinuke women had built on Greenham Common— tarps flung over shrubbery to form a network of crude warrens.

She was astounded. "Where do they come from?"

"All over. Germany mostly, at the moment. I saw some Dutch girls too."

"Is it always like this?"

"Usually more," said Susan. "This is the tail end of the season."

Like pilgrims in a cathedral, they kept their voices low as they passed through the encampment. Here and there, women's faces beamed up at them in the lantern light.

Sappho's tribe, thought Mona, and I am a part of it.

Susan, it seemed, knew a woman in one of the benders: a young German named Frieda, square-jawed and friendly, with a blond ponytail as thick as her forearm. She poured vodka for her visitors and cleared a place for them to sit on her sleeping bag. There were

726

faltering efforts at an English conversation before Susan and the girl abandoned the effort and broke into frenetic German.

Unable to join them, Mona downed her vodka, then let her eyes wander around the bender. There was a battered leather suitcase, a bottle of mineral water, a pair of blue cotton panties hanging out to dry on a branch. On the ground next to her knees lay a pamphlet for something called Fatale Video, printed in English; the headline FEMALE EJACULATION leapt out at her.

She glanced at it sideways and read this:

FATALE VIDEO—By and for women only.
Thrill to Greta's computer-enhanced anal self-love!
Sigh with scarf play, oral and safe sex with Coca Jo and
    Houlihan!
Gasp at G-spot ejaculation and tribadism with Fanny and
    Kenni!

She smiled uncontrollably, then looked up to see if she'd been noticed. Susan and the girl were still nattering away in German. The return address on the pamphlet was Castro Street, San Francisco. While she'd been becoming a simple English country dyke, her sisters in the City had been building their own cottage industries.

The conversation across from her grew quieter, more intense. Then Susan said something that made the girl laugh. They're talking about me, thought Mona.

"Well," said Susan, addressing Mona again. "Ready to mosey?"

"Sure."

Susan spoke to the girl again, then led the way out of the bender. Mona's leg had gone to sleep, so she felt a little shaky as she left. Smiling at her, the girl said: "Bye-bye."

"Bye-bye," said Mona.

They didn't talk until they were out of the thicket and walking back to town on the moon-bleached sand.

"How long have you known her?" asked Mona.

Susan chuckled. "Since . . . oh, four o'clock."

They had seemed like old friends.

"I met her coming back from the beach today. She paints houses in Darmstadt."

"Why was she laughing just before we left?"

Susan seemed to hesitate briefly. "She thought you were my lover. I told her you weren't."

"Oh."

"She wasn't laughing at you."

Mona accepted this, but she had the uncomfortable feeling she was cramping Susan's style. "Well, look," she said, "if you wanna go back . . ."

"No, no." The broad smile seemed brighter by moonlight. "She didn't want *me*."

Mona stopped in her tracks.

"Or *just* me, anyway. She was looking for a couple."

"You're shitting?"

"No."

"Both of us?"

"Exactly."

"Christ," said Mona.

"Welcome to Lesbos," said Susan.

Just before midnight they drank thick Greek coffee at a restaurant near the square. The breeze off the sea was chillier now, and Mona was sorry she hadn't brought a jacket.

"It's almost winter," said Susan. "You can practically smell the rain coming."

"Yeah."

"I always come this time of year. I like it when I'm right on the cusp. When the tourists are leaving, and they start to batten everything down. There's something so poignant about it. And so purifying." She stirred her coffee idly. "All those leaves being washed clean." She looked at Mona. "What's it like where you are?"

"Right now?"

"Well . . . anytime."

Mona thought for a moment. "It's in the country. Gloucestershire."

"Oh, that's magnificent."

She nodded. "It gets cold and damp any day now, but I really don't mind it."

"Sure. You can sit by the fireplace with a cup of tea."

More often than not, Mona stood *in* her fireplace with a cup of tea, but it seemed pretentious to say so. She flashed for a moment on winter at Easley House: the lethal drafts, the frost on the diamond-shaped panes, the smoke curling out of the limestone cottages in the village. Then she saw the silly grin on Wilfred's face as he dragged some lopsided evergreen into the great hall.

Susan asked: "Do you live alone?"

She shook her head. "I have a son."

"How old?"

"Twenty. I adopted him when he was seventeen."

"That's nice. Good company."

Mona nodded. "The best."

"I have a daughter myself. She starts at Berkeley next year."

Mona smiled and sipped her coffee. If they weren't careful, they'd start dragging out snapshots.

Later she got another joint from her room and shared it with Susan as they strolled through the maze of deserted streets behind the promenade.

"This is nice," said Susan, holding a toke.

"It's Northern Californian."

"No." Susan laughed, expelling smoke. "I mean this. Getting to know you."

"Well, thanks." Mona gave her a wry smile. "Futterwoman."

After another leisurely silence, Susan said: "You think she's found her couple yet?"

Mona had been wondering the same thing herself. "Maybe not."

"Poor baby."

729

"I know. Must be tough, being so specialized."

Susan seemed lost in thought. "Did you know that whales do it in threes?"

Mona mugged. "Pardon me?"

"It's true. Certain types of whales perform the sex act in threes. The gray ones, I think. The third whale sort of lies against the female and holds her steady while the other two are fucking."

Mona mulled this over. "Is the third whale male or female?"

"I don't know."

"Well, what good are you? We need *facts* here, Futterwoman."

Susan chortled, obviously feeling just as giddy as Mona. "It was only a footnote."

"Are you sure you heard her right?"

"Absolutely," said Susan.

"What would she want with a couple of old dames?"

"Fuck you."

Mona laughed.

"She's not that young, anyway. It's just the ponytail."

"Yeah . . . but . . ."

"But what?" said Susan.

"If we go back . . ."

"Yeah?"

"Well . . . I don't wanna be the third whale."

Susan laughed. "Who does?" She stopped at an intersection, got her bearings, and reversed her course.

"The tents are back this way," Mona told her.

"I know. I have to get something in my room."

"What if she doesn't want us? I mean . . . what if she requires actual lovers?"

"We'll fake it," said Susan, picking up steam.

Her room was in a boardinghouse off the square. Mona waited for her downstairs while Madonna serenaded the patrons of a nearby taverna. Susan returned about three minutes later with an oblong box in one hand.

"Saran Wrap?"

Susan winked. "Don't leave home without it."

"What do you mean?"

"C'mon. Where have you been?"

Mona started to answer, but "Gloucestershire" didn't seem to cover it.

"Better safe than sorry," said Susan.

"Oh." The light dawned. "Right."

They hurried arm in arm down the pitch-black beach, giggling like a couple of teenagers.

Disguises

In the sun-splashed courtyard at Presidio Hill School, Brian knelt amid the other parents and children and applied the finishing touches to his five-year-old. "Stop squirming, Puppy. I'm almost through."

"Hurry up," she told him. "He's gonna be here."

"Yes, Your Majesty."

He dabbed his forefinger in the gunky green makeup and obliterated the last patch of white on her cheek. "This is looking pretty good, actually."

"Lemme see."

"Hang on."

She had brought along a little hand mirror, something from a doll's wardrobe, and was consulting it to the point of obsession. She had already used it to check the angle of her "shell"—two shallow cardboard boxes he had covered with green garbage bags—and to adjust the roll of her turtleneck sweater.

"Where is he?" she asked. "He's gonna miss it."

"He has to open the nursery first." He checked his watch and saw that Michael was half an hour late. He'd probably hung around the place too long and gotten entangled in a sale.

Shawna pawed through her bag of costume supplies. "Where's my ninja mask?"

"In my pocket. You don't wanna put it on yet. The parade won't start until . . ."

"I wanna have it on when Michael gets here."

"Oh . . . OK. Good thinking." He produced the mask—really an orange blindfold with eyeholes—and knotted it behind her head. "Can you see?"

"Yeah."

He drew back a little and appraised her. "I think we've got it."

She grabbed the little hand mirror.

"See?" he said. Out of the corner of his eye he spotted Michael climbing the stairs from Washington Street.

"Puppy . . . he's coming."

Shawna tossed the mirror aside and assumed what was apparently the stance of a Teenage Mutant Ninja Turtle.

"Where's Shawna?" Michael asked, playing along.

Shawna giggled and gave his leg a halfhearted little karate chop.

"Oh, no," said Michael. "The dreaded Michelangelo." He knelt and Shawna attached herself to his shoulder, laughing wickedly. "You look fabulous," he told her.

"Thanks."

"You're welcome." Michael turned back to Brian. "Sorry I'm late."

"No sweat. It hasn't started yet."

"Yeah," said Shawna. "No sweat." She let go of Michael's shoulder and darted across the courtyard to the spot where her classmates were assembling for the parade.

"How was it?" asked Brian.

"OK." Michael stood up. "Polly's there with Nate and the new guy."

"I thought it might have gotten busy on you." He hoped this sounded conscientious enough. He had already begun to feel guilty about leaving Michael in the lurch.

"No," said his partner. "It was slow. I got the shits, that's all."

"Oh."

Michael smiled ruefully. "Nothing dramatic. Just . . . garden variety."

"Well, look . . . nobody's gonna hold you to this."

"I know."

"If it gets too much . . ."

"I'll tell you. Don't worry. I'm over it, anyway. Shawna looks great."

"Doesn't she?"

"Did you make the costume?"

"Yeah."

"Not bad, Papa."

Brian said: "She's been waiting for you. You're the one she did it for."

"That's nice."

"She's gonna miss you, guy."

Though Michael didn't respond to this, something registered in his eyes. Brian couldn't decide what it was. Embarrassment, maybe? Sadness? Resentment?

"Where does the parade go?" asked Michael.

"To Saint Anne's," Brian told him, glad to change the subject. "The old folks' home."

The procession included a fairly predictable array of witches, ghosts, pirates, Hulks, and Nixons. To her delight, Shawna was the only Teenage Mutant Ninja Turtle. Brian and Michael tagged alongside with the other grownups, like paparazzi at a royal wedding—there but not there.

The general idea was to cheer up the old folks, but most of the functioning inmates of Saint Anne's were off at mass somewhere when the kids arrived. The deserted halls were modern, devoid of soul and pungent with piss. Nuns in white habits—the Little Sisters of the Poor, Michael said—smiled the tight smiles of sentinels as the parade of tiny pagans passed them by.

Michael touched Brian's arm. "Look."

A ghost in a white sheet had left the procession long enough to stop and stare in stupefaction at one of the white-habited sisters. From this angle, the child and the nun looked like a pair of Mutt-and-Jeff Klansmen.

"Saint Casper the Friendly," said Michael.

Brian smiled.

"This is sort of surreal, isn't it?"

"Sort of?"

At the core of the building lay a mini-mall meant to suggest a city street. There were flimsy aluminum lampposts and plastic plants and an assortment of pseudoshops providing amenities for the residents. At the ice cream parlor one of the ghostly sisters was constructing a cone for a nearly hairless old woman in a wheelchair.

Michael leaned closer to Brian's ear. "Sister Mary Rocky Road."

The old woman heard the chatter of the children and stared, slack-mouthed and uncomprehending. One of the teachers yelled, "Happy Halloween." The old woman squinted at the alien invaders, then turned away, clamping a palsied claw on her ice cream cone.

"Christ," Brian murmured, almost involuntarily.

"What?"

"Is this what it comes to?"

"If you're lucky," said Michael.

Brian left it alone.

"Oh, no." Michael made a face suddenly.

"What?"

"I gotta find a nun."

"Huh?"

"Or a toilet. Whichever comes first."

Brian looked around. "There's a nurses' station up ahead."

"See you later."

"I'll meet you out front. In case we get separated."

"Right."

Michael all but bolted to the nurses' station.

● ● ●

They reunited on the lawn at Saint Anne's, twenty minutes later.

"Are you OK?" Brian asked.

Michael nodded, looking decidedly pale. "I made many new friends. Where's Shawna?"

"They just headed back. We can catch up with them, though." He threw his arm over Michael's shoulder. "Sorry you're feeling bad."

"Thanks."

"You wanna get some breakfast after this . . . or would that just make it worse?"

"No. I'm hungry, actually. Ravenous."

"Good," said Brian. "I've found a great new place on Clement."

It was time they talked.

Back at the school, climbing out of her shell, Shawna pronounced the parade an unqualified success.

"We're doing a pageant at Christmas," she told Michael. "Wanna come?"

"Sure." Michael looked uncomfortable. It had obviously occurred to him that Shawna wouldn't be here then.

Brian swiped at her face with a Kleenex. "You're gonna be green till Christmas. I think you'd better try some soap and water on this."

"No," she said. "Cold cream."

"Great. But we don't have any cold cream."

"Nicolas does."

"See if you can borrow his, then." He gave her behind a pat as she darted off to one of the classrooms. When she was gone, he said: "We haven't told her about the move yet."

Michael nodded but wouldn't look at him.

"You think that's unwise?"

"Brian . . ."

"Well, you look like it does."

"It's none of my business." Michael's tone was reasonable enough, but something was bugging him.

"Mary Ann hasn't firmed it up with Burke yet, and she thinks Shawna might spill the beans."

"Yeah, well . . ."

"Plus I don't wanna hit her with this until we can be . . . you know, more specific about her new home. So she feels like she's moving *to* something instead of just away."

Michael shrugged.

"If you think it's a rotten idea, tell me."

"I don't think anything."

"You're lying." Brian said this jovially, then smiled, hoping it would get a rise out of him. "You're right, though. It's her life too. She has a right to know what's going on."

He had always believed that kids could sense it when you held out on them. At least on some subliminal level. Secrecy was unhealthy in the long run. He would talk to Mary Ann again and insist that they tell her.

Shawna returned breathlessly, clutching a jar of cold cream. "We have to give it back," she said.

"Sure thing," he said, and winked at Michael.

Michael ordered dry toast and ate it slowly.

"There's a bug going around," Brian assured him. "A lot of people have it."

His partner nodded.

For a moment, perversely, Brian's imagination went berserk. He saw Michael at ninety pounds, the way Jon had been, an old man at thirty-two. "Sometimes," he added hastily, "when you change your diet or eat too many fruits and vegetables . . ."

Michael gave him a small, indulgent smile as if to tell him to drop it.

"OK," said Brian.

"What time is it?"

He looked at his watch. "Eleven."

"We should be going. I told Polly we'd be back by now."

"I have to say something first."

736

Michael looked uncomfortable. "What?"

"I just . . . I want you to know that this isn't easy for me."

"What isn't?"

"Leaving."

"Oh."

"You're my best friend, you know, and . . . being your partner has meant more to me . . ."

"Brian, c'mon . . ."

"No, wait a minute, dammit. I have to say this."

Michael looked down at his toast.

"If you're embarrassed, I'm sorry but . . ."

"I'm not embarrassed."

"I've thought about this a lot, Michael. We've been through so much together. I'm really aware of . . . what it must be like for you right now."

"Look, don't exaggerate the . . ."

"I'm not, OK? I'm looking at the way things are. I couldn't handle it if you thought I was . . . you know, deserting you."

"You're not. I don't feel that way. Stop overanalyzing things."

Brian smiled dimly. "That's what Mary Ann always says."

"Well, in this case, she's right."

"But something's bothering you," said Brian. "I can tell."

"Look, my stomach . . ."

"Not your stomach. C'mon. I know you, man. I love you. Tell me what's on your mind."

Refusing to meet his gaze, Michael picked up a piece of toast. "It's got nothing to do with you and me."

"I know that's not true."

"It is. Can't you just leave me out of this?"

"Nope," Brian told him, smiling. "Sorry. You're in my life. There's nothing I can do about it. C'mon now. Tell me."

Michael sighed and set down his toast.

Completely Amicable

The show that morning had been about modern witchcraft, but the broomstick graphics and spooky music that accompanied it had not exactly jibed with the panelists: three paisley-clad crystal enthusiasts from Oakland. They had been desperate last-minute replacements; all the really serious occultists had defected to the networks for Halloween.

As she passed this funky trio afterward in the green room, Mary Ann fully expected a complaint to be lodged. Witches were a minority group nowadays, and one of these aging hippies was bound to accuse her of negative stereotyping, or possibly even "witchist" behavior.

But they were all smiles.

"That was a ball," said the oldest one.

The other two agreed, grinning like idiots.

"Good," she told them. "Let's do it again soon."

Well, it figures, she thought, heading for the dressing room. They had gotten high off their first dose of television, and all other potions had paled by comparison. Witches were just as susceptible as anyone else.

The phone was ringing when she reached her inner sanctum.

"Yeah?"

"It's Burke, Mary Ann."

"Oh, hi." She collapsed on her sofa, toed her shoes off. "You're back. How was LA?"

"Good. Useful. I've lined up some more talent."

"Terrific."

"Is this a good time?"

"Sure."

"Have you had time to think it over?"

"Uh-huh."

"And?"

"I think we can do business."

She wasn't sure what she'd expected. Maybe a small preppy cheer of some sort. Or at least a burst of boyish laughter. What she got was a brief silence and the sound of breath being expelled. "Well," he said. "All right."

She said: "I think we've got a hit on our hands."

"You bet."

"What's our timetable?"

He didn't hesitate. "I need you in New York by the end of the month."

She'd expected this but gave a whistle, anyway.

"I know. I'll make it as easy as possible for you. I'll get you the best movers in the business."

"Actually," she said, "I won't need to move that much."

"You're gonna sell your stuff?"

"No. Brian wants to stay here with Shawna."

"But, I mean, eventually . . ."

"No," she said. "They'll stay here for good."

Silence.

"He thinks it's best," she said, "and so do I."

"Well . . ."

"It's not fair to uproot Shawna, and he's got his own business." She paused, wondering how Burke was taking this. "I'll really just need a furnished place for the time being."

He seemed to hesitate. "Is this resolved?"

"Yes."

"Completely?"

"Yes," she said quietly. "This has been coming for a long time."

"I'm sure you understand." He cleared his throat. "There's a contract involved here."

"I know."

"Are you getting a divorce?"

"Does it matter?"

After a moment he said: "No. Not really."

"It's all completely amicable. You don't have to worry about it."

739

"All right . . . OK."

"Shall we meet?" she asked.

"No. I'm flying back to New York tonight. There's nothing we can't work out on the phone."

Another call came in. "Hang on," she said. "Would you?"

"That's OK. I'll sign off. We'll talk at the beginning of the week. I'm delighted about this, Mary Ann. I've got a great feeling about it."

"Me too," she said. "Talk to you later."

She punched the flashing button. "Yeah?"

"It's Security, Mary Ann."

"Yeah?"

"Your husband's here."

What the hell was this about? "To pick me up?" she asked.

"I dunno."

"Well, ask him, please!"

"I can't. He's on the way up."

"Terrific." She slammed down the phone, suddenly filled with panic.

The rap on her door came moments later.

"Yes?" she called evenly.

"It's me."

She opened the door, to find him looking wretched and drawn, like a lost man stumbling into a ranger station.

"What is it? What's the matter?"

"You tell me," he said.

"Huh?"

"Michael says you don't want me to go with you."

That little snitch, she thought.

"Is it true?"

She eased the door shut and gestured toward a chair.

He sat down at once, obedient in his shock, and gazed up at her with red-rimmed eyes, waiting for an answer.

"He shouldn't have said that," she told him.

He nodded slowly, obviously taking that for a yes. "I thought maybe that . . . ?" He cut himself off as his eyes filled with tears and overflowed.

She sat on the arm of his chair and touched his arm gently. "Please don't think . . ."

There was a rap on her door.

"Yes?" she called irritably.

Raymond's head poked through the doorway, prickly with mousse. "Sorry. Need some autographs for the studio audience."

"Come back later, please."

"But they're leaving in . . ."

"Raymond . . ."

"Right. Sorry." He shut the door.

"I'd hoped we could talk tonight," she told Brian.

"How long have you felt like this?"

She didn't answer.

"A month? A year? What?"

She stroked his arm and used the gentlest tone she could muster. "I think you've felt it too."

"No." He shook free of her and stood up, his cheeks slick with tears, his voice choked with anger. "I don't think I have. I don't think I've felt that at all."

She paused for a moment, still on the edge of the chair. "I'm sorry you had to hear it like this."

"Yeah, well . . ." He was flailing around for something to hurt her with. "What else is new? I'm always the last fucking one to know anything. Of course, I realize that when you're destined for stardom . . ."

"Brian . . ."

"What did I do? Embarrass you in front of those lounge lizards at Stars?"

"You've never embarrassed me."

"Bullshit!"

She kept herself centered by smoothing the material on the arm of the chair. "If it makes you feel better to cast me as the villain . . ."

"Oh, yeah! It does. It makes me feel fucking great! I'm on a major high right now!"

"If you would just . . ."

"Goddamn that asshole!"

She had been waiting for this and resolved to remain calm. "You know perfectly well Burke and I . . ."

"He's taking you away, isn't he? He's paid for your expensive ass, and you're outa here!"

"Lower your voice, please."

"Does he know about this?"

"About what?"

"That you're dumping your husband and child."

She flinched. "I'm not dumping anybody."

"You got that right! That's one luxury you're not gonna enjoy." He lunged toward the door.

"Stop, Brian. Don't be silly. Where are you going?"

"What the fuck do you care?"

"C'mon. Sit down. We can have lunch somewhere."

"Fuck your lunch!" He flung open the door, then turned to face her for his parting shot. "You're one coldhearted bitch, you know that?"

He slammed the door so hard that it knocked one of her awards off the wall.

She took off her makeup, then called the nursery.

"Plant Parenthood."

"It's me, Michael."

"Oh . . . hi." He sounded guilty already.

"Brian was just here," she told him.

"Yeah. I kinda figured."

"I just want you to know I feel totally betrayed by you."

"Well, I'm sorry. What was I supposed to do?"

"You were supposed to keep your mouth shut. You promised me you would."

"And how long ago was that?" he snapped.

"What difference does that make?"

"You told me you'd tell him, that's what. It's been days. The poor bastard was making plans about New York. He was apologizing to *me*, for God's sake. I couldn't just pretend I didn't . . ."

"Why couldn't you? I asked you to."

"Oh, well," he said snidely, "in that case . . ."

"You've hurt him very deeply. I think you should know that."

"Me?"

"How do you think it felt for him to hear that from you? To know that you and I had discussed something so personal before he even knew about it."

"Well, OK, but . . ."

"If you had seen how destroyed he was . . ."

"You have got one helluva goddamn nerve!"

"Well, think about it."

"I am thinking about it! You're the one who's leaving him, sister, not me!"

He hung up on her.

She sat at her vanity and cried.

Sooner or later, men were all the same.

A Long Evening

"If it rains a lot this winter," said Thack, "it'll be nice and weathered by spring."

He was talking about his pink triangle trellis, now a fait accompli. All that was left was to plant the pink clematis, or maybe roses (they hadn't decided which), and wait for nature to do her stuff. "It looks great," Michael told him, standing back to admire the carpentry. "I really like the way you've joined the corners."

"It's not bad, is it?"

Michael didn't have the heart to tell him that the whole thing might not read, that flowers—roses especially—might refuse to conform to the perimeter of the triangle.

They admired it together in silence. Eventually, Thack said: "I'm worried about Brian."

"Me too."

"He didn't come back to work at all?"

"No."

"You'd think he would've called, at least."

"Well, she said he was really upset." Michael felt awful about this. Maybe Mary Ann was right. Maybe he had only made it worse—actually contributed to Brian's humiliation—by spilling the beans. "You think he's pissed at me?"

"No. Is that what she said?"

"No, but . . . if he sees me as her ally . . ."

"What did he say when you told him?"

"Nothing, really. He was just kind of numb."

Thack nodded.

"Do you think I fucked up?"

"I don't know, baby."

"Well, thanks for the vote of confidence."

"It doesn't matter. He had to find out." He slipped his arm around Michael's waist. "How's your stomach?"

"Still there," Michael told him.

"Why don't you run a hot tub and relax?"

Michael did so for half an hour. He was changing into his nightshirt when the phone rang.

"Hello."

"It's me, Mikey."

"Oh . . . hey, Mama." He collapsed on the bed and slipped into his mother mode.

"I hadn't heard for a while, so . . ." She stopped there, as she always did. He had never known her to finish this sentence.

"I've been really busy. I'm sorry."

"I left a message on your machine."

"I know," he said.

"Didn't Thack tell you . . . ?"

744

"Yeah. I just forgot. I've had a lot on my mind. How are you?"

"Oh . . . can't complain."

"Well, that's good."

"How are you feeling?"

"OK. I seem to be responding to the AZT. My T-cells are holding steady."

She was quiet for a moment. "Now which are they?"

He'd expected this, but he was still annoyed. "Mama, did you get the pamphlet I sent you?"

"I got it. It's mighty confusing, though."

"Right."

A long silence. "You haven't got it though, have you?"

"No, Mama," he explained one more time. "I have the virus. I'm OK now, but I could get it eventually. I probably will." God, how he hated this "it" talk. How could he ever explain to her that he had had "it"—or it had had him—from the very moment he learned of Jon's diagnosis, over seven years earlier? Most people thought you got this thing and died. In truth, you got this thing and waited.

"Well . . . I think you should be positive about it."

How like her not to know that she'd made a pun. "I am, Mama."

"Your daddy's worrying killed him, sure as I'm sitting here. More than that cancer ever did."

"I know," he said. "I know you think that."

"I just can't help thinking if you found yourself a nice church, with a pastor you liked . . ."

It never took her long to get back to this. "Mama."

"OK. Never mind. I've had my say."

"Good."

Thack passed through the room naked, bound for the tub with a bottle of Crabtree & Evelyn bath gel. "Is that Alice?" he asked.

Michael nodded.

"Tell her I said hey."

"Thack says hey," Michael told his mother.

"Well, tell him hey back."

"Hey back," he told Thack.

Thack leaned over the bed and sucked Michael's big toe. Michael yanked his foot away and tried to slap Thack's butt, but his lover dodged the blow and gamboled off to the bathtub, laughing under his breath.

"So what have you been up to?" he asked his mother.

"Well . . . me and Etta Norris went to the new multiplex and saw that movie with Bette Midler you told me about."

"Oh, yeah? What did you think?"

"I liked her."

"I told you."

"I guess I didn't like her near as much as Etta. She like to laughed herself silly."

Michael hollered into the bathroom, where Thack was splashing about like some creature at Marine World. "She likes Bette Midler."

Thack laughed.

"What was that?"

"Nothing, Mama. I just told Thack you like Bette Midler."

Thack yelled back. "I knew this would happen when they fucked up the ozone layer."

"What did he say?"

"Nothing important, Mama."

"Listen, Mikey, they finally put in Papa's tombstone last week. It looks real nice."

"Well . . . good."

"I took some pictures of it, so you can see."

For a moment all he could picture was the floral arrangement that had stopped him short at his father's funeral the year before. Some doting, Bible-toting aunt from Pensacola had sent it, and his mother had displayed it proudly—and conspicuously—at the funeral chapel.

A bed of white carnations formed the backdrop for a child's toy telephone, also white. JESUS CALLED was written across the top in fat, glittered letters. Down below, it said: AND HERB ANSWERED. To Michael's dismay, no one else there that day—not even his younger

746

cousins—had found the slightest humor in this. He had ended up calling Thack from a neighboring Taco Bell, just to laugh with someone about it.

He tried, and failed, to picture his mother's idea of a "nice" tombstone. "I'm glad it turned out," he told her.

"It's so pretty there."

Apparently she meant the cemetery.

"Your papa was a smart man to buy that plot. You know they're so expensive now you can't hardly afford 'em at all."

"That's what I hear."

"And he made sure there was room enough for the whole family."

For her, this was subtlety. Not to worry, she was saying, we've saved a place for you. He let it pass without comment, knowing she meant well, the way she had years before when she'd lobbied annually for him to spend Christmas "with the family" in Orlando. It had never even occurred to her that his family might be elsewhere.

She rambled on for another half hour, filling him in on people he hadn't seen for at least fifteen years. Most of her gossip was second generation, since his high school buddies were now the parents of children old enough to drink and take dope and "get into trouble with the law."

It wasn't the same Orlando anymore. He'd seen as much when he went home for the funeral. In the years since his departure, the trees at Disney World had thickened into plantation oaks. The Mickeys and Goofys who plied their trade there could now be found off duty at Parliament House—the PH to those in the know—an antiseptic gay mall offering a choice of leather, western, or preppie saloons.

The cemetery, as he recalled, had been two minutes off the interstate, with a broad avenue of palms and a heart-stopping view of the Piggly Wiggly.

No, thank you, ma'am.

● ● ●

Thack emerged from the bathroom in his terry-cloth robe. "How was she?" he asked.

"Fine."

"What's she been up to?"

"Well . . . among other things, trying to bury me in Florida."

"Huh?"

"My father's tombstone arrived, and she's working on a family reunion."

Thack rolled his eyes and sat on the edge of the bed. "Leave it to me," he said.

"She'll fight you over it."

"No she won't. She likes me."

"That has nothing to do with it. Trust me."

Thack picked at the comforter for a moment. "Did you tell her what you wanted?"

"No."

"Are you going to?"

"I guess I'll have to write her," said Michael. "It's kind of hard to get chatty about."

Thack smiled. "Turn over."

Michael turned over. Thack straddled his back and kneaded the muscles at the base of his neck.

"These people are serious Christians," Michael told him. "They'll put me in the living room and bring casseroles."

His lover laughed. "Shut up."

"I mean it. You don't know."

"Yeah, yeah."

"And next to me there'll be this huge philodendron on a spinning wheel . . ."

"Just relax."

"Lower," said Michael. "That feels wonderful."

"There?"

"Yes."

Thack seized the tightest rope of muscle between his thumb and forefinger. "What is this, anyway? Mary Ann?"

"Do you have to name it?" said Michael. "Can't you just rub it?"

The new doorbell made them both jump. This particular model had caught Michael's eye at Pay 'n Pak with its simple design and lyrical name—the Warbler. What this meant was that it fired away like a machine gun as long as there was a finger on the bell. Only the briefest poke would produce the lone dingdong usually associated with a doorbell.

And the damn dog went nuts over it.

"Harry," said Thack, springing off Michael's back. "Shut the fuck up."

"Who are we expecting?"

"Nobody."

Harry was in the living room now, yapping like crazy. Michael scooped him up and stashed him in the guest bedroom. Peering through the spy hole in the front door, he saw Brian's distorted face, golden as a carp's under the orange porch light. He was the only person they knew who never remembered not to lean on the doorbell.

Michael opened the door. "Hi."

"Hi. Sorry I didn't call first."

"No problem."

"Is it a bad time?"

"Not at all."

Thack let Harry out of the guest bedroom. The dog did a barkless little jig around Brian—the one he saved for members of the immediate family.

"How's it going, Harry?" Brian let the dog sniff his hand for a moment, then gave it up, seemingly drained of energy. "You guys were in bed, weren't you?"

Thack shook his head. "On it. Back rub."

"Oh."

"Sit down. Can we warm up some polenta lasagna for you?"

"No, thanks." He sank into the armchair as if he might never get up again.

749

"There's some wine," said Michael. "Sauvignon blanc." He had just noticed how wrecked Brian's eyes were.

"Any Scotch?"

"Not really."

"How 'bout rum?" Thack suggested.

Michael looked at his lover. "Where do we have rum?"

"Under the sink, next to the cleaning stuff."

"Since when?"

"We bought it for the eggnog last year."

"Oh, yeah."

"Rum would be great," said Brian.

Michael brought back the bottle with a glass. Somehow, the mission seemed fraught with urgency, like serum being dogsledded across the Yukon. "There's not much to mix it with. Diet Cherry Coke, maybe?"

"Straight up's fine."

Michael poured several inches. Brian downed it in one gulp and handed the glass back. "I know that's a cliché, but it had to be done."

Michael smiled. "Want another?"

"Nope. That was it. Thanks."

"No problem."

Brian looked down at his hands, dangling between his legs. "I talked to her," he said.

"Did you?" It was best, Michael decided, not to tell him she had called. That could only lead to trouble. He put down the glass and sat next to Thack on the sofa.

"Why didn't I see it coming?" said Brian. "How out of it could I have been?"

There was a long silence, during which Harry hopped onto the armchair and settled his chin against Brian's leg.

"I was actually picturing it, you know."

"What do you mean?" asked Michael.

"New York," explained Brian. "We had a brownstone on the Upper West Side. And a cat. And Shawna and I knew the museums by heart." Brian stroked the dog's back. "I was just cruising along like everything was copacetic."

"Why shouldn't you?" Thack said quietly.

"But . . . if I'd communicated more . . ."

"Look," said Thack, "it's not your fault."

Michael, who was thinking what a straight word "copacetic" was, cast a nervous glance at his lover. Neutrality was in order here, and Thack, as usual, seemed on the verge of blowing it. "I don't think it's a question of fault, really."

Thack gave him a dirty look.

"I can't go back to the condo," said Brian. "Not while she's still there."

Silence all around.

"Somebody's gotta talk to Shawna, I know, but . . ." Brian's face balled up like a fist, rubbery with grief. He began to sob soundlessly.

Michael and Thack remained still.

"I'm sorry, guys."

"That's OK," said Michael.

"It's just there, you know?" Brian took a couple of swipes at his eyes. "I thought I had it under control."

The doorbell fired off another sally, making them all jump. Harry sprang off Brian's lap and barked vigorously at the latest intruder.

"Who the fuck is that?" Thack looked at Michael.

"Got me." Michael picked up the poodle, causing him to downgrade his yap to a low growl. Brian gave Michael an apprehensive look, as if he thought Mary Ann herself was waiting behind the door.

Thack peered through the spy hole. "Christ."

"What?" said Michael.

"What day is this? Think."

It took Michael a moment. "Oh, shit."

"Do we have anything?" asked Thack.

Michael racked his brain. There hadn't been candy in the house for months. None, at any rate, that had survived their last tumble off the sugar wagon. There weren't even any apples. This was the second year in a row they had forgotten to stock up on treats for the kids. In this neighborhood it wasn't just the grownups who did Halloween.

The doorbell rang again.

"Maybe they'll go away," offered Thack.

"We can't do that," said Michael. He dashed to the kitchen and found a package of dried apricots in the back of the cupboard. "How many are there?" he hollered.

"Just one," yelled Thack. "At the moment."

Michael returned with the apricots and opened the door to a three-foot Roger Rabbit. "Well, hello there."

The kid held out a Gump's bag without a word. In a single, guilty movement, Michael deposited the apricots, hoping they would sound like Tootsie Rolls. The kid said "Thanks" and ran back to a cluster of older children waiting on the sidewalk. Michael closed the door and leaned against it, feeling like a total fraud.

"If you'd done that to me," said Brian, "I would have TP'ed your house."

There were bound to be more trick-or-treaters, so Michael made an emergency run to the Noe Hill Market, where he found a giant assortment of miniature candy bars. If they didn't give them all away, he could always throw them out in the morning.

Back at the house, while Brian played listlessly with Harry in the living room, Thack confronted Michael in the kitchen. "Shouldn't we offer him the guest room?"

"I don't know, sweetie."

"We can't just . . . send him off."

"Yeah, but it would seem like taking sides."

"Who cares?"

"I care. Mary Ann's my friend too."

"Some friend. She just blamed the whole damned thing on you."

Michael threw him a medium-sized dagger. "We'll just make it worse if he stays here."

"For God's sake," said Thack, "he's your partner."

752

"Don't preach to me, all right? I know who he is."

"OK, fine. Call the Motel 6."

"It's no problem," said Michael. "Really."

He and Thack were back in the living room. Brian was still on the floor with Harry. "Are you sure?" he said, looking up. "I can get a motel."

"Nah. That's ridiculous."

Brian shrugged. "I've done it before."

"Well, it's . . . You have?"

"Sure. Couple of times."

"When?"

"I dunno. Last year." He raised his brows sheepishly.

"You should stay here," said Thack.

Michael nodded. "Yeah."

"OK, then. Thanks."

Thack looked at Michael. "Are there sheets on the guest bed?"

"No, but . . ."

"The couch is fine, guys."

"Don't be noble," said Michael. "We've got a guest room for just this purpose. Well, not *exactly* this purpose . . ." The doorbell rang.

"Shit." Michael peered out through the spy hole. This time there were five of them. More plastic capes and plastic faces.

"It's gonna be a long evening," said Thack.

Brian helped Michael make the bed in the guest room.

"What about Shawna?" Michael asked. "Who's gonna take her to school in the morning?"

"Nguyet can do it."

"Are you sure? I'd be more than happy . . ."

"No. That's OK. Thanks." He looked at Michael earnestly. "Can we not talk about this for a while?"

"Sure." Michael finished tucking in the top sheet and plumped a feather pillow into place. "There are some little hotel toothbrushes in the top of the medicine cabinet."

"Thanks." Brian smiled feebly. "Trick toothbrushes."

"What?"

"Isn't that what you used to call 'em?"

Michael chuckled. "What a memory."

"I'm sorry about this, Michael."

"Don't be."

"I can't go back there. I can't just . . . wait for her to leave."

"I understand."

"I knew I could count on you," said Brian.

The Kastro

Mona felt a twinge of homecoming when her cab rounded the sea-front bend and Molivos sprang into view. The bright shutters and stone terraces, the smokestack of the old olive oil factory, the Geno-ese castle crowning the hill—all had lost their exoticism and become suddenly, ancestrally familiar. She had been here before and now she was back, an Amazon returning from the Sapphic Wars.

It pleased her somehow to be able to identify the noise coming from the esplanade. It was the laundry truck, which announced itself by what appeared to be a top-mounted gramophone, and which, once or twice a week, transported the dirty clothes of tourists into Mit-ilini, sixty kilometers across the mountains. The people of Molivos were a proud lot, who did their own washing but no one else's.

The first time she'd heard the blare of that loudspeaker, she'd held her breath and waited for word that a coup had been declared. Even now, almost three weeks later, she suspected it of fascist lean-ings. Who knew what it was saying, anyway? Maybe it wasn't *just* a laundry truck. Maybe it was issuing some sort of public edict.

Attention all dykes, attention all dykes. The season is officially over. Please vacate the streets immediately and return to your home coun-tries. This is your last warning. I repeat: This is your last warning . . .

She smiled and peered out the window. A lot of the shops and restaurants had been boarded up in her absence, now citadels against the coming rains. In the tiny high street, the sea-green grotto of Melinda's Restaurant harbored the last of the tourists. The men at the Old Guys' Café—her name for the place where Stratos usually ate—seemed tickled to death that Molivos was about to be returned to them.

Who can blame them? she thought. I wouldn't want to share it either.

She disembarked at the wisteria-covered end of the high street and paid her driver. She had chosen this approach to the house, rather than the easier one from the esplanade, for the sheer navigational thrill of threading her way down the maze of cobbled walkways. She enjoyed knowing where she was going in such a completely foreign place.

When she reached the Turkish fountain that identified the base of their terrace, she stopped and, looking up, saw the flutter of silk against the sun. Anna cooed a greeting. "You're home."

"I am," said Mona, and smiled at her, one seasoned traveler to another.

"It was truly elemental."

They were on the terrace now, under big hats. The waning sun had turned the sea to blue Mylar, and there was a breeze. The wisteria on the terrace had lost its thick coat of dust in what Anna said had been a torrential rainstorm.

"No shit?" remarked Mona. "It barely drizzled in Skala."

"Indeed?"

"How long did it last?"

"All night. We were giddy on the ozone. We flung open the shutters and let it just tear through the house." Anna smiled winsomely. "I was quite the madwoman."

"Did it knock out the electricity?"

"No. Why?"

"There are candles all over the place."

"Oh. Those were for"—Anna dropped her eyes—"atmosphere."

"Atmosphere?"

"Yes."

Mona didn't pursue this, but the image that leapt to mind was of Anna buck naked in a thunderstorm, head wreathed in laurel, arms aloft, like some transcendental Evita. "Did you enjoy the house?"

Anna nodded.

"You didn't throw him out, just because I was . . ."

"No, dear. We both wanted a little distance for a while."

"A breather," said Mona.

Her parent glowered.

"He seems nice."

"He is. Very."

"How was the birthplace of Dukakis's father?"

"Lovely."

Mona tilted her hat and gave Anna a friendly smirk. "You never even went, did you?"

"We most certainly did."

"For how long?" She wasn't letting her off the hook this easily.

Anna hesitated, then said: "Most of a day, at least."

"You could've just asked me to leave, you know. I wouldn't have minded."

"Dear, I *assure* you . . ."

Mona laughed.

"How was Sappho's birthplace?"

"Fine."

"Did you meet any nice people?"

"Several," said Mona, and let it go at that.

When Mona woke to the three o'clock church bells, the air was much cooler, and there were fat, bruised clouds lolling outside her window. This had been her last siesta; tomorrow she'd be back in Athens, sitting on her luggage, waiting for her flight to Gatwick. Wilfred had insisted on meeting her plane, so she felt compelled to be strict about her schedule.

"What haven't you done?" Anna asked her over tea.

Mona rolled her eyes. "Don't ask."

"I mean here," said Anna, smiling. "Have you seen the *kastro*?"

"They have gay boys here?"

"The castle, you philistine."

"I know."

"It's extraordinary, if you haven't seen it. Fourteenth century."

"Fine. Let's do it."

"It's a bit of a walk."

"Something told me," said Mona.

Higher and higher they trekked through the cobbled labyrinth, until the houses fell away and the castle gate loomed above them. Two black-sweatered old ladies with apple-doll faces were on their way down, so Anna chirped a cheery "*Kalispera*" before taking Mona's arm and pointing to the squiggly writing above the gate. "The Turks ruled this place for over four hundred years. They didn't leave until 1923."

Mona imagined Stratos on the same spot, telling Anna the same thing. And the goofy look in Anna's eyes when he said it.

"The *kastro* itself is Genoese, built by a titled Italian family."

Mona grunted and followed her through the gate and up a scrubby incline to another entrance, more mammoth than the first. Thirty feet above their heads, a gnarled fig tree grew from the very stone itself. The ground was sticky from a recent bombardment of fruit.

The door to the keep was ironclad on the outside, but its wooden inside had proved vulnerable to tourist graffiti. It was Greek, for the most part, and the quaint fraternity lettering of the ancients somehow reduced its offensiveness. The only English word she recognized was AIDS, emblazoned in red against the medieval wood.

She averted her gaze and kept walking, her temples pounding as she strode into the open air of the inner fortifications.

Her parent seemed unaffected. "They use this part for a stage," she explained. "Stratos says they did a production of *The Trojan Women* several summers ago."

"Oh, yeah?"

Anna forged ahead, ignoring the lackluster response, climbing until the castle began to resemble an opera set—all turrets and fragments and stony niches framing the sea. There were Wagnerian clouds to match, and the wind had picked up considerably, invading Anna's hair to create a sort of Medusa effect.

She looked at Mona, then swept her arm toward the distant Turkish coastline. "Troy," she sighed. "Imagine."

"That's it, huh?"

"That's it."

Mona leaned against the battlement and studied her parent's face, struck suddenly by its radiance. "You've enjoyed yourself, haven't you?"

"Oh, yes."

"I'm glad."

"I've never known anyone like him."

Mona hesitated, surprised at the sudden appearance of "him."

"He's asked me to stay, in fact."

"For how long?"

Blinking at her, Anna made a vague gesture in the direction of Troy. "This long."

Mona laughed, suddenly tickled. "Really?"

Anna nodded.

"A Lesbian wedding?"

"Heavens, no!"

"OK, then. A Lesbian shack-up."

They laughed together, sharing their distrust of institutions.

"Is he rich?"

"Mona!"

"I just meant . . ."

"He's comfortable. We'd have plenty between us. His brother-in-law is a Dukakis."

Mona smiled.

"I forgot to tell you," said Anna. "He lost."

"Who?"

"Dukakis. Stratos told me this morning."

"Oh." She wasn't in the least surprised. America was already fucked.

"Stratos is really rather bleak about it."

"What did you tell him?"

"About the election?"

"About you." She smiled. "Don't be coy."

Anna raked her Medusa locks with her fingers. "I haven't told him anything yet."

"Is he . . . important to you?"

Anna nodded.

"Enough so that . . . ?"

"Oh, yes. More than enough."

"What would you do?" asked Mona. "Sell the house?"

"I suppose."

"Could you do that?"

"I don't know. The Treachers have made me an offer."

"Who are the Treachers?"

"They're on the third floor."

"Oh."

"They're a nice young couple. They're looking for a place to buy. I'm sure they'd take good care of it."

"You'd probably get a fortune for it."

"I'm not interested in a fortune."

"I know, but . . . it wouldn't hurt. You could travel all over Europe, visit me at Easley. Hell, I'd come see you here. I'd make the sacrifice."

Anna chuckled, then held Mona's arm and gazed down at the toy-boat harbor, the train-set village flung against the mythic hillside.

"I can see you here," said Mona.

"I am here," said Anna.

Mona smiled at her. "You know what I mean."

"Yes."

"Are you afraid he's not for real?"

"No. Not at all."

"Don't you want a companion?"

"In my old age?" A smile darted across Anna's lips.

"C'mon."

"I have plenty of companions. Wonderful company. Just like you."

"You want to do this," said Mona. "I can tell you do."

Anna fidgeted with the sleeve of her caftan. "The children would never understand."

"If you mean Michael, he's got his own life. You should do the same."

"And there's Mary Ann and Brian . . ."

"They're all gone, for God's sake."

"Nevertheless . . . I have responsibilities."

In her mind's eye Mona saw the writing on the castle wall. She knew exactly what Anna was thinking. "Look," she said, "Michael would never forgive you if you passed this up on his account."

"Dear . . ."

"If that's the reason, I'll tell him, so help me."

"You'll do nothing of the kind."

"You've spent your whole life telling other people to live and be free. Why don't you stop blowing smoke and take a little of your own advice?"

"That's quite enough."

"You know I'm right."

"It's starting to rain . . ."

"Go home and tell them. See what they say, at least."

Her parent didn't answer as she scurried along the battlement, in flight from the downpour.

Cock-and-Bull Stories

When Brian pulled up in front of The Summit, Shawna was downstairs as arranged, scribbling furiously in her coloring book.

"How's it goin'?" asked the doorman, leaning into the Jeep. He was obviously curious as hell about the change in their daily routine. This was the fourth morning in a row Brian had arrived from somewhere else to pick up his daughter.

"Not bad, not bad." He made a point of sounding jaunty.

"Hey, are those rumors true?"

"What rumors?"

"Mary Ann taking her act to the Big Apple."

"Oh." He shrugged. "Looks like it." He opened the door and let Shawna in. "Where's your lunch box, Puppy?"

"We don't have to," Shawna told him. "Solange's mom is fixing burritos."

"I guess we'll be losing you guys." The doorman wasn't giving up.

"Well, it hasn't really been . . ."

"We don't have to go with her," Shawna offered brightly.

"Puppy." Brian gave his daughter a scolding look before turning back to the doorman. "Nothing's really definite."

He pulled away from the curb, causing his interrogator to slap the side of the Jeep and say: "Hang in there." There was a sympathetic, man-to-man air about this, which made Brian wonder if the guy had already guessed the score.

"What did I do wrong?" his daughter asked.

"Nothing." He couldn't bring himself to reprimand her for telling the truth, or at least her slant on it.

"When is she going?"

"Next week, Puppy."

"Will you come back then?"

"Sure. Of course. I told you that." He reached across and wiggled one of the tight little braids Nguyet had woven for her. "Where else would I go, silly?"

"I dunno." Shawna ducked her eyes. "Are you still mad at Mary Ann?"

"No. I'm just . . . I've never been really mad at her, Puppy. We had a misunderstanding. It makes me sad to be around her now, so I'm gonna stay with Michael and Thack until she leaves."

"Will you be sad when she's gone?"

He hesitated. "Some. Yes."

"I don't want you to be."

He looked at her. "I'll give it a shot."

She was distracted by a passing station wagon. A black Lab was in the back seat, poking his rubbery nose through a crack in the window. She waved at it briefly before turning back to him. "Does Michael have AIDS now?" she asked.

"No, Puppy. Michael is just HIV positive. Remember when he explained that to you?"

"Yes."

"Why'd you ask, then?"

The child shrugged. "Mary Ann said he was sick. She said you were taking care of him."

"Oh." So that was the excuse she'd used. "He had an upset stomach for a while, but he's fine now."

"Oh."

"It was just a regular ol' upset stomach. Just like you have sometimes."

She looked out the window again.

"Michael would tell you if he was really sick. Don't worry about that."

"OK," she said.

That afternoon, as they clipped the brown spikes off the yuccas, he told Michael about Shawna's distress. "She was so confused, poor kid."

"I'm not surprised," said Michael.

"What do you mean?"

"Well . . . she's pretty much in the dark about this, isn't she?"

There was the suggestion of negligence to this, which annoyed Brian. "Look . . . I've been perfectly straight with her. I wasn't the one who fed her some cock-and-bull story about taking care of you."

"I realize that."

"Well . . . you sounded pretty judgmental."

"Sorry."

"It's typical of her not to level with the kid, to make it even worse by . . ."

"She's got to tell her something, Brian."

"Tell her the truth, then. Tell her I'm hurt and pissed. What's so difficult about that?"

"Is that what you told her?"

"No . . . not exactly . . ."

"OK, then. She's just trying to spare Shawna's feelings."

"And I'm not, huh?"

"Brian . . ."

"It's *my* fault her mother's running off to join the goddamn circus. I get it."

"I'm not talking about fault, Brian. If you would just sit down and hash this out with her . . ."

"Have you talked to her or something? Did she tell you to say this?"

"No."

"She's been giving you grief, hasn't she? What did she do? Accuse you of defecting?"

Michael rolled his eyes. "I haven't talked to her once since you left."

"Well . . ."

"I do think it's time you grew up a little and talked to her. You're only making things worse."

"Is that right?"

"The longer you put it off . . ."

"Thanks, Michael. I get the point. Just what I needed—another nagging wife."

Michael stuck his clippers in his belt and began to walk away.

"Wait," said Brian. "I'm sorry, man. Don't listen to me. I don't mean this shit."

"I can't handle it, Brian. I don't know what to tell you anymore."

"You don't have to. I don't expect you to."

"You haven't stopped pumping me all week. I can't keep playing middleman like this."

"When have I ever . . . ?"

"Oh, Jesus, Brian, for years and years. I'd like to have a nickel for every time you've asked me what she really thinks about something."

"Because she talks to you, man. She never tells me shit. You know stuff about my life that I don't even know."

Michael gave him a long, steely glance. "It helps to get her trust first."

"What's that supposed to mean?"

"Oh, Brian . . ."

"No. Tell me. I wanna know."

Michael gave him a weary little smile. "You fucked around on her so much."

"If you mean Geordie . . ."

"No. Not just Geordie. What about that woman from Philadelphia?"

"What woman from Philadelphia?"

"You know. Brigid Something. With the tits and the saddle shoes. You said she was your cousin. Give me a big break."

Brian remembered. He had brought her by the nursery one day years ago, long before he'd become a partner here. He had just come off an incredible nooner and wanted to show her off a little. Michael had still been a bachelor, still a trusted co-conspirator in matters of lust.

"Did you tell Mary Ann about that?" he asked.

"Hell, no," said Michael. "She told me. I had no idea. I thought the cousin bit sounded too obvious to be an out-and-out lie."

"Then how could she have possibly . . . ?"

"She's got eyes, Brian. You're not as subtle as you think you are."

Brian took this in, smarting a little. "Did she just tell you this?"

"No. Years ago."

"Then why are you bringing it up now?"

His partner heaved a sigh. "Because you keep acting so wronged."

"I am wronged."

"Fine."

"When did you get to be such a little Calvinist, anyway?"

"I'm not talking about sex; I'm talking about lying."

"I haven't fucked around for years, and you know it."

"Since Geordie, right? Since you got scared shitless. Sorry, but no cigar."

Brian's face was aflame. "This is really ironic coming from you."

"From me? Why is that?"

"You were the Whore of Babylon, Michael."

"Maybe so, but I wasn't married."

"Only because you couldn't be. You and Jon were a couple. If he were still alive . . ." He cut himself off, horrified by the careless ease with which he'd waded into these waters.

"If he were still alive, what?"

"Nothing. I'm sorry. I shouldn't have said that."

Michael regarded him with cow-eyed melancholy, then walked back to the office without a word.

They avoided each other for the rest of the day.

Remembering's Different

"I wouldn't count on him," Michael told Thack that evening. "Not for dinner, anyway."

Thack looked up from the chicken breasts he was breading. Behind him, beyond the big window, the fog tumbled into the valley like white lava. "What happened?"

"We had a fight."

"Over what?"

"Nothing much. We called each other sluts."

Thack arranged the breasts on a baking dish. "How tired."

"I'm well aware."

"Was it over Mary Ann?"

Michael paused. "Somewhat."

"Thought so."

"Well . . . he was getting so sanctimonious. He hasn't exactly been a saint. She's had plenty of reason to . . ."

The phone rang.

Michael picked it up, pulling out the antenna. "Hello."

"It's me, Mouse." It was Mary Ann.

"Hi."

"Is he there?"

"No."

"Is that her?" asked Thack, not exactly *sotto voce*.

Michael gave him an annoyed nod and turned away. "I'll tell him you called, OK?"

"No. Don't. You're the one I wanted."

"What for?"

"She's gonna suck you in." Thack was being a real pain. Michael gave him a dirty look and walked out of the kitchen. The cordless model came in handy sometimes.

"How 'bout a date, Mouse?"

In the living room, he collapsed on the sofa and kicked off his shoes. "Come again?"

"Don't make this hard on me," she said.

"Well, what are you talking about?"

"I've got tickets to this open house tonight." She paused dramatically. "Would you like to go with me?"

"Babycakes . . . look . . ."

"I feel so ganged up on, Mouse." Her voice was small and plaintive.

"Well, you shouldn't," he said, melting fast.

"How can I not?" She sounded almost on the verge of tears. "Come with me, Mouse. Just so we can talk. We don't have to stay long."

"If you just wanna talk, can't we just . . . ?"

"I have to be there. I'm committed. I thought Brian would be here when I told them . . ."

"Oh . . . so you need a walker."

Her response was grave and wounded. "You know that's not true. I just thought we could . . ."

"Kill two birds with one stone?"

The silence was so long he wondered if she'd hung up. "Why am I so awful?" she said at last. "What did he tell you?"

"Nothing."

"Well, why are you acting like this?"

He heaved a sigh of resignation.

"I thought you'd enjoy it," she said. "It's black tie, and it's in this beautiful house out at Sea Cliff."

Thack, of course, saw his acquiescence as something just short of betrayal.

"Give me a break," Michael argued. "I can't stop seeing her just because they're . . ."

"Why not? She dumped him, didn't she? That's clear enough."

"And we men have got to stick together. Is that it?"

Thack frowned. "What do our dicks have to do with it?"

"A lot, if you ask me."

"You think I'm being sexist?"

Michael shrugged. "Maybe unconsciously."

"Well, you're full of shit, then."

"I didn't say . . ."

"Is that what she told you? That this was the men versus one poor little woman?"

"No."

"She's jerking you around, Michael. Just the way she does him. She'll say anything to get what she wants."

"And women aren't supposed to do that."

"Nobody's supposed to do that! It's got nothing to do with sexism. You know I'm not a sexist. Why are you so blind about this? I don't get it."

Michael let him calm down for a moment. "You haven't known her as long as I have."

"Well, maybe I can see her more clearly, then."

"Maybe you can." He sighed. "You want me to cancel?"

"Do what you want to do."

"Oh, right."

"I'm not gonna lie to Brian about it."

"I don't expect you to." Michael's tone was glacial as he left the room. "I hadn't planned to myself."

His tux was spotted in several places and required major sponging. His dress shirt was clean, but he ended up stapling the cuffs, since he couldn't find his cuff links and he wasn't about to ask Thack for his. His beeper went off in the middle of this procedure, causing him to fling down the stapler and skulk off in search of water.

Back in the bedroom, he sat on the bed and finished dressing. As he put on his socks, he spotted something on his ankle—his lower calf, really—that he hadn't noticed before. He leaned over to look at it.

"Hey," said Thack, walking into the room, "if you wanna wear my red cummerbund, go ahead."

Michael didn't answer.

"What is it?"

"Come here a second. Look at this."

His lover came to the bed. "Where?"

"There."

Thack studied the purplish inflammation, touching it lightly with his forefinger.

"Does that look like it?"

No answer.

"It does to me."

"I don't think so," said Thack. "It looks like a zit or something. Something healing. Look at the edges of it."

When had he ever seen a zit down there? "The color seems right, though."

"Go see August, then, if it worries you. Isn't tomorrow your day for pentamidine?"

"Yeah."

"It'll put your mind at ease, anyway."

"Yeah."

"I'm sure it's nothing," said Thack, shaking Michael's knee. "I'll get the cummerbund."

Mary Ann had done a show that morning on baby evangelists, so that was what they talked about on the long drive to Sea Cliff. His guess was that the heavier stuff would come later, when they were both feeling a little more sure of each other.

The fog in Sea Cliff was as dense as he had ever seen it. The house was seventies modern, a cluster of multileveled metallic boxes with thick glass walls overlooking the ocean. Flashcubes of the Gods, he thought, as Mary Ann turned the Mercedes over to a valet parker.

"What's the deal here?" he asked. The lights along the path glowed soft and spongy in the fog. Out on the darkling plain of the Golden Gate there were horns bleating like lost sheep.

"We just walk through and look at it," she said. "It's a benefit for the ballet."

"Whose house is it?"

"I don't know, really. Some guy who died. He left a provision in his will that they could let people see it after he died."

"How odd."

"Well . . . he was a realtor." She shrugged as if this explained it.

Suddenly it hit him. "Arch Gidde. Was that his name?"

"Yeah," she said. "That's it."

"Christ."

"You knew him?"

"Not very well. Jon did. He used to come here all the time."

"This Gidde guy was gay?"

"What did you think he died of?"

"Prue said it was liver cancer or something."

"Right," said Michael.

"Well . . . I guess he has a right to his privacy."

Michael knew what Thack would have said to that.

• • •

The house was nicer than he'd imagined, but this was hardly the night to show off its view. The fog pressed against the windows like a fat lady in ermine. While Mary Ann sought out "somebody in charge," he loitered in the living room and gave the place an embarrassed once-over. It seemed a little callous to be checking out the digs of a dead man, even with the blessing of the deceased.

He remembered the day the realtor had propositioned him at the nursery—back when it was still God's Green Earth. Arch had come in for primroses and recognized Michael as an ex-lover of Jon's. Moving in for the kill, he had stuffed a business card into Michael's overalls and made an overt and clumsy reference to owning a Betamax.

Now "Betamax" had the ring of "Gramophone," and the travertine reaches of Arch Gidde's living room, circa 1976, seemed as quaintly archival as a Victorian parlor preserved in a museum. The focal point was a gleaming chrome fireplace (with a matching chrome bin for the logs). Facing the hearth was a pair of enormous Italian sofas—pale arcs of buttery leather, burnished over the years by the endless buffing of gym-toned asses. The only thing missing was a lone anthurium in a crystal vase.

He could picture Jon here easily, sprawled in the golden light like some surly sweater spread out of *GQ*. He had been a mess in those days, but he had changed dramatically toward the end, and that freer, more forgiving person was the one Michael chose to remember.

"Wait till you see the bedroom."

Mary Ann was back, taking his arm at the bar as he ordered a Calistoga.

"Is it nice?"

"The walls are brown suede. And padded. It's such a *womb*."

"What are you drinking?"

"Nothing. No, fuck that. A white wine."

"Hey," said Michael. "Wild woman."

She smiled at him. "I'm so glad you're with me."

When their drinks came, he lifted his to hers. "To things getting better."

She took a sip, then said: "Why am I no good at this, Mouse?"

"At what?"

"Ending things."

"Oh."

"I wanted so much not to hurt him . . . to do it the right way . . ."

"You think there is one?"

"One what?"

"A right way."

"I don't know." She took a sip of her wine. "I guess if I'd told him earlier . . ."

"Yeah."

"I know I'm doing what has to be done. But even so . . . I feel like such a piece of shit, you know?" She looked at him almost reverently, as if she was expecting absolution.

"Well, c'mon . . . you're not a piece of shit."

The room was beginning to fill up. It seemed to make her uneasy. "Why don't we get away from the bar?" she said.

"Fine."

They found a quieter spot—a den of sorts—on a lower level. "The thing is," she said, continuing where she'd left off, "I can't ever remember what it was like when I did feel something toward him. I wake up some mornings, and I look at him, and I think: How did this happen?"

What did she expect him to say to that?

"I mean . . . I remember feeling it, but I don't remember how it felt. Like that time at the candlelight vigil . . ."

"Harvey Milk's?"

"John Lennon's."

"Oh, yeah." He smiled, remembering it too. Brian had bought strawberry-scented candles to invoke "Strawberry Fields." He and Mary Ann had spent hours on the Marina Green, paying homage to the world's most celebrated househusband, then returned to Barbary Lane bleary-eyed and exultant.

"He was so sweet," said Mary Ann. "And afterwards he left this note on my door that said: 'Help me if you can, I'm feeling down, and I do appreciate your being 'round.'"

Michael nodded.

"It was so completely him. So overblown and corny and really nice." She smiled wanly. "I wish to hell I could feel that now."

"You must. You're telling me about it."

"Only what I remember. Remembering's different."

"But you must at least feel . . ."

"Not a thing, really." She paused and gazed bleakly out at the fog. "Just a little sorry for him sometimes." Turning, she looked directly at him, her eyes brimming with tears. "If that makes me a bitch, I can't help it."

He took her hand. "It doesn't make you a bitch."

She began to weep quietly. When he tried to take her in his arms, she pulled away. "No, Mouse, I can't. I'll come unglued."

"Be my guest."

"No. Not here."

A clubby-looking woman appeared in the doorway. "Oh, isn't this nice? Is this the study?"

"The orgy room," said Michael.

The woman tittered briefly, nervously, before her face fell like a soufflé and she retreated.

"You're terrible." Mary Ann wiped her eyes.

"Well . . . it probably was."

"Let's get out of here."

"Fine by me," he said. "You wanna get some coffee in the Avenues?"

"Oh, that sounds wonderful."

"I know a perfect place."

"I knew you would," she said, squeezing his arm.

● ● ●

They were nearly out the door when Mary Ann spotted the shining, sculpted faces of Russell and Chloe Rand, floating through the crowd like a pair of beacons. She stopped in her tracks. "Mouse, look . . ."

"Yeah."

"We should say hello, don't you think?"

"I thought we were . . ."

"They must be back from LA."

"Must be."

He followed dutifully as she plowed through the throng. For a fleeting moment, when she reached back to take his hand, he thought he knew how it felt to be her husband.

Nickel-Dime Stuff

It was a generic valley, a dark bowl twinkling with porch lights and undistinguished by landmarks. There was neither bridge nor bay nor pyramid to tip you off that this was San Francisco, but—to Brian, at least—it couldn't have been anywhere else in the world.

Thack joined him on the deck, gazing out at the fleecy fog. "They must be socked in out at Sea Cliff."

"I guess so."

"There's some Häagen-Dazs in the freezer."

"Maybe later."

"Don't worry about it, Brian. He wasn't upset."

"Are you sure? I know I shouldn't've brought up Jon like that."

"Why not?"

"Well . . . you know . . . a dead guy."

Thack smiled at him. "We talk about dead guys all the time."

Brian nodded absently.

"It's just the way it is."

"I guess so."

"He was defending Mary Ann, right? And it got out of hand."

"More or less," said Brian.

"Well . . . serves him right. He shouldn't walk the fence so much."

Brian was surprised by this cavalier reaction. "He's known her a long time," he said in Michael's defense.

"Yeah."

"I don't expect him to take my side, just because . . ."

"He knows that," said Thack. "He also knows you're getting a bum deal. The trouble is he wants everyone to like him. He works at it way too hard. He's spent so much time being a good little boy that he's never figured out which people aren't worth it."

Brian figured this was said for his benefit. To convince him that what he was about to lose was nothing of value, nothing worth crying over. He didn't buy it.

Thack kept his eyes on the fog bank. "Where'd you go after work? We were worried about you."

"Just out for some brews."

"You holding up OK?"

"Yeah." He looked at Thack sideways. "You must be tired of hearing me piss and moan."

"Nah."

"It's nickel-dime stuff, though, compared to what you and Michael have to deal with."

Thack shrugged. "We've all gotta deal with something."

"Maybe, but . . ."

"If Michael were leaving, I wouldn't consider it nickel-dime." He gave Brian a sleepy smile. "You're entitled to be miserable."

There was another long silence.

Brian asked: "Doesn't it scare you?"

"What? Michael?"

"Yeah."

Thack seemed to sort something out for a moment. "Sometimes I watch him when he's playing with Harry or digging in the yard. And I think: This is it, this is the guy I've waited for all my life. Then this other voice tells me not to get used to it, that it'll only hurt more later. It's funny. You're feeling this enormous good fortune and waiting for it to be over at the same time."

"You seem happy," Brian ventured.

"I am."

"Well . . . that's a lot. I envy you that."

Thack shrugged. "All we've got is now, I guess. But that's all anybody gets. If we wasted that time being scared . . ."

"Absolutely."

"You ready for that ice cream?" said Thack.

In the Loo

The Rands, bless their hearts, had greeted her like an old friend, obviously tickled to see a familiar face at yet another alien benefit. They were a little slow in coming up with Michael's name, so she let them off the hook right away.

". . . and you remember Michael."

"Of course," said Chloe.

Russell extended his hand. "Sure thing. How's it going?"

"Great," Michael told him.

"Were you on the way out?" Chloe asked.

"Well . . ."

"Oh, don't be. I'm sure we don't know a soul."

"Yeah," said Russell, addressing Michael. "Stay and keep us company."

"Well, OK," said Mary Ann. "Sure."

"Fabulous."

"How was the benefit?"

Chloe's high ivory forehead furrowed.

"Didn't you go to some AIDS benefit in LA?"

"Oh, sure," said Russell. "It was very nice. Very moving."

"Right," said Chloe. "I spaced out for a second." She perused the crowded foyer. "Is it this packed everywhere?"

Michael replied: "It's better once you get past the bar."

"Actually," said Chloe, "I have to pee like crazy. Know where the loo is?"

"C'mon, I'll show you." Mary Ann took her hand, feeling sisterly and conspiratorial all of a sudden.

Chloe looked back at her husband. "Can you boys play on your own for a while?"

"Sure," said Russell.

Michael shot a glance at Mary Ann. One of those stranded puppy-dog looks that Brian was so fond of giving her.

"We won't be long," she told him.

The bathroom designated for women was gleaming black onyx, huge.

"So," said Chloe, "I'm dying to know. I didn't wanna ask in front of your husband."

This threw her for a moment. "Oh . . . Michael's not my husband."

"Oh. Shit. The other guy . . ."

"Right."

"I'm sorry."

"It's OK," she said. "Really."

"So . . . what's the verdict on the show?"

Mary Ann gave a sheepish shrug. "I'm gonna do it."

Chloe squealed and hugged her. Though she had never actually experienced it, Mary Ann felt like a freshman at a sorority rush night. "Tell me I won't be sorry," she said.

"You won't be sorry. How's that?"

Mary Ann smiled at her gamely.

"Is . . . what's your husband's name?"

"Brian."

"Is he OK about it?"

She faltered for a moment, then decided to come clean. Chloe had felt like an ally from the moment she met her. "He's not going with me," she said. "We're getting a divorce."

Chloe nodded slowly. "Uh-huh."

"It's been coming on for a long time."

"Was this your idea or his?"

"Both, really."

"Well, that's good."

"I'm kind of freaked out about it. I mean, I know it's the right thing to do, but . . . it's a lot of new stuff all at once."

"You'll be OK. Look at you. You'll land on your feet like a cat."

"Think so?"

"Absolutely."

"It's not just him I'm leaving, though. It's my whole life here, my friends . . . Michael out there . . ."

"They can come see you. This isn't Zanzibar you're moving to."

"Oh, yes it is."

"Look, you're talking to an Akron girl, remember? If I can do it . . ."

"But you did it with somebody you care about . . ."

"Yeah . . . well . . ."

"I am so envious of that. Having somebody on your own wavelength. Who loves the same things you love, laughs at the same jokes. Goes to things with you."

Chloe looked as if she didn't quite understand.

"It's never been that way with me and Brian."

"What has it been?"

"I don't know. Sex, mostly."

Chloe fixed her lips in the mirror. "Poor baby."

Mary Ann laughed uncomfortably. "I don't mean we did it all the time. I mean that's what . . . you know, kept us together."

"Is that what you married him for?"

"No, not completely."

"Then what?"

"He was also . . . very gentle." Mary Ann paused. "Plus he didn't have a name for his dick."

"Excuse me?"

She rolled her eyes. "For the longest time every guy I dated had a name for his dick."

"You're not serious?"

"Yes."

"Like what?"

"I dunno. Ol' Henry or something."

Chloe snorted. "Ol' Henry? Was this here or in Ohio?"

"Here! It was so depressing!"

They laughed together raucously.

"So," said Chloe, recovering. "Ol' Brian came along with this nameless wonder between his legs . . ."

Someone knocked on the door.

Muffling their giggles, they composed themselves. "Come in," said Chloe with exaggerated mellifluousness.

The door swung open slowly and a face appeared. Mary Ann recognized her as one of the pillars of the ballet board. "Oh, I'm sorry," the woman blurted. "I thought . . ."

"No problem," said Chloe. "It's all yours."

She recognizes us both, thought Mary Ann. Won't she have something to tell the girls?

They were in a sort of glass gazebo now, high above the water.

"Shouldn't we look for the guys?" Mary Ann asked.

"Fuck, no. Let 'em look for us."

Mary Ann chuckled. She felt a little guilty about deserting Michael, but she knew he could handle himself. Besides, he was probably thrilled to death to be hobnobbing with Russell Rand.

"This house is weird," said Chloe. "So seventies."

Mary Ann nodded, though she wasn't quite sure what Chloe meant.

"This looks like one of those elevators at the Hyatt Regency. You know?"

"It does, doesn't it?"

"I guess it was pretty hot shit once upon a time. Russell said it was, anyway."

"This house?" said Mary Ann. "He knows it?"

"He knew the guy who lived here."

"Oh."

"Not well, but he came to a few parties."

Mary Ann nodded.

"If you know what I mean," said Chloe.

That Eternity Crap

"Isn't this where we started?" asked Russell Rand, grinning boyishly.

They had wandered from one crowded level to another in search of Mary Ann and Chloe. So far, all they'd come up against were slack-jawed fashion victims, people who simply stopped what they were doing and gawked when the famous New Yorker appeared.

"I think you're right," said Michael.

"I know I've seen that one before." Rand nodded toward a champagne-blond matron in gold lamé knickers.

"You're right. Maybe she moved, though."

"No. She's been there the whole time. A veritable beacon. I'm sure of it."

"Well . . ."

"Oh, Christ." The designer spun on his heels, ducking his head in the process.

"Who is it?"

Rand seized Michael's elbow and steered him away from the advancing menace, all the while pantomiming a surprised, jovial greeting to an imaginary person in the other room. Michael played along, waving vaguely to the same phantom.

When they had made their way to a lower, less populated level, Michael laughed and said: "Who was that?"

"Prue Giroux."

"Oh."

"You know her?"

"No. I know of her."

"Don't *ever* know her. You'll regret it deeply."

Michael laughed. "She likes to talk, I hear."

"Oh, Christ. I thought we could get through here without seeing her this time." He gazed imploringly at Michael. "Let's get some air. This is too much for me."

Without waiting for a response, the designer opened a door leading out to a cliffside rock garden. A pink spotlight beamed through the fog at a bank of succulents. At the end of the path was a stone bench, where Rand sat down with a sigh of relief. "The people in this town are carnivores," he said.

Michael joined him on the bench. "Not everybody."

"Well, everybody here."

He couldn't argue with that.

"What do you do?" asked Rand.

"I'm a nurseryman."

"Oh, yeah?"

"Uh-huh."

"That's a nice solid profession."

"Well . . ." Michael shrugged, not sure what to say about that.

"Have you known Mary Ann long?"

"Years."

"Has she told you about her new show?"

"Oh, yeah."

"Why isn't her husband here tonight?"

Michael decided not to elaborate. "He doesn't like this kind of stuff."

Rand nodded ruefully. "But you do."

"Not really. She asked me as a special favor." He hoped he hadn't come off as her walker.

After a pause Rand said: "You're not married, then?"

Michael smiled. "To a woman?"

His interrogator obviously hadn't expected this.

"I have a lover." It was hardly necessary to specify the gender.

Rand nodded.

"Three years."

"That's nice."

"Yeah . . . it is."

The silence breathed heavy with suggestion.

"Is it an open relationship?"

"Oh, sure." Michael smiled at him. "Everybody knows about it."

Rand shook his head. "That's not what I meant."

"Oh . . ."

"I've got a suite at the Meridien. You could be home by midnight."

Well, well, thought Michael. How do you like this? "What about your wife?"

Rand's lip curled handsomely. "She's got her own suite."

"Right."

"Ours is open."

"Your suite?"

"Our marriage."

"Oh."

"How 'bout it?"

"No, thanks."

"Sure?"

"Yeah."

"We'd play safe," said Rand. "I believe in that."

"It's cold out here," said Michael. "I'm gonna look for Mary Ann."

"C'mon, sport. Stay for a minute."

Michael stared at the ground for a while, then said: "You're really amazing, you know."

The designer's brow furrowed.

"How can you live with yourself?"

"Look, if you mean Chloe . . ."

"No. I mean your own self-worth. What do your friends think when you start spouting that crap?"

"What crap?"

"You know. About the love of a good woman. The joys of being straight. I saw you on the *Today* show last week. I've never heard such a line of shit in my life. You're not fooling half as many people as you think."

Even in the fog, and under a pink light, Rand colored noticeably. "Look, you don't know me . . ."

"I know you're a hypocrite."

Rand took a long time to react. "You run a nursery, for Christ's sake. Nobody expects you to be straight."

"You think they expect dress designers to be?"

Rand nodded dolefully. "The world doesn't want to know. Trust me."

"Who cares?"

"I do. I have to."

"No you don't. You're just greedy. Keeping up a front while your friends drop dead."

Rand gave him a flinty glare. "I've raised more money for AIDS than you'll ever see."

"And that lets you off the hook? Entitles you to lie?"

"I think it entitles me to . . ."

"You had a chance to make a real difference, you know. You could've shown people that gay people are everywhere, that we're no different from . . ."

"Oh, get real!"

"Why not? Are you that disgusted by yourself?"

"Why should the public know about my private life?"

"We sure as hell know about Chloe, don't we?"

Rand grunted and stood up, obviously beating a retreat.

"You're a dinosaur," Michael said. "The world has moved on, and you don't even know it."

Rand glowered back at him as he headed for the house. "What do you know about the world? You live in San Francisco."

"Thank God for that," yelled Michael. "And good luck getting laid."

When Rand was gone, Michael remained there in the rose-tinted fog, filling his lungs with the stuff as he collected his thoughts. Then, remembering suddenly, he leaned over, lifted his pants leg, and examined the purple spot again.

● ● ●

When he found Mary Ann, she was in the act of autographing a cocktail napkin for an ecstatic fan.

"Are you about ready to go?" he asked.

She handed the napkin to the fan, who looked at it disbelievingly, then backed off, bobbing like a court servant. "I guess so," she answered. "Are you bored?"

"No. I've just sort of . . . done it."

"Right." She perused the crowd. "We should say goodbye to Russell and Chloe."

"No," he said. "We shouldn't."

She frowned. "What's the matter? What happened?"

"We had sort of a scene. I'll tell you about it later."

"Mouse . . ."

"I'll get the car."

She followed him up the path to the valet parker. "What sort of a scene?"

"He made a move on me."

"What do you mean?"

"He invited me back to his hotel."

"Well, that may not have been . . ."

"I think I would know," he said.

In the car, after a weighty silence, she asked: "What did you tell him?"

"Not much. That he was a closet case and should go fuck himself."

"You didn't."

"In so many words, yes."

"Mouse . . ."

"What was I supposed to say?"

"It isn't what you say, it's how. Were you rude to him?"

"Does it matter?"

"It does to me, yes."

"Why?"

"Because they've been very nice to me. Chloe's helping me with my move, and . . ."

He laughed as bitterly as he could.

"I mean this," she said.

"What was I supposed to do? Suck him off to show your gratitude?"

"Don't put words in my mouth."

"The guy is a slimeball."

"You've been hit on before," she said. "You know how to turn somebody down in a pleasant way."

"I can't believe this."

"Where do you get off being so sanctimonious, anyway? You picked up plenty of guys before you met Thack."

As usual, she had missed the point entirely. "This has nothing to do with picking up guys," he said.

"Then . . . what?"

"He's a liar, Mary Ann."

"He's a public figure."

"Oh, I see. Can't have Amurrica knowing he's queer. Anything but that, God knows."

"There are practical considerations," she said. "You're not being at all reasonable."

"I haven't got time for people who don't like themselves."

He peered sullenly out the window. Pale stucco façades slid past in the darkness. It made him sad to realize that she hadn't grasped this fundamental concept in all their years of knowing each other. If she, of all people, didn't get it, was there any hope for the serious bigots?

She turned and looked at him. "You sound so strident. It isn't very becoming."

He kept quiet.

"You liked Russell the other night. Did Thack bad-mouth him or something?"

"No."

"Then what's gotten into you?"

His beeper went off, answering her question more eloquently than anything he might have said.

784

She looked flustered for a moment. "Do you want me to stop for water?"

"No."

"Are you sure?"

"Yes. I'll take it when I get home."

"I can always . . ."

"I'm fine, all right?"

They were silent for a while, staring out of different windows. As they dipped into Cow Hollow, he turned to her and said: "You're the one who's changed, you know."

"Have I?" Her voice was surprisingly gentle.

"Yes."

"I'm sorry if my leaving . . ."

"It isn't that. It happened some time ago."

"Oh."

"I wish there was some way to convince you I'm not dead yet." She gazed at him, blinking.

"That's the way you've acted," he added. "Ever since I told you I was positive."

She pretended not to understand. "What do you mean? Acted how?"

"I don't know. Careful and distant and overpolite. It's not the same between us anymore. You talk to me now like I'm Shawna or something."

"Mouse . . ."

"I don't blame you," he said. "You don't wanna go through Jon again."

"What do you think tonight was about? And that day at the Wave Organ?"

He shrugged. "Insecurity."

"C'mon."

"You needed somebody to hold your hand. Somebody to listen. Nothing more."

"That's not very kind."

"Maybe not," he said. "But it's true."

"If I can't count on you, Mouse . . ."

"Hey, it works the other way too."

She looked wounded. "I know that."

"You're leaving more than one man, you know."

She seemed to be composing her words. "Mouse . . . you and I will always . . ."

"Horseshit. You scrapped our plans tonight as soon as that closet case walked through the door. Don't gimme that eternity crap. You've got your new friends now. The rest of us are just an interim measure."

"I know you don't mean that."

"I do mean it. I wish to hell I didn't, but I do. You don't give a shit about anybody." He looked away from her, out the window. "I'm amazed it took me this long to figure it out."

"I don't believe this," she said.

"Believe it."

"Mouse, if I've said something . . ."

"Jesus, why are you always so innocent?"

"Look, if you'd tell me where this coffee place is . . ."

"Fuck that. Stop at the next corner. I'm getting out."

"Oh, for heaven's sake."

He turned and gave her a look to signal his seriousness. "I said stop, please."

"How will you get home?"

"A bus, a cab. I don't care."

She pulled next to the curb at Union and Octavia.

"This is so unnecessary," she said.

He opened the door and left the car without looking back. As the Mercedes sped away into the fog-fuzzed corridor, he stood on the curb and wondered bleakly if she even cared, if she was feeling anything at all.

Love on the Machine

He woke at dawn the next morning. The only dream he could remember had been a real doozie, a full Dolby extravaganza involving
dead turtles, vintage biplanes, and a brief, heart-stopping walk-on by
the Princess of Wales. Out of old habit, he lay there for a while re-
constructing this epic, honoring it with his stillness, like a moviegoer
who remains in his seat until the credits are over.

Leaving Thack in bed, he slipped into jeans and a corduroy shirt and took Harry on his morning walk—the abbreviated
version—before sorting the laundry and fixing a breakfast of apples
and yogurt. His pentamidine appointment was at nine, but the office
opened at eight. He knew from experience that August wouldn't
mind squeezing in an unscheduled examination.

As he left, Thack was lurching toward the shower in his morning muddle. "Want me to come with you?"

Michael told him no.

"Are you coming home afterwards?"

This was a hard one to call. "I dunno."

His lover pecked him on the shoulder. "Call me, then. Or I'll
call you at work."

"OK."

"And don't worry," said Thack.

August's office was in a black glass building on Parnassus opposite
UC Med Center. Michael parked in the basement garage, then rode
an elevator smelling of disinfectant and the hot dogs in the fourth-
floor snack bar. On the fifth floor he was joined by a bulky Samoan
lady who smiled pathetically and held up a splinted forefinger. He
offered his condolences, then got off at the seventh floor.

In August's waiting room the receptionist behind the glass re-
strained her smile enough to hide the braces he'd seen many times
before. "Morning, Michael."

787

"Hi, Lacey."

"You're early, aren't you?"

"I've got pentamidine at nine, but I was hoping August could take a look at something."

She nodded. "He's out till noon."

"Oh."

"He's testifying in Sacramento."

"Oh, yeah."

"You know, funding . . . something like that. Joy is here. You wanna see her?"

Joy was a nurse practitioner. "Sure. I guess. It's just a place on my leg."

"OK." Another camouflaging smile. "Have a seat. She'll be free in a little while."

He sat down, grabbed a copy of *HG*, and thumbed through it mechanically. One of the featured homes was Arch Gidde's house at Sea Cliff, almost unrecognizable amid the jungle of exotic flora imported for the photograph. He checked the date of the magazine— two months back. The realtor must have been close to death when it hit the stands.

"Hey," said Lacey, "did you see where Jessica Hahn is making a video?"

Michael managed a chuckle.

"Is that disgusting or what?"

"That's pretty bad."

"They say she's had a boob job."

"Chances are," he said.

He returned to his magazine and, feeling his palms begin to sweat, studied the lucite-framed cavalry uniforms in Arch Gidde's bedroom.

Five minutes later, Joy met him at the door and led him down a sunny hall lined with August's collection of Broadway show posters.

"By the way," she said, "that was me who honked at you yesterday."

He drew a blank.

788

"On Clement," she explained. "You were leaving your nursery, I think."

"Oh, yeah." He pretended to remember. At the moment he couldn't focus on anything. Certainly not on yesterday.

"I hate it when people honk at me and I can't see who they are. It fucks up my whole day."

"I know what you mean," he said.

When they reached the examining room, she said: "What can I do for you?"

He sat on the table and rolled up his pants leg. "Is that what I think it is?"

She studied it in silence for a moment, then straightened up. "How long has it been there?"

"I don't know. I haven't noticed it before."

"When did you find it?"

"Last night."

She nodded.

"Is it?"

"It looks like it," she said.

He made himself take a deep breath.

"I'm not a hundred percent certain."

He nodded.

"August'll be back at noon. He should look at it. We can take a biopsy."

"Whatever."

"Are you feeling OK otherwise?"

"Fine."

"I'm not completely sure," she said.

"I understand." He smiled faintly to show that he wouldn't hold her to it.

He loitered in the waiting room until nine, then went to the third-floor lab for his pentamidine. While he sucked away on the phallic plastic mouthpiece, the nurse who attended him carried on his usual monologue.

". . . so George went to this big, fancy gay and lesbian banquet in Washington, only the airlines lost his luggage with all his leather in it, and . . . well, you can imagine . . . he had to get up in front of everybody in wool pants and a white button-down shirt . . ."

Michael smiled feebly under the mouthpiece.

"He was totally upstaged by this S-and-M dyke, who made her entrance in a merry widow . . . with *visible lash marks* on her back. Is that a fashion statement or what?"

Michael chuckled.

"Are you OK, guy?"

"Yeah, fine."

"Am I talking too much? Just tell me, if I am."

"Not at all."

The vapor, as usual, left a bitter, tinfoilish taste in his mouth.

He left the building just before ten and walked down the hill to the park, where he wandered amid people frolicking with Frisbees and dogs. Three years of daily fretting had left him overrehearsed for this moment, but it still seemed completely unreal. He had vowed not to rail against the universe when his time came. Too many people had died, too many he had loved, for "Why me?" to be a reasonable response. "Why not?" was more to the point.

And there were lots worse things than KS. Pneumocystis, for one, which could finish you off in a matter of days. August had assured him the pentamidine would prevent that, if he did it faithfully. And KS had been known to disappear completely with the proper treatment. Unless it spread, unless it got inside you.

He remembered Charlie Rubin when the lesions moved to his face, how he'd joked about the one on his nose that made him look like Pluto. They had covered him eventually, forming great purple continents. Charlie was blind by that time, of course, so at least he was spared the sight of them.

He sat on a bench and began to cry. It wasn't major grief at all, just another pit stop in the Grand Prix of HIV. He still felt fine, didn't he? He still had Thack and a home. And Brian and Shawna. And Harry. And Mrs. Madrigal, wherever she might be.

He tilted his head and let the sun dry his tears. The air smelled of new-mown grass, while what he could see of the sky seemed ridiculously blue. The birds in the trees were as fat and chirpy as the ones in cartoons.

As soon as he returned to August's office, Lacey's face grew soft with concern. She had obviously gotten the word.

"August is back," she said. "He's expecting you."

He found the doctor in the first examining room, washing his hands. "Young man," he said, smiling. "Sorry we missed each other."

August was in his late forties, not that much older than most of his patients, but he called them all "young man." Over the years he had watched his peaceful little dermatology practice grow into something that seemed more like a fraternity than a medical venture.

"How's that handsome husband of yours?"

"Fine," said Michael.

"Good, good. Sit on the table for me." He tore off a paper towel and dried his hands.

Michael sat.

"Where is it?"

He held out his leg and pointed.

August leaned over the place and squinted at it. "Does it hurt?"

"Not really."

"Yeah." August shook his head. "I wouldn't say so."

"What?"

"I don't think that's a lesion." He let go of Michael's leg and left the room, returning moments later with his nurse practitioner.

"Hi again," said Joy.

"Hi." Michael was sure he could feel his heart beating.

"There's a sort of ring around it," Joy said, looking at the spot again. "That's why it seemed to me . . ." She didn't try to finish this.

"I can see why you'd think that," August said evenly, "but there's only one of them."

She nodded.

"They almost never come singly."

"Yeah . . . I see." She gave Michael an apologetic glance.

"It doesn't really warrant a biopsy," the doctor told him. "If it's not gone in a week, we can talk again, but I'll be surprised if it doesn't clear up on its own."

Michael nodded. "There's nothing I need to do, then?"

"You might try a little Clearasil," said August.

Like the other false alarms he'd experienced over the years, this one sent him on his way with a noticeable spring in his step. He felt an irresistible urge to buy something. Clothes, maybe, or furniture. Or maybe he'd just go ride the circular escalator at the new Nordstrom store and see what occurred to him. Nothing extravagant; just something useful and commemorative.

He knew this feeling well. When his T-cells soared to six hundred following his first six weeks of AZT, the orgy of consuming that ensued had not been a pretty sight. Limiting himself to the bare essentials, he had pushed his Visa card to the limit in the linen department at Macy's before going berserk with his pocket cash at the Fair Oaks Street garage sale.

He phoned Thack at home from the garage of the medical building. "It's me, sweetie."

"Oh, hi."

"August says it's just a zit."

"Well . . . great." He could hear the relief in Thack's voice. "Told you."

"You working today?" Michael asked.

"No."

"I thought I might call Brian and tell him I'm taking the day off."

"Good idea. Do it."

"You wanna have lunch somewhere?"

"Sure. You pick."

"It doesn't matter. Someplace cozy and lesbian."

His lover laughed. "Sounds like you're on the verge of buying things?"

Michael chuckled. "I might be."

"Can we do it together?"

"Sure."

"What's it gonna be?"

"I dunno," said Michael. "I thought maybe chairs."

"Chairs?"

"You know . . . for the kitchen table. Like we decided."

"Oh, yeah."

"We could go down to the Mission, check out the junk stores."

"OK."

"Mrs. Madrigal swears by that one at Twentieth next to the organic food . . ."

"Oh," said Thack. "She called."

"Mrs. Madrigal?"

"Yes."

"What did she say?"

"Nothing. Just sent her love. It was on the machine. She was in Athens, apparently."

"She must be on the way home."

"Yeah," said Thack. "I guess so."

D'orothea's Grille was a little short on celebrities that day, so their people-watching centered around the bubble-butted boy who brought them their Chinese chicken salads. DeDe emerged from the kitchen when they were almost done, kissing Michael's cheek, then Thack's. "Hi, boys. Like the new decor?"

"Not bad," Michael told her.

"Not finished either. We've still gotta knock out that back wall, open the whole thing up. God, it makes me tired just thinking about it. How were the salads?"

"Great," said Thack.

"You should've come earlier. Chloe Rand was here."

Thack grunted.

"You know her?"

"No," said Thack. "But her husband tried to fuck my husband last night."

DeDe turned to Michael and let her jaw drop comically. "No!"

Michael chuckled.

"Did you do it?" asked DeDe.

He smiled cryptically.

DeDe glanced at Thack. "I think he did, don't you?"

Thack laughed.

"Where was this?" asked DeDe.

"Out at Arch Gidde's."

She nodded. "We were invited to some brunch thing at Prue Giroux's, but D'or didn't think she could stomach it. She used to model for him, you know, back when he was still gay."

This got a hoot out of Thack.

An hour later they scored big in a junk store on Valencia Street: two matching wooden dinette chairs, covered in cruddy white vinyl but displaying an unmistakably Deco silhouette. They paid an old man ten bucks for the pair and tied them onto the VW, fussing like nuns with a fresh busload of orphans.

Back at the house, they set to work with hammers and crow-bars, ripping away two, three, four layers of plastic and stuffing, until the original chairs were revealed. Their peaked backs and oval hand-holds conveyed a sort of Seven Dwarfsish feeling, which Michael thought suited the house perfectly.

At dusk, as the fog rolled in, they lay on the deck completely spent, staring at their treasures.

"What should we paint them?" asked Michael. "A Fiesta color, maybe?"

"How about turquoise?"

"Perfect. God, look how many tacks there were!"

"Yeah."

"They must feel better," said Michael.

"Who must?"

"The chairs. To have all those tacks out."

"Right."

"Well, think about it. It was like a crucifixion or something."

Thack gave him a sleepy smile. "You're such a weird guy," he said.

Michael reached over and took hold of Thack's cock. It felt fat and warm through the padding of his sweat pants. Holding on, he slid closer and kissed Thack softly on the lips.

"Feeling better?" asked Thack.

"Much."

"I want you to stick around, OK?"

"OK," said Michael.

They heard the hiss of a pop-top in the kitchen and realized without looking that Brian had come home.

Inheritance

On her way back to New York the morning after, Chloe had left a chirpy see-you-soon on Mary Ann's machine, so whatever nastiness had transpired between Michael and Russell must not have made its way back to his wife. Thank God for that, anyway. Four days after the debacle in Sea Cliff, Mary Ann still hadn't heard from Michael, and knowing him, he wasn't likely to relent anytime soon. His tantrums had a way of lasting.

Ditto Brian. Yesterday she'd left a message on Michael's machine, telling her husband that she'd be gone by the end of the week, that Shawna should not be deprived of her father any longer than necessary. He hadn't called back. She'd begun to wonder if he was deliberately trying to screw up her departure, knowing she couldn't leave in good conscience without turning over Shawna to his care.

Shawna, thankfully, had taken all this grownup childishness in stride. (If anything, she seemed more distressed by her father's current absence than by Mary Ann's impending one.) The same could not be said for Mary Ann's bosses at the station. Their ill-disguised resentment over her new position had been gratifying only to the degree that it confirmed—or betrayed, rather, since they'd always kept it a secret—her real value to the station.

As she'd sat there outlining her new duties and watching a vein throb in Larry Kenan's temple, it was all she could do not to pull a Sally Field and blurt out the revelation that had finally come to her after all these years:

You like me . . . you really like me.

She had endured *Mary Ann in the Morning* for one last program— "The Truth About Breast Implants." Now she was home in her walk-in closet, dragging out a trunk, which had been there unopened for ages. It was crammed with things from Connie's apartment in the Marina. Connie's little brother, Wally, had brought it by Barbary Lane only days after he'd shown up with the newborn Shawna. "She might want this someday," he'd told them somberly, bestowing a sort of heirloom status on stuff he'd simply been too soft-hearted to throw out.

When Mary Ann pushed back the lid, Shawna all but dove into the musty interior.

"Hey, Puppy. Take it easy."

"What's this?"

It was a filthy terry-cloth python with plastic eyes that rolled. She remembered it all too well. Connie had kept it on her bed, next to her giant Snoopy. "It's a snake, see?" She made the eyes roll for Shawna.

"Was that hers?"

"Sure. All of this stuff was."

"Gah!" Obviously impressed, the kid lunged into the trunk again and pulled out a little cardboard crate that Mary Ann recognized immediately.

"What's this?"

"Open it."

Shawna did so and frowned. "It's just a dumb rock."

"No, it's a Pet Rock."

"What's that?"

"Well . . . people used to have these."

"What does it do?"

"It's kind of hard to explain, Puppy. Look at this, though." She removed a satin pillow, maroon faded to rose, and read the inscription: "School Spirit Day, Central High, 1967."

"What is it?"

"Well, that's where your . . . birth mommy and I went to high school in Cleveland. She was head majorette. You know what that is?"

Shawna shook her head.

"She marched in front of the band. With a baton and this really neat uniform. It was a big deal. Everybody saw her. You know, I think maybe . . ." She foraged through the trunk, hoping that Wally had rescued Connie's *Buccaneer*.

Sure enough, there it was, tucked behind an atrocious painting of a bullfighter on black velvet. The raised medallion on the front cover had been rendered medieval by mildew. "I'll show you a picture," she said.

It was a full-page photo at the front of the sports section: Connie strutting her stuff, buttons gleaming, teeth and tits to the wind. At the time, Mary Ann had written it off as slutty looking, but she had probably just been envious. It seemed almost virginal now.

Sitting Indian style on the floor, Shawna took the yearbook on her lap and studied the page. "She was pretty," she said at last.

"She was," said Mary Ann. "Very. I think she looks a lot like you. Don't you?"

Shawna shrugged. "Did you move out here with her?"

"No. She was here a long time before I was. But I stayed with her when I came out here from Cleveland."

"How long?"

"Oh . . . a week." It had been a long week too, what with Connie dragging home guys from Thomas Lord's and Dance Your Ass Off. She had moved out with a sense of profound relief, putting all that tackiness behind her. Or so she thought at the time. Who would have dreamed she would end up as the custodian of Connie's memory?

"Didn't you like her?" asked Shawna.

This caught her off guard. "Of course, Puppy. Sure I liked her. Why would you say a thing like that?"

The child shrugged. "You left her."

"I didn't leave her."

"But you said . . ."

"I found a place at Anna's house. I wanted my own apartment. I was only at your birth mommy's place for the time being. She knew that."

Shawna seemed to weigh this, her blue eyes narrowing. She looked down at the yearbook again. "Are you in this?" she asked.

Mary Ann found her ridiculous class picture with the ironed hair and showed it to the child, wincing privately at the meager credits and the condescending epigram: "Still Waters Run Deep."

"Is that all?"

"That's it." What could she say? She'd been a nerd.

Shawna closed the book and laid it aside. "Can I play with this stuff?"

"Sure. It's yours, Puppy. That's why . . . your mommy left it for you." She had almost said "birth mommy" again, but it sounded a little stingy somehow.

For a moment, remembering, she felt a rush of unfettered affection for Connie, something she'd never been able to manage while her old classmate was still alive. She flashed on Connie looking radiant in her BABY T-shirt—the one with the arrow pointing to her bulbous belly—and it struck her again how much single parenthood would have suited Connie.

When Shawna had repaired to her room with Connie's python, Mary Ann dragged out her suitcases and made a few decisions about the stuff she would take to New York. Burke had reserved her a suite at the Plaza, and Lillie Rubin was furnishing her wardrobe, so she resolved to pack light and ship the rest of her things later. Anyway, Chloe had promised to take her shopping as soon as she arrived.

It would be cold, of course, so she went mostly for the tweed and cashmere. She made choices that were businesslike and neutral, so they would see she was an empty canvas, not the finished product. She would work on her look later, after she'd been able to analyze the setting they had planned for it.

Shawna seemed to sense that this was a good time to ask for the moon. It was by her decree that they drove to Mel's Drive-In for chocolate shakes that night, following a roller coaster of a route, which included the steepest slope of Leavenworth.

"Look!" said Shawna, pointing, as they passed the Barbary Steps. "There's Daddy and Michael."

"Sit down, Puppy."

"Look, there . . . see?"

"I see." They were trudging up the steps, their backs to the street. She saw Thack's pale, feathery head under the streetlight at the top. She decided that Mrs. Madrigal must be back from Greece.

She felt a brief pang of paranoia, knowing they would talk about her tonight—distorting the facts, no doubt—making her seem like an unfeeling monster. It wasn't a bit fair.

Shawna made a lunge for the wheel. "Honk," she ordered.

She held the kid back with an arm. "Sit down, Puppy. That's very dangerous."

"Honk the horn."

"No. This isn't the time. Put your seat belt on."

The child threw herself back against the seat and pushed out her lower lip.

"We'll call them when we get back."

Silence.

"OK?"

"When is he coming home?"

"Soon."

Shawna turned and looked out the window. "I want extra malt," she said.

Not That

"She sounded funny," said Michael, as they picked their way along the ballast stones at the head of the lane. "Didn't you notice it?"

"Not particularly," said Thack.

"Well, she did to me."

"It's probably jet lag," said Brian. "Unless you mean funny about . . . ?"

"No," said Michael, knowing he meant Mary Ann. "Not that. Something else."

As they passed through the lych-gate at Number 28, a cat leapt from the mossy roof, clambering for safety up an ivy-wrapped tree. The windows of the old shingled house seemed to glow with gratitude for their mistress's return.

There was music—a pleasant sort of new age ragtime—coming from Michael's old apartment on the second floor. He had never met his successors and really didn't want to now. Tonight he hoped it would just be family. He didn't want to share Mrs. Madrigal with people he didn't know.

When the landlady opened the door, the first thing that struck him was her tan. Her Wedgwood eyes went wide and actressy as she hugged them one at a time, in order of their appearance: Michael, Thack, Brian.

"You all look gorgeous!" she said, leading them into her parlor. "Sit down. There are joints on the table there. Some sherry if you like. I have a few adjustments to make in the kitchen. I'll be back in two shakes of a lamb's tail."

Brian and Thack took the sofa. Michael remained standing, unconvinced and a little unsettled by this flurry of ferocious hostessing. "Can I give you a hand?" he asked.

The landlady seemed to hesitate. "If you like."

• • •

In the kitchen, after slipping several cottage pies into the oven, she gave him another hug and said: "That was from Mona. She made me promise."

"How is she?"

"Lovely. A very charming, grown-up person."

"Mona?"

The landlady smiled and closed the oven door. "I tried to get her to visit us, but, as usual, she's completely wrapped up in that house of hers."

"Can't imagine where she gets that."

Her smile turned a little wan. "I've missed you, dear."

"I'm sorry I didn't call before you left."

"Don't be silly."

"No," he said. "I promised."

"Well, you had so much on your mind. Oh . . . here, before I forget." She dashed off to the bedroom and returned with a small cardboard box. "Lady Roughton said to tell you this is the last trace of Sappho on the island."

It was a key ring with a green enamel medallion bearing the poet's likeness. He smiled and enjoyed the smooth feel of it beneath his thumb. "Did she fall in love?"

"She wouldn't tell me," said Mrs. Madrigal.

"I'll bet."

"I don't blame her, really."

"How about you?"

"What do you mean?"

He shrugged.

She batted her eyes at him in a way that suggested he was being impertinent. "I had lovely walks in the hills."

He chuckled. "Good."

She turned away and began rinsing spinach leaves under the tap. "I've some pictures to show you later."

"Great."

After a silence, she asked: "Is she leaving for good?"

"Looks like it."

She gave a little murmur and continued rinsing.

"It's a big break, really."

"Is he all right?"

"No," he answered. "Not particularly."

"When does she leave?"

"Day after tomorrow, I think."

The landlady dried her hands on an Acropolis dish towel. She had about her such an air of quiet competence that he imagined for a moment she would set to work fixing things. Like a doctor who'd been given all the symptoms and was ready to prescribe the cure.

Instead, she opened her ancient refrigerator and removed a tray of stuffed grape leaves. "Take these in for me, would you, dear?"

Snaps

". . . and in Petra, which is the next village over, there is something they call a tourist collective, which is made up solely of women. They sell crafts and rent out their homes and such. And it's the first time the women of that village have ever made a penny—or a drachma or what have you—independent of their husbands. They just sit there with their little trays of lace, with these enormous grins on their faces . . ."

After several joints and a long dinner, Brian's mind had begun to wander, but this part of the landlady's travelogue, drifting toward him out of nowhere, seemed somehow pertinent to his pain. He wondered if she'd intended it to be.

"I thought you had snapshots," said Michael.

"Now, dear . . . are you sure you want . . . ?"

"Absolutely," said Thack, flicking his worry beads vigorously. The landlady had given them each a string, marking their places at the table with them. Blue ceramic for Brian, orange for Thack, olive-wood for Michael. Somewhere, undoubtedly, there was a string for Mary Ann.

Mrs. Madrigal left the room, apparently in search of her snapshots.

Across the table Michael smiled drowsily. "She looks good, doesn't she?"

Brian nodded.

"Something agreed with her," said Thack.

Mrs. Madrigal returned with the photographs, fanning them out like playing cards on her velvet-draped sideboard. "I'll let everyone look for himself. You can do without my narration for a while."

Brian joined the others at the sideboard.

"I didn't know you owned a camera," said Michael.

"I don't, actually," said the landlady. "Someone else took these."

The shots were largely what Brian had expected, except maybe for the absence of whitewash. Parched hills above vibrant blue water. Random donkeys. Brightly painted fishing boats. Anna and Mona squinting into the sun, the family resemblance more evident than ever as they held up middle age from either end.

"The villa looks wonderful," said Thack. "This is it, isn't it? With the terrace?"

"That's it."

"This is Mona." Michael showed one of the snaps to Thack.

"Yeah. I recognized her."

"How?" Michael asked.

"That shot she sent us last Christmas."

"Oh, yeah."

Brian was drifting again, dwelling morosely on the consolation of "us" and how it was about to vanish from his own vocabulary. Mrs. Madrigal locked eyes with him and smiled with excruciating kindness.

Michael held up another snap. "Is this the one who took the pictures?"

"Which?" said the landlady.

"This guy who looks like Cesar Romero."

Brian was sure he saw the color rise in the landlady's cheeks.

"Yes," she replied demurely. "That's Stratos. He showed us around."

Michael nodded, giving her a sly look.

"Who needs sherry?" asked Mrs. Madrigal, holding out the bottle and looking everywhere but at Michael.

"Here," called Thack, reaching toward her with his glass. He had noticed Michael's teasing, apparently, and was helping her change the subject. "This stuff is great, by the way. So nutty."

"Isn't it?"

"Mmm."

"It was new down at Molinari's . . ."

"I'll take some," Brian put in.

"Lovely." As she poured she looked directly at him and spoke in a low, even voice. "Let's take ours to the courtyard, shall we?"

Somehow, he felt as if he'd just been summoned to the principal's office.

"You boys will excuse us, won't you?"

Michael and Thack answered "Sure" in unison.

The bench where they sat was usually referred to as "Jon's bench," since his ashes had been buried in the flower bed just beyond it. The soil there was bare now, but by the end of winter, the air would be narcotic with the scent of hyacinths.

"Michael told me," the landlady began.

"I know." He smiled at her a little. "He told me he told you."

"Are you all right?"

He shrugged.

She paused awhile, then said: "I won't tell you it'll get better . . ."

He finished it for her. ". . . because you know I know that."

She chuckled ruefully. "Oh, dear. Am I that easy to read?"

"No. Not really."

"I hate old ladies who have homilies for everything."

"Don't worry," he said. "You're not like that."

"I hope and pray not."

He smiled at her wearily.

804

"Have you spoken to her?" she asked.

"Not lately."

She took this in silently.

"You think I should, huh?"

Mrs. Madrigal arranged her long fingers in her lap. "I think there are some scenes . . . we're simply required to play. If we don't, we rob ourselves of ever feeling anything at all."

"Oh, I feel something."

"I know."

He snatched a little pinecone from the ground and flung it into the shrubs. "She's leaving day after tomorrow. I was planning to be back then."

"What about Shawna?"

"I'm still taking her to school every day."

"I meant afterwards."

"Oh. I'll manage. That's no problem."

"If you need help during the day, you know how glad I'd be to keep an eye on her."

"Thanks."

The landlady cast her eyes around the courtyard. "She loves it down here, you know."

He nodded. "Yes."

"She's a smart little girl." Mrs. Madrigal looked at him. "She'll know how to deal with this."

Another nod. "She's already doing better than I am." His embarrassment finally got the best of him. "I'm sorry we stopped bringing her by."

"Don't be silly."

"No . . . I mean it."

She reached over and took his hand.

They sat there in silence, staring into the shadows. Finally he said: "You think I oughta do it, huh?"

"What's that?"

"Go up there and say goodbye like a man."

She nodded.

"Bummer."

"I know." She sighed a little. "I just had to do it myself."

He was thrown. "With Mary Ann?"

"No. In Lesbos."

He thought about it for a moment. "The man in the picture?"

She nodded.

"So you had a little . . . ?"

"Yes."

"And you miss him."

"Like a sonofabitch," she said.

Stay, Then

No show tomorrow meant no homework, she realized. With Shawna in bed and her bags packed, she felt oddly like a sixth grader on Saturday morning. Determined to enjoy it, she had taken a long bath, then curled up in her bathrobe on the sofa with the Linda Ellerbee book. She'd been trying to finish the damned thing for almost a year.

When a key rattled in the front door, she knew that Brian was home.

"Hi," he said.

"Hi." She laid the book on her stomach and yawned so unexpectedly that "Excuse me" followed as a reflex. It must have sounded idiotic to him.

He walked past her and down the hall to the bathroom. She heard him taking a leak, then splashing water on his face. She sat up on the sofa but didn't rise. If he wanted to talk to her, he'd be back.

He was, and he took the chair across from her. "I was down at Mrs. Madrigal's."

"She's back, then."

"Yeah."

"Did she feed you? There's some turkey salad if . . ."

"No, thanks. I'm full."

She nodded.

"I'm not staying."

After a pause she said: "I wish you would."

He shook his head.

"I hate that it's happening like this."

He shrugged.

She gave him the gentlest look she could manage. "Please don't be mad."

"I'm not mad."

"Stay, then."

"It's not a good idea, OK?"

He was obviously hurting, so she didn't pursue it. "I picked up the laundry," she said instead.

"Thanks."

"I thought you might be low on shirts."

He nodded. "Is Shawna OK?"

"Fine. Did she tell you she got a part in the Presidio Hill Christmas play?"

"Uh-huh."

"I have a feeling it's not the lead, *but* . . ." She widened her eyes as winningly as possible.

"It's an atom."

"Adam?" She frowned. "A girl plays Adam?"

"No. *An* atom. Like . . . a nuclear particle."

That school, she thought. "Doesn't sound very Christmasy."

"It's about . . . you know, saving the planet." He smiled at her, sort of.

"When can I tell her you'll be back?"

"Friday."

After she was gone, in other words.

"She knows that already," he added.

"Oh . . . OK."

"She won't be alone, will she?"

"No," she answered. "Nguyet'll be here. I've explained everything to Shawna. She's OK about it."

He nodded.

"The logistics have all been worked out."

"I'm sure," he said. "What time are you leaving?"

"There's a limousine coming at six."

"P.M.?"

"A.M."

He winced, apparently empathizing. "You have to get up early for this job too."

She smiled. "I guess I'm in the habit."

Their eyes met for a moment, then sought safer places to rest.

"I'm really sorry," she said.

He held up his palm. "Hey."

"I think you're such a great guy . . ."

"Mary Ann."

"I don't know what to say. I feel so awful."

"Fuck it," he said quietly. "I'm over it."

He didn't look a bit over it.

"Michael's the one you should talk to," he added.

"What do you mean?"

"Well . . . this is kind of it for you guys."

"What?"

"I mean, if he got sick . . . You've thought about this, haven't you?"

"What is this? What are you saying? I shouldn't be going, because he might get sick and I should be here to . . . ?"

"Did I say that? I didn't say that."

"Well, good, because Mouse would never . . ."

"I know that."

"Let me finish. He would never, ever, accuse me of . . ." She felt close to tears, so she collected herself. "He knows what I'm doing and why I'm doing it, and he wishes me well. I'm glad he's going to miss me, if that's what he told you, because I'm going to miss him too. But that's what happens, Brian. Life just sort of does this sometimes."

He looked at her blankly and said: "Your life."

"Yes. OK. My life. Whatever. Just don't accuse me of running away from . . . his illness."

"I didn't."

"I would be back in a second if . . ."

"You can't. How could you?"

She hated thinking about this. He knew it too. Michael was his last card, and he was determined to play it. "This is the lowest, Brian. If Michael knew you were using him to . . ."

"Talk to him. That's all I'm saying."

"No it isn't. You're laying this big guilt trip on me."

"I can't help how you take it."

"You don't know what goes on between me and Mouse. You don't know how much we understand each other."

He gave her a dim, mournful smile. "No," he said, "I guess not."

She could see the effect this had and tried to undo it. "I didn't mean it that way."

"Just call him, OK?"

"Sure."

He rose.

"Don't go yet," she said.

He smiled faintly. "I'm getting my shirts."

She stood by the window and stared out at the bay. He was back in less than a minute, his laundry flung over his shoulder like a cavalier's cape.

"You could sleep on the couch," she said, "if the bed bothers you."

He leaned over and pecked her on the top of her head. "That's OK."

At the door, for some stupid reason, she touched his arm and said, "Drive carefully."

Another Letter to Mama

Dear Mama,

When you were talking about Papa's headstone the other day I noticed you mentioned there was room at the plot for the entire family.

No. Awkward. Start again.

Dear Mama,

It was wonderful talking to you the other day. Thack says you and I should talk more, and I guess he's right, since it always makes me feel better.

Stop lying and get to the point.

Dear Mama, I'm glad we talked the other day. There was something you mentioned, though, that concerned me. You seemed to think that someday the whole family would be buried at the cemetery there. I know how you meant this, but frankly, the idea of Christian burial strikes me as unnecessary and a little ghoulish.

Real subtle, Tolliver.
Keep writing. You can change it later.

I don't know how much time I have left—whether it's two years or five or fifty—but I don't want to be taken back to Orlando when it's over. This is my home now, and I've asked Thack to make arrangements for my cremation here in San Francisco.

This wouldn't be so important to me if I didn't believe in families just as much as you do. I have one of my own, and it means the world to me. If there are goodbyes to be said, I want them to be here, and I want Thack to be in charge. I hope you can understand.

If you still want to do a memorial service in Orlando (assuming you can't come here), Thack can send you part of the ashes. I think you know I'd prefer not to have a preacher involved, but do whatever makes you comfortable. Just make sure he doesn't pray for my soul or ask the Lord's forgiveness or anything like that.

Please don't get the wrong idea. I'm fine right now. I just wanted this out of the way, so we don't have to think about it again. I'm not too worried about how you'll take it, since I know how much you like Thack. He sends his love, by the way, and promises to send pix of the new chairs as soon as we get them painted.

I'll try to call more often.

All my love,
Michael

PS. My friend Mary Ann Singleton (you met her once years ago) has a new syndicated morning talk show. It starts in March, so watch for it. She's a good friend of mine, and we're all really happy for her.

Relief

With winter came precipitation, but not nearly enough. The puny mists and drizzles drifting in from the ocean barely dented the parched reservoirs of the East Bay. Michael watched the nightly forecasts with a sense of mounting dread for the nursery. By the end of February the weatherman was leading off the news again, speaking darkly of the stringent water rationing to come.

Then, on the day after Saint Patrick's Day, huge flannel-gray clouds appeared over the city like dirigibles, hovering there forever, it seemed, before dumping their cargo on a grateful population. The rain came with sweet vengeance, making things clean again, sluicing down the hills to whisk away the dog shit like logs in a flume.

It kept up like this all week, until Harry's running meadow in Dolores Park had become a bog, impenetrable to man or beast. When the skies cleared temporarily on Saturday morning, Michael stuck to the concrete route along Cumberland as he gave Harry his first real exercise in twenty-four hours. The blue rip in the clouds was about to be mended again, so they would have to make it quick—a fact that even Harry seemed to grasp.

At the top of the Cumberland stairs, while the dog squatted ingloriously in the wet weeds, Michael sat on the rail and looked out over the rain-varnished valley. There were lakes beginning to form on the flat roofs of the non-Victorians.

A tall, thin man with a little blue backpack came toward him up the stairs, taking his time. When he reached the landing, Michael recognized him as the guy from the Rawhide II. Eula's son. With the six T-cells. "How's it going?" he asked, recognizing Michael.

"Pretty good. Isn't this air great?"

The man stopped next to him and filled his lungs. "Beats pentamidine."

"Doesn't it?" Michael smiled. "How's your mother?"

"Fabulous. They asked her to judge the Bare Chest Contest."

He chuckled. "She must be in hog heaven."

"She is."

"You live around here?"

The man shook his head. "I was just down at the Buyer's Club."

"The one on Church?"

"Yeah."

"What did you get?"

"Dextran. Some freeze-dried herbs."

Michael nodded. "I did Dextran for a while."

"No good?"

"Well, I heard your body can't absorb enough to make any difference."

"I heard that too." The man shrugged. "Can't hurt. The Japanese take it like aspirin."

"Yeah."

"Have you heard about this new thing? Compound Q?"

Michael hadn't.

"It's been killing the virus in lab tests. Without damaging the other cells."

"Oh, yeah?"

"They haven't tried it on people yet, but there's a lot of . . . you know."

"Cautious optimism."

"Right."

Michael nodded. "Wouldn't that be something?"

"Yeah."

"What is it? A chemical?"

"That's the amazing part. It comes from the root of some Chinese cucumber."

"No shit."

"It's a natural thing. It's right here on earth." The man gazed out over the valley for a while, then looked back at Michael. "I try not to get too hopeful."

"Why the hell not?"

"I guess you're right," said the man.

They swapped names again. His was Larry DeTreaux, and he was on the way to Metro Video. "My lover told me to get *Mother Teresa* and *Humongous II*. Does that tell you about my life or what?"

Michael smiled. "Which do you watch first?"

"Good question."

"*Humongous II* is pretty good."

Larry nodded. "We just keep the sound off and use it as background."

"Yeah. Same here."

"The voices are the worst."

Harry pawed impatiently at Michael's leg.

Larry smiled. "This is yours, huh?"

"Yeah. It's hard finding time to walk him in this rain. Mellow out, Harry."

"Poodles don't know the meaning of the word."

Michael clipped on the leash, peering up at him. "You're not a poodlephobe, are you?"

"No. But I know these dogs. Eula's had a few in her time."

I'll bet she has, thought Michael. "I'll walk with you," he said. "My house is just over there."

Thack was in the garden when they arrived. He was bent over his trellis, examining the new growth. He did this at hourly intervals, it seemed.

"You remember Larry from the Rawhide II."

"Oh, yeah." Thack smiled and shook hands with him. "Thack Sweeney."

"New trellis?" asked Larry.

"Fairly."

"Interesting shape."

"We're growing clematis on it," said Michael, "so it'll be a pink triangle this summer." He was certain more than ever that it wouldn't read, but he was trying to be supportive.

"What a great idea! Who thought of that?"

Thack puffed visibly. "Me."

Larry glanced up at the clouds, which had turned threatening again. "Better haul ass."

"Need an umbrella?" Michael asked.

"Got one here." He patted his backpack. "You guys take care."

"You too," said Thack.

Michael added: "Say hi to Eula for us."

"Sure thing."

"Eula," said Thack, as soon as Larry was out of earshot. "*That* was her name."

Michael let Harry into the house and closed the door. "How could you forget?"

"We should fix her up with your mom when she visits."

"Don't you dare."

"She could take her to all the piano bars . . ."

"Look, if you know what's good for you . . ."

His lover laughed. "You're just afraid it'll agree with her."

"Damn right."

"She'll move here and we'll have to drag her out of the Galleon every Sunday afternoon."

Michael opened the mailbox. "Hasn't the mail come yet?"

"I took it inside."

"Anything good?"

"A postcard from Mona."

"Oh, yeah?"

"She wants us to visit this summer."

"Really? At Easley House?"

"Yep."

Michael caught his breath at the thought of it. "Should we do it?"

"Sure! You won't believe this place, Thack!"

"What about you know who?"

He felt a sudden pang of guilt, vaguely parental. "Oh, yeah."

"Dogs have to be quarantined for six months before they'll let them in."

"Forget it," said Michael.

"Elizabeth Taylor used to keep hers on a barge in the middle of the Thames. That way it was only subject to maritime law."

Michael rolled his eyes. "Now there's a travel tip I'll be sure to remember."

"What about Polly?"

"What about her?"

"Hasn't she offered to house-sit?"

"You're right," said Michael. "And Harry loves her."

"You don't think she'd mind?"

815

"Are you kidding? She can drag babes home from Francine's."

"Good point," said Thack, grinning.

The rain drove them indoors. They made tea and watched the downpour from the kitchen table. Michael thought of his rainy spring at Easley House, over five years before. It was there, at the folly on the hill above the house, that he had finally told Mona about Jon's death. Now, more than anything, he wanted her to meet the man who had made him happy.

He picked up her postcard and studied it again. It was a garden view of the great house. A ballpoint-penned arrow on one of the gables was labeled: "Your Room, Gentlemen."

"We should really do this."

"Then we will," said Thack.

"I know you'll love her. She doesn't take shit from anybody."

Thack smiled and poured more tea for him.

That Much in Love

"Now roll it up really tight . . . like so . . . then take one of those rubber bands and put it on the end there . . . that's right, lovely . . ."

It was a sunny May Sunday in Mrs. Madrigal's courtyard. Stretched out on the bricks in his Speedos, Brian listened while the landlady taught Shawna how to tie-dye. To his amazement, his daughter had actually requested this; tie-dyed stuff was cool again, she said. It made him tired just thinking about it.

"OK, now put some more rubber bands on."

"Where?"

"Anywhere."

"Point, OK?"

"No, dear. I mean put them anywhere you like. That's what makes them beautiful. The designs are all different."

"But I want one like you just did."

"Well, what good would that be? Then it wouldn't be yours, would it?"

Silence.

"Go on, now. You'll see."

Sitting up, Brian shielded his eyes from the sun as he watched the child coax the rubber bands onto the rolled T-shirt. "How's it going?" he asked the landlady.

"Beautifully."

Shawna rolled her eyes like the great Drew Barrymore. "I haven't done anything yet."

"Well, go to it, then."

His daughter donned rubber gloves that were much too big for her, then dunked the trussed T-shirt into Mrs. Madrigal's big porcelain tub.

"These are for Michael and Thack," Shawna volunteered.

"That's a good idea."

"They can wear them to the May Festival."

"Hey . . . there you go."

"Are they both mediums?"

"Think so, yeah."

Shawna turned to Anna. "Told you."

"Yes, you did," said the landlady, turning back to Brian. "How is Michael, by the way?"

"Fine."

"He had strep throat the last time I talked to him."

"It's gone now."

"I'm making the green one for Thack and the blue one for Michael." Shawna raised her voice to get back their attention.

"Yeah," said Brian. "I think green looks better on Thack."

"Can we take them by there tonight?"

"If you want to, sure."

"Michael says he'll show me the parrot tree."

"Don't count on it," Brian warned her. "You can't be sure of them."

"I know."

"Anyway, it's more special when it's a surprise. When they just swoop down out of nowhere."

The child turned back to Mrs. Madrigal. "If we add more salt it makes it brighter?"

"Yes, indeed."

"Let's add some more, then."

"All right, dear. Now watch very closely . . ."

Shawna gazed at her mentor with a look of such adoration that Brian felt a brief stab of jealousy.

Later, while his daughter was inside napping, Mrs. Madrigal sat on the bench and talked to him as he sunned. "How is her new place?" she asked.

"Didn't you see *People* this week?"

"What people?"

"The magazine."

"Oh. No."

"She's in it. There's a picture of the apartment."

"Ah."

"It looks good. Old-fashioned, with high windows."

"That does sound nice."

"Not much furniture, of course . . ."

"No."

"They call her the new Mary Hart."

"The who?"

"Just this woman on *Entertainment Tonight*."

"Oh."

"I'll bring you the article."

"Don't go to any trouble, dear."

He smiled a little.

"You've lost weight," she remarked. "Your tummy looks so flat."

"I've been working out again."

"Where?"

"At home. I made her old closet into a weight room."

She chuckled. "There's a clever boy."

"I thought so," he said.

His goal was to be back in shape by the end of summer.

When Brian arrived at the nursery the next morning, Michael was in the office, watching television in the tie-dyed T-shirt.

"Hey," said Brian. "Looks good."

"Doesn't it?" Michael swiveled his chest for an instant, then turned his gaze back to the set. "Guess who she's got on."

Brian looked up and saw a very tanned Russell Rand, arranged with studied elegance on the near end of Mary Ann's couch. He had just said something funny, apparently, because Mary Ann was laughing merrily.

"But it was such a natural idea," she said, composing herself. "Designer wedding rings. You wonder why no one thought of it before."

The designer's expression was appropriately modest.

"And you and Chloe, of course, are your own best ad."

Rand ducked his head. "Well . . ."

"I mean it. It's just so damned nice to see two people that much in love." There was scattered applause from the studio audience, so she egged them on a little. "Isn't it? Isn't it nice for a change?"

"Gag me," said Michael.

Brian smiled. "You think she's got Chloe behind the curtains?"

"Probably. So Russell can kiss her on camera."

"And let me tell you . . ." Mary Ann was on a roll now, developing her theme. "Those of us who haven't had such good luck in matters of the heart . . ."

"Fuck me," Brian said.

". . . can't help but feel a little envious."

"Fuck me fuck me fuck me."

Michael gave him a rueful look.

"She can't do one goddamn show without talking about it. Not one. She's a professional divorcée."

"Yeah . . . seems like it."

Brian swatted off the set. It felt curiously satisfying. "You'd think she'd at least wait until the divorce was final."

His partner gave him a half-lidded smile. "I think she wanted to start with a new persona."

Brian grunted. "Have you talked to her lately?"

"Not lately, really. Last week."

"That's lately." He glanced guiltily toward the blank screen. "I'm sorry, man. If you wanna . . ."

"No. Who cares? I just thought she might do a Lucy tribute."

"Well, here . . ." He reached toward the set. "Let's turn it back on."

"No. Really. I'm Lucyed out."

How could he not be? thought Brian. Only yesterday his partner had passed an impromptu memorial at Eighteenth and Castro and been so moved by the sight that he'd bought a small box of chocolates ("for my favorite episode") and laid it ceremonially among the flowers.

"Are you sure?" asked Brian.

"Yeah. All they ever show is the grape–stomping scene."

He leaned against the counter. "So what did she say?"

"Who?"

"Mary Ann."

"Not much. Just stuff about the show."

"Nothing about me?"

Michael looked annoyed.

"Sorry . . . I promised I wouldn't do that."

"That's right. You did."

"OK." Brian nodded. "Point taken."

"Life goes on, sport."

"I know."

"You wanna do a movie tonight?"

"Sure."

"Thack wants to see *Scandal*."

"What's that?"

"You know. The Christine Keeler thing."

He shrugged. "Sure. Whatever."

"Can you find a sitter?"

"Yeah. I think Mrs. M is probably . . ."

"Well, well, well." Michael was suddenly distracted by something out the window. "Look at that, would you?"

He looked.

"Jessica Rabbit is back."

Sure enough, she was. This time in a pink cotton blouse and khaki short shorts. Brian moved to the window and watched as she strode down a sun-dappled aisle, her rust-colored hair swinging like draped satin. He could practically smell her.

Then, out of nowhere, Polly bounded onto the scene, taking a shortcut through the Burmese honeysuckle to head off her quarry at the pass. He couldn't hear what was said, but both women smiled a lot, and Polly reached out at one point to touch Jessica's arm.

"I knew it," he said with quiet resignation.

Michael regarded him with sympathetic spaniel eyes.

"I had her spotted the minute she laid eyes on Polly."

"Oh, well."

Brian turned his gaze from the women and tried to be a good sport about it. "What the hell. More power to 'em."

"I dunno," said his partner, still watching.

"C'mon. That's a pickup if I've ever seen one."

"Then what's she doing now?"

Jessica, in fact, was walking away from Polly, a purposeful glint in her slanting cat's eyes. When she reached the end of the aisle, her creamy legs pivoted and scissored smartly up the path to the office.

"I'm outa here," said Michael.

"Where are you going?"

"Just in back. I've got some reorganizing to do."

"Michael . . ."

But his partner had already ducked into the storeroom and closed the door. By the time Brian had turned around again, Jessica Rabbit was at the door of the office. "Hi," she breathed, gliding in.

"Hi."

She came to the counter and gave him a languid smile. "Remember me?"

"Sure."

"The bushes are doing great," she said.

"Well . . . good. Glad to hear it."

She studied him for the longest time, looking wryly amused.

"Is something the matter?" he asked.

"Oh, no." She wet her lips. "Not a thing in the world."

He did his damnedest not to squirm.

"Your friend out there"—she jerked her head toward the window, but didn't take her eyes off him—"says you're a free man again."

He gazed uneasily out the window. Polly stood by the door of the greenhouse, watching them. She grinned at him for a moment, then thrust out her thumb triumphantly. He was certain he was blushing when he turned back to Jessica.

"Yeah," he told her. "Looks like it."

THE END

About the Author

ARMISTEAD MAUPIN is the author of the nine-volume Tales of the City series; his other books include *Maybe the Moon* and *The Night Listener*. Maupin was the 2012 recipient of the Lambda Literary Foundation's Pioneer Award. In 2014 he received an honorary Doctor of Letters degree from the University of North Carolina at Chapel Hill. He lives in San Francisco with his husband, the photographer Christopher Turner.

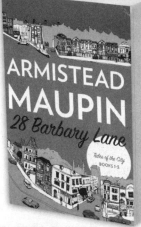
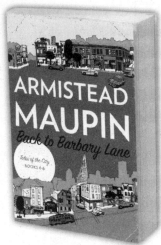
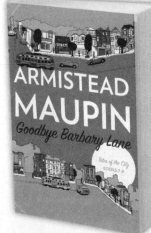